Son of the
Silvery Waters

Son of the
Silvery Waters

Alan Firstone

Chris Auney
aka Alan F.

Rutledge Books, Inc. Danbury, CT

ALL RIGHTS RESERVED
Rutledge Books, Inc.
107 Mill Plain Road, Danbury, CT 06811
1-800-278-8533
www.rutledgebooks.com

Manufactured in the United States of America

Cataloging in Publication Data
Firstone, Alan

    Son of the Silvery Waters

    ISBN: 1-58244-148-0

    1. Fiction.

Library of Congress Catalog Card Number: 00-112202

Acknowledgments

When you grow up in a beautiful small village with plenty of excitement, it's the best of all worlds. My formative experience was exactly that situation. Growing up in Sodus Point, NY, in the 1950s and 1960s was thrilling and enjoyable. As I wrote this book, I reminisced about those days, being thankful for the wonderful people in the village, my relatives, neighbors, classmates, and friends. My grandfather George Arney was a commercial fisherman on Lake Ontario. He and the other village elders taught my generation and me so much about life, nature, and values. So I must acknowledge their inspirational and developmental help. Also adding to my inspiration were the members of the Sodus Bay Historical Society. This group has grown and become a valuable part of the Sodus Bay area. Congratulations to the Society for its success and tremendous contributions. Sincere thanks to many special people who gave me further seasoning as I undertook my military career—my mentors Frank Giordano, Dave Cameron, and Jack Pollin; my friends and fellow mathematics professors, Jim, Jack, Gary, Rick, John, Kathi, Joe, PJ, Kelley, Bill, Rich, Steve, Doyle, Dave, Lida, Don, Brian, Fred, Joe, Gabe, Wade, Peter, Marie, and many, many more; my fellow math historians, Joe, George, Jim, and Fred; my students (West Point cadets are very special and unforgettable); my teachers (at Sodus Central School, West Point, and Rensselaer Polytechnic Institute); my friends, coaches, officers, civilians, and colleagues. For almost 20 years, I was a member of a marvelous organization, the Department of Mathematical Sciences at West Point. Its history and tradition are stimulating, and study of the Department's history gave me insight into the issues and mindset of the United States in the early 19th century. I thank the Academy's leaders who gave me the opportunity to serve in the education and development of the future leaders of our nation. I hope for the same opportunities in my new position at the College of Saint Rose. Whenever and wherever I needed help on this project, I found the right people willing to lend a hand. Thanks to Elizabeth Samet and the staff at Rutledge Books for their expertise. Finally, I wish to acknowledge my family who kept encouraging me as they sacrificed for the good of this writing adventure. I have been blessed with a wonderful family, and I thank them all—sister Jo Ellen, brother John, father George, my deceased mother Harriet, my children Kristin, Dan, Lisa, and Kate, and my wife Sue. Sue is a terrific artist, and I thank her for the artwork on the cover as well.

Preface

Son of the Silvery Waters is set in early nineteenth-century frontier America. It is the story of an amazing person—Soso Washington. Born and raised in an influential Indian family, he encounters the world of white people. As an adult, he calls the shores of Sodus Bay his home, although he travels to many places including New York City, Albany, Sacketts Harbor, West Point, and Washington, D.C. Soso becomes a talented fisherman, hunter, boat builder, and farmer. He learns to appreciate the white man's culture while maintaining his native roots. As a minority, he has to overcome fear, prejudice, and discrimination to survive and grow. As a strong, viable role model, he leaves a legacy for others to follow. Soso's acquaintances include frontier settlers, Indians, farmers, fishermen, slaveholders, slaves, underground railroaders, ship builders, political leaders, army officers, bankers, famous people, and ordinary citizens. As an older man, Soso marries a Black woman whom he earlier helped escape from slavery and helps the Americans win battles during the War of 1812. Through his eyes, we see the wilds of the frontier, the chaos of the cities, the vastness of Lake Ontario, and the beauty of Sodus Bay, as the 19th century unfolds.

Alan Firstone is the penname of a former resident of Sodus Point. He recently retired from the Army after spending 34 years in military service, 22 of them as a mathematics professor at West Point, an important location for many activities in this book. Alan and Soso share a tremendous love for the spectacular beauty that nature has bestowed on the Sodus Bay area and the Hudson Valley region of New York State. *Son of the Silvery Waters* portrays the lives of frontier settlers as they struggle to survive and search for beauty in their world. Firstone dedicates this book to his deceased mother, Harriet Arney, who provides him inspiration, and to his wife, Sue Arney, who gives him love and understanding.

Chris Arney (a.k.a. Alan F.)
West Point, NY

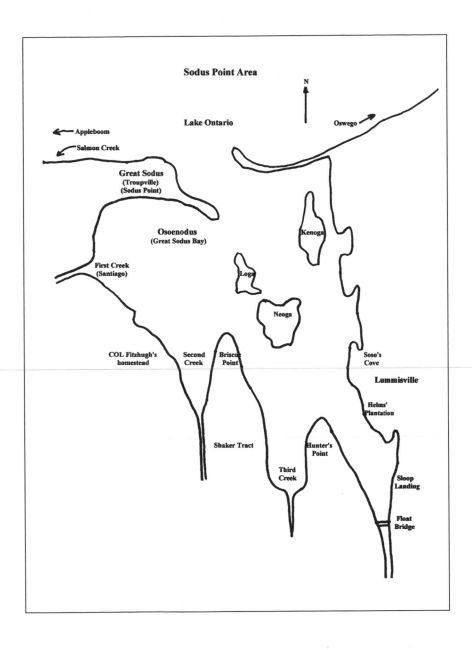

Sodus Point Area

N

Lake Ontario

Oswego

Appleboom

Salmon Creek

Great Sodus
(Troupville)
(Sodus Point)

Osoenodus
(Great Sodus Bay)

Kenoga

First Creek
(Santiago)

Loga

Neoga

COL Fitzhugh's
homestead

Second
Creek

Briscoe
Point

Soso's
Cove

Lummisville

Helms'
Plantation

Shaker Tract

Hunter's
Point

Third
Creek

Sloop
Landing

Float
Bridge

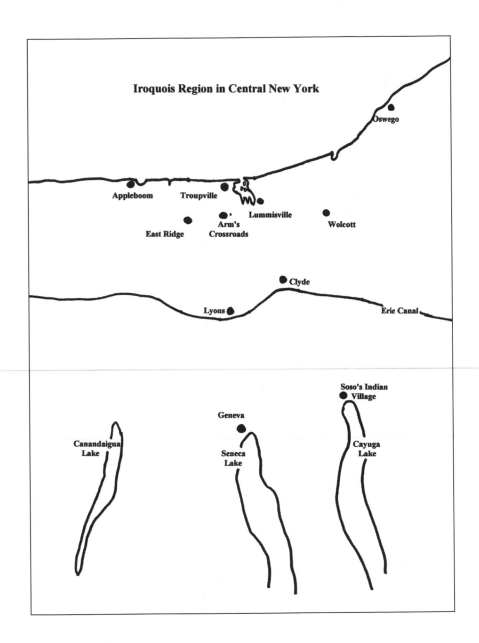

Iroquois Region in Central New York

Part I

Settling the Frontier

The Boy

The young boy loved to climb high up the hill and look down on the sights far below him. From his lookout, he could see the splendor of the long clear lake, the vast greenery of the forest, and the blue clarity of the sky. Whenever he was here, on his hill, his thoughts became clear and easy, his dreams grew exciting and lively, and his entire body felt cleansed and energized. He knew that he must be the most fortunate person alive. After all, he was a Cayuga Indian living in the village of the tribal chief, the great warrior *Juggetea*, the Fish Carrier. His family was one of the most important in the entire village. His village was the best of the tribe, his tribe was the best of the Iroquois, the Iroquois were the best and strongest of all Indians, and the Indians were the chosen people of the Creator. He was truly sitting on top of the world.

He carefully watched the birds and the animals, just as they watched him. He had a special sense and awareness that made him feel at once part of the wilderness, yet also the wise, benevolent master of all the animals around him. He was not an intruder here; he fit into the environment without disturbing its tranquil balance.

Even at 11 years of age, he was a special Indian brave. His name was *Sosoenodus*, son of the silvery waters. His mother, father, and friends called him Soso, but the village elders, who included his grandfather, called him by his full name.

Soso was special in many ways. His grandfather, Trout, was the chief provider for the village. Trout was appropriately named since he was the best fisherman the tribe had ever had. He knew exactly when, where, and how to fish and hunt. For the most part, the tribe had eaten well during Trout's tenure as chief provider.

Soso's father, Gar, was a warrior and *Schema*, a nonhereditary tribal leader. The talk in the village was that the brave warrior Gar would be the next battle chief. He would have to be appointed to that position by Cornstalk, the matriarch of the village, because it was the women who actually ran the Iroquois villages and made the important decisions. Soso was very proud of his father and grandfather, but he was never one to brag about their positions. What Soso liked best was working with, and learning from, them, especially his grandfather, who in Soso's opinion knew more than anyone else about the important things in life.

Since Gar was often too busy with the activities of the braves to spend much time with Soso, Trout took his grandson everywhere: fishing on the lake, hunting in the forest, going to meetings of the village council. Soso knew more than most Indians twice his age about hunting, fishing, and politics. He understood the habits and instincts of the fish and animals. He also possessed exceptional physical abilities for such a young boy. He could run faster, jump higher, throw farther, and shoot an arrow better than any boy under 16 years old in the tribe. Recently, Trout had let him fire a flintlock rifle, a powerful weapon of the white man. Stories of Soso's performance in the Indian game of *bagataway*, called lacrosse by the white man, were often told in the neighboring Cayuga villages and throughout much of the Iroquois nation. Soso, however, was content simply to learn more about the techniques of hunting and fishing and let others boast of his athletic achievements.

Soso continued to look down on the lake from the hilltop. He could see the small, birch-bark canoes of the village make their slow progress from the south up toward his village, which was hidden in the forest below. He wondered how many and what kinds of fish they had caught. By leaving the hilltop now, he could be at the shore to help them unload the catch of the day. Then he could help clean and lay out the fish for drying. Those were some of the jobs he liked best because he was so good at them, and he was often put in charge of many of the squaws and other children. While the women and children worked at their duties, the men under the direction of Trout would plan the next days fishing or hunting, cleaning and repairing the nets, sharpening their harpoon spears, and making arrows for the hunt.

Later that same day, after he had cleaned fish for several hours, Soso heard some important news from his grandfather. The annual fishing party would soon be leaving for the bay of Osoenodus and the lake of Ontario. Soso was filled with anticipation for his return to the silvery-watered bay for which he was named. He and his family had been in the fishing party to the bay for the past three years, but because the Cayugas had been forced to sell much of their land to the Americans as a result of the Revolutionary War, Soso had been afraid that the annual trip would be canceled. He loved every minute of time spent on the beautiful bay and the great lake. The fish were bigger, more plentiful, and easier to catch at Osoenodus than here at the lake of the Cayugas. The water of Osoenodus was clear, deep, and cold. But most of all, Soso liked to go to Osoenodus because he could see more white men there. He saw very few white men in his own village and never was able to get close enough to talk to them when they were there. During the last two summer trips to Osoenodus, he saw the white men who fished, trapped, and hunted on the bay. One year he even saw the big fishing boat owned by the white man John Fellows that could carry many men and supplies.

After dinner, while Soso was dreaming of new adventures at Osoenodus, Trout called him to his side. Whenever Trout talked with Soso, he began with a fishing story. Soso loved Trout's stories and always listened intently to every word, no matter how many times he had heard the same story. Soso always learned something new and important from Trout's stories.

"Sosoenodus, remember last year when you fished the creek of Santiago and your father and I took a fishing party on to Ontario? The wind blew lightly from the direction of the setting sun. That morning we left Sodus with four canoes and paddled toward the morning sun." Trout always used the white man's words—Sodus and Ontario—for the bay of Osoenodus and the huge lake the bay drained into, whenever he talked to Soso. The rest of his words were in Iroquois. He had been teaching Soso some of the white man's words for several moons. Soso was a quick learner and enjoyed the challenge of learning the new words.

Trout continued with the story that Soso had heard several times before and wished he had witnessed firsthand. "Just after passing the bluff pointing to the sky, we fished our nets close to shore where the shad were jumping from the water. In just one haul we filled all our canoes with fish and left fifteen more canoes of fish on shore. We spent all day hauling the whitefish that come from the big sea back to our camp. There was enough of the delicious fish to feed the entire village for several days. Because these fish are no longer easily found here on our lake of the Cayugas and the fish are still plentiful at Sodus, the bay of the Cayugas, this year we are going to set up a permanent village at Sodus."

This was big news because the tribal leader, Fish Carrier, knew that this would violate the treaties that he had signed with the Americans. However, the leader had little choice, since he had to feed the Indians that lived in his village. The fishing village at Sodus was essential for the survival of the main Cayuga village.

Soso could hardly believe his ears, a Cayuga village at Sodus. His mind and heart began to race. Questions began to pour out from Soso. Who would go? When would they go? Where would the village be located? Would he be able to go and fish the big Lake Ontario?

All the questions came to an end when his grandmother, Secanda, interrupted their discussion with the possibility that his family might not go to Osoenodus. Gar wanted to stay at their current village where he had a chance to become the battle chief, but Trout and Soso certainly wanted to go to Sodus. Trout believed that his son should be content to be battle chief of the new village even though it would be much smaller in size than the main village. Gar, Trout, and Secanda continued to debate well into the night, but everyone knew the final decision would be up to Secanda. Secanda was the oldest woman of the *ohwachira*, the family group that was made up of her female offspring and their families. Soso kept dreaming of the possibility of moving to Osoenodus until sleep finally overtook him late into the night.

Old Village

Soso's current village had been moved and rebuilt after the American white man General John Sullivan had burned the old village and the tribe's fields during the white man's war of rebellion against the redcoats. The Cayugas and many other Iroquois had supported their friends the redcoats, but since the Americans had won the war, the Cayugas were just trying to exist in peace with the American white men. The British war agreement with the Americans left no local lands for the Cayuga Indians. Some of the tribes felt betrayed by the British, who had promised the Indians much land for helping them. Other tribes blamed the Americans for their problems and were still hostile toward all American white men.

The war had severely divided the six tribes of the Iroquois nation after over 200 years of unity and peace with one another. The six tribes, Cayuga,

Seneca, Onondaga, Oneida, Mohawk, and Tuscarora, were in bitter disagreement and acting as separate tribes instead of providing the united front
needed to bargain with the Americans. Up to this time, the Iroquois had
been the strongest Indian opposition to the whites in North America because
of their large size and strong political unity. They had also been able to dominate neighboring Indian tribes by banding together to form large armies
and using firearms procured from the Dutch at the city of Albany. Now, this
recent divisiveness was weakening the once-powerful Iroquois nation.

After the war, Fish Carrier had signed many treaties with the
Americans in order to keep some of the land of the Cayugas. Most of the
Iroquois tribes, including many of the Cayugas, had lost all of their land
and supplies and were moving to Canada, where the British were giving
them land on large reservations.

Soso's Cayuga village had been in its present location for 13 years, and
because of the new treaties with the Americans, it would not be possible to
move it again soon. In previous times, whenever the fishing, hunting, and
farming became unproductive because of over-harvest, the villagers would
simply move their entire village to a new location. This proposed move of
some of the villagers to Osoenodus was an attempt to reduce the main village's population and to provide food for the village instead of moving the
entire village. Fish Carrier knew that moving part of his village was probably forbidden under the new American laws, but it seemed to be the tribe's
only chance at survival. Despite Trout's success as chief provider, the
prospects for continued success in hunting, fishing, and farming were
becoming slimmer each day. Fish Carrier and Secanda also worried that the
Senecas would take over their best fishing area by establishing their own
permanent village on Osoenodus. Because Secanda would be the matriarch
of the new village and would serve the new residents of the village as their
leader, she decided it was best to move her ohwachira to Osoenodus. Trout
and Soso were happy and eager to go. Gar was disappointed with the decision and very reluctant to go. However, once Secanda gave her final decision, there was no choice. Her entire ohwachira was moving to Osoenodus.

New Village

A week later in early April, the ohwachira moved out of their long
house and started the forty-mile trek to Osoenodus. They carried all their

possessions including a great deal of fishing equipment, canoes, nets, spears, and line. Several women and braves would have to make a second trip in order to move all the supplies they needed for the new village. The route followed the lowland valleys and streams to avoid as many hills as possible. The path still had to circle and weave around many marshes and swamps and the densest parts of the forest. In all, there were four ohwachiras, consisting of around 120 Indians, moving to Osoenodus. This trail had been traveled many times over the last several hundred years by both the Cayugas and Senecas, so, despite the rough terrain, it was easy to follow the well-worn trail and very few obstacles impeded the path. Soso was excited during the entire trip. When he passed over the last Indian trail on the tall east-west ridge, he became full of anticipation to see the waters of the magnificent bay that he would soon call home. It was a truly beautiful sight as they overlooked the last several miles of land to view the vast, blue Lake Ontario. While it was difficult to get a clear view of the entire landscape from the wooded, rugged ridgeline, through numerous glimpses of different areas, Soso could visualize the beauty and details of the geography that lay before him.

Gar and another brave from another ohwachira had selected the location of the village. They had traveled ahead to check several possible locations. Of course the location would have to be approved by Secanda. When she arrived, she agreed that the recommended location was perfect. The new village would be located almost a mile up the creek of Santiago, called First Creek by the white trappers. This creek would provide easy access to the bay by canoe, yet it was protected from direct attack from the water of the bay by the mile of winding stream and numerous marshes. In order to protect themselves from direct attack from the sea, the Iroquois never built their villages right on large bodies of water. This was an important consideration, especially since white men were fishing and trapping in the Sodus Bay area. Many of the Indians had seen the big boat of the white man named "Fellows." This big boat had been sailing on the bay for several years, and they were afraid of its return. The Indians were protecting themselves not only from the white man, but also from hostile Indians, especially the Huron from across the Lake Ontario. None of the Cayugas, who called themselves "the peaceful people" and "farmers of the mucky land," enjoyed the prospect of an attack by fierce Huron braves.

This location had the additional benefit of being near a large natural salt spring on First Creek that could supply the village with sufficient quantities of salt. The salt would be used to preserve the fish, a technique that the Native Americans had learned from the white man. The Iroquois hung their dried, salted, or smoked fish on the ceiling of their longhouse for storage. Without adequate salting, the odor of rotting fish was often overpowering in the longhouses. Sometimes during times of poor hunting and fishing, the Indians had no choice but to eat rotting fish. Very seldom was any food wasted or thrown away. The Indian culture and lifestyle insured that they caught or killed only what they could use. The easy availability of the salt would be a vital advantage to this Indian village and provide the Cayugas with the opportunity to send plenty of the fish caught in Osoenodus back to the main village.

The first order of business was to clear the land and build living places for each ohwachira. This construction took considerable effort. An entire ohwachira would live in one large rectangular building called a longhouse. The typical longhouse was about 100 feet long and 20 feet wide, with small partitions inside for the different families. The roof was made of bark tied to bent saplings, as a result it often leaked in many places.

The longhouse was the traditional home for all the Iroquois. The name the Iroquois called themselves was *Hodenosaune*, the people of the longhouse. But by 1792, longhouses were declining in popularity with the Cayugas and only two of the four ohwachiras in the village were going to build traditional family longhouses. The other two ohwachiras decided to build several smaller individual family cabins along with one larger hut constructed as a meeting and storage place. Secanda oversaw the construction of the longhouse for her ohwachira. Almost everyone worked on the effort, but Trout and Gar were excused from the construction work since they were needed to provide food for the village by hunting and fishing in the area. Palisades, walls of logs designed for protection from enemy attack, would be built after the longhouses and huts were finished. While he diligently worked at gathering bark and saplings for the longhouse, Soso's mind nevertheless wandered to visions and dreams of fishing and canoeing. He couldn't wait to see the open water of the bay and go on an exciting fishing trip.

Fishing the Bay

Trout selected a small party of braves to go fishing each morning. There were only four canoes in the village, so only eight braves could go fishing at any one time. More of the small elm bark canoes would be built when the village construction was completed. Soso was usually included in the eight fishermen selected by Trout. He was selected because, despite his young age, he was one of the best fishermen in the village. He could paddle a canoe, find fish, set nets, and spear fish as well as any of the older men. Soso considered it an honor whenever he was selected to go in Trout's canoe. Gar did not go fishing since he was in charge of the hunting party and usually took four or five braves to the west of the village to try to obtain venison.

On the first day of fishing, and only the third day after their arrival in Osoenodus, it was windy and cold. The wind was blowing heavy and hard from the west. The canoes of the fishing party had to hug the southwest shore of the bay near the mouth of First Creek to avoid the stormy winds and white-capped waves. Trout, Soso, and two fishermen in another canoe decided to try to move along the south shore to the next major stream and fish in its mouth. The fishermen in the other two canoes decided not to venture out that far and stayed in close to fish in the marshes of Santiago at the mouth of First Creek. Trout knew from a quick survey of the marsh that the other two canoes would spear enough catfish, eels, frogs, turtles, and bass to feed the village. The main reason for his trip to Second Creek was to scout out the sea trout that spawned in the creek. The trip down the south shore of the bay was uneventful, except that Soso was so excited he lost his rhythm in paddling the canoe several times causing Trout to continually adjust the canoe's direction. Trout wasn't really annoyed at this and didn't say anything to Soso, because he sensed the boy's excitement. Besides, he felt much the same way himself.

After they arrived at Second Creek, they decided to put out their hand-woven nets near the east shore. Trout knew the sea trout were there, but it was often difficult to catch many of these elusive fish this early in the season. Numerous seagulls circled the area, searching for easy prey, fighting the stiff wind, and generally causing a commotion. The net was set out in an arc, and then the ends were hauled together to encircle the fish. Next, the net was moved into shallow water, where it was carefully checked for entrapped fish. The fish were pulled out of the net and put into boxes in the canoes. Soso jumped into the water to check the net for fish, but found the depth of the water to be several inches over his head. Soso was tall and slender for his age, but he was still several inches shorter than the adult Indians were. He was a very good swimmer, but it was impossible to work the heavy nets while treading water, so a taller brave from the other canoe took over the task of pulling the fish out of the nets. First one, then several more of the big sea trout were found in the netting and thrown into the boxes in the canoes. But, in the end, only two dozen or so fish were caught. The load of fish and equipment was equally split between the two canoes. It was not a big haul, but Trout had discovered the information he sought. The sea trout were still returning to Second Creek to spawn, and in the next ten days or so the Indian fishermen could fill their nets with as many fish as they wanted. This was a good sign of *orenda* from the Creator, the Iroquois god of good things, for the new village. They would eat well and be able to send plenty of fish back to the main village, even as they finished building their homes in the new village.

The return trip to the village was much more adventurous. The wind had shifted more to the northwest and had picked up considerably. The little canoes had to fight against the white-capped waves in their western trip. Progress was slow and tedious. As canoe partners, Trout and Soso had never faced a blow like this, but Trout was an experienced waterman and kept the canoe steady by heading directly into the wind and waves. The Indians in the other canoe had serious difficulties from the very start. Catching the waves at the wrong angle, their canoe kept taking on water. Finally, their small canoe became completely swamped: nets, spears, paddles, and fish floated away. Trout and Soso tried to help their friends, but the wind prevented them from maneuvering their canoe into a proper position. The two drenched Indian fishermen had no problem getting to shore because of its proximity, but it appeared that all the equipment and the canoe itself would be lost.

White Men

Just then, Soso saw four white men appear on the shore. The four men immediately saw the predicament of the two Indians and jumped into the water helping to retrieve the canoe, paddles, and most of the nets and dragged them onto shore. At about the same time, Trout was also able to get his canoe to shore to help with the rescue. Once all the equipment was found and hauled up on the bank, the eight men—actually seven men and one boy—four Indians and four whites, were soaked, cold, and extremely tired. Not a word had been said between them until then.

Now Trout, who could speak some of the white man's language, expressed his thanks to the rescuers. "Thank you for your help. You are good friends."

"Lucky thing we saw your friends. This is quite a wild wind. I've never seen such big waves on this part of the bay." One of the white men talked with Trout.

"We fished too long and caught too many of the big fish. One always pays for being greedy." Trout explained why the Indians had exposed themselves to the dangers of the rough bay.

"We never catch too many fish. But we have had a good year trapping beavers and muskrats. We hope our luck will continue." Trout had already figured out that these men were trappers and fishermen, and that they had no grudge against Indians.

As the eight of them sat on the bank of the stormy bay to rest and dry off, Trout continued to talk with the four white men. Soso knew only a few of the words used by the white men, but occasionally Trout would tell the other three Indians what was being said. The four white trappers were relatively new to the area, having recently arrived at Sodus Bay from the lake streams to the east. They had spent the last several days looking for several other trapper friends who, they thought, were in the Sodus Bay area. Trout, wanting to keep on friendly terms with the whites in the area, asked them to return to the village with the Indians. Besides, they had all the fish and heavy equipment to carry back to the village and could use the additional help. So the group of eight fishermen stored the two canoes in the tree line along the bank near the shore and started the one and a half-mile trek back to the new Indian village, carrying some of the fish and most of the fishing equipment.

The return trip back to the village was uneventful for everyone except Soso. He listened intently and tried to figure out every word spoken between the white men and Trout. Soso was able to determine their names. Jim was the leader, or at least the one who spoke the most. The other three were brothers, George, Tom, and Bill. Soso noticed that none carried the white man's firearms, and he also sensed that they were friendly, but slightly afraid of the Indians. Soso wanted to ask them many questions but did not know their language well enough. Therefore, he was content to listen to their words for now, but he vowed to learn more of the white man's language as soon as he could.

Their arrival at the village caused quite a commotion. The dogs were barking, and the Indian children ran alongside the visitors. Some of the Indians were afraid that these white men would cause them harm by bringing others back to attack the village. Gar was among those who advocated killing the white men, but those in agreement with him were in the minority, so the trappers were safe. When the white men arrived in the village, the construction of the longhouses and huts stopped and the talking began. The white men and the Indians swapped many stories about the Sodus Bay area. For many days after the whites left, these stories would be retold and exaggerated by the Indians. Soso wanted to hear everyone's version of the white men's visit.

After a feast of sea trout and venison stew prepared by Soso's mother, Clear Dawn, and of meat and fish provided by Trout and Gar, the white men retired for the evening, sleeping in a corner of Soso's longhouse. They left early the next morning. They headed for the Salmon Creek along the lake about three miles west of the bay, where they hoped to find their trapper friends. They intended to trap and fish in that area for about 30 days before returning to their homes in the big city called Albany.

The rest of the summer went fast for Soso. He was busy fishing, working, and learning. Trout had predicted good fishing and the summer's catches didn't disappoint. The daily catches were large enough not only to feed the entire Osoenodus village but also to supply plenty of fish to the main Cayuga village they had left. Trips were made almost daily to deliver salted fish to the old village, where Fish Carrier was pleased to see the food arrive. Fish Carrier now felt that he had made the right decision to establish a fishing village on Sodus Bay.

The hunting in the Osoenodus area was also good, and there were venison and deer hides for everyone. The creek and marshland also provided numerous beaver, which were easily trapped for their hides. However, there were still many problems and challenges. The tribe was less fortunate in the activity of farming. The Indian spirits of agriculture had not been kind to the new village. The land was not as rich and fertile as the productive, mucky land they had near their main Cayuga village. Despite long and hard work, the farming in the area was much more difficult and less productive than desired. It had taken a long time for the land to be cleared in the spring, and the crops were seeded late. The harvests of corn, squash, and beans were small.

Learning the Language

Most of Soso's spare time was spent with the Indians who knew the language of the white man. Soso learned many new words from his mother, Clear Dawn, and his grandfather, Trout. By his twelfth birthday, which fell at the end of summer, Soso was ready and able to ask many of the questions that he had wanted to ask the four white fishermen in the spring. However, he would have to wait until the following summer for the next opportunity to talk with a white man.

Fishing the Lake

One opportunity that Soso did have was to fish the big Lake Ontario. Since the fishing had been so good on the bay, the Indian fishing parties did not need to go out on the big lake to catch fish. One morning in the early fall, however, Trout decided it was time to investigate the lake fishing and led his fishing party out on the lake. Soso went with Trout and six other braves across the bay and through the natural channel outlet to the lake. Soso's heart raced as they made their entrance onto the vast, seemingly endless lake. It had been a long paddle of over two miles just to get to the lake. They paddled their canoes about two miles further west before Trout decided it was the proper time and place to release their nets. The smooth, clear water stood out from the white sandy beach lining the shore, the brown rugged cliffs behind the beach, the lush green forests on top of the cliffs, and the bright blue sky. The omni-present seagulls squawked more than ever as they reached this magical fishing spot. It was the right time and place indeed. They were just 200 yards off a place the white men called Boulder Point, appropriately named for the giant boulder that sat at the end of a point of land. Nature had blessed this spot with both beauty and plentiful resources. Soso believed in many of the powerful and benevolent Indian spirits that guided the ways of the Iroquois, but somehow he just couldn't fear the Serpent Spirit of the lake. This beautiful place was just too inspiring to be haunted by an evil spirit.

Soso had never seen fishing like this before. Each haul of a net brought dozens of the big lake trout and many more of the delicate, smaller white-fish. The Indian fishermen could easily see schools of the big fish in the clear lake water, and they set their nets accordingly. The fishing was excit-ing, the lake was dazzling, and Soso was enthralled with the experience. It was a feeling that he would never forget. As they began their long journey back to the village at First Creek, Soso took time to sense all the spirits of nature and to absorb all the elements of the spectacular environment. The setting sun glistened from the bright sky and illuminated the deep blue water of great Lake Ontario.

When he returned to the village that night, Soso was exhausted from the hard work but nevertheless ready to go again. It had been a magnificent day for this young boy. As he was lying on his mat to sleep, Soso reflected on the waters and sky of the lake. He sensed that no evil lake serpent could ever live in such a beautiful place. Unfortunately, he would have to wait until the next summer to repeat his fishing experience on the lake. There were enough fish in the bay to keep the Indian fishermen satisfied for the rest of the year. The usually rough water of the lake and the longer trip to get to there influenced Trout from making any further plans to fish the lake during the rest of the summer. Despite Soso's constant suggestions to his grandfather to return to the lake to fish, Trout had to do what was best for the village.

Capture

The four white fishermen had quite an adventure after they left the Indian village. They never found the friends they had expected to meet at Sodus Bay. It turned out that a week before they had rescued the two Indians at Sodus Bay, their friends, out west in the Niagara frontier trap-ping beaver and muskrat, were attacked by a band of hostile Iroquois. The Indians had surprised and overwhelmed the hapless trappers. Other trappers found the remains of six victims about a week later. Word of the killings eventually spread eastward causing anxiety for white frontier settlers in the northern states. Such killings and raids were becoming more and more common in the Niagara region in 1792, and the white set-tlers and their governments were becoming frustrated over these acts of terror. Unfortunately, the violent actions of a few renegade Indians and disdainful white trappers were damaging the white-Indian relations on the frontier.

The Iroquois were the fiercest of all the Indians in eastern North America. Their presence in New York and Pennsylvania had slowed the western movement of settlers into and through that region. The settlers in the southern colonies and states faced the less feared and more peaceful Indian tribes of the Algonquin, Cherokee, and Shawnee. The southern settlers also had legendary and heroic frontiersmen Daniel Boone and Davy Crockett to lead the way west. No such hero was to appear in the North to subdue the Iroquois. Therefore, westward progress was slow in this area, and the few whites bold enough to settle in western New York lived in constant fear of Indian attack.

However, what happened to Jim, George, Tom, and Bill, the four white fishermen and trappers who rescued Soso's friends, as they fished near Great Sodus, was a very strange story indeed. While spearing lake trout in the Salmon Creek near Great Sodus Bay, they were surprised and captured by a band of hostile Indians. They were blindfolded, taken down to the shore of Lake Ontario, and put into canoes. They were taken by these canoes a long way to the west. Resting on shore during the nights, they paddled during the days. The westward trip continued for three days until they suddenly stopped and were taken into a cave near the shore. Only then were the blindfolds removed from the four white men. The Indian captors kept guard at the entrance of the cave at all times.

The four prisoners had no idea where they were or what their fate would be. After about two weeks of captivity, while Jim lay awake at night, he heard the unmistakable voice of an Englishman. Jim couldn't make out the entire conversation, but the Englishman seemed to be arguing with an Indian over the price to be paid for the abduction of the four white fishermen. It seemed to Jim that their capture had been arranged for, or at least instigated by, the British soldier to whom the Indian kept referring as Captain Longknife. From what he heard, Jim surmised they were being held somewhere in Canada along the northwest shore of Lake Ontario. He also decided that they were in grave danger and had no choice but to attempt to escape past the Indian guards as soon as an opportunity presented itself. He sensed that their fate would be much worse were they to be handed over to English soldiers.

Escape

The opportunity for escape came the next night. The Indians were celebrating wildly and drinking whiskey, probably obtained from the British
soldiers. Even the guards of the cave seemed quite drunk, so Jim decided to
attempt an escape later that night. It was almost too easy. By late night,
every Indian in camp had fallen asleep in a drunken stupor. Jim and the
three brothers were able to move quietly out of the cave into the darkness
past the sleeping Indians. They followed a footpath through the darkness
of a dense forest and fortunately came upon the Indians' canoes along the
lakeshore. As they searched for paddles and attempted to launch two
canoes, several Indians who were supposed to be guarding the canoes
woke up and saw what was happening. Jim and George were able to jump
into a canoe and slip away into the darkness unhurt. However, Bill and
John were not so lucky. They had to fight off a couple Indians just to get into
the canoe and were badly wounded by arrows before their canoe disappeared into the darkness on the lake. Bill and John had only one paddle,
and their canoe was leaking badly. But now luck was on their side. It was
an extremely cloudy, dark night, and the drunken and angry Indian pursuers in their canoes were unable to find the drifting canoe of Bill and John
despite passing within 200 yards of it.

Jim and George had not seen Bill and John since their escape, but by
sunrise they had found the shore. They decided to hide their canoe on shore
and travel the rest of the way by foot. They were afraid that they could be
easily spotted on the water and caught by their pursuers if they continued
to travel in the daylight by canoe. As near as Jim could determine, they
were close to the extreme western end of Lake Ontario in Canada. They
would have to travel eastward along the south shore of the lake past the
Niagara River to reach the Sodus Bay area where they had been captured.
There they felt that they could find help from other white trappers they
knew in the area. They were concerned about evading, not only their previous captors, but also other hostile Indians and British troops. They had
heard rumors that the British were trying to stir up Indian hostility in the
western part of New York that had just been purchased from
Massachusetts. It had been rumored that England was going to claim this
disputed land as theirs. From the discussion that Jim had overheard the
night before between the Indian leader and the British Captain, Longknife,

he was convinced the British were definitely stirring up hostilities. This entire region along the lake was a disputed area, since the British still maintained a small fort in New York east of Sodus Bay at Oswego called Fort Ontario.

Jim and George had a long, dangerous 150-mile journey on foot ahead of them, but Bill and John had other, more pressing, problems. Their wounds were severe, and they realized they would not survive for long in the open canoe. They had just enough strength to keep the leaky canoe afloat, but they had no way to maneuver it. Not only that, they did not know where they were or exactly which way to go to safety. All day long, seemingly hundreds, maybe thousands of seagulls flew overhead, marking and squawking out the location of the sinking craft and its exposed, vulnerable occupants. The two trappers could only lie in the drifting canoe and hope for help from friendly winds and currents. Fortunately, they received the friendly winds they needed. The wind blew steadily and softly from the northwest for the next two days, depositing the canoe and its severely wounded passengers at the harbor of the Irondequoit Bay. Both men were near death, but the next day a fisherman found them just in time to save their lives. Amazingly, both men were almost fully recovered from their ordeal when nearly three weeks later Jim and George arrived on foot at Sodus Bay. Jim and George were reunited with their two companions after their own hazardous journey on foot through hostile territory. They had narrowly evaded capture several times. One time they had to spend five days hiding in a small cave waiting for an Indian war party to give up their search and move away from the area.

This incident of the four fishermen was just one of several episodes of terror spawned by hostile Indian bands in western New York during that time. This incident was unusual in that most of the hostile Indians' misdeeds were much further west than Sodus Bay. Much of the Indian harassment for the next 20 years, until the War of 1812, was to be instigated by the British in hopes of reclaiming this land as part of their Canadian colony. The captivity and escape of Jim Davis and his three companions was just one in the sequence of events that would eventually provoke another war between England and America.

A White Friend

As fate would have it, the next white man Soso would talk with was none other than Jim Davis, whom he had met the year before. Soso, older and wiser at age 12 and now able to speak many more English words, had questions for Jim. They met for the second time during the late summer of 1793, while both were fishing the narrow and shallow strip of water between the islands of *Neoga* and *Loga* on the bay called Osoenodus. Soso had been fishing alone on the days when Trout was ill, which seemed quite frequent now. Jim had decided to return to Sodus Bay for a summer of fishing after staying in Albany the previous winter. Because of their adventure the previous summer, the three brothers, who usually fished and trapped with Jim, decided to stay home and live a safer and quieter life in Albany. Jim knew he was taking a big risk working in this potentially dangerous area without a regular partner.

Soso and Jim Davis immediately developed a mutual respect for one another. Jim remembered how impressed he had been with the young Indian boy when they had first met a year earlier. Over the next several weeks, Jim told Soso many things about the white man's world—life in the big city of Albany and the great lands of Europe and Asia across the big oceans. Soso was very interested when heard about the big ships that brought the whites across the ocean and the big fish that lived in the huge seas. Soso told Jim about many of the Native Americans' methods and secrets of catching fish and trapping animals. Jim taught Soso how to shoot the flintlock gun. Soso taught Jim the techniques of making and shooting a bow and arrow. The communication between the two of them could have been difficult, since Jim spoke little Iroquois and Soso only some English. Nevertheless, they somehow seemed to understand each other quite well and were working hard to learn each other's language.

This strange partnership lasted throughout the rest of the summer and fall. In many ways they were very different—age, race, experience—and in many ways they were the same—interests, personality, needs. The thirteen-year-old Indian boy and 23-year-old white man became constant fishing companions. Often, they would go out on the big lake to catch trout and salmon. The fishing was always good, but the weather never seemed to cooperate. The rough waves of the lake often produced problems for the small canoes. The more fish they caught and tried to carry home, the less freeboard for the canoes. Soso and Jim had several close calls—swamped or capsized canoes, broken paddles, and lost equipment. Even though these incidents were common occurrences on the lake, they never dampened Soso's enthusiasm to go back again. Soso loved the big clear lake and its never-ending supply of big fish.

Jim, on the other hand, enjoyed fishing the calmer waters of the bay. His favorite fishing spot was the deep hole on the east side of the bay called the "pork barrel." Jim was the better of the two at catching the big jaw-protruding gar fish, pike and muskellunge. When the big fish were not biting, Jim loved to fish in the shallows near the shore for the abundant and eager-to-be-caught perch and bass.

Either setting, however, bay or lake, was fulfilling for both. The beauty of this area and its waters was inspiring and refreshing. Nature had bestowed a special touch of splendor to this area that these two men of nature treasured and loved.

Some days Trout would come along, whenever his failing health permitted. Several times when Trout was along, Soso invited Jim to return to the Indian village with them. During that summer, Jim was the only white man who was allowed the privilege of entering and staying in the Indian village. Several other white trappers and fishermen would come to the village to trade, but they were never allowed the total access to the living areas of the Indians that Jim had. By the end of the summer, all the Indians of the village knew and trusted Jim because he had helped them so many times before.

More Trouble

The construction of the Indian village was now complete. It was small and well-built. There were three longhouses and over a dozen small huts and cabins. Two ohwachiras lived in the longhouses, and another longhouse was used as a village meeting place and community storage shed. One of the initial four ohwachiras had returned to their old Cayuga village after finding the first season's farming on the shore of Sodus Bay too difficult and unproductive. The Cayugas were used to farming in the rich, mucky inland soil. Secanda reluctantly had let the ohwachira with the most farming success leave Osoenodus and return to the inland village. Survival for this small village was going to be difficult, given the slow start in producing crops. The Cayugas' primary sources of food, their life supporters, were the "three sisters": maize, beans, and squash. None of these crops did very well during the first summer of planting in the more compact soil of Osoenodus.

The palisade was complete, but it was not very high or protective. The small village still worried about an attack from their enemies, especially since many of the braves of the village had become disgruntled and frustrated with the poor farming, leaving to join hostile bands in the west. With each passing week, there were fewer and fewer warriors to protect the village and provide food.

Among those braves who had left the village was Soso's father, Gar. Gar had been at the new village for only a few weeks when he realized that the small village held no promise for him to become a great warrior. He knew that many of the Cayuga, Seneca, and other Iroquois braves had left to join the renegades so when he discovered a renegade raiding party moving through the area with some braves he knew, he joined up with them. It just so happened that the raiding party Gar joined was the one that had captured the four white fishermen, including Jim Davis, at the Salmon Creek near Sodus Bay.

Gar had returned to the Indian village on Sodus Bay several times over the past few months. He stayed only briefly to rest and eat before moving back west to rejoin his hostile band. Each time he returned, he would talk with his young son Soso. Gar wanted Soso to join him as a renegade. Gar was a strong, brave warrior who was gaining power in his war party. He promised Soso adventure if Soso would return with him to raid the white settlers and trappers. Gar would tell Soso stories of raids against the American white men and the riches that the Indians received from the British redcoats for such actions. Gar explained to his son about white men. To Gar, the whites were a people completely apart from the Indian world. The Indians would never understand whites; the whites would never understand Indians. Despite his father's persistence and vehemence, each time Soso refused his father's invitation. He preferred to remain at the Sodus village where, despite his youth, he was now the chief provider with Gar gone and Trout ill. Soso also had no desire to fight against the whites. He had decided that he wanted to cooperate with them, to learn from them, and to become their friend. Gar often left the village disgusted and frustrated with his son's senseless and inexplicable attitude.

Trout's Illness

During a late fall fishing trip to the head of the bay, Trout became extremely ill. He was paddling the canoe with Soso when his hands and arms went numb. Soso realized that he had to get Trout back to camp, but the day was so cold and windy that the return trip across the angry, rough waters of the bay would take several hours. Instead of returning all the way to the Indian village, Soso decided to take Trout to Jim's camp, which was at nearby Hunter's Point. Since the day was so miserable, Jim was still in his small hut skinning the beaver and fox that he had trapped that morning near Second Creek. They laid Trout on Jim's straw bed and tried to warm him using the heat from the open fire. Soso gave Trout some of the herbal medicine that he carried with him, but Jim thought the chances of Trout's recovery were slight. There were several other white trappers and fishermen living in nearby huts on Hunter's Point. That night several of them visited Jim and the Indians with offers of favorite medicines and help of any kind needed for the old man.

Soso had met all these white men before on fishing or hunting trips. But that night, in sensing their concern for his grandfather's health, he developed an appreciation for their sincerity and compassion. Soso and Trout ended up staying at Jim's hut for several weeks while Trout underwent a slow, but remarkable recovery. The winter weather had become severely cold by then, and it was not until the bay had frozen over completely that Trout was strong enough to make the return trip back to the Indian village. A litter was placed behind a trapper's horse, and Trout was carried across the frozen bay and up First Creek back to his home in the Indian village.

On Their Own

Several of the trappers and fishermen spent the rest of that winter in the Indian village. It turned out to be a rough winter for all—Indians and whites. The weather was severe, the hunting and fishing were poorer than anyone remembered, and the vegetable stock was poor because of another small harvest from the farm fields. The one bit of good fortune for the village was the recovery of Trout. By early spring the old man had returned to full health, ready to fish and hunt in order to provide for the village.

However, it turned out that the village would not need the services of the talented provider Trout for the next year. Because of the miserable conditions over the winter, the other two remaining ohwachiras decided in the early spring with Secanda's approval to return to their old village along the lake of the Cayugas. The one remaining ohwachira, that of Secanda, had only two remaining working men, the old man Trout and the young man Soso. All the other braves had gone off with Gar to make war on the whites and live as renegades. Secanda's health had also failed, and, when she died in the late spring, most of the remaining squaws of her ohwachira also decided to return to their old inland village.

Soso had loved his grandmother, and he mourned her loss. She had shown Soso how to lead people using wisdom and dedication. She always had taken time to nurture her family and listen to her grandson. Her body was returned to the inland village and buried with a traditional ceremony. Trout and Clear Dawn went to the ceremony, but Soso and his brother and sister stayed at Osoenodus. Everyone prayed to the Great Spirit of Death that Secanda's soul would travel safely across the bridge over the raging river of evil and far along the road of eternal peace.

The structure of Soso's life was changing rapidly causing him feelings of anxiety and worry. How things had changed in just a few short months.

He no longer thought of himself as the most fortunate person in the world, but he was still thankful to the Creator for the good things he did have. That he still had his mother and grandfather was a great comfort for the young brave, and that gave him strength, courage, and faith.

The disintegration of the village precipitated a surprising decision by Trout, Soso, Clear Dawn, and two other squaws. They decided to stay on their own in Osoenodus Bay instead of returning to their old village. They moved their camp near the shore of the bay at the mouth of First Creek to facilitate fishing. Several white men trappers and fishermen, including Jim Davis, also built small cabins there on the shoreline of the bay and the marshy creek. These whites lived with the Indians. The three male fishermen, Jim, Trout, and Soso, lived in a small cabin together. Three Indian women and their children lived with three other white trappers. Soso's mother, Clear Dawn, his younger brother, Perch, and his older sister, Water Lily, lived in the cabin next to Soso's. It wasn't much of a village, but all the inhabitants liked their new community.

Great Sodus

This turned out to be the beginning of an amazing summer. It was the white man's year of 1794, and settlers were beginning to arrive in the region of Osoenodus. The two main reasons they had not come sooner were their fear of the violent Iroquois in the region and the ambiguous terms of the British government's treaties with these Indians. But in this year under the new laws on American land rights, Captain Charles Williamson had the land along the northwest shore of Osoenodus surveyed into lots that settlers could purchase and occupy. This land was part of the vast Pultney Estate, or Phelps and Gorham Purchase, bought by Sir Pultney from the United States, New York, and Massachusetts governments. The intent of the estate was to encourage the development of several villages in the area. Under this plan, the village at Osoenodus would be called Great Sodus and, would, it was hoped, develop into a prosperous city.

The land near Osoenodus had originally belonged to the State of Massachusetts, but eight years earlier the Treaty of Hartford mandated its sale and eventual control by the State of New York. In 1791, the surveying of the dividing line between the states called the Pre-emption Line, stretching from Pennsylvania north to Lake Ontario, cost one English surveyor his life. Surveyor A. N. Briscoe died from the fever at the end of the survey line near a cove and point on Sodus Bay. The two landforms on the bay near that place would thereafter be called Briscoe Cove and Briscoe Point.

The settlers began arriving at Great Sodus in the early part of the summer of 1794, after long, dangerous journeys along the Mohawk River and the rugged overland roads and trails from Albany. Much of the land throughout this area was heavily forested or marshy. Trees, shrubs, grasses, and vines of all varieties seemed to grow everywhere, constantly clogging roads and trails. The lots in the village of Great Sodus were filled with trees and shrubs that needed to be cleared before any settlement or construction could begin. It took considerable effort for a frontier family to get to Great Sodus, to build a home, and to plant crops. It was tremendously difficult just to notice the natural beauty of the area. The settlers were in the survival mode, not in the enjoyment mode, and for many of them the beauty of the area was an extraneous item that barely played a role in the day-to-day lives of the frontier families.

Most of the settlers were tough, hardy men with strong wives and growing families. There were a few single men, but no single women in a frontier community like Great Sodus. Fortunately, the initial settlers had skills that every growing village like Great Sodus would need. John Wafer was the blacksmith. Dan McNutt was the shoemaker. Jabez Sill built and kept a small tavern, which eventually would become a hotel. Captain William Wickham was building a general store and arranging for transportation of supplies for the little village. Other settlers to arrive during the summer were Moses Sill, James Kane, John Gibson, Thomas Wickham, and John McAllister. All of them had bought their land through Captain Williamson, agent for the Pultney Estate. Many were simple farmers who wanted the freedom to sow seeds and build their lives from the strength and bounty of mother earth. The land of the area was rich, but it would take tremendous effort to clear the land, to prepare it for farming, and to survive the challenges of the frontier.

The cold winter posed significant problems for the settlers. The initial dwellings were small flimsy cabins with many draughts and no insulation. Fortunately, there was plenty of wood in the area, so the settlers kept the fires in their stoves burning hot. The occupants of the homes spent much of their time during the winter crowded around the hot stoves trying to stay warm.

Captain Williamson was a gracious man who helped the settlers of the area any way he could. He allowed them to make late payments for their land or gave livestock and seeds to those who couldn't afford their own. His dream was to make the magnificent bay of Great Sodus the best port on Lake Ontario. He was also responsible for developing several other villages in the area. He lived with his wife, Abigail, and his four children in the village of Bath, some 55 miles south of Great Sodus. However, he visited Great Sodus on numerous occasions, usually staying at Jabez Sill's newly built, but rustic hotel. He also arranged for a larger, more refined hotel to be built at the new settlement at Geneva, laid out and constructed many roads in the area, and provided post riders to deliver mail throughout the area. It took him two days to travel from Bath to Great Sodus, but he loved to ride along the trails he had designed and see first hand the villages he was helping to develop. He had a vivid imagination and could envision their eventual growth into large, civilized cities, as the area prospered in the future.

Although the area surrounding Great Sodus showed great potential for development, it was, in the 1790s, the frontier. The trails between villages were rugged and often steep. There were no real roads, only narrow wagon or foot trails. Danger, in the form of wolves, bears, or fierce Indians, lurked around each bend or over every hill. Help in the form of other settlers was often miles away. Even though the conveniences of civilization were missing, beauty was everywhere and natural resources were plentiful. There were huge trees, flowering meadows, majestic hills, and pretty valleys. The streams were pure, and the wildlife abundant. The soil was rich, and the sources of life-giving water were seemingly unlimited. This was a land blessed by nature, and the jewel of the area was the magnificent bay called Great Sodus by the whites and Osoenodus by the Indians.

Even with the help of Captain Williamson, however, the challenges ahead for these first settlers were enormous. They had to clear land, build their homes, feed and clothe their families, protect their property, and pay their debts. These initial settlers may not have survived their first year had it not been for the small community of Indian and white fishermen, hunters, and trappers of First Creek. This small group was able to catch enough fish to easily feed the entire population of the small village. Every day during that first summer and fall, the three Indian women living with the white fishermen would travel the mile from First Creek to the homes of Great Sodus. They would bring fish and sometimes venison for the settlers.

They saw to it that all the settlers were well provided for during their initial days in Great Sodus. The free food supply allowed the settlers to concentrate on other important tasks.

By summer Trout had recovered fully, and he, Soso, and Jim had become the best of friends. The three were constant companions and expert fishermen. Actually, their fishing expertise didn't matter too much because almost anyone could have caught fish in Sodus Bay during the summer of 1794. However, because of their talents, they were able to give large amounts of fish to the settlers and expected nothing in return.

At his advanced age, Trout was often too tired to travel into the village of Great Sodus, but Soso made the one-mile trip often by foot or canoe. He had learned enough English language to talk with the settlers, and he often discussed with them the lands in the east that they had come from. The settlers welcomed Soso because he would always bring food and would help them with their work. Soso cherished their company and wanted to learn white man's knowledge. He wanted to learn all about the white's world that he knew so little about. He especially enjoyed stories about cities, big ships, and the vast oceans.

One day, Captain Williamson sought out Soso, who was delivering fish to the villagers. Captain Williamson had heard stories of the kindness and support given to the villagers by Soso and Jim.

"I hear that you're a talented fisherman. It would take me a week to catch the amount of fish you give away every day. How do you do it?" asked Captain Williamson.

"Luck of the Indians. It's a secret trick known only to those who learn and understand nature's ways. If you and your people watch and learn, someday all these fish will grow big and delicious just for the white man's plate." Soso's reply was half-fun and half-serious. He was proud to reply in the newly learned language of the whites.

Captain Williamson then made his point. "Thanks for all you do for the village. Without you and Jim Davis, Great Sodus would still be just a dream. You're the best friend this village could have. If you ever need a favor from me, just ask."

Soso was thrilled to have the whites' chief as his friend. He wanted to be friends with all the whites. Soso could tell that Captain Williamson was a wise leader. Captain Williamson respected the maturity of this fourteen-year-old Indian boy, who seemed to give so much without asking for anything in return. Soso was not only tall and strong, but also bright and caring. But his most obvious characteristic was his maturity. Soso was honest, hard-working, and responsible.

Soso and Jim also spent some time that summer working on the construction of the roadway from Great Sodus to the southwest. Soso amazed the foreman by the way he quickly learned the tasks of digging ditches and clearing trees and how he worked so hard for so little pay. Soso truly felt that he was a good, close friend of the white men of Great Sodus. He had no way of knowing that things would change drastically in the days ahead.

Indian Raid

It was one of those dark, cloudy days that often arrive along the shores of Lake Ontario in early November. The settlers still had considerable work to do before winter took its icy grip on the area, but the chill of this day drove most of the settlers inside their small cabins or shelters. Word had just arrived at Great Sodus that General Anthony Wayne had soundly defeated the hostile Indians, mostly renegade Iroquois braves, west of the Niagara frontier. The settlers were thankful for the military's intervention, and most believed this military victory in 1794 would end the Indian harassment in the area. The settlers began feeling a sense of security. Little did they know that the pioneers living in Great Sodus were to feel one last blow of Indian hostility on that very day.

Ed and Tom Newton were two young farmers who had recently bought fifty acres of outlands at the western end of Great Sodus near the Salmon Creek. On this miserable day, the two rugged brothers were clearing trees from the land and building a small cabin which, when completed, would house their families. They were anxious over their work since their families, already en route from Albany, were expected within a week. Much hard work had to be done before their families arrived. No time could be wasted waiting for better weather. Earlier in the day, they had been helping to build a sawmill on Salmon Creek for Captain Williamson in order to earn extra money to pay for their land and for their families' travels. They didn't actually get money for their work. Instead they traded their work for the land that they had obtained from Captain Williamson.

Suddenly, appearing out of nowhere, 20 war-painted, hostile Indian braves attacked and easily killed the two unarmed farmers, who had no warning of the danger. The Indians set fire to the cabin and moved off to the east toward Great Sodus. The renegade band next came to the small dwelling of Paul Sage, who was inside his cabin preparing a dinner of fish, which had been given to him that morning by the Indian squaws from First Creek. Paul didn't even have time to grab his gun from the wall before the Indian arrows again found their mark. The war party ransacked Sage's home before setting it afire.

The smoke from Paul's house was the alarm that warned the other settlers of Great Sodus of the danger. John Gibson was the first to see the smoke, and then he saw the Indians coming his way. He and his wife Daisy grabbed their guns while sending the rest of their family throughout the village to warn others. Luckily, the other villagers had also seen smoke and were already on their way to help. A quickly organized defense was all that was needed to turn the Indian raiders away from Great Sodus. John and Daisy Gibson got off several shots that injured two renegades, but no Indians were killed in the action. The hostile war party had no reason to press the attack by confronting any organized resistance. This was a renegade band, not very organized or well-equipped. They had hoped only to cause some trouble and obtain enough food and supplies for travel to the west. They really wanted only to escape from the whites' interference and find a better life with and among their own people.

To avoid any further contact with the armed and alerted settlers of Great Sodus, the Indian raiders moved quickly toward the south away from the village along the shore of the bay. Then at the mouth of First Creek, they discovered the huts of their next unsuspecting victims. Their tactics were the same as before. They attacked the helpless, unarmed people and burned their homes. But this time the Indian attackers were surprised at what they found: Indians were living with the whites.

Soso was out in his canoe spearing the big frogs in the Santiago Marsh when he saw smoke billowing from his and his neighbors' homes on the banks of First Creek. Within minutes Soso was at his burning home trying to save it from destruction. He was too late to save the dwelling but just in time to pull its two occupants, Jim and Trout, out of the blaze. Both men had been shot with arrows and were badly burned. They were unconscious and near death.

Soso ran to the other burning cabins nearby only to find them so engulfed in flames that he could do nothing. The only survivor that he found was his mother Clear Dawn, who had been badly beaten. She told Soso that the white fishermen had been killed and left to burn in their cabins. She also told him that the other Indian squaws and the children had been taken captive by the Indian attackers. Soso searched the area, but soon he and Clear Dawn realized the worse, Water Lily and Perch were among those kidnapped.

Soso and Clear Dawn returned to Jim and Trout, both of whom had miraculously gained consciousness. Jim's arrow wounds were deep in his leg and shoulder, but they would not be fatal. Trout's wounds were much more serious. An arrow had struck his chest and penetrated his lung, and he was badly burned. Trout knew that he would not survive, but Soso wasn't about to let his grandfather die without a fight. However, Trout would not let Soso tend to his wounds, claiming that Jim needed Soso's attention more. Soso tried to stop Trout's bleeding and seal the wounds. It was no use. Trout's last words to his grandson Soso were, "Sosoenodus live here to catch the big sea trout of Sodus and teach the whites about the ways of the Indian."

Momentarily stunned by his grandfather's death, Soso soon recovered to help the others. He began to put the situation into perspective. Now was not the time to panic or to grieve. He built a litter to take Jim into the village for care by the white men. However, before he could leave, several villagers and Nathan Sargent, who was building a sawmill about a mile up First Creek, arrived. They had seen the smoke from the burning cabins and had come to see what was happening. Soso explained what he knew of the attack to them, and the settlers left taking Jim back to the village with them in order to treat his wounds properly.

Soso's life, which had been grand and orderly, suddenly was ugly and confused. Soso had always believed in the role of the good spirits, and he had tried to ignore the existence of evil ones. He had been taught to believe in many powerful spirits by his elders. But he had serious doubts about these spirits. Certainly, he had seen the goodness in the lake and knew no evil lake serpent could exist in those beautiful waters. However, he now wondered; maybe there were evil spirits, and maybe Flint, the Iroquois god of evil, had for some reason brought this misery into his life. He mourned deeply for his grandfather, who had taught him so much. He worried about the fate of his best friend Jim, who was now in the care of others. He tended to the wounds of his badly beaten mother, who for some reason was reluctant to tell him the complete story of the attack. It was too late to follow the war party or search for his siblings. He worried about them and wondered about their condition. Would he ever see them again? Why had this happened? How could Indians do this to their own people?

He buried Trout in the mound of land near the mouth of First Creek. He asked the great spirits of death to take care of his grandfather. He was confident that his grandfather's soul would be as powerful in death as the man had been in life. While he grieved, he thanked the good spirits for all they had given him and his family and asked that they continue to support them in their time of need.

Soso stayed with Clear Dawn in a small storage shed that was not destroyed by the attackers. For a couple of days Soso did not hear anything about the condition of his friend, Jim, since he was consumed by his own tasks. He wanted to go into the village to find out about Jim's condition, but Clear Dawn still needed his full attention to care for her wounds. Finally, two days after the attack, Soso felt Clear Dawn was recovering sufficiently and went into town to learn what he could about Jim.

Outcasts

Soso was not greeted with the warm smiles he usually received in the village. Instead he sensed a cold, hostile feeling from the villagers. Soso inquired about Jim and eventually was told that Jim was being cared for in the house of John Gibson. Even Captain Williamson, who had just complimented him on his contributions, ignored Soso's inquiries. Soso went to John's house and knocked on the door. No one came to the door. He knocked again, and again there was no answer. Yet he knew someone was home because he heard talking inside and the curtains on the window had moved. Soso did not understand this rejection. He had helped John many times and probably knew him better than any of the other villagers. Soso was Jim's best friend and was deeply concerned about Jim's health, yet he couldn't even get into the house to see his wounded friend. Without finding out anything about Jim, Soso reluctantly returned to First Creek to continue caring for Clear Dawn.

While Soso was in town, several villagers had come out to the fishermen's cabins to pick up the fishermen's remaining possessions. The settlers that had come by gave Clear Dawn the rest of the news of the Indian raid.

When Soso returned to Clear Dawn, he found out the information on the Indian raid that he did not know yet. Besides the three fishermen, three villagers had also been killed by the raiding Indians. Clear Dawn also told Soso the rest of what the villagers told her. The two Indians, Soso and Clear Dawn, were no longer welcome in the village of Great Sodus. The villagers had told Clear Dawn that even Jim Davis didn't want to see them again. This news, combined with Soso's experience in the village, convinced him that they were indeed not wanted. Soso wondered how friends could change into enemies so quickly. Couldn't they see that he and Clear Dawn were victims, just as badly hurt as the others? Their only similarity with the murderers was their race. Maybe these whites had never been their true friends.

Soso and Clear Dawn found themselves without a home, and winter was approaching. The small storage shed would not provide sufficient shelter from the cold, snowy winter weather along the shore of Osoenodus. They had only one option—go back to their old Cayuga village. The winter journey along the Indian trail was difficult. By then the snow was deep in some places, and Clear Dawn had difficulty walking the long distance with her injuries. They slowly retraced the well-established trail they had taken to Osoenodus three years before. But they were completely surprised at what they found at the site of their old village. No one was there. The entire village had been abandoned for at least several months. It was overgrown with vines and many of the deserted structures were already in ruin. What a terrible shock and disappointment. Their people were gone, and they didn't know where. This was as depressing as their unwarranted and surprising treatment by the whites back in Great Sodus.

Lonely Winter

Completely exhausted from their journey, Soso and Clear Dawn were forced to spend the rest of the winter in one of the huts that was left standing in the village. Almost all their possessions had been destroyed in the fires at First Creek. Although he had very little equipment for the tasks, Soso knew he could find enough fish and game for them to eat. Both Indians were confident they could survive the winter in the deserted village, but it would be a long, cold, difficult ordeal.

It was a rough winter for Soso and Clear Dawn, but they managed to survive on their astute wilderness skills. First, they made spears, traps, bows, and arrows out of wooden branches; nets and line from vegetable fiber; and fish hooks from the bones of small animals. Then Soso found and caught fish, trapped several beavers, and managed to kill a small deer. Fortunately, Clear Dawn recovered fully from her injuries. She foraged for roots and nuts and collected wood for their fire. She made moccasins and clothing from the hides and pelts that Soso had obtained. They struggled against the elements and survived. In the process, the bonds of their mother-son relationship grew even stronger.

There was no traditional, festive Midwinter Rite for Soso and Clear Dawn that year. The festival, which celebrated all the good things the Creator had brought and thanked the good spirits, was completely forgotten. There were no friends or relatives with whom to visit and celebrate. All the days of that winter seemed cold, dark, and miserable. There was one question foremost in Soso's mind. Why had the whites turned against them? Soso and Clear Dawn had not hurt anyone. They had not helped the hostile Indian raiders. They were victims just like the villagers of Great Sodus. Certainly, Jim knew that Soso had nothing to do with the tragic incident. Jim knew that there were both good and bad Indians just like there were good and bad whites.

In the spring, they tried to find out what had happened to the people of their old Indian village. They thought that if they traveled south along the west shore of the lake they might find other Cayuga villages. As they traveled, they could sense something was wrong. There were surprisingly few signs of other travelers or activity in the fields or forests. Finally, after several days of searching, they found a small band of Cayugas living in a camp near the southwest corner of the lake.

After greeting their fellow tribal members, Soso queried them about the old Cayuga village. The other Indians seemed surprised that Soso and Clear Dawn had not heard of the extensive and final Cayuga migration of the previous summer. The Indians told them of the mass exodus of the remaining Cayugas from all the local villages to the lands provided by the redcoats across the Ontario Lake and Niagara River to the Grand River of Canada. The redcoats promised plenty of food and warm shelter to the Cayugas who came to live on this new reservation land. The redcoats threatened war and famine to the Indians who remained with the Americans in the old land of the Cayugas. In any case, the Americans already had forced many Indians to leave their lands, which now belonged to American white men after the war. Many hostile Indian bands sided with the British and through threats of violence forced village chiefs to take their entire villages to Canada. The only Cayugas that stayed were those too weak to travel and the few willing to fight against the Americans to stay in their homeland, like the great Cayuga warrior Fish Carrier. The elderly Fish Carrier was the chief of this small band of Cayugas.

The small band that Soso and Clear Dawn had found contained a strange mix of Indians. Several braves loved the land of the Cayugas and decided to stay and fight alongside their leader, Fish Carrier. However, most of the Indians in the camp were old and weak. They were just too tired to move over a hundred miles to a new home. It would be a struggle for this small band of Indians to provide enough food and sufficient protection to survive. Soso and Clear Dawn inquired about Perch and Water Lily, but none of their new friends knew anything about the kidnapped children or the Indian raid at Great Sodus.

New Village

Soso and Clear Dawn were without any home, so they decided to stay with this group of Cayugas on the shore of the lake of the Cayugas. It was good to see their old chief, Fish Carrier, who they knew to be a wise and caring leader. Fish Carrier was happy to see them as well. He had always admired the maturity and dedication of the young brave named Sosoenodus. Soso could help supply fish and game, and Clear Dawn could help farm the land. Clear Dawn and Soso built a small hut to live in and began to make contributions to their new village. However, this was hardly a powerful, efficient village like the one Soso had grown up in. This was much more like a poor, run-down camp. They had little food and no protection from enemies.

Despite the myriad of problems, Soso enjoyed this summer back on Cayuga lake. He made fishing nets, spears, hooks, and line, and he caught plenty of fish for the villagers. He was a natural leader and a tremendous contributor. Nevertheless, it was not the same as Sodus Bay or Lake Ontario. He missed the bigger fish of the lake and the silvery waters of the bay that he had called home just one year before. Clear Dawn also longed for her old home and the lifestyle that she enjoyed in the Sodus Bay area. She had liked living near the whites and learning their ways of life. She had especially enjoyed the conveniences of their inventions, which made life more pleasurable and productive. Ever since Gar had left her life, she had concentrated on developing and caring for Soso. Clear Dawn was a strong, wise woman, and a loving mother.

The summer of 1795 went by slowly. The Indian women in the rugged village managed to plant and harvest their meager crops. Most of the meals consisted of corn-cakes and fish. Soso spent most of his time with two young braves, He-Runs-Far and Nothing-But-Dreams. Both boys were a bit older than Soso, but neither possessed his hunting or fishing skills or his maturity. At fifteen years of age, Soso had become a strong, handsome brave. He usually wore deerskin pants and moccasins. Unlike his friends and most of the other braves, he kept his hair short.

As the summer progressed, some additional Indian braves returned to join this village with stories of the life in the Grand River region where the redcoats had established the Indian reservation. The returning braves had not found life in Canada under the care of the redcoats to their liking. They reported that many of the British promises had never materialized. They preferred to fight for their freedom in the original land of the Cayugas than to live as protected slaves on a reservation. Once again, none of the new arrivals had seen Water Lily or Perch. Only Clear Dawn's great optimism and will kept Soso confident. She had lost her husband to the evils of the changing world. She had no intention of letting her son turn sour or evil.

As fall began, Soso found himself depressed and homesick. This had been the first summer in the last seven that he had not spent most of his time on Sodus Bay. He wondered about his old friend Jim Davis and whether he would ever see Jim again. He still questioned why he and his mother had been treated so poorly by the whites of Great Sodus after being their friends for so long. They had to understand that Soso and Clear Dawn were their friends, not their enemies.

Recovery

It turned out that Jim was wondering similar things about Soso and Clear Dawn. After Jim had recovered from the wounds that he had received during the Indian attack, he went back to First Creek to find Soso and Clear Dawn. During his recuperation at the Gibson's, he had repeatedly asked the villagers about his Indian friends, but no one could or would tell him anything about them. When he found out that they had left First Creek, he wondered where they could have gone and why they had left. Jim didn't know of Soso's visit to John Gibson's house or about the false message the settlers had told Clear Dawn about Jim not wanting to see the Indians. This deception left Jim confused about why his good friends had suddenly left him. He worried for their safety.

Jim considered returning to Albany for good, but instead he decided to restart his life again in Great Sodus. He loved the beauty and challenges of the frontier. He just couldn't leave the bay and lake he loved. Jim negotiated with Captain Williamson to buy one of the small lots in the village on the shore of the bay. He then set about to clear the land and build a small wooden cabin. He also started fishing again. He repaired the small canoe that he and Soso had used. Remembering all that he had been taught by the Indians, he was able to catch enough fish in just a couple of hours a day to feed many of the people of the small but growing village of around sixty settlers. This year instead of giving away his fish, he started to sell or trade them to the other settlers for the household and business items that he needed. Jim had started a successful small business as the village fisherman. He had a new beginning, but still he wondered about the strange occurrences the year before. What had happened to his friend, Soso?

By the fall of 1795, Great Sodus had developed into a busy little village. The roads, more accurately described as improved trails, to the neighboring settlements in Lyons and Palmyra, were complete, and traffic in the form of horse-riders or walkers traveled on these rugged highways on an almost daily basis. In many places the trails were just wide enough for wagons or stagecoaches, but that didn't stop the settlers who were ready for frontier life. There was a nice, well-stocked general store and a small, but busy tavern. The businesses included a blacksmith, a shoemaker, and Jim's fishing operation. Many of the lots in the village had been cleared of the huge trees that had occupied this land for hundreds of years. It was beginning to look like a civilized community. Several sawmills and gristmills were ready for operation. A well-kept street ran by the homes and businesses in the village and ended at the waterfront where several boat docks were built. After all, this was just the beginning of what was being planned for the village by Captain Williamson and the other operators of the Pultney Estates. Captain Williamson had good reason to be proud of his beginning efforts to develop Great Sodus. If only its growth could match its beauty, it would soon develop into a booming, prosperous city.

The operators of the Pultney Estate envisioned Great Sodus as the hub of business in western New York State. They dreamed of the large well-protected harbor as the finest port of commerce on Lake Ontario. They all knew that Great Sodus was destined to become a great city that was why the name, Great, was always used. Pultney Estates had plans to manage and control the growth and development of Great Sodus. Its prosperity and eventual growth into a large city seemed certain, and several people were willing to bet their future on Great Sodus.

Captain Williamson had been elected to the New York State Assembly representing the western frontier and through that position he began an advertising campaign to encourage and support more settlers to move into the region. He also continued to ensure the current residents were satisfied and well-provided for. His gifts to the village and its residents included building equipment, tools, livestock, lumber, public water wells, and even a small fishing boat for the settlers to share. He financed several sawmills and gristmills that were being built on creeks and rivers in the region.

The Choice

Soso, Clear Dawn, and other the Indians living in the small village with them had an uneventful winter. Despite the lack of able-bodied braves, the villagers managed to obtain enough food to survive the cold winter. Soso, as chief provider for the village, led several successful hunting parties that brought venison into the village. There was also always plenty of fresh or dried fish thanks to Soso.

The coming of spring brought new hope for the Indians in the village. However, this hope was short-lived. Officials of the American government and soldiers from the Army came to the small village to meet with Fish Carrier. The Indians were going to have to move again, this time to a small reservation, which would hold all the Cayugas remaining in New York. Fish Carrier would be the chief of the village, but the new laws of the whites of America would be enforced on the reservation. The reservation was not on the water, but in a marshy area several miles north of Cayuga lake, and the fishing and hunting opportunities for the Indians on the reservation would be limited. The government promised some food, general supplies, farming tools, and protection. The Indians were expected to farm for their sustenance and to obey their white leaders.

Like the other Cayugas, Soso and Clear Dawn faced a decision about where to live. Both had little desire to move onto a reservation away from water. From what they had heard, life on the reservations in Canada was not what they wanted. Their only other alternative was to find a remote area to live where no one would bother them or to buy land of their own from the white men. Soso still had some of the American money that he had earned when he worked on the road construction crew two years before. Although it was a start, Soso was sure it was not enough to buy land. The two of them agreed to stake their future on a return to Great Sodus to try to find a camp in a remote area along the bay or lake to live on. They hoped the white men would not bother them there and that eventually they would make enough money to buy some land of their own. Maybe there they could again obtain the respect and friendship of the whites. Considering the alternatives, it was certainly worth a try. At least they would be back on the bay that they both loved. Soso couldn't wait to go. Clear Dawn saw it as another opportunity for her son to take on the new challenges of the modern world. They sorely missed the beautiful, silvery waters of Osoenodus Bay and the vast, dazzling waters of huge Lake Ontario. They both happily agreed to this risky, but exciting adventure.

Soso and Clear Dawn again traveled along the Indian trail to Sodus Bay hauling all that they owned with them. They carried a small elm bark canoe filled with their fishing equipment and their clothes. Four days later they found themselves on the hill overlooking the south shore of the bay. Once they saw the waters of the majestic Sodus Bay, they both knew that they had made the right decision to return. The beauty of the silvery waters of the bay enthralled the two Indians once again.

Their first task was to find a place to live. Soso began by scouting around the bay to find a remote, preferably hidden, location for their new home site. They intended to stay away from white men as long as they could. Clear Dawn dragged the canoe down to a marshy area near Second Creek, built a temporary camp there, and tried to catch some fish for supper.

Homecoming

Soso went west toward First Creek where his old home had been. He walked past the spot on the south shore of the bay where he first saw Jim and the three other white men who had helped the Indians in the capsized canoe. Next he reached First Creek where he had lived just two summers earlier. There were two new cabins near the burned remains of the cabin that Soso and Jim had built. He stayed a good distance from these new homes so that the occupants would not discover him. Soso remembered his last encounter with the villagers of Great Sodus and was unsure of the type of reception he would receive if he met any of the whites that he knew face-to-face. He saw and stopped by the gravesite of his grandfather Trout, and all the horror of that terrible day returned. Maybe there were evil spirits. He finally forced himself to travel further up First Creek and found the sawmill and salt factory of Nathan Sargent in full operation. Again Soso kept his distance.

Soso decided not to travel any closer to Great Sodus. He realized that this area was already too congested for his purposes and liking. Any possible home site would have to be found on the east side of the bay. Soso returned along the same path he came on, eventually finding Clear Dawn at the camp near Second Creek. He briefly helped Clear Dawn complete the building of a small shelter before continuing along the shore to the east. He first considered a location near Briscoe Point and Briscoe Cove, but this area was too visible to the white men who fished and trapped in the region to be suitable for the Indians' new home. Similarly, he realized that too many white men frequented Hunter's Point and Third Creek. He also found a couple of cabins and boats up near the head of the bay, so he crossed the shallow water passage through the vast marsh area at the head of the bay and went north along the east side of the bay.

At first, Soso considered the possibility of living on one of the three large islands of the bay. But as he stood on the shore across from Loga Island, he could see evidence of some settlement there and a new building was being erected near the narrows between Neoga and Loga islands. By process of elimination, the only area Soso found close enough to water, yet remote enough for the Indians, was on the east side of the bay, across from the south end of Neoga Island. There was a small cove hidden behind a point, which seemed ideal for his new home. To insure their privacy in every direction, Soso went inland for quite a distance and couldn't find any signs of settlers, since this area was mostly swamp. He determined that this location would not be in any white man's way. With vigilance and a little luck, they should be able to hide there for a long time.

Soso couldn't wait to tell Clear Dawn about his findings. In fact, in his haste to return to notify his mother, he didn't notice the small fishing boat sitting just off the shore at the Pork Barrel. Soso would have been very interested in recognizing its occupant, because it was his friend Jim Davis. As he often did, Jim was fishing just 300 yards off shore at his favorite spot. Similarly, Jim was too busy working his fishing line to notice the Indian brave run along the wood line near the shore on the way back toward Second Creek. The old friends, Soso and Jim, were just 300 yards apart, but they were completely unaware of each other's presence.

Soso returned to the temporary shelter at dusk. Clear Dawn was cleaning several bass that she had caught, and the two Indians cooked and ate their meal on the shore of the bay they loved. They spent the evening talking about the new home they would build and all the fish they would catch. It was an exciting time for the two Indians. Soso even wondered whether he would meet his old friend, Jim, again. Both of the Indians, mother and son, were happy to return to Sodus Bay yet apprehensive of what the future might bring. They were confident in their own abilities, but, with good reason, they still wondered how the whites would treat them.

Homestead

The next day dawned bright and beautiful. It was an exceptionally warm day for April. The wind was still, and the bay was completely flat without any ripples. The morning sun reflected off the mirror-like bay, and everything glowed brightly from its rays. The two Indians loaded their canoe with all their belongings and paddled directly toward the rising sun. Soso could feel simultaneously the deep warmth of the sun and the deep chill of the cold water as he traveled toward his new home. Orenda, the good fortune from the Creator, was again with Soso and Clear Dawn. Osoenodus was once again their home.

Despite their slow pace in paddling the overloaded canoe, they reached the cove in less than an hour. Soso knew exactly where he wanted to build the cabin. The location would completely hide the cabin from view from the water, yet it was only fifty yards from the cove. Clear Dawn agreed with Soso's selection, and the two immediately began clearing the land and building a small cabin. The structure would consist of two log sides, much like a log cabin, two sides of animal hide, and a roof of bark and dried leaves, much like a longhouse. After seven days of hard work they had completed the structure. Each day Soso took a break from the construction work just long enough to fish for the day's meals. The house had room for a cooking area in the middle and sleeping areas on two of the sides.

They were proud of their new home and were ready to start fulfilling the rest of their dreams. The two Indians felt the orenda, and it gave them great spirit. The Creator, through the beauty and splendor of Sodus Bay, had restored their energy and enthusiasm.

They still hoped to somehow find their missing family members, Perch and Water Lily. Almost daily, Clear Dawn and Soso asked the spirits for help in that endeavor, but, sometimes, Soso doubted that the spirits would be able to deliver on such a difficult feat. He began to question the power of the spirits, but not of nature itself. He could plainly see nature's considerable work, but in his eyes there was little evidence that the other spirits were at work. Soso secretly hoped for his father's return as well, but he knew that his mother didn't share that desire. She never allowed him to talk about his father, Gar, or to mention his name to her at all. Also, he would never question the role of the spirits to his mother. She was deeply spiritual and always credited the spirits with the circumstances of her and Soso's lives.

Clear Dawn selected a spot for a vegetable garden. She had plenty of corn seeds, but she had been able to obtain only a few squash and bean seeds before she left the Indian village. Her garden area needed only four medium-sized trees to be cleared out before the ground could be worked and sufficient sun would reach her plants. Soso cleared the trees in a couple of days, and the Indians began working the soil in hopes of a plentiful harvest of vegetables during the late summer and fall.

Soso began making plans for providing the rest of their food, in particular, meat and fish. He knew that he would have no trouble catching plenty of fish. He also wanted to hunt for deer and trap beaver. He realized that a bigger canoe and other new fishing equipment would have to be made to continue good fishing for next year. First, he went inland to check the deer hunting grounds. He knew that this area would be harder to hunt than the lands near Cayuga Lake. There were fewer bears, fox, and wolves, but that didn't bother Soso. He preferred to hunt for deer, but there were also fewer signs of deer, and now he had no one to help drive the deer in the manner that he was used to hunting. His first few hunts produced no kills, but it was more important for now that he was learning the habits of the deer in the area. There was plenty of fish to eat now, and venison wouldn't be needed until the late fall and winter when the fish were more difficult to catch.

While Clear Dawn worked on the garden, Soso began fishing and trapping Sodus Bay again. It was as if he had never left. He caught fish around the islands and near the east shore. He trapped muskrat and beaver in the cove and along Neoga Island. He was careful not to venture too far from his home and tried to avoid discovery by any white man. During the summer, he saw only a few whites in boats or canoes on the east side of the bay, and he always managed to keep a safe distance from them or to hide along the shore until they passed. Soso wished he could risk communication with the whites because he wanted to trade with someone for the items he needed. He could have used trapping and fishing equipment such as metal hooks,

metal beaver traps, fishing spears, and fishing line. Clear Dawn also wanted better cooking utensils and metal pots like the one she had when she
lived as neighbors with the white trappers and hunters on First Creek.
However, neither Indian wanted to risk their still tenuous position by meeting with any whites. The activities of this summer had made their lives
enjoyable again, and time passed quickly. For now, they remained happy
and thankful for what they did have.

Hunting

There were two times during the year when catching fish on Sodus Bay
was difficult for Soso. The periods of freezing and thawing of ice in the fall
and spring, respectively, made travel on the bay treacherous and fishing
practically impossible except in the small area of open water near the bay's
outlet to the lake. However, even in that area the fishing was never very
good during those periods. Therefore, for a short time each fall and spring,
Soso would have to hunt for deer instead of fishing. Once the bay was
frozen thick enough to walk on, it was possible to fish through the ice during the rest of the winter. Soso had some trouble chopping holes through
the thick ice because of his poor equipment for that task, but he still preferred ice fishing over having to hunt for meat.

Soso had prepared himself well for the fall deer hunt. He had studied
the habits of the deer in the area near his cabin. On the first day that icing
in the cove prevented Soso from launching his canoe and going fishing, he
decided to hunt for deer. Actually, the fall's hunt was over almost before it
started. He had noticed a deer run from the east down to the shoreline
across from Neoga Island. His plan was to go along the shore to the deer
run and then follow it to the east. However, when he approached the inter-
section of the run and the shoreline, he found his prey waiting for him. Two
large deer, a ten-point buck and a large doe, had attempted to cross the thin
ice from the east shore to Neoga Island and had broken through the ice less
than 25 yards from shore. The two deer were struggling in vain to get back
onto the shelf of ice, but the ice was just too thin to support their weight.
Soso with his keen sense of nature felt the misery and futility of the deer.
However, he had no choice but to seize upon the opportunity to end their
misery and complete his hunt. His two arrows quickly found their mark,
and the struggling ended. In order to retrieve the deer, he carefully crawled

out on the ice shelf and looped a rope around the animals' heads. One at a time, he cautiously pulled them ashore.

Clear Dawn was surprised to see Soso return just a little over an hour after his departure with two dressed out deer. The meat would be enough to keep the Indians fed for several weeks of the winter. The meat usually kept well in the freezing weather of December and January at Sodus Bay. Great orenda was flowing into their lives.

Preparations

The cold days of December and January eventually brought a thick layer of ice covering almost all of Sodus Bay. Soso had fished through ice before, but this year he intended to perfect his ice-fishing techniques. He wanted to supply Clear Dawn with plenty of fresh perch and pike to supplement the venison and fruits and vegetables in their diets. Each day Soso would fish just long enough to catch what was necessary for that day's meals. When he was through, he worked in a small shed that he had constructed in the fall just 100 feet from the house. There he was trying to build canoes and boats, which he hoped to sell or trade to white men in the spring. Soso still had the dream of owning land so that no one could make him move again. He reasoned that by selling boats and canoes he might be able to earn enough money to buy land. Clear Dawn worked just as hard clearing land for their garden and improving their house.

Soso was building three deep, wide, heavy canoes that not only could go on the bay, but also could take the rough waves of the lake. He planned to keep one of the canoes for himself in order to fish on the lake next year. He was also building a flat-bottomed boat similar to the one he remembered Jim had used. Soso didn't have the tools or equipment that a white professional boat maker would have. However, he was able to use the Indian techniques of carving, digging out logs, and fastening with fibers that Trout had taught him. He carefully chose the best soft pine logs he could find to use in these boats. Soso realized that harder wood would make better boats, but he was constrained by his lack of tools and fasteners. By necessity, he worked every available minute. Determined to build these boats by spring, he slept just a few hours before getting up in advance of sunrise to start work again. Amazingly, all three canoes and the boat were completed by the end of the winter. More amazingly, they were built as well as any boat on the bay. Soso only hoped that he would have the opportunity to sell or trade them to white men in the spring. He liked this kind of work, and the winter passed by quickly for both Soso and Clear Dawn.

Soso and Clear Dawn agreed that when spring arrived, they would come out of hiding in order to make contact with whites to try to sell or trade the canoes and boat. On just his third day of fishing after the ice broke up in the spring, Soso saw two white fishermen in a small canoe near Kenoga Island. The wind was blowing hard out of the west so the men were fishing in the calm waters on the east side of the island. He carefully watched these two men to determine if it would be safe to talk with them. He went ashore on the mainland and hid in the bushes across from Kenoga Island. Soso watched the two of them fish for the entire day without catching a single fish. He also discovered that the small canoe they were using leaked badly because one of the men had to bail out a considerable amount of water every several minutes.

The two men returned to the same spot the next two days with nearly the same results. On the last day, they did manage to catch two small trout. Soso sensed that they were friendly men—inexperienced but dedicated fishermen. They had kept their sense of humor and patience during their long, unproductive days of fishing. They often laughed at one another's jokes and even stayed good-natured when the leaky canoe filled with water and nearly capsized because they had forgot to bail it out.

The Sale

After three days of watching these men, Soso decided to trust them and made plans to approach them the next day if they returned. Later the next morning, Soso traveled north along the east side of the bay fighting a strong crosswind to reach the protection of the island. As he approached the island, he saw the two men faithfully fishing in the same spot, so Soso continued his progress right toward them. In the narrow passage between the island and the shore, Soso's small canoe had to pass within fifty yards of the fishermen, who were still in their small, leaky canoe. At first, the two men looked surprised and a bit apprehensive about seeing the Indian brave approaching, but they both waved and gave Soso a warm greeting. Soso stopped his canoe near the fishermen and cautiously began talking with them. It had been quite some time since he had talked with a white man.

But he had practiced using the words often with Clear Dawn. He hoped the men would understand him.

"Are you from Great Sodus?" Soso asked.

"Yes, settled there last summer. We work for the fish market during the summer and cut ice during the winter," the bearded fisherman named Sam answered. Sam was a bit surprised and pleased to hear the Indian speak English. This calmed his fears a little. Then he asked Soso, "Where you from? I've never seen any Indians around Great Sodus before."

"I live on the east side of the bay," Soso responded and then quickly tried to change the subject. "How's the fishing?"

The three men continued their discussion with remarks on the status of each other's fishing. Soso didn't use his name, just referring to himself as a boat-builder. The two men mentioned that they had caught only two fish in three days of fishing and their boss was getting a bit angry at their failures. Soso advised them on where and how they could catch some early season trout and gave them the five nice trout that he had already caught earlier that morning near his cove. Soso noticed that the canoe they were using was too small for fishing and very poorly built. So he took the opportunity to ask, "Do you need a bigger canoe?"

"Yeah. This old canoe is owned by the fish market. The boss is going to have new canoes and boats built when he gets some money. We've sure been having trouble with this canoe leaking pretty bad in rough water. She capsized on us about ten times last fall. We thought we had the leaks fixed, but it's still leaking just as bad as it did last year."

Soso pursued the possibility of a sale by asking, "Do you think your boss would like to look at canoes and a boat I have built?"

"Might be. Our boss is coming out fishing tomorrow with us. Why don't you ask him then?" answered Carl, the fisherman without the beard.

"I'll see you tomorrow then," Soso said, as he began to paddle north toward the sand bar where he wanted to check some traps that he had set and look at the condition of the lake. Soso found nothing in his traps and a rough, swollen lake with lots of ice still built up in mounds along the shore, but he spent the time to catch a couple trout on the bay side of the sand bar before returning home.

He was very excited as he told Clear Dawn all about his meeting with the white fishermen. The two Indians made their plans for the next morning. They would take the new boat and one of the new canoes down to

Kenoga Island in the morning and wait for the boss of the fishermen. The boat and canoe were finished and ready for sale, but one thing still bothered Soso as they made their plans for the next day. He had very little knowledge or understanding of the white's money system. He still had money from working on the road construction crew several years before, but he had no idea what it was worth. He, like most Indians, understood trading, and although the money he already had was worth value, to him it seemed worthless. He had seen the adults in his tribe use wampum. But money with numbers and symbols was very confusing. How could you trust such a system? How could you be sure your money would always be worth value? How did you set a fair price on something like a boat or canoe?

Jim had taken care of Soso's money matters. Jim used to tell him not to spend the money unless Jim was with him and could explain its worth. Soso had no idea how much money to sell the boat and canoe for or what they were worth in trade. He wanted to get money because he realized that money was needed to buy land. He also wanted to trade several furs for some of the hunting and fishing equipment he needed. Soso wished that Jim was still around to help him learn about money and other ways of the whites. Jim would know how much to charge for the boat and canoes.

Soso and Clear Dawn awakened early the next morning. They wanted to get the boat and canoe to Kenoga Island early so that the owner of the fish market could look at them both. They left their cove before sunrise. Clear Dawn paddled the big canoe, and Soso rowed the boat which was towing his older small canoe. Soso brought the small canoe along to fish in during the day, while the boat and canoe for sale were kept clean and ready on shore. Besides, he hoped to sell both boats and would need a way to get back home.

Soso and Clear Dawn pulled the boat and canoe onto shore at the south end of Kenoga Island. Then they began fishing on the west side of the island close to shore. Soso kept one eye looking to the west toward Great Sodus hoping to see the fishermen as they came across the bay.

Reunion

The sun rose high in the sky as the two Indians continued to fish. They became increasingly anxious as time passed. They were having a good day fishing, both caught several trout by noon, but they were more concerned about selling the boats. Finally, Soso noticed two small canoes slowly approaching from the west. After a while he could recognize the two fishermen that he had met, Sam and Carl, in the lead canoe. The other canoe with only one person was going a little slower. As Carl and Sam approached near to Soso and Clear Dawn, they yelled their greetings.

"Sorry we didn't get here earlier, but we had to fish up near First Creek for perch this morning. We got the boss to come look at your boats, though."

"Glad to see you come. I hope he…" Soso stopped in mid-sentence. His face lit up as he recognized the fishermen's boss in the other canoe. It was Jim Davis.

Jim saw Soso and Clear Dawn at almost the same time. He yelled for joy and almost jumped out of his canoe. The two fishermen sat bewildered as their boss and the two Indians greeted and hugged one another like long-lost relatives. It took several minutes of excitement and craziness before the three old friends could explain to the two bystanders the reason for their happiness. The two fishermen had heard many stories from Jim about his Indian friend Soso, but they had no idea that this boat builder could have been him. As they slowly paddled the three canoes back toward the end of Kenoga Island, Soso began to relate the story of his last three years to Jim.

"After the Indian attack, I tried to see you at John Gibson's house, but they wouldn't let me in the house. Other settlers told Clear Dawn we were no longer wanted in Great Sodus, so we returned to our old Cayuga village for the rest of the winter. Last year, men from the American government were forcing all Indians to live on a reservation. We came to Sodus Bay instead. We have been living in a cabin we built on a cove on the east side of the bay for the last year. During all this time, we've never heard anything about Perch or Water Lily, who were kidnapped during the raid. Trout died from his wounds, and I buried him over by First Creek."

Jim was completely puzzled by Soso's story. He never knew that the villagers of Great Sodus had forced his two Indian friends to leave town. Jim then told Soso about his last three years. "I'm real sorry to hear about your family. I recovered from my wounds after several weeks and went looking for you. No one seemed to know where you had gone. I decided to stay in Great Sodus and build a home there. I bought some land near the tavern, married Karen, and now have a baby girl named Hannah. Carl and

Sam work for me in our fishing business. We sell fish and ice to the villagers of Great Sodus and even travel to other nearby villages."

"Jim, it is a great comfort to see you and know that we are still friends."

"Yes. I have thought about you and Clear Dawn every day since that terrible day of the raid." The two old friends continued to catch up on the news of their lives over the last three years. Then the subject changed.

"Wait until you see the boat and canoe I've built." Soso was anxious to show Jim his work.

Jim took one look at the boat Soso had built and could not believe his eyes. It was just like the one he used to have. Unfortunately, Jim's old boat had capsized and was destroyed in a storm on the lake the previous fall. Jim decided that the best way to test out the new boat was for him and Soso to take it out fishing on the lake. Jim was sure that this would interest his friend Soso, whom he knew loved to fish in the deep rough water of Lake Ontario. Jim and Soso rowed toward the lake's outlet, while Clear Dawn, Carl, and Sam stayed near Kenoga Island to continue fishing.

The new boat handled the chop on the lake just fine. The two friends stopped their rowing and began fishing off the shore of the Chimney Bluffs. It was like old times. The friendship had survived their tragic separation. They caught several trout in just an hour or two of fishing. Then they returned to Kenoga Island to meet with the others. Carl and Sam went back to Great Sodus rowing the new boat, which pulled their canoe and all the fish. Jim, Clear Dawn, and Soso returned with three canoes back to the Indians' cabin. As instructed, Carl and Sam told Karen the news of Jim finding Soso and Clear Dawn and that Jim would return with the Indians to Great Sodus in the morning.

The three friends spent that evening at the Indians' house celebrating their reunion. Soso related his and Clear Dawn's search for a place to live, and Jim told them all about Great Sodus, his family, and his fishing business. Jim asked Soso and Clear Dawn to come live with him at Great Sodus and work in his fishing business. Jim felt certain he could get Captain Williamson to sell Soso some land in Great Sodus. However, neither Soso nor Clear Dawn was sure they wanted to leave their new home on the east side of the bay. They liked the isolation and quiet there and still didn't know what to expect in Great Sodus. In any case, Soso agreed to fish with Jim again. Actually, from that moment on, the two men decided to become business partners. Soso would be in charge of fishing, and Jim would be in charge of marketing the fish and as well as other operations of the business. It was an evening of tremendous joy and exciting dreams. Soso was thankful for the opportunities that the spirits had brought him. He hoped to make the best of them.

During the next day, the three of them took two of Soso's big new canoes to Great Sodus. They pulled the canoes ashore near Jim's fish market and home. Several people, including Jim's family, Carl, and Sam were there awaiting their arrival. Soso recognized several faces in the group from his days in Great Sodus. John Gibson, William Wickham, and Frank North were there and welcomed Soso and Clear Dawn back to Great Sodus. There were several others whom Soso did not recognize. The new faces were those of new settlers who had arrived in the village during the last three years. Soso and Clear Dawn were very surprised at the village itself. They saw many new homes, roads, and businesses that weren't there just three years earlier. As predicted, Great Sodus was growing and prospering. They met Jim's baby daughter, Hannah, and wife, Karen. Karen was eager to meet Soso and Clear Dawn since she had heard so much about them from Jim. Jim's house and fish market were well-built structures since Jim had constantly improved them over the past couple of years. Soso and Clear Dawn were amazed by all the changes. They found an improved village of Great Sodus. More importantly, they felt welcome.

Those whom they knew before greeted Soso and Clear Dawn very kindly. There seemed to be no hostility left from the incident of three years before. In many ways, it was as if nothing bad had ever happened. Time had healed most of the wounds of that terrible tragedy of November, 1794. However, those who lost loved ones, like Soso and Clear Dawn, could never forget. Trout had died; Perch and Water Lily had been taken away from them. For those kinds of wounds, even large amounts of time could never completely heal them.

Business

During that afternoon, Jim held an informal business meeting with Soso, Clear Dawn, Karen, Carl, and Sam. Despite their kind reception in Great Sodus, Soso and Clear Dawn had decided to stay at their home on the east side of the bay rather than move to Great Sodus as Jim had suggested. However, both of them would work in the fishing business. Soso would be in charge of the fishing operations, and Sam and Clear Dawn would help him fish. Karen would sell fish from the market in Great Sodus. That way she could care for Hannah, who was an active one-year-old toddler, full of considerable energy and a little mischief. Carl would help process the fish by filleting, smoking, salting, and icing them, and he would also deliver them to the farms in the area and to the citizens of the neighboring villages of Lyons and Sodus. Jim was going to oversee all parts of the business, while personally trying to spend some time fishing with Soso, Clear Dawn, and Sam.

Jim had another job that was going to keep him rather busy that summer of 1797. He had been hired by Captain Williamson to be the captain and caretaker of the luxury yacht that had been built for use on the bay. It was an exquisite boat—22' long, sleek with a tall single mast. It could hold six to eight people comfortably. Captain Williamson was going to use it to entertain prospective settlers and investors in Great Sodus. The yacht was sitting on shore next to Jim's dock and was ready for launching on the next day, so Clear Dawn and Soso decided to spend the night at Jim's house in Great Sodus to see the launching and maiden voyage of the wonderful boat. Soso was fascinated with the smooth and sleek design and precise workmanship of this magnificent sailboat. The boat had been built in New York City and assembled and rigged at Great Sodus, at enormous expense, under the supervision of the builder from the city.

A large crowd gathered near the village dock the next day to see the launching of the yacht. Captain Williamson and several dignitaries from the Pultney Estate were on hand for the ceremonies and ready to take the maiden voyage. A big cheer went up as the boat slid down the planks into the silvery waters of Sodus Bay. Soso was amazed at the way the boat rode in the water. It seemed perfectly balanced, and when Jim put up the resplendent heavy-cloth sail for the first trip around the bay, Soso watched in amazement. He had never seen anything travel as smoothly or as fast. Soso was among the crowd that stayed for several hours to watch the sleek yacht cruise round and round the bay. Jim was also enthralled by the boat. He knew from the start that he was going to enjoy his new duty of sailing the boat for Captain Williamson.

Visitors

It just so happened that there was another spectator in the crowd that day who would someday have considerable influence on Soso and Jim. He was a visitor named Dr. William Lummis. A well-dressed, well-educated young man from Philadelphia, he was respected as a fine doctor and gentleman in his city. However, William was growing tired of city life, especially its stuffy social events and crowded existence. He was in Great Sodus on vacation with the additional motive to look for a new place to live and work. He longed for a quiet rural life, and he certainly could find that in Great Sodus. His vacation was taking him throughout western and central New York, where he was looking at potential places to move. The things that he would remember most about Great Sodus Bay were the beauty of its silvery waters as the yacht sailed its course around the bay and the well laid out streets of the village that showed signs of good planning by the developers.

During the summer of 1797 there were several other visitors to Great Sodus and its surrounding region. Some came in response to advertising by the Pultney Estate, while others were just following the new roads that led through the region on their western migration for open land and freedom. The majestic natural beauty of its bay impressed those that came to Great Sodus. Nevertheless, it seemed that only a very few of the visitors actually settled in the village. Despite Captain Williamson's attempts to civilize the area and to develop its villages, this was still the harsh, spartan frontier of civilization. There were very few of the amenities of eastern city life in Great Sodus. The age of enlightenment that modernized the culture of England and the northeast cities of America seemed to have no effect on the lifestyles of the residents of the western frontier. Life was rough in nearly every respect. The houses were mostly small and crudely built because of lack of building materials. Simple but important items, like the whale oil to keep lanterns lit, were always in short supply. There were never enough items like cloth to make clothes and bedding. Culture and luxury, except for Captain Williamson's yacht, were virtually nonexistent. Residents suffered not only the hardships of frontier life, but also the continual threats and rumors of hostile Indian and British invasion. It seemed as if Captain Williamson's dream of prosperity for Great Sodus would take much longer than he or his employers had originally thought. By 1797, they had planned that Great Sodus would be well on its way to living up to its name. In reality, it was far from it.

Soso, Jim, and Clear Dawn fished and enjoyed the summer of 1797. Their strong friendship was rekindled. Soso and Clear Dawn continued to learn and appreciate the civilized ways of the whites. They made new friends and were again accepted into the village of Great Sodus. It was a remarkable summer for these close friends. None of them minded the lack of progress and growth of the area. They thoroughly enjoyed the open spaces and clear waters of the bay and lake.

New Resident

On a hot day in June, a wealthy English gentleman, William Helms, arrived at Great Sodus with his family and an entourage of over seventy slaves. He had been living in Virginia for a few years and had decided to move north to find a better life and to build a large plantation. They had traveled by Pennsylvania wagon from Virginia and were hoping to settle on a prime location on the Genesee River. A miscalculation on the route at Phelps, however, had brought them to Sodus Bay instead. Helms and his family checked into Sill's tavern while he scouted out the area. At first he was upset over the miscalculation, thinking that it had cost him several days of travel time. His large entourage traveled very slowly. However, one trip around the bay in Captain Williamson's yacht convinced him it had been his good fortune to have gotten lost and in doing so to have found the impressive area of Great Sodus.

Helms fell in love with the bay and the region. The area he found most to his liking was on the east side, just about a half-mile north of Soso's cabin near the head of the bay. He negotiated a fair price for the 128 acres of land in lots 112 and 114 of the Pultney Estates and became the first white settler and major land owner on the east side of the bay. Soso would have a rich, racist slave-owner for a neighbor.

Helms immediately put his slaves to work clearing the land. However, this type of heavy labor was not what his slaves were used to doing. They had been used to picking crops on southern plantations. Many of his slaves became ill, and some died of the combination of hard work, excessive abuse, and poor medical care during the first summer. The cold winter weather was even worse on the slaves' health. But the brutality of Helms toward his slaves was the cause of most of their health problems. He whipped and tortured them for minor infractions of his strict rules. It was no wonder that many of his slaves fled from his plantation whenever the opportunity arose and many others died before they had a chance to escape.

Helms had other problems. Due to lack of seeds, he was able to plant only a little corn and grain during the first summer. Most of that didn't grow. Luckily, there were plenty of fish and deer in the area. Because he didn't allow his slaves to hunt or fish, he had to buy his fish from Soso and Jim and his venison from other hunters. They were happy to sell fish and meat to Soso's new neighbor. Helms also bought two of Soso's canoes and ordered two new boats from Soso for spring delivery. Helms' attempt to build a majestic plantation on Sodus Bay was a failure from the very start. However, despite his loss of large amounts of money and wealth, Helms and his relatives loved the area and stayed for many years on the east side of Sodus Bay. He may not have built the vast plantation that he had dreamed of, but he did have a nice comfortable homestead on the spectacular bay that he now loved. Partly due to constant prodding from Soso and Jim, Helms eventually freed all of his slaves. That act alone seemed to help him become a happier, healthier man, and, eventually, a respected citizen of Sodus Bay.

The summer was very successful for Soso and Jim. Their business was doing well in all areas. Soso always caught plenty of fish of all types even when other fishermen were unsuccessful. Like his grandfather, Trout, he knew just where and how to fish. Sam had learned well from Soso and was fast becoming an excellent fisherman. Jim had established a growing market throughout the area. Everyone seemed to want to buy fish from Jim. Every day, many pounds of fish were sold directly from their market in Great Sodus, and even more were delivered inland by Carl and Jim. Everyone admired the canoes and rowboat that Soso had built. Soso had orders for several more with delivery in the spring. Soso was going to have plenty of boat-building work to do over the winter in order to complete all the orders. This time Soso would have much better equipment and materials to build the new boats. He spent much of his summer fishing and dreaming of the enjoyment that he would have building boats over the winter. He selected the best white oak trees for most of the planking and several tall, straight white pine trees for the masts. He carefully cut enough wood for several boats. Soso had hopes of building boats for a good long time.

Hunting

Before winter arrived, Jim and Soso took a break from fishing to pursue another activity, duck hunting. The two men were expert marksmen who had taken the time to learn the habits of the migratory visitors. In the late fall when the skies became crowded with ducks and geese, they would place out on the water hand-made floating duck decoys and hide along the shore. As the ducks and geese came into the decoys, the two shooters would take aim with their crude, but functional flintlocks. It took enormous expertise to hit the fast moving birds with these inaccurate and heavy firearms. This was much more difficult than fishing, but the two men would never miss their duck hunts. They had hunted together several times before. The intense hunting and shooting usually only lasted two or three weeks, but it was always productive. The demand for wild ducks and geese was high, and Soso and Jim sold their harvest at top prices. William Helms was especially fond of wild duck and had a standing order to purchase at a fair price any ducks that Soso and Jim cared to sell.

Another rewarding part of hunting was the camaraderie and communication the two men shared as they patiently waited for their next migratory visitors. They told stories, taught each other details of their own languages, talked about the customs and culture of their people, and developed their own frontier philosophies.

The Hunt

The arrangement of the decoys was an important task, and one of great debate between the two men. The flocks of ducks were quite sensitive to any decoy that was either of out place or acting strangely as it bobbed in the water. Soso and Jim made sure every one of their carefully carved and painted decoys was set out perfectly before settling into the blind to wait for the first arrivals. This day's hunt, on the end of Kenoga Island, was no different.

"The last decoy is out too far and is swinging too far along its line. Shorten up the line and bring it in some," Jim suggested to Soso, whom Jim knew didn't agree with that assessment.

"It looks fine to me. The first flock will barrel right in on these decoys," Soso answered. "You'd better get ready for some fast shooting."

"Well, it's near light now anyway. Let's get ready, but if that decoy scares the ducks away, you'll have to change it." Jim figured that they had argued long enough over the decoys and that it was time to start hunting.

Once the first flock came into range, the fun began. Depending on the direction of flight, the two men knew exactly when to shoot and which bird to shoot at. Way off in the distance, almost directly into the spectacular sunrise over the east shore of the bay, the two men could faintly see a big flock slowly heading over the sandbar and onto the bay. With luck, these ducks would come close enough to investigate the decoys. It was feeding time, and this hungry flock had left its night of sleeping on the lake. They were heading for the best available location for a breakfast feeding.

"Coming this way," Jim whispered.

"Flock of canvasbacks—they look big and hungry," Soso whispered back.

Jim worried over what he thought was the misplaced decoy. He teased his partner, "They're probably wondering what that stupid decoy is doing way out by itself. They'll break off in a second."

Soso was confident. "Quiet. Here they come."

Nothing was said until two loud and accurate shots broke the silence. The next sound was the distinctive plop of two dead ducks striking the water. Both men watched silently as the rest of the flock turned back out into the bay and flew away from the noise.

"Nice shooting," Jim congratulated Soso. "I guess I'd better go get these two beauties. They liked this spot so much, they didn't care how we set out the decoys." Jim wouldn't admit he was wrong, but there was no reason to change the decoys. It was time to continue the hunt and enjoy the spectacular day.

The entire day's hunt brought six flocks of ducks from ten to fifty into the two hunters' decoys. Total harvest for the day was eleven ducks, mostly bluebills and canvasbacks, although one flock each of redheads and buffleheads had come by and were added to the day's bag. It had been another enjoyable day on the bay with great orenda and success. The argument over the decoys was just part of their hunting ritual. Because of Jim and Soso's tremendous skills, the Helms family would have wild duck for dinner for the next couple of nights.

More Business

One problem in the fishing business was lack of ice to cool the fish and keep them fresh for a longer period of time. Ice was crucial for delivery of fresh fish to inland villages since transportation via horse and wagon was very slow. Jim, Carl, and Sam had cut hundreds of ice blocks from the bay the previous winter that now filled Jim's icehouse and several small ice caves. But the ice had lasted only to late August. Jim decided they needed a bigger and better insulated icehouse. Captain Williamson agreed to help finance part of the construction if Sill's tavern and other local businesses could also use the ice. Jim and Captain Williamson struck an agreement, and construction began in October. The new icehouse was more than twice as large as the old one, with thicker walls for better insulation and a big storage section dug deep into the side of the hill between Jim's house and the tavern to make use of the better natural insulation. The icehouse had a small vent opening in the roof to allow warmer air to escape, and the exposed front of the building was painted white to provide maximum reflection of the sunlight. To provide more insulation, the ice was packed in sawdust, which was brought in from the sawmill on First Creek. By the time ice began to form on the bay near the end of December, the icehouse was completely built and ready to receive the blocks of ice cut from the bay for storage. Jim, Carl, Sam, and workers from Sill's tavern were going to have a busy winter cutting ice trying to fill this huge icehouse.

Boat Building

Soso fished right up until the day the winter cold completed its thin, but firm ice cap of the bay. Then he turned over all the fishing duties of the business to Sam, Clear Dawn, and Jim. They would have to wait for a few days until enough ice formed to walk safely on top of the ice to fish. As planned, Soso spent the winter concentrating on his new job of building boats and canoes. He had definite orders for four boats and three canoes. That was a lot to do during the four months of winter, but Soso intended to put all his energies into the project. This year he had the significant benefit of using the white man's modern tools and equipment that he had bought from Wickham's general store or borrowed from Jim. He also had all his wood already prepared. Use of metal screws, nails, and fittings made his work much easier and the finished product much better. He truly enjoyed his carpentry work and intended to improve this year's vessels over those that he had made previously. During that winter Soso came to realize that he probably liked boat building even more than he liked fishing. It would turn out that he was as adept at boat building as he was at fishing.

Jim also had a similar experience during the previous summer. In taking care of the yacht and sailing it around the bay and lake for Captain Williamson, he realized that he enjoyed sailing as much as fishing. There was no one in Great Sodus who could put that yacht through its paces like Jim. He was a natural sailor and always enjoyed time at the helm of the sleek yacht.

The First Catch

Winter doesn't give up its grip on Great Sodus easily. During the months of March and April, the weather is unpredictable and often extreme. It can be sunny and warm one day and then cloudy, stormy, and cold the next day. The one constant element is the vast sheet of ice that sits over the bay. Even on the warmest, sunniest day in early April, the wind that blows across the frozen bay turns cold and biting. Then suddenly, in only a few minutes time, the ice covering the entire bay disappears completely as the thin, honeycombed sheet of ice gets blown onto the windward shore and crushed. It's on that day that you can finally say spring has come to Great Sodus. Because from that day on, the winds blow warmer, the waters feel soft and friendly, and the shoreline becomes alive with activity.

Every fisherman worth his salt tries to be the first of the spring with a load of fresh trout. So it was with Carl, Sam, Jim, Clear Dawn, and Soso in the spring of 1798. All five of them were fishing during the very afternoon of the day the ice went out. It was a warm, sunny day and by afternoon the wind that had pushed the ice away had died down considerably. Soso fished with Clear Dawn off Hunter's Point in one of the new boats he had built during the winter. Carl and Sam fished in their favorite spot near Kenoga Island. Jim took Karen and Hannah along on their first fishing trip of the spring. Karen wasn't all that fond of fishing, but she was happy to go with Jim a few times each year. They didn't go far, preferring to stay close to the shore of Sand Point just off the village itself. Hannah was two years old and enjoyed spending time in the boat. However, Hannah's energy level made for a hectic and nervous fishing trip for Jim and Karen. The water was extremely cold, and Hannah's parents tried in vain to keep her calm, bundled up, and warm.

It probably could have been easily predicted which of the three boats would bring in the largest catch of trout. Jim Davis and his family returned empty handed by early afternoon, having enjoyed their ride on the bay despite their lack of success at fishing. Hannah preferred the boat to be moving, instead of stopped in a fixed location to fish. This hampered Jim's fishing efforts, but he didn't mind, as long as he got to spend an enjoyable afternoon with his family. Carl and Sam returned at dusk with stories of several near misses but only one fish. Soso and Clear Dawn arrived at Jim's dock just after darkness set in with 20 big fresh trout. They were met by the others, who by this time were no longer surprised by Soso's fishing accomplishments. But there was one surprise at the dock when the two Indians landed their boat that evening. It was the beauty and workmanship of the boat that Soso had built during the winter. Everyone was amazed at the fine detail and style of this practical and efficient fishing boat. Jim was impressed with its sleek design; it was narrower, lighter, and longer than any boat previously built by Soso. Jim could see some of the structures and features from Captain Williamson's yacht in this new fishing boat. All there congratulated Soso on his accomplishment and adjourned to Jim's house to warm up and enjoy fried, grilled, and roasted trout, discussions about the upcoming fishing season, and stories about last year's season.

"Soso, your boat is designed like a pike, long and sleek. It almost looks too nice to use for fishing." Jim teased Soso as they relaxed from their afternoon on the water.

"I wanted to make it bigger and longer, so I could carry more fish. Just about reached its capacity today. Noticed that you didn't need a very big boat," Soso countered with a tease of his own.

Karen rescued her husband. "Hannah liked to keep moving. I think we had a hook in the water for a total of 10 minutes all day. Today we took a boat ride. Tomorrow Jim catches fish."

Since Karen rescued Jim, Soso let him off the hook. The two fishermen took their fishing competition seriously, especially on the first day of the season. Soso knew that Jim would have caught many more fish had he been alone. He also knew that it was important for Jim to spend time with his family. The teasing stopped, and the celebrating began—fishing season was here.

Good Business

Jim and Soso's fish business was much the same in the summer of 1798 as it had been the previous year. The new icehouse worked out well. There was ice available all the way into early October, and this enabled the fresh fish to be delivered to the neighboring villages throughout the summer and fall. Soso, Clear Dawn, and Sam caught enough fish to keep the business supplied with ample quantities of all varieties: trout, salmon, bass, perch, pike, sturgeon, whitefish, and catfish. Soso particularly liked catching the large sturgeon and the good-tasting whitefish from the deeper waters of the lake. Even though he was only eighteen years old, Soso was more than an experienced fisherman. He was an expert. In addition to his fishing talents, Soso was perfecting his shooting eye with the flintlock. No one spent as much time or as focused on learning how to accurately fire his flintlock as Soso. To Soso, practicing shooting the flintlock was as natural as practicing with a bow and arrow, something he had done almost daily for many years. No one thought of Soso as a teenager. To all his friends and acquaintances, he was a mature, responsible man.

The village of Great Sodus didn't change much in 1798 either. There were a few new settlers in the village and neighboring region. More trees were cleared in the village, and the two roads that ran through the village were improved by making them a bit wider and smoother. There did seem to be more people settling in some of the neighboring towns like Phelps, Palmyra, Clyde, Lyons, and Rochester. Captain Williamson kept making improvements in the area by building new roads, streets, and mills; improving and maintaining the old structures; and lending money to needy settlers and businessmen. Despite this help, several families decided to leave the frontier life in Great Sodus and return to the big cities in the east. Still others left to venture further to the west seeking more isolation and cheaper land than what they had at Great Sodus. The land at Great Sodus was more expensive than most other frontier land because of its tremendous potential. Many prospective settlers couldn't afford the extra cost or desired more farmland than what was available in the Great Sodus area. Elevated land costs plagued the area for many years, considerably restricting the growth along the shores of Great Sodus Bay. The average settler simply couldn't afford the difference in cost between the more expensive Great Sodus land lots and the land in the surrounding communities or further to the west. Many people didn't fully grasp the new concept of mortgages, interest rates, and inflation; so they still bought only what they knew they could afford. Unfortunately, for many, Great Sodus was out of their price range.

Soso spent time during the summer rebuilding and improving his and Clear Dawn's log cabin. Using nails that he bought from Wickham's store, he replaced the hide walls and straw and bark roof with solid wood. He already had some excellent carpentry tools that he had purchased earlier to help with the boat building. Soso was also learning all about the American money system from Jim. Although Jim still helped him purchase some of the items that he needed, Soso was beginning to understand the convenience and value of money. He was saving most of the money that he earned from the business to buy his plot of land. Captain Williamson was unaware or possibly uninterested in Soso's squatting in his home on Pultney Estate property, but, through the efforts of Jim, Captain Williamson had agreed to sell Soso the parcel of land. Soso's payment would have to be made in full at $3.50 per acre for the 40-acre parcel. Because Soso was a Native American, he was not allowed to borrow money from the Estate as many of the white settlers did. By the fall of 1798, Soso had saved almost $30, which he kept safely hidden in the walls of his cabin. He was well on his way to fulfilling his dream.

Tragedy

The winter of 1798 was extremely cold from the very start. Ice covered the bay by early December and the weather stayed cold and damp throughout the entire month. Jim, Carl, Sam, and a worker from Sill's tavern named Bob were harvesting thick blocks of ice for storage by the middle of December. Usually it was January or February before the ice was thick enough to harvest. No sooner had they started the demanding work when tragedy struck their operation. On the day before Christmas, while sawing an ice block, Bob fell through a hole in the ice and into the cold, nearly frozen water. He struggled to grab the ledge of ice but the weight of his clothes and the numbness in his frozen hands prevented him from pulling himself out of the water. Carl and Sam eventually heard Bob's cries for help and hurried over to the water hole to help rescue him. But they arrived too late. They could no longer see Bob. Carl and Sam dove into the freezing water but were unable to find him. The cold water numbed their hands and bodies, and after several minutes they were unable to continue their search. Jim arrived by wagon just in time to pull the two tired, frozen men from the water. He quickly took the shivering men back to his house.

Carl and Sam were in severe pain as their frozen limbs began to thaw. They had suffered frost-bite on their toes and ears, but a worse ordeal was yet to come. The next day, the two men were stricken with terrible fever. Carl had the worst of the disease from the start. There was no doctor in Great Sodus, so Jim and Karen cared for the stricken men in their home the best they could. The wives of the two men came over to Jim's house to help with their care. Carl's temperature was so high that Karen and Jim were never able to reduce it. After three days of delirium and hopeless struggle, Carl died.

Sam had a high fever for a couple days, but it slowly lowered over the next few days. However, the fever left Sam in poor health for the rest of his life. His muscles became weak, and his bones brittle. He wouldn't be able to continue the rough outdoor work required to survive in Great Sodus.

Carl was not the only victim of the fever in Great Sodus during that winter. Several others in Great Sodus and other people in the surrounding region contacted the fever and died. Many of those who fell to the terrible disease were young children. Without proper care and medicine from doctors, this illness always took a greater toll in the rural frontier regions. Great Sodus had no doctor, and winter fever took a tremendous toll.

The illness of Sam and deaths of Bob and Carl left Jim depressed and without workers for the winter's ice harvest. Soso was planning to build several boats during the winter months, but he had to discard that plan and help Jim with the harvest. It was a rough, sad, dismal winter for everyone. The residents of Great Sodus mourned over their losses and hoped and prayed for better days ahead.

The bitter cold and stormy weather made the winter of '98-'99 one that would not soon be forgotten in Great Sodus. For many settlers this extreme winter was just one hardship too many to endure. The next spring saw many villagers leave Great Sodus to return to the eastern cities or to move south hoping to find less austerity and better weather.

Frontier Life

The progress to develop Great Sodus into a busy city had been slowed again. The cold, damp winters, combined with no medical care in the village, killed several people and left many seriously ill. These conditions continued for several years and made life in Great Sodus harsher than its planners had ever imagined. Despite continued support by Captain Williamson and the Pultney Estate, the population of this tiny village leveled off at around 95 residents from 1799 to 1801. A few Seneca and Cayuga Indians stayed in temporary camps near Great Sodus to hunt and trap, but they usually moved on after a couple months. Soso always took time to visit his people to help them with their work and ask if anyone knew anything of Perch and Water Lily. Over the entire six years since their kidnapping, Soso and Clear Dawn took every opportunity to ask about their missing family members. They had never heard one word about them. It seemed as though the two children had just vanished into thin air.

A few new settlers moved to Great Sodus, but just as many left their homes to start anew elsewhere. Jim and Karen delivered fish to Carl and Sam's families while they were in Great Sodus. Soso gave them all the money that he had saved. However, none of that was enough. Sam and his family had to move back east after his failing health prevented him from working. Carl's family had returned east earlier, unable to support themselves in Great Sodus. Jim and Soso had tried hard to help the two families, but their support was not enough to overcome the added hardships the tragedy had caused. The two families needed to reestablish their lives back in the civilized world. The frontier was no place for the weak, the sick, or the depressed. Yet, often, frontier hardships produced these symptoms in the healthiest of its inhabitants.

Jim was unable to find any reliable, hardworking employees to replace

Carl and Sam in the fishing business. Therefore, he and Soso were busier than ever. For the next couple years Soso was able to build only a few more boats, and Jim was so busy that he was eventually unable to continue as captain of the luxury yacht. He reluctantly gave up his sailing job to concentrate on catching and selling fish. Most of his fish-buying customers lived inland, so transportation was a very important, and, unfortunately, a tedious and time-consuming part of his business.

Celebration

On July 4th, 1801, the nation's 25th birthday was celebrated in grand style in the village of Great Sodus. As the celebration took place in the village, three distinguished men were passengers aboard the Pultney Estate's luxury yacht as it sailed around the bay. The host of the cruise was Colonel Robert Troup, who had just taken over as the area land agent with the Estate replacing Captain Williamson. Captain Williamson had worked hard to establish and develop the communities in this frontier region and had sold many acres of land. Despite all his efforts, he had lost nearly $100,000 of the Pultney Estate money and had not developed the small villages like Great Sodus into the booming cities his superiors had envisioned. Captain Williamson and the Pultney Estate mutually agreed to end their relationship. Captain Williamson retired to a homestead in Rochester to enjoy his own family and the beauty of the frontier.

The Estate had hired a new land agent to try his hand at this challenging job. Colonel Troup had just arrived at Great Sodus and was fascinated, as many before him had been, by the natural beauty of the bay. His excitement and commitment to his mission grew as they sailed further around the bay. He could see vast potential in the region and could envision a grand city being established on the fertile bay. He was committed to the task and excited about its prospects. He was also a pretty good sailor, and he captained the vessel himself as he discovered the enjoyment of sailing on Great Sodus Bay.

The second passenger on board was Colonel Peregrine Fitzhugh. He was an elderly and distinguished man who had been General Washington's aide-de-camp during the Revolutionary War. Colonel Fitzhugh had recently bought vast acreage on the south shore of the bay, and he was having the land cleared at that time. He had plans for a great house overlooking the bay for his family. Colonel Fitzhugh's current home was in Geneva, but he had always been impressed with Great Sodus and couldn't wait to move into his new homestead on the highlands overlooking the bay.

The third passenger on board was Dr. William Lummis of Philadelphia. Dr. Lummis was a distinguished young doctor, who had recently decided to spend his summers in the lovely village of Great Sodus, which he remembered fondly from his visit to the region four years earlier. He had studied medicine under the tutelage of the famous Philadelphia teacher and statesman, Dr. Benjamin Rush. Lummis was in Great Sodus to buy land for his homestead. He was negotiating with Colonel Troup for a nice lot in the center of the village of Great Sodus.

Peregrine Fitzhugh was impressed with Colonel Troup's sailing abilities. "It seems like you know your way around this bay already. Where did you learn to sail?"

"I began sailing as a boy on Long Island Sound. But I've never had the pleasure of sailing in such a majestic location as this. I could spend my life sailing along the shore of this lovely bay. This water is so shiny, silvery, and clean," Colonel Troup answered.

"I've been dreaming about this delightful spot for four years since I first saw this beautiful bay and the village. It hasn't changed much, but that is part of its charm. I hope you have a nice lot for sale right in the heart of the village. I'd like to build a big home so I can enjoy summers and still survive these harsh winters that I keep hearing about. Is there a place where you can get a nice view of both the bay and the lake right in the village? I'll let Colonel Fitzhugh keep his peace and quiet on the south shore of the bay." Dr. Lummis wanted to get down to negotiations. He already knew that this was where he wanted to be. Of course Colonel Troup was especially delighted and eager to have such an outstanding citizen—a physician—interested in moving to his village. It was a friendly and easy negotiation, which resulted in Dr. Lummis buying a prime lot in Great Sodus. The best news was that the citizens of the area would now have some medical care, at least during the summer, which partially solved one of the biggest problems preventing expansion of the village.

All three men were thinking the same thoughts. A finer piece of water could hardly be imagined. Lush green shrubs lined the water's edge, and the winding shore was broken by numerous coves, creeks, and rivers. Parts of the bay were filled with shoals and reeds, while others parts held deep clear water. There were marshes teeming with birds, frogs, and turtles. The shallows held innumerable fish and minnows. The three islands were majestic and gave the bay even more diversity and beauty. It was a paradise for the outdoorsman and the gentleman, and these three considered themselves both.

While the three men sailed around the bay, the anniversary of American independence was being celebrated in the village. Settlers from all around the area flocked to Great Sodus to take part in the festivities. The entire village area was crowded with people who had come from miles away. Well over two hundred people squeezed into the tiny village. Tents were present in every open space and flat area. There were several Indians from around the area who came to enjoy the celebration. Colonel Troup couldn't help but wish that Great Sodus looked like this every day. The idea and plan for this celebration and others like it in the region had originated with Troup's predecessor, Captain Williamson. The first day's activities in these celebrations of independence often started with a parade though the village and concluded with a crude torch lighting and fireworks display. There were contests and games of all kinds for men, women, and children. Especially popular in Great Sodus was the shooting contest, which featured Soso and Jim as the chief contenders for the first prize. There were also cooking contests such as cherry pie baking. Millie Smith won that contest for the third straight year. Clear Dawn was in the running for growing the largest squash, but she lost out to an entry from Helms plantation for the second year in a row. All in all, this was great fun and gave everyone a brief break from the serious and dangerous work that characterized life on the frontier.

During Captain Williamson's years, the winners of these local fairs brought their entries to a county-wide fair that was held in the fall. Colonel Troup intended to keep this county-wide celebration in place. This year the county fair was to be in Lyons during the last week of August. Soso, Clear Dawn, Jim, and Karen were all planning to go to the county fair for the first time this year, but unfortunately a dreadful incident would prevent their attendance.

This year's celebration at Great Sodus lasted three days with each day becoming a bit wilder than the previous one. The third day was more like a drunken brawl; only the wildest celebrants remained. Soso, Jim, and Clear Dawn fished during that last day, since this was the busiest time of the year for their business. In addition, they didn't care to be around for all the wild and drunken partying. On the morning of the third day, two new Indian celebrants arrived at Great Sodus already quite drunk and disorderly. They spent the day at Sill's tavern drinking and sometimes fighting with other drunken men. One of the Indians kept asking for information about any other Indians who lived in the area. Eventually, he was told about Soso and Clear Dawn and their fishing jobs at Jim's fish market.

The celebrating finally ended the next morning, and peace and quiet returned to Great Sodus, as the wild celebrants returned to their homes. Once again the streets of the tiny village were nearly deserted. Soso and Clear Dawn spent the day fishing the fertile waters off the mouth of First Creek catching a boatload of bass. They returned to Jim's dock in the late afternoon to unload the fish. After carrying the fish into the market to be cleaned, Soso remained at the dock to clean his boat. Clear Dawn went into the market to help Jim clean and fillet the fish, which were to be delivered to Helms Plantation, the workers at the Fitzhugh Estate, and other customers early the next day.

Family Tragedy

Soso was very proud of his fishing boat, which was still the envy of all the boatmen on the bay. Even after four years of hard use, it was still as good as new. Soso had refurbished and improved the vessel each winter. As he cleaned the gunwales and floorboards, he dreamed, as he had many times before, of building a bigger, better boat than this one, a boat that could be used for both sailing and fishing. As he continued, noises and shouts from the direction of the fish market interrupted his thoughts. At least he thought that he heard shouting. He paused a moment from his work to listen for the noise. This time he was sure he heard shouting and banging from inside the market. Soso headed for the market to see what was the matter. As he grew nearer, he heard the voices of Jim and Clear Dawn and the voice of a third person that at first he didn't recognize. As he came closer, he realized that the voice he heard was that of his father, Gar, whom he hadn't seen in several years. Soso ran for the door as he determined that the three were involved in a bitter argument. When he burst through the door, he heard the sounds of struggling and a cry of pain. The first thing Soso saw as he entered was his father lying on the floor in a pool of blood. Gar clutched a fillet knife in his hand. Soso ran to his father's side, but Gar only looked at his son with disgust, refusing any help for his knife wounds. Soso then looked at Clear Dawn whose expression was mixed with hatred, terror, and pain. Soso then realized that Jim and Clear Dawn, although both still standing, had also suffered severe knife wounds. Clear Dawn had a deep gash in her back, and Jim's hands were badly cut and bloody.

Soso quickly picked up his mother and carried her next door to Jim's house, while helping Jim follow along. Karen, who was in the house preparing supper, was shocked to see the three come stumbling into her house covered with blood. She immediately began treating her husband and Clear Dawn.

After insuring that Jim and Clear Dawn were being treated, Soso returned to the fish market to help his father. Gar had propped himself up on one elbow but didn't have enough strength to get all the way up. Soso again tried to help him, but the response of the wounded, angry, drunken Indian was to lunge with the knife at his son. Soso caught his father in his arms as Gar's feeble, dying attempt to strike out at Soso and the changing world fell far short of its mark. Gar dropped the knife and died in Soso's arms.

Soso was overcome with grief and confusion. He hadn't experienced such emotion since as a 13-year-old boy he witnessed his grandfather's needless death. He had often thought about his father, wondering where Gar was and if he would ever see him again. Soso had always hoped Gar would return. Now when he finally saw his father again, it was only to see him die. Gar looked so old and tired, Soso had hardly recognized him. Over the years, whenever Soso had talked to Clear Dawn about Gar, she would change the subject and not answer any of Soso's questions. Clear Dawn had never shared Soso's dream of having his father return. Now Soso, a mature 21-year-old man, was confused and hurt over the death of his father.

Soso carried his father's body to his boat and rowed across the bay to First Creek. There he buried Gar next to Trout. At deeply emotional times like this, the spirits in his life seemed to awaken. He needed to talk with these spirits. Soso spent the evening in ceremonial Indian prayer at the gravesite before returning to Jim's house later that night. It's strange how the spirits were there to serve him when he needed them the most. The prayers and chants to the Great Spirits of Death had helped him, and through them, he began the slow recovery from his confusion and depression.

Karen had taken good care of Jim and Clear Dawn, but their wounds were severe. Clear Dawn was sleeping soundly when Soso returned, but Jim was lying awake in bed. Soso went to his friend's bedside and asked, "Jim, how are you?"

"I'll be OK. It's Clear Dawn that's hurt pretty bad. How's Gar?"

"He's dead. I buried him over near First Creek next to Trout. What happened?" Soso was a little hesitant to ask that question so soon, but eventually it had to be asked and answered. There was no avoiding knowing the reason for this calamity.

"I don't know exactly. Clear Dawn will have to tell you." Soso felt anxiety in Jim's voice.

Then Soso noticed the strange shape of Jim's bandaged left hand. Soso held up Jim's hand and saw that two of Jim's fingers were missing, completely cut off in the fight. Soso let out a cry of sorrow, "Oh, Jim. No! No!" The two men embraced. Then Soso left the room to let Jim rest. He was in deep anguish. His father was dead; his mother was severely wounded; and his best friend had lost two fingers.

Soso spent the rest of the night by Clear Dawn's bedside. She was restless and uncomfortable, but she was able to sleep through some of the night. She was usually so bright and beautiful, but in her suffering, she looked old and tired. It was a shock just to see her in such a condition. In the morning Soso re-bandaged the wounds on Clear Dawn's back. After insuring that Clear Dawn was comfortable, Soso reluctantly spoke with his mother. "Gar is dead. Jim was badly hurt. What happened?"

"Your father was a great warrior and a strong man. But he was a bad husband to me, a bad father to you, and a bad son to Trout. He didn't understand white men and hated them all. He was very drunk and came at me with a knife yelling about me being a traitor and a white Indian. Jim tried to help keep him away from me, but I had no choice but to stop your father before he killed Jim. So I picked up the knife from the table and stabbed Gar. He deserved what he got. Not just for yesterday, but for long ago, when he killed Trout, wounded Jim, and stole your brother and sister away from me."

Soso was completely numbed by what Clear Dawn had just said. His father, Gar, had killed his own father and Soso's grandfather, Trout, and for all these years his mother had never told him about it. Now he needed to know why. Clear Dawn's response was simple and direct. "I wanted you to forget about Gar and remember Trout as your father. The less you knew and heard about Gar the better. He was evil. Now that he is dead, we can all forget about him. He never was a real father or husband."

That wasn't going to be easy for Soso. He had never understood the meanness that was in Gar, but Gar was still his father and a great warrior. Clear Dawn's words made Soso feel even more uncomfortable. He needed time to think, so he went to a place where he had always found comfort and understanding. He rowed his boat toward the Great Lake named Ontario.

It was a hazy and windy day, but even the 3-foot, white-capped waves couldn't stop Soso's determination and progress. It took him over an hour of rowing just to get a little over a mile from shore. His concentration on rowing the boat was easing the pain and mental anguish that he had felt over his father's death and the terrible news that he had just heard. Suddenly, he was surprised by the sight before him. He looked up from his rowing to see a large sailing ship bearing down right at him. The sailing ship was the largest that he had ever seen; its two giant masts of full sails reached high into the sky.

Soso had no time to react as the boat skimmed right by the shocked Indian in the tiny rowboat. Obviously, neither the skipper nor the crew of the huge ship saw Soso. The boat disappeared almost as fast as it appeared. Soso sat stunned for a moment as he tried to understand what had just happened. His thoughts were completely scrambled. The size, speed, and magnificence of the boat had temporarily overwhelmed his remorse and grief. He only wanted to rush back and tell Jim about the magnificent boat he had just seen. As he refocused his thoughts, Soso realized that he must get over his grief, help his mother and Jim recover, and get on with his life.

Troupville

If it was possible, Colonel Troup had even more ambitious plans for the Sodus Bay area than had Captain Williamson. In fact, during the early spring in a ceremony in the park near the tavern, Colonel Troup renamed the village of Great Sodus after himself. The grand city envisioned on Sodus Bay would be called Troupville. Unlike Captain Williamson, who lived 55 miles away in the village of Bath, Colonel Troup would spend his summers in Troupville and actively take part in the development of this grand city.

He sold village lots to several investors who were going to spend their summers in Troupville. Among those was Dr. Lummis, who was spending the summer of 1802 overseeing the construction of a house in the village and beginning to care for the medical needs of the citizens of Troupville. By August Dr. Lummis had developed such a love for the little village that he wished he could stay there permanently. However, his medical practice back in Philadelphia needed his attention. Before he left Troupville that fall, he made himself a promise that someday he would make Troupville his year-round home.

Smooth Sailing

1802 was a good year for Jim and Karen Davis. Hannah was an energetic six-year-old girl. She was becoming a big help to her parents and a tremendous joy to all who knew her. In May, their first son, Jamey, was born. Then in June, Jim was offered and accepted a job as captain of the lake-transport merchant ship *Bluff Runner*. The ship was to be home-ported at Troupville and would carry cargo to ports along the south shore of Lake Ontario, like Oswego, Rochester, Pultneyville, Sackets Harbor, and Cape Vincent. This was the opportunity that Jim had dreamed about since he first sailed the Pultney Estate yacht for Captain Williamson. The *Bluff Runner* was an old but gracious and sturdy vessel, 42-foot long, with two tall masts and plenty of sail. She had a cargo hold of several tons, yet when empty she could sail like a dream. Soso immediately recognized the ship as the one that had just missed him a year before when he was rowing on the lake after his father's death. Jim couldn't wait to take over the helm of such an impressive sailing ship. Soso was equally excited for his friend's opportunity. This was the largest boat that Soso had ever seen. He was sure it could sail the big oceans that the whites had told him about.

Jim's new job put the burden of running the fishing business on Soso's shoulders. Soso was able to handle the responsibility, both as a fisherman and as a businessman. He was now comfortable with handling money and with the negotiations needed to sell the fish. He finally understood and trusted the American monetary system, which is something that few Indians—let alone every white settler—had mastered. The 22-year-old Indian was a well-trained, competent businessman. He normally wore the clothes of the whites, talked their language, and knew their culture. The only question was whether the residents in the area were ready to accept a young Indian as a prominent businessman.

Soso's first task was to find two new employees, one to help catch fish and one to deliver fish to neighboring villages. Finding the fisherman turned out to be quite easy. A trapper and fishermen named Tom Reese, who had spent the last several years in the Niagara frontier, recently had decided to settle down in Troupville. Tom had been a scout for Colonel Troup and General Anthony Wayne during the Revolutionary War. Because of his relationship with Colonel Troup, he had the opportunity to purchase a small lot near First Creek and was looking for a job suitable to his talents. Soso had known Tom for several years because Tom had brought his animal hides to Troupville to trade at Wickham's store, and several times Tom and Soso had fished together on the lake. Soso trusted Tom and respected his fishing abilities. Soso knew he was lucky for he couldn't have found a better man for the job.

It also turned out to be quite easy to find a new deliveryman. Soso hired Carl's 14-year-old son, Herman. Herman had just returned to Troupville, since he didn't like the city life back in Albany. Herman's family had lived in Albany for the past three years since Carl's death while harvesting ice on Sodus Bay. Herman had been unable to find a good job in

Albany and felt more comfortable on the frontier than in the city. Herman, as a young child, had ridden with his father for several years when Carl delivered fish for Jim, so he knew the region and the buyers as well as anyone. Herman was going to live with Jim and send some of his earnings back to Albany to help support his family, which had struggled to survive back in Albany.

Soso had put together all the necessary parts for the business, and they had a good year. Tom, Clear Dawn, and Soso supplied plenty of fish. Karen continued to help by selling fish from the market in Troupville as she cared for Hannah and her new baby, Jamey. Young Herman delivered the fish and ice to customers all over the region, sometimes as far away as Lyons and Palmyra. Soso did have problems bargaining with a few people. Several men tried to take advantage of his financial inexperience and tried to underpay for fish. Soso quickly caught onto their schemes and made them pay full price. Others didn't want to do business with an Indian and took their business to other fishermen. Included among those was Soso's neighbor, Helms. As a slaveholder and southern gentleman, Helms's prejudice prevented him from treating Soso as a business partner. The other fishermen in Troupville were quite unreliable, and even those who left as regular customers would often buy fish from Soso when the other fishermen couldn't deliver. All in all, Soso proved he could handle the management of the fishing business, even though there was still prejudice in some of the residents of the Sodus Bay area. While this bothered Soso, he didn't let it affect his business or personal life; it just made him more determined to get along with everyone.

Jim also had a successful summer. He turned out to be an excellent skipper who was able to sail the *Bluff Runner* in any weather and to keep to the tight and demanding delivery schedule. Over the summer, he logged many hundreds of miles on Lake Ontario. He made good money for his boss and boat owner, Roy Harper, who lived in Syracuse. Roy spent considerable time in Troupville, staying at Sill's Tavern. Roy had bought the boat through some shady dealings with slave traders in the southern port of Charleston. He had hired a crew to sail the ship up to Lake Ontario, but the members of the original crew had quit shortly after they arrived on Lake Ontario over what they claimed was improper payment for their services. Roy was not very organized in arranging the cargo schedule, and Jim frequently had to correct Roy's mistakes or make up for his inefficiencies.

Jim and his crewmen, Bill and Steve Brewer, were, by far, the best sailors on the lake. Their reputation as excellent sailors and honest businessmen was well deserved. Unfortunately, Roy's reputation wasn't nearly as good.

In carrying out their fishing job for Soso, Clear Dawn and Tom Reese spent considerable time together. They were a perfect match both to accomplish their duties and in their personal lives. Clear Dawn was always at peace with herself. Her beauty was radiant and refined. Tom, on the other hand, was a rugged frontiersman. He was tall, lanky, and wore a full beard that covered most of his face. While spending so much time together, their relationship blossomed and by the end of the summer, Clear Dawn had married Tom Reese. They were a fine-looking couple, but some of the whites couldn't or wouldn't let themselves understand this inter-racial marriage. People talked about them, but Tom and Clear Dawn didn't care. They were happy and lived their lives together in peace and quiet in a small cabin overlooking First Creek. They fished together; they spent their time together. They were the happiest and most contented couple on Sodus Bay. While Soso missed having his mother stay with him, he was happy for her and really liked Tom. Soso had to get used to being alone and independent.

Philadelphia

After Dr. Lummis returned to Philadelphia, he immediately started work again in his medical practice. The rugged, exhausting 300-mile journey on horseback had taken him twelve days. Travel in the early 1800s was slow and uncomfortable. The roads and trails were abominable. Often he had to ford streams and rivers, because there was no bridge or ferryboat. However, even after he had arrived back in Philadelphia, his heart and dreams remained in Troupville. He had enjoyed his summer on the beautiful silvery waters, so much so that he couldn't wait to return there the next summer.

Dr. Lummis had many highly respected and distinguished friends in Philadelphia. The closest was his teacher and mentor, Benjamin Rush, who was much older than William and more like his father. Rush was also a medical doctor in Philadelphia and had a distinguished reputation as a leader in many fields. He was one of the signers of the Declaration of Independence and a former Surgeon General of the Colonial Army. Rush seemed to have great influence on the policies of the federal government and wrote numerous essays on the abolition of slavery, temperance, education, health, and disease. He was a world expert on many diseases and studied in great detail the cause of yellow fever. One of his special interests was the medicines and diseases of the Indians of North America. He had discussed this topic often with Dr. Lummis, who also had interest in this subject. Dr. Rush was one of the savants of Philadelphia and a member of the American Philosophical Society. In 1799, he had become the Treasurer of the United States Mint in Philadelphia having left his medical practice, but he still kept a significant interest in medicine and science. William Lummis felt himself indeed fortunate to know such a great man and spent considerable time at the Rush home, just around the corner from his own home at the corner of Walnut and Fourth Streets.

They often discussed some of Dr. Rush's medical treatments and medications. New for 1802 were laxatives that Rush had just developed. They had various names—"Rush's pills," "Magic pills," and "Magic potion"— but Dr. Lummis gave them a name that stuck, the "Thunder-clappers."

Benjamin Rush saw to it that Dr. Lummis was invited to all the high-society social events in the city. Dr. Lummis didn't consider himself a handsome or dignified man. He had a light complexion and dark blond hair. He certainly disliked getting dressed up in fancy clothes. Lummis usually felt a bit uncomfortable at elaborate, formal affairs. Being a bachelor, he was always being introduced to eligible ladies by his friends in hopes that a relationship would result. However, the type of woman that Dr. Lummis was interested in meeting was not usually found at gala social events. He was looking for a strong, independent woman who would welcome a harsher, more exciting life in the frontier village of Troupville.

It was just by chance that Dr. Lummis found such a woman. Her name was Sara Maxwell, daughter of the Revolutionary War hero Colonel John Maxwell. The place and coincidence of their first meeting were appropriate considering their interests in life.

Dr. Lummis often spent his lunchtime fishing on the Delaware River, which ran through Philadelphia less than a mile from his house. The few minutes of nature's peace and quiet reminded him of his summer home and frontier living in Troupville. One day he decided to extend his lunch-break and fish the entire afternoon several miles up river, north of the city. He rode out to a pleasant spot he had seen before, but had never fished, and began his afternoon of fishing. He seemed to have no luck. Yet less than 200 feet up river, a man and woman seemed to be able to catch trout at will. He watched as they landed a dozen fish, while he didn't catch any. As the afternoon wore on, Dr. Lummis became more and more amazed. He finally went over to the man and woman to ask how they were fishing. However, he hardly heard the answer that the man gave him. He was completely taken by the beauty of the young woman who was so adept at catching fish. She was attractive, yet at the same time strong, intelligent, and fascinating. She had long, dark hair, and was beautiful and elegant even while standing in water fishing for trout.

Dr. Lummis was so taken with the young lady that he quickly introduced himself to the couple. He was delighted to find out that they were father and daughter, Colonel John Maxwell and Miss Sara Maxwell.

"You are experts at catching these fish. I haven't caught a fish all afternoon." Dr. Lummis continued to talk with the couple.

"We have fished here every day for a week. We are getting to know these waters and the fish here quite well," answered Colonel Maxwell.

"You certainly know more about fishing here than I do. In any case, it's been an enjoyable afternoon for me. I always like to fish and relax along this pretty river." Dr. Lummis directed his next question to Sara. "Do you and your father live nearby?"

"We live right in the city of Philadelphia. But we both like the country much better. Someday, I hope to move out of the city and into the country. I prefer fishing and farming to sitting in my parlor." Sara was as adventurous as she was beautiful.

Dr. Lummis invited the Maxwells to his home for supper that evening, and everyone had an enjoyable time. Very soon thereafter, Sara was attending many of the social events in Philadelphia with Dr. Lummis. They had a lot in common and enjoyed each other's company. Dr. Lummis was enthralled by this wonderful woman.

Marriage and Honeymoon

Benjamin Rush was also completely taken with the young lady whom William found so charming. He considered William and Sara a fine couple and encouraged their relationship. Sara was strong and caring. Over the winter and early spring, William Lummis and Sara Maxwell were constant companions. The only rough spot during the exciting courtship occurred during the late spring, when Benjamin Rush was doing a favor for President Thomas Jefferson. Jefferson had asked Rush to help educate and equip the President's personal secretary, Captain Meriwether Lewis, in medical care before Lewis launched an expedition to explore the west. Dr. Rush, with assistance from Dr. Lummis, showed Meriwether some basic medical procedures in the few weeks that Meriwether had to prepare. Dr. Rush gave Meriwether over a thousand "Thunder-clapper" laxatives to take on his journey. The difficulty came when Meriwether Lewis met Sara Maxwell at a formal ball given by the Rushes. Meriwether fancied himself a ladies man and took to pursuing Sara. After just one dance, Dr. Lummis stepped in and confronted the rugged Army officer over his interference with his fiancée. After the confrontation, Meriwether understood the situation and decided to pursue other young ladies in Philadelphia. The confrontation, however, left a scar on the relationship between Dr. Lummis and the explorer Meriwether Lewis.

By the late spring of 1803, nuptials were planned, and in June, William Lummis and Sara Maxwell were married in Philadelphia. Both the Maxwell and Lummis families were delighted.

Dr. Lummis could think of no better place to take his new bride on their honeymoon than Troupville. So the newlyweds headed for Sodus Bay with William describing over and over again to Sara the beauty of the bay and the fun and excitement they would have there.

Sara did enjoy her summer on the frontier in the small yet exciting village of Troupville. Troupville was the ideal spot for this woman who enjoyed the outdoors and could fish as well as her husband. Their summer home was rustic but pleasant. It had a nice view of the bay, and the Lummises liked their neighbors, the Olsons. They often took long morning walks on the beach along the lakeshore. They also liked to ride their horses far into the countryside although they were always careful to travel on well-marked paths. Their favorite place was the mouth of Salmon Creek, just three miles west of Troupville, where there were always plenty of fish and pleasant surroundings. The scenery was lovely there, and Sara liked to sit and look at the two pretty little mills which had been built through Captain Williamson's financing nine years before. They never had any trouble catching fish in the stream. Their summer together in Troupville was like a wonderful dream for both of them.

William's medical talents were a tremendous addition to Troupville. He cared for the ill, delivered several babies, and improved the general health of the community. Everyone felt safer and happier when Dr. Lummis was staying in Troupville and available to treat residents in need of care. Likewise, Sara made her contributions as a community volunteer and nurse for many of William's patients.

Colonel Troup entertained the Lummises on the Pultney corporate yacht several times during the summer. On each trip they noticed several of the sleek fishing boats that Soso had built several years before. They both admired the workmanship and seaworthiness of these small craft. On the last trip of the summer—a voyage in honor of their imminent return to Philadelphia—Dr. Lummis inquired as to the origin of these remarkable boats. He was amazed to learn that the young Indian fisherman Soso had built them. Dr. Lummis knew Soso quite well and had bought fish from him several times during the summer. He had fond memories of his meeting with the Indian boy when he had spoken with Soso on his first trip to Sodus Bay in 1797. He was pleased to discover that the young man had such a marvelous talent.

A Commission

The next morning, just prior to the Lummises' departure for Philadelphia, Dr. Lummis approached Soso about building a boat for him over the winter. "Soso, I found out yesterday that you are the builder of those fine fishing boats that I keep seeing on the bay. You've done some splendid work on them."

Soso was flattered by Dr. Lummis's remarks, for he admired and respected the doctor very much. "Thanks, Dr. Lummis. I do enjoy building boats, and I try to make them sturdy and safe for fishing on the bay and travel on the lake."

Dr. Lummis got right to the point. "Well, that's perfect. It's just what I need. How about building a boat for me this winter? I'd like a boat that Sara and I could sail on the lake once in a while and row around the bay to fish and enjoy the sights."

Soso had long dreamed of building just such a boat. It would be a tough challenge to build one large enough to sail on the lake in comfort yet also small enough to sail or row around the bay easily. Soso had spent a lot of time thinking about that problem and had a design almost completely thought out. However, Soso had another problem; he didn't have enough time to build a boat over the winter and still run the fishing business.

Soso tried to explain this to Dr. Lummis. "I'd love to build you a boat, but I'm too busy with the fishing business. It could take me as long as two years to finish it by working a little each winter." Soso really wanted to build the boat, but he had to explain his problem to Dr. Lummis. "If you don't need the boat for two years, I'll build you one for $115." Over the years, Soso had become a confident and shrewd businessman.

Much to Soso's surprise, Dr. Lummis agreed with the offer. He also left Soso an advance of $45 to start work and promised $70 more when the boat was complete. Soso was glad for this opportunity and thanked Dr. Lummis for his support.

Soso bid Dr. and Mrs. Lummis a pleasant return trip to Philadelphia. Then he rushed over to Wickham's store to order the necessary materials and some new tools needed to build the boat. It would be a big challenge to build such a boat, but he was willing to try.

Soso had a very busy fall. Clear Dawn had become ill and no longer fished with Tom. Because of this situation, Tom often had to spend days at home caring for Clear Dawn. Jim was gone on sailing trips almost every day. This meant that Soso had to do most of the work of the fishing business by himself. He spent part of each day fishing, but also he had to return to the dock each afternoon to fillet fish, load fish for delivery by Herman and to conduct the business deals. There was no time left to work on Dr. Lummis's boat.

Trouble

On a stormy, windy day in October, Soso was called over to the tavern to see Roy Harper, Jim Davis's boss. Jim was two days late returning from a trip to Cape Vincent. Roy was very drunk, which was often the case, and immediately began bad-mouthing Jim to Soso and others in the tavern. "Your buddy, Jim, is late again. He probably got lost or can't handle the little swell on the lake. That's what you get with a bay-sailor." Bay-sailor was a derogatory term that Roy and others used to describe boaters who preferred to stay only on the bay, protected from the heavy winds and waves that often occurred on the lake.

Roy was more obnoxious than ever and continued with his annoying comments. "Jim probably learned to sail from you Indians. Everyone knows Indians are scared to death to go on the lake."

Soso very seldom went to the tavern, and, when he did go, he never drank liquor. Roy asked Soso to have a drink with him, but Soso tried politely to refuse the offer. Roy took offense at the refusal and began degrading Soso. "I thought all you Indians liked whiskey. I heard your dad died of the drink. Is that why you're afraid of taking a drink? Or you just too good to drink with the likes of me. I guess I've seen it all; an Indian fishermen refuses to drink with a merchant fleet owner." Roy continued his harassment of Soso and even physically prevented him from leaving the tavern. Soso had always tried to avoid situations like this. He knew firsthand that nothing good could come from a confrontation or drunken argument with a white man.

Soso was a very patient man, but Roy's behavior and remarks finally struck a sensitive spot. Soso was about ready to strike back at Roy when Jim arrived at the tavern. Jim was late and upset because Roy's mismanagement had again necessitated his making an extra trip from Cape Vincent to Oswego which had caused the two-day delay. The drunken ship owner, Roy, denied that he had made a mistake and continued his verbal attack on the two men, until Jim's temper erupted. Not only did Jim defend himself and Soso, but he also quit his job. Before Jim and Soso left, Jim had decked the belligerent and over-matched Roy with one punch to the chin.

Jim always had a bit of a temper, but in this case his outburst was justified. Jim was 32 years old and had mellowed a bit from his earlier days of frequently displaying his short temper. Despite his age, Jim was as strong as a bull and able to defend himself from the likes of people like Roy. Jim was tall, strong, and rugged. He wore a full beard and always dressed more like a frontier trapper, which he once was, than the sailing captain he had become. The physical confrontation was hardly a match. Jim could have taken on four or five men like Roy without worry. On the frontier, physical strength was an important asset in coping with the harsh lifestyle. Not only was Roy Harper unfit to be a merchant businessman, he hardly belonged on the frontier.

Three days later, a captain from Oswego arrived at Troupville to see Jim Davis with papers signed by Roy to release the boat to him. The captain sailed the *Bluff Runner* out of Sodus Bay to its new homeport of Oswego. Jim was sorry that he had lost his sailing job, but he had never gotten along very well with Roy. He actually felt relieved that he no longer worked for this corrupt man. Maybe another opportunity to sail a transport ship would come his way, but for now, he was ready to return full-time to the fishing business.

With Jim's resignation from the sailing job, Soso was able to turn control of the fishing business back to his partner. In that sense, the ugly incident was not all bad, for it unexpectedly freed Soso to spend considerably more time during the winter working on Dr. Lummis's boat. Now that Clear Dawn was living in Troupville, Soso was alone in his cabin on the cove. He had built a large workshop next to his cabin, which allowed him to continue working on the boat on even the coldest days of winter. He completely dedicated himself to the effort of building the finest boat on the bay. Several times during the winter, Jim and Karen, and even Clear Dawn and Tom, worried over Soso since they did not see him for several weeks at a time. Soso was clearly concentrating on his work.

A Masterpiece

On a cold, bright, sunny day in February, Jim took Karen, Hannah, and Jamey on a horse-drawn sleigh ride across the frozen bay to visit Soso. The bright sun made the ice sparkle, and the extreme cold kept the ice surface solid. The snow crunched under the home-built cutter as it sped across the frozen bay toward Soso's house. It was spectacular to watch and feel the cutter glide along and to sense the cold, crisp air blowing against the faces of the riders. The sky was bright blue and so big that it seemed to fill the entire world. From the middle of Sodus Bay, the world was filled with blue sky, bright shiny ice, and many of the sensational features of nature.

When Jim and his family arrived at Soso's home, Soso was in his usual spot—his shop—working on the boat. Soso was so engrossed in his work that he didn't even hear the visitors come into the shop. He suddenly looked up to see Jim, Karen, and their children studying his boat. Jim was completely astonished by the boat that he found in Soso's shop. The hull of the boat was completely finished; it was long, sleek, slender, and perfectly shaped. Soso was producing in his small crude shop a product that before this was built only by master craftsmen in the large professional shipyards of the big coastal cities of Boston, New York, or Philadelphia. It was a marvel that an unschooled Indian could ever produce anything so attractive, so complicated, and so advanced. Jim knew firsthand that Soso was a true genius.

Soso was surprised and happy to see Jim and his family. He warmly welcomed them, "Hello everybody. What are you doing way over here?"

Jim sincerely praised the boat and complimented Soso. "Soso, it's beautiful. How did you do it? It looks perfect. The design is so sleek. This boat looks like it will go very fast."

"I hope Dr. Lummis will like it. You don't think it's too big, do you?"

Soso was concerned that the 23-foot long boat would be too big for the combination fishing-sailing boat that Dr. Lummis had desired.

Jim could only shake his head in amazement. His Indian friend was truly a remarkable man with an exceptional talent. Jim could hardly wait until spring to see this boat move though the water. But now, he was here to get Soso to have some fun. "The children came over here to go sledding with their Uncle Soso. What do you say; let's have some fun."

Jim, Karen, Hannah, Jamey, and Soso spent the rest of that day picnicking, tobogganing, and ice skating on frozen Sodus Bay. The snow was crisp and hard, and Jim's toboggan skimmed down the slope near the shore of the bay and then along the smooth, slippery ice of the bay for hundreds of feet before stopping. It was a day of fun for everyone and allowed Soso some relief from his arduous work on the boat. As an eight-year-old tomboy, Hannah loved the outdoors and the winter activities. Two-year-old Jamey was trying hard to keep up, but eventually wore out and took a long nap at Soso's house. It was a special day of great fun.

As winter passed, Soso spent more and more time working on the boat. The only reason he would leave his work was to travel over to Troupville to buy or order tools and materials from Wickham's store. He had plenty of food stored away and didn't need to hunt or fish for the rest of the winter. Whenever he was out for a trip, he always stopped to see the Davises in Troupville and then went over to First Creek to see Clear Dawn and Tom. Clear Dawn was still weak from her illness, but she was always happy to see her son. Jim and his family were the only ones, other than Soso, to see the boat, and they had seen only the hull. By spring, the boat was almost done. Soso hoped that it would be as good as he envisioned and that Dr. Lummis would be satisfied with his work.

In mid-April 1804 the ice went out, and with that event, fishing started in earnest. However, even the first day of spring fishing didn't get Soso out of his workshop. After fishing on the second day after the ice went out, Jim went across the bay to check on Soso. It wasn't like Soso to miss the first two days of spring fishing. Soso met Jim at the small dock in the cove. "Hi, Jim. How's the fishing? Did you get anything today?" Soso asked his best friend.

"I must be getting better, Soso. I pulled in about forty trout over the last two days. Look at this beauty." Jim held up such a nice trout that Soso had to take a closer look at it. Usually, the spring trout were smaller than those caught in the fall. But this one, weighing over twenty pounds, was a huge trout for any time of the year.

Soso admired Jim's catch and asked, "Where'd you get him?"

"Caught him over by the outlet to the lake. I fought him for ten minutes before I brought him in. What's going on over here? Why aren't you out fishing?" Jim asked.

"I'm still working on the boat. There's lots to do, and I want to get it done before Dr. Lummis gets here. I saw Colonel Troup last week and he said the Lummises will be here in about three weeks," Soso answered.

"How's it looking? I haven't seen it in a couple months. Let me look it over?"

"Not yet. I'll let you see it in three weeks when I put it in the water. Do you think you could get about three or four men to help put it in when it's ready? And I'd like to use Herman in the afternoons to help me with the final touches."

"You bet I can find some helpers. The whole village is talking about this boat. I'll bring over John Gibson, along with Sam and Will Hill, whenever you need us. I'll send Herman over every afternoon. I'd better get back now and clean these fish. I promised Colonel Fitzhugh some fresh trout for his supper." Jim waved to Soso as he left the dock and headed back to Troupville across the cold, choppy water of the bay. Soso immediately returned to his shed to continue working on the boat.

The Launch

Soso worked harder than ever over the next three weeks. The only other person to see the boat was Herman, who was spending his mornings fishing and his afternoons helping Soso. On May 10th Herman brought news to Soso from Colonel Troup that Dr. and Mrs. Lummis were expected to arrive in Troupville in two days. The timing was perfect since Soso was ready to launch the boat. Soso sent Herman back to Troupville that evening to ask Jim to bring over a launching crew the next day.

As is usually the case in small towns, it's impossible to keep exciting news like this secret. The information is often exaggerated, and rumors run rampant. By morning, all of Troupville had heard about the launching and about the beauty of the boat. As Jim and his launching crew of Herman, John Gibson, Will Hill, and Sam Hill left Jim's dock early in the morning, a parade of five other boats joined them. All the occupants of the boats had heard stories from Herman about this boat and wanted to see it for themselves. Of course this large audience was not what Soso wanted or anticipated. As he greeted Jim and the others at the dock, he was shocked to see a crowd gathering to witness the launch. When Soso asked why the others were there, Herman very sheepishly admitted that he had spread the word about the beautiful boat and had invited a few people to see the launching.

Soso asked the spectators to wait by the bay shore while the boat was launched in the cove. He promised them that he would then sail the boat out onto the bay and bring it around close to the shore so they could get a good look at it.

The launching went smoothly. The six men were able to roll the boat out of Soso's shed on the logs that he had laid out. Then they slid the boat across the lawn down a small ramp into the cove. Even though they had heard about the beauty of the boat, its magnificence and workmanship impressed the men who were seeing the boat for the first time. However, as the boat settled into the water, Jim and the other boatmen knew this was no ordinary boat. Soso had built a masterpiece. The boat settled gently into the water and floated softly in the still water of the cove. As Soso returned to his shed to get the sails, the others admired every detail of the boat. The woodwork was perfect, and the finish was smooth and finely shaped. The boat was perfectly balanced as it sat in the water. Soso brought out the sails that had been sewn locally by Jabez Sill, and he and Jim rigged the mast and sail before the two of them set sail out of the cove and onto the bay.

Test Ride

Soso was at the helm, and Jim handled the sail. The boat cruised quickly out of the cove and onto the open, choppy waters of the bay. Soso sailed along the shore directly in front of the spectators standing on the shore. Despite everyone's high expectations because of Herman's bragging, none of them were disappointed in what they saw as the boat skimmed smoothly and silently by them. This was truly an impressive and innovative boat, and none of them had ever seen anything quite like it before.

As Soso and Jim sailed farther out onto the bay, they headed around

Loga Island. Jim complimented Soso on his work. "This is the finest boat I have ever seen. It's so fast and easy to handle, and the workmanship is perfect. You know you really ought to do this full time."

Soso was pleased with Jim's praise, but he quickly responded, "No, I want to return to the fishing business with you again. This boat is the last one I'll build for awhile. Do you think that Dr. Lummis will like it?" Jim's only answer was to nod his head in the affirmative.

They headed back to Soso's cove. Half way back Jim lowered the sail, and Soso rowed the sleek boat back toward the cove and the spectators who were waiting to get a better look at the boat. And look they did. All those present on the shore admired the boat and congratulated Soso on his excellent work. The boat launching had turned into a celebration. All day long, people from Troupville and the surrounding area arrived at Soso's cove to see the boat. Soso spent most of the day showing the boat and explaining how he had built it.

Early the next morning, Soso sailed the boat to Jim Davis's dock. He wanted to make sure it was ready and waiting when the Lummises arrived in town. Soso spent the entire day at the fish market in Troupville repairing nets, spears, hooks, lines, and fishing rods, while Jim, Herman, Clear Dawn, and Tom went fishing on the lake. Of course, Soso would have preferred to be with them because lake fishing was what he enjoyed the most, but he felt it was more important to stay with the boat so that he could show it to the Lummises as soon as they arrived.

Opportunity

Colonel Troup came by Jim's dock during the afternoon to see the boat that everyone in town was talking about. He, too, was amazed at its beauty and immediately approached Soso. "Soso, you'll have to build me one of these lovely boats. In fact, if you build one for me, I'll give you that lot on the east side of the bay you've been wanting to buy for such a long time." Soso had approached Colonel Troup several times about purchasing the lot, but no deal could be arranged because Soso didn't have enough money or valuable possessions to offer for the land and, as an Indian, no credit to buy the land through a mortgage.

This opportunity was more than Soso had ever expected. His excitement and anticipation were enormous. He could think only of finally owning his own land. Soso quickly responded, "I'll make you an even better boat than this one by next spring."

"Then it's a deal. You build me the boat by July 4th next year, and you get ownership of lot 107." Then Colonel Troup mounted his horse and left Troupville to travel out to Salmon Creek to check on the conditions of the mills. There was some concern that they might wash out with the high water and spring flooding. The mills were very important to the area, and Colonel Troup wanted to be sure everything possible was done to save them.

Soso was a little disappointed, but not surprised, when the Lummises didn't arrive that day. He decided to leave the boat at Jim's dock that night while he borrowed Jim's boat to return across the bay to his house. Soso spent that evening thinking about the new boat that he would build for Colonel Troup. What he had in mind would take a lot of expensive materials, but he figured that he would have just enough money from his savings and the money he would receive from Dr. Lummis to build the new boat for Colonel Troup. He had already spent most of his previous savings for the materials for the Lummis boat. However, the most difficult task facing Soso was to tell Jim about his plans to build another boat instead of working full-time for their fishing business. Soso certainly did not want to let down his best friend, but he wanted to own his own land. It had been his dream for many years, and now it was very close to happening.

Long Trip

It really wasn't surprising that the Lummises were late in arriving at Troupville. The few roads in the region were still rugged, and overland travel was slow, uncomfortable, and full of delays. The wet spring didn't help, since streams and rivers were overflowing and washing out bridges and fords in the area. This long trip was especially difficult for Sara because she was pregnant. Sara was six months into her pregnancy, and because of that, she rode in a small buggy instead of on horseback, as she had the year before. Neither form of transportation was very comfortable. She had considered not returning to Troupville, but her wonderful experience the previous summer gave her motivation to make the trip. It turned out that they spent that evening in the hotel in Geneva instead of Troupville. They planned to make the remaining 30 miles of their trip to Troupville the next day. With luck, they would be safely in their summer home by the next evening.

Illness

As the Lummises traveled the next day, another event interrupted Soso's thoughts and consumed all his energies. The day before, Clear Dawn had become very sick after she had returned from fishing on the lake. She had been feverish all night. Tom Reese sent his friend and neighbor Bob Whalen across the bay to get Soso early in the morning. Soso came quickly to his mother's side, but she had turned much worse by the time he arrived. She looked old and tired, and he knew that she was seriously ill.

Soso spent the entire day with his mother, treating her with many of the special herbs and roots that his grandfather, Trout, had shown him. It was a fretful day for Soso and Tom, since they both thought Clear Dawn was too sick and would not recover. Both loved her in the special ways that only husbands and sons can love such an extraordinary woman. Clear Dawn was a proud and talented woman, and she was an exceptional wife and mother. She also was a determined woman. There was some hope for her recovery as long as she kept her determination.

Late that evening, the Lummises finally arrived in Troupville. By the time they had settled into their house, Herman had heard of their arrival and went over to greet them. He told the Lummises all about their new boat. Dr. Lummis didn't expect his boat to be completed already. Soso had promised him a boat in two years. After hearing Herman's glowing reports, Dr. Lummis couldn't wait until morning to see the boat. He and Herman went down to Jim's dock carrying torches to light their way through the darkness. Through the dim torch light, Dr. Lummis immediately fell in love with the beautiful boat. It was much more than he had expected. Soso had done a magnificent job.

As they left the dock, they were met by Jim, who informed them about Clear Dawn's illness. Dr. Lummis immediately offered to help care for her. Since the fastest way to travel over to Tom's cabin was by boat, they decided to sail the new boat over to Tom's. Herman ran back to the Lummises to tell Sara about the bad news of Clear Dawn's illness and the emergency plan to help her. He also picked up Dr. Lummis's medical bag. After Herman returned to the dock with the bag, Jim raised the sail and took Dr.

Lummis for his first ride in his new boat across the bay toward First Creek. It was barely over a mile. The ride in the dark went quickly, and it was a short walk from the shore up to Tom's cabin. When Dr. Lummis knocked on the door, a worried and tired Soso opened the door to greet him. "Dr. Lummis, I am relieved that you are here. It's my mother. Her fever won't go down."

Dr. Lummis could tell right away that Clear Dawn's condition was serious. "What have you given her?" he asked Soso.

"Some roots and leaves of the Yarrow. It hasn't helped her at all." Soso's answer concerned the doctor even more. The Yarrow was as effective as any medication that he had and should have controlled the fever if anything could.

Just then the doctor felt a swelling on Clear Dawn's neck and glands. As soon as he felt the swelling, Dr. Lummis realized the cause of her illness. He treated it immediately by bleeding the infection from Clear Dawn's glands.

Recovery

After one more night of worrying and caring by Jim, Tom, Dr. Lummis, and Soso, Clear Dawn awoke feeling a bit better and on the road to recovery. Before Dr. Lummis left the cabin the next morning, however, he warned that Clear Dawn's recovery would take a considerable amount of time and may never be complete. Her fever had been severe, and Clear Dawn would need attention for quite some time before her strength and energy would return. She was in a very fragile state and needed rest and care. The good news was that her life was no longer in danger, but she would probably be sickly the remainder of her life.

It was an exhausted and relieved group that left Tom's cabin that morning. Considering the circumstances, the three men had a rather pleasant and relaxing sail back across the bay to Jim's dock. With the apparent recovery of Clear Dawn, they were able to discuss the attributes of the new boat, as Soso and Jim put the boat through its paces to show Dr. Lummis its capabilities. It was a spectacular morning to sail the fastest boat ever to cruise on Sodus Bay. By the time they reached their destination, Dr. Lummis was most pleased to accept the boat and paid Soso $80 even though the contracted price was for only $70 more. Dr. Lummis insisted that Soso take the additional money since the boat was worth much more. Nor would Dr. Lummis accept any money from Soso for his care of Clear Dawn. Dr. Lummis also agreed to pay Jim $10 for use of Jim's dock during the summer to tie up the new boat. All in all, it was a most pleasant trip with all three men enjoying the others' company. This trip across the bay marked the beginning of an exceptional friendship that would last for the rest of their lives.

After the boat landed at Jim's dock, Dr. Lummis, exhausted from his medical duties and lack of sleep, still found the energy to get Sara to show her the boat. She loved it. It was just what she needed to enjoy her summer days fishing and sailing on Great Sodus Bay.

Soso and Jim went to the fish market to discuss their plans for the summer. One consequence of Clear Dawn's disability was a reduction in the capacity of Jim and Soso's fishing business. Since Clear Dawn was going to have to stay in bed for at least several weeks on Dr. Lummis's recommendation, Tom would have to spend most of that time caring for Clear Dawn. Without Tom and Clear Dawn, it appeared the summer would be extremely busy for Jim and Soso. Soso also had the extra task of building a boat for Colonel Troup.

New Opportunities

Soso came right out and told Jim about his boat-building commitment to Colonel Troup. "Jim, I must tell you about an agreement I made with Colonel Troup yesterday. I agreed to build him a boat like the Lummises in exchange for ownership of the lot across the bay. In order to get the boat done by next summer, I won't be able to fish much this summer or even next winter."

Jim's reply really surprised Soso. "That's great, Soso. You'll finally get that land you've always wanted. It turns out I have an opportunity to return to sailing this summer. So, maybe it's best we just close the business for this year since we have these other opportunities and there is no one else to help us with the fishing."

Soso was surprised at Jim's idea and quickly added, "I'll hire Herman to help me with the boat. He can live over by me if he wants. So who are you going to sail for?"

"You know that Roy's new captain ran the *Bluff Runner* on the rocks near Cape Vincent last fall. So Rob Fellows bought a new boat, which he plans to run on supply routes between the New York State harbor-towns and across to Canada. It's an old, small boat, called the *Lake Queen*, but at least I'll be back on the lake," answered Jim.

The two men were pleased that their own opportunities weren't going to have an adverse effect on their best friend's plans. They wouldn't be working as closely with one another, but they would be working in jobs they enjoyed as much as fishing. And, in the end, Soso was finally going to have ownership of the land that he had wanted for so long.

Vacation

The summer of 1804 was a period of enjoyment for William and Sara Lummis. They used their new boat to sail all around the lake and the bay, and they fished the silvery waters of the bay with tremendous success. The two of them became expert sailors and fishermen. The only interruption of their sporting life on the water was for the birth of their son.

New Arrival

Benjamin Rush Lummis was born on a hot afternoon in late August at the Lummises' summer home in Troupville. The baby was named after William's teacher, the famous doctor Benjamin Rush. William and Sara were blessed with a healthy baby and a normal delivery. They were excited parents who took special pride in the addition to their family. They planned to take good care of Benjamin and to teach him well. Just five weeks later, their baby, whom they nicknamed Ben, went for his first boat ride on Sodus Bay. Then just two weeks later, when the harsh winds of October fell upon the area, the Lummises left Troupville to return to Philadelphia. It was a journey that none of them would soon forget. At Dr. Lummis's recommendation, Clear Dawn went back to Philadelphia with them to receive expert treatment for her illness. She had not recovered from her illness as quickly as expected. In fact, she had spent the entire summer bedridden. Dr. Lummis thought that with his care and that of other Philadelphia doctors that Clear Dawn could recuperate over the winter and return to Troupville with them the next summer.

In order to accommodate the baby, Sara, and Clear Dawn, William sold his small buggy and purchased a larger wagon built by Herman especially for the trip. Dr. Lummis rode his riding horse alongside the two-horse wagon, while Sara and Clear Dawn took turns driving it. Travel was extremely slow, and they already had a late start. The rugged roads with their steep grades made every mile of the trip long and tedious, and the cold, foul weather didn't help. William tried to arrange the traveling route and schedule so they could stay in hotels or rest in village areas or near rural homes during the night, but sometimes the distance between neighboring villages was too far to travel in one day. Therefore, they were forced to spend several nights on the road in desolate and wild country surroundings.

More Adversity

It was on a dark, cold October night in the mountains of Pennsylvania that danger and misfortune entered the lives of the travelers. They were forced to make camp along a rugged, mountain trail because they were still many miles from the next village when the sun began to set. They got things situated, set up camp, and ate their supper. Just as things quieted down for the evening, a hungry, rampaging bear decided to ignore the dangers of humans and their campfire and charged into the camp. William tried his best to fight the bear off with a small knife that he had used to prepare dinner, but no man was a match for such a ferocious bear. William was badly mauled and knocked unconscious. As the wounded bear turned toward the others, Clear Dawn, who was resting in the wagon at the time of the attack, managed to grab one of William's guns and shot the bear just as it extended its heavy paws in the direction of the little baby, Ben.

There was blood everywhere. William was in very poor shape. Sara and Clear Dawn treated his wounds the best they could and managed to travel the rest of that night along a dark and sometimes treacherous, mountain trail to get him to a doctor's treatment in the nearest village the next morning. Luckily, they found a doctor in the small town in the morning.

After over three weeks of care and rest in that village, William had recovered enough to continue the journey to Philadelphia, but he was still weak and sore. The small wagon carrying the wounded man, the sick Indian woman, the small baby, and Sara finally arrived at the Lummises' Philadelphia residence in the bitter cold of December, just in time for

Christmas. It had been a terrible trip, filled with tremendous hardships and grave danger. It was a grim reminder that the frontier could still be very wild and very dangerous.

Progress

Under a doctor's care in Philadelphia, William recuperated enough to resume his medical practice by February. Clear Dawn's illness was treated, not only by Dr. Lummis, but also by several other noted Philadelphia physicians including Dr. Rush. During the winter, Sara enjoyed her time with Ben, who seemed to get a healthy start on life.

In Troupville, Soso continued to work on the boat he was building for Colonel Troup. Herman helped him, while he learned many of Soso's ship-building techniques. This new boat was a couple feet longer than the Lummises' boat at 24-foot long and slightly narrower. The boat was also a bit deeper and heavier to provide more stability. If it was possible, the woodwork was even better than the previous boats he had made. There were several reasons for these improvements. One reason was the type of wood being used for this boat. Soso had found a hard, tough wood, perfect for this kind of boat building. The wood came from rock elm trees, which were in a small stand just a few hundred yards from Soso's house. Soso selected the best trees in the stand for his purposes, always taking care to insure that he harvested only the trees he needed. Soso hoped to use plenty of this perfect wood for many years, while leaving nature's rock elm forest healthier than when he had found it.

The mainsail, which the Sill brothers made from heavy cloth to Soso's specifications, was larger and better shaped. Soso had designed this boat specifically for speed. He hoped that Colonel Troup would like the superiority of this boat over any other on the bay in both speed and handling. He wanted to make sure the boat was worth more than the valuable land he was to receive in trade.

Whenever Soso worked on the boat, he thought about this land. He made plans for rebuilding his rustic home and workshop and eventually building even bigger and faster boats. Soso had wonderful dreams that were much more like those of a white man than an Indian. Why not? Soso now knew his way around the white's world. He could learn, adjust, and succeed. He made plans. He aimed high in both his hopes and his life's work. The white men had taught him these things. Soso knew that he had the potential to accomplish his lofty goals, if he was only given the chance. However, this was still a big if. Despite his recent successes, he was still an Indian, whom some whites considered a crude, ignorant savage, trying to live and work in the white man's world.

The boat was completed right on schedule, and on July 4th, 1805, Colonel Troup took the vessel, with Soso and Jim aboard, for its first voyage around the bay. Although the Colonel had sailed before, he now found himself a bit overwhelmed by the capabilities of this fine boat. He was very tentative at the helm and let the sails luff some in the brisk wind. However, when Colonel Troup let Jim take control of the rudder and sail, the boat seemed to jump ahead and cut through the clear water with astounding speed. For sure, no boat had ever traveled so fast on Great Sodus Bay before. Even if Colonel Troup didn't realize it yet, Jim and Soso knew that this boat was something really special. Best of all, its delivery fulfilled Soso's dream of owning land. He was now an integral part of the civilized white man's world—a landowner and a successful businessman.

The July 4th celebration that took place in the village had special meaning for Soso. It was gratifying to be in the land called America, even if, because of confusing laws that he could never understand, he couldn't be an American citizen, taxpayer, or voter. He owned land, and for now, that was good enough for the 25-year-old Native American. He had a bigger smile than normal as he won the shooting contest during the festivities and took home a big, plump turkey as first prize.

During that summer and fall, Colonel Troup was busy with the many activities associated with managing the area's municipalities and developing the region. His boat spent most of the time tied to Jim's dock alongside Dr. Lummis's boat. Dr. Lummis had decided to remain in Philadelphia that summer. William and Sara had wanted to return to their summer home, but, after the near disaster of their previous trip, they were apprehensive about exposing young Ben to the dangers of the long rugged journey. Besides, William was still feeling some of the effects of the bear attack and had not regained full strength. Unfortunately, the citizens of Troupville missed their summer doctor and were disappointed at having a season without medical care. This was another setback for the village with enormous potential, but little progress toward becoming a populous city.

Clear Dawn had made some progress under the care of Drs. Lummis and Rush, but she was still too weak to travel on her own. So she also stayed in the city for the summer. She had been confused, yet intrigued, by her strange surroundings in Philadelphia, and at first, she had longed to return to the wilderness that she understood and loved. However, the longer she stayed in Philadelphia, the more she appreciated some parts of the civilized life of the whites. She especially enjoyed the modern conveniences. She helped Sara cook and loved to shop in the markets and stores. The white's city-life was a complicated experience for a 43-year-old Indian woman who had never seen a bustling city. However, Clear Dawn was able to adapt, and she enjoyed the beneficial and exciting parts of city life. Of course, her heart and love remained on the frontier, so she had to cope with her homesickness and separation from loved ones.

New Opportunities

Dr. Lummis had given Jim and Soso permission to use his boat, but the two men had such a busy summer that they rarely had a chance. Jim's sailing job took him all around the lake with only short stays in the homeport of Troupville. While Jim seemed to be living on the water, Soso was spending all his time on land. The 25-year-old Indian was now the registered owner of lot 107 on the east side of Great Sodus Bay. Colonel Troup had delivered the deed to the land as promised, and ever since that day in July, Soso had worked continuously at improving his property. He started by rebuilding much of his house. He strengthened and insulated the walls, floors, and ceilings. He expanded and improved the garden and produced a bumper crop of vegetables, which he canned and stored away in order to survive the winter. Soso's hard work had paid considerable dividends, and now he was exploiting his opportunity. Soso no longer had to hide. While it was a strange concept for an Indian, Soso was feeling good about ownership of his land. In his heart, Soso knew that he was just renting it from nature, but he didn't reveal that idea to any white man. He planned to enjoy the use of the land and to care for it as long as nature allowed him to work the land.

As if by design, opportunity again stalked Soso, as two distinguished-looking visitors arrived at Troupville by horseback in late September 1805. They checked into the tavern under the names of Forman Cheesman and Henry Eckford. Early the next day, they met with Rob Fellows and Jim at the latter's house. Rob Fellows had managed a shipping business for the last two years and needed to expand to keep up with the demand. Rob was interested in buying a new transport boat with twice the capacity and speed of his current ship, the *Lake Queen*. By the end of the summer of 1805, the *Lake Queen* had been booked to capacity, and a larger, faster ship would be needed to satisfy the overwhelming demand for shipping goods on Lake Ontario. Rob was hoping to select a design from these two shipbuilders and then make a deal with them that included trading in his old ship. First, the four men discussed the plans that the young marine architect Henry had drawn up. These drawings looked very impressive to Jim and Rob. But the price for such a ship had Rob worried. It was a lot more than he had wanted to, or could, pay for a new boat. Also, Rob didn't like the fact that the boat would be built in New York City and, then, sailed up the ocean to Nova Scotia and then up the St. Lawrence River to get to Troupville. Sailing up the rapids of the St. Lawrence was always risky, and the delivery time would add a significant delay and cost to his plan to expand his shipping service on the lake.

After viewing the drawings, the men went down to Jim's dock where they took a small rowboat out to see Rob's *Lake Queen*, which was moored about 200 feet off shore. The two shipbuilders inspected the old cargo boat from bow to stern, and much to everyone's surprise they were impressed with what they saw. They had a buyer in Canada who wanted a boat like this and were quite sure they could sell it to him if Rob agreed to trade it for the new one.

As the four men returned to shore, Forman noticed the two other small boats tied to Jim's dock. He asked Jim, "Whose boats are those?"

"They belong to Colonel Troup and Dr. Lummis. I'm using the doctor's boat this summer since he's staying in Philadelphia," replied Jim.

As they reached the dock, Forman got a better look at the boats. "These are magnificent. I've never seen a design or a construction quite like this before."

Because Forman was aware of all the boat designs in the New York City area, he knew they weren't made in New York. So he asked Jim Davis,

"Where were they made, Boston or Philadelphia?" Forman expected such elaborate and professional work, so obviously evident in the boats, had to be done at one of the other two major shipbuilding centers in the nation. Shipbuilding, like many other activities involved with the crucial commerce of water transportation, was one of the most important skills in America. All transportation of heavy materials moved by water, so Americans like Cheesman and Eckford always thought about water and its use for transportation. Forman thought he knew all the important and skilled shipbuilders in America; he was about to be surprised at what he would hear.

"Neither, they were made right here, just across the bay," answered Jim. Both Forman and Henry were amazed by this response. These impressive boats had been made out here in the wilderness. They wondered who could have built such beautiful boats, and why was he living way out here on the frontier.

Henry took over the questioning from Forman, "Who made these?"

This time Rob answered, "Jim's Indian friend named Soso. He lives across the bay on the other side of the islands."

The expression on the two visitors' faces was now one of complete astonishment. How could an Indian build such splendid, refined boats? By that time, the two shipbuilders were inspecting the two boats and asking more questions about the Native American boat-builder. As Jim continued to answer their questions, he volunteered to take everyone for a ride in Dr. Lummis's boat. The four men continued their discussion of boat building as they sailed around Sodus Bay in one of the most advanced and modern boats in all of America.

The winds were light, and the boat was burdened with the weight of the four men, yet the shipbuilders were very impressed with the boat's performance. Despite these handicaps, with Jim at the helm, the boat glided swiftly and smoothly through the water. The northwest wind seemed to take the boat naturally toward the southeast corner of the bay. When it rounded the southern tip of Neoga Island, Jim asked the two men if they wanted to meet the man who had built the boat. Henry answered in the affirmative, so Jim steered the boat directly toward Soso's hidden cove.

Soso was in his root cellar storing vegetables from his harvest when he heard Jim's yell from the direction of the cove. Soso met the four men half way up the path to his house. Jim introduced Henry and Forman to Soso, who, dressed in his gardening clothes of work pants and an open vest, looked much more like a common Indian brave than a master shipbuilder. At first, the two men doubted that this Indian could build such excellent boats. However, they asked about Soso's shipbuilding, especially his designs and construction techniques. Soso took them into his boat-building shop and showed them his drawings, tools, and materials. Immediately, they were impressed with several of Soso's shipbuilding inventions, especially some of the tools that shaped the wood. They poured over his roughly sketched plans, which were crude in that they contained none of the standard specifications, but nevertheless revealed Soso's genius for his craft. After thirty minutes of conversation about boat building, Forman Cheesman was so convinced of Soso's talents that he made Soso an offer that Soso would never forget: a job as a marine engineer and master shipbuilder at Forman's shipyard in New York City.

"You would be able learn all the latest techniques and use the most modern equipment. You can design and build small boats or even work on the larger ships that sail across the oceans," offered Forman.

"How many people work at building one of your big boats?" Soso asked.

"We just finished a 180-foot schooner. We had over twenty workers on the hull, and many others working on the deck and rigging." Forman thought this would impress Soso.

"Hard to know whether you really helped to build a boat like that or not. I'm sure you don't need my help, but I'm sure I can help the people who need boats here on Sodus Bay." Of course, Soso could never leave his newly purchased land and home. "I must stay here with my land and friends. Sodus Bay is my home. Maybe someday I will build big boats right here on this bay." Again, Soso was making big plans, but a trip to New York City was not part of the plan at this time.

Before Forman left, he took, with Soso's permission, several shaping tools and several drawings. Soso wouldn't take any money for these items, so Forman promised that he would send Soso tools and plans from his own shipyard in trade. Henry left with the promise to return someday to learn more from Soso by watching the Indian work at his craft.

As they walked down the path to the cove, Forman saw Soso's pile of lumber, the essential raw material for any boat-building enterprise. Forman couldn't believe the magnificence of what he saw.

"Soso, I see you have some nice rock elm. Where do you get such fine specimens? Canada or out West?" Forman asked, as he carefully inspected the pile of lumber.

"About 300 yards due east there is a large stand of rock elm. This wood is strong and never splits. It shapes out real well. I use a little white oak, but I prefer the elm," Soso answered.

"This is some of the best timber I've ever seen. I had no idea that there was any rock elm this far east or south. Someday, I'd like to see your trees or maybe get a plank or two for some of my special projects. We usually bring cherry or mahogany in from overseas for our best boats. I think your rock elm is as good as our imported wood."

After the men left, Soso reflected on their visit and the praise that they had given his work. He felt more confident than ever that he could build boats and sell them to the boatmen of Lake Ontario or even to the sailors of the great seas. He wanted to make contributions that would last forever.

Unfortunately, the negotiations between the two ship builders and Rob Fellows were unsuccessful. Rob just couldn't afford to buy the size boat he wanted. Before he left, Herman suggested to Rob a potential method to rebuild and expand the *Lake Queen* and left ideas and rough plans for increasing its capacity and speed. Henry and Forman may have left Troupville without a contract to build a new ship; however, because of their discussion with Soso, they left much richer in their boat-building knowledge. Both men were amazed. One of the most talented boat builders in the world was a Native American living and working on the frontier without benefit of modern tools, equipment, and materials.

Poor Hunt

On a crisp autumn day in October, with a stiff wind out of the northwest at 15 knots, Rob Fellows went to find Soso. Rob took his small rowboat, an older model built by Soso several years before, across the choppy bay. As he rowed the cold spray from the boat slapping the waves hit his back and the cold water numbed his hands. Even so, he was able to make good time with the wind at his back.

He arrived at Soso's cove quite cold, but in good spirits. Rob had an offer to make to Soso, and he could hardly wait to get the Indian's response. He tied the boat at Soso's dock and walked up the path to the house. It was

Herman who answered the knock on the door. "Hello there, Mr. Fellows. Soso's not here right now. He's gone hunting."

"When do you expect him back?" asked Rob.

"Well I'm not quite sure. He could be back tonight or tomorrow. He usually hunts in this area, but for sure he won't be back until he has a deer."

"Please tell him I stopped by. I have some business to talk with him about." Then Herman invited Rob to come inside and warm up. The two of them drank coffee and talked about boats. Both men respected Soso's talents in boat building and shared stories about some of the astonishing boats that they had seen him build.

After warming up, Rob left the protected cove and returned across the angry bay. This time he rowed directly into the wind and rough waves. The spray battered his back when the waves broke against the bow of the boat. However, the little boat was designed for just such weather, so Rob was able to make his return trip without incident or worry. A poorly designed or weakly constructed boat would have left Rob in grave danger as he crossed the cold, swollen bay. The strength and design of his little boat made him appreciate Soso's talents even more. He tied the boat securely to his dock and headed off to Sill's tavern to warm his nearly frozen body with a drink much stronger than Herman's coffee.

Soso didn't return home for five days. Herman was getting a little worried because it had never taken Soso that long to bag a deer. Soso finally returned with more than just a deer; he also had an adventure that demonstrated erosion of his Indian heritage and skill.

During his hunting trip, Soso had been frustrated over his poor performance in the woods. On several occasions he had been unable to follow a fresh deer trail. He missed several clear shots at walking deer. One time he had failed to notice another hunter who surprised him as he walked through the forest. He was even slow in reacting to a wolf attack, which was a mistake that almost cost him his life. So, despite bagging a small deer on the fifth day, Soso's hunting trip had been a complete failure. Soso began wondering if he still had the instincts to live with nature. Had he traded them for the ways of the white man? It was important to have both the Indian's understanding of nature and the white man's knowledge of technology and civilization.

Soso didn't pay much attention when Herman gave him Rob's message. He focused on dressing out the deer. Soso was concentrating on his plans to return to the woods to revive some of his lost Indian instincts for the wild. He asked Herman to continue to watch his home and quickly left still dressed in his Indian hunting clothes.

Return to the Wild

Soso decided to head south toward his childhood home near Cayuga Lake. He took his time trying to rediscover his instinct to live in harmony with the wild that surrounded him. He dug roots and picked berries to eat. He carefully tracked game as he had many years before. He visited the rich, lush marshes in the area to see nature in its purest form. Several days after leaving his home, he found himself at the lookout on the hill near his childhood village. His thoughts went back to those days. He remembered his family, their longhouse, their village, and its people. His thoughts were pleasing and refreshing. During that brief moment, it didn't seem so long ago that he sat at this very spot and watched as his father and grandfather led fishing parties across the lake. Slowly, however, the realities of the present began to invade his thoughts. The hill and the lake seemed to shrink in size from the ones he remembered in his dreams. There was little sign of the Indian village that had been abandoned over ten years before. His father and grandfather were dead. His mother was ill and far away from him. He no longer lived in a world of Indians. Instead, his world was back on Sodus Bay living among the whites. This was the reality he couldn't avoid, and it was the life that he had chosen. He also knew it was what he wanted, and he would never again regret his decision. He was still very much an Indian, but that didn't mean that he had to live like his parents. Progress could and should be made, and he considered what he was doing as progress.

Before he left, he watched a small sailboat as it seemed to crawl its way across the lake. It was heading toward a dock along the east side of the lake. Inland from the dock he could see the trails of smoke coming from several cabins. This was the beginning of another settlement of whites being carved out of the wild land that had once belonged to the Indians. He knew that wasn't fair. What the white men had done to the Indians, in forcing them from their lands, was wrong. However, that was a different issue—one that he hoped to confront later in his life. He could still learn from the whites, while keeping his Indian culture and pride.

Refreshed

The next day, Soso returned to Sodus Bay. He was refreshed from the week's vacation in the wild. He was ready to go back to work. He completely surprised Herman as he walked into the house carrying another deer he had taken only a few hundred yards into the woods from his house.

Soso was also excited about his discovery of a large stand of white oak trees about three miles east of his house. These trees were large, tall, and straight—perfect for boat construction. This lumber resource would complement his rock elm wood to give him superb materials for building his future boats. With proper care and restrained harvesting, this stand of trees would stay healthy and produce high-quality trees forever.

Herman gave Soso messages from both Rob and Jim to come over to Troupville as soon as possible. This time Soso responded by quickly cleaning up, changing from his Indian hunting clothes into the normal work clothes of a frontier settler, and heading over to Rob's house in Troupville. Before he left, he asked Herman to finish dressing out the second deer and to take the meat to several neighbors and people in Troupville who needed the meat.

Rob was eager to talk with Soso about rebuilding the boat, and he got right to the point when Soso arrived. "Soso, I'd like to have you rebuild the *Lake Queen* using these designs," Rob stated as he handed Soso the drawings left by Henry Eckford.

At first, Soso didn't completely understand the offer or the plan. He looked over the drawings. "These drawings aren't of the *Lake Queen*," responded Soso.

"Yeah, but they are the way Eckford said to convert her to gain speed and carrying capacity," replied Rob.

Soso finally understood Rob's offer and the plans left by Henry Eckford. "The plan looks fine, but how could I do this. I don't have the facilities to work on such a big boat. It would take a shop or dry dock four times bigger than mine."

"I can pay you most of the money for the work up front, so you can build the facilities you need first. And Jim has an idea about where to build a workshop. Let's go over to his house and talk with him."

Jim was happy to see Soso and Rob come across the yard because he knew what they had been discussing. Jim suggested they go to the tavern, and there he laid out his plan. Soso could build his workshop by adding onto the existing fish market. It was the ideal location because the water depth was perfect for a dry dock and there was lots of room for a large work area. Soso also needed labor and supplies, which were available in Troupville. This plan would make Soso and Jim partners again.

By the time the three men left the tavern, a deal had been struck. Soso and Jim would spend the winter reworking Jim's fish market into a shipyard by building a crude but functional dry dock for the *Lake Queen* and a shop for the wood working. Rob would lead another crew that would work on the interior of the ship at its mooring at the inlet of the bay to prepare it for reconstruction. At the first thaw in the spring, work on the ship would begin in earnest. They hoped that the *Lake Queen* would be ready for service by the end of August, but it seemed more likely that the project would last at least until late fall, making it ready to sail in the spring of 1807. Rob was going to pay Soso some of the money now, in order to convert the fish market into a workshop. The rest of the money would be paid in the summer.

Soso stayed up late reviewing the plans of the shop and planning all the work that had to be done. He was so excited about the project that he was aboard the *Lake Queen* at sunrise the next morning. He wanted to check several details of the ship that weren't completely clear on the drawings. By noon he was satisfied that he understood the reconstruction, so he loaded his fishing boat with fishing gear, picked up Jim, and the two of them went fishing on the lake. It was a relaxing trip during which both men renewed their commitment of friendship to each other. It would be exciting being partners again.

Great Expectations

The thaw of 1806 brought great expectations to Troupville. Colonel Troup was in fine spirits since he had heard by letter that Dr. Lummis was moving to Troupville permanently. Having a doctor in town would certainly help the growth of Troupville and the surrounding area. Soso was even more pleased since Clear Dawn would be returning to Troupville with the Lummises.

Soso was extremely busy with his job of rebuilding the *Lake Queen*. He worked full time on the ship and lived right in Jim's shop so he wouldn't lose time in traveling across the bay. Herman was staying at Soso's house, taking care of the crops and rebuilding Soso's dock, which had been destroyed by the ice push over the winter.

The work on the *Lake Queen* was progressing right on schedule. The dry dock and shop were excellent facilities for this work. The ship was being reworked by a crew of two men. Soso supervised and did all the delicate and important work such as the re-seaming of the stringers along the bottom of the ship.

The Lummises and Clear Dawn were expected in Troupville by the first of June, but, as usual, they were late. Soso tried to wait patiently for their arrival, but it was difficult to do so, because he was so excited to see his mother again. The letters that he had received from Dr. Lummis warned him not to expect a full recovery for Clear Dawn. In any case, he just wanted to see her again. However, that was not to be.

Great Grief

June seventh was a cold, damp day along the lakeshore. It felt more like March than June. At noon the Lummises arrived in Troupville. When Soso heard the news, he hurried from the dry dock at Jim's toward the Lummis house. Halfway there he met a solemn Dr. Lummis on the path. Soso knew immediately from the expression on the Doctor's face that something was wrong. Dr. Lummis spoke first, "Soso, I have bad news. Clear Dawn died on the trip. She passed away two days ago near Geneva. She…"

Soso didn't hear the rest. His grief was overwhelming. One more time he had a member of his family taken away. He turned back toward Jim's and did as he had done before when he lost his father. He got into his boat and rowed straight for the lake. He hoped that exhaustion would eventually overtake his feelings of grief, but this time his feelings were too strong. He had lost his mother who had loved and supported him through all his years. Her courage had given him the strength to become an independent man and the confidence to enter the world of the whites. Now without her, he began to doubt his abilities to continue with this lifestyle. Maybe, he had set his sights too high. Maybe the evil spirits were too strong and were causing him pain and suffering. Or maybe there just weren't any good or real spirits to help his people. Without his mother he couldn't continue.

Then it happened again. He must have been several miles from the inlet to the great bay, when suddenly there were huge sails only a hundred yards away from his small boat. This time it was a British warship with the red and white flag of England flying from the top of its tall mast. The ship completely overwhelmed Soso's little boat and its passenger. Soso's rowboat had been sighted by the ship's lookouts. Soso had no choice, so in his exhaustion, he simply stopped rowing to avoid a collision with the massive ship. As the ship approached his boat, he looked up on the ship's deck to see its crew at full battle stations. The guns were manned and the officers and troops were standing at the ready.

Soso's feeling of grief disappeared, but this time it was replaced with a sense of fear and intimidation. The huge British ship seemed directly on top of him. All Soso could see was a wall of wood with thick cooper protection on the hull of the immense ship. Shouts from the top of the wall rang down for him to surrender. Soso knew what the word surrender meant and he would have complied. However, he had no idea what he needed to do to accomplish it. He certainly had no thought of resisting or escaping, so he just sat there.

Finally, the warship slowed and stopped. It lowered a small dinghy from its side with three armed sailors aboard. The dingy came up along the side of Soso's boat. As the dinghy approached, the sailor in the bow yelled at Soso, "What's your name? Why are you way out here?" This was a threat as much as it was a query.

Soso was so startled and confused that he didn't answer immediately. However, by now the sailors recognized that the boatman was an Indian and saw all the fishing gear piled up in the boat. The sailor yelled his findings back up to the deck of the warship. The dingy was rowed back to the spot along side the ship and was raised back up onto the deck. Within seconds the big ship jumped into motion and sailed directly away from Soso. It moved quickly to the west down the lake and after several minutes disappeared from view. Soso had not said a word.

Soso's senses and emotions slowly returned to his body and mind, which had been completely numbed by the preceding events. As he slowly rowed back toward Troupville, his direction in life became clearer. He began to put his mother's life into perspective. She had always encouraged his ambitious plans and his life with the whites. She would have wanted him to continue to strive to succeed in their world. The white man's world was one she could never completely understand, but one that Soso was beginning to understand, and Clear Dawn had been proud of his accomplishments. He vowed to continue his hopes and to make a contribution. The good spirits had always been there to help him through the difficult times. He would succeed. It was what his mother wanted, and what he had to do.

There were plenty of things in his new, civilized world that bothered Soso. In the white's world, power did not come from physical strength or wisdom. Power was formed from possessions. Possessions were obtained through any manner possible. Dishonesty was bad only if the person wronged had more power than the other person did. People in the world of the white man were never good or bad, they were always both. There was never black or white, there were always shades of gray. Soso sensed this was unjust, but it was reality. He would have to learn about power, possessions, and shades of gray. It wouldn't be easy, but he knew he could do it.

Soso returned to Troupville to bury his mother next to the graves of his father and grandfather. Dr. Lummis and Tom Reeve went with him. Soso reflected on the lives of the three family members he had buried there. There was his grandfather, Trout, the distinguished Indian chief who had been successful in the Indian world yet had also recognized the changes that were occurring in the modern world. Trout had encouraged Soso to interact with the whites. Buried next to Trout was Soso's father, Gar, who could have been just as successful as his grandfather, but suffered from his misunderstanding of the whites. That confusion caused Gar misery, failure, and death. Now there was his mother, Clear Dawn, who was buried next to his father. She was able to adjust to both the Indian and white lifestyles, even though she never completely understood the strange world of the whites. She had been successful as a strong, caring woman in both cultures. Soso knew that he had learned from all three of them and possessed a blend of their characteristics. He wondered how his life would turn out. He wondered when he would join with his family again. The spirits never answered his questions, but he still had to keep faith. Somehow he knew they were there, and they would help him in times of need.

Soso's only comment to Dr. Lummis on their return trip across the bay was a request, "Please make sure that when my day comes I join my family here at the mouth of First Creek."

Rebuilding the Ship

The next day Soso and his crew were back working on the *Lake Queen*. They were in the midst of reinforcing the hull and reworking the storage hold. This was a critical time in the rebuilding and Soso's expertise was needed to accomplish the ongoing work. The work had progressed ahead of schedule, and everyone was hopeful for a summer launching. Fortunately the tools that Forman Cheesman had promised Soso had arrived in the spring. Soso made good use of these sophisticated tools. They were very valuable in performing some of the complicated hull work necessary for this job.

About a week later, unusual visitors came to Troupville and Soso's dry dock. The United States Navy had its Lake Ontario fleet at a base in the port of Oswego. The Navy needed a strong force on the lake because of the continued squabbling with England over borders with Canada and property rights. The British ships like the one Soso had encountered still cruised around the lake harassing American ships. The Oswego area was more developed than Troupville and had a large, well-protected fort for the troops' protection. The port was a deep, narrow river with some good facilities for ships. However, the port at Oswego wasn't nearly as large or beautiful as

Sodus Bay. The Navy was conducting maneuvers on the lake and brought its two largest ships into Sodus Bay for a couple of days. Some of the sailors were given shore leave for the day and visited Troupville. After spending some time at the tavern, several sailors came over to the dry dock to see the work being done on the transport ship. Some of the sailors had seen the *Lake Queen* before and wondered how the rebuilding would change her. Everybody liked watching Soso and his work crew perform the amazing transformation taking place right before his or her eyes.

One young sailor in particular was curious about the rebuilding effort. He asked many questions about the plans and Soso's wood working techniques. Soso was very impressed with the young man's brilliance, enthusiasm, and knowledge of ships. The two men continued their discussion over dinner at the tavern. Soso was amazed to find out that although the sailor, James Cooper, was only seventeen years old, he knew a great deal about ships and the rest of the world. After dinner, Soso showed James the smaller boats he had built for Dr. Lummis and Colonel Troup. The rest of the evening was spent in an interesting discussion between the two men. The knowledge of each impressed the other. They talked about ships, sailing, fishing, Indians, whites, and politics. Finally, James had to return to his ship. He had enjoyed his day of liberty in Troupville and the time that he spent with his new Indian friend. He told Soso that he would try to return to Troupville some day to talk more about ships and the attributes of the Indian culture.

Settlement's Development

Colonel Troup had asked Dr. Lummis and Colonel Fitzhugh to help him establish regular transportation and postal routes into the Troupville area. This task required the two men to travel throughout the area to establish potential customers, to determine efficient routes, and to convince government officials of its utility. During a week in early July 1806, Dr. Lummis was scheduled to ride with Colonel Fitzhugh to neighboring villages and towns to drum up support for the plan and determine the requirements that would be needed to make the plan operational. However, Colonel Fitzhugh was in ill health and decided the trip would be too much of a burden. Jim and Soso agreed to ride along with Dr. Lummis instead. Soso figured a short break from the shipbuilding would do him and his crew some good. They had worked every day for three months without a break. So he gave everyone three days off work. Early on Monday morning the three men started out riding along the lakeshore heading west.

The first settlement they came to was Appleboom. John Halett was a new settler there. He called the area Pultneyville. It was a quiet, charming spot overlooking a small river. They rode quite some way further through the rough landscape before they found another settlement. It was on a pretty river on which Colonel Nathaniel Rochester had established a series of mills. They spent the night at Colonel Rochester's home, where after dinner Dr. Lummis discussed with Colonel Rochester the need for regular stagecoach and postal service. This area was very rough and hilly, and the river valley was steep. There seemed to be little hope that it would develop like Great Sodus, but Nathaniel Rochester was a friendly man, who was willing to help develop a regional transportation system.

With their business to the west completed, the three travelers headed back east the next morning. This time they ventured about 15 miles farther inland from the southern shore of the lake. Along the way, they talked about the Native American culture. Both Jim and Dr. Lummis had learned the Iroquois language and appreciated the way the Indians incorporated their understanding of nature into their way of life.

They followed an old Indian trail along the east-west ridge. They visited villages and townships called Freetown, Palmyra, Williamson, East Ridge, Lyons, Clyde, and Wolcott. Palmyra and Lyons were well-developed settlements, each with several hundred residents. Soso was surprised at what he found in Lyons. As Dr. Lummis talked transportation business with Judge Daniel Dorsey, Soso wandered the streets. On Williams Street he found several Indian huts and behind the huts a bagataway field. There were over thirty Indian braves playing a fierce game. Most of the Indians were Senecas, but Soso met a couple Cayugas. One older woman was from Soso's old village and remembered him as a small child. Soso enjoyed a few minutes reminiscing with the woman. As was always the case, she had no knowledge of his missing siblings, Perch and Water Lily. However, it was very exciting for Soso to meet someone from his childhood life.

The players talked Soso into joining the bagataway game even though he hadn't played since his childhood. For just a moment on the field he relived his childhood dreams. He was surprised how some of his skills at bagataway came back after all these years. But a group of the younger braves eventually ran him down. There was no doubt that Soso was in good condition. He was 26 years old and had deceptively strong muscles and excellent coordination. He was a natural athlete, and he also had the intensity to excel in a contact sport. His skills with a bagataway stick may have eroded, but he still maneuvered and ran as though he were an experienced player.

Soso's fun ended when Jim and Dr. Lummis called him over so that they could continue with their journey. Jim and Dr. Lummis were astonished at Soso's talents. Even the little bit of play they watched had conclusively demonstrated that he was a superb athlete. And they weren't the only ones impressed with Soso's play. Several older braves congratulated Soso on his performance. One remarked how he had only once before seen a player with such natural skills in bagataway—a brave named Gar who played in the tribal contests at the Onondaga council many years before. The brave was surprised when Soso told him that Gar was his father.

After the exciting afternoon in Lyons, the three men continued their journey and after several more miles of travel arrived at Clyde to spend the night. The next morning they traveled southeast to Webster's Landing. There they met with Father LeMoyne, who maintained a processor near a large salt spring. Father LeMoyne's support and influence would be important to the success of their plans. Dr. Lummis had no difficulty in convincing Father LeMoyne of the benefits of their transport and mail-delivery plan. He was a visionary leader who was dreaming of big things for his frontier community.

All in all, it had been a successful trip. The key hubs of the transportation network had been established. Now Colonel Troup just needed to obtain the men and the equipment and soon regular mail and transportation would be part of this growing region. The three men had done their job to help the area develop, and they had certainly enjoyed their trip around the region together.

"We have plenty to be thankful for. This area is rich and beautiful. I had no idea so many people had moved into the region in the past few years," Jim Davis commented to his companions. Jim remembered how wild and desolate this area had been when he first starting trapping, hunting, and fishing here over 15 years before.

"I had no idea there were so many white men in the world," laughed Soso. "It was nice to see some Indians and play a game with them. It had been a long time since I played the game or even spoke with Iroquois."

"I wonder what this region will be like in the future. I worry that so many people will live here that it will lose its natural beauty. Great Sodus Bay is big, but it could become so crowded that no one will enjoy it. I worry that big businesses and government might ruin all that we now enjoy in this area." Dr. Lummis was always thinking about the future. The three founding fathers of the Sodus Bay area continued their discussion as they rode back home to the bay they loved.

Launching

By the middle of August, the reconstruction of the *Lake Queen* was complete. The boat was ready for launching. The placement of the rigging and the final sewing of the mainsail were the only details left to be finished. A large crowd gathered at the dry dock at Troupville to see the rebuilt ship slide down the ramp into the silvery waters of the bay. The ship's owner, Rob Fellows, was pleased with the work that Soso had done, and he was proud of his ship as it settled into the water. Now the *Lake Queen* was a large, sleek, modern transport ship. Rob took several merchants, politicians, and customers onto the *Lake Queen* to show her off. The next day the rigging and the sail were finished so Jim took the ship out for an initial test sail. Rob and Soso were aboard, anxiously awaiting the result of this test of performance and handling. In just a few minutes time they all knew they had a winner. The ship handled like a charm, and Jim was sure her speed had more than doubled. The cargo capacity had more than doubled. Rob had already contracted for some immediate cargo hauling, so the very next day the *Lake Queen* resumed her old routine. This time she would be the envy of the lake—no longer a tired, bulky, slow scow, but an efficient, fast, modern transport. All this thanks to the genius of an Indian brave and master shipbuilder.

Soso went fishing each day for the week following the completion of the *Lake Queen*. He did this to relax and unwind after the preceding hectic days and weeks. He was glad for the opportunity to work on the big ship and thankful for the ability to transform it into a majestic vessel. The ship was now in the capable hands of his friend Jim and no longer his worry. He also spent some time working on his garden. Herman and his new wife Catherine had worked the field for him during the spring and summer. Soso was left to harvest the vegetables and clear more land for a larger garden and an orchard of fruit trees.

Friendship

A rather hot fall afternoon in early October brought a visitor to Soso's field. The stranger approached Soso just as he was trying to dislodge a big tree stump from its roots, which were buried deep into the ground. Soso was having an extremely difficult time. This stump looked determined to stay in the ground forever. The man pitched right in to help Soso pull out the stump. After pulling, prying, chopping, and wedging for several intense minutes, the stubborn stump gave up its grip on mother earth and finally popped out of its hole. The two men were exhausted from their efforts but quite pleased at what they had accomplished.

Soso spoke to his helper as they both sat down to rest and catch their breath on the old stump. "Thanks for the help. That was a tough one. I'd probably never have gotten it out of there by myself. You are a good friend."

The stranger responded, "Glad to help you out. You are Soso aren't you?" The man continued as Soso nodded yes. "I hear you're trying to start a fruit farm here on your land. It sure seems like excellent soil for that plan."

Soso noticed right away that this man was a bit strange. He was wearing tattered clothes and carried a large satchel with him. He was extremely strong and well conditioned. He appeared to be a few years older than Soso and in very good health.

"You heard correctly. I hope to increase the size of my garden and I'd like to plant some fruit trees right here where I'm clearing this land. How did you know about my plans?" asked Soso.

"I've been over at Troupville talking with Dr. Lummis. He said you may need some of the same kind of help I gave him."

"What kind of help is that?"

"I have plenty of seeds for apple trees and a few cherry tree seeds as well. They'll produce the best apples you've ever tasted. Especially here along the lake where the weather is just right for these hardy trees. Here's enough seeds for a couple acres. They'll be ready for planting in the spring." The man reached into his satchel, pulled out a large bag of apple seeds and a small bag of cherry seeds, and gave them to Soso.

Soso had always enjoyed eating big, red, juicy apples. However, he had noticed that only a few select trees produced such high quality apples. Most other trees that he'd seen produced smaller, sour-tasting apples. Shocked by the man's offer, Soso accepted the seeds. They were just what his orchard needed. He asked the man, "Don't you want some money or a trade for these seeds?"

"No money. My pleasure is that I know you'll have a productive orchard of apple and cherry trees in a few years. I passed through this area a few years ago and always thought it had potential to produce the best apples I've ever seen. Take good care of the trees, and they'll produce good apples. I have to go now. I'm traveling back west to Ohio. I have a long journey ahead and only a few weeks to make it in."

"Thank you very much. I hope to fulfill your wish." Soso was taken by this man's kindness and sincerity.

Soso had to give this strange man something to show his thanks. All he had available with him were some of the vegetables that he had picked earlier in the day and a couple of smoked fish fillets. Soso gave them to the man suggesting that they would make a few good meals for his trip. The two thanked one another before the stranger headed off on his journey. Soso could tell by the man's walk and mannerisms that he was at peace with himself and nature. This white man was more like an Indian than any other white whom Soso knew. Soso realized that he didn't even know the man's name so he yelled out just as the man reached the woods, "what's your name?"

"John. Johnny C. from Ohio."

Soso took the seeds into his storage area. He had plenty of vegetable seeds already prepared for next spring's planting. He added the apple and cherry seeds from Johnny C. to his stock and promised himself to have another four acres of land cleared for an apple and cherry orchard by the spring. There would be more than a few stubborn stumps to tangle with before he could accomplish that goal.

Homemaking

Since William, Sara, and Ben Lummis were now year-round residents of Troupville, William was deeply involved in two major projects. He was building a new home for his family and establishing a small farming business. Of course, the majority of his time was devoted to medicine; caring for the sick was his main contribution to the village. His new house would be located on his own land in Troupville. He had plenty enough room on his lot to build a nice large permanent house next to the temporary one that they had been living in. He was planning on renting out the temporary house once they moved into the new one. He hoped that the new house would be ready by the middle of the next summer. He was already in negotiations with a buyer for all of his property in Philadelphia. He promised Sara that they would use the money from the sale to send their children to the best schools when the time came. It was the one condition Sara demanded, if she was going to move her family to the frontier. She knew that she personally would enjoy her frontier life. She had never been comfortable with the fancy socializing and idleness that city life offered a young woman. Sara was active and hard-working by nature. She was much happier confronting the challenges of the frontier than the boredom of the city.

The Lummises' farm would be located out of the village, several miles from their home, at a location near Salmon Creek. This was an area that William and Sara both loved for its splendor and excellent stream fishing. He and his father-in-law were also purchasing the two mills, which were located along the creek. His farm would be small, but he had plans for many different kinds of crops. He planned on planting wheat, several varieties of vegetables, cherry trees, and apple trees as a start. Dr. Lummis knew very little about the details of farming, so he planned to hire a farm manager. In the meantime, he was actively involved in clearing the land for both projects.

A Friendly Hunt

Winter hit early and hard that year of 1806. Nevertheless, the bitter cold and icy water didn't prevent Soso and Jim from their annual duck and goose hunt. This year they had invited Dr. Lummis to come along on the first day. However, they figured that the nasty weather and the fact that the Lummises had a houseguest would prevent Dr. Lummis from coming. So as Jim and Soso walked toward the point of land near the outlet to the lake they weren't really expecting to find Dr. Lummis. Instead Dr. Lummis and a friend of his from Philadelphia were already waiting at the duck blind when Soso and Jim arrived. Dr. Lummis introduced the two frontiersmen to his city friend, James, from Philadelphia.

"I hope you don't mind my bringing along an extra hunter," Dr.

Lummis said after the introductions. "James knows a lot about ducks and has hunted some before. He wants to learn more about the birds in our area."

"He's welcome to hunt with us. We have plenty of room in the blind, and there'll be plenty of ducks for all of us," Soso said. Both Dr. Lummis and James carried a firearm so all four hunters could shoot at the waterfowl.

Soso and Jim went right to work. They set out about thirty hand carved and painted decoys. Of course, there was the traditional disagreement over the placement of a decoy or two, but soon the argument was over. They put some final touches of camouflage on the blind, and Soso took the boat about a hundred yards down the shore to hide it behind some trees. The four men situated themselves in the blind. It was cozy, but there was just enough room for all of them to shoot. Now it was time to wait for the light of the coming sunrise and the waterfowl to fly toward the decoys. The time was spent in idle chat, anticipation of the action, and enjoyment of nature's spectacular awakening for the day.

"Doctor, you sure you know how to shoot that gun?" Jim teased Dr. Lummis.

"I'm a little better than my teacher," joked Dr. Lummis. Soso had taught Dr. Lummis to shoot a gun in the fall. Dr. Lummis was at best a fair shooter; Soso was the best there was. William took tremendous pride in his newly acquired ability to shoot a flintlock, but it took a real expert to hit a fast flying duck with a flintlock. William would have to improve miraculously or be very lucky to hit many ducks on his first day of hunting.

"Where did you hunt before, James?" Jim asked Dr. Lummis's guest.

"I tried to hunt in Philadelphia. Well, actually a place near there called Mill Grove. But the hunting there was never too good, although there were some ducks on the Delaware River. So I had to travel into the interior of Pennsylvania and along the New Jersey coast to hunt. Now, I'm used to traveling to hunt and find waterfowl and birds. However, I'm not sure I know all your species of duck." James answered in perfect English with a bit of a French accent. James had grown up in France and had been in America for only three years.

"Well if all goes right, you'll see plenty. There's been several hundred ducks feeding in this area for about a week now." Jim was boasting about this location for the blind since he had selected it. Soso had preferred hunting over in the narrows between Loga and Neoga islands. But since they invited Dr. Lummis to come along, Soso had agreed that this was a better place to hunt the first day since it was so convenient. Besides, there should be plenty of action wherever they went. Sodus Bay was filled with migratory birds of many species.

Their discussion was first interrupted by the splendor of the morning sunrise. As the sun began to edge its bright colors through the horizon and onto the faces of the hunters, it enhanced and highlighted the rest of nature's beauty. Nature always seemed to give her best and brightest bounty to the shores of Sodus Bay. There was a distinct moment of overwhelming silence as all of nature's living creatures were in awe of this majestic sight. That brief pause occurred every morning on Sodus Bay as nature announced the wakening of another day. Then suddenly, another wakening for the hunters occurred as the distinct sounds reached them of wing flutter and splashes in the water. Ducks were settling into their decoys, but it was still a bit too dark to shoot. The four men were completely quiet for several minutes as the scene in front of them began to unfold. The sky lightened as the sun grew in size and climbed steadily in the sky. The mist along the water rose to reveal a raft of over fifty ducks feeding around their decoys. Jim very quietly whispered the shooting instructions to the others. The four men would stand and shoot at the same time, each taking a different sector. At the count of three, it happened.

The four shots rang out in the stillness of the morning. The noise of the wings seemed even louder than the shots as ducks took off in all directions. All four were happy at the results as four ducks were floating in the water. None of them had ever seen such success. Dr. Lummis obviously had beginner's luck, and it was evident that James was an excellent shot. Soso went down to get the boat and to retrieve the four birds. When he returned with the kill, James was quick to ask to see the waterfowl, and he studied each of them quite carefully.

"Healthy and well-fed birds," James commented as he studied them in detail. "Mallards are a strong, magnificent species."

"These ducks like this spot. The bay has several regions of celery weeds, but the most plentiful area is right here." Soso knew exactly why these birds had come by in the dark to join their decoys for a breakfast of celery.

"They were beautiful. I had no idea that ducks could be so noisy when they flew." Novice hunter Dr. Lummis was still in awe of the morning's activities.

"Get ready. Here comes another flock," Jim Davis whispered, as an another cloud of ducks raised up from the lake and headed their way.

The hunt continued for several hours in much the same manner. The ducks seemed to be cooperating by flying low and directly over the decoys. The shooters were unusually accurate, including a couple more successful shots by the novice Dr. Lummis. It was not easy to bring down fast flying birds, but the numerous opportunities allowed Dr. Lummis to practice. Eventually, he developed enough skill to hit a lucky shot. In any case, it was very exciting for the city-raised doctor to participate in the challenging activity of hunting waterfowl.

Soso and James compared notes on the habits and features of various types of ducks. After a while James stopped hunting and just studied the ducks instead of shooting at them. Then James began to make pencil sketches of the ducks on paper that he had brought as the other three men continued to hunt. The beautiful sketches fascinated Soso. He couldn't believe how detailed and accurate they were.

After the hunt, the hunters returned to Jim's house to warm up by the fireplace and eat large bowls of steamy hot soup. The soup had become the traditional meal provided by Karen on the first day of waterfowl hunting by Jim and Soso. This was the fifth year she had provided hearty soup to hungry hunters.

After the four men were warmed up and quite full of the delicious soup, Jim took the ducks out to his shop to clean them, while Soso and Dr. Lummis went over to the Lummis house to clean the guns. James continued drawing ducks on his sheets of paper. He showed Soso some of the drawings he had made during his trip up from Pennsylvania. They were wonderful. Soso could tell this man had a special talent to capture with accuracy the details and posture of the birds. Soso was especially taken by a magnificent sketch of a snowy owl. The bird seemed so real that it was ready to take off from the branch it was perched on. Soso was astonished at such talent. He had never seen pictures like the ones that James produced.

The pattern of activity was the same for each day of that week. The four men got up early and went hunting together. They did go to a couple other locations around the bay. The locations were selected by Soso based on the speed and direction of the wind. Two days were spent at the narrows between Loga Island and Neoga Island. That location was Soso's favorite. He always had good luck there. One day they went over to the sand bar across from the outlet to the lake. And one day a hole opened in the ice off the end of Briscoe Point, so they hunted there. The rest of the time they hunted where they did the first day. The week's total kill was an astonishing 94 ducks and seventeen geese. All the birds were used in meals for the hunters and their families and friends, except for the geese, which were taken over to the tavern and cooked for a community dinner celebration. Soso and Jim had provided geese for the tavern on several occasions.

James spent a considerable amount of time during that week drawing sketches of ducks, geese, and other species of birds. He was especially excited whenever a bird of a species he had never seen before was sighted or killed. James seemed to know all about the unique species of gulls, terns, plovers, ospreys, and sandpipers. He also loved to watch the waterfowl of the old squaw species fly along the lakeshore. James left Troupville after staying eight days. He had to return home to tend to his farming business and court his girlfriend, whom he missed and talked about almost as much as the waterfowl. James was very appreciative of the invitation and hospitality given to him by the Lummises. He was also very thankful of the opportunity to hunt with the two waterfowl experts, Jim Davis and Soso. He had learned a lot from them about waterfowl habits that would help him during the rest of his career as a wildlife artist. Before he left Troupville, he gave to each of his companions one of his bird drawings. Soso received the drawing of the snowy owl that he had admired so much. James was as generous as he was talented.

Spring Flood

Spring came too early. The fall and winter had been wet and cold, and the snow cover was deep. Then for three straight days in early March the sun shone brightly and the temperatures soared past sixty degrees. The water runoff was extensive, and that, combined with the already high water, was more than many of the streams could bear. The hardest hit stream was Salmon Creek. The two old gristmills had no chance against the tremendous force of flooding water. Both mills were completely washed away. Dr. Lummis' dream of owning a milling venture on that stream vanished. He lost the money that he had placed as a down payment on the mills, but it was Colonel Troup who suffered the biggest losses during this disaster. Several other mills owned by Troup on different streams were also washed out that spring. Many homes and barns were flooded, and several structures were washed away completely. Nature had a strange way of cleansing itself. But those who knew nature's ways, also knew that from nature's perspective there were good reasons for this occurrence.

The high water also hurt fishing that year—especially the stream fishing, since high water kept the currents in the streams too fast for the spawning fish. Soso and Jim fished a little, but both men were still busy with their other activities. It was a rough time for those who depended on catching fish for their livelihood. No one could remember the fishing on the streams, the bay, or the lake ever being so bad.

Business

Jim was now sailing the *Lake Queen* full time. Rob Fellow's business connections had blossomed, which meant the ship was busy transporting goods around the lake the entire season. The dry dock by Jim's shop had been converted into a cargo area and loading dock. It seemed Troupville was fast becoming a significant shipping port for Lake Ontario. Increasingly, area farmers and businessmen who needed goods shipped into and out of the area used Rob's shipping service.

Meanwhile Soso was back in his own workshop across the bay building boats. He was simultaneously building two boats similar to the one he built for Colonel Troup. His shop was crowded with the two 24-foot long hulls. However, he and Herman, who was working part-time for Soso, were managing to make good progress on both boats. Soso concentrated on the most crucial parts of the construction, while Herman worked on the easier tasks. This way both men kept busy, usually alternating their work between the two boats. The construction had started in earnest during December, and the hope was that both boats would be finished by July. One of the boats had already been sold to Tom Hornsby. The other was still available. Soso wasn't worried about selling the second boat, but he did hope that he would sell it soon because he needed money to buy parts and equipment in order to finish the boats. Soso was a trusted businessman in the village, but he had never asked for credit. He had always paid cash or traded for everything that he needed.

During that spring and summer, Soso also kept busy in his garden and orchard. He had planted more vegetables than ever, and he had about 75 superb apple tree seedlings sprouting from the seeds that Johnny C. had given him the previous fall. Soso's busy schedule kept him from missing his family. He was now a 27-year-old man, strong and independent. However, he took time to remember his deceased family members, and he was very emotional about their loss. Every month he would visit his family's graves at the west side of the bay. His ritual for the visit was short and simple. He walked to the burial ground and stood there for a couple minutes remembering the best times that he had with each member of his family. Often, he would speak a few words, as if they were still able to hear and reply. Then he would leave to return to his own activities. Sometimes he would combine his trip to the gravesite with a fishing trip into the marshes of First Creek. He always caught plenty of turtles, frogs, perch, and bass in those waters. Fishing there brought back memories of his first visit to Osoenodus almost 20 years before and enhanced his memories of the family that he missed and loved.

The Lummises were as busy as Jim and Soso. The plans for developing their fruit farm near Salmon Creek were delayed because of the flooding, but the building of their house in Troupville was continuing at a rapid pace. Dr. Lummis had a couple of full-time carpenters working, and he and Herman were doing some of the interior work. Herman was an excellent wood worker thanks to the training that he received in boat building from Soso. On the other hand, Dr. Lummis was inept at carpentry; however, he tried hard to contribute to the effort. Usually, Herman ended up spending some time redoing what Dr. Lummis had messed up. Sara realized her husband's limitations and tried her best to keep William away from the construction. She was also making some of interior decorations and designing the home furnishings. Herman usually spent half a day at the Lummises and then went over to Soso's to work the rest of the day on boat building.

One source of pleasure for everyone was the growth of little Ben Lummis. The three-year-old was a bundle of activity. He was an intelligent, cheerful child who was friendly with everyone. He seemed to go nonstop from one end of the growing house to the other. Little Ben was already an avid fisherman and swimmer. Sara and William spent time with him in their boat and at the beach near their home. Sara had always been an attractive, strong women—perfectly suited for frontier life. Her happiness added to her beauty. She was still a young 28 years old. William was a caring husband and father. He was starting to show his age as he approached his 50th year. His hair was graying. Despite the contrast in their ages, the two made a stunning, distinguished couple. Everyone in Troupville looked up to and respected the dedication, commitment, and humility of the Lummis family. Troupville was blessed with their presence.

Residents of the area celebrated these and other blessings at the 4th of July festivities of 1807. As usual, there was plenty of intense celebrating that took place over a three-day period. Troupville may not have developed into a big city, but its residents truly appreciated its treasures and enjoyed each other's company. The big social event of this year's celebration was a party at William Wickham's house—the biggest and nicest house right in the middle of the village of Troupville. Guests began arriving at 3 P.M. Most were farmers dressed in their best clothes—blue tunics with big buttons and high black boots. These were made of too heavy cloth for this hot time of the year, but it was the dressiest clothes that were owned. The women were adorned in colorful cotton dresses with many ribbons and bows. Many came via carriages or buggies, others on foot or by boat. It was about

200 yards from the shore of the bay to the party house. The guests brought bottles or jugs of their best spirits—whiskey, corn liquor, apple cider, or heavy beer. Most of the women brought some food to share—breads, desserts, or fruit platters.

If the celebrants wanted to talk, they went inside to converse since the loud music was played outside. The food was set up inside. The big table held the beef, fish, and cooked vegetables—all this provided by the Wickhams. Another table held the desserts, and another held the bread and fruit platters brought by the guests.

The Wickhams had a large yard. In the middle of the yard a small platform held the fiddler. All around the fiddler, guests danced. Actually, a couple fiddlers alternated to keep music available continuously. This was a noisy, riotous, and happy bunch of partygoers. At dusk, lanterns hanging from trees were lit and a small bonfire was started. To an outsider, it must have looked like complete chaos. To a native of Troupville, it was just another Independence Day party.

About midnight, the partygoers began to leave. Most negotiated their departure fine, but a few had to climb aboard boats that were tied to posts along shore. It was nearly impossible for a sober person to perform this task without getting good clothes wet. It was completely impossible for the drunken celebrants. There was a big full moon to shed some light on the boats, but it didn't make the task of climbing aboard the boats any easier. It was a humorous sight, but eventually the boats were boarded with soaked, drunken guests as the party drew to a close. People of all ages and all social standings had tremendous fun at Wickham's party. The Troupville area residents showed that they could party as hard as they worked.

By late July, Soso was ready to launch his two new boats. Tom Hornsby would be over in two days to pick up his, but the other boat still had not been sold. Soso didn't have enough money for the second sail, which was being sewn by the Sills. If he didn't sell the boat soon, he would try to trade furs, meat, and vegetables to the Sills in return for the sail.

Old Friend

Soso was putting the final touches on the boats when he heard a knock on his house door. To his surprise it was his sailor friend, James Cooper, whom he had met at Troupville a year before. James was accompanied by two other Navy sailors. James introduced Soso to his friends, Roger and John. The three of them were on liberty for a week from their port in Oswego, and they had decided to spend the time on Great Sodus Bay. Roger had an additional motive for coming to Sodus Bay; he wanted to buy a boat. Upon meeting Soso, Roger got right to the point, "Do you have any of those boats that James told me about for sale?"

Soso showed him the way to the shop. "The one on the far side is still for sale. She's almost ready to go now. All I need to get is the mainsail, which is waiting for me over at Sill's Tavern in Troupville."

"This is a beauty. James, you're definitely right. These are the best fishing boats I've ever seen." Roger was wide-eyed looking at the boat that he wished would soon be his.

Roger couldn't believe his good fortune. He had expected to have a long wait while a boat was made. This boat was everything James had said and more. Roger had spent his life on the waters of Long Island and Lake Ontario, and he had never seen such a well-built boat of this size. Roger was going to leave the Navy in three weeks to start his own fishing business on the St. Lawrence River. His only concern now was the price of the boat. Certainly, a boat like this would be too expensive for him. He had saved $190 from his Navy pay and his inheritance, but he needed to have enough money left to buy a parcel of land that he liked up in Cape Vincent after he purchased the boat.

Roger timidly asked Soso, "How much is it?"

Soso was charging Hornsby $95 for the other boat so he stated that price to Roger, "95 dollars, and I will accept money or any items I need in trade."

Roger was relieved. He had budgeted $100 for a boat. So he quickly responded, "I'll buy it then. I have $95, but I'll need to return to Oswego to get the money. I can be back tomorrow."

Soso was also delighted. "I'll have it in the water for you by then. The only problem is that I owe $14 for the sail so I have to wait for your money before I get the sail." Soso had spent all his other money on farming equipment and tools.

James interrupted, "I have $14 that you can borrow until Roger returns. We can go over to Troupville and get the sail right now."

Roger and John left immediately for Oswego. They borrowed Soso's old fishing boat, which had good freeboard and a big sail. They left the small canoe that the three of them had used to paddle down from Oswego for James and Soso to use. Their plan was to make the 25-mile trip to Oswego that afternoon, pick up Roger's money at the Naval Base in the morning, and return to Sodus Bay by the next afternoon or evening. Of course all that would depend on the status of the weather and waves on the lake. Soso's boat could handle some rough weather, but a big storm could postpone the completion of their journey. The lake was calm now, but you could never tell about its future temperament.

Soso and James took the canoe across the bay to Troupville. They stopped by Jim's house when they noticed the *Lake Queen* was docked there taking on cargo.

Jim remembered James Cooper from his visit a year ago, and they also had seen each other in Oswego earlier in the spring when the *Lake Queen* had made a delivery there. Jim knew that James was a naval officer, so he related to James his latest encounter with the British Navy.

"Those meddlesome British ships have been harassing the *Lake Queen*. Just yesterday I was coming out of Cape Vincent when their big warship, *Royal George*, blocked my path. They actually came aboard the *Queen* claiming they were checking for contraband and guns. It's the second time that's happened. What's our Navy going to do about this?"

James' response was disappointing to Jim. "They probably won't do anything. It seems right now that we're afraid of those big British ships. We don't want to start a war, so we just avoid them whenever we can. I'd sure like to see us take them on though. I'm sure we could drive them right off this lake."

"They'd better not interfere with me again. Next time I'll just run away from that bulky tub. I know I have more maneuverability and speed than the *Royal George*. My boat was built by Soso." Jim was being boastful and brave, but knew that such an action could turn into a serious affair, if the British Navy decided to push the lake sailors too much. Running away from a warship was probably not a very smart action. Jim had no way to defend his ship from the big guns of a ship like the *Royal George*.

The three men then went over to Sill's Tavern where Jim and James continued their discussion about the current problems with the British Navy. Soso left after a while to buy his sail from Jabez Sill. After loading the sail in the canoe, he returned to the tavern. He was planning to wait until the next day to launch Roger's boat, but James had assembled a launch crew ready to get the job done now. James had convinced Jim, Herman, Dr. Lummis, and Rob Fellows to come over to Soso's to launch the boat that afternoon.

Soso and Jim took the small canoe back across the bay, and the rest rode in Dr. Lummis's boat. James took control of the helm for part of the trip. He was amazed at the boat's performance. He loved the sensation of speed as the small boat rode up on its keel and cut through the water. James Cooper had sailed on large Naval vessels, which gave little sense of speed and maneuverability. He couldn't wait to give Roger's boat a test sail.

More Launchings

The members of the launch crew were familiar with Soso's boats. However, the splendor of these two boats sitting in the shop was extraordinary. Finding himself with all this manpower, Soso asked them to launch both boats. He had the launching sequence well designed. Once the two boats were in the water, Soso and Jim stepped the masts, finished the riggings, and prepared the sails.

Then it was time for sailing. A new boat always needed testing and checking. Dr. Lummis and Rob went in Dr. Lummis's boat. Soso and Herman went in Hornsby's new boat. James and Jim took Roger's new boat.

The wind was southwest, varying from about 12 to 20 knots. It was almost a perfect day to go sailing on the bay. The two new boats and their crews were evenly matched in capabilities. Dr. Lummis's older boat was fast but couldn't quite stay with the newer boats. Dr. Lummis and Rob were capable sailors, but they were not of the same caliber as Soso and Jim. Dr. Lummis's boat was able to stay close when it was going with the wind, but whenever it was heading into the wind it fell behind.

Jim and Soso put the two new boats through tough tests. Soso wanted to make sure everything was just right before turning them over to the new owners. They were also having fun racing these boats and testing their sailing skills against one another. Jim was having an enjoyable time and wanted to continue racing, but Soso needed to perform some more finishing work on the boats. Therefore, the boats were docked.

James Cooper spent the evening helping Soso finish the woodwork on the boats. Dr. Lummis took the others back to Troupville. However, before they left, James had organized another sailboat race for the next day. Soso and James worked on the two boats in the cove until dark. While they worked, they talked about all the news associated with the recent return of the frontier explorers, Meriwether Lewis and William Clark. Cooper saw this whole adventure as imperialism by the United States government and believed that the country wouldn't be happy until it owned all the land on the continent and the Indians were driven to complete submission and annihilation. Cooper was disappointed with President Jefferson, whom he had originally supported. Cooper disagreed with the President on issues involved with the expedition: westward expansion, empire building, and Indian affairs. Soso was more optimistic about the results of this expedition. He had enjoyed hearing the reports of the vast wilderness, the tremendous resources of land and animals, and the various Indian tribes that populated the area. Soso saw the potential for Indians to have their own land, free of the evil influences of the whites. Cooper realized that could never happen. No matter how vast the lands were, the whites would eventually want them all. The topic was controversial, not just with Soso and James, but with most people in the United States. For many, it meant another opportunity to grab free land and use it until they could move further west for even more land.

When James and Soso were through, they took a late night sail in Roger's boat. Night sailing was difficult and a bit scary. You had to know your way around the bay very well to attempt to sail in the darkness. However, with a little moonlight like there was on that night, it was no problem for Soso. He knew thoroughly the shoreline and the invisible features of Sodus Bay. They went to the marsh near Second Creek where the two of them speared frogs by lantern light. After a couple hours, they had over forty frogs. Soso always gave any extra frogs to Sara Lummis, who fixed the best froglegs in town. So the two men ended their evening cleaning the frogs in Jim's shop and leaving the froglegs at the tavern for Sara to pick up in the morning. Then they returned to Soso's cove, arriving there well after midnight.

The next morning Soso and James prepared the boats for their new owners. Tom Hornsby arrived at 10 A.M. ready for the occasion. He had brought his entire family and all seven of them got into the boat, which sailed off from Soso's cove under its heavy load. Roger and John returned with Soso's boat at a little after 2 P.M. The two men were tired from their overnight trip to Oswego, but the excitement of seeing the new boat in the water re-energized them. Roger was very happy to pay Soso for his new boat and take delivery of his dream.

The Race

Roger, John, and James sailed out of the cove to go to the race that James had set up for 5 P.M. They went directly to Jim's dock, which was the meeting point for any boats wishing to race. James went over to the tavern to recruit any boatmen who hadn't yet heard.

To everyone's surprise there was quite a large turnout. Seven of the boats entered were built by Soso—those of Mr. Hornsby, Dr. Lummis, Colonel Troup, Roger, Jim, Rob, and Soso. The eighth entrant was a boat built in Albany and owned by Colonel Fitzhugh. There were two sailors in each boat. The crews consisted of Mr. Hornsby and his son, Dr. Lummis and Herman, Colonel Troup and Tom Reese, Roger and James Cooper, Jim and Karen Davis, Rob Fellows and Daniel Dorsey, Soso and John, and Colonel Fitzhugh's foreman Jake and Jabez Sill.

It was a wild time. The races were all close. Roger and Mr. Hornsby, each won two races, but the surprise winner of the other race was Dr. Lummis, whose boat was most competitive when the wind died down. The only boat that was not competitive was that of Colonel Fitzhugh. He had a well-built, expensive boat with a nice, fancy manufactured sail and rigging. The sail was an important item in this kind of racing, and Colonel Fitzhugh's boat had a better sail, made of stronger, yet lighter material. However, the Fitzhugh boat was too wide and too heavy to keep up with the narrower, lighter, more streamlined boats built by Soso.

After the races, all the participants except Karen went to the tavern to tell stories about the races and boast about the exploits of their boats. Soso and Jim had to leave early in the evening. Jim had to sail the *Lake Queen* across the lake the first thing in the morning, and Soso had to go fishing early the next day because he had promised Colonel Fitzhugh thirty pounds of fresh sea trout by noon.

The three Navy sailors, James, Roger, and John, had a grand time in Troupville during the next few days. They sailed all over with Roger's new boat. They fished the streams, the bay, and the lake. One day they went horseback riding with Colonel Troup on a circuit of the area's farms. On the last day of their vacation, they stopped by Soso's to pick up their canoe and thank Soso for all he had done. James Cooper vowed to return again, and Roger said he would let everyone know where he got his beautiful new boat.

Controversy

Since his return to the area ten years before, Soso had always been friendly and cooperative with the residents of Troupville. However, in this ever-changing world of the whites there were things happening that profoundly upset Soso. Several fishermen, especially one named Jack Porter, were continually wasting fish and other natural resources. They seemed to have no respect for the laws of nature. Jack was a good fisherman, and he had taken over many of Soso and Jim's fish-buying clients when they went out of business. However, Soso felt that Jack and others continued to violate the intrinsic laws of caring for nature and the environment. They would net more fish than they could haul back to the dock or use. Often, they would just dump the extra dead fish in the water or on shore.

In the fall, Soso discovered several nets filled with rotten, spoiled fish in Second Creek. The seagulls had a field day with these rotting carcasses. Wasting animals and damaging the environment were foreign notions to Soso. The owner of the nets had not bothered to check the nets for over two weeks. This type of waste was also happening with some hunters and trappers. Soso often saw hunters kill birds, ducks, geese, and deer that they had no intention of keeping or eating.

Soso refused to tolerate such behavior any longer. Whenever he saw people violate the laws of nature, he confronted them and hoped that they would change their ways. However, he had wanted to do something more about this for a long time. Didn't these so-called intelligent and civilized people understand the most basic laws of nature? The continuation of these activities with their devastating effects on the environment finally pushed Soso into action.

Soso was fishing in Third Creek for bass when he smelled something unusual and overpowering. It was the distinctive smell of rotting fish. He saw a swarm of seagulls that were always attracted to such delights. With a little searching Soso easily discovered the cause of the foul odor—a pile of dead fish and animals over five feet high on the shore of the creek. Soso could see rotting fish, hundreds of dead frogs and turtles, a deer carcass, dead beaver, and several dead birds including his favorite bird, a Bald Eagle. The sight of this violent crime against nature made Soso both sick and angry. He immediately suspected Jack Porter because this was a place often fished by Jack, his employees, and his friends.

Soso went directly to Jack's cabin, which was located on Hunter's Point. Jack wasn't there, but his workers were. Soso confronted them with his discovery. Their reaction angered Soso even more. They admitted their role in producing the pile of dead animals and joked about Soso's concern, claiming that he was just jealous of their success.

Soso's next stop was Colonel Troup's cabin in Troupville. By the time he arrived back in Troupville his emotions had calmed slightly, but he still was angry and upset. Colonel Troup listened intently to Soso's story. There had been other complaints by concerned citizens about these kinds of incidents before. Colonel Troup agreed with Soso—this time the waste and slaughter had gone too far. Colonel Troup immediately posted a notice for a village and area meeting for the next evening at the tavern in Troupville. He wrote on the notice that the meeting's purpose was to discuss the waste and slaughter of wild animals and fish. Word about the meeting spread quickly to residents throughout the area.

Jack and his friends found out that Soso had reported their fun to Colonel Troup. Before the meeting had even started, the villagers were taking sides in the dispute. Jack wasn't all that popular with the villagers. Many people knew about his actions and felt it was time to make him stop. Others disliked him because of his lack of reliability in providing fish and game to them when he promised. However, Jack and his co-workers were trying to drum up support for their cause by claiming that an Indian had no right to make any claim against them.

By the time the meeting started everyone was in a highly agitated state. Colonel Troup tried to keep order, but tempers flared as speakers debated what to do about the problem. When Soso started to talk, Jack tried to interrupt him. However, with help from Colonel Troup, Soso finally had his say. "All people must live within the rules of nature. Since we have more abilities to kill and more intelligence to reason than other animals, we must conserve not waste. If we waste our fish and animals, soon there will be none. Then we will have no way to support ourselves and we'll have to move, but since there are people everywhere, there are no longer many good places to move. With such waste, we cause severe problems for ourselves. Somehow we must make ourselves abide by nature's ways."

Soso's statement virtually ended the discussion. Soso was right, and everyone there knew it. It didn't matter that Soso was an Indian, speaking out against whites. By now he was a trusted, respected, and wise resident of the area, and he had earned and deserved the support of his friends and neighbors on this issue.

Colonel Troup determined the punishment for Jack and the other violators. They would have to clean up the mess they had created and repair and maintain the village docks for the next year. Colonel Troup also drew up a new law for policing such deviant activity. From that day forward, the hunters and fishermen in the Sodus Bay area would have to respect the laws of nature or pay for their violations.

Colonel Troup personally thanked Soso. "Soso, thanks for showing us the path to progress. Sometimes we have to rely on your Indian values in taming our civilization, so we won't violate the laws of nature. You have taught us all a valuable lesson. I hope we don't forget it."

Soso felt good about the role that he played in setting up this new law. Maybe the white man's world could learn something from the Indians after all, especially, from an Indian with the goal of making a difference in the world. Not only had he initiated the action that brought about a new law to conserve natural resources, but also he had the support and respect of his neighbors and friends in the Sodus Bay area. Soso, in effect, was being told that he was no longer an outsider. He was a full-fledged member of the community. Soso liked the feeling. Many people had congratulated him on his actions. Even Jack Porter held no hard feelings. Jack told Soso that he understood Soso's actions and from now on he would be more careful in conserving wildlife. Everyone agreed Sodus Bay and its natural habitat were far too important to let careless people destroy its beauty. It had been a great day for Sodus Bay and its residents.

Journey

For 55 days James Pollock had looked out in all directions and had seen the same thing, water. Even though the view of the water in the Atlantic Ocean was always slightly different, it had become a boring sight. One day the water would be blue and clear. The next day it might be gray, green, or even brown. Sometimes the waves would disappear, only to come back the next day bigger and more threatening than ever.

A big storm had lasted for eight days. The sea had come down on them from all sides. James was on a small single deck ship that was not built to take such punishment. However, the Captain and crew kept their heads and saved the ship. Somehow they survived the storm and continued their journey across the vast, seemingly endless ocean.

The eighteen-year-old had started his journey in Wigtown, Scotland over two years before. He had spent over a year and a half in northern Ireland working and searching for an affordable passage to the new world, the land of freedom called America. Finally, an opportunity came for him to travel aboard the *Sea Bird* to the city called New York in America. Captain O'Hara planned to put the ship into the port of New York just 40 days after sailing from Ireland. However, from the start of the voyage, nothing had gone right. The winds seemed to alternate between the two extremes: either there was not enough to make good progress or there were violent storms that blew the ship far to the north of their planned route. Now all the Captain wanted to do was to reach the shore of the American continent. His boat was leaking badly and may have sustained permanent damage. Fortunately the bailing efforts using the hand pumps were able to keep up with the leaks, and the boat was not in any danger of sinking as long as another big storm didn't hit and damage her further. Experienced as he was, O'Hara had never endured such misery.

The Captain steered the ship straight west hoping to make landfall as quickly as possible. His plan worked, as the ship headed directly into the Gulf of St. Lawrence, finding the shores of the North American continent in the British Commonwealth of Canada.

A brief stop was made at the first small port, where the ship's hull was given a temporary patch after it was determined that the Sea Bird was seaworthy enough to continue her voyage. The Captain then continued the cruise up the St. Lawrence River heading for the first great lake, Lake Ontario. James and the rest of the passengers actually enjoyed this part of their journey. Some were upset that their destination was no longer New York City, but most were happy to be heading for anyplace in New York State or even the United States. After all New York State couldn't be so big that they couldn't easily get to New York City from wherever they landed.

The scenery along this remarkable river was gorgeous. It was a startling contrast to the drab ocean view of the last 65 days. There were trees and plants of many varieties, and the edible fruits were delicious. There were plenty of fresh fish to eat, and, best of all, hunting parties from the ship brought back fresh venison and moose. After a few calm and peaceful days on the river, the violent and frightful days on the ocean were nearly forgotten. This time good luck rode with the *Sea Bird* as it passed up the river rapids without incident. Several passengers liked what they saw on the river so much that they persuaded the Captain to let them off right there. Since the Captain was under obligation to deliver his passengers to New York, when they arrived at Lake Ontario he declared their passage had ended. Even though he didn't have any charts of the lake, O'Hara knew that New York State lay on the south shore of the lake. As far as he was concerned, anywhere in New York State would fulfill his obligation to sail the passengers to New York. There would be no refunds or complaining. His decision was the final word, and the passengers knew it.

Captain O'Hara's only other consideration was to find a port with an adequate shipyard to repair his vessel. His inquiries of people along the river indicated that a port called Oswego was the most likely to have such a ship-repair facility. He followed their directions. He liked what he saw as he entered the port. Surely, the large Navy Base had a shipyard that could quickly and easily handle the repairs to his ship.

While arrangements were being made to unload his passengers and their belongings, Captain O'Hara queried the sailors and dock workers for the whereabouts of the best shipyard to make the necessary repairs. No one seemed to be able to help him. It seemed that all the Naval facilities were closed to civilian ships. Finally, he happened to ask the sailor named James Cooper for advice on getting the *Sea Bird* repaired. Cooper told him quite emphatically that the best, and probably the only, shipyard nearby that could handle his repairs was in Troupville, and for a small fee James would direct him to that port the next day.

Arrival

Captain O'Hara made the last 25 miles of his journey with his eight crewmen, only ten remaining passengers, and his guide, James Cooper. The ten passengers, including James Pollock, figured if they had survived the miserable 79 days on the ship, they might as well travel for one more day. James Cooper had told them good things about Troupville, and besides, Captain O'Hara offered them $.25 per day pay for helping to reload the ship with provisions for the return trip.

Cooper was happy to see his friends in Troupville again. The *Sea Bird* had practically followed the *Lake Queen* into port, so he was able to find Jim Davis as soon as they moored off Jim's dock. Soso happened to be visiting Dr. Lummis, so he was easily found. James arranged for a meeting at the tavern with Captain O'Hara, Jim, and Soso.

After the three men were introduced to one another, James left them to talk business while he went to see if he could borrow a boat to go sailing. He had missed the excitement of sailing one of Soso's boats around the bay. He persuaded Tom Hornsby to let him borrow his boat for a while and then convinced Dr. Lummis to come out in his boat to race against him.

A Big Opportunity

Captain O'Hara was surprised to find that the shipbuilder recommended by James Cooper was an Indian, but he got right to the point. "I understand that you have a shipyard. I need some repairs done on my ship right away. I have to return to Ireland immediately." He had already lost a considerable amount of money on this voyage because of the delay and damage and needed to make another voyage to make up the difference.

Soso was excited about the prospect of working on an ocean-going ship, but he had no idea if he could make the repairs. He hadn't even seen the boat. He worried that the boat would be too large for the facilities at Jim's dry-dock or that the repairs would be too complicated for his skills and tools. But he told O'Hara, "Captain, let's go see your ship."

When Soso saw the ship, he was amazed. The ship was barely larger than the *Lake Queen*, and hardly the type of ship that Soso had imagined could cross the ocean. However, the good news for Soso was that he could easily handle the repairs. The ship only needed re-caulking, reinforcement of the hull and deck, and a few repairs on the rigging. Soso figured the job would take at most two to three weeks provided he could get a few people to help him. Captain O'Hara and Soso struck a deal for the repairs. Soso, Herman, and three crewmen from the Sea Bird would do the work. Captain O'Hara would pay for all the materials needed, and Soso and Herman would receive $25 to share for their pay. Soso figured it would be the easiest $25 they had ever made. Unfortunately, Jim couldn't help because he had to make a run with the *Lake Queen* to eight different ports on the lake over the next two weeks.

Soso and his work crew began the job the next morning. This work was a lot easier than the rebuilding of the *Lake Queen*. James Cooper also helped for two days before he had to return to Oswego. Soso used James to supervise the repairs on the rigging while he and Herman concentrated their efforts on the hull. Meanwhile Captain O'Hara was making the necessary arrangements to replenish the ship's provisions for the return trip. He had contracted with William Wickham at the general store for the essential items and most of the food. Other food items, like vegetables and meat, were bought from other local merchants and farmers. Captain O'Hara had hired former passenger James Pollock, who the Captain knew as a reliable worker, and two local men to help transport and load the supplies onto the ship.

All the activities proceeded on schedule during the first week. The only disruption occurred when one of the crew helping Soso decided that he wanted to stay in America. He left town and headed west with a couple local hunters and trappers. James Pollock was substituted for the man on the repair crew, and that turned out to be very fortunate for Soso. James had considerable talent for woodworking, and Soso quickly saw James' potential as a ship builder and carpenter.

Soso completed the last of the repairs just fifteen days after the *Sea Bird* had arrived at Troupville. Captain O'Hara had all the provisions on board and had hired a replacement for the missing crewman. Also, a family of six from Geneva had heard about the Irish ship at Troupville and had arranged for passage back to Ireland. They were returning in order to bring back more of their relatives and friends from the old country and start a new town in the wilds of western New York. The return passengers were an unexpected bonus for Captain O'Hara. He was also transporting a few furs and other products back to Europe for Wickham and several businessmen.

All in all, Captain O'Hara was glad that he had found the little village called Troupville after his arduous and inauspicious voyage across the ocean. As he climbed aboard the *Sea Bird*, he waved to the villagers who had gathered to wish him and his ship well. The ship's sails were raised, and she headed out of port for the long journey across the ocean. 1808 had been a catastrophic and eventful year for the Captain. He hoped for a much better return voyage than the original crossing.

A New Opportunity

Former Scotsman James Pollock was now an American, living in Troupville, New York, and looking for a job. He was excited and anxious about his new village, state, and country. He already believed it was much better here than where he had come from. He considered himself a very lucky man. Because Herman had recently decided to find full time employment as a carpenter in Troupville, Soso was looking for a shipbuilding apprentice. Both men recognized this opportunity, so Soso hired James Pollock as his new apprentice. Herman, who had been valuable help for Soso, could find plenty of jobs right in the village building new homes and repairing old ones. It would be much more convenient for Herman to stay in the village instead of continually traveling across the bay to Soso's for work. Additional motivation for Herman to stay in the village was provided when Herman's wife gave birth to their son, Charles. James Pollock was the perfect substitute for Herman.

Neighbors

Soso had new neighbors. Norman Sheldon, Norman's wife, Margaret, his six sons, and his four daughters had moved from Connecticut into a small cabin only 300 yards from Soso's house during the fall. They had survived the harsh winter thanks to Soso's generosity, large purchases of food and supplies from the Helms plantation, and the helpful care of Dr. Zenas Hyde, who lived on the east side of the bay about a half mile from Soso in an area called Sloop Landing.

Soso had supplied the Sheldons with plenty of fresh fish and meat, and although he had only a few fruits and vegetables put away for the winter, he shared what he could with his new neighbors. The Sheldons bought the rest of their food from the Helms plantation.

During the winter, Margaret Sheldon had contracted a severe case of the fever. She had been sick for over three months. Dr. Hyde checked her condition every other day all winter. Through his care and her strong will, she finally recovered and returned to near full strength by spring.

A bright, spring afternoon brought all twelve of the Sheldons to Soso's house. Since it was the first day of open water, the ice having blown away the day before, Soso had already been out fishing that morning. Soso was cleaning ten nice trout, and James Pollock was working in the shop when the Sheldons arrived. Mrs. Sheldon brought Soso fresh baked bread, and Norman had another special gift for Soso.

"I can't tell you how much we appreciate all your help over the winter, Soso. You're the best neighbor, and the best hunter and fisherman we've ever seen," said Norman.

Soso had taken Norman and his oldest two sons hunting and fishing several times over the winter. However, the Sheldons weren't very good at either activity. They were gentlemen farmers from Connecticut who had come to this place on Great Sodus Bay to build a prosperous farm. They had never intended to hunt or fish for a living. However, Soso taught them what he could, while providing them food from his own hunting and fishing.

Norman gave Soso the gift. It was a bag of seeds. "We've noticed you have some nice apple and cherry trees growing in your garden. We'd be pleased if you added some pears to your orchard. These are the best pear seeds in Connecticut. The boys and I will help you plant them when it warms enough. We're planning on planting some ourselves in a couple weeks."

"Thank you. I've never eaten pears before, but I'd love to try to grow some. I've heard they're delicious," replied Soso.

The conversation changed to the building of the Sheldons' new home. Norman and his sons were going to build a new, larger, and more comfortable house and barn. They had already started by clearing land and collecting lumber for the job. James Pollock became excited as the plans were being discussed. Finally, James asked Norman, "I'd sure like to help you build that house and barn. I'm a pretty good wood worker. Just ask Soso."

Soso was a bit surprised by James' remarks. He had planned to use James to work on a big boat that he was going to build as soon as the small one they were working on was finished. Nevertheless, Soso figured the house-building experience would be good for James. So he gave his recommendation of James' abilities and his consent for James to work with the Sheldons. "Can't find a better young carpenter than James. He can help until July 4th, but then I need him back to help me work on a new boat."

Shipbuilding

Soso's next project was to build a transport boat for Sam Ledyard of Appleboom. He had to enlarge and renovate his shop and collect the wood and supplies before he actually started work on the big boat. It was going to be 35 feet long with two tall masts. The new ship would retain the sleek lines of Soso's smaller boats. He already had a deposit for half the $600 price of the boat, so he could buy the materials and supplies needed for the construction.

The first thing in Soso's construction process was to select the perfect wood from his stack of lumber. The hull would be constructed from his select stock of rock elm, and the deck and bracing would be white oak. Two long white pine logs would be prepared for the masts. Then Soso spent two days carefully re-supplying his woodpile. He selected mature trees, carefully cut them to insure continued good health for both his rock elm stand and white oak stand. The white pines were available at numerous locations, so Soso searched and found two of the tallest and straightest trees to replenish his supply of masts. Soso knew full well how important the right wood was for building a strong, fast sailing boat.

Sam wanted the boat to transport small items quickly. His friend, Captain Samuel Thropp, already owned and sailed a larger ship, the schooner *Nancy*, around the lake. The *Nancy* was the biggest local competition for the *Lake Queen*, although many small schooners and sloops carried cargo out of Sodus Bay periodically. Sloop Landing, the area just south of Soso's cove, got its name because various sloops came in there to pick up and deliver goods around the lake. Soso promised Sam Ledyard a quality boat, well-built enough to handle the rough waves of the big lake and fast enough to shorten the long trips across the lake. If a boat were going to have less cargo capacity, it had to make up for that shortcoming by traveling faster.

There was also some good news for the residents of the Troupville area in 1809. Colonel Fitzhugh and Dr. Lummis had managed to establish the village as a regular stop on the route of the Western New York Stage Company. On alternate days there was an eastward or westward stage stopping in Troupville. Along with this new service was the need for an official United States Post Office in the village. July 4, 1809 marked the official opening of the Troupville Post Office. Its first postmaster was Dr. Lummis, who set up a small office on the side of his house for handling official mail delivery. Progress was coming to the rural frontier, and these were big steps in making Troupville a modern, progressive community.

There was quite a celebration in the village on July Fourth that year. The new nation was 33 years old, and the beginning of stage service and the opening of a post office gave the villagers and area residents even more reasons to celebrate. Soso attended some of the holiday festivities. He enjoyed the games and contests the most, and he didn't disappoint his supporters. As everyone expected, he won the shooting competition for the tenth straight year. And the runner-up was also no surprise. Jim Davis finished second for the tenth straight year as well.

During the festivities Soso found out why James Pollock was so intent on helping the Sheldons build their house and barn. James was infatuated with one of Norman Sheldon's daughters. However, James wasn't the only one courting April Sheldon. There was a long line of young men waiting to dance with this eligible young lady.

After the July Fourth celebration, Soso and James Pollock began in earnest their task of building the new boat. This would be Soso's largest undertaking. He hoped to finish the boat within a year. The two men knew it would take complete dedication on their part to finish on time. Soso hired two of the Sheldon boys to take care of his crops so he could concentrate full time on building this boat.

The only interruption to their boat building that Soso allowed was the barn raising at the Sheldons. This turned out to be quite an affair. Almost every resident in the area was there to help. Everyone enjoyed the festivities except James and a few other young men who lost out in the courting of April Sheldon. She and Slim McNab announced their engagement at the party. James was heart-broken, but he didn't allow this to effect his work. He was as reliable and productive as ever.

Growth of Civilization

The little settlement on the east side of the bay called Sloop Landing was coming alive. The area just south of Soso's cove and the Helms plantation was full of activity in the spring of 1810. Dr. Hyde and Norman Sheldon were both building log taverns in the village. The structures were small and crude, especially in comparison to the more substantial Sill's Tavern over in Troupville, but they were sufficient for the travelers along the ridge road, which passed east-west through the village. Both tavern keepers and the other merchants were counting on an increase in passenger traffic once a floating bridge was completed across the narrow part of the bay.

The Sheldons, Hydes, and workers from the Helms' plantation had already built the sections of the bridge the previous winter. A crew of many of the residents of the area worked to assemble the sections in the water across the narrow part of the bay. The sections were very heavy. They were almost twenty feet long and made of six to eight heavy logs with a wooden plank deck built over the top. Soso was one of the volunteers helping to assemble the bridge. He headed a group of twenty men who carried the sections from where they had been built down to the water's edge and launched them into the water. It was hard work to carry more than thirty of the awkward sections almost 100 yards over the bumpy ground. However, the job was finally accomplished after two days of exhausting, back-breaking work.

Another crew of ten men was floating the sections into place and connecting them with one another. They also drove pilings alongside the bridge to keep it from bending and splitting in the middle. It took five full days to complete all the work on the bridge.

Once the bridge was completed, the two main supporters and financiers of the effort, Dr. Hyde and Norman Sheldon, crossed the bridge together. It may not have been an elaborate bridge, but it was surrounded by a myriad of beautiful water lilies which were prevalent in this section of Sodus Bay. Both men had high expectations for the benefits of the bridge to the area. They believed, as did many others, that this was the beginning of good things for the new village of Sloop Landing. Maybe the great city expected for Sodus Bay would originate from the little village beginning on the northeast corner of the bay, instead of from the more developed community of Troupville.

The residents of the area had a neighborhood party to celebrate the opening of the bridge. The Helms plantation provided two pigs, which were roasted by Dr. Hyde, and Soso donated two dozen trout, which were cooked by the Sheldons. Several area farmers provided vegetables. Dr. Hyde and Norman Sheldon provided home-brewed beer and plenty of corn liquor. The corn liquor produced by Dr. Hyde rivaled the best in the state, and those who really knew their beer considered Sheldon's beer the finest in the entire area. The partygoers dined, danced, and drank well into the night. It was a happy time for the residents of Sloop Landing.

The floating bridge was an immediate success. Travelers, mostly families moving west, began using the ridge road, which was more convenient than the interior east-west routes. The Western New York Stage Company began using this route and steadily increased the number of trips. It seemed as if the two taverns were busy nearly every night. Both tavern keepers were more than satisfied with their business. However, a friendly rivalry developed over which tavern was the first to open its doors. Both taverns laid claim to being first and tried to use that distinction in their advertising. Both taverns benefited from the late night arguments that developed over this issue. All through the controversy and competition, the Hydes and Sheldons remained good friends and respected community leaders.

Soso and James Pollock had a busy winter and spring working on the new boat. The two men worked every day, often remaining in the shop until late at night. The construction of this boat was the biggest challenge that Soso had faced. He was adapting the design that had worked so well on smaller boats to this much larger boat. It wasn't obvious how this could be done on such a large scale. However, Soso again set an ambitious goal and had confidence in his abilities to adjust the plans to obtain the proper dimensions for this ship. Additionally, James Pollock was a tremendous help. The young man had natural wood working skills that were nearly equal to Soso's, and his experience of crossing the ocean on the *Sea Bird* helped Soso in making some of the critical decisions. Soso's rock elm wood was perfect for the hull of this ship. It was strong and tough wood. It gave a distinctive look to Soso's boats. The tall masts were made from select white pine trees that were over ninety feet of perfectly straight, strong wood.

By early June both men realized that they were creating an exceptional boat. Soso called this design a "knock-about." The launching of this ship would be another remarkable step in the development of Soso as a master shipbuilder. The boat had taken its final shape with only small cosmetic details remaining to be performed, when its completion was delayed for about a week by a rather strange incident.

Another Scare

Late one evening near the middle of June, Soso and James were working in the shop when Joe, one of the young Sheldon boys came running into the shop. Joe was around Soso's house often because he helped take care of Soso's crops. But, he had never come over so late at night and had never entered Soso's shop, which was off-limits to the Sheldon boys until the boat was done. At first Joe was stunned at seeing the massive boat right there before his eyes, but then he remembered his mission. He had come to sound an alarm. "Indians are coming. Hundreds of Indians are attacking Troupville," shouted Joe. Soso and James looked at one another in disbelief. It didn't seem possible that Indians could or would attack Troupville. It had been over fifteen years since the last Indian problem in the area. Of course, Soso remembered that attack on Troupville very well as the source of his greatest sorrow. Certainly, too much progress had been made for something like that to happen again.

The boy continued his warning. "My father says everyone is moving south. We're going too. The Indians could be over here anytime. I have to go home to help pack. My father says you can come with us if you want." With that, the boy left as quickly as he had arrived, and he didn't stop running until he was home.

Soso and James stopped working and walked back toward the house to contemplate their actions. James spoke first. "I sure hope Joe is wrong. I'd hate to have a bunch of savages ruin all our work." James realized what he had said only after he said it. He had never thought of Soso as an Indian or a savage, and he didn't mean to offend him with his remark. Soso's reaction relieved James' embarrassment.

"If those savages try to ruin this boat, they'll have to fight this savage," returned Soso. "I just can't believe that there are enough Indians in this area to try to attack an entire village like Troupville. Indians would never make a foolish attack on an organized village."

Soso sent James to help the Sheldons and then to see what was happening in Sloop Landing. James was to return to Soso's in a couple hours and stay there to guard the boat and property, although not at the risk of his life. Soso hated to leave his home unguarded until James returned, but he decided to go over to Troupville right away to find out what was really happening. So he closed up everything he could on his property and headed across the bay toward Troupville in his boat. Soso left his flintlock for James in case he needed it.

It was a quiet night with very little wind, which meant Soso had to row all the way. It was cloudy and pitch dark. Soso thought that he heard several other boats rowing away from Troupville heading across the bay, but he couldn't be sure. One time he thought he heard a boat nearby so he called out asking if someone was there. There was no answer. Soso sensed something was very wrong. There was a kind of disturbance on his bay that he had never seen or experienced before.

Flight

Soso arrived at Jim's dock just as Jim and his family were loading their boat with their belongings. Jim was relieved to see Soso. Jim had the same uneasy feeling that Soso had. He, too, remembered the events of fifteen years before.

"What's going on?" Soso asked.

"A rumor has been spreading around all evening about an Indian attack on Troupville. A couple of Jack Porter's trappers were supposedly captured by about 150 Indians in a raiding party just south of the lake between here and Appleboom. One of them escaped, and the other was killed. The survivor claims he overheard the Indians talking about attacking Troupville. I guess he is in pretty bad shape. Anyway the rumors have sent almost everyone out of the village looking for safety. We were planning on staying, but since everyone has fled I thought maybe Karen and the children could stay over at your place."

"Sure, I have plenty of room. Aren't you coming over, too?"

"No. I told Dr. Lummis I'd stay here with him to help protect the village. He has about ten men willing to stay. He's waiting for Jack Porter to come by with the latest news on the attack." Jim was disgusted over the panicked reaction of most of the villagers to the rumor. First of all, he doubted that any Indians were going to attack Troupville, and second, he was disappointed that so few decided to stay and protect the village that they had worked so hard to carve out of the wilderness. Jim Davis was a fighter, but he needed a force to lead.

"I'll stay here and help Dr. Lummis. You take your family across the bay. James should be over at the house. He went over to Sloop Landing to find out what was happening there, but he should be back at my place by now," Soso answered, as he helped Jim finish loading the boat.

Karen interrupted with a plan of her own. "I will take the children across the bay. James can help us once we are over there. Both of you stay here with Dr. Lummis. He can use all the support he can get." Her logic couldn't be refuted. Karen Davis could easily handle the trip across the bay in the dark.

As Karen headed out from the dock rowing the small boat filled with children and belongings, Jim and Soso waved good-bye and headed up the road to the Lummises. Hannah was fourteen-years-old and a big help to her mother. Jamey was just eight years old and very scared of the potential danger. His vivid imagination gave his mind many things to think about as they rowed in darkness across the bay.

William was glad to see his two friends come into the yard. It turned out that only six other men were staying behind to defend the village. If there really were 150 Indians preparing to attack Troupville, this miniature defense force didn't have much of a chance. In reality, Troupville had surrendered to just the threat of an Indian attack.

Sara and six-year-old Ben Lummis had already left with Herman and Mary Smith by horse-drawn carriage toward the Fitzhugh Estate. They joined with a large group of evacuees, which included about half the residents of Troupville.

Defenders

"We're here to help, Dr. Lummis. What's the plan?" asked Jim, who was carrying his flintlock musket. Soso also carried a musket that Jim had gotten for him.

"Glad to have you. That makes nine of us." Dr. Lummis called them together. "All I can tell you is that we have heard rumors that a group of 150 Indians have assembled about ten miles to the west and intend to attack Troupville. We are waiting for further word from Jack Porter who has gone out to confirm that information. In the meantime, we need lookouts on the west side of town to give us early warning and defense." Dr. Lummis was not a military man, but neither were any of the others. With the exception of Soso and Jim Davis, the others who stayed behind were young, single men. All the older and married men of the village had taken their families to safety. Soso was 30 years old and had experienced enough surprises not to get flustered over this alarm. Likewise, forty-year-old Jim had experienced enough confrontation as a frontiersman to realize the risks and dangers of holding their ground. However, they also realized the need to be there to protect their property.

Just having the rugged frontiersmen, Jim and Soso, with the defense force boosted the confidence of the other defenders, who had never faced a situation like this. Jim's rugged and tough features made it look as if he were ready to take on an attack. Of course, they also knew Soso was skilled in the arts of soldiering and fighting. First, the two frontier partners helped Dr. Lummis put together a plan. They set up two lookouts along the west side of the village with two men each. Three men, including Dr. Lummis, stayed at the tavern, which served as the command post and allowed them to react to any situation. The tavern was in the center of the village, and Troupville was small enough so that the three men at the tavern could hear and see if anything was happening at the outposts. Soso and Jim were employed as a mobile scouting party, riding on horseback about two miles to the west of the village. Their intent was to find out what was happening and to provide early warning for the others. This was the best they could do, but they still had no chance of repelling or surviving a forceful attack by 150 Indians.

Soso and Jim rode through the darkness along the lakeshore. They stopped at Salmon Creek to check on the homes in the area. All the people who lived there were gone, indicating how quickly the rumor had spread. It was past midnight, so they decided to hole up in this area until first light. Soso stayed on horseback down near the lakeshore, and Jim stayed by the houses along the creek, which was a couple hundred yards south of Soso's position.

At first light, Jim heard a noise from one of the nearby houses. He quickly ran to investigate and then slowed down as he approached the house. As he carefully walked around the side of the house, he was afraid he might discover Indians from the war party. Instead he saw several wolves ready to attack two pigs and a calf in a small corral behind the house. Jim took an instinctive action by shooting the wolf closest to the calf. The rest of the wolves quickly disappeared into the surrounding woods. Then suddenly another shot rang out in the tree line where the wolves had disappeared. Jim jumped to the ready, but relaxed as he saw Soso walking out of the woods dragging a second dead wolf. Soso also had been investigating the noise and the wolf had run right by him. Ordinarily two wolves would be quite a valuable prize. Dr. Lummis paid a bounty of $10 for a wolf carcass as part of his governmental duties with the post office. However, under the circumstances of an impending Indian attack, the two dead wolves were merely thrown into the woods to allow Soso and Jim to leave the area quickly in case the attacking Indians were nearby and had heard the shots.

Soso and Jim decided to scout about two miles farther to the west. They kept about a half a mile between them in order to cover more ground. Soso rode near the lakeshore and Jim stayed more to the interior. They rode very slowly and carefully to insure that they wouldn't miss any activity or become captured by hostile Indians. All they found were a few more deserted cabins. There was no sign of any Indians.

The two men returned to the outskirts of Troupville around noon. They were suspicious when they didn't find anyone at the two outposts, so they quickly rode to the tavern to check out the situation. There, they were met by Dr. Lummis who, by now, had the real story of the impending Indian attack that had sent the villagers into a panic.

Dr. Lummis told the story to Jim and Soso. It seems that the two trappers who were supposedly attacked by Indians had been drinking and arguing over ownership of some furs and one had killed the other. In order to cover up the crime, the killer had made up the whole story about the

Indian attack. The rumor had spread so fast that a third trapper, who was a witness to the murder, didn't have enough time to report it to the authorities before everyone in the region had run away in panic. The witness finally found the regional sheriff at Daniel Arms' house at Arms' Crossroads. The sheriff got the trappers' boss, Jack Porter, to confront the trapper who eventually admitted his guilt and the falsehood of the report of an impending Indian attack. Just as Jim and Soso had suspected, there were no Indians and no attack.

Jack and the sheriff had sent out men in all directions to sound the all clear and to persuade people to return to their homes. Jack himself had brought the news to Troupville just before noon. And by the time Soso and Jim had cooled and corralled their horses, the first residents of Troupville were returning to their homes. The celebrated Indian attack on Troupville was over without a shot being fired, except for the two shots that killed the wolves near Salmon Creek. Everyone was relieved that there had been no bloodshed, and Soso was especially happy at the outcome since he remembered all too well the aftermath of the real Indian attack on Troupville.

Later that day, Jim rode back down to Salmon Creek to pick up the carcasses of the two dead wolves, but they were gone. The dead animals had either been carried off by other animals or found by the returning settlers and turned in for the bounty. It didn't matter much to Jim, who by now was thinking only of returning to his normal schedule of sailing the *Lake Queen*. He was, of course, relieved that there had been no attack but disappointed in the response of his community to the threat. Somehow, they had to get organized so they could respond properly to a real emergency.

It took several days for all the residents to return to Troupville. Several had fled to villages far to the east or to relatives and friends as far as fifty miles away. However, after a week or so, the threat of an Indian attack had become just a humorous story and things returned to normal in Troupville and the surrounding area.

Launching

Soso and James Pollock returned to their boat building. Only a few details on the hull and cabin had to be finished along with the construction of the masts and some of the rigging fasteners. The two of them completed that work in about ten days. When the ship was ready, Soso asked the

Sheldons and Hydes to give him a hand launching it. The launch crew slid the big boat along the logs into the water of the cove, while Dr. Hyde guided their effort. Then they carried the two tall white pine masts down to the cove. It took a couple hours to step the masts into their position in the hull. When the work was done, Soso treated the workers to fresh perch, fried up crispy in a skillet, and some bear stew from a bear that he had killed a couple days before. The eight men had enjoyed their day of hard work because of the beauty of the boat they had launched. They ate and drank heartily for the rest of the evening.

At daybreak the next morning, Soso headed for the cove to finish his work on the boat. He was surprised to find several people already there looking at the ship. Ralph Sheldon, one of Norman's sons, had returned to Sheldon's Tavern at Sloop Landing and told everyone there about Soso's newly-built boat, as had Dr. Hyde. Word had spread overnight, and by now almost the entire community had heard about the size and beauty of the ship. The people at the dock were curious residents of the area who had come by to see the boat for themselves. Everyone there was impressed with the ship and congratulated Soso on his and James Pollock's accomplishment. Soso had plenty of volunteers from the onlookers to help set up the rigging and get the sails into place on the booms. By that afternoon, word of the launching had spread over to Troupville, and several people, including Herman, had come across the bay to see the boat.

Later that afternoon, Soso assembled a crew of three, Herman, James Pollock, and Norman Sheldon, and set sail for Troupville. Before landing at Jim's dock, they cruised around the islands and over by First Creek. Jim, Karen, and Dr. Lummis met them at the dock. There was barely enough water for this ship to come into shore, but, since the water level was a bit higher than normal because of the heavy spring rains, Soso took it all the way up to the dock. The Troupville viewers unanimously declared this boat Soso's finest. He made several trips around the bay giving many people rides. Then he returned to his cove at nightfall. There were a few people from Sloop Landing still waiting to see the boat when Soso returned. For them, it was worth the wait. They, too, were impressed with the ship.

The next afternoon, the new owner, Sam Ledyard, arrived to take possession of the boat. He was very pleased with Soso's work and gladly paid the remaining $300 before sailing the ship out of the cove, through the outlet, and down the lake to Appleboom. Designed by Soso, the ship had no problem negotiating the choppy waves and rolling swells of the lake. Now there was a new, fast, light transport on the lake. The new vessel, named *Pultney's Pride*, would tie up to the pier in Appleboom next to Sam Thropp's schooner *Nancy*. Most of the business for the two ships came from the new cannery, distillery, and tannery that just opened in Appleboom. The businesses in Appleboom also began building a large warehouse near the pier in order to store goods before shipping. Soso's expertise had helped launch a new industry in the village of Appleboom.

Farewell

The cold days of fall brought bad news to the village. Colonel Peregrine Fitzhugh had died. He had been one of the leaders of the village and an inspiration to many in the region. General Washington's aide-de-camp during the Revolutionary War, he was the most famous resident in the area. He was also one of the richest. His home on the hill overlooking the south shore of the bay was elegant and magnificent. His farmland was the envy of all the farmers in the area. His widow, Elizabeth, decided to keep his uniforms, sword, and military awards as treasured family keepsakes and left them fully displayed in his room. The entire area would miss this great man and famous military leader.

Newcomer

Colonel John Maxwell, the father of Sara Lummis, had maintained his residence in Philadelphia. However, he always enjoyed his yearly summer visits to Troupville and finally decided to spend more time than just one month a year on the frontier. Over the winter he had bought the remaining land next to Salmon Creek, his favorite fishing spot. Now, between himself and his son-in-law, William Lummis, they owned over 3500 acres of land on both sides of one of the best fish and mill streams that emptied into Lake Ontario.

Colonel Maxwell had been busy since his purchase of the land and by the spring of 1811 was ready to build one sawmill and two gristmills on the creek. They would be built near the location of the mills built by Captain Williamson that had been washed out in 1807. Daniel Arms was also building a small mill upstream on Salmon Creek about five miles near the crossroads of the ridge road and the road to Troupville. Colonel Maxwell hired James Reeves as millwright and Isaac Davidson as miller. At the first spring thaw, those two and several workers from Troupville began the mills' construction. Herman was hired to do carpentry for the mills.

At the same time, Dr. Lummis was beginning in earnest his farming venture on the land adjacent to Salmon Creek. He had several workers clearing the land and others preparing the existing fields for planting. He planned on planting trees of several fruits including apples, cherries, peaches, and pears, and vegetables including corn, peas, and beans. Also, he would be raising a small cattle herd and chickens. By the fall of 1811, Dr. Lummis's farm became the largest in the area, surpassing the farming acreage of the Fitzhugh homestead and Helms plantation.

Dr. Lummis hired many of the slaves who had been freed from the Helms and Fitzhugh farms. He paid the black workers well and provided housing for their families. The cabins built for the workers were small with meager furnishings, but Dr. Lummis insured that these workers were provided with the necessities and treated with the dignity of free men. The freed slaves enjoyed their freedom and worked hard for the man who gave them the opportunity to better themselves. Dr. Lummis sold some of the housing and farm lots to his good workers on credit. The area of Salmon Creek was becoming a viable village.

Shipping

During that summer of 1811, Jim Davis continued sailing the *Lake Queen* for Rob Fellows. Even though there now was considerable competition for the shipping business in the Troupville area, all the ships were busy, several working at capacity. Rob's *Lake Queen* was hauling bulk material around the lake, including deliveries and pickups in Canada. Sam Thropp's schooner *Nancy* performed the same services out of Appleboom. Sam Ledyard's *Pultney's Pride* was smaller and faster than the other two ships. Her cargo consisted mostly of smaller, lighter products and mail. Another new ship, the *Enterprise*, was launched in Appleboom by her maker and captain, Russell Whipple. She usually carried cargo further to the west to the numerous small ports opening on the south side of the lake. The port of Appleboom outgrew its initial name. The merchants and residents there decided to call their growing village Pultneyville. Now that the floating bridge was the main attraction at Sloop Landing, that area was more popularly known as Float Bridge.

Since there was such a large demand for shipping, Rob Fellows decided to expand his business to include another ship ported at Float Bridge. Rob took in a partner, Slim McNab, who was a good carpenter and had some knowledge of ship building. Slim began building a warehouse on the shore of the bay between Float Bridge and the Helms plantation, and Soso began working on a new transport ship for Rob. The new ship would be forty feet long, just slightly larger than *Pultney's Pride*. Over the winter Soso had expanded his shop in order to build ships of this size more efficiently. James Pollock remained in Soso's employ although James' parents, who had emigrated from Scotland, had bought a farm west of Troupville and wanted him to stay there to help tend the farm. Slim McNab also worked part time for Soso on the ship.

"Noticed that you and James put in a bunch of half ribs up near the bow. Why so many half ribs in that region?" Slim was always asking Soso about the design details of the ships.

"Need to have more support there because of the cargo load, but I don't want that many whole ribs, because they stiffen the hull and reduce performance." Soso was a master at balancing considerations of utility with performance.

"Soso, I left the chisels up on the bow deck so you can finish the detail work on the deck and bow spirit. I never can figure out how you get that to look so good. When you do that work, let me watch. I have to learn how to do that." James Pollock was a conscientious apprentice and always wanted to learn more about the fine points of woodworking and shipbuilding. Soso enjoyed having both James and Slim in his workshop. They were a productive team, and the long days of work were fun with plenty of conversation and good-natured teasing.

With three workers, the ship building proceeded quickly. The boat was launched in September, 1811 and immediately started its shipping service. The newest member of the Sodus Bay shipping fleet was named the *Sodus Belle*. Her job would be delivery of forest and farm goods produced near Float Bridge to locations throughout Lake Ontario.

Progress

The area around Great Sodus Bay had been growing during the last decade. The village of Troupville had been settled for eighteen years. It hardly qualified any longer as the American frontier. However, it was not keeping pace with many other areas of western New York. Troupville still had fewer than 200 residents, and the entire Town of Sodus, which included Troupville, East Ridge, and Arms' Crossroads, and the surrounding area, had only 900 full time residents. During the summer, the region had a tendency to grow larger with an influx of visitors and vacationers. Many of the summer visitors were relatives of the residents of the area like Colonel Maxwell who, before this year, had come to Troupville for a month or so every summer. The population of many inland villages like Lyons, Williamson, Palmyra, and Geneva were over double or triple that of Troupville. One explanation for the slow growth of Troupville was the higher cost of land there. Since the developers like Captain Williamson and

Colonel Troup knew the property near the bay was more desirable, they charged more per acre for this prime property than for inland property. Most quarter or half acre lots in Troupville sold for $250 or more. Outlying lots of ten acres, but near Troupville, sold for over $300. Lots in inland villages usually sold for only $10 per acre or less. Even farm land was more expensive near the lake and the bay. Farmland was over $4.50 per acre near Troupville, and less than $1.00 per acre inland. Settlers were generally hungry for land. The more land they could buy, the happier they were. Many settlers, who could afford the land prices in other inland villages, were unable to pay for the expensive land in Troupville. Unless a settler was wealthy or intended to use the waters of the bay and lake for his livelihood, he was better off living farther inland. The practical nature of the frontier settlers made it unlikely that Troupville would soon progress to the lofty state envisioned by it founders and developers.

For the most part, the residents of rural western New York paid little attention to state, national, or international politics. They had read with great interest about the opening of the new west as a result of the Lewis and Clark expedition beyond the Mississippi River, but that had been an exception. Big city, multinational politics usually had no effect on the inhabitants of rural America. Most people had come to rural frontier to get away from politics, governments, and laws. However, the happenings of 1811 placed politics foremost in the minds of many residents in the area. The actions of the British Navy had the residents practically up in arms. As part of their blockade of France, which was at war with Britain, the British Navy had been stopping and boarding American ships. They would confiscate cargo and sometimes press American sailors into duty for the British. Some of this activity even occurred on the Great lakes. Most, if not all, of the residents of Troupville thought the United States had the right to declare war on Britain and should have attacked those offending ships. They considered the illustrious French General Napoleon, who had challenged British supremacy, a real hero. Many figured they had suffered enough and now was the time for action. Others wondered whether this would be advisable. They questioned whether the United States could win a naval war against the great sea power of Britain. These people worried that they would be caught in a terribly lop-sided war and pay a steep price for their country's aggression, even if it was defending their rights.

It was a tense, frightful time. The residents of western New York readied themselves for an eventual conflict. Militias were formed, and many men of the area volunteered to serve. In Pultneyville, a company formed under Major Rogers with Russel Whipple, Sam Ledyard, and Sam Thropp as officers. In Float Bridge, John Hyde and Norman Sheldon led the citizen soldiers. Lieutenant Colonel Philetus Swift commanded the First Regiment, which included the volunteers from Troupville with officers of Moses Sill, Jacob Hallet, William Rogers, and Timothy Axtell. The residents of the Troupville area were eager to join the fight, but there was legitimate question over whether or not they were ready. Very little real combat training took place, and the few officers who had seen action in the Revolutionary War over 35 years before were too elderly to be viable military leaders.

Part II

Fighting the Wars

Declaration of War

War broke out. On June 17, 1812, the United States and her Navy had taken too much abuse from the British Navy and declared war against Great Britain. President Madison had decided that enough was enough. With Lake Ontario largely surrounded by the British territory of Canada, there was no doubt from the start that the conflict would have considerable impact on western New York State. Even though this area of the state was vulnerable to direct attack, the small frontier villages were almost completely on their own. There were no large fortifications or regular army units to protect them. America had neither Napoleon nor an army to match the British regulars. Their only defense was the small American Navy force on the lake and their own militias. The regular army and most of the largest and most powerful navy ships took up duty protecting the big east coast cities.

In 1812, the American Navy was still growing and actually no match in numbers or firepower with the British Navy. Having recently defeated the navies of the other European powers, the British Navy was queen of the seas and by far the most powerful force in the world. The British had six ships with a total of over 100 powerful guns on Lake Ontario. Their force included the 22-gun *Royal George*, 16-gun *Prince Regent*, and 14-gun *Earl of Moira*. All were classified as frigates, the smallest type of warship. However, by the relative standards of the Great Lakes, these were large, powerful ships. On the other hand, the American Navy, under the command of Commodore Chauncey, had six smaller warships with about thirty smaller guns. The prize of the American force was the Oneida, a slow, crude warship with sixteen guns. This certainly wasn't an even match, but, if possible, there was an even worse match for the Americans on the high seas of the oceans.

The War of 1812 on the Great Lakes was not one of decisive battles or steady conflict. Instead, it was a contest of shipbuilding and small, sporadic skirmishes. The shipbuilding effort would not be easy for the Americans, although Commodore Chauncey was the right man to lead the effort. He had just come from commanding the shipyard at New York City and brought many of the most competent people with him. Most of the supplies and material, except for wood, had to come from New York City, up the Hudson and Mohawk Rivers, across Oneida Lake, and down the Oswego River to get to the Great Lakes. There was plenty of hardship in that journey including several rugged, overland portions of travel. Also, many of the American shipbuilders were like Soso and Russel Whipple, knowledgeable in building small sloops and schooners but ignorant in the methods of constructing large naval gunships. The center for American shipbuilding on the lakes was Sacketts Harbor on Lake Ontario, and Henry Eckford was put in charge of the shipbuilding operations there. He would have to staff shipbuilding crews at Sacketts Harbor with workers from the shipyards in the cities along the eastern seaboard supplemented by a few shipbuilders and carpenters from the frontier.

Threat of Danger

It appeared at the outset that the British would have an easier time building ships for use on the lakes. They could build new ships in Canada at existing facilities for large ship construction in Kingston at the east end of the lake and in York, the shipping port next to Toronto at the west end of the lake. Their supply lines from Great Britain to these ports were longer but in many ways more direct. There were many experienced shipbuilders in these two Canadian ports.

Moreover, the British already had a viable fleet on Lake Erie consisting of the *Queen Charlotte*, seventeen guns, *Lady Prevost*, thirteen guns, *Hunter*, ten guns, and three smaller ships. The United States had a lot of catching up to do on Erie, and because of the barrier at Niagara Falls, no large ships could be moved between the lakes. Therefore, in order to catch up, the Americans had to reallocate their staff on Lake Ontario to send some of their shipbuilders to the west to build ships for Lake Erie.

Many vessels built and employed by the Americans were far from classical warships. To save time and effort, American schooners were converted to warships by adding one or two guns. These small new warships were named the *Hamilton, Governor Tompkins, Growler, Conquest,* and *Pert.* Others that followed in their path were named the *Ontario, Scourge, Fair America,* and *Asp.* Special gun barges were built to beef up harbor protection. Many of the salt barges were converted to troop transports to move the Army's soldiers and militiamen around the lake. It seemed that the best and most popular strategy for the Americans to win the war was to attack and conquer Canada overland. That would leave the British without a base in North America and cause a British withdrawal. However, the present state of the American Navy to support the attack and of the American Army to make an attack made aggressive strategy impossible. The Americans had no means to take an offensive posture against the enemy at this time.

Now that the war had begun, everyone had to do his or her best to support the country in its hour of need. Few wanted to return to British rule. Independence and freedom were too valuable to lose. The residents were behind the cause and willing to do anything they could to insure success.

Ready for War

The residents of Troupville began preparations in case of enemy attack, which, of course, would likely come from the water. They were very interested in all reports of naval activity on the lake. Now that hostilities had begun, the merchant fleet was extremely vulnerable. The British Navy had stopped many American merchant ships before the war; now everyone expected that activity to increase with more dangerous results. Certainly no supplies were being shipped to Canada, and the ships in the area like the *Lake Queen, Nancy, Enterprise, Pultney's Pride,* and *Sodus Belle* began working to support the war effort. They traveled in small convoys near the south shore of the lake, often carrying war supplies between small villages and Sacketts Harbor.

The *Lake Queen* was actually commissioned as an official naval transport vessel. Her assignment was the transport of material and passengers between the two major naval ports on the lake, Oswego and Sacketts Harbor. In order for supplies and troops to get to Sacketts Harbor, they came along the inland rivers and overland portages to Oswego. Then ships like the *Lake Queen* transported them the last forty miles east on the lake to Sacketts Harbor. This was a dangerous forty miles because the British knew this was the exposed and, therefore, vulnerable link in the main American supply line for Lake Ontario. Direct overland travel through the 150 miles from Albany to Sacketts Harbor was nearly impossible because there were no roads across the rugged, heavily wooded, mountainous terrain.

Soso quickly realized that his role in the war effort would be the same as it was in peace, building ships. Since the Navy was using many existing ships, more transport ships were needed for regular civilian shipping. Soso had several people ask him about building them a new boat. He decided to build another large transport ship for Rob Fellows and Slim McNab. He expanded his shop so he could build bigger ships. His work crew consisted of James Pollock, Herman Smith, Slim McNab, and a shipbuilder from Ohio named Levi Johnson. By early fall the five men had laid a keel for a 45' sloop and started shaping the hull. This was the largest ship Soso had ever designed and built. It was a major undertaking for the five frontier shipbuilders.

Levi was a talented carpenter and quite a character. A shrewd businessman, he had several deals brewing with the Army for goods needed for the war out west in Ohio. He was temporarily working for Soso because he enjoyed carpentry and shipbuilding and wanted to learn more about the trade. His only other experience in shipbuilding consisted of a few months with Robert Fulton building the steamboat *Clermont*. Levi had plenty of stories to tell about Fulton and his steamboats. Levi continually made strange claims that someday all boats would be powered by steam engines. Of course this prompted laughter and doubts from the others, but Levi truly believed that the steamboat was the way of the future. Soso enjoyed Levi's stories and gladly taught him some of the basic skills of shipbuilding.

Despite his support for the war, Dr. Lummis did not volunteer for the local militia. Instead, he accepted an appointment as chairman of the town committee for safety. He felt that he could contribute more in this position. His fellow committee members were Rob Fellows, Byram Green, and William Wickham. Their job was to learn about enemy movements and to warn the local populace about prospective enemy approach so that they could protect themselves and their property. The committee had authority to call out the militia in case of imminent attack. Dr. Lummis was a natural choice to head this committee because of his roles as postmaster and government agent, which meant that he was usually the first to receive news about official military activities and happenings in the area. Dr. Lummis also continued his farming effort at Salmon Creek that summer and contributed much of his produce and wheat to the war supplies. The flour produced from his mills was a major portion of the supplies kept at the small government warehouse at Troupville. He had taken over the mills upon the death of his father-in-law Colonel Maxwell in the spring. In honor of Colonel Maxwell, the settlement around Salmon Creek was now called Maxwell, and the creek was thereafter known as Maxwell Creek.

Rob Fellows was on the committee because of his contacts with the various American merchant ships, which provided the area with the information about British ship movement. William Wickham, the general store owner, probably had the most possessions vulnerable to any British attack. Byram Green was the militia's representative on the committee. He was a lawyer who had just moved to the small settlement called East Ridge about six miles southwest of Troupville. He had come from Williamstown, Massachusetts by way of Beaufort, South Carolina with nineteen other family members including his brother Dr. Joseph Green. Their families lived in six log cabins built along the Indian trail on the ridge. Byram worked hard on the area's war preparation and organized the effort in the Town of Sodus, which now included the villages of Troupville, East Ridge, and Arms' Crossroads, and numerous other smaller settlements with only a few residents. Many of the thousand or so residents of the township lived on isolated farms, often a mile or more from other settlers, which made communication and organization very difficult.

The War Effort

The most critical effort for the American Navy was the building of the huge gunship, *Madison*, at Sacketts Harbor. A crew over 25 ship's carpenters, under the supervision of master shipbuilder Henry Eckford, had begun work on the 24-gun ship in August. When completed, this mighty warship would have a crew of over 200 sailors and would help the Americans even out the strengths of the two warring navies on Lake Ontario.

With respect to the fighting at the initial stages of the war, the Americans did much better than they could have expected or hoped. The American sailors seemed to be more spirited, and even though they were outnumbered, they held their own. They repelled a weak British attack directly on Sacketts Harbor, which fortunately was well fortified at the time. And the only naval skirmish of 1812 on Lake Ontario occurred on November 9th near Kingston. The Americans under Commodore Chauncey again had held their own and kept the British tied up in port until navigation closed for the season because of the ice build-up along the shorelines on both sides of the lake in late December.

Call for Help

In early November, Dr. Lummis received a rather strange dispatch in the Troupville mail. It was official mail from the Navy addressed to Mr. Soso, Shipbuilder, Troupville, NY. Because of the importance of such official mail in war time, Dr. Lummis immediately went across the bay to deliver the letter to Soso. Soso could read only a little English, so Dr. Lummis opened the letter and read it to him.

> Dear Mr. Soso, Shipbuilder, Troupville:
> I have recently taken over the shipbuilding operations at Sacketts Harbor. We are building several warships for spring launching. I have designed a large, fast sloop, and we just laid out the keel for the boat this week. I am so involved with the building of another ship that I need an experienced shipbuilder like you to oversee the work on this one. I believe that you will find this a superb ship worthy of your effort. Your skill is much needed here, even though I understand that you are currently building a ship on your own for use in the war effort. There will be ten ship's carpenters working on this boat. If you are available, please join our effort here at Sacketts Harbor. It is of great importance to our nation. I am sending the *Lake Queen* to Troupville on November 12 for supplies; if convenient, you can travel to Sacketts Harbor on that ship. Of course, you will be paid for your services as a master shipbuilder, $2.00 per week, by the United States Navy.
> Sincerely,
> Henry Eckford

Soso was shocked that Henry Eckford or the U.S. Navy would want his services as a shipbuilder. He wasn't trained or schooled and really knew very little of the finer shipbuilding techniques or the construction of large warships. Certainly, there were many other white shipbuilders more qualified than he. However, he was confident in his ability to learn quickly and wanted to learn more about modern shipbuilding, especially the construction of large vessels. One thing worried him, however. How would he be treated and accepted by his work crew and the other shipbuilders? He was still an Indian, and he had not forgotten the ugly incidents of the past. He felt accepted and safe in the local area around Sodus Bay, but would it be the same at Sacketts Harbor?

Soso asked Dr. Lummis for advice. "Should I go? I'm sure they can find someone else much better than me."

Dr. Lummis was quick to respond, yet was sensitive to Soso's reluctance to leave his friends. "It's a great opportunity, and I know you'll do well. You know you'll be able to see Jim a lot up there. Our government needs workers like yourself, and the building of good ships is very important if we are to win this war. I definitely think you should go." Dr. Lummis knew that Soso was the best shipbuilder that Henry Eckford could have as an assistant.

Soso didn't have much time to prepare for his departure. November 12th was the next day. He informed the others working with him of his new job and the need for them to continue work on the boat without him. Soso had no idea how long he would be gone, but he promised to return as soon as possible. Slim was put in charge of the work crew, and Soso gave him as much guidance as he could before he left. James Pollock would take care of Soso's home and farm. Soso packed his bags that night after a nice dinner party was held in his honor by the Lummises. Soso was waiting on Jim's dock the next morning when the *Lake Queen* arrived in Troupville.

Jim Davis was happy to see Soso waiting at the dock. Henry had told him about his letter and Soso's possible return to Sacketts Harbor on the *Lake Queen*. The two friends had a brief reunion on the dock before Jim went to see his family for a few hours. Jim hadn't been back to Troupville in over a month, and he missed his wife and children. Jim relaxed with his family in his comfortable home. The *Lake Queen* was going to sail later that afternoon after all its cargo was unloaded and the new supplies loaded into the hold. Soso helped William Wickham and a crew of several workers load the ship with barrels of foodstuffs, mostly flour, and bundles of uniforms and clothes from the government warehouse. By three in the afternoon the *Lake Queen* was loaded, the Captain and his passengers were aboard, and the ship was headed back out of Sodus Bay toward the port of Sacketts Harbor.

It was a rough, cold trip. The winds were southwest, perfect for making good time down the lake. But the cold temperatures and bitter wind made the cramped quarters of the ship very uncomfortable. Soso had plenty of questions for Jim about the naval shipyard at Sacketts Harbor. Jim described the enormous size of the facilities and the rapid pace of the work there. But those things were difficult to explain since neither man had really ever experienced such a place before. Also, there really wasn't much time for conversation, since Jim and his crew were busy during most of the trip. They had to be aware of any British ships nearby, and they warily made their way along the shoreline of the lake. They weren't in any serious danger since the *Lake Queen* was fast enough to outrun any British warships as long as they had an early enough warning and the seas did not get too rough. But at night captains had to be very careful not to give away their position or miss seeing an enemy ship and let it get too close.

Jim Davis brought the *Lake Queen* into Sacketts Harbor at first light. They had made good time and had not seen any enemy ships. Jim identified his ship by setting and waving the correct signal flags to the blocking ships and the heavily manned fortifications protecting the harbor. Soso was amazed by all the guns that seemed to be pointing at them as they entered port. Jim pulled the *Lake Queen* up to the unloading wharf, gave his crew and dockmaster their instructions, and guided Soso to Henry Eckford's office at the Naval shipyard. As they walked along the road, Soso was further amazed by this place. He had never seen so many big ships, so many guns, such huge fortifications, and so many soldiers and sailors. The once sleepy village of Sacketts Harbor was now a beehive of activity.

Building the Fleet

Jim left Soso at Henry's office and went back to his ship; he had plenty to do and wanted to make sure the unloading went smoothly. Henry had a small, cluttered office, which was filled with stacks of papers that contained the details of several ships' plans. There were piles of papers everywhere. Excited and anxious, Soso waited about fifteen minutes before Henry arrived. Henry was extremely pleased to see Soso. It was a tremendous relief for the exhausted Henry to turn over the building of the sloop *Lady of the Lake* to such a fine shipbuilder.

Henry wasted no time in showing Soso the plans for the ship. He was proud of the design, which would make a fast, sleek dispatch sloop to cut through enemy blockades and outrun enemy ships. He quickly sorted out a stack of diagrams from his desk and gave them to Soso. Then Henry asked Soso to follow him. Soso carried the papers with him down the hall and followed Henry into an office similar to Henry's except neat and clean. "This will be your office," Henry said to Soso.

"But I don't need an office. Just show me the ship. Where is she?" Asked the overly excited and eager frontier shipbuilder. Soso didn't think he had any need for an office. He intended to spend all his time working on the boat.

"Just as soon as we review these plans." Henry then went through the entire set of plans with Soso. He explained every detail of the design. Soso was impressed. The *Lady of the Lake* was going to be a marvelous ship. It really was a design suited for Soso's talents with emphasis on speed and maneuverability.

Finally, Henry spoke the words that Soso had been waiting for, "Let's go see the ship." Soso followed Henry out the door, and there in front of him was an amazing sight. Four huge boats in various stages of construction were right before his eyes. The largest ship, the *Madison*, was overwhelming. Soso had never seen or imagined such a huge ship. It was almost ready for launching. And since it was on land, it towered above them, even more than if it had been in the water. Next to the *Madison*, the keel of an even larger ship was just beginning to be laid in place.

The *Lady of the Lake* or at least her keel was next to the much larger *Madison*. Soso was immediately enthralled by the prospects of building this sloop, even though her construction had just begun and was much smaller than the ship next to her. Soso could already picture the sleek sloop gliding through the water, faster than anything else on the lake.

Henry introduced Soso to his work crew of ten ship's carpenters. All of them seemed so young and eager. They had been brought up from New York City over the past few weeks. For most of them, Soso was the first Indian that they had ever seen or talked with. Of course, he was nothing like they had pictured. Henry had already told them about Soso, but still they were surprised at the dress, regular white man's clothes, and the mannerisms of the highly civilized, intelligent Indian. It seemed to them he was just like a white man, with maybe a little darker skin and rougher, blacker hair. Certainly, they thought, not all the savage Indians that they had heard about during their youth were like this one. Soso shook their hands and asked each their name. Henry then left Soso to acquaint himself with his crew and the facilities. Henry had plenty enough to do to get the *Madison* launched this winter and fully equipped by the spring and another new 28-gun ship built by the next summer.

By the end of that day, Soso was exhausted. He was assigned a bed in a small cabin located next to the fort. His roommates were three other master shipbuilders, Jim Davis, and another civilian merchant ship captain. After supper Jim showed Soso the rest of the fort, shipyard, and village. Despite all the activity there, Sacketts Harbor wasn't really that big a place. Certainly, the harbor at Troupville was bigger and probably better-suited for a busy navy base. Except for fate, this important Navy base could have been located in Troupville.

Over the next few days, Soso assessed the abilities of each of his crew members and the nature of the tasks to be accomplished in building the boat. Then he assigned each man a task, leaving some of the most demanding tasks for himself. He selected each plank of wood that would be used in the remaining section of the hull. Soso had never seen such strong and light wood. It was called mahogany, and it was even better than the rock elm that he had used in his own boats. Henry explained that it was imported from overseas. Soso also learned his administrative duties and the procedures for using the shipyard's tools. Within ten days of his arrival, Soso had his crew well organized and making significant progress on the construction of the *Lady of the Lake*.

Another Launching

The workers, sailors, soldiers, and area residents took a day off from their usual activities to watch and celebrate the launching of the *Madison*. Soso and his crew were called upon to help. Their job was to insure the lines holding the huge ship did not tangle during the launching. Soso enjoyed watching the ship glide gently down the extensive ramp and float in the cold water of the harbor. They had already chopped some thin ice off the shoreline to allow the launching to take place. Henry Eckford took a little time during the day to celebrate before he assumed responsibility for construction of the next huge ship whose keel was already laid.

Soso was helped considerably at Sacketts Harbor by having his friend Jim Davis there. Jim's routine with the *Lake Queen* usually took him to Oswego and back every day. Sometimes, due to bad weather, poor winds, or special cargo, he would have to stay in Oswego overnight. And one time Jim got to make another run back to Troupville to obtain flour and food from the warehouse there. Jim liked making that trip because he got an opportunity to see his family for a few hours. Despite his rugged appearance and rough experiences as a trapper, Jim was a loving, caring family man who missed his family as much as they missed him. Jim was almost done with his work for the year, since as soon as the ice clogged the harbors, he and his crew would be released for the winter. They planned to return to Troupville as soon as that happened. On the nights that Jim was back at Sacketts Harbor, he and Soso would spend their evenings talking about their old times on Sodus Bay. These discussions were relaxing for both men and provided Soso the level of support he needed to continue at his own hectic pace.

Trouble at Sea

The Americans tried to run their supply ships along the lakeshore as long as they could. However, near the end of December, it was so cold that ice was forming in the harbor and along the shore of the lake. Commodore Chauncey figured that the *Lake Queen* could run two more trips to Oswego before being released for the winter. So it was on the second to last run for the *Lake Queen* that disaster struck. The ship was on the return trip from Oswego about twelve miles out from Sacketts Harbor. There was almost no wind, and the *Lake Queen* was barely making any headway. The problem was the small ice sheets that were everywhere around the ship. Ice was forming on the hull, making it heavy and awkward to maneuver. Jim knew that every minute in that ice flow brought the possibility of severe damage to the hull. He tried to steer the ship further from shore, but it seemed as if the ice was everywhere. The dark night didn't help their efforts. They couldn't tell which direction had the least amount of ice. Then the worst thing possible happened to the ship. The hull was punctured and split wide open from a razor-sharp sheet of ice, and water began to gush in. There was nothing the crew could do except hold on and hope for the best. Jim and his three crew members managed to climb aboard some of the floating debris. But the ship and her cargo plunged to the bottom of the lake. It was so cold that the four men had little chance of making it back to shore before they succumbed to hypothermia. They paddled with some small boards they found floating in the debris, but by morning they had made only a couple hundred yards. Miraculously, they were still alive, and the bright sun of the new day was unexpectedly warm. Then a little later in the morning, a strong south wind began to blow them further out to sea despite their efforts. By then their lives were in serious danger. It was mid-morning, when Jim saw a sail approaching them. He could only think of the warmth that rescue would bring as the British warship took the four men aboard. Jim and his crew may have been civilian sailors up to that time, but now they were prisoners of war.

The four prisoners were taken by their capturers down to the western end of the lake to the Canadian port of York, near Toronto. They were questioned by British intelligence officers at the port about their knowledge of the fortifications at Sacketts Harbor, Oswego, and Troupville. The four men told the British nothing, so they were put in prison. They were forced to work with some other prisoners chopping and cutting ice from the frozen streams and lakes to fill area icehouses. Several times they made the claim of being civilians to the British authorities, but they were denied any consideration. The British maintained that they were American sailors and were now military prisoners of war.

It took the American forces at Sacketts Harbor a few days to learn the fate of the *Lake Queen*. A group of Oneida Indians who patrolled the shore between Oswego and Sacketts Harbor for the American Navy found parts of the wreckage on shore four days after the accident. The pieces of wood and items they found were identified as belonging to the *Lake Queen*. Neither the Indians nor the naval investigators sent to the site found any bodies. Since the crew would have no chance of survival in the icy water, the Navy personnel believed that the crew had probably gone down with the ship. Soso was grief stricken when he heard the news. He didn't want to believe that his friend Jim was gone. Once again, confusion and despair rushed into his life, and this time he had nowhere to go—no friends to console him. Official notification was sent to Karen Davis and the families of the other crewmen of the crew's probable death. The entire village of

Troupville mourned over the loss of their good friends and patriotic sailors.

Good News

However, three weeks later momentous news arrived from Canada. The crew was alive and held prisoner in York. It turned out that Jim Davis had gotten word to Captain O'Hara of the *Sea Bird*, the Irish ship that had been repaired at Troupville. Several years before, Jim had seen that ship when it had come into Troupville, and when he saw her arrive in York he had asked to see her captain. Captain O'Hara remembered Jim and promised to get word of the crew's capture back to Troupville. Captain O'Hara sent a messenger from York around the west end of the lake to Troupville.

The messenger arrived in Troupville to tell Karen Davis of her husband's imprisonment in York. What a relief it was for her to hear the news. She had lived almost a month thinking that her husband Jim was dead. Now the new information gave her and the entire village reason to celebrate and to be hopeful. Her husband was still alive even though he was being held captive by the enemy on the other side of the icy lake.

Soso received the good news about two weeks later, when the mail from Troupville reached Sacketts Harbor. Overland mail took quite some time to travel seventy miles through the frontier. Dr. Lummis wrote to him telling the story of Jim Davis and the *Lake Queen* as he knew it. Soso felt like a new man. His spirits were uplifted. It had been a rough winter for Soso, thinking he had lost his friend and being away from his home. This good news gave him the confidence and energy to complete his shipbuilding task. The progress on the *Lady of the Lake* had been slow and sporadic up to this time. Several of his ship builders had been incapacitated by sickness. And two other workers from Soso's crew had left Sacketts Harbor along with about twenty other ship's carpenters to return to New York City to work there. Because there were very few new supplies coming in over the winter, the material for the ships had to be used carefully. Priority of men and equipment went to the big ship being built by Henry, but Soso made do with what he had. He was used to working with shortages and hardships. Somehow, he would accomplish his mission and get the *Lady of the Lake* ready for launching in the spring.

Heroes

Captain Oliver Hazard Perry was assigned to the Naval forces on lake Erie. He had been at Sacketts Harbor for a while without a ship to command. He had even spent several days with Soso discussing details on the rigging for *Lady of the Lake*. Then, Perry traveled overland from Sacketts Harbor through Troupville to Lake Erie. Soso learned a great deal from Captain Perry, especially how to consider the perspective and needs of the Navy crew that would sail the ship. The *Lady of the Lake* would be a better ship because Captain Perry had shown Soso how to accommodate the capabilities of the crew that would soon sail this sleek ship through the waters of Lake Ontario.

The *Lady of the Lake* was completed during the last week of March. She was a magnificent boat, and the all the workers in the shipyard congratulated her builders. Henry was especially pleased with both the effort and the product that Soso and his crew had made. They had done the impossible by completing the ship on schedule under extreme hardships. Soso was proud of their accomplishments. Additionally, he was amazed about the quality of the sail that had been sewn for this ship. With this sail, Soso knew that this sloop would be really fast and maneuverable, just the type of ship that could help the Americans win the war on Lake Ontario. The plan was to launch the boat just as soon as the ice broke out of the harbor. Henry gave Soso the option of staying at Sacketts Harbor and working on the big ship or returning to Troupville. It wasn't a hard decision for Soso. He wanted, and needed, to return home. He briefly considered staying around a couple weeks to see the *Lady of the Lake* launched, but he decided not to wait and to head home right away. If he left immediately and had good fortune, he could make the seventy-mile overland journey in four or five days.

Soso arrived back at his home in time to see the spring thaw and ice melt on Sodus Bay. The boat in his shop that his crew had worked on in his absence was coming along fine. However, one of the builders, Levi Johnson, had left shortly after Soso had gone to Sacketts, so there was still a couple months more of work to be done. To celebrate his return, the Lummises invited him over to dinner. Most of the evening was spent in discussion over Jim's condition and health. Jim's friends and family in Troupville were still very worried about him. Soso had brought gifts from Sacketts Harbor for his friends and their children. Troupville, Float Bridge, and Sodus Bay were all happy to see their friend Soso return. The first day of open water on the bay found Soso right where he wanted to be. He caught a mess of trout over by Second Creek, and he cherished every minute of his day on the beautiful bay that he was named after.

At the end of April, Dr. Lummis received bad news in the mail from Philadelphia. His old friend and mentor Dr. Benjamin Rush had died. William and Sara were still grieving over the death of Sara's father, Colonel Maxwell, and this bad news was very upsetting to the Lummises. Even though he was in the process of building a new home for his family at Maxwell and wanted to stay and help defend his community, William decided to take Sara and Ben back to Philadelphia for a while. That way, he could pay his respects to the Rush family and leave Sara and Ben at a safer place until the war was over. He sensed real danger for them in Troupville and felt that his family would be better off in Philadelphia. He personally planned to stay in Philadelphia only briefly and to return to Troupville as soon as possible to help defend his community. The Lummises left for Philadelphia on May 5; William hoped to return to Troupville by the middle of July.

Back to War

By the spring of 1813, the two naval forces on Lake Ontario were at even strength, even though they were very distinct in their complement of ships. The key ingredients of the American force were the *Madison*, which was the strongest ship on the lake, and the *Lady of the Lake*, which was the fastest. The assignment of Captain Yeo as the British fleet commander gave both sides competent leadership. Through good intelligence agents at one another's ports, both leaders knew quite well the other side's strengths, weaknesses, and intentions.

The spring of 1813 brought the first big engagement on the lake as the American force got the early start in April and attacked the city of York, which was the second largest British naval port on the lake. The attacking force consisted of the two big ships, *Madison* and *Oneida*, ten converted schooners, a transport squadron of converted salt barges carrying 1700 troops, and the *Lady of the Lake*. The American force surprised the British and destroyed the 24-gun ship being built in the naval facility there. This loss was a major setback for the British. The Americans also captured a ten-gun ship named the *Gloucester*. However, there was a price paid for this success. The Americans lost over fifty Army soldiers including their commander, General Pike, in an explosion that occurred while they were burning the warship the British had under construction. Fortunately, all the prisoners being held there were rescued. Jim Davis was relieved to see the American force and to obtain his release from captivity. He had bad memories of his last imprisonment at the hands of the Indians under control of the British some twenty years before. That time the escape had been very adventurous and dangerous. Jim and his fellow crew members couldn't wait to leave Canada and return to their homes in Troupville.

The Americans continued their attack on the western side of the lake by taking Fort George on the Niagara frontier. The British force manning the fort retreated into the wilderness after the American forces executed Commodore Chauncey's attack plan to perfection. This success was important since it gave the Americans the opportunity to control the Niagara River. They wasted no time in transporting five medium-sized ships overland past the falls, back onto the Niagara River, and finally to Lake Erie. This operation was commanded by Captain Oliver Perry, the new American commander on Lake Erie, and was important step that helped even out the strength of the opposing naval forces on Lake Erie.

While the American fleet was engaged on the western half of the lake, the British finally got busy on the eastern half. They formed their attack fleet around the their newly built 24-gun ship, *Wolfe*, at the Kingston harbor and attacked the unprotected and vulnerable port of Sacketts Harbor on May 28. The British, as well as the Americans, knew that completion of the big American ship, now named the *General Pike* in honor of the American Commander killed in the battle at York, would give the American naval forces clear superiority on the lake. Such superiority would probably force the British into port and give the Americans full use of the lake until the British could build more ships to even out the force strength.

A British land force of over 800 regular soldiers under Sir George Prevost landed on shore and attacked the fortifications of Sacketts Harbor. They were supported by fire from several British gun ships. The American militia fled in the face of the vicious initial charge, but the regulars held their positions and eventually thwarted the attack. The Oneida Indians harassed the British rear area and flanks so much that the redcoat army finally was forced to withdraw to avoid the harassment. Unfortunately, the *General Pike* was temporarily set on fire by some of the American troops who panicked when they thought the British attack would succeed in capturing the ship for their own use. However, the fire was extinguished before any permanent damage to the hull occurred. Repaired by Henry Eckford's crew within two weeks, the injury to the *Pike* wasn't a huge setback. The report of the British attack on Sacketts Harbor brought Commodore Chauncey's forces racing back across the lake to protect their homeport and the powerful ship under construction there. Chauncey's new plan was to hole up in port at Sacketts Harbor until the *General Pike* was ready for operation. Then the Americans would have clear superiority on the lake. There was no reason to risk leaving port until then. Meanwhile, Chauncey thanked Henry Eckford for his superb work. The *Madison* and the *Lady of the Lake* had seen their first action and had proven to be superior ships of war.

Homecoming

Jim Davis and his crew returned to Troupville on June 2nd. They had been transported around the lake on a warship for over a week. Then after a week's stay at Fort Niagara, they met up with the *Sodus Belle*, which was headed back to Troupville. They made passage down the lake on tranquil waters and through a pleasant voyage. Almost the entire village came out to greet them once word was spread that they had arrived at Jim's dock. Soso came across the bay to see his friends as soon as he received word of their return. The village was excited to have their sailors home, and the good news of the American success at the battles at York and Fort George added to the celebration.

More War

However, the celebration didn't last long. The dangers of war still existed, and all the villages on the American shore of the lake were more vulnerable than ever with Commodore Chauncey's naval force holding in
Sacketts Harbor. Captain Yeo had no choice but to do as much damage as
he possibly could now, before the launching of the *General Pike*. So, in the
beginning of June, Yeo assembled most of the British fleet on Lake Ontario,
leaving small, defensive forces at Kingston and York, and set sail for the
south shore of the lake. His intention was to interrupt the vulnerable
American supply line and to harass the small undefended American ports.
He planned to capture or sink as many small merchant vessels as he could
chase down and destroy the supplies in the warehouses of the small,
unprotected American villages.

Captain Yeo met his first success on June 8 by capturing a small military camp and a warehouse fifty miles west of Troupville at Forty Mile
Creek. On Sunday, June 13, his forces captured two unarmed merchant
schooners running supplies to Army forces along the lakeshore. Then his
forces destroyed a depot containing hundreds of barrels of corn and flour
at the settlement of Charlotte at the mouth of the Genesee River on Tuesday,
June 15. Yeo's plan was working perfectly.

Ready the Militia

The Town of Sodus Committee for Safety heard the news of these
attacks and was concerned about these British actions at nearby villages
and the enemy's possible intentions toward Troupville. The committee's
chairman, Dr. Lummis, had gone to Philadelphia, but the rest of the committee took action on Thursday, June 10, and called out the militia. Over 290
part-time soldiers assembled at Troupville over the next few days. The
British fleet was nearby, and the Committee didn't want the same thing that
had happened at Forty Mile Creek or Charlotte to happen to Troupville.

The large militia force at Troupville was ready for action. The British
had worked their way down the lake, and many felt Troupville would be
their next stop. This time the American forces would be ready and waiting
for the redcoats. However, the British fleet didn't appear as expected. The
militia waited for eight days, and there was no sign of the enemy force and

no report of where they were hiding. The militia had been called out to Troupville about ten times since the start of the war. Each had been a false alarm. Each time, they would stay in a camp on the outskirts of the Troupville village for a few days, and when nothing happened they would be dismissed to return to their regular work. Most of these citizen-soldiers were farmers who couldn't afford to be away from their farms for too long. So even though the British could still be nearby, the militia commanders, Colonel Swift and Major Rogers, reluctantly decided to release their troops to return home after eight days of waiting. The local militia and village leaders hoped that the British either had returned to Canada or skipped by Troupville because they were more interested in Oswego or Sacketts Harbor.

Before the militia left, they carried most of the military supplies out of the government warehouse in the village and hid them in a ravine about a hundred yards into the woods behind the building. Lieutenant Merrill, who lived in Troupville, was left with five soldiers to guard the supplies in the ravine. All the other militiamen headed for home on either Friday night, June 18, or Saturday morning.

Enemy Arrives

Late in the afternoon of the June 19, the inevitable happened. The fleet of British warships arrived on the horizon of Troupville. The sentries watching the lake from the bluff above town sounded the alarm. It was no coincidence that the British had arrived the day after the militia had been released. The British fleet had been signaled the night before by the "blue light" federalist spies. This group consisted of Americans who were still loyal to the British, and they had arranged a system of light signals to keep the British informed of the status of the American forces on the lakeshore. There was obviously a blue light federalist in Troupville, and he or she knowing that the militia had been dismissed had sent the "all clear" signal to the fleet the night before. The bright blue lights could be seen for many miles over the water, so the fleet could stay out of view from shore and still see the signal.

Five big British warships sailed up to within a quarter mile of shore directly in front of the inlet to the bay. There they stopped and waited. About thirty smaller ships carrying British Army troops and supplies joined the fleet by late afternoon. Captain Yeo wondered if any American warships were hiding in the bay, and, just in case, he decided to act cautiously in his attack on the village. The last thing he wanted was to be caught in an ambush by a strong American naval force.

The Defense

As soon as Lieutenant Merrill heard the alarm, he ran out to warn the rest of the villagers and the militia soldiers guarding the government stores hidden in the ravine. He ordered his soldiers to hold their position and to prepare to defend themselves and the government property. All the women and children in the village were evacuated. Many of them headed south on Geneva Road toward Arms' Crossroads and beyond, while others planned to go to the Fitzhugh homestead on the hill overlooking the south shore of the bay. On Fitzhughs' hill they would be safe, but they could clearly see the activity in the village and the actions of the British ships.

Lieutenant Merrill didn't dare send any of the militia for help. He needed the few men he had to stay where they were to guard the supplies and man the outposts. As he headed back toward the village center, he met Jim Davis and Herman Smith. They had already sent their families to safety and were reporting to help the militia. Even though neither man was a member of the militia, Lieutenant Merrill knew that they were reliable and capable. If any viable defense was to be established, Lieutenant Merrill needed help from the rest of the militia that had just left Troupville over the last 24 hours, so he sent Jim and Herman to ride into the interior to recall whomever they could find from the militia and sound the warning to the area residents. The two of them rode together up the Geneva Road to Arms' Crossroads. Then Jim turned west along the ridge toward East Ridge and beyond. As he rode by houses and farms, he yelled the warning. "Turn out! Turn out! The British have landed at Troupville!" Herman went east riding past Float Bridge shouting the same way. Some of the recently released militia heard the call and came running back toward Troupville. Bill Danforth, Byram Green, Lyman Dunning, Bob Paddock, and the Reverend Seba Norton came from East Ridge. Charles Terry and Hoarse Terry came from a small settlement further south. Daniel Arms and Asher Warner came from Arms' Crossroads.

Meanwhile Lieutenant Merrill was organizing the men in the village.

He assembled everyone at the ravine at the edge of the village, leaving only two sentries to watch the British ships. Luckily, the British took their time in scouting out a suitable landing sight on the lakeshore. Captain Yeo also sent a small sloop into the bay to scout around for any American warships hiding between the islands or in the coves. By the time the ship returned to the fleet with the "all clear," it was dark. Captain Yeo decided to wait until midnight to make his attack on the little village.

The extra delay gave the Americans time to assemble and organize their force. Seba Norton took over for Lieutenant Merrill when he arrived. Then Captain Hull relieved Seba when he arrived at Troupville about ten o'clock that night.

Jim had ridden over twenty miles to the west when he decided to turn around and head back toward Troupville. He turned north, rode to the lake, and came back along the shore. His voice was hoarse and weak from shouting, but he continued to ride hard. He had twice changed horses. By the time he reached Maxwell, he realized that the people in that area must have already heard the warning. There was no one to be found in the little settlement. He rested his horse for a while, letting it drink a little from the stream. It had just gotten dark. He was just ready to leave when he heard muffled shouts coming from one of the gristmills. Jim carefully approached the building and finally got close enough to understand the shouts. It was Isaac Davidson, the miller, who had accidentally been locked in the mill. He had heard the warning of the British attack, and being a member of the militia he had returned to the mill to prepare himself for the fight. However, in the haste to evacuate the area, someone had locked the door of the mill with Isaac still inside. The mill had no windows, and the lock on the door was secure. Isaac had spent over two hours trying to get out of the mill to no avail. Isaac was really itching to fight the British by the time Jim unlocked the door and released him from the mill. Jim helped Isaac ready his horse, and the two of them rode hurriedly toward Troupville. They wondered what they would find when they arrived.

Herman's ride to the east to sound the warning had not gone as smoothly as Jim's ride to the west. Herman was following the ridge trail about three miles past Float Bridge when he rode too close to a tree, and an overhanging branch knocked him off his horse. Although the spill left him with a banged-up head, he was not hurt badly enough to stop his ride. However, less than a mile further on, his horse threw a shoe and came up lame. Herman had no choice but to walk his horse back to Float Bridge. By the time he returned there, the settlement was almost completely empty. Herman had no idea where everyone had gone so quickly, but he was happy to find the militiamen of Float Bridge preparing defensive positions along the shore of the bay. By that time, Herman's only thought was to get back to Troupville to join his neighbors and the militia in defense of the village. He figured it was too late to continue his ride to the east to call out more men. The word would spread fast enough now that so many people were fleeing to the interior.

Herman asked Norman Sheldon if he could borrow a horse to get back to Troupville. Norman gladly obliged but suggested Herman check on Soso first before riding back to Troupville. Norman had sent his son Joe over to Soso's house to give him the news earlier, but Soso hadn't been at home, so he was probably unaware of the attack.

It was dark by the time Herman arrived at Soso's house. He called out and heard a response from Soso's workshop. Herman found Soso busy at his usual activity, working on the hull of a boat. Herman told Soso the news of the British sighting off Troupville. "The word is out. The British are ready to land at Troupville. The militia is being called back, but the situation looks hopeless." Everyone had worried about this eventuality, and now it was happening.

"We'd better get over there right away. They'll need every man to help. We can't let the British get ashore. They'll burn everything, if they do." Soso headed out of work shed with Herman right behind him.

"Troupville has to be saved. Everyone will lose their homes." Soso was hoping for a miracle, and he wasn't the only one.

Out fishing during the evening, Soso had missed Joe's visit. But Soso had seen a strange boat on the bay, and the news of the British ships in the area now explained the unusual behavior of the boat. Soso had watched that small boat search all the coves, inlets, and gaps around the islands. And while he noticed it was a fast, deep draft sloop, he had not noticed any British sailors on board or a British flag. However, Soso now knew that he had seen a British scout boat.

Soso figured the fastest way to get Herman and himself to Troupville was by boat. He had the use of Dr. Lummis' boat while the doctor was in Philadelphia. It was dark so it would be no problem getting by any British ships in the bay undetected. Soso grabbed his flintlock and his bow with a quiver full of arrows. Then, the two of them set sail for Troupville. They landed about half way between First Creek and Jim's house, beached the boat, and covered it with branches and leaves. Heading up the ravine to where the government stores were hidden, they quietly walked right up to the American militia assembled in the tree line next to the ravine. The sudden appearance of the two men coming toward their position nearly triggered several nervous men to fire, but luckily they recognized that it was Herman and Soso before any fatal mistakes were made. Lieutenant Merrill shouted out for everyone to hold his fire.

It was after eleven that night, and the British had not yet attacked. Captain Hull, who was now in charge of the militia, placed Herman on the end of the skirmish line next to Jim and Isaac Davidson. The pair had arrived about an hour earlier. Captain Hull then sent Soso out to check on the sentries. Soso carried his own gun, having left his bow and arrows back with the hidden boat. All the militiamen were anxious and nervous. While rugged men were able to cope with the frontier hardships, most of them weren't well trained for military combat and had no idea what to expect. They realized that they would be hopelessly outnumbered in any skirmish and would possibly face the regular soldiers of the redcoat army. Nervous sentries watching the ships lying off shore had delivered several false reports that the redcoats had landed. These reports only added to the uneasiness and confusion of the citizen-soldiers.

Just after midnight the Americans decided to take action by advancing their line through the village to near the shoreline. They hoped to ambush the redcoats before they got into the village. However, the British had already started their amphibious assault on the village. Captain Yeo loaded over 300 of his best regular soldiers into twenty landing boats and sent them ashore. As soon as Soso saw the British actions, he ran back toward the American formation in the ravine. The American militia was already advancing through the village toward the redcoats.

Attack

The British landing party quickly organized into their attack formation along the shore. However, their use of lanterns to help them avoid confusion in assembling gave the Americans the advantage. Now the Americans knew the location and intention of their enemy. On the other hand, the

British had no idea if there was an enemy force facing them, or its size, location, or intentions. The Americans also had other advantages of knowing the terrain and holding the higher ground. The British started their advance up the slope from the water's edge through some shrubs and bushes toward the village. The only thing the Americans were unsure about was the enemy strength. Soso arrived just minutes before the two forces would meet with the information about the number of boats and number of soldiers that he saw coming to shore. Now the puzzle was complete. The Americans had maximized their intelligence gathering and that temporarily helped even the odds, although an engagement of regulars against militia was never an even match.

Captain Hull now realized his force of 130 men was outnumbered almost three to one. Therefore, his orders stood as given. The militiamen were to stay in their positions in the narrow tree line next to the village, deliver one round of well-aimed fire, and then retreat. Each man would be on his own to reload and fire as he fell back through the village. They would meet and reassemble back at the ravine to form another defensive line in order to attempt to hold the government supplies.

Remarkably, the inexperienced and frightened American militiamen were ready, and they held the advantage of surprise. The British Regulars were not ready. Each militiaman huddled behind a tree or shrub, and his nerves and muscles tensed as the drum roll of the British advance got louder and louder. As the British approached close to the American line, two sharpshooters, Jim Davis and Amasa Johnson, fired at two British soldiers carrying the lanterns along side the drummers. The British land force commander panicked and shouted to return fire. Their massive volley was totally ineffective. They didn't realize the position of their enemy, and most of their shots were way off-target. Some rounds went high over the Americans' heads, while others buried into the ground yards in front of their intended targets. Only a couple of shots hit the Americans. Soso saw Charles Terry and Lieutenant Merrill fall from gunshot wounds from that first barrage.

Counterattack

Now, it was the Americans turn. They knew the exact location of their targets from the lanterns and the flash of over 200 British guns. Several

Americans were wounded, several others were helping the wounded, and a couple had fled at the first sound of gunfire. However, over a hundred well-aimed flintlocks shot down at short range on the exposed and well-defined British line. The result was devastating. Eight British soldiers were killed instantly, and over fifteen others including their commander were badly wounded.

What followed was complete confusion. The British orders were to continue to advance, but in the wake of the devastating American fire, they were slow and timid. Only a few British soldiers actually continued all the way into the village. The Americans fled in all directions. Herman and Isaac Davidson helped Lieutenant Merrill and Charles Terry back to the ravine. Three Americans accidentally ran the wrong way and found themselves face to face with soldiers on the British line. The three—Chris Britton, Harry Skinner, and Gil Saulter—were surrounded by redcoats and captured immediately. The only American unable to flee was Asher Warner, who had been mortally wounded by the first British gunfire. Soldiers from the British advance element picked him up, placed him in Merrill's tavern, and left him there.

The British advance stalled at that point. They didn't know where their enemy was now, and they feared another attack from out of the darkness. Their flanks were being harassed by accurate gunfire, which killed another two red-coated soldiers. The British soldiers were shocked to meet a partially organized American force. The attack had not gone as planned.

The wounded British commander figured they must be facing a well organized, powerful defensive force—possibly Regular Army soldiers. He decided to withdraw to their ships until the light of morning. The late night attack had not surprised their enemy as they had planned. At least in the light of the morning, they would be able to see the Americans. The British troops gladly scrambled back to the shore, boarded their boats, and returned to the safety of their ships. They took back ten dead, fifteen wounded, and three American prisoners. If they had only known the current status of the American militia, they could have safely stayed in the tiny deserted village or pushed ahead to overwhelm the weak and disorganized resistance. The American withdrawal was utter chaos. Most of the soldiers had scattered to the woods. Some didn't stop their retreat until they had traveled for miles.

Regroup

Of the 130 original militiamen and villagers on the skirmish line, only thirty managed to reassemble at the ravine as ordered. Militia leaders Captain Hull, Byram Greene, and Seba Norton were there. Many villagers, including Herman, John Nicholas, and Captain Wickham, were there. Several of the men there were wounded, including Lieutenant Merrill, Charles Terry, and Charles Eldridge. Soso and Jim Davis were a little late getting back to the ravine. They were the only Americans who had stayed back in the village to fight. They had separated from one another. Soso ended up on the west side, and Jim Davis on the east side of the advancing British line. The few shots they had fired at the British flanks must have been just enough to raise doubts in the British commander's mind about the American withdrawal.

After the first volley was fired by both sides, Soso noticed the incapacity of his wounded colleague Asher Warner and tried to prevent his capture by the British. However, there were too many redcoats to scare off. Soso did get a good shot off at a British soldier, who ventured a few yards off the flank of the main British line, killing the redcoat. Jim was able to do the same on the other side of the British line. They both took a couple of shots at the British as the redcoats climbed back into their boats, but the distance was too far, and their fleeing targets escaped unharmed.

When Soso returned to the ravine, he reported to Captain Hull the information of the capture of Asher Warner and the three other Americans and the withdrawal of the British force back to its ships. But the real prize was his own prisoner. One of the British soldiers had been accidentally left in the village unable to find his way back to the boats on the shore. Soso had almost run right into him. Upon seeing Soso, the red-coated soldier knew any resistance was futile and immediately threw down his gun. Soso gladly obliged the redcoat and brought the prisoner and his weapon back to the ravine. Soso remained calm and effective just as he had learned to do through intense, emotional experiences. Of course, things were quite a bit different. He was in a real life-and-death, combat situation. He had just killed another person, one of the soldiers of the enemy. Killing another person wasn't the same as killing animals for food. But he convinced himself for now that killing the enemy in self-defense was justified. He had to stay focused on the present. If he was successful, there would be time to reflect on his past actions at a later time.

By the time the Americans reorganized their defense in the ravine, it was past four in the morning. They all wondered and worried about what would happen later that morning. They hoped the British would leave Troupville and head back to Canada, but each man knew that was very unlikely. Captain Hull and Seba Norton made plans for the next day. They certainly didn't have a strong enough force to defend the village if the British attacked again. However, if they stayed hidden in the woods near the ravine, they probably could protect the supplies hidden there. Two soldiers were released to take the prisoner back to Pollock's farm about two miles up the Geneva Road. Two others were sent to take Lieutenant Merrill and Charles Terry to the same place to have their wounds treated. Five men, led by Timothy Axtell, were sent back to a position near First Creek to act as lookouts and a rear guard in case the British landed on that side of the bay. That left about twenty men to stay in assigned positions in the woods and ravine. The plan was to fire only if British soldiers entered the woods, thereby directly threatening the Americans' defensive positions.

Naval Maneuvers

Soso, Jim, and Herman were assigned the mission of becoming the American Naval force on the bay. They were to put to sea to scout around and notify the militia of any British activity on the bay.

Everyone knew that if a large British force attacked again there would be little they could do to save the village. The entire village of Troupville and all the supplies would certainly be lost.

Soso, Jim, and Herman went back down to the shore to pick up Dr. Lummis's boat from its hiding place. Their plan was to hide between the islands and watch out for the British ships. If more than one or two ships headed into the bay, they would make a run for the shore to notify the militia leaders. Soso also had an idea in the back of his mind of a way to trap the British sloop that he had seen the day before. That is, if it came back into the bay again. After discussing his idea with Jim and Herman, it became their plan of action. By daybreak, the three Americans had hidden their boat between the islands with a pretty good view of the British ships on the lake.

Just after daylight a cannonade of the village started. Three big gun-ships had moved into a direct firing position, and their guns were firing point blank at the empty, unprotected village. The firing was slow, but methodical and devastating. It lasted for an hour or more. Every shot ripped through the homes, streets, or trees of Troupville.

About half way through the firing, Soso saw a British sloop round the point and head into the bay. It was the same one that he had seen the day before. The skipper sailed the fast, small ship up the bay and into shore near First Creek. There really wasn't any concern about this one small boat con-ducting an attack on the rear of the American position. The small rear guard at First Creek could have repelled any attack from the five or six men that such a small sloop held. It turned out the ship was just returning the three American prisoners, who were captured the day before, back to shore to deliver a message. However, at that time, Soso had no idea what it was doing down by First Creek. It didn't stay on shore very long before it head-ed back down the bay. It seemed to be heading straight for Soso, Jim, and Herman, and as it approached, they decided to put their plan into action.

As the boat approached them at a distance of about 400 yards, Jim pulled Dr. Lummis's boat out into the open. Would the British take the bait? Jim stopped the boat dead in the water, the sail completely limp and useless, hoping to attract the attention of the British skipper. It worked. Now the British boat was coming directly toward them, only a hundred yards away. They could see the British crew, two sailors and one red-coated soldier.

Now it was time to set the hook. Just as Jim brought the boat about at full sail, Soso shot his gun directly toward the British. The sloop was still out of range, but now a full-fledged chase was on. The Americans took off at full speed toward the narrows between the islands. The British were barely 25 yards behind. Jim tacked to the port and heeled Dr. Lummis's boat up on her side and cut right over the shallow sand bar between the islands. The small keel of the boat skirted inches over the bottom in less than three feet of water. The deeper-keeled British sloop didn't have a chance; it plowed right into the underwater sandbar at full speed. The British boat had run hard aground. There was no way the British could get their boat off the sandbar without considerable effort and plenty of help. And the only help around was Soso, Jim, and Herman, who had in mind a different fate for the British.

So far their plan had worked to perfection. Soso knew that the British sloop had over a foot or two more draft than Dr. Lummis's boat, which he had built with a shallow draft for use in the bay. They had checked their path carefully so their keel would just pass over the underwater ridge. Now phase two of their plan went into effect. Would the British surrender peaceably, or would the Americans have to persuade them to become prisoners?

Jim brought the boat around and approached within fifty yards of the British sloop. He called out to the British, "throw your guns into the bay, and put your hands on your heads." Jim's invitation was answered with a shot from the redcoat. The two British sailors began rocking their boat trying to dislodge it from the sand on the bottom of the bay. But they eventually realized the futility of their work.

Soso took one final pervasive step. He took out his bow and launched a flaming arrow toward the sail of the enemy boat. The sail burst into flames. The sailors quickly threw water on the sail and eventually put out the fire. But the sail was now nearly useless with a large hole near its top.

The British sailors on the boat finally realized that further resistance was futile. They threw their guns into the bay, held up their arms, and gave up to the three Americans. It could almost be said without a shot being fired. Since Jim had recently been a prisoner himself, he knew all about keeping them. He tied the three prisoners together in the American boat, while the Americans dislodged the British boat by lightening its load and pulling it off the sandbar with Dr. Lummis's boat.

Jim Davis spoke briefly with the captives. "I guess we fooled you with the sand bar trick. Why are you attacking little villages like Troupville? We can't hurt the huge British Navy."

"We never know where we are attacking. We thought this must be a big city. I was surprised to see such a small village in such a big, beautiful harbor. We thought you must be hiding more people or an entire city along the shore of the bay, but we never found any large population," the Navy sailor, who commanded the ship, answered Jim.

"You have a big Navy, but it is wasted on attacking such small villages. Why did you go down the bay and then come right back this way?" Jim continued the questioning.

"We dropped off the prisoners. The Commodore wanted to impress upon all villages in the area that we will not tolerate the stiff resistance that our land forces received last night. The prisoners have a message to that effect for your leaders." Jim had heard enough. He told the captives to be quiet, while the Americans decided what to do next.

Burning

About the time the boat came free of the sandbar and they finished their parley, Herman noticed the large cloud of smoke above Troupville. He pointed it out to the others. They all realized what it meant. Their worst fears were being realized; the village of Troupville was being burned to the ground.

It didn't take the British soldiers long to destroy what had taken settlers over twenty years to build. The British landing force of 150 redcoats had slowly moved across the same ground as they had the night before. This time they could see there was no opposition. The Americans had left Troupville undefended. The redcoats took everything of value in the village. A few villagers had left in such a hurry that they had abandoned all their family property. Others, having taken everything of value that they could move with them, were only a bit more fortunate.

First, Captain Wickham's store and warehouse were completely ransacked. The tavern was wrecked as the British carried their plunder down to the shore, then ferried it out to their ships. After taking everything of value, the British started burning all the structures. First, the store was set afire; then Sill's tavern, the Lummises' house, Jim Davis's house and warehouse, the other houses and buildings, the icehouse, and the government warehouse were torched by the revengeful British. One by one the structures of Troupville were set on fire and destroyed.

Captain Yeo intended to make it clear to the Americans that resistance like that in Troupville the previous night would not be tolerated. The burning and destruction of Troupville would be an example of the power of the British fleet long remembered in this area.

The families that had retreated to the Fitzhugh homestead tearfully watched as their houses went up in flames. They could see the redcoats romp through their village unopposed. This was a depressing sight for these hard-working settlers. Within just a few minutes, their entire life's possessions were gone. Several men were on lookout, protecting the Fitzhugh homestead from British attack and similar destruction, even though as far as anyone could tell the nearest British soldiers were over two miles across the bay from their location. The few militiamen of Float Bridge worried over the next possible British action. They could see the thick cloud of smoke over Troupville. Their small force of citizen soldiers lined the shore, knowing that they stood little chance if the British decided to enter the bay and treat Float Bridge as they had Troupville.

Soso, Jim, and Herman towed the captured boat toward Float Bridge. As they went down the bay, Jim and Herman realized by the huge cloud of smoke over Troupville that their homes and property had been destroyed. After delivering the captured boat and the three prisoners to Norman Sheldon, they set sail for Jim's dock to see if anything could be saved. As they approached the dock, they could see that there was nothing left of the homes and buildings but smoldering ashes. The British were gone, and the village was deserted. As they walked up the road, they noticed that the only building left standing was Lieutenant Merrill's small tavern. They went inside and found the body of Asher Warner laid out on the floor next to a blood covered wooden table. He had died from the gunshot wounds that he received in the fighting the night before. Apparently the British had spared the tavern because the dying or dead man, Asher, was inside.

They continued to investigate the ruins of the once picturesque village. When the three men reached the bluff overlooking the lake, the British ships were just small dots on the eastern horizon. The actions at Troupville showed Captain Yeo to be a desperate man who realized with the imminent launching of the *General Pike* that this engagement could be his final victory of the year. Now he had to head back to port in Kingston to make his plans and hide his fleet for the rest of the year. However, from now on during the war, many—but not all—small American villages would remember the fate of Troupville and not resist the British attacks on government supplies.

The British left Troupville with ten dead soldiers, fifteen injured soldiers, and four captured. The American troops suffered one dead, four wounded, one of which, Charles Terry, would later die, and none captured. The British had returned the three men whom they captured in order for them to tell the Americans that any further resistance like that in Troupville would result in similar destruction. The British had also lost the small dispatch sloop that Soso, Herman, and Jim had captured.

The American militia had done better than they expected. For one brief encounter, they had actually inflicted losses on the British Regulars. Even though they had lost the homes and buildings of the small village, they had made the British forces pay a price for their victory. It had been a painful way for the small village to become involved in the war.

Rebuilding

The residents of Troupville slowly began returning to see the extent of the damage to their property. Lieutenant Merrill's tavern was used to store some of the property that was saved. Most of the residents decided to move somewhere else temporarily. To some it seemed senseless to rebuild immediately, only to risk another British attack. Others, thinking that the British surely wouldn't attempt another attack on a recently destroyed village, figured they might just as well rebuild now.

Soso invited the Smiths and Davises to stay with him until they could rebuild. It turned out the three men, Soso, Jim, and Herman, stayed over at Troupville working at clearing out the rubble and rebuilding the homes, while the two wives, Karen Davis and Mary Smith and their children stayed over at Soso's. Soso did take a couple of days to work on the boat, and with a concentrated effort by Slim McNab, the new transport boat was launched on July 10.

Dr. Lummis returned to Troupville on July 13 and found his village and his home in ruins. He had heard rumors of a British attack on Troupville, but he had no idea of the extent of the devastation. He had lost his home, all his furniture, and his small barn. Luckily, he had already started building a new home at Maxwell, but now he had plenty of cleaning up to do in Troupville and help to render to his neighbors. Residents from the surrounding area helped in the clean up of the burnt homes. Every day for a month, several of the Sheldons and Hydes sailed over from Float Bridge to work in Troupville. Soso, Herman, and Jim sold the boat that they had captured from the British to the American Navy for $150. They divided the money among the needy residents of Troupville who had lost their homes and would need money for the rebuilding. Several families decided to make permanent moves away from the dangers of frontier living. Others decided to wait until the end of the war to return and rebuild. However, many people, like Herman Smith, Jim Davis, Captain Wickham, and Rob Fellows, rebuilt immediately and moved into crudely built new homes in the late fall.

More War

Later in the fall, Soso was happy to receive a letter from his old friend, Henry Eckford. In the letter, Henry again thanked Soso for all his work at Sacketts Harbor and sent his sympathy for the destruction of Troupville. He also indicated that there was a standing invitation to Soso to come back to Sacketts to build more ships. Henry related the exploits of the *Lady of the Lake*, which had captured the British schooner *Lady Murray*, her crew of 20, and a boatload of ammunition on June 18 while on a raid up near Kingston.

The *General Pike* was operational on July 21. Commodore Chauncey immediately showed his confidence in the powerful ship by attacking the British forces on the western end of the lake. The American force destroyed eleven transport ships and captured five cannons at York on July 30.

Commodore Yeo timidly ventured forth with his fleet to test the Americans' resolve to use the *General Pike*. On August 7 the two fleets faced off at Fort Niagara. For the entire day the two fleets maneuvered with the Americans holding the advantage because of the strength of the *General Pike*. However, the British managed to avoid any decisive engagement. On August 8 a sudden squall sank two American gun schooners, the *Hamilton* and the *Scourge*. The maneuvering continued another two days until, on the evening of the August 10, the two fleets briefly exchanged fire. Unfortunately, the Americans lost two important ships, the *Julia* and the *Growler*. The brief engagement was a tremendous victory for Commodore Yeo, who had won despite being out-gunned.

The importance of this battle was that it left the two fleets at even strength. This parity kept both fleets active on the lake, but usually well away from one another. Both seemed to prefer to avoid any decisive engagement, while claiming it was the enemy that was afraid to fight. Because of the individual strengths of the two fleets, the Americans wanted to engage in light winds and the British hoped to fight in heavy winds. Each force avoided contact when the weather was unfavorable to its side.

Henry Eckford once again aided the American cause with the launching of another ship, the ten-gun *Sylph*. As predicted, the real war on the lakes was being waged by the shipbuilders. Thanks to Henry Eckford and his shipbuilding crew at Sacketts Harbor, America was more than holding its own in this regard.

The two fleets finally engaged again off the Genessee River on the eleventh of September. As soon as the Americans held the advantage, the British evaded and ran off. Action so close to Troupville again brought concern to area residents. They knew all too well the consequences of a British attack. The militia was no stronger than it had been before. The militia was put on alert by the Committee for Safety for seven days during the nearby sea battle, but no British ships were sighted so the men were released.

The last major naval action on the lake for the year finally showed the strength of the *General Pike*. The powerful American ship did extensive damage to several British ships off York on September 28. Then seven British ships were trapped and captured by the *Lady of the Lake*, while fleeing the *General Pike* a couple of days later. These setbacks kept Commodore Yeo and the British Navy hiding in port for the rest of the year. The Americans had finally won the battle of Lake Ontario during 1813 and could now rule its waters for the rest of the season. Their greatest asset had been shipbuilder Henry Eckford—with assistance from an unheralded shipbuilder from Troupville, Sosoenodus.

It was a rough winter for the few stalwarts who spent the winter in Troupville. There were a few hastily built homes, and Merrill's tavern was used to house a couple of families still working during the winter to finish rebuilding their homes. However, it was a cold, desolate village much like it had been twenty years earlier, when the first settlers arrived. Captain Wickham had not started to rebuild his store, so there were shortages of food and other goods. Soso and Jim Davis became the village providers just as they had twenty years before. It wasn't a pleasant winter for the residents, but they had plenty of fresh fish and meat to eat.

Renewed Spirits

Spring, however, brought renewed life to the village. Many of the old residents who spent their winter back East or in the interior returned to rebuild, while those who had remained throughout the cold, bleak winter regained their commitment to the Troupville lifestyle. A sense of optimism returned to Colonel Troup, who visited the village in May, and many of the other area businessmen. The little village was quickly regaining its charm and prosperity. Captain Wickham's store was being rebuilt. Spring was nature's time of renewal and growth. The spring of 1814 definitely brought renewal and growth to the village of Troupville.

Dr. Lummis had spent the winter working on his house at Maxwell. It was almost complete by spring. Maxwell had become an active little settlement. Several of the previous residents of Troupville had begun rebuilding at Maxwell. Dr. Lummis was building a dock at the mouth of the stream, which would enable small transport ships to pickup and unload supplies right at Maxwell, instead of carrying supplies for import and export back and forth over the three miles to Troupville.

Once again the spring thaw brought more than just good fishing to Sodus Bay; it also brought the threat of war. The two hostile forces had spent the winter preparing more formidable ships for the summer's battles. Henry Eckford had accomplished the impossible by producing two 22-gun ships, the *Jefferson* and the *Jones*, and he had nearly completed a huge 62-gun frigate, the *Superior*. The hard work had taken its toll on the shipworkers, who even went on strike for a brief period. However, the most disastrous event of the winter had been the onslaught of the plague on the workers at Sacketts Harbor. The sickness had nearly wiped out Henry's work force, and by spring he was desperate for help. More so than any battle loss, the loss of the ship-building capability put the American war effort in great danger.

War Returns

Thanks to Henry's miraculous efforts, the Americans started the season with a slight advantage on Lake Ontario. However, the British took to action first on May 3, 1814.

Their target was the small, weakly defended naval port of Oswego, just 25 miles east of Troupville. The British knew this port well having recently controlled it and maintained it as a fort for over a hundred years. They sent in small, fast gunboats to draw fire from the six guns in the fort in order to divert attention. Then they attacked in earnest. Eight-hundred soldiers stormed the small fort, quickly capturing it. The redcoats took a few cannons and one small schooner, burnt some of the buildings, and left. The American forces were fortunate that the British did not pursue them because they were in complete confusion and vulnerable to being overrun and annihilated.

The British fleet intended to build upon the advantage of their early start by pursuing tactics similar to the ones that they had used the year before. Fortunately for the residents of Troupville, Commodore Yeo bypassed the small, rebuilding village as he sailed west down the lake and went on to the next unprotected lakeside village, Pultneyville.

Knowing that the British fleet was nearby, the militias were ready in both the port villages of Troupville and Pultneyville. Captain Hull headed a force of over 75 militia at Troupville, while Major Rogers' battalion of 75 men protected Pultneyville. General John Swift's unit of 130 volunteers spent several days reinforcing at Troupville and then moved down to Pultneyville on the night of May 14. As General Swift paraded his troops in the fog on the lakeshore on Sunday, May 15, he had no idea that the British fleet was standing just offshore, outside the fog bank, waiting to attack the tiny village. Of course Commodore Yeo likewise did not realize that the tiny village had been reinforced with a unit of General Swift's troops. The blue light federalist spies had signaled the British ships of Pultneyville's vulnerability the previous night, before the unit had arrived. The dense fog had prevented any further communication intended to warn the British fleet of American reinforcements.

The fog finally lifted later in the morning and revealed the huge British fleet set up in battle positions directly threatening the village. Pultneyville was even more exposed to sea attack than Troupville. The women and children were immediately sent away to the interior. Commodore Yeo sent a small row boat carrying the flag of truce to shore to convey his terms. His only demand was "surrender the government supplies, remember Troupville." Everyone knew what that meant. In the current ranks of the militia at Pultneyville, there were several who had been at Troupville a year earlier. Neither they, nor anyone else, wanted a repeat of the destruction that had occurred at Troupville.

Russell Whipple and Sam Ledyard received the message from the British and agreed to let the enemy fleet carry off the supplies from their private warehouse. However, General Swift, the senior Army officer in charge, steadfastly refused to allow the British access to government supplies.

Despite the reinforcement of the militia with General Swift's force, resistance would have been foolhardy. The village of Pultneyville wasn't as protected from a lake attack as Troupville. It was right next to the lakeshore on low ground, wide open for slaughter by the British ships' guns or by troop assault. After the British delegation returned to their ship, Russell Whipple, Sam Ledyard, and other village and militia leaders eventually convinced General Swift of the folly of his stubbornness. He finally agreed to allow the British to remove the supplies from the government warehouse, as well. This really wasn't a big loss for the Americans since all the good products had been removed from the warehouse the day before and hidden in the woods, much like had been done in Troupville. Russell and Sam quickly rowed out toward the British fleet under a flag of truce. As one rowed the other made up the agreement, which Commodore Yeo readily signed. Only the warehouses were to be emptied, and no British soldiers were allowed to take or destroy other private property in the village.

The British sailors and soldiers came ashore to accomplish their task. However, the temptation to loot the ripe village was too much for some of them. They remembered the plunder in Troupville and other small lakeside villages. After only a fraction of the warehouse had been emptied, several redcoats decided to wander through the village to find better pickings than the stale, rotting flour stored in the warehouse. The American militia that had been hiding in the woods on the outskirts of the village noticed the infraction of the agreement and took action. They fired at the red-coated intruders, and, just like that, the battle began.

British soldiers came running from all directions when the firing began. Some of the officers came running out of the tavern unaware that fighting had broken out. The redcoats headed back toward their ships in the small landing boats firing back at the Americans in defense. The Americans shot wildly at the fleeing redcoats. Several prisoners were taken by both sides. But, just as the Americans thought they had the upper hand, the strength of the British fleet was unveiled. Unaware of the cause of the fighting, Commodore Yeo figured to make Pultneyville another example of foolish American resistance. Pultneyville was soon to become another Troupville.

The big guns on the ships began firing. First, they were aimed deep inland past Pultneyville to keep any reinforcements from coming to the village. Then the cannon fire was directed right into the tiny village. Cannon balls rained down on homes and streets. But suddenly after only a brief volley, the firing stopped as quickly as it had begun. The militiamen held their breath, expecting an all out land assault by British regulars. Such an attack would have been devastating. Instead, the British ships put to sail and headed off to the east.

The battle of Pultneyville was a short one. The British suffered two killed and two wounded. The Americans had four wounded, two taken prisoner, and several houses and buildings destroyed. However, thanks to an important message delivered to Commodore Yeo during the firing by a dispatch sloop, which had been on the east end of the lake, the village was saved from certain destruction. The important message that sent Commodore Yeo heading for Sacketts Harbor was that the Americans were trying to transport guns for their big ship Superior from Oswego to Sacketts Harbor. Commodore Yeo had no intention of letting that big ship get its armaments. Commodore Yeo's plan was to cut the Americans' lake supply line by completely blockading Sacketts Harbor. There was no time to finish the destruction of the tiny American village. However, once he had accomplished his mission of isolating Sacketts Harbor, he could then bring his forces back to finish the job of destroying Pultneyville.

Recall

On the morning of the attack on Pultneyville, the fastest ship on the lake, the *Lady of the Lake*, came sailing through the inlet into Sodus Bay. Her captain brought the ship up near Troupville and laid anchor just offshore of

Jim's new house and dock. He immediately rowed to shore with the small boat on board and inquired as to Jim's whereabouts. Karen gave the captain directions to First Creek, where Jim and Soso were out fishing.

It was quite a sight for Soso to see the *Lady of the Lake* sail across the bay. He recognized the boat as the one that he had built as soon as he noticed her sail way across the bay. The fastest and sleekest sloop on the lake sailed right up to the small fishing boat. The ship was so close that Soso could clearly see the select mahogany planks he had placed in the hull. The captain of the *Lady of the Lake* called out to Jim as he came along side, "I have a message from Captain Woolsey for Jim Davis."

"I'm Jim. What does the Captain want?" asked Jim.

"Request for your service, sir." The captain of the *Lady of the Lake* gave a sealed message to Jim.

Jim opened Captain Mel Woolsey's letter and read:

> Dear Jim,
>
> I've been given a mission of considerable importance for our success in the war. It involves transport of sensitive cargo from Oswego to Sacketts, and that is why I need your help. You know I wouldn't ask unless it was very important. By the way, bring along Soso and any other watermen of Troupville worthy of such a mission. Please return on the *Lady of the Lake*. I need you now.
>
> Sincerely and faithfully,
> Mel Woolsey

Jim respected Mel Woolsey more than any other ship's captain on the lake. Captain Woolsey had commanded the slow but powerful *Oneida* throughout the war and had recently taken over the faster and more powerful *Sylph*. He had made the most out of the limited abilities of the *Oneida*. Mel had also purchased the *Lake Queen* for the Navy and hired Jim to sail her on the Oswego-Sacketts Harbor run.

Jim told Mr. Hinn, the captain of the *Lady of the Lake*, "I'll meet you over by my dock in one hour."

Then Jim turned to Soso. "Ready to go on an adventure?" he asked his friend.

"Why not? It must be important," Soso replied. "It sure is a good-looking boat." Soso watched intently as the *Lady of the Lake* sailed off toward Troupville. He was extremely proud of his creation, and he had every right to be. The *Lady of the Lake* was a dazzling, modern boat, years ahead of its time in design and construction. Jim was equally impressed, because he had also seen the boat in action at the battle of York a year before.

Jim took Soso over to his house to pack up; then the two of them returned to Jim's dock. By the time they arrived, word of their departure on a mission for the Navy had spread through town. Jim said good-bye to Karen, but before they left the dock, Herman and Dr. Lummis were there asking to go along. If Captain Woolsey wanted watermen for an important mission, then Herman and Dr. Lummis were volunteering. Jim told Mr. Hinn that he couldn't find any better watermen than the two volunteers, so the four sailors from Sodus Bay boarded the *Lady of the Lake* and headed east.

The American sloop met a few British ships on the way. One was a large, powerful gunship, called the *Labrador*. But Mr. Hinn used the speed of his ship to sail around and through the pursuing enemy ships, staying well outside the range of their guns. Little did they know that the entire British fleet was just leaving Pultneyville and following them up the lake.

Adventure

Captain Woolsey met them at the dock at Oswego harbor. He had a fleet of nineteen small transport ships lined up at the docks and along the shore. He also had the port well protected with his ship, the *Sylph*, and his old ship, the *Oneida*, used as the center of the harbor defense. He was happy to see his two friends from Sodus Bay and immediately assigned one transport boat to Jim Davis and another to Soso. Dr. Lummis was assigned to ride with Soso, and Herman would serve on Jim's boat.

That night Captain Woolsey gave the orders to the captains of all nineteen transports in his fleet. Their mission was critical if Commodore Chauncey was to regain control of the lake. They would be loading the nineteen boats with 34 large-caliber ship's cannons and ten huge cables over the next few days. This cargo was too heavy to go overland, and therefore had to go by sea to Sacketts Harbor. He expected either a British attack on Oswego before they left or a blockade of Sacketts to prevent the delivery of the valuable cargo. Somehow this cargo had to get through.

Once the boats were loaded, they would leave Oswego at night and try to make it to Sacketts, or at least Stoney Creek, by morning. If they didn't make it to Sacketts, they would unload at Stoney Creek, which was only three miles overland on established roads to their destination. The *Lady of the Lake* would provide some sea cover and protection for the transports, and Major Appling would lead a ground force in support of the operation. The ground unit consisted of 120 regular Army soldiers, around thirty militiamen, and sixty Oneida Indians, who had been patrolling this area for the Navy throughout the war.

Over the next few days the transports were loaded with the heavy cannons and thick metal cables. These 24-pound guns were state-of-the-art weapons. They actually weighed over a ton and it took a crew of eight men to load and fire them. The new cannons had a longer range and more firepower than the existing guns used on either the American or British ships on Lake Ontario. Getting them to Sacketts and mounted on ships would make a big difference on the balance of seapower on Lake Ontario. Since there was no attack on the port of Oswego, the Americans knew that the British ships were blockading Sacketts Harbor. It wouldn't be an easy trip. With the help of the islands off Sacketts as obstacles, the British were able to seal the harbor pretty tightly.

On May 28 the small transport convoy sneaked out of Oswego harbor in the dark. It was only a quarter moon, and the sky was mostly cloudy, so the little moonlight was not significant—the darkness was in their favor. There was very little wind so the boats were rowed carefully and silently by their crews of sailors. They quietly edged their way along the shore. At daybreak they were still about ten miles short of Stoney Creek so they put into Big Sandy Creek. This was a small, shallow, weaving stream, but it was the only protection they could find from direct exposure on the lake. The *Lady of the Lake*, which had stayed with the transports up to now, was unable to negotiate the creek, so she returned to Oswego, powerless to help the transports any further.

At best, the *Lady of the Lake* tried to divert attentions to herself instead of the transports. It didn't work. Unfortunately, one transport boat had ventured off line of the others, and when daylight broke, it was in the midst of the British ships of the blockade just to the right of Stoney Island. The small transport made for the shore of Stoney Point, but it was easily captured by a British warship. Fortunately, the cargo was dumped before the boat could be boarded by the British. One transport was lost, but that left eighteen available to deliver their valuable cargo.

Commodore Yeo personally interrogated the captured sailors. Despite their resistance for quite some time, he eventually gathered the information he wanted from them. By late afternoon, he knew the location of the American convoy. He sensed the vulnerability of a helpless convoy of small transport ships hiding up Big Sandy Creek. He quickly dispatched two shallow draft gunboats and four small sloops, each with a small gun and around forty soldiers. The British commander could almost taste the sweet flavor of this important victory as he sent his forces out to meet the trapped Americans. This action alone would make the blockade a success. He knew that without these new cannons for the *Superior*, the Americans would have to stay helpless in their port, and he would control the lake.

The Trap

However, Commodore Yeo failed to consider the strength of the American ground force or the wisdom and cunning of the American water-men with the convoy. The American force knew that they had been discovered when scouts told them of the British ships assembling at the entrance to the creek. Under Captain Woolsey's orders, Soso, Jim, and the other boat commanders took their boats quite a distance up the stream and hid the boats in overgrowth along the banks.

Soso and Jim presented a plan to Captain Woolsey. It was a modification of the plan they had used to capture the British sloop on Sodus Bay. They planned to unload one of the boats and use it as bait to lure the British forces upstream into a trap set by the soldiers and Indians in the ground force. Captain Woolsey and Major Appling accepted the plan, and the soldiers and sailors went into action.

Soso's boat was unloaded in order to make it faster and more maneuverable. Soso and Jim used a hand picked crew to row it down the creek. First, they made as if they were going to try to break through the British blockade at the mouth of the stream. When the British reacted, they quickly turned about and headed back upstream. The chase was on. The lightened transport boat traveled quickly back up the stream. Five British ships were right behind it, not paying enough attention to their flanks. They did unload some of their soldiers to lighten the boats, and the soldiers also charged after the American ship by running along the banks. The British soldiers and ships ran right into the ambush. They didn't suspect a thing. The American ground force waited until the entire British force was trapped and fired a devastating volley. The few British soldiers who were not wounded or killed by the initial volleys fled right into the Oneida Indians, who easily captured them. All the British sailors on the ships were captured. The total result was sixteen British soldiers killed, 32 wounded, and over 120 captured. Three Americans were wounded.

That night, under the cover of darkness and through the utter confusion of a devastated enemy, the American convoy completed its mission. The cannons were delivered, and the outfitting of the *Superior* proceeded on schedule. Soso and Jim were happy to see some old friends at Sacketts Harbor. Henry Eckford talked Soso into helping with some of the shipbuilding while he was there. But a few days later, the unsuccessful blockade of Sacketts Harbor was withdrawn by the British, and Soso, Jim, Herman, and Dr. Lummis safely returned to Troupville on the *Lady of the Lake*. They received considerable thanks from Captain Woolsey, Henry Eckford, and Commodore Chauncey for their daring exploits.

Rebirth

Troupville spent the rest of the summer of 1814 rebuilding itself. By fall it had almost regained its population and appearance before its burning. The region was still vulnerable, but for some reason the residents felt much safer than they had the year before. Maybe they held the false belief that such terrible destruction could happen only once. In any case, Troupville residents knew that they were survivors, and they cherished their beautiful homeport. Of course, there were still shortages of food, especially vegetables, and some special supplies for rebuilding homes and businesses.

Life went on almost as if nothing had happened on that fateful day in June, just a year ago. Dr. Lummis and Soso's orchards of apples, cherries, and pears were producing tasty fruit. Soso and James Pollock completed another boat for Rob Fellows and Slim McNab. Jim and Karen Davis had a baby girl named Susan, and Herman and Mary Smith had a son named Karl. Dr. Lummis finished building his house at Maxwell, and Sara and her son Ben returned from Philadelphia to live there. Troupville, and the rest of the area, was beginning to bloom again even though the war wasn't over.

When Colonel Troup visited the village, he was amazed by its rapid recovery. He was confident that the war had resulted in only a temporary delay in Troupville's evolution into a grand city.

It was a bitter cold wind that blew hard from the northwest on the first day of December, 1814. The two opposing naval forces had just ceased operations for the winter. There were rumors that a peace treaty was being negotiated, and both navies were hopeful of a quick and lasting peace. Both sides were worn out from the three years of shipbuilding and fighting. They realized that nothing could be accomplished by continued fighting on Lake Ontario, where there was a permanent stalemate.

Hidden Treasure

The British Navy had sent a payship from Kingston to York to pay the sailors, soldiers, civilian shipworkers, and other government employees in the York and Toronto areas for the fall, winter, and spring. The ship was heavily loaded with British money, silver, and even gold. Unfortunately for the British captain, his ship floundered in the terrible storm and suffered severe hull damage. The northerly winds had blown the troubled ship to the south shore of the lake and into enemy territory. The captain's only hope of survival was to sail very slowly towards Niagara following close to the shore or to attempt to hide in a protected cove out of the wind until the storm subsided. However, the captain panicked when he saw the sails of an American ship closing in. He didn't know that the American transport had suffered nearly the same fate as his ship and was also sailing for the protection of the shore.

The British captain saw no other alternative but to seek refuge in Sodus Bay. But the hard sailing to make the Sodus inlet and hide from the American ship caused the hull to split open even further. By the time the ship arrived in Sodus Bay, there was no longer any way to keep it afloat. The ship was taking on water and slowly sinking. The Captain sensed the end was in store for his fine ship with its valuable cargo.

It was dark, but as Soso looked out from the shore of the bay he could see the faint outline of the ship as it went down just southwest of Neoga Island. Most of the ship's crew went down with the ship, but a few survivors were able to swim to the island. Soso searched the area the next morning, but he found no trace of the ship or its crew. A couple of

Troupville residents had also seen the shadow of a ship come into the bay and had almost sounded an alarm of a British attack. But they didn't see what happened to the ship. Soso was the only American who knew the fate of the ship, but even Soso didn't know the value of its cargo. Soso had no reason to tell anyone of this mystery. The British ship, or whatever it happened to be, was surely no danger to anyone, given its current position on the bottom of Sodus Bay.

Peace

The message everyone had been waiting for reached Troupville on the last day of February – the war was over. A treaty had been signed in Ghent, Belgium by the United States and Great Britain. The result was that the United States had won its grievance against the British searches and impressments. Even though America had not punished Britain for her wrongs by taking Canada, the young country had held its own against a much superior military force. More than likely with just a little preparation before the war, the U.S. forces could have taken Canada. The United States had shown its resolve and resourcefulness in building a powerful navy from almost nothing in only three years. America had gained status as a world power in less than forty years of existence. It had won the war, and Troupville and the other lakeside communities were again safe from attack.

Now it was time to use the same characteristics that won the war to rebuild the country. The immense energy and confidence of the young country was especially strong in small villages like Troupville. The residents were both relieved over the end of difficult times and enthusiastic for a prosperous future. The reconstruction of Troupville was now being performed in earnest. The old residents returned, and new ones arrived. Trade and commerce returned to the lake villages as ships began sailing freely around the lake. Jim captained a new boat, the *Clear Dawn*, built by Soso for Rob Fellows and Slim McNab and named for Soso's deceased and fondly remembered mother. Dr. Lummis' farm at Maxwell was an impressive business and a productive farm. He had hundreds of acres of orchards and cultivated fields. His mills were busy grinding wheat into flour. Small transport ships took products from the Lummis dock in Maxwell throughout the lake. The same could be said for Troupville, Float Bridge, and Pultneyville. Soso had enough boat orders to keep him busy for years. And the fish kept returning to spawn, leaving Troupville the well-fed, happy village it was before the war, and Sodus Bay the big, clear, silvery-watered bay it had always been. It was amazing how the devastation of war was overcome and nearly forgotten in such a short period of time.

Progress

The summer of 1816 was one long remembered by the residents of Troupville. Snow actually fell several times in May and June, and a frost hit in August. Despite poor weather, progress in rebuilding the area continued, although the short summer was hardly refreshing for the tired residents. Ridge Road underwent a refurbishment. The east-west Indian trail had developed into one of the heaviest trafficked roads in the area, but it had not been improved in many years. The stage company and mail riders had always complained about its poor condition. Now through a cooperative effort of local businessmen, local government, state government, the stage company, and the federal post office, the road was widened, leveled, and straightened. Dr. Lummis headed up local businesses, which provided workers for the effort. Soso volunteered to help with the reconstruction of the floating bridge across the head of the bay at Float Bridge. The old bridge had worn out from use and from the yearly abuse of taking it out in the fall and putting it back across the bay in the spring. When the improvement of the Ridge Road was completed, daily stagecoach runs replaced the horse-back riders who delivered mail only twice per week.

There were two new businessmen in Troupville. Their business was the revival of Jim and Soso's old fishing business. The two were talented and dedicated fishermen, who loved to spend all day at this occupation. Each day they worked hard to find the best location and the best technique to catch fish. Their marketing system was better than Soso and Jim's because they were able to use the improved transportation systems of the stage line and Rob Fellow's transport ships. The names of these two new business-men were Jamey Davis, age 15, and Ben Lummis, age 13. Their fathers were very proud of them. They had developed into fine, young men—or at least mature boys—with tremendous energy and ambition. It seemed that they were on the waters of the bay every day from sunup to sundown. They were natural born fishermen, just like their fathers. Their best days on the water were when they were able to talk Soso into fishing with them. Soso taught them the tricks of the trade. They learned where and how to fish. Soso also taught them which fish to keep and which to let go to breed to maintain an abundant supply. Whenever, they went fishing with Soso their catch was twice as much as usual, and they learned more about their new profession. The two boys also learned all about the Iroquois. Soso taught them his native language, the Indian customs, and the cultural beliefs of the Native Americans. The boys were both fascinated and impressed by what they learned. The Indians had a perspective of life that the whites had missed or had somehow forgotten. With Soso's help, these two whites were beginning to see life in many new ways. Their own philosophies were forming, and they were being empowered by a lifestyle that had evolved successfully for many centuries.

William Lummis and Jim Davis were both busy men, but they always had time for their sons. Jim's schooner, the *Clear Dawn*, was a beauty. It made continual runs on a loop from Oswego, though Troupville, to Niagara and back. Sometimes, Jamey would go with his father, but normally he preferred to stay at Troupville to fish. Jamey had little interest in becoming a ship captain like his father, but he did enjoy some days on the lake helping him. Similarly, Dr. Lummis was busy with his farm and mills. He also helped care for the sick, but Troupville now had another full-time doctor, Dr. Donald Andrews. So Dr. Lummis only helped his colleague during busy times. Ben Lummis also had very little desire to become a businessman, farmer, or doctor. He definitely enjoyed fishing.

Soso's orchards were thriving. His land was excellent for the apple, cherry, and pear trees that he had planted. No one disputed that Soso's fruit was among the best in the area. However, Soso refused to accept credit. He always gave the credit for his farm's success to his helper, Joe Sheldon, who at age fifteen knew how to work the soil much better than Soso.

A Grand Idea

For quite some time, Colonel Troup, along with several other land investors, had an idea of a sure-fire way to develop western New York State. Their idea, a lifelong dream for some of them, was to build a canal from Albany to western New York. They reasoned the canal would increase business and settlement in the area which would lead to increased land prices and progress. Colonel Troup had been one of the original owners of the Western Inland Navigation Company. This company had built several small canals and locks and had helped open up the military supply route from New York City to Oswego during the war. However, Colonel Troup realized that a small private company could never build a canal of the size that he and others had envisioned. So he and others went to Albany to push for New York State government sponsorship of the canal.

DeWitt Clinton was the primary ally for their cause and the main advocate for the canal in the state government. The struggle for state and federal support for the project was long and rough, but when Clinton was elected governor of the state in 1817, the dream of building a canal quickly became reality. New York State would build a canal to connect Albany with the western frontier. Most of the businessmen of the Sodus Bay area applauded the decision and dreamed of increased business and vast profits.

One unanswered question was the path of the canal. Should it link with Lake Ontario or Lake Erie? Should it pass through or around Oneida Lake? Many of the original backers in western New York wanted the canal to connect to Lake Erie with its destination at Buffalo. But there were many others who argued, with good reasons, to turn the canal north from Oneida Lake and either follow the Oswego River or build a short canal along the Cayuga Indian trail to Sodus Bay to end the canal on Lake Ontario. These other options would save time and money and still result in a boom to all of central and western New York State.

Several western New Yorkers—John Nicholas, John Greig, Nathan Rochester, Colonel Robert Troup, and Dr. William Lummis—joined the canal commissioners in debate over the path of the canal at a meeting in Canandaigua. After the meeting, Colonel Troup arranged for Jim to sail the commissioners and several other dignitaries on the *Clear Dawn* down the shore of Lake Ontario. They got to see first-hand how the lake portion of a westward journey would proceed. They were worried about rough weather and disappointed in the tiny village of Troupville. How could such a great canal end at such a small, rural village?

The debate over the path of the canal continued for months, and the commissioners finally narrowly decided on the longer, more expensive route to Lake Erie. If only Troupville had grown as expected or not been burned during the war, it might have been the destination of the great New York State canal. But the commission could see no reason to terminate the canal at such a small village. They were enthralled by the more populated village further to the west called Buffalo.

Reunion

A hot summer day brought a couple of old friends back to Troupville. Henry Eckford and Levi Johnson arrived on horseback on the first of July. They brought along another shipbuilder by the name of Cadwallader Colden. Henry, Levi, and Cadwallader checked into rooms at Merrill's Tavern. Henry was amazed to find the village had been rebuilt so quickly. It looked better than the village that he remembered from ten years before. The new homes that lined the pretty streets were nicer than the old ones that had been burned during the war. Troupville may not have grown much in the last ten years, but it had improved considerably—no matter what the canal commissioners thought. Henry was impressed by the miraculous work done by the residents over the past two years.

Henry and Levi met up with Jim down at the dock and introduced Cadwallader to Jim. Cadwallader was famous for building steamboats and taking over Robert Fulton's steamboat business on the Hudson River when Fulton died in 1815. Cadwallader owned the *Clermont*, which was still steaming on the Hudson River, and had helped Fulton build the *Demologos*, which was the first steam powered warship. Jim remembered that Levi Johnson had told numerous stories of the renowned Robert Fulton and his friend, Cadwallader Colden, when Levi had been working with Soso during the war. Being a sailing man, Jim had serious doubts about the steamship, but he was still impressed to meet a man who had designed and built such strange ships.

The steamship and its on-land relative, the steam locomotive, were on the verge of changing the world. This was the start of a revolution in transportation systems. As far as transportation was concerned, there had been little change over the ages. Before the steamship, boats relied on wind or oars just as they had for over a thousand years. On land, still nothing moved faster than a horse, and on most roads in America that meant a slow walk of four to six miles per hour. But thanks to scientists, engineers, inventors, and even businessmen, steamships were moving people and their equipment and supplies over ten miles per hour upstream and against the wind. Soon, locomotives would travel on land over 25 miles per hour, up hills, over rivers, and through bad weather. The world was about to change.

"You must have a huge dry dock and ship-building facility. You could probably build the world's largest clipper ship. Why do you build those bulky steam boats that make such a terrible noise?" Jim was as enthralled with clipper ships as he was opposed to steamships.

Cadwallader was used to comments like this, so he was tactful in his response. "Steamships go without the wind and easily go where wind powered ships can't go. The ideal is to have a sailing ship that would only need power when there is no wind."

"It will take a brilliant genius like Soso to build such a boat," Henry chimed in. "Let's get over to see the master himself. Can you take us across the bay, Jim?"

Jim quickly agreed to take the visitors across the bay to Float Bridge to see Soso. He had the *Clear Dawn* unloaded and sitting at the dock. His next lake run wasn't for two days. So they boarded Jim's ship for a quick trip across the bay. As they went, Henry and Levi pointed out to Cadwallader some of the unique design and construction features found on Soso's boats. Cadwallader was impressed by the *Clear Dawn's* features and performance. He couldn't wait to meet the Indian shipbuilder.

After landing at Float Bridge and walking down to Soso's, they found him in his workshop. There, in all its glory, was another Soso original. The nearly complete ship was a 45-foot sloop, sleek and elegant. The men gazed up at the magnificent sight. As experts, they quickly recognized the beauty of the work, the innovation of the design, and the distinctive rock elm wood of the hull. Soso intended for this boat to be the fastest that he had ever built. He had selected perfect planks of strong, lightweight rock elm. When it was launched, it was likely to be the fastest sailing ship in America.

Master shipbuilder Henry Eckford couldn't have done better. Soso was indeed a masterful shipbuilder. Soso was introduced to Cadwallader. This was a special day for Soso to see his old friends again and to meet the famous steamship builder.

Soso showed his visitors a few of the details of the nearly completed boat and the designs for the next ship he was going to build. But the real discussion started when Henry showed Soso plans for a new, ocean-going steamship. It was a grandiose plan that Henry was ready to implement, if he could get the right help. Cadwallader Colden and the famous Robert Fulton, himself, had supported the design, and Levi was going to help with some of the construction, but the key ingredient for its success was still needed—Soso.

The five men spent the rest of the day sailing around the bay and on the lake in the *Clear Dawn*. It was a marvelous day, and they all had a good time discussing boats and their construction. Levi and Jim had some heated discussions over the merits of the steamship. However, before the day was over, Henry had accomplished his mission of persuading Soso to come to New York City for the winter. Soso would be arriving in October, 1817, and staying there until May, 1818. Soso was eager to find out what steam power was all about. He also wanted to see the big shipyard that he had heard so much about. Soso, the 38-year-old Indian, would be traveling to the largest city in America.

The three visitors left Troupville the next day. Henry and Levi were looking forward to their reunion with Soso in October. They had accomplished their mission. They now had the best boat builder that they knew as part of their team.

Big Chance

It was very late on a breezy, rainy night in July 1817 when Dr. Lummis finally heard the knock on the door. He had been expecting the signal for hours and had been getting more and more impatient and nervous as he waited. He opened the door and saw Peter, his foreman for the orchards of the farm. Peter motioned for Dr. Lummis to climb aboard the carriage next to the driver, and they drove off toward the dock down at the mouth of Maxwell Creek. Dr. Lummis looked up at the light shining through his bedroom window and thought about Sara. And at the same instant Sara let her worry get the best of her and she peeked out the window down at her husband. She supported him and shared in the dangers that he faced as he helped these desperate people. They could barely see one another, but their senses of one another's feelings were stronger than ever. Her support gave him strength and courage. He wouldn't back down now.

It was a dark night, and the wind swept through the treetops. When they arrived at the dock, Dr. Lummis jumped off the carriage and for the first time saw his passengers. Four men, two women, and three children were huddled together hidden on the floor of the enclosed carriage. The escaped slaves looked back at Dr. Lummis. Their expressions showed both fear and hope. He helped them out of the carriage and into the small boat. Once everyone was in the boat, Peter untied the lines and pushed the boat away from shore. Dr. Lummis expertly raised the sail and away they went. Their destination was Canada and freedom for the nine passengers on the underground railroad.

The little boat was crowded with the ten people, and the west wind was pushing the waves up to three feet. However, this boat was designed by Soso to accept this kind of load and water condition. No one said a word for the first hour. Dr. Lummis was concentrating on his bearing for York, Canada and nervously checking for possible pursuers. His passengers couldn't afford a mistake this close to the end of their journey. There was a tremendous weight of anxiety in the hold of the small sailboat.

Finally, after the first hour, Dr. Lummis felt a little more confident and relaxed. He talked with his passengers about their journey to freedom. It had begun over two months before in North Carolina. They had traveled in wagons, carts, boats, but mostly on foot through Virginia, Maryland, Delaware, Pennsylvania, New Jersey, and now New York. They had hidden in cellars, attics, secret rooms, hollow trees, and holes in the ground. Most of their travel had been at night in darkness. Dr. Lummis listened intently to their stories.

Just as the first rays of sunlight fell on the boat, there was the land they had been waiting for—Canada. Dr. Lummis figured he was still quite a ways east of York so he swung the boat to the west. He sailed close to the shore. If anything were to happen now, he would at least get them to shore. The runaway slaves, nearly free people, peered silently at their land of freedom. They could taste freedom, and with it, feel the new sensations of happiness and joy.

After almost a half hour of sailing to the west, Dr. Lummis finally saw the port of York just ahead. The larger city of Toronto was also in view. His instructions were to drop his passengers about a mile east of York near a rocky point with a white house on top of the cliff. Suddenly, there was their destination just as it was described. Dr. Lummis brought the boat to shore.

"Be careful on your way off the boat. You are now free people. Enjoy your freedom. Good luck and God bless you all." Dr. Lummis was as excited as the passengers were.

"Thanks for the fun ride," the smallest girl told her captain. She smiled for the first time in months, or was it years.

"Thanks for our future," her mother told Dr. Lummis, as they left his boat.

No longer slaves, the nine people disembarked the small boat and walked up the steep path toward the white house. He could see his Canadian contact and their new friend coming down the hill to meet them. Dr. Lummis saw a sense of relief in their eyes and even smiles on the faces of the children. As Dr. Lummis set sail back across the lake, he didn't look back. He had never prayed so hard for anything as he did right then for their success. He was consumed by the plight of these desperate people. He told himself he would do this again and keep doing it until he had done all he could to help these special people to obtain the basic right of all people— freedom.

Long Journey

That September as Soso rode eastward in the stagecoach, he noticed the hubbub of activity all along the route to Albany. Everyone was talking about the canal. It was a subject of controversy with Soso's fellow stage passengers. One lady in particular kept criticizing Governor Clinton calling the effort "Clinton's folly." Several passengers tried to convince her that the canal was a good idea that would open the frontier of the state and the country to new settlement and development. They reminded her of the success of the steamboat once called "Fulton's folly." She would have none of their arguments and insisted on continuing her criticism. Soso rather enjoyed listening to the debate, since it seemed to make the time go by faster. He began to consider the costs and benefits of technology. This type of consideration was foreign to his people. The Native Americans had never thought about technology as a tool to advance society and improve the lives of the people. To the Indians, technology was like magic or a gift from the spirits. The powerful things were spirits, not things that could break or die like technology or people. Certainly, good spirits were able to support the people who developed technology. But he was almost sure there was no great spirit within technology. He was beginning to realize the impact of science and technology and how the whites had become so powerful. He realized that technology, when used correctly, could help people.

But, he had also seen its evil use by the whites to take advantage of and overwhelm his people. He listened intently to the debate. He had to learn about technology if he was going to succeed in the white man's world. He had no spirit to guide him, but he had to find a way to learn and grow.

Other than the discussions, the ride was tedious and uncomfortable. The coach bumped and rattled along at an awkward pace. Progress was slow, and Soso's 160-mile stagecoach trip was going to take over seventy hours of riding on a hard seat or waiting for changes in the team of pulling horses.

Soso found Albany a delightful city. Its population in 1817 was about 20,000 people. It was busy, but the people were friendly. The endless streets and huge buildings amazed Soso. Albany was just what he imagined a city to be like. There was one place in particular that immediately caught Soso's attention—the riverfront. Even though it was a cold day during the last week of September, the riverfront was a lively place with people scurrying everywhere. Suddenly, all the activity stopped for a brief moment as everyone looked south down the river. Soso followed their lead and saw the impressive steamship *Chancellor Livingston* chugging up the river toward the dock without any sail on its mast. It was an intriguing vessel designed by Robert Fulton in 1814 and built by Henry Eckford in 1816, right after Henry had completed his duties at Sacketts Harbor during the war. It was five times bigger than the *Clermont*, which was Fulton's first steamboat and had traveled the Albany-New York route until 1815. The *Chancellor Livingston* was one of about 15 steamboats on the Hudson River route in 1817. It was owned by Soso's new employer Cadwallader Colden as part of the North River Steamboat Company. This company still held a monopoly on the steamship business in New York that the founders of the company, Robert Livingston and Robert Fulton, had obtained in an agreement with the state government. Cadwallader had been the heir to the company and its valuable monopoly.

Steamships

The steamship was the first American invention of earth-shaking importance and the real beginning of technology's impact in America. In 1817, the Hudson River was the world's focal point of steamship activity. The three main contributors to the invention of the steamboat were John

Fitch, James Rumsey, and Robert Fulton. The first two were men of genius, rivals, enemies, and eventually business failures. Although the latter, Fulton, was an able scientist and inventor, his boats never reached the quality of the other two, despite being built almost twenty years later. Yet Robert Fulton was born to succeed, because he was also a good businessman. He became rich and famous from his steamboats. The other two didn't. The amazing thing was that all three were Americans, and the steamship was the most obvious product of America's new role as a powerful nation. In any case, Americans, and soon thereafter Europeans, were traveling upstream and against the wind and still moving faster than ever. The world was going to change dramatically during the 19th century.

Robert Fulton had been an artist before becoming a shipbuilder. He had experimented with other naval ideas such as submarines, torpedoes, and sea mines. In 1807 he built the *Clermont*. It was almost 150 feet long, only thirteen feet wide, and it made the Albany-New York run in about 30-35 hours. He later went on to design 20 more steamboats. Other Fulton ships on the Hudson River had been the *Car of Neptune*, *Fulton*, *Paragon*, and *Richmond*. The last two still ran the same Hudson River route along with the *Chancellor Livingston* in 1817.

After watching the *Chancellor Livingston* land at the city pier, Soso introduced himself to the boat's ticket agent as he had been instructed to do in a letter from Cadwallader. Soso was dressed in his finest clothes. He had bought them new for this trip from Wickham's store in Troupville. However, the ticket agent had no time to waste on an Indian who obviously couldn't afford the expensive fare of the steamboat. This was a very expensive trip. The *Chancellor Livingston* was the luxury boat in the fleet of Hudson River steamboats. The minimum fare was $25 and with additional luxury accommodations the price went as high as $35. The ticket agent was used to receiving only the wealthiest people and had been instructed by his boss Cadwallader Colden to be ready to receive an important shipbuilder for passage to New York today as Cadwallader's personal guest. So the ticket agent paid no attention to the Indian's introduction, poked some fun and criticism at the misinformed native, and sent him down the pier to book passage on a cheaper sailing boat.

Soso knew that he still had to get to New York City so he did as the agent suggested. He booked passage to New York on the sailing ship, *Maid of the Hudson*, for $6 with a departure the next morning. Then he proceeded to check out the sights of the riverfront. He was amazed at the number of boats and amount of freight that came into and out of the port in the few hours that he watched. He noticed the shallow draft of all the boats, which he figured the designers had done to accommodate the shallow water in the river. He enjoyed his day of sightseeing. Albany was a busy city, and the Hudson a pretty river, but Soso still preferred that quiet village and beautiful bay in western New York that he called home.

Soso spent the night in a small room in the tavern nearest the riverfront. The tavern was quite a wild place where many of the sailors hung out and drank away their few free hours between trips on the river. Soso listened to stories of adventures on the river before he went up to his room to go to sleep. He especially enjoyed the stories told about the *Clermont*. One story he listened to with particular attention was about the first steamboat race. The storyteller claimed to have been a passenger on the *Clermont* during the race. The race was in 1811, the year that John Stevens' boats, the *Hope* and the *Perseverance*, challenged Fulton's monopoly on the Hudson. The *Hope* raced the *Clermont* from Albany to New York. The *Hope* got the early lead and kept blocking out the *Clermont* whenever she tried to pass. Both boats had a top speed of only five miles per hour. Finally, the *Clermont* made its move and didn't back down as the Hope tried to cut her off. The two boats collided in a loud crash that made both captains stop their boats. It turned out there was little damage to the boats, but the passengers were so scared that the captains called off the contest. Of course, both sides cried foul and accused the other of poor sportsmanship. It was still an extremely emotional issue. Even then, six years after the race, the storyteller claimed it was the *Hope's* fault, while several others in the audience argued that the *Clermont* was to blame.

Soso was so anxious to get going that he was waiting on the dock near the *Maid of the Hudson* long before departure time. He was watching the working of a large boom unloading heavy digging equipment from a barge when he was surprised by a voice from behind him. "Soso, glad to see you've made it. Welcome to Albany." It was Cadwallader Colden who had spent the last few days in Albany. "I'd like to have you meet someone."

"Hello Mr. Colden. What an exciting port. I love to watch all this action and these magnificent boats."

"Soso, this is Dewitt Clinton. Governor of this fine State of New York," Cadwallader introduced his colleague to Soso.

"Governor, this is Soso. The talented Indian shipbuilder that I've been telling you about."

"Good day, Governor Clinton. I certainly have enjoyed my stay in your fine capital city."

Cadwallader introduced Soso to Governor DeWitt Clinton as one of the premier shipbuilders in the nation and soon to be the builder of an ocean-going steamboat. Cadwallader was running for mayor of New York City and had been in Albany politicking. Cadwallader was on the dock early to take the Governor on a tour of the *Chancellor Livingston*. He invited Soso to come along.

As instructed, the ticket agent came running up to meet his employer Cadwallader and Governor Clinton as they approached the ship. He was excessively polite as he greeted the two dignitaries. However, when he noticed that the third member of the group was the Indian he had made fun of and turned away the day before, a look of fright came across his face. Cadwallader asked the ticket agent if he was all right and introduced him to Soso, his personal guest and the shipbuilder the agent had been instructed to watch for. The ticket agent stood in disbelief while the three men moved onto the boat to start the tour. How could he have known that the important shipbuilder was an Indian? The agent wondered if his behavior during the previous day would cost him his position.

Cadwallader showed his two guests everything on the huge ship. The *Chancellor Livingston* had a 157-foot long, 33-foot wide, wooden hull. It drew eleven feet of water. The pilot house was in the bow and overlooked the river. The engine and paddle wheel were amidships. The main cabin and state room were astern. Finely decorated with paintings, fine furniture, and fancy trim, the main cabin was a floating palace. There were over 150 berths which were covered by elaborate curtains. They weren't very comfortable, but they looked quite elaborate. There was also a big galley in which many foods could be prepared, but the centerpiece of the cabin was the bar. It was a resplendent, long, wooden counter that ran along an entire wall. This was as fancy a ship as Soso could imagine. He wondered why anyone would make a ship so extravagant. After all, it had to work hard to transport its cargo. Fanciness and elegance just got in the way of performance and efficiency.

The *Chancellor Livingston* was the first Fulton ship to burn coal, which made it more powerful than the previous wood-burners. The propulsion system was able to push the 180-ton ship to speeds of six and a half miles per hour. The huge ship had cost an unbelievable $125,000 for Henry Eckford to build in 1816.

After the governor left, Soso stayed on board the *Chancellor Livingston* with Cadwallader. The ship stoked up its steam engine and left for New York City later that morning. A large column of smoke and pollution belched from its tall smokestack. Soso knew that steamships were efficient and fast modes of transportation, but he wondered if the world could survive the effects of this terrible smoky pollution.

Soso never did tell Cadwallader about his unused ticket for the *Maid of the Hudson*. After all, how would the ticket agent know that the shipbuilder that he was waiting for was an Indian. Soso didn't want to cause the man any embarrassment or trouble with his employer. Besides, Soso figured, that man would never make that mistake again.

Luxury

The 150-mile trip on the Hudson River was a complete contrast with the first 160 miles of Soso's trip on the stagecoach. It was a relaxing, smooth ride through the breathtakingly beautiful scenery of the river valley. The Hudson River was gorgeous in the fall. The leaves were just starting to turn color, and the waterfowl were beginning to fill the sky and river banks as they made their southerly migration. Geese, swans, and ducks of all varieties paid little attention to the steamship as it cruised right past these majestic birds, down the middle of the river. Soso gaped at the stately mansions that overlooked the river. The ship traveled by several small islands in the river and it brought back memories of the first time he had seen the islands of Sodus Bay over 25 years before.

Soso stayed up late into the night as they slowly passed the little villages along the river. These villages were lit with small lanterns lining the street that came to the river's edge and ended on a small wharf. He slept for only a couple of hours so he was up early in the morning to see more of the river. At the place where the river took a sharp turn around a point, Soso wondered the reason for a fort with soldiers encamped there. He asked his host Cadwallader about this spectacular place. "Why is there a fort here in the middle of the state? Are there enemies nearby?"

"This is our country's military school. The place is called West Point,"

Cadwallader answered. "The soldiers train and study to become officers in the Army. During the Revolutionary War, this fort protected the Hudson River from the British."

Soso shook his head in confusion over the purpose of the fort, but was still intrigued by the school. "What do they study?"

"The Military Academy is like a college. They study mathematics, science, and engineering. Then they do military training by learning horse riding, how to shoot guns, and how to fire large cannons. After four years of training, they become officers."

"Who are these soldiers? Where do they come from?" wondered Soso. He had never heard of a military academy or knew that the United States had army soldiers stationed at forts in the east. Soso knew that there were Army soldiers out west to fight a war against his people, the Native Americans. But why a fort to train soldiers so far from the war?

"They are young men from all over the country. Anyone who is intelligent enough and wants to serve in the Army can go to West Point." Cadwallader knew all about the West Point system, since he had helped several young men get into the Academy and knew several of the officers who that had served there. "They get to go there free. They actually receive money so they can buy their uniforms and books. It is a great place for developing our country's leaders."

The beauty of this place called West Point rivaled that of Sodus Bay. The river waters glistened and contrasted with the tall, rugged mountains and the large, green plateau. This place made a lasting impression on Soso, who couldn't help think of the similarities between West Point's Hudson River and Troupville's Sodus Bay.

The City

Almost twenty hours after they had left Albany, the skyline of the city of New York appeared on the horizon. This city was an amazing example of man's power to build and create. Unlike Albany, which seemed to live in harmony with nature, there was very little left of nature's work in New York City. Everything there seemed to be man-made. There were tall buildings, numerous piers, huge ships, and people everywhere. As the *Chancellor Livingston* docked at the pier, the passengers and dock workers sprang into action. Everyone seemed to know exactly what to do and did it at a rapid pace. Carriages picked up passengers and whisked them away onto busy streets. The dock workers unloaded the cargo and baggage. Soso watched the activity and confusion for a few minutes until he saw his friend, Henry Eckford, pull up to the pier in a fancy, horse-drawn carriage.

Soso loaded his bags into the carriage while Henry talked with Cadwallader. Then Henry took Soso across the island of Manhattan and across a long bridge to a place called Brooklyn. Soso was amazed by the number of people and the way they were all crowded together. It seemed as if there wasn't room left for another person to live in this city. There were already 150,000 residents in this enormous city. One thing Soso knew for sure was that no more people could possibly fit into this city, nor would they want to live there. Dirt and garbage would eventually accumulate to be so high, people would be forced to leave the city.

Henry took Soso to a hotel next to the shipyard. Soso put his things in his room and immediately went over to the shipyard. It was a huge building that Henry had modernized in order to build the new steamboat. There were several sailing ships being constructed, but there was plenty of room in the center of the building for the new steamboat. It would be a large ship capable of crossing the ocean. Soso could barely conceive of such a ship or of such a large body of water.

Henry had finished the details of the plans and showed them to Soso. Soso would be in charge of the first stage of the operation, the hull construction. Soso liked what he saw on the drawings. This was going to be a high performance ship, quite unlike the river steamers he had seen on the Hudson River. The engine and paddle wheel design were completely foreign to Soso. However, those components were immaterial to his role in the construction. He concentrated on formulating a plan to construct the hull. After he reviewed the plans, he toured the facility. Henry's operation had all the modern tools, equipment, and expert workers to get the job done.

Even though he wasn't enthralled by his first impressions of New York City, Soso was excited about the project. He couldn't believe that people wanted to live in such crowded conditions. Nature seemed to have no role in the living conditions of this overgrown city. Everything was man-made. There was no quiet place. No place to hear the wind in the trees or the sweet songs of the birds and insects. The whites of the city didn't seem to notice the stench in the air and the poison in the waters.

Soso immersed himself in his job. He often worked over fifteen hours a day every day for several weeks straight. He found very little in the crowded city to enjoy except his work. He did go fishing several times on the East River, but he found it as dirty and polluted as the land. There were so few fish in the river that even Soso had a difficult time catching many. He worried about civilized people and their destruction of nature. Surely, these people had at least one thing yet to learn from the Indian culture. Yet very few people paid any attention to Soso when he talked about conserving natural resources. Everyone acted as though there was no end to the things nature could provide. Soso knew better, and the conditions in New York City were obvious examples of nature's limits. Man had to live in harmony with nature to survive and grow. Soso felt that New York City was doomed to failure if the residents didn't change their wasteful ways very soon. Even technology couldn't help the whites if they didn't start conserving and protecting their resources.

Soso ate his meals at the hotel or at the shipyard. He had only a few friends in the city besides Henry, who was as busy as Soso working on other ships. Soso liked his chief assistant, Forman Cheesman. Forman was a talented ship builder and had a great sense of humor. Forman's humor helped Soso cope with the urban existence that he really disliked. Soso's only social engagements were a couple of parties put on by Cadwallader, who was busy with his campaign for mayor. Soso enjoyed the parties, except for the tendency of a few guests to mock or tease him because of his race. To Soso, his race or his background had no bearing on his current position in New York City. Most people he met at the parties had no idea that Soso was an Indian until they were told. His dress, his mannerisms, and his speech were as refined as the whites. His skin was different, but that was not always noticeable in the dimly lit party rooms.

At 38 years old, Soso was more than just a survivor. He was a contributor. And that's what he did during his ten months in New York City. He returned to Sodus Bay in July 1818 having been in charge of the construction of the hull of the most advanced ship built up to that time in America. He had made a contribution to shipbuilding that would last for a long time. That was enough for Soso. Most of his other remembrances of New York City were negative. He was glad that his time in the city was over so he could return to the more comfortable, more friendly, and more natural surroundings of Great Sodus Bay. Soso could only hope that Troupville would never become such a dirty, depressing place as New York City.

Canal

The residents of Troupville were excited about the canal being built some 25 miles to the south. Many of the men in the area had already signed up to work on its construction, which started in earnest in the spring of 1818. The laborers received $8 to $10 for a month of work, or less than 50 cents per day. If they also brought a horse, which was used to pull dirt-hauling carts, the pay was an extra 10 cents per day. It was hard, demanding work, consisting of clearing land, digging ditches, hauling dirt, and leveling banks. By the summer, over 3000 men and 700 horses were working on the middle section of the canal between Seneca and Oneida Lakes. The men who worked on the canal considered themselves lucky to have an opportunity to earn so much money.

The canal's engineers were self-taught and had to use good old American intuition to accomplish this demanding job. Considerable surveying and construction planning were needed to build such a long canal with so many locks. Locks were needed to raise or lower the boats as the level of the local terrain changed. There were very few formally educated engineers in America, and none were available in New York for this job. The nation's first engineering school had just begun at West Point, and there had been very few graduates of the Academy. Unfortunately, none of these graduates was readily available to be employed by the canal commissioners. The engineering work was done by trial and error and on-the-job training. The foremen relied on the hard work of the laborers to make progress and adjust for any mistakes or errors made by the engineers.

The influx of canal money into the area gave Troupville and all of western and central New York State optimism and prosperity during the spring. Troupville was shedding its winter cocoon and blooming with the spring flowers. The bay and its creeks ran heavy with fish, and the mills again began to grind grain. This spring was especially joyous in the settlement of Maxwell because Sara Lummis was pregnant. Sara and William were pleased, and Ben was looking forward to having a little brother or sister.

Friends

Ben Lummis and Jamey Davis knew that this was going to be their last season in business together. Ben was fourteen years old, and in the fall would be returning to Philadelphia for formal schooling, which had been arranged by his parents. He might be able to get back to Troupville for a few weeks during the next few summers, but continuation of the business partnership would be impossible.

It was a bit ironic that Ben would go off to school, while Jamey Davis would stay in Troupville. The two boys had been attending school together in Troupville for over two years, and Jamey was a much better student than Ben. It wasn't that Ben was a poor student; Jamey was just naturally gifted.

Ben had done well in school when he was in Philadelphia with his mother during the war. Of the fourteen students that attended the Troupville School, Ben and Jamey were far superior to all the others. Jamey was going to be sixteen years old in the fall, and this would probably be his last year of schooling. There wasn't much else of importance that he could learn at the one-room Troupville schoolhouse. It was time for Jamey to begin his adult life, get a job, and leave his schooling behind.

Mary Smith was a good teacher, but she had trouble staying ahead of Jamey or challenging him with assignments. He did well in reading, writing, spelling, language, history, and arithmetic. Mary especially marveled over Jamey's mathematical abilities. He was far ahead of the mathematical subject matter that she could teach and had gone on to read from two algebra and trigonometry books written in French, which he also knew quite well. Jamey had surpassed the opportunities offered at the Troupville School.

The two boys spent their summer fishing and reading. They missed having Soso there to teach them more about fishing. Their independence and their ability to handle the responsibilities of running their own business had turned the two boys into young men.

William Lummis was busy but nevertheless found time to spend with

Sara. He would be sixty years old that summer, and Sara was almost 39. Both worried about having a child at their ages. They still went into Troupville once a week to sail around the bay and to enjoy its beauty. They would also check on Ben who was spending most of the summer living at the Davises' house with Jamey. By the middle of August, Sara had become uncomfortable with the heat and her pregnancy so she decided not to travel into Troupville anymore with William. The first day William went into Troupville alone he met up with Byram Green. The two spent the day fishing for bass around the islands. Byram was an impatient, unlucky fisherman, but he enjoyed traveling to Troupville and spending a day on the bay. Byram had traveled all around New York State, but Sodus Bay was still his favorite spot. He and William enjoyed their day fishing together even though they caught only a few fish.

The Judge

Byram was the circuit judge for Ontario County, which included most of central New York and extended all the way to the Pennsylvania border. He had been the State Assemblyman from the Ontario County district, which included Troupville, for a couple of years. Byram would ride from village to village on a fixed schedule to hear the cases for trial in the county. He had a reputation as a fair judge who was knowledgeable in the laws of the land. Byram often asked other men from the area to ride the circuit with him in order to help write up the cases and to keep the court running smoothly. Therefore, it was no surprise when Byram asked his friend William Lummis to join him for the next several days as he made a circuit through Geneva, Auburn, Skaneateles, and Otisco. William had looked forward to such an opportunity so he agreed to go despite being quite busy and concerned about Sara's pregnancy. Sara supported William's travel plan and promised to be careful during his absence.

Byram traveled the circuit on horseback because many of the routes he traveled had no stage lines. He and William met at Arms' Crossroads early in the morning and made the 25-mile trip to Geneva by early afternoon. Geneva was a pretty village over-looking one of the magnificent, long, slender lakes in the area. Byram called these lakes the Finger Lakes, because of their shape. The area near the village had been the home of the Seneca Indians just thirty years before. In Geneva, Byram held court in the local meeting house in the center of the village. He started the cases right away, and by nightfall he had convicted two men of thievery and one woman of breach of contract. He had also acquitted the two town drunks of assault on one another when both apologized and repaid the damages done to the local tavern during their fight. William was amazed with the efficiency and thoroughness with which Byram conducted the proceedings. There was no time for long, drawn-out pleas by lawyers. Byram wanted only the facts and a statement from the accused, and from that information he made his decision. Frontier justice was swift and efficient, and Byram was a master of the trade. Elegant, long-winded, legal talk was wasted and unwanted by this common-sense, country judge.

Later that night in the hotel, Byram showed William the paperwork associated with the cases and asked for administrative help from his friend. After a couple of hours, the two men had completed the paperwork and retired for the day at around midnight.

Early the next morning, they were on horseback again. This time it was only a fifteen-mile trip to Auburn. This day was nearly an exact duplicate of the previous one. Byram convicted three men of public disorder and one man of forgery. Another man was acquitted of horse thievery. Byram also settled a property dispute between two brothers by having them agree to the present property line instead of making them move a heavy wooden fence to a compromised location. The two bothers agreed it was easier to live with their current situation than to move the fence. It was a mystery to Byram why the two brothers hadn't figured this out for themselves, but he was glad to help resolve the family feud.

That night's activities were also the same as the previous night's. Now that he had an idea of what needed to be done, William had a head start on some paperwork. However, the two men still needed a couple of hours of work to finish filling out the necessary legal forms. By midnight the two men were asleep after another long, exhausting day.

The next day's trip was 25 miles to Skaneateles. Byram knew a difficult case was awaiting him there. The case involved the tragic death of a young girl who had died while drinking a cup of medicine provided by a traveling doctor. Claiming the medicine was poison and caused the girl's death, the father was suing the doctor for murder, negligence, and fraud. The case took all day as several witnesses testified for both sides. Many locals felt that the medicine was tainted or fake. Samples of the doctor's medicines had been confiscated and were made available to Byram. He had given the samples to William, who as a qualified physician, analyzed them during the day. By late afternoon, Dr. William Lummis, now the court's expert witness, was ready to testify. William's testimony was revealing. The medicine was not poison, and its main ingredient was plain drinking alcohol. While the traveling doctor's brew had not killed the girl, it surely was not going to cure her. Byram found the doctor guilty of fraud and negligence, but innocent of murder.

He sentenced the charlatan to two years in jail and confiscated his possessions. Dr. Lummis saw to it that the liquor-filled medicine was destroyed. The doctor's wagon was given to the village to sell, and the horses were given to the family of the dead girl. While the exact cause of the girl's death was still unknown, by the end of the case, everyone believed that justice had been done.

The two men again spent the evening discussing and writing the disposition of the case. Byram thanked William for his expert help and admitted this case had influenced his invitation to William to accompany him on this circuit. As they retired for the evening, Byram reminded William there was one more stop on their trip. William remarked that he hoped that the remaining cases would have nothing to do with him. He had not expected to be an expert witness and was a bit uncomfortable with the idea of doing it again.

Slavery

They arrived in Otisco after a 15-mile trip in the morning. The area surrounding the Finger Lakes was full of natural splendor and life. This splendor was one reason that the Indians had established many of their settlements in New York State near these lakes. By the time the two men rode into Otisco, a large crowd had formed at the schoolhouse where the trial would be held. William had not asked Byram about the case up to then. However, the presence of such a large, intense crowd spurred his own interest. "What's this case about, Byram? Don't tell me another murder."

"No. Just harboring a run-away slave," answered Byram as they dismounted from their horses.

A shudder of fear ran through William's body—"just" harboring a runaway slave. His next thought was that this could be him. Was this another setup by Byram letting William know that he knew of his helping slaves? After his first trip to Canada, William had made many more trips. Several times he had hidden runaways in his basement for a couple of days when the weather was too poor to cross the lake. Even though the New York State Legislature had passed a law in 1817 to ban slavery in the state completely by 1827, it was still against the law to harbor runaways. William tried not to show his concern and calmly asked Byram, "What's the maximum sentence for the offense?"

"Two years in jail and $1000 fine."

Byram met first with the prosecutor, the sheriff, and Walker Cornby, the slave owner from North Carolina. Then he talked to the defendant, Pete Smith, and Smith's lawyer. The slave stood in the corner of the room and seemed to be completely ignored by the others. Finally, Byram went over to the young black boy, about fourteen years old, named Tom, and talked with him for about five minutes. Byram asked William to take care of Tom during the trial. As was usually the case with efficient Byram, within thirty minutes of their arrival the trial started. It was obvious to William that the crowd was in sympathy with, and in complete support of, the local man, Pete. It seemed to William that things could get ugly if Byram found Pete guilty.

The beginning of the trial was peaceable enough. The identity and ownership of the slave were established according to papers that Walker had brought with him. The sheriff explained where he and Walker found the slave on Pete's property. Then Byram had Pete take the stand. Pete didn't deny hiding Tom from Walker and the sheriff on his property. But Pete did deny knowing that Tom was a slave. Pete thought he was just helping a friend in need.

The next witness was Walker. As soon as he took the stand, several of the thirty or more people that crowded into the small schoolhouse became belligerent. They hurled cat calls and shouts of abuse every time Walker began to talk. Finally Byram had the sheriff take most of the rowdy, disruptive crowd outside. The noise and demonstrations were even worse out there. However, Byram still seemed to have control of the situation in the courtroom. He allowed some interruption, but, whenever he pounded his gavel, everyone, both inside and outside, settled down. William admired how Byram handled this difficult situation. The situation was not helped by the fact that Walker Cornby was an arrogant, obnoxious man. Even though he was asked specific questions about the case, he went on to ridicule Pete, Tom, and the entire justice system in the north. Finally, Byram had heard enough abusive and extraneous comments from Walker and threatened him with contempt of court.

After Walker finally finished with his testimony, Byram had William bring Tom to the stand. The questioning focused on whether Tom had told Pete that he was a slave. Every time Pete's lawyer tried to get Tom to describe his life of slavery or his flight to the north, Byram stopped the testimony and made the questioning return to the relationship between Pete and Tom. Byram saw no need to put the questions of slavery or the mistreatment of slaves on trial. He had enough problems determining the accuracy of the evidence within the scope of this specific case. Tom was quite articulate and told a vivid account of how he met Pete and what had transpired between them. His story matched Pete's testimony and refuted Walker's accusations.

Byram's decision was ready immediately. He found Pete guilty, but, because Pete was unaware that Tom was a slave, the sentence was only a $20 fine and two weeks in the local jail. Pete would also have the privilege of a four-hour absence from jail each day to tend to his farm. Walker exploded with anger over the light sentence and rushed toward Byram. William and the sheriff managed to stop the mad man just as he reached Byram's makeshift bench. Finally, order was restored when Walker was tied and gagged. Byram then pronounced the rest of his decision. Walker was found guilty of assault and contempt of court. His sentence was a $200 fine and three months in jail. However, the punishment would be waved if Walker freed Tom, by signing official court papers, and left the state immediately. Walker flushed again with anger but eventually knew he had no choice. He reluctantly signed the papers, freeing Tom from his slavery and himself from a jail sentence.

By the time Byram left the schoolhouse he was a local hero. Everyone, including Pete, who now had to pay his $20 and spend a couple of weeks in jail, thanked the judge for his fair and just decision. Byram left instructions for the sheriff to keep Walker for a couple of hours while he, William, and Tom left for the hotel back in Skaneateles. Tom spent the night in William's hotel room in Skaneateles. The next day Byram went on to Geneva to finish his paperwork to send all the trials' results to Albany. He asked William to see to it that Tom had someplace to go, and William offered Tom work on his farm. William and Tom returned directly to Maxwell. Tom was a free person with a new life to start and enjoy. William hoped to give him a good chance to succeed.

By the time Byram had returned to Sodus, the exploits of the cases, especially the slavery case, had spread among the residents. He was a hero to some, and a villain to others. While the slave issue was not often discussed or debated in the daily routine of the residents of western New York, the publicity of a case like this one had everyone's attention. There was no avoiding the fact that slavery was a highly emotional issue.

New Addition

After William's return to Maxwell, he had more pressing things on his mind than Byram's cases or the slavery issue. Sara was in her last month of pregnancy and was having a difficult time. He worried about her condition considering her advanced age for childbirth. Finally, after a month of worry and care by William, Sara gave birth to a baby girl on a chilly day in October, 1818. She was named Elizabeth Fries Lummis. Sara and William felt especially blessed with the arrival of Elizabeth, given the difficulties of her birth.

The Lummises threw the biggest party ever remembered in the Sodus Bay area. Hundreds of people came, some from over fifteen miles away, to celebrate. It was like the three days of a county fair all rolled into one. As a special treat for his guests, Dr. Lummis had hired the first steamship on Lake Ontario, appropriately named the *Ontario*, to give twenty people at a time rides from Maxwell to Troupville and back. The *Ontario* was tiny compared to the ocean-going steamship that Soso had built or the big steamboats of the Hudson River, but it still was a thrill for the Lummises' guests to get a ride on a real steamer. The ride was slow and noisy. It took over an hour to make the eight-mile round trip. However, everyone enjoyed the ride and the inspiring sights along the shore of the lake. Progress and technology had come to the frontier.

Soso had returned from New York City and was thankful to be back home on Sodus Bay. Now it was his turn to tell others, especially the children who had spent their entire lives on the rural frontier, all about the big city and its huge ocean-going steamships, crowded streets, mounds of dirt and garbage, and tall buildings. Some parts of the story were exciting and full of good news; other parts were just plain bad news.

Jim was thankful for the happiness and health of his family. Jamey had grown into an intelligent, strong young man. Hannah was an attractive, mature young lady ready to be married in two weeks to Mike Porter, Jack and Jenny Porter's oldest son. Jim's youngest child, Susie Davis, was a rambunctious, enthusiastic five-year-old. Almost everyone seemed to have plenty to be thankful for—the two young friends, Ben Lummis and Jamey Davis, excepted.

These two were about to be separated. Ben was leaving the next day for school at a private academy in Philadelphia. Each wondered what life would be like without his best friend. Jamey was going to work for Soso, who had brought back plans for a new clipper ship. The construction was to begin in the winter. Both boys promised to keep in touch by writing often and to maintain their close friendship. Ben realized that the best way to contribute to his friend's happiness was to send him schoolbooks. Jamey loved to read and study new subjects, and so Ben vowed to keep him well supplied with schoolbooks and technical journals.

New Partner

Another interesting addition to Soso's life occurred over the winter. The Sheldon families always had several dogs. These impressive and intelligent animals would wander through the neighborhood and sometimes visit the houses in the area. They were all friendly, well-behaved dogs, and everyone liked them, especially the children. Over the winter, one of the Sheldon's dogs became more than just a good, friendly neighbor to Soso. A one-year-old male dog named Mac liked Soso's house so much that he wouldn't leave. Eventually, with the agreement of Soso, Joe Sheldon, and Mac, the dog became part of Soso's family. Joe had plenty of other dogs of the same retriever breed, so he didn't mind that Mac had found a new home. Now, Soso's house on the east side of the bay had two occupants, Soso and Mac.

Mac was a big, dark brown dog. Always friendly toward Soso and Jamey, he had a warning bark for any other visitor, including his former master, Joe Sheldon. After the initial bark, however, Mac got along well with visitors. He followed Soso everywhere during the day and slept in front of his fireplace at night. Soso and Mac became a close-knit team. Both respected and cared for one another, and neither really played the role of master. They were partners. Mac did just what he wanted, which was to be with Soso. Soso did what he wanted, which was to have Mac hang around his house and workshop.

Apprentice

Soso knew from the start that Jamey had special talents. The young man was quick to learn the shipbuilding craft. He understood many of the reasons for the design of the new boat. Jamey possessed intelligence beyond that ever seen by Soso. Soso gave Jamey several books about marine engineering and ship design that Henry had given to Soso. Soso couldn't understand the technical writing in these books, but he did use the drawings to help him with his own designs. Jamey dove into these books with tremendous enthusiasm and energy. Sometimes, he would study from a book most of the night and come to work the next day with questions for Soso. Soso helped Jamey by answering some of the questions. Jamey helped Soso by explaining some of the technical details of ship design from the books that Soso had given him. There were important ideas and principles that Soso never knew existed.

The two men worked hard on the new ship. It was taking shape by late winter. Jamey missed his friend Ben, but he used the shipbuilding and reading to keep himself occupied. Ben's letters from Philadelphia were special treats for Jamey. He enjoyed hearing about the exciting activities in the city and the subjects that Ben was studying in school. Ben sent Jamey several books, one on ship design and the others on advanced mathematics topics called algebra, geometry, and calculus written in French by Biot. Jamey attacked these books with energy and confidence. The book on shipbuilding was useful in his work with Soso, but the mathematics books were the ultimate challenge that his clever mind needed. At first, Jamey didn't understand anything about these topics of higher mathematics, and sometimes the more he read the more confusing it seemed to get. However, he never went a day without spending a couple of hours reading his books and making some progress in understanding these difficult, advanced subjects.

Jamey arrived later than usual on a Monday in April. Soso had already been working for several hours, but he didn't say anything to Jamey when he entered the workshop. Soso knew that the ice had blown off the bay the night before and fishing could begin in earnest. After working for about an hour, Jamey finally brought up the subject of fishing. "Wasn't much sense going fishing today. I only hooked one small trout and it got away," admitted Jamey. Then he added, "The bunch of men fishing from that large boat off the southwest end of Neoga Island must be getting some. They've been out there since first light."

"It was a pretty day, though. The bottom of the bay was probably too riled up for the fish near the shore. Did you try out in deeper water?" Soso asked, because he would have fished the deeper areas of the bay on a day like this.

"No. You know I like that spot over by Second Creek." Jamey had a couple favorite spots and preferred to fish them whenever he could.

"What did you say about someone fishing off Neoga?"

"There were a bunch of men fishing from a large boat with heavy equipment off the southwest end of Neoga Island. They must be getting a lot of fish. They've been there all day."

British Return

It took a while for Soso to understand the possible impact of Jamey's remark. Once he realized what could be happening he sprang into action. Soso and Mac immediately went down to the shore to see exactly what Jamey was talking about. It was immediately clear to Soso that these men were not fishermen. He knew from the size of the rig, the type of equipment on deck, and where the boat was located, that these men were searching for something other than fish. He recalled that night five years before at the end of the war, when he saw the faint outline of a British transport ship as it sunk in the same spot.

Soso asked Jamey to stay at the shop and to continue his work. Then Soso launched his fastest bay-sailing boat and headed over to Troupville. His course took him a couple hundred yards from the strange boat. It appeared that the workers on deck had hooked onto something underwater with their rigging and hoist and were trying to lift it, but Soso couldn't be sure.

Soso deliberately lingered a few hundred yards from the foreign boat. Despite Soso's best efforts to keep him quiet, Mac barked a couple times alerting the strangers of Soso and Mac's presence. They looked up to see Soso and Mac, but immediately went back to work. Eventually, Soso got close enough to see their actions. He watched carefully as the lift cable suddenly broke from the heavy weight they were lifting, causing the boat to lurch severely. Two workers on the deck lost their balance and fell into the bay. Another worker was hit by the flying cable. Luckily, the fourth worker was fine. Soso continued to watch, but then realized that the worker hit by the cable could be severely injured. He decided to help. He sailed directly over to the boat. First, he helped the two men who fell into the water climb into his boat. They were freezing from the extremely cold water, but otherwise fine. The water had been ice just the day before. Then he pulled along side the other boat. By then the healthy worker was caring for the injured man. He was cut along his side, and the cut looked to be bloody, but not too serious. He had been extremely lucky.

Mac jumped into the water to retrieve the men's hats and gloves, which were floating on the surface. The men finally got things organized, cared for their colleague, and thanked Soso and Mac for their help. They seemed to take to Mac right away, which allowed Soso to linger around for another couple minutes.

Soso figured he just had to ask the obvious question, "What are you doing, trying to raise a boat from the bottom?"

"Yeah, but it looks like we lost it in the deep water now. We'll probably never get hooked to it again. We were lucky to hook onto it before. But, I think we're done now." The healthy, dry man was obviously the leader and he was doing the talking.

Soso confirmed their belief. "Yes. This is one of the deepest parts of the bay. If it's down there, it's probably staying there. Anything else I can do to help? You're welcome to come dry off and warm up over at my place. It's just over there." Soso pointed over toward his house.

"No. Thanks for the help. We'll go over to the tavern to dry out. Then we'll head back home. Nothing more we can do here." The men were very disappointed, but still friendly.

"Good luck," Soso replied as Mac barked out his own farewell. Soso knew these were good men, who had hoped to claim a treasure, but were not greedy enough to kill for it. Mac was a good judge of character, and he liked these men.

Soso went over to Troupville to talk briefly with Jim. When he returned, he sailed right over the spot where the men had lost their prize a few hours earlier. It really wasn't the deepest part of the bay. But, whatever they were looking for, Soso figured it was best to let it stay right where it was. Maybe someday in the future, someone else would find what these men were looking for. The next day, Soso heard the story about some Canadians who got drunk at the tavern and told everyone of losing a treasure that was buried in a sunken boat on the bottom of the bay. They had left for Canada in the morning, hung over and disappointed. Everyone had laughed about the good story, and no one took them seriously. They were too friendly and open to be secretly hunting for a real sunken treasure. To everyone else, it was just a good story. However, one man, Soso, knew the truth, and he wasn't talking.

Horserace

The celebration of America's 43rd anniversary of independence on the Fourth of July, 1819, was especially exciting. Along with all the usual activities and contests in the villages was a special horserace. This race was a supreme test of endurance for both horse and rider since the course was from Float Bridge all the way to Troupville. This year's contest was longer than any ever held before in the Sodus Bay area and was wide open for all entrants, since Ben Lummis, the usual winner of most horse races in the area, was still at school in Philadelphia. There were over twenty entries including Jamey Davis, Soso, Wendell Troup—son of Colonel Troup—Ralph and Joe Sheldon, and even Byram Greene—who was riding William Lummis's horse Easy Street, the finest and fastest horse in the area.

Race day was on July 5. The previous day and night had brought wild celebration to both little villages. Traditionally, Troupville had plenty of meat and wine for their festivities. The meat came compliments of Dr. Lummis's smokehouse, which had been purposely stocked with plenty of smoked beef and pork during the proceeding weeks. The wine had come directly to Wickham's store from a winery near Geneva. Similarly, Float Bridge traditionally had plenty of fish and beer. Soso provided the fish, and Mrs. Sheldon cooked it with plenty of spices in big pots over open fires. Dr. Hyde made and sold the beer. It was a special brew he made for the Fourth of July party. The local residents of Float Bridge had been worried that this year that they would have to do without this treat because Dr. Hyde had been bedridden most of the spring. But when the day came, plenty of the best brew in the area was available for the revelers. Dr. Hyde had supervised its preparation despite his illness, and the Sheldons had helped as well.

By race time on the afternoon of the fifth of July, most of the people in the area were lined up to watch the action at the starting line on the west side of the narrows of the bay. The start was on the west side so that the horses wouldn't have to cross the floating bridge at full gallop. That would have been too dangerous for the horses and riders and potentially damaging to the bridge. The course was set to follow the ridge road west to Arms' Crossroads and then turn to the north toward Troupville finishing in front of Wickham's general store. Dr. Lummis was stationed at Arms' Crossroads to insure all the riders traveled the entire course. William Wickham was the judge at the finish line. The course was nearly twenty miles long and took nearly two hours for the average contestant to complete. The plan of most of the spectators was to see the start of the race at Float Bridge and then to ride over to Troupville by boat to see the finish. That short boat trip would take less than an hour if the winds cooperated.

The start was exciting. The twenty mounted horses immediately raced for the lead when Colonel Troup dropped the flag. By the time the horses had disappeared, it appeared to most of the spectators that the oldest and most distinguished rider, Judge Byram Greene, had established a lead over Soso in second place.

Plenty of excitement occurred in the race that was conducted by the boats as they headed away from Float Bridge and across the bay toward Troupville. There were over forty boats of various sizes and shapes heading into the west wind. Several boats bumped into one another to get the most favorable winds and to begin their tacking into the wind. The rowboats took a straight path but were too slow to keep up with the faster sailboats, which were tacking back and forth to catch the maximum wind and making the most headway toward Troupville.

All the spectators from Float Bridge arrived within an hour and a half, and it turned out that was just in time to see the first horse finish. The winning horse and rider came into view just one hour and 35 minutes into the race. It wasn't Byram Greene or Soso. Instead, Jamey Davis had taken the lead at Arms' Crossroads and widened it to almost a half of mile by the finish. The young agile boy wasn't just intelligent, he was very athletic and his endurance and careful riding had spelled the difference in his victory over riders with superior horses. He was mobbed with congratulations when he crossed the finish line.

It turned out that the two initial leaders, Byram and Soso, had both run into bad luck near Arms' Crossroads. Soso's horse had come up lame after he had ridden too fast through a streambed trying to catch up. And Byram had actually fallen off his horse and had to spend over ten minutes catching the horse before remounting to rejoin the race.

Jamey was excited about his victory. Everyone had always thought he was intelligent, but not as strong as some boys his age. This victory dispelled all doubts about Jamey's strength and endurance. This excitement also erased the disappointment that he had felt over the fact that Ben was not coming back to Troupville that summer. If Ben had been riding the

Lummises' fastest horse, Easy Street, he probably would have won the race quite easily.

Soso's ship was not ready for launching that fall. He had hoped to have it in the water by October, but there was still too much work to do, so he delayed the launching until spring. That was disappointing, but the boat was taking shape and he was generally pleased with its condition.

The bitter cold winter brought the bad news of Dr. Hyde's death to Float Bridge. The likable doctor, innkeeper, and brew-master had suffered through severe pain for several months which had weakened his health, and the cold winter drafts brought his death. His loss not only left the Float Bridge area without a doctor, but also without its community leader.

Part III

New Generation

Decision

Soso was involved in two special decisions over the winter. The first decision was made by Dr. Lummis after consultation with Soso. Dr. Lummis decided to buy 300 acres of land surrounding Soso's lot and move his farm and home to the east side of Great Sodus Bay. Soso recommended this action, since he knew the Lummises would enjoy the opportunities to fish, farm, and boat on the east side of the bay. Dr. Lummis was just the type of person the area needed with the recent passing of Dr. Hyde. Float Bridge would inherit the services of a doctor and community leader. Soso looked forward to having the Lummises as his new neighbors. While Dr. Lummis enjoyed his farm at Maxwell, he had restricted the further growth of his farm by selling a considerable amount of the land on the perimeter, mostly to his employees and many freed slaves who had moved into the area. Besides, he had become uncomfortable with the rapid increase in the overall population in the Maxwell area. This was especially dangerous considering his continued activity in the transport of run-away slaves to Canada. Dr. Lummis knew that he would have considerably more privacy and protection for that activity on the east side of the bay, which was less settled. Soso and William talked it over, and the two men liked the idea of growing old together as they lived as neighbors and friends on the shore of Sodus Bay.

The other decision was made by a committee on which Soso served. The committee was made up of the watermen of the Sodus Bay area. Jim Davis was the president, and Rob Fellows was the vice-president. Colonel Sentell had approached several members of the committee about building a lighthouse on the shore of the lake to mark the entrance to Sodus Bay. The committee of watermen unanimously agreed with Colonel Sentell's proposal. The fund-raising for the lighthouse went well, so the plan for the construction of a lighthouse was developed and refined. The work was scheduled to commence as soon as Colonel Sentell's land, which was on Ontario Street next to the bank overlooking the lake, was cleared. Several people volunteered their time for this project. Soso was one of the leaders in both the design and construction. This was a big step in making Troupville an important port on the lake. Passage in and out of harbors like Sodus Bay was extremely dangerous at night. Now with a lighthouse marking the entrance, Sodus Bay would be a safer harbor.

School Work

Ben Lummis had studied hard and quickly made up for his frontier schooling. The extra work that Mary Smith had given him enabled him to surprise his new teachers with his considerable knowledge. As promised, Ben didn't forget the education of his friend, Jamey. Ben accumulated as many books as he could. Then after a month or two, he would send the material to Jamey. There was usually a book or two in each package. The arrival of a package in Troupville from Ben was special for Jamey. New Troupville Postmaster, William Wickham, made sure Jamey got word of the arrivals, and Jamey quickly went to the Post Office to pick up his package. Then, the 17-year-old would practically devour the contents of the books and notes over the next week or two.

Soso could tell when such a package arrived because Jamey would arrive at work a bit late or show up tired from studying all night. Whenever this happened, Soso gave Jamey a few days off to read and study. Soso recognized the value of this activity for Jamey. Soso knew Jamey had the exceptional ability to learn important things and to possess valuable knowledge, and he hoped that someday Jamey would have the opportunity to utilize his knowledge to do great things.

Soso enjoyed the arrivals of these packages. Although much of the technical information in science and mathematics was beyond Soso's educational background, he still enjoyed listening to Jamey discuss those subjects. It provided Jamey the opportunity to teach Soso some of the elementary concepts from the books. Soso especially liked the things that Jamey told him from the books about the history of the white men. Soso tried to make comparisons with the history of the Indians as told by his elders, especially Trout. Soso enjoyed telling Jamey about the history of the Indians, and likewise Jamey liked to listen to Soso's stories.

While Jamey didn't realize it, he was getting through the books from Ben an education that was the equivalent or even better than what could be had at a fine preparatory school. This, combined with Jamey's tremendous academic abilities, prepared him for even more advanced schooling. Even though he was highly qualified for further education, he lacked one necessary ingredient, the money to pay for such schooling.

There were very few colleges in America in 1820, and they all were expensive. But, mostly through Ben and Soso's encouragement, Jamey still maintained hope of attending college. Sometimes, he even dared to dream of attending a fine school like Harvard, Yale, or Columbia. It was Soso who first told Jamey about a school that he could attend for free. At first, such an opportunity seemed impossible. However, the only requirements were to be an American citizen and to be smart and physically fit. In the opinion of Soso and everyone else in the area, Jamey satisfied all of these. Everyone considered Jamey brilliant. He was tall and physically strong. The school that Soso recommended to Jamey was the United States Military Academy at West Point. Soso told Jamey all that he knew about the Academy, and Jamey listened intently.

Soso had seen the military school at West Point first-hand two years before during his return trip from New York City. The steamship on which he was traveling made a stop for two hours at the Academy. He had been impressed with the natural beauty of the location called West Point, which he remembered as the only other place that he had ever seen with the splendor to rival that of Sodus Bay. Soso remembered the cadets in their impressive and distinctive uniforms. Cadwallader Colden had told him that anyone could attend the school, and it was free. However, no one knew exactly how to apply to the Academy, so Jamey waited for Ben's return to ask for help.

Reunion

It was a hot day in July, and most of the people of Troupville and Maxwell were assembled in the yard of Dr. Lummis's home to witness the marriage of James Pollock and Mary Riggs. Since his arrival at Troupville on the ship *Seabird* twelve years earlier, James Pollock had become one of the leaders in the community. He now owned a large plot of land in

Maxwell and was considered the area's best carpenter. Mary's family had recently moved to Lyons, and she had become an accomplished farmer. She was going to tend to the crops on their farm while James continued carpentry. They were a fine, strong couple, and everyone wished them a successful future.

Ben arrived at his house, completing his travel from Philadelphia, about half way through the ceremony. He realized what was taking place, so he waited quietly in the back until the marriage ceremony was over. However, for some reason, Jamey turned his head away from the service and noticed the arrival of his old friend. Jamey couldn't hold back his excitement and immediately ran back to greet Ben. The two young men had a joyous reunion in the back of the congregation just as the preacher declared James and Mary husband and wife.

"Jamey, you look great. It feels so good to be home and see you. It seems like I've been away for years." Ben hugged his best friend, Jamey.

"Do you look handsome and grown up! What did that school do to you? You look like some fancy city slicker." Jamey had to tease his friend, who hadn't sailed, fished, hunted, farmed, or rode a horse in almost two years.

"It may take me a couple days to get back to the Troupville lifestyle, but I can't wait. How about you and I go fishing tomorrow?" Ben wanted to experience everything he had missed. It sure was good to be home.

Ben's arrival added more celebration to the festivities of the day. He had been away from home studying in Philadelphia for two years. Everyone had missed the bright, friendly, young man. Now sixteen years old, he had grown taller and stronger, yet he was still several inches and many pounds shy of Jamey. He wore his dark hair long and stylish, and he was dressed in fancy city clothes. Jamey still had light short hair and wore the clothes of a hard-working country boy, although Jamey was dressed in his best clothes for the wedding. Dr. Lummis showed his son around Maxwell, and Jamey reacquainted him with Troupville. The two friends had a lot of catching up to do. Ben couldn't believe the rapid growth of Maxwell. However, he was most amazed by his two-year-old sister, Elizabeth. When he had last seen her, she had been a newborn baby. Now she was walking and talking and was already a delightful girl with a pleasant personality.

Ben had only a one-month vacation before he had to return to

Philadelphia. He kept busy during that month fishing, boating, and riding. He and Jamey picked up their friendship immediately, and the two were constant companions once again. Ben had one more year of schooling in Philadelphia before he would be ready for college. He had been in contact with Columbia College in New York City, and arrangements were being made for him to attend that fine school in a little over a year. It would be expensive, but Dr. Lummis through his promise to Sara had planned ahead and saved enough money for his son's education. Jamey asked Ben about the Military Academy at West Point that Soso told him about. Ben was excited about this potential opportunity for his friend. He promised to check on the admission procedures when he returned to Philadelphia, where he figured this kind of information would be available. Ben hoped that Jamey would have a chance to attend the Academy.

The future home of the Lummises was being built on the east side of Sodus Bay by James Pollock, who had assembled a crew of the region's best carpenters. The site of this magnificent structure was located only 300 yards from Soso's house and would overlook the bay and its islands. Whereas, Soso's home was completely hidden from view from the water, the Lummis house would stand out in majestic splendor from nearly every spot on the east side of the bay. While the house was being built, the planting fields were being cleared by work crews from Float Bridge. Dr. Lummis planned to move into the new house by October, and he spent a busy summer supervising the construction and selling off his property in Maxwell.

Ben's last day at home was spent on Sodus Bay. Postmaster and storekeeper, William Wickham, organized a fishing tournament for that day. All the famous fishermen in the Troupville area participated in the event. There was no entry fee, except all the fish caught that day went to Wickham, who cooked the fish for a party held at the tavern for the entire Sodus Bay community.

As expected, Soso won the fishing derby by catching both the largest fish and greatest total weight of fish. All the participants were successful, and there was plenty of fish for the party's feast. With all the food and friends assembled at the small tavern, a good time was had by all.

Ben left for Philadelphia early the next morning. He said good-bye to his parents and little sister, Elizabeth, at Maxwell and rode to Troupville to see Jamey. Jamey returned the books that Ben had lent him over the summer. Thanks to Ben, Dr. Lummis, Mary Smith, and William Wickham,

Jamey had assembled an impressive library of books and notes. He had copied word for word many of the books Ben had lent him through the years. The two young men said their good-byes. Both promised to keep in touch with the other, and Ben promised that he would check on the application procedure for the Military Academy.

New Home

By mid September 1820, the Lummis house was taking final shape. It was a large, elegant farmhouse that rivaled in beauty and size the old Fitzhugh house on the south side of the bay. Those two homes were by far the biggest and nicest on the bay. This new home far exceeded the now run-down Helms homestead. The details in the workmanship and design were what set this house apart from the others. Everything was exquisite. Sara Lummis had everything she dreamed—the luxury and convenience of civilization and the excitement and enchantment of the country. Dr. Lummis was pleased as he personally put the finishing touches on the porch that wrapped half way around the house and the grand balcony outside the master bedroom. From that balcony, one could see a good portion of the bay, although the islands blocked some of the view of Troupville. He could sit and watch as boats moved across the bay from place to place. He could see the flocks of ducks and geese rise up in the sky off the silvery water and move to their next feeding grounds. He could watch his favorite fishing spots to see if anyone was catching his fish. He felt considerable peace as he sat watching nature's beautiful world of Sodus Bay. The splendor of the bay served as William Lummis' inspiration and peace of mind.

The construction of the house had been a cooperative effort of Maxwell, Troupville and Float Bridge craftsmen and professional workers. It seemed as if everyone had contributed in some way. Certainly everyone in the area had come by at some time to see this masterpiece being built.

The month of October was used to finish the painting and interior woodwork and to move furniture and farm equipment from Maxwell to Float Bridge. That in itself was a major undertaking. Fortunately, much of the heavy equipment and materials were transported by boat.

Everyone in the three communities of Maxwell, Float Bridge, and Troupville came to the house warming party on the first day of November, 1820. While everyone dressed in fine clothes for the party, it was not exactly a formal affair. The Lummises had friends and neighbors from all walks of life. Some had never seen the conveniences of civilization up close and were enthralled by some of the luxuries, while others pretended to be accustomed to such elegance. Dr. and Mrs. Lummis were going to do their best to see to it that everyone had a good time. The men took time out from the eating, drinking, and dancing to hold a turkey shoot and toss horseshoes. The women, after a tour of the house, barn, and fields, all took turns weaving on Sara Lummis's new loom and sewing on her fancy foot-powered sewing machine.

"I could make some fine clothes for Herman and the children with that loom and machine. This is the exact kind that I saw in the catalog over at Wickham's store. This is the best you can get in any city in the country." Mary Smith was a talented seamstress and knew good sewing equipment when she saw it.

"With this machine we could sew sails so they would never rip out. It would cut my work in half. It sure would be nice to have a machine like this one." Susan Sill helped her husband sew sails and probably did more sewing than anyone in Troupville.

Mary Gibson wasn't thinking of sewing. She loved the house with all its splendid furnishing and elaborate woodwork. "They sure did a remarkable job in building this house. It's big, but feels so warm and cozy. I could just sit on the porch and look at the bay all day long."

Sara Lummis was proud of her new home and glad her friends approved of its design and construction. "Please come and visit often. I'd love to help you sew with this new machine, and I'd love to have you come over to sit on the porch. Let me show you where the gardens will be."

The house stood three stories above ground. There was a full basement below ground with wooden flooring and walls. Most of the cooking would take place in the huge oven in the basement, although there was a small kitchen on the first floor where Sara could prepare meals and eventually teach Elizabeth the art of cooking. What a great day. What a fantastic house. It was a celebration that everyone would talk about for years to come.

Disaster on the Lake

Just 25 miles from the warmth and joy of the celebration in Float Bridge, cold reality was setting in on the waters of Lake Ontario. Just a few miles out into the lake off the village of Oswego, a life and death drama was unfolding for the fifteen men in the crew of the sloop *Ontario*. This sailing ship shared its name with the only steamship on the lake. Rough, windy weather had pushed the waves on the south shore of Lake Ontario to over six feet from trough to crest. Each mammoth wave had its own characteristics that took their toll on the helpless ship. The transport ship was overloaded with heavy grain from Canada. As the rain and lake spray continued to come into the hold, the grain was getting wetter and heavier every minute. For some reason, which none of the crew could determine, the ship had started taking on water shortly after they had left port in Canada several hours earlier. Until darkness set in, the crew's tedious work at the pumps had kept pace with the inflow of water through the leak, but suddenly everything went wrong. The constant battering of the waves broke loose a major support in the hold causing the load to shift and puncture the hull. After that, the leaking water quickly overwhelmed the pumping capacity. Within minutes after the puncture, the captain realized that his ship was lost. He had no idea of their exact position, but he hoped they were close to Oswego. He believed with luck the ship could hold together until they were close enough to shore to swim to safety. But luck wasn't with the *Ontario* that night. Before much progress could be made, a big wave hit her broadside and flipped the ship completely over. The crew and cargo were tossed into the foaming, cold lake waters too far from shore. There really wasn't much of a struggle in the cold water. The only evidence of the disaster was a few broken planks and wooden ship fixtures that floated onto shore several miles west of Oswego harbor the next morning. The violent lake had taken another victim.

It took a few days before the evidence of the disaster was found and the *Ontario* and her crew declared lost. This unfortunate vessel wasn't the first, nor would she be the last victim of the lake that shared her name. Several days later, when news of the casualties reached Troupville, the citizens of the area mourned the loss of the proud ship and their friends. Sometimes it was difficult to determine which was more hostile, the wilderness or the vast waters of the lake. Both were unforgiving to those who weren't completely prepared, and even to some who were.

All of the sailors knew that safe navigation along the shores of the lake was nearly impossible during the night or in foggy or foul weather. In 1820, very few harbors had marked channels or a lighthouse to help guide ships' captains. Only a few of the bigger cities like York and Sacketts Harbor had candle-powered lights. In November, 1820, Troupville was added to the list. A new lighthouse with its small light and crude lens was ready to mark the entrance of Sodus Bay. Just maybe this light would save the life of a sailor or guide a distressed ship like the *Ontario* to safety. The feeling of security given by the light in the wake of the *Ontario* incident made the work of the men of Troupville and the planning of Colonel Sentell worthwhile. Given the recent loss of life, it wasn't the proper time for celebrating the completion of the light, but everyone knew the Sodus Bay lighthouse was more than just a sign of progress and civilization. It was a key in the future of the bay and the nearby villages.

The Troupville lighthouse was relatively small, but it stood on the high bank overlooking the lake and the entrance to the bay. Its lens magnified the candlelight so it could be seen for miles out into the lake and along the shore. Even though the lighthouse was only three stories high, it reached above most of the village. A birds-eye's view of Troupville could be seen from the light's tower. Throughout the winter and spring, residents of the area climbed the crude stairs and ladder to the top of the tower to look down upon the village and to gaze out at the vast open water of the lake. There was no problem finding caretakers for the light. Everyone gladly volunteered their time to keep this valuable resource fully operational and well-maintained. The Sodus Bay lighthouse was a great source of pride for the tiny lakeside community.

Canal Boats

After the arrival of the new year, Jamey and Soso moved to a work camp on the shore of Oneida Lake to join a small group of shipwrights building canal boats. The twenty workers had plenty to do. The central section of the canal would be opening in the spring, and the canal company needed boats to transport people and cargo between Syracuse and Albany. Soso and the other shipbuilders followed the established plans for the awkward and bulky canal boats. Soso did what he could to improve the seaworthiness and capacity of the boats within the constraints of the standard design. He also made several suggestions to the foreman, but the man had no insight into the art of shipbuilding. Soso feared that these canal boats would be doomed as slow, inefficient transportation. The construction crew completed four boats by the spring thaw, and Jamey and Soso returned to Sodus Bay. Neither man thought much of the canal or its bulky boats. From now on, their efforts and thoughts would remain on the lake and bay that they loved. To lake sailors, the canal wasn't a real body of water. It was a narrow, man-made river with all of nature's challenges eliminated. The canal was a strange and foreign transportation system that had little to do with their own experiences on the water.

Application

It was late March when Byram Greene returned to his home in the small village of East Ridge, a few miles southwest of Sodus Bay. He had just completed his duties as a state legislator in the state capital of Albany. He had been elected to this new position after his tenure as a circuit judge. He brought along an important paper for 19-year-old Jamey Davis. Byram headed off immediately to Troupville to deliver the document personally.

Byram found Jamey, Soso, and Jim at the dry dock making repairs to the *Clear Dawn* before the shipping season started.

Jamey smiled a nervous smile as Byram approached, for he had hoped the local political leader would have news of the West Point application procedure. Ben had told Jamey that the local congressman would have to help Jamey get into West Point. Byram had said that he could help with that coordination. Without saying a word, Byram handed the envelope to the excited boy. Jamey read through the contents. It seemed too easy. All he had to do was submit in proper format his name, birthday, family information, and send the completed application with four letters of recommendation to the Academy. If selected, he would then go to West Point on the first of July for an entrance test and enrollment in the program.

The work on the boat stopped as the four men discussed Jamey's application and his chance for selection at such a distinguished school. It was determined that Byram and Soso would write letters of recommendation and that Dr. Lummis and Colonel Troup would be asked to write the other two letters. Jamey was both excited and anxious. Up to now, college had been a dream. Now it was a goal. It was time to do something to make his dream come true.

Jamey eagerly read all about the Military Academy and its rules. It was established in 1802 by then President Thomas Jefferson. The cadets, the name given to the student-soldiers who attended the Academy, studied both engineering and military subjects. After four years of study, the graduates went into the Army to serve. All of this was exciting to Jamey, and it seemed to be just the kind of school to fit his personality.

That afternoon Jamey went across the bay with Soso to see Dr. Lummis. Soso sailed the boat up to the dock in front of the stately Lummis house. The two men moved quickly up the walkway. When they reached the house, Sara told them that her husband was out in the field supervising the planting of apple trees in the new orchard. Soso stayed at the house to play with little Elizabeth, while Jamey searched the field for Dr. Lummis. Jamey finally found him, with a work crew, planting seedlings.

Dr. Lummis knew of Jamey's dream to go to West Point, so he wasn't surprised when the excited young man ran up to him and explained the application procedure. Jamey confidently asked, "Dr. Lummis, would you please write a letter of recommendation for me to go to the Military Academy?"

Dr. Lummis also knew of Jamey's immense abilities and believed that Jamey would do well at the school. "I would be honored and pleased to write such a letter for you, Jamey. Let's go to the house, and I'll write the letter now."

By the time they reached the house, Soso had finished playing with Elizabeth and had walked back to his own house only 300 yards away. Soso was anxious about writing his letter for Jamey. He had only recently learned to read and write, and he certainly had never written a formal letter to the United States government. He wanted to help, not hinder Jamey's chances to obtain this opportunity. Soso was honored that Jamey had asked him for a letter. However, he was worried. What could he say that would help this talented young man achieve his life-long dream? Soso followed an outline for a letter that Byram had given him. He very carefully wrote out the words in his letter for Jamey. The letter read as follows:

To whom it may concern, this 29th day of March, 1821:

I recommend Jamey Davis of Troupville, State of New York, for appointment as a cadet at the excellent military academy located at West Point. Jamey Davis has worked hard to learn as much as he could from books and from master workers. He is a natural leader and an honorable young man. He is intelligent and has expert skill in firearms, horse riding, and construction. Jamey Davis will make an outstanding military officer. I have been blessed to know this mature and dedicated young man. He will succeed at everything you ask him to do.

Your faithful patriot,
Sosoenodus

The other three letters were written on the formal stationary of the three powerful, and well-known men. Each letter presented similar ideas—Jamey was worthy of an appointment and he would make a fine officer in the Army. Jamey and his father put together the application letter. On the first day of April, Byram mailed the complete packet of application material to the Academy. Then it was only a matter of waiting for the decision by the leaders of the Academy.

Acceptance

When the Academy's admissions committee met in late April to consider applications from over 700 young men wishing appointment to the Academy, Jamey received the break he needed. General Joseph Swift, the very first graduate of the Academy in 1802, was the chairman of the committee. As he perused the files of all the applicants, he couldn't help notice the rough lettering on Soso's crude stationary. As he read the letter in support of Jamey Davis, a smile of fond remembrance came upon his face. General Swift had been the senior regular Army engineering officer at Sacketts Harbor during the War of 1812. He had always been impressed and amazed by the Native American boat-builder, whom he had credited with producing the finest ship in the Lake Ontario fleet, the *Lady of the Lake*. General Swift also remembered the dedicated boat captain Jim Davis, from the lovely, little village of Troupville, his favorite harbor on the lake. If Soso was recommending Jim Davis's son, then that was good enough for General Joe Swift. Jamey Davis's name was added to the select list of potential cadets. All he would have to do to become a cadet was come to West Point and pass the entrance exams.

The letter from the Military Academy arrived at Troupville on May 24. Postmaster William Wickham sent Susie Davis, Jamey's seven-year-old sister, who was in Wickham's store, to go get her brother Jamey. Jamey came running into the store just three minutes later. William and Jamey both took deep breaths as Jamey opened and read the formal letter. His only reactions were to yell "yes" and run out of the store at full speed.

Word of Jamey's acceptance to West Point spread like wildfire throughout the area. Soso and Dr. Lummis heard about it together that afternoon as they worked on several of Dr. Lummis's boats. Joe Sheldon came by the Lummis's dock in a small rowboat and yelled the news as he passed by them just twenty yards off shore.

The next day, the Davises held a party to celebrate the good news. A special guest came—Ben Lummis had arrived at his family's new home in Float Bridge earlier in the day and, he went immediately to Troupville and Jamey's house as soon as he heard the news. The two men had a joyous reunion. They soon would be freshmen at two prestigious colleges just fifty miles apart—Jamey at the Military Academy at West Point and Ben at

Columbia College in New York City. Both were excited and happy for the other. Their dreams were coming true.

Travel

Jamey left Troupville on June 19. He had made arrangements to travel the Erie Canal and Hudson River to West Point. It was eleven days of discomfort—sitting, waiting, and anticipating his first day of college. His letter of acceptance had included instructions on what to bring and how and when to get there. About all that Jamey knew about West Point was that he would wear a uniform, be trained as an Army officer, and have to take entrance tests in mathematics and writing when he arrived.

Jamey's trip was long, but certainly not boring. He was seeing new places, meeting new people, and experiencing new situations. He actually enjoyed riding the slow, awkward canal boats. The slow pace enabled him to see everything as they passed by the countryside. He wondered if he had helped build the boat on which he was riding. They all seemed to be identical, so it was hard to tell. He immediately liked the city of Albany when he arrived there. It seemed that man and nature had worked together to make it both busy and beautiful. His trip down the Hudson River on the steamship *Full Moon* was full of excitement and anticipation.

Jamey met two of his soon-to-be classmates on the steamship. They were both younger, smaller, and more timid than Jamey was. The younger was Thompson Brown, only fourteen years old. The other boy was Horace Smith. Both knew more about West Point than Jamey did, so they told him all about being a cadet and how difficult the training and discipline were. They worried about the tests they would have to take and about how rough the summer training would be. Since they both had attended a regular secondary preparatory school, Jamey, too, began to worry about taking the tests and enduring the rigors of cadet life. He hadn't been concerned about those things until then. He had never worried about his future. He had always taken care of business as it happened. It was part of his frontier upbringing. If a frontiersman worried about all the things that could happen, he would have no time or energy to accomplish what he needed for survival.

"My father told me only half the candidates passed the entrance exams last year. He said the mathematics test is nearly impossible to pass. I don't know if I can talk at all about my mathematics. I never talked about mathematics before." Thompson Brown was really worried about the oral exams they would have to take.

"I heard that you had to march and even shoot a flintlock on the very first day. I hope I get to do that. I've never shot a gun before." Horace Smith was optimistic about his tests, but wondered if he could keep up physically with the rough, tough cadets and soldiers.

"It sure has been fun traveling and meeting all the people. I would love to get to stay and learn about being a soldier and an engineer. My father says if you do your best, you'll get rewarded. That's all I'm planning to do. I'm sure both of you will do fine, and in four years all three of us will graduate and become soldiers." Jamey was doing his best to stay optimistic and to encourage his new friends to show some confidence. West Point couldn't be any tougher than living and working on the frontier.

First Impression

As the steamship docked at the West Point landing, a bit of apprehension overtook Jamey. He wasn't sure where to go or what to do. After asking around, he finally got situated into a room in the hotel at the fort. He wasn't supposed to check in to the cadet area until the next morning, so he spent that afternoon and evening walking around the fascinating countryside. He walked back down the path to the river and watched several boats, steam and sail, make their way from one side of the bend in the river to the other side. Then he climbed up the side of the mountain that overlooked the fort. From that vantage point, the area's name, West Point, was obvious. He could look down from the mountain and see how the land protruded out from the west bank into the river. He knew that he would like this place. The landscape was breathtaking. As Soso had told him, the natural beauty of West Point rivaled that of Sodus Bay. He felt right at home.

Jamey could see the fortifications that had protected the area. He also saw the cleared-out area on a small plain where the cadets lived and trained. There were several buildings of various sizes that were used for cadet activities. Most of the other buildings were houses for professors and staff officers. The most impressive building was the Superintendent's quarters.

Jamey returned to his hotel and ate a light meal with his two new friends from the steamship ride. The two boys were intimidated by their strange military surroundings. Jamey again tried to bolster their confidence. However, they were overwhelmed. Jamey then went to his room to write a short letter to his parents. He went to bed early in expectation of a busy next day.

Beginning Days

The following day, the first day of July, was definitely a busy one for Jamey and the rest of the cadet candidates. It was nonstop confusion from the time he arrived at eight in the morning at the cadet guardhouse until he fell exhausted onto his mattress on the floor of his new cadet room at eleven o'clock that night. During those fifteen hours, he and his 84 classmates, selected from the pool of nearly 700 applicants, had been herded like cattle from one place to another. They learned how to salute, march, and talk in "the proper manner of a gentleman cadet." Jamey still wondered what that meant. They performed physical exercises several times and even got to hold a soldier's rifle for a few minutes. Sometime during the day, they had eaten and been assigned their rooms. Jamey couldn't recall everything that had happened, and despite his excitement, he fell fast asleep from complete exhaustion.

Many of Jamey's fellow new cadets were concerned about the main event of the second and third days—testing. Each cadet would be drilled in oral examinations by the professors of the academic board. While the questioning was at a basic level, the outcome was very significant. Failure to show adequate knowledge, confidence, and ability would send the perspective cadet back home. The professors also used these exams to gauge the abilities of the survivors, and many academic reputations were formed during these short, intense, initial testing sessions.

The testing was done alphabetically by the candidates' last names. For the first half of the alphabet, mathematics was tested the first day; language and history were tested the second day. Around midmorning Jamey found himself standing in front of three stern-faced professors in a small, rather dark classroom. His inquisitors—Professors Jared Mansfield, Charles Davies, and Claudius Crozet—were seated at a long wooden table at the front of the room. There were blackboards along all four walls and plenty of chalk on the shelves under the blackboards. Jamey was nervous, yet as confident as he could be under the circumstances. He wondered what his fate would be. Determined as he was, he had no idea if he could meet their standards.

The questioning started harmlessly. The first few questions involved simple arithmetic. These first questions seemed too easy to Jamey. They weren't the type of problems he was prepared for. His only difficulty was that he tended to make more of them than was there. The next few questions tested the more advanced subjects of geometry, algebra, and trigonometry. This was more to Jamey's liking. His correct and direct answers surprised the three questioners. They saw nothing in the file of this boy from the rural frontier to indicate that he had such a solid education in mathematics. Professor Mansfield's next question simply asked, "Where did you learn these things?"

Jamey's response shocked the three men. "I read and worked the problems from the books of Legendre and Hutton. I really enjoyed their algebra and trigonometry books. They are my favorite subjects."

The professors wanted to know more about Jamey's readings and where he obtained these advanced mathematics textbooks. These were the same books used by cadets during their first two years. They had never had a candidate who had studied these advanced subjects on his own and done so well. Jamey explained how his friend Ben Lummis had given him the books to use. "Then I would copy the book word-for-word and do all the problems. The book I liked best was Biot's *Calculus*."

This last revelation completely amazed the professors. Could this young man have learned calculus on his own. After Jamey answered a couple calculus problems correctly by writing the solutions with chalk on the blackboard, the professors dismissed Jamey. They smiled and laughed in amazement after their new protégé left the room. It was an understatement that Jamey had established a positive reputation for himself in mathematics. They all suspected that Jamey Davis would be a special cadet, capable of doing remarkable things at the Academy and in the Army.

During the next day, the language and civics oral examinations were conducted under the same format. Jamey held his own on the questions in grammar, history, and literature. Many of Jamey's answers were based on the discussions that he had with his father and Soso on the history of the revolution and the recent war against the British. Even though Jamey didn't shine as brightly as he had the previous day, the professors, including Thomas Picton, Claudius Bernard, and Superintendent Sylvanus Thayer, were satisfied with Jamey's performance.

After Jamey passed the medical exam and a test of his physical strength and conditioning, he was officially made a new member of the Corps of Cadets of the United States Military Academy. Uncomfortable gray uniforms were fitted and given to the 67 new cadets who survived the two days of testing. They were from places all across the growing country. Jamey's roommate Alex Bache and his two acquaintances from the ship ride, Horace and Tom, also passed the tests and were admitted into the Academy. What a relief, the first major hurdle had been cleared. Jamey knew there was plenty more work ahead, and he was ready for the challenge.

A little older and physically stronger than most of his classmates, Jamey felt reasonably comfortable in his new environment. Although he wasn't from the same social and economic class as some of his classmates, they respected Jamey's abilities and immediately looked to him for leadership and advice.

After a busy week of indoctrination and training, Jamey took some time to write letters to his parents, Dr. Lummis, and Soso. In each letter, Jamey explained about his new friends and the military surroundings. His new close friends, along with Horace and Tom of New York, were three of the youngest cadets—Joe Clay of Georgia, Bill Bibby of New York, and his roommate Alex Bache of Pennsylvania. Even though there was very little privacy, Jamey liked the arrangements in the barracks. He shared a small room with Alex Bache. Both cadets had a thin, straw-filled mattress on the floor and shared a table for a writing desk. They had two small oil lanterns on the desk and on a platform near the door. Their clothes and other belongings were stored in chests that stood at the base of their mattresses. These accommodations were what Jamey was used to from living in a fisherman's family on the frontier. Some of the other cadets complained about these sparse accommodations and the lumpy mattresses.

After the first week's testing, there was very little academic work during the summer. After two weeks at West Point, Jamey hadn't fired his weapon, but he had learned to march with it and take it apart, clean it, and reassemble it. It was with him all the time. It seemed that this weapon was becoming a part of him.

Summer Training

The rest of Jamey's summer as a plebe—one of the terms used for first year cadets—went fast and furious. Everything was done at a nearly impossible pace. The days started at six o'clock in the morning and didn't end until after ten at night. The meals were ordinary, yet well prepared. The staple was "meat pies," often cooked with little or no meat. However, the plebes were too busy to enjoy — or even eat—much of their food. At every meal, the plebes had to sit at attention on the edge of their seats. The upperclass cadets made sure the plebes were kept disciplined and challenged, both mentally and physically, and the harassment of their underlings was often most severe during the meals and on the parade field. That was fine with Jamey. He liked the little bit of food that he was able to eat, and it was enough to survive. He was used to living a rough, disciplined life.

Summer training consisted of drill in marching and parade, physical conditioning, training in weapon skills, and basic military tactics. The highlight of the summer for Jamey was the three days of artillery training. The new cadets got to sight in and fire the large cannon artillery pieces. This training was quite technical, and Jamey used his knowledge in mathematics to help produce accurate firing of the guns. Having very little success in that endeavor, Jamey's classmates were so impressed and amazed with his skills that they elected Jamey their class leader when they joined the upperclass cadets for a long road march at the end summer training.

Jamey appreciated the letters that he received from his friends and family in Troupville. These letters helped subdue homesickness, which periodically struck during the summer. Finding time to write home wasn't easy. Jamey used his free time to write letters. Jim and Karen Davis weren't the only ones proud of their son. The entire Troupville community was proud of their favorite son and wished him well in his future adventures.

"Mister Ducrot, 25 pushups!" The unknown upperclassman ordered Jamey to serve his punishment for not standing tall enough to suit his fancy. Jamey quickly obliged, as he did many times each day to develop his self-discipline and physical conditioning.

"Mister Ducrot" was the name used by the upper-class cadets for the plebes. This enduring name came from the author of the French grammar books, which were used at the Academy to teach French to all the plebes. The cadets had to learn French to read some of their textbooks in mathematics, science, and military tactics. Jamey quickly became used to being called "Ducrot" and being harassed by aggressive upperclassmen. He recognized these as just part of the program. The tough times would pass, and eventually he could return to a less harried lifestyle. However, many of

Jamey's classmates were stressed to the breaking point from this harassment. Jamey clearly saw that his major duty was to help his stressed classmates survive their tough summer training.

Jamey's cadet dress uniform looked splendid. The gray coat had a high, tight collar; long tails; and large, brass "bell" buttons. The trousers were white with buttons along the sides. The hat was heavy, uncomfortable, and outlandish. The "tar bucket" hat had a tall plume that stuck up over ten inches. Overall, the uniforms were as uncomfortable to wear as they were impressive to see. Jamey disliked wearing the stuffy uniform, but managed to keep out of trouble by looking tall and straight in his well-kept uniform.

Another area of cadet training where Jamey excelled was horseback riding. There were only twelve horses for the 65 or so new cadets to share. The riding instructors always assumed that their students had no riding experience, so the instruction was slow and methodical. After the first class, the instructor asked Jamey to help put the horses in their pen. Jamey quickly mounted the nearest horse and maneuvered his mount around the others to drive the horses into the pen. The instructor was amazed. He had seldom seen such expert horsemanship by a new cadet, nor had he any idea that the old riding horse had so much agility. From then on, Jamey was the assistant instructor for the other new cadets' riding lessons.

March

As the leader of the new cadet class, Jamey was called to the office of the chief tactics instructor, Major William Wroth, along with several upperclass cadets in similar leadership positions. The "spit-and-polish" Major carefully explained the details of the cadet march to Boston that was to begin the following week. The plan was for 160 of the 210 cadets in the camp to leave West Point by steamboat and travel up river to Albany. Then, led by the Army band, the corps of cadets would march directly east to Boston and back to West Point via a more southern route through Providence, New London, and New Haven. The 350-mile trip was scheduled to take over a month, with a four-day stay in Boston. This tough trip brought the cadets together in close-knit units and gave them experience in moving army units across long distances.

Jamey loved the journey. During the steamboat ride, he explained to his classmates the principles of the design and production of a boat's hull.

Jamey was fascinated by a fellow cadet's explanation of the steam engine and propulsion system. He also enjoyed learning about the topographic measurements that were being taken by the upper-class cadets during the march. Tactics instructor Lieutenant Griswold explained how the measurements were used to make maps. Jamey used this trip to prepare himself mentally for the study of his academic courses, which were to start when the cadets returned to West Point. The very idea of using mathematics to survey the ground features and make maps fascinated Jamey. He dreamed that someday he would be able to produce maps for others to use.

Academics

The beginning of the fall brought a special event for Jamey. Ben Lummis visited West Point on his way to Columbia College in New York City. Stopping off from his steamboat ride from Albany, Ben arranged to catch another steamboat heading south to New York City the following day. Fortunately, Ben's visit came on a Sunday, when Jamey had several hours of free time. First, Ben teased Jamey about his stuffy uniform. Then, Jamey showed Ben all the historical sights at West Point and explained the details of his summer of military training. The time went by too quickly. It was exciting for Jamey to share his new experiences with his old friend, Ben.

After saying good-bye to his friend, Ben spent the night in the hotel at West Point and left on the steamboat for New York City and Columbia College the next morning. Ben was as excited about his prospective life in college as Jamey had been when he arrived at West Point a few months before.

Another thrill for Jamey was the beginning of academic classes. Jamey had never experienced anything like the classes conducted by the West Point faculty. Everything that happened in the classroom had a definite purpose. The instructors orchestrated the instruction hour after hour, day after day, week after week. The cadets were graded every day in all their subjects. Adjusting to this disciplined, demanding academic program was a challenge for every cadet, including Jamey. While he enjoyed his studies and all that he was learning, his first semester was a constant struggle adjusting to the strict and rigid system of learning. He was being challenged to learn the most he could, but it was done the military way. He had always learned on his own and at his own pace. Now, learning, along with every other activity at the Academy, was done in cadence. The entire system had been developed by the Superintendent of the Academy, Captain Sylvanus Thayer. Many of his ideas had been borrowed from the famous French military academy in Paris, the Ecole Polytechnique. There was no doubt, Jamey was receiving a first-rate education.

Columbia

After Ben left West Point, he arrived in New York City ready to face the challenges of Columbia College. He was ready. His experiences at the preparatory school in Philadelphia made his transition to college smooth and natural. Columbia was a typical liberal arts finishing school. The courses and environment were designed to develop the manners of the young men who attended this expensive school. Teaching was conducted in the liberal, free-thinking style of ancient Athens, quite different than the Spartan-approach Jamey was experiencing at West Point.

Ben liked city life, although at times he missed his rural lifestyle. He was able to attend school during the day and tour the exciting places in the city at night and during the weekends. He enjoyed this freedom and made the most of it. Meeting many of the rich and powerful people of New York, Ben had an excellent start on the road to success.

West Point

Fifty miles up the Hudson River, Jamey was undergoing a significantly different experience. His environment was austere, and in place of freedom was discipline. The academic courses and military training were practical and intended to develop military engineers who could build the infrastructure of the growing nation. West Point truly defined the Spartan, disciplined lifestyle of the military. The high standards were a reflection of the leadership and insight of Superintendent Thayer, who had been at West Point since 1817. He had designed and implemented the most technical and demanding curriculum of any school in the country. Only special, military-minded, disciplined, intelligent young men could survive such a program.

Thayer and his faculty had implemented an American version of the successful French educational system. The courses were demanding, rigorous, and practical. The cadets attended class in small sections supervised by a tough, unbending Army officer or experienced civilian instructor. The most important subject was mathematics, which formed the foundation for the practical military application of science and engineering. There was no room at the Academy for the weak or the lazy. Cadets resigned or were separated when they couldn't keep up with the pace.

Jamey worked hard, but still struggled in several areas. He was slow in learning the fine points of spoken French and was a poor writer. Luckily, Jamey's knowledge and aptitude in mathematics compensated for his problems in French and writing. Cadets were ordered in their sections by their grades in each subject. Jamey proudly sat in the first seat of the first section in mathematics, just ahead of roommate Horace Smith. He sat in the middle of his class in both French and writing. Since mathematics was weighted considerably more than the other two subjects, Jamey was in very little danger of being dismissed and stood quite high in his class after the first semester. However, Jamey still worried about his progress. His instructors considered him the hardest worker in his class.

Loss of a Friend

Schooling was also a major topic of discussion in the Sodus Bay area. The school at Troupville was reopened and a new school started up at Arms' Crossroads. The eleven children in the Arms' Crossroads area were blessed with a new building and new teacher. The Troupville school had seventeen children but no regular schoolhouse. Therefore, classes met in alternate private houses and barns.

The Troupville area had developed in some ways, but in most respects it was still rural frontier. It appeared as though the expansion of civilization with its modern technological conveniences were going to pass it by. A few new settlers arrived in the area, but just as many current residents left to head further west or return east. Land was cheaper in the new states of Illinois, Indiana, and Missouri. It was as if time and progress were at a dead stop in Troupville. This didn't bother the faithful residents of the area, however. They were satisfied with the peace, quiet, and charm of their community. They also felt secure now that the war had resolved the problems with the British and the Canadians. Generally, they were happy citizens of the great nation of the United States. President Monroe was making it stronger every day. Soon the rest of the world would have to leave the United States alone, and there would be permanent peace and safety in the land.

Soso had a difficult time adjusting to working without Jamey. Thank goodness, faithful dog Mac still kept him company. Soso had relied on Jamey's knowledge and experience to maintain a sufficient pace to complete the work on the sloops and knock-abouts that he had been building. He now realized that it would be impossible to continue to build larger ships without an assistant. Mac was just no substitute for Jamey in regards to the shipbuilding work. Soso decided that once he completed this last sloop he would return to his earlier style of building small sailing boats for use around the bays, rivers, and harbors of Lake Ontario. He would leave the bigger ships to be built by other boat builders.

As Soso struggled to finish the last sloop in his yard, he received bad news from Henry Eckford in New York—Soso's shipbuilding friend, Forman Cheesman, had died. Soso had learned considerable about his craft from Forman. Forman had been a good friend and had helped Soso adjust to life in New York City. This loss reminded Soso of man's frailty and mortality. Soso realized how fortunate he was to have lived 41 years and experienced so much. He was no longer just an Indian living in the strange world of the whites. Soso and his friends considered him an equal citizen and productive resident of the community. They had overcome the prejudices that cause people to mistrust those of a different color or race. Soso had taught them much about life and respect. Soso had overcome his own prejudice against the mysterious world and strange customs of the whites. Soso may not have become a Cayuga chief or a powerful warrior, but he had become a remarkable and wise man nonetheless.

Math Class

"Class, attention." The twelve cadets came to rigid attention. "Sir, all present," Jamey reported, as he gave a firm, crisp military salute to the officer, who instructed this class of top cadets.

"Take seats," commanded the instructor. "Any questions?"

There was a brief moment of silence, while the cadets nervously wondered if they dare ask a question or if any of their classmates would ask something. There was just a moment to hope and pray that someone would ask a question. However, since no one said anything, they expected to get right to work.

"Take boards," commanded Jamey's strict and tough mathematics instructor, Lieutenant Ross.

"Cadets Davis and Smith report to the front desk," continued Ross.

Just as Jamey prepared to take his position next to Lieutenant Ross' desk, he noticed a visitor come into the small classroom. It was the Superintendent, newly promoted Major Sylvanus Thayer. Jamey took his position at parade rest facing the front of the classroom on the left side of the desk. His roommate, fellow student, and for today his competition, Horace Smith, stood at the other side of the desk.

Jamey didn't realize the significance of this visit. The Superintendent had come to see the best of his new crop of cadets in action. He had heard that the new plebes had started off well. Now it was time to see for himself whether or not his reforms were working. In Thayer's mind, mathematics class was the ultimate challenge—the place where he could best gauge the progress of his school. Thayer was first and foremost a mathematician. He sometimes taught a math class, as he had done earlier in his military career as a newly commissioned officer. He knew that in mathematics class, the seeds were sown that could produce bold, illustrious technical leaders for the growing country. On this day, he came specifically to see if the two seeds with the most potential had started to grow.

Jamey and Horace were prepared to face off in an academic competition called question boards. While their classmates would spend time writing solutions to instructor-assigned problems with chalk on the blackboards, the two competitors would take turns responding orally to questions asked by the instructor. The challenge of question boards was one of the most demanding and stressful activities that cadets had to contend with. Normally, a cadet would have a question board once a month or so. The question boards on this day were extra special in two ways—the presence of Major Thayer and the face off between the two top cadets.

By the time that Lieutenant Ross got the other cadets busy with their board work and he had taken his seat at the desk, Jamey and Horace were nervous. There was no place to hide and no way to avoid exposing your knowledge—or lack of it. In a few short minutes, everyone in that room would know precisely what you were made of as both a student and a potential military officer. Lieutenant Ross turned to Jamey and asked him the first question. Jamey snapped to attention and quickly answered the easy question. Then Lieutenant Ross turned his attention to Horace. Jamey returned to parade rest and Horace jumped to attention. Horace also easily answered the next question. These first questions were just a warm-up to insure both cadets understood the format and rules of the game. It was a way to ease some of the tension, but not all of it.

Now that the competition was underway, the pace and difficulty of the questions increased. Alternately, the two young men correctly answered several questions. Finally, a tough question stumped Jamey. After thinking for a moment, Jamey reluctantly, but emphatically, responded to Lieutenant Ross, "Sir, I do not know."

Lieutenant Ross repeated the question for Horace. Horace thought for a while and then tentatively answered the question correctly. The questioning continued with Lieutenant Ross pushing his two best students to their limit. After several more correct answers from each cadet, Lieutenant Ross abruptly interrupted one of Horace's answers with the dreaded statement "wrong, Mr. Smith." This time Lieutenant Ross repeated the question for Jamey, who confidently answered that question. The two cadets were even—one mistake each.

The cadets at the blackboards were having difficulty concentrating on their own work. They were trying to follow the battle of question boards taking place in the classroom behind their backs as they stood facing the wall, trying to work out their own problems. After all, this was the first time the two top-ranked cadets had faced one another, and the Superintendent was witnessing the battle. Because of the strict cadet honor code restricting any help from others, they had to stand facing their own blackboard. Therefore, they could only listen carefully and envision the scene that was unfolding behind their backs.

The pace had been so fast that Lieutenant Ross had nearly exhausted all the questions that he had prepared, but he did have the two most difficult questions remaining. The first one stumped Jamey, whose response was only half-right. Horace correctly finished the problem. In turn, Lieutenant Ross's last problem stumped Horace, and Jamey returned the favor by pulling out the correct answer at the last moment. For a moment it looked as if the contest had ended in a draw. Lieutenant Ross concluded the question boards and board work by commanding all the cadets to "Cease work and take seats." However, before the two cadets at the front of the room could return to their seats, the Superintendent interceded with his own question. Major Thayer wasn't about to let the results stand. He wanted competition between cadets and that meant that someone had to win.

"Do either of you know how many cannon balls can be stacked on a 'n by n' rectangular base of cannon balls?" asked the Superintendent to the mentally exhausted cadets.

Both cadets hesitated for a moment. Horace was unsure of how to approach the problem. He had never studied a problem of this type before. Jamey, on the other hand, was confident that he could compute the answer, if he had a moment at the blackboard to perform the calculations. Jamey decided to give it a try and asked the Superintendent for permission to use the blackboard. "Major Thayer, sir, may I write the solution on the blackboard?" Permission was granted.

The entire class watched as Jamey quickly sketched the situation and carefully wrote out its solution. When Jamey finished his calculations, he took a long, slender wooden pointer from the rack under the blackboard and explained each step of his solution method to his classmates, his instructor, and Major Thayer. When Jamey was finished, Major Thayer complimented Jamey. "That was a very fine performance, Mister Davis. Your solution is correct, and your explanation was clear and concise. Your recitation today gives your classmates an example to follow in doing their own work."

Fortunately for the other cadets in the class, because of the additional time it took for the competitive question boards and Major Thayer's extra problem, there was not enough time for them to explain their own sub-par work on the blackboards. They knew that Lieutenant Ross would still grade their work after they left. They would see their poor grades posted at the beginning of the next class. But at least they weren't going to have to explain their distracted performance to their instructor or the Superintendent. Major Thayer left the classroom as Lieutenant Ross took the remaining five minutes to explain the next day's lesson and then dismissed his excited section.

After class, each the ten other cadets in the section recounted their own versions of the proceedings that had taken place during the class. For a brief moment, Jamey and Horace were elevated to folk heroes. They had taken the best Lieutenant Ross and Major Thayer had offered and survived. The presence of the latter gave the ordeal the makings of a legend. The exploits of the two mathematically gifted cadets would be told among cadets of all classes at the Academy for several weeks.

Last Stop on the Underground Railroad

The Lummis estate on the east side of the bay had grown substantially over the past two years. The house was completely finished by the finest artisans, carpenters, and craftsmen in the area. It was the most splendid home in the Troupville area. The fields of the farm were also extensive and now established. Dr. Lummis had supervised the planting of the over a hundred acres of fruit trees and had put in a fine vegetable garden near the shore of the bay. He had the best apple, cherry, pear, and peach trees to be found anywhere. Dr. Lummis was a master at grafting the best fruit producing branches onto the best root-stock to produce healthy trees with excellent tasting fruit. He was truly an expert farmer, who used the most modern and scientific techniques to improve his produce.

The estate's waterfront contained a large boathouse and dock for the four ships used to transport goods to and from the farm. The property overlooked the bay and its three islands, which were also part of the Lummis estate. The islands had lost their traditional Indian names, and now were called Arron (old Neoga), Islay (old Loga), and Bute (old Kenoga), although some people used other names for the three impressive structures that defined the beauty of Sodus Bay.

The Lummis family had several domestic servants and numerous field laborers. Some of these employees were black, but the Lummises had no slaves. All of the employees were well paid, well cared for, and free to live independent lives. New York had passed a law in 1817 that would make it completely free of slaves by 1827. While no one would be able to own slaves in New York after that date, until 1827 it was illegal to harbor run-away slaves or aid their escape in any way. Nevertheless, despite the risks, once Dr. Lummis had his new estate established, he became one of the key final links in the underground railroad. This organization had established success at moving run-away slaves from the southern states to freedom in Canada.

Dr. Lummis now had a near-perfect system to safely hide and transport numerous runaways across the lake to Canada. The slaves came to the Lummis estate by several different means. Sometimes Dr. Lummis had one of his employees, usually Ron Johnson, pick up runaway slaves from a farm, another underground railroad station, in Geneva where Dr. Lummis often bought fruit trees. A special wagon had been constructed with a false, hidden compartment under the floor that held five adults lying flat. The trees were then piled on the bed of the wagon. It was an uncomfortable ride for the runaways, but it was the safest way to transport these important passengers. Slave hunters were always more aggressive and desperate as their prey approached safety and freedom, so maximum precautions were needed. Other run-away slaves came to the Lummis estate by other means—foot, horse, wagon, or boat.

Once on the Lummis farm, the slaves were usually hidden in one of three places. The most elaborate hiding place was behind a false wall in the basement of the Lummis house. The home construction had been based on providing this hiding place. The other two hiding spots were on the islands of Bute and Arron. Dr. Lummis now owned both islands and maintained cabins and boathouses there. The two cabins had large, hidden basements that could accommodate up to fifteen people. The hidden basement of the cabin on Bute Island had a tunnel that connected it to the covered boathouse. With this setup, the runaways could move to and from the island's hiding place without being seen, exposed to detection, or captured by law enforcement officers. Dr. Lummis had established a nearly fool-proof system.

Dr. Lummis personally met and prepared the desperate people for the last leg of their journey to freedom. The passengers were given food, extra clothes, and some Canadian money to help their start in a new country. Then as soon as possible, Dr. Lummis would dispatch one of his four small ships to carry his passengers to safety and their freedom. The vessels held between five and fifteen passengers in enclosed compartments. For most of the trips, Dr. Lummis himself captained the ship. However, Ron Johnson or Soso sometimes captained these freedom voyages.

After several months of building up the underground operation, Dr. Lummis was able to maintain a pace that moved over twenty slaves to freedom per month throughout the spring, summer, and fall of 1822. The usual stay of a railroad passenger on the Lummis farm was only a few days. However, during the last days of November, an unusually high number of slaves had arrived at the farm. The three hiding places were filled to capacity. There were a total of forty slaves on the Lummis property waiting for a break in the cold, windy weather so the boats could make one, last fifty-mile trip across Lake Ontario before the boating season ended. For five more days, the bad weather continued, and several more slaves arrived during that time. The hiding places were cold, damp, and uncomfortable in these harsh conditions. Dr. Lummis decided to move about 25 of the youngest and oldest slaves into the bedrooms in his house. The increased warmth and better ventilation helped everyone's spirits and health. However, this action resulted in a significant increase in the risk of detection for the fugitives.

While everyone was concerned about discovery during this vulnerable time, Dr. Lummis' confidence kept everyone at this station of the underground railroad in good spirits. Even when the Lummises had several neighbors over to their home for a Fall season feast, none of the dinner guests suspected that the basement and upstairs bedrooms contained a different sort of houseguest. Of course, to Dr. Lummis and his family, these other guests had a more compelling reason to be there than those who dined at the elaborate dinner table, eating a meal of select meat, fine wine, and delicious dessert.

Among the guests at the dinner table were the local constable, Joe West, and circuit judge, Ken McCarver. While both men were sympathetic to the plight of run-away slaves, they were staunch enforcers of the law. Probably the only persons who would receive any special consideration from either man were Dr. William Lummis and possibly, Jim Davis. As added insurance for his railroad passengers, Dr. Lummis had fostered a strong friendship with these two men, who could endanger his operation. He hoped that he would never have to rely upon it, however.

Long Voyage

When the wind finally let up several days later, Dr. Lummis, Soso, Ron Johnson, and Jim Davis each set sail in one of the Lummis boats loaded to full capacity. Under normal conditions, the four boats could hold a total of 40-45 passengers. For this voyage, the boats were overloaded to take all 55 of those awaiting transportation. Fortunately, the trip across the lake was uneventful. The four boats stayed within 200 yards of one another, and no one bothered them during the trip.

The 55 newly freed people were set ashore just before sunrise at the Canadian city of York after a twelve-hour boat ride. The four captains immediately turned around and started back across the cold, dark water. Dr. Lummis captained the largest and slowest of the vessels. He had the help and company of Dan Colling, one of his farm hands. Soso had his trusted companion Mac with him. The other two captains were alone on their smaller vessels. It was cold, but the daylight coupled with the satisfaction of having completed their mission gave them the energy to continue the trip home. All were tired, but none realized that he was sailing into serious trouble.

First, the winds died down to a complete calm. The four sailing vessels were becalmed, dead in the water. Then the temperature dropped dramatically. It was well below freezing. Even the ever-present seagulls retreated from the cold waters of the lake. The men tried to keep the four boats close to each other by paddling, but the currents moved the lighter boats faster and further, and the current was more powerful than paddling. By noon the four boats were barely visible to one another, and none of them had proceeded more than ten miles from the Canadian coastline. One by one, the captains dozed at the wheel of their ships. There wasn't anything else they could do, and the exhaustion and tedium eventually overcame all of them. As they awakened from their sleep at sunset, they saw more than darkness had fallen upon them. A thick fog had settled on the cold, still, freezing lake. The men had a full-time job trying to keep warm and survive this trip, and now the boats were completely out of sight from each other and without accurate means to guide them.

About midnight the breeze picked up slightly, and the four boats made slow progress to the south. The lighter boats made more headway, but by morning they were still in the middle of the lake, 25 miles from land ahead and astern. The men had been at sea for 36 hours without any real sleep. Dr. Lummis and Dan Colling were able to provide relief for one another. However, the larger ship often took both men to handle the sails, rigging, and steering. Soso talked with Mac, who was cold and shivering, but never complained. None of them had any protection from the cold. When they dozed at the helm, they endangered their vessel and themselves, although there was little except the cold to cause problems on the huge lake. Anything that got wet in the exposed air immediately froze. The ice kept building up on their rudders, and it had to be chipped away constantly.

Daylight brought a return to the conditions of calm and bitter cold temperatures. At times, a frozen mist or light snow fell on the stranded ships. The four boats sat perfectly still on the eerie and foggy lake. Their captains were unable to see each other or any signs of life.

By sunset the wind picked up a little, and the boats again began slow southerly movement. As experienced boatmen, Soso and Jim were aware that the easterly current had pushed them quite a way off course. The two of them sailed their boats more due south than planned in order to head for Sodus Bay. Dr. Lummis and Ron Johnson, however, had not taken the current into account and tried to sail in a more southeastern direction, the normal route to return to Sodus Bay from York.

It was a tribute to Soso and Jim's sailing instincts that they brought their two ships directly to their intended destination. Soso spotted the Troupville light about a half mile through the darkness and fog about an hour before sunrise. Seeing the beacon was a tremendous relief for the tired captain. He hoped the others would have the same good fortune. Jim happened to be following fairly closely behind, yet out of sight, and spotted the light, Soso's boat, and the shoreline just at sunrise. However, it was only then that the two men realized the serious trouble that the boats faced.

Danger on the Lake

The bay was frozen and a thin shelf of ice extended some 200-300 yards into the lake all along the shore. While the ice was thin and could be easily broken by chopping at it, if a boat ran straight into this ice sheet, its hull could be sliced apart. The ice sheet would act like a giant razor blade and could make a cut completely through the boat. Soso carefully maneuvered his craft up next to the ice sheet. Then by knocking on the surface of the ice with a long oar, he broke out large areas of the ice sheet. Then he carefully moved forward through the broken ice, right up next to the remaining ice shelf. This type of maneuvering for one man in a sailing boat required considerable skill. Soso was able to do it, but he worried about the others.

Since Soso's progress was slow, Jim was able to catch up to him. The two men pulled their boats alongside each other to plan what to do next. While Soso was concerned about getting their boats through the ice, into the bay, and up to the Lummises' dock, he worried even more about Dr. Lummis and Ron. He guessed that their two boats had drifted farther east, because of the effects of the current. If the ice sheet continued farther down the lake, the other two boats also would be in danger of running into it.

Soso and Jim agreed to the following strategy—Soso would sail down the lake to intercept and warn the other two captains, while Jim would remain at the entrance to Sodus Bay to help the boats should they arrive at their intended destination. The wind was still light, and Soso's progress was slow. He stayed a couple hundred yards from the glimmering ice shelf. He hoped that the wind would pick up and break the shore ice, thereby eliminating the danger.

By early afternoon, Soso saw the sails of two boats almost directly ahead of his path. As he closed in on the boats he identified them by their sails and hulls—it was Dr. Lummis and Ron Johnson. Soso was still a little too far away to warn them of the ice danger. Unfortunately, just then his worst fears were realized. The boat captained by Ron Johnson hit the edge of the ice sheet at full force. The boat's hull was sliced for about three to four feet along the starboard side of the bow. The cut was so narrow that initially very little water leaked through the cut. Despite Ron's reaction to steer away, the boat's momentum continued into more of the ice shelf producing several more short cuts in the hull on the starboard side. About the time

Ron managed to lower the sails, the boat began taking on water in earnest. By the time Dr. Lummis saw the danger and steered his boat around, Soso's boat had also arrived next to Ron's. Ron had to abandon the sinking ship. Luckily, Ron was in the water for just a few seconds before Soso held out an oar and hoisted his frozen friend into his boat.

There was nothing that could be done to salvage the sinking boat. Luckily Ron was safe, but the boat was the bottom of the lake under nearly forty feet of water. Soso helped warm up Ron by removing his wet clothes and covering him in a blanket he had brought along. Mac also huddled next to Ron, keeping each other warm. Dr. Lummis followed Soso back toward Sodus Bay. It wasn't until the third day of the journey that the three surviving boats made their way slowly through the icy bay back to the Lummis dock. The mission was accomplished at the cost of one boat and the complete exhaustion of five sailors and one faithful dog.

Sarah Lummis, relieved to have her husband and friends safely return, cooked the men a big dinner and sent the word out of their return. The men were so exhausted that they ate very little before falling asleep right in the Lummis' living room. Partially recovered, the men returned home the next morning. Before they left, they made sure their stories were straight. Each man realized that someone might ask questions about the extended voyage. The only thing the men needed to say was they were carrying important cargo from the Lummis farm to Canada and ran into bad weather, which, of course, was the truth.

Summer Duty and Fun

Jamey Davis finished his first year at West Point in grand style. He was selected to spend the summer working on the fortifications in the New York City harbor area with the chief of engineers for the entire US Army. This duty enabled him to apply his mathematical abilities in new and interesting ways. Each part of a fortification was built with a specified shape to accomplish a special purpose. Both the design and construction were precisely checked and rechecked mathematically. It was valuable summer duty for the mathematically gifted cadet.

To a young man from the frontier, New York City was alive with excitement. Jamey worked hard on his military duties, but every weekend during the summer he and his friend Ben Lummis would meet for socializing and enjoyment. Both young men found girlfriends to enjoy their activities with. They spent time boating around Manhattan, visiting the beaches of Long Island, and attending parties with some of Ben's friends from the high society of New York City.

By the end of the summer Jamey was considered a capable engineer and an outstanding mathematician and surveyor by the officers in his unit. He had made real contributions over the summer and took back glowing reports to West Point for his efforts. It was a summer to remember for the frontier-born boy, who was fast becoming a military man.

Captain David Douglass, head of the Mathematics Department, welcomed his protégé back to West Point. Jamey and Captain Douglass spent over an hour discussing the summer assignment. Jamey had assembled a portfolio of engineer drawings of the fortifications that he had visited and worked on. Professor Douglass intended to use some of Jamey's work in the Academy's course on descriptive geometry. Douglass himself had accumulated numerous drawings of shapes of engineer structures and, along with assistant professor Charles Davies, intended to write a textbook on the subject. Engineers relied upon this branch of mathematics; therefore, it was important for it to be part of the West Point program.

Jamey's second year at West Point was going to be very similar to his first. He would study mathematics every morning and English and French in the afternoons. Although as an upperclassman, he would have more free time and fewer menial chores. Studying engineering under Thayer's academic system nevertheless gave all cadets plenty of challenges. Fortunately, Jamey flourished under the Spartan lifestyle of the military and continued to meet the challenges that cadet life posed.

More Passengers

The winter of 1822-1823 in New York was unusually cold and long. The bay had frozen solid earlier than normal and stayed frozen later than anyone remembered. The long winter presented two serious problems for Dr. Lummis. Over the winter the number of runaway slaves at his station had built up to over capacity, as it had in the fall. And the bad weather had severely affected the potential of his fruit harvest. He had hoped for a mild year to help mature his young trees. He could only hope that the spring and summer weather would cooperate and not cause further damage.

The last leg of the Underground Railroad had ground to a halt over the bitter winter. Dr. Lummis couldn't risk moving his cargo overland, so he and the fugitives awaiting transportation had to wait for the bay to thaw to make the trip to Canada.

After all the regular Lummis hiding places were filled, Soso volunteered to help keep several of the freedom seekers in his house and workshop. His guests included a family of five —father, mother, and three young children, four boys from different families, and an older single woman who had lost her hand in a farming accident.

For the most part Soso and his visitors enjoyed the rest of the winter and the beginning of spring. Soso had plenty of food in his vegetable cellar to supplement his daily catch of fish, usually caught just a few yards offshore through the sheet of ice that covered the bay. Mac kept guard over the guests while Soso was gone, in case of intruders.

The runaway slaves stayed indoors to prevent detection. You could never tell if someone suspected something or if a runaway had been followed to this location. Soso enjoyed the company of his guests. He taught the children how to carve designs in sticks and how to sand and smooth the hull of the boat that he was in the process of finishing. The mother and the father of the family spent most of their time caring for the baby who was quite sickly. The older single woman, Betty, was a lovely person. She cooked meals and generally helped Soso care for the house. She was exceptionally bright; she surprised Soso by her ability to read and write. Because she had lost her hand and was limited in the physical labor that she could perform, her master educated her and made her a teacher on his plantation. She loved to read Soso's books, and she helped Soso write letters to friends. He wrote letters every week to Jamey and Ben, and with Betty's help, these letters were very informative and detailed.

By spring Soso had developed strong feelings for his new friends. He wished they could stay as his neighbors and help build up the area, now referred to as Lummisville, having earned a name separate from Float Bridge. He was especially fond of Betty. She was attractive, smart, and hard working. She also liked Soso. He had been the first man to show her respect without pitying her for the loss of her hand. He was the only Indian whom she had ever seen, and she was surprised at how different he was than what she expected. He was tender and caring, instead of wild and savage as she had heard and read. His shipbuilding work was magnificent and artistic. She had found a man who liked her and in many ways needed her. Even though she was close to freedom, in her heart, she really didn't want to leave on the last leg of her journey. If it were up to her, Betty would have opted to stay in Lummisville near Soso and take her chances. She loved Soso so much that she was willing to risk her freedom.

During the first week of April, 1823, the ice started breaking up. Jim Davis stayed over at Soso's house during this time, and he and Soso spent their days readying Dr. Lummis' boats. The plan was to launch the boats on the day after the ice broke and to move the passengers the following day. Dr. Lummis now had three boats, which would be captained by Jim, Ron Johnson, and Dr. Lummis. Soso would captain Jim's smaller sailboat, which would hold the ten visitors staying at Soso's house.

Everything went according to plan. The day after the ice broke, the four boats were launched. Jim sailed his boat over to Soso's cove and helped with the launch of the other three boats. All the boats checked out fine, and the four captains were ready for a trip across the lake. This time they hoped for better winds and no dangerous ice jams. No one was anticipating problems.

The sun rose bright and clear the next morning. It was a perfect day to sail. The boatmen carefully loaded their cargo. The day brought mixed feelings for Soso and Betty. Neither had told the other of his or her deep feelings for the other. As Soso carefully loaded the other passengers into Jim's boat, Betty stayed back at his house to prepare food for the trip. Soso returned to meet Betty and express his feelings, but Betty was the first to speak. "Soso, I prefer to stay. I like it here and I can help you so much. This is where I belong."

This expression of emotion actually put Soso on the defense. He responded in an entirely different way than he had expected, "Betty, you must get your freedom. You can never be safe here. Your freedom is what I want for you now. Please, hurry. We must leave now." Those were the toughest words that Soso had ever spoken. Inside, he wanted to consent to Betty's request and have her stay with him forever.

More Trouble

Then, they both heard a commotion from the cove. Mac was barking wildly. People were shouting and running. Soso feared the worst and told Betty to hide in the root cellar. He started running toward the cove, but he was met halfway by Constable Joe West. West grabbed Soso and escorted him back to the cove. The slaves were all standing on the dock, surrounded by several agents of southern plantation owners, often referred to as slave-hunters. They had suspected these kinds of voyages to Canada and had searched Soso's boat and found the stowaways.

Joe confronted Soso with the obvious crime of harboring fugitive slaves. He explained the gravity of the situation—the maximum fine was $100 with a prison term for up to two years. Joe had always liked Soso, but this was a serious situation. State laws had been broken, and justice would have to prevail. No Indian could break the law and get away with it. Joe tied Soso's hands and began interrogating him. Joe then sent his assistant to search Soso's house. The slave hunters began shackling the slaves and loading them into their wagon.

Soso was considerate and respectful to the lawman, but he didn't tell him any of the secrets of the underground-railroad operation. Joe's assistant searched Soso's house without any success. Soso breathed a huge sigh of relief when he saw the man return without Betty.

Joe was ready to cart off Soso when Jim Davis arrived on the scene. Jim came right up to Joe and asked him to explain what was going on. Joe explained what he had discovered in the boat. Jim then explained to Joe that the boat belonged to him and that he was responsible for the hidden cargo.

This made things a lot messier for Joe. Jim was one of his best friends and a pillar in the community. While he knew that he could bully Soso and convince a jury of an Indian's guilt, convicting Jim in such a case would be impossible! Joe took Jim over to the side and struck a deal. If Jim promised never to involve himself in such activities again, Joe wouldn't press this case. The slave hunters had what they wanted, their slaves, and that would end the case right there. Unknown to the constable, just as Jim agreed to the constable's conditions, three boats overfilled with important passengers rounded Bute Island under full sail heading for Canada.

Jim and Soso quietly returned to Soso's house. Constable West, his assistant, the slave hunters, and nine shackled slaves headed south back toward Float Bridge. Soso wondered how Jim had come along just at the right time. Jim explained how Betty had run over to the Lummises and alerted Dr. Lummis and Jim, just as they were ready to leave the dock. Dr. Lummis obtained another captain to replace Jim, and Jim came over to rescue Soso from his predicament. Soso had been saved by Betty's quick thinking, and now he wondered if she was on her way across the lake. Jim assured him that Betty was safely on her way to freedom and happiness in Canada. However, Jim did not realize that Betty had not climbed aboard one of the boats and was still staying with Sara Lummis. Jim disappointedly sailed back to Troupville on his boat, and Soso headed over to the Lummis house to talk to Sara and to see if she was all right and to find out what else he could do.

Soso arrived at his neighbors in a very depressed mood. Friends in need and under his care, had been caught, arrested, and were now returning to a life of slavery, and the woman he loved was on her way to a new life in a different country. Soso was shocked when he entered the Lummis house and saw Betty standing there with Sara. They embraced, and Sara quickly realized the special feelings that they had for each other. Relieved to see one another, their discussion quickly turned to what could be done to save their friends.

It was decided that Betty had to stay hidden in the Lummises' basement. Sara volunteered to ride to Float Bridge to find out what was happening to the slaves who were caught. Several men would be needed for the activities that Soso had in mind. Soso went to gather others who could help.

Fortunately, the trip across the lake for the other three boats went without a hitch. This time the wind and currents were favorable, and the three empty boats returned to Sodus Bay just twenty hours after they had left. When Dr. Lummis, Ron Johnson, and substitute captain Walter Hill entered the Lummis house before sunrise, they found a group of men already assembled and making plans.

The Rescue

The rescue plan that Soso had devised was bold and daring. It would take perfect timing and tremendous bravery. Everyone hoped and prayed that no one would get hurt. The consensus was that it could work and was worth the risk. Now that Dr. Lummis, Ron, and Walter were there, Soso laid out the plan for them. First, Soso and five others would ride with four extra horses to the valley along the road near Geneva that morning. There, they would ambush the slave-hunters and their confiscated cargo of the nine runaway slaves. Once the slaves were rescued, they would ride or be carried by horseback back to Briscoe Point on Sodus Bay and loaded on Dr. Lummis' boat. Then, the boat ride to freedom would depart for Canada. Betty would go on the boat as well. Both of them knew that it was much too dangerous now for her to stay in Lummisville.

There wasn't much time to debate and discuss the plan. The duties were assigned to all men present, and the ambush party, carrying all of Soso's bows and arrows, departed immediately for Geneva.

By noon, everything was ready. It was just a matter of waiting for the slave-hunters' wagon to arrive at the designated place. After about two hours of waiting, the time came. Soso sprang out of the bushes directly in front of the wagon. Arrows flew out of the woods and struck the side of the wagon. The sight of a fierce Indian brave, dressed in war paint and battle dress, and the impact of arrows coming out of the shadows, caused complete terror in the hearts of the slave-hunters. Soso and his colleagues screamed and shouted. The slave hunters threw down their weapons and put up their hands in surrender. Soso motioned for them to climb out of the wagon and walk up the road ahead. The three southern men were terrified. They never had seen such a savage warrior, and they envisioned others like him hiding in the woods.

Once the men were out of sight, the rescuers unshackled the slaves and loaded everyone on horseback for the ride to Sodus Bay. They left on their flight, just about the time Soso was tying the hands of the three men and attaching them by rope to a tree along the road. Soso was careful not to show his face, although he was covered with thick war paint and make-up. Once all were tied, he let out a piercing scream and war-whoop and ran back through the woods.

Soso mounted his horse and rode quickly and quietly through the forest, rather than along the road. He didn't want anyone to see him. Despite his delayed start and rougher travel route, he arrived back at Briscoe Point just when the slaves and the other rescuers arrived. There was no time for long emotional good-byes. But Soso, still dressed in war paint and Indian clothing, and Betty took a moment to wish each other well and to promise to see each other and to write faithfully. Betty then joined the others on the ship, and Dr. Lummis set sail for Canada and freedom.

While the other rescuers took a few moments to celebrate their success, Soso immediately went back home to change out of his costume and destroy all the evidence. As it turned out, there was very little to worry about. The slave-hunters were set loose by a passerby about an hour after their ordeal. They were still so frightened that they immediately headed south and never bothered reporting their Indian attack to the authorities in New York. The way they figured it, they were lucky to be alive after being attacked by a band of hostile Indians. And if anyone ever questioned their story, they had plenty of arrows sticking out of their wagon to prove it.

After this terrifying episode, the "Lummis station" of the underground railroad stayed out of commission for a couple of months. However, by the middle of the summer, passengers began arriving again. Although Jim Davis kept his word and never participated in the activities, Soso volunteered to make the boat trip across to York whenever possible. As it turned out, Betty settled right on the lakeshore in York. York was a small village that served as the shipping center for the growing city of Toronto. Toronto was a well-organized and growing city on the shore of the lake. From then on, Soso had a special feeling in his heart for the village of York.

When traveling the lake, Soso often stopped for a meal or for some pleasant conversation with Betty and her new family of the four young boys. Sometimes they would travel into Toronto to see the exciting sights of the growing city. Soso and Betty were destined to have a long-distance relationship, but a caring one nonetheless. Both knew that was better than never having met and known each other. It was both frustrating and exciting at the same time. These two strong people understood full well the realities of the world and were satisfied for now with dreaming about the ideals.

Joe West didn't come around Lummisville very much after that day. He was always pleasant to Jim, Soso, and Dr. Lummis whenever he saw them. But Lummisville was no longer one of the regular stops on his rounds through the area.

Discipline and Punishment

Springtime put color and life back into the dark gray walls of the fortifications at West Point. Jamey liked the spring. Its arrival enabled him to get outside to go horseback riding and take hikes. He watched fishermen net the abundant shad in the Hudson River. These fish were different than any that he had seen in Lake Ontario. In the fall, another fish specie called striped bass was caught by hook and line. These were big and beautiful fish, and the fishermen were thrilled to catch these elusive fish. Jamey liked the trout and salmon of Lake Ontario better, but he had to admit that the striped bass were superb game and eating fish as well.

The fun planned for the spring of 1823 was short-lived. Jamey encountered his first major problem at West Point. He had been caught returning to his room late after a dance at the hotel. He had danced several dances with a pretty girl named Mary. After the dance finished, he sat and talked with his new friend, and lost track of time. By the time he noticed the candles and lanterns in the barracks being extinguished, which meant it was time for taps, he was too late. Now, Jamey had to face the consequences of his lapse of self-discipline.

After the report of his delinquency was given to the Superintendent, Jamey reported to Major Thayer to receive his punishment. Major Thayer had great hopes for Jamey and liked the potential that he saw in the young man. However, to Major Thayer, this situation called for a more severe punishment than usual. He always demanded more from those who could achieve more. Thayer's entire method of development was based on the goal to develop each cadet to his potential. Therefore, every cadet at West Point felt challenged. There was no easy way through the Academy, even for a talented young man like Jamey Davis.

"Cadet Davis, do you understand the charges against you?" asked the Superintendent.

"Yes, sir," answered Jamey.

"Do you have anything to say in your defense?"

"No, sir."

"Then you receive the maximum punishment of a '12 and 8'," Thayer proclaimed. "Case concluded. Cadet Davis, you are dismissed. I never want to see you back here for such purposes again."

"Good afternoon, sir." Jamey saluted and left Thayer's office in a sweat. He was relieved that it was over, but disappointed at the severity of his punishment.

Thayer's punishment of a "12 and 8" for Jamey may have been harsh, but it would be a constant reminder to him to stay aware of his duties at all times. Jamey would have to perform 12 hours of extra labor each week for eight straight weeks. Since there was no extra time during the weekdays, this meant that Jamey would work six hours each on Saturday and Sunday. His job would be to dig and move dirt using a wheelbarrow from the mountainside above the Academy to the valleys and gullies on the Academy grounds. The Academy was using cadets, especially those serving punishment, to flatten and expand the plateau overlooking the Hudson River called the "plain." Jamey's dream of a fun spring had been transformed into tedium.

This incident made Jamey even more determined than ever to do well and to develop to his full potential. The West Point curriculum was adapting to accommodate the few really advanced students like Jamey. Previously, there were very few students in America who were prepared for such advanced mathematics or science, but the generally poor, rural country was beginning to find a way to improve itself through the education of its youth. Jamey was a prime example, and under Thayer's direction, West Point was determined to lead the way in improving America's college-level education.

Jamey had spent the year at West Point discovering the concepts and techniques of the advanced mathematics of calculus. He intuitively understood the potential uses of this subject. His success in mathematics produced further success in other subjects—Natural Philosophy, English, and French.

The new Head of the Department of Mathematics, Charles Davies, was pleased with Jamey's progress. Davies taught Calculus to a section of five of the most advanced cadets. Jamey appreciated Professor Davies as a caring and competent instructor, but Jamey thoroughly enjoyed his instructor in Descriptive Geometry, Claudius Crozet. Crozet was a native French mathematician who had served on Napoleon's staff in France. Crozet spoke and taught in a half-French, half-English language. He motivated his students by including real-life situations in his instruction. Crozet's stories included the engineering aspects of Napoleon's campaigns and tales from the czar's court in Russia. Crozet told stories about notable mathematicians whom he had worked with in France. Claudius Crozet and Charles Davies were ideal role models for the talented young cadet.

Crozet used the blackboard to draw in precise detail the engineering designs and fortification plans that were included in the Descriptive Geometry course. Then the cadets would draw their designs in their own drafting books. Jamey took great care in producing his drawings, knowing first-hand from his summer's experience how important they were in designing and building fortifications and other structures like bridges, canals, and buildings. Jamey was a motivated and talented student, and Crozet enjoyed teaching him engineering and problem solving.

Jamey's enthusiasm and aptitude in academics left him with a 2.91 average out of 3.0 for the year. This performance vaulted Jamey to second in his West Point class after two years of study, trailing only his former roommate, Alex Bache.

New Neighbors

After the British attack on Troupville during the War of 1812, Jim Davis had bought several plots of land next to Judge Nicholas's land on the south shore of the bay with the intent to start a farm. However, it became apparent over the years that Jim was a sailor and a fisherman, not a farmer. So late in the year, when two men from Chatham, New York, arrived at Troupville looking for farmland, Jim Davis was happy to talk to them about selling his unused and unwanted land.

The two men, John Lockwood and Jeremiah Talbot, were interested in obtaining about 2000 acres of prime farm land for their small religious community. Jim only owned about 300 acres. However, Judge Nicholas held over 1600 acres that he wanted to sell. The judge was away on business, so

Jim and Dr. Lummis showed the two visitors both tracks of land.

They were impressed with the location and the quality of the land. They wanted a rural, fairly isolated tract of fertile land with access to water, and this land filled those requirements. Jim and Dr. Lummis liked the two men and appreciated their plan for the development of a religious community. Neither Jim nor Dr. Lummis knew anything about the religion they practiced. They called it "The United Society of Believers in Christ's Second Coming." However, if all the followers were as kind as these two men were, they would be an exceptional addition to the Sodus Bay communities.

Jim agreed to the price offered by the two men. However, the deal was contingent on the men obtaining Judge Nicholas' land. They were unsure of Judge Nicolas' price for his property.

Jim spent the next week sailing his last circuit of the lake for the year, distributing goods and produce from Dr. Lummis's farm. Just as Jim had promised Joe West, none of the cargo came from the underground railroad. Jim was a man of his word, and he would do exactly as he had promised. Soso accompanied Jim on the voyage in order to see Betty during the short stay in York. When they returned to Sodus Bay, Dr. Lummis was waiting to deliver the news to Jim. Judge Nicholas had sold his land to the two religious men so that the sale of Jim's land was now official.

The paperwork was finalized during the next month. Jim had gained a nice profit from his land speculation and now planned to re-enter the fishing business on a part-time basis. He also used part of the money to improve his home in Troupville. By next spring, there would be an addition of a nice sunroom, with several windows that overlooked the bay so that he and Karen could sit in their house and see the activities on Sodus Bay. Actually, Jim spent very little time in his house, but Karen would really enjoy the view of the bay.

Young Lovers

His punishment for being late for taps had long since been served and forgotten. Jamey, meanwhile, had developed into a handsome, brilliant young man. He was well liked by his fellow cadets. His professors also respected him as a dedicated student. Jamey's courses for his third year included chemistry, astronomy, natural philosophy, and drawing. But the most exciting news was that Jamey had the opportunity to teach one section of mathematics. Because the new freshman class was larger than anticipated, three upper class cadets were chosen to teach the algebra and trigonometry topics to the plebes. The three cadets chosen were Jamey, Alex Bache, and senior cadet Dennis Hart Mahan.

Jamey was a natural at teaching. The time he spent in the classroom was the best part of the day. His students enjoyed his enthusiasm, dedication, and sense of humor. As a teacher, Jamey's only anxious moments came when Major Thayer or Captain Davies visited his class to check on his teaching. Jamey always sent his cadets to the boards as soon as Thayer or Davies arrived. Then the visitor would wind up spending his time helping and questioning cadets instead of listening to Jamey's instruction. Jamey also relied on the talents of his star pupil, Albert Church, whenever distinguished visitors stayed in his classroom. Cadet Church was always ready to recite on his board work. He was a brilliant, articulate cadet, who always put on a good show for important visitors, and Jamey knew to utilize Church's talents to impress visitors with the knowledge and skill of the cadets in the section. Jamey also used Cadet Church to help other cadets who were falling behind. All in all, Jamey's experience as a teacher was highly rewarding and successful.

The other big news in Jamey's life was his new girlfriend, Carin Roe. They met at a dance at the hotel. Carin lived just 5 miles north of West Point in the Canterbury Village. She was pretty, smart, and well-educated. She was Jamey's age and had already attended a women's finishing school for one year. Carin had studied in previous years at home under the tutelage of her brother, Peter, who was a schoolteacher. After one year of higher-level work, however, she had decided to stay home and help in her family's farming business.

A year before, Peter Roe had married and moved onto a farm in New Windsor. Carin spent considerable time helping her brother on the farm. However, every weekend she tried to make enough time for the ride over the big mountain to West Point. Whenever she came to West Point for an evening dance, she was escorted by her brother or father. However, she would usually just ride over by herself to spend Saturday or Sunday afternoon with Jamey. Their afternoons together were fun and exciting. They were falling in love.

Jamey was able to take a short trip off post during two of the weekends in the spring, and he asked to spend that time visiting Carin. Jamey came out to Peter's farm in New Windsor on Saturday and spent the day working with Carin. That night Jamey stayed at the farm, while Carin returned to her home in nearby Canterbury. Then the two spent Sunday riding around the area and meeting Carin's friends.

Jamey's second weekend trip was similar to the first. On Saturday, they were playing "hide-and-seek" on the farm when Jamey found a hidden room under the barn. When he entered the room, he was surprised to find several black people hiding there. By the time Carin came along to "find" Jamey, he understood the situation that he had unwittingly discovered. The barn was being used as a stop on the underground railroad for fugitive slaves. Carin was worried that she had exposed her family to danger. She loved Jamey, but didn't know his feelings towards slavery. This was a very serious moment of decision for Carin and her family.

Carin's family were abolitionists, and she wondered what Jamey would do and say in response to this situation. However, she quickly found out that there was nothing to worry about. Jamey praised Carin and her family for their actions. He realized that talking about it could endanger Carin, so nothing more was ever said about the incident. Of course, Jamey didn't realize that his father had been involved in similar activity in Troupville. Jim Davis had never told his son about his past involvement in the final leg of the underground railroad.

Sunday afternoon was especially pleasant for Jamey. One of Peter's friends invited them for a sailboat ride. They rode over to Cornwall Harbor and met Mr. Cyler. Mr. Cyler's boat was a beautifully built classic sloop. Jamey had sailed and helped Soso build several boats like this one. Cyler's boat was built from mahogany, whereas Soso's boats were constructed from rock elm. Otherwise, Cyler's boat was nearly identical in shape and size to some of Soso's older sloops. That afternoon Jamey helped sail Mr. Cyler's boat and explained its characteristics to the others. It was a marvelous day for sailing, especially for Jamey and Carin. For Jamey, in particular, it brought back vivid memories of his days on Sodus Bay.

"Cornwall is a pretty place. It reminds me of my hometown of Troupville. But we don't have such big mountains right next to the water. It's the contrast of the rugged mountains, next to the smooth, flat river, that makes this such a beautiful place," Jamey commented to Carin as he sat next to her on the deck of the sloop.

"I like the way the river winds around West Point. Look, you can see the plain and the fort of West Point right from here." Since the sloop was in the middle of the river heading south, Carin noticed the distinctive buildings of the Academy at West Point several miles away.

"With this steady north wind and this fast boat, we could sail to West Point in 15 minutes. However, I'd love to stay on this river sailing in circles all day. This is a fast boat, but I've seen faster ones up on Sodus Bay. Maybe we could sail up there and I could show you. Actually, by following the Erie Canal, you can almost get to my village. Unfortunately, it would take several weeks to get there. That would be quite a ride on the boat like this, or better yet, we could take a steamboat." Jamey was thinking crazy thoughts and dreaming about future technology, because the current state of the Erie Canal didn't support steamship travel. His rambling, nervous talk was caused by his love for Carin.

Jamey spent his third year at the academy enjoying himself and making the most of his opportunities. He slipped in academic standing to third in his class of 46 cadets. He was poised for success in the Army. He continued to feel very fortunate to have the tremendous opportunity of a free education and a career in the United States Army.

Sodus Bay Shakers

The two elders of the church brought the first part of their flock to the shores of Sodus Bay. The 200-mile trip from New Lebanon, near Albany, was long, tedious, and uncomfortable. Most of the men walked the entire distance because they had few horses or wagons to ride. The initial settlement consisted of 28 people who would spend time over the next few years preparing fields and building dwellings so others could follow.

When the first group arrived at their new home on Sodus Bay, they were pleased with what they found. The deep blue water of the lake and the silvery waters of the bay enlivened the already lush green countryside. The view from their hilltop land was spectacular. They could see the entire bay and look through the open channel far out into the lake. As the final wagon of religious followers completed their journey, it was time for them to celebrate. The whole flock of 28 people, eighteen from New Lebanon and ten recent converts from Lyons, who had joined the others, rejoiced in celebration and prayer. Their new homestead on the heights overlooking Sodus Bay was the answer to their prayers to find a peaceful place to live without prejudice and harassment.

Everyone in the Troupville area was aware of the arrival of these new residents. After all, the arrival of 28 new people significantly increased the population of the Sodus Bay area. Not only that, but these people were strong and hardworking. Within days, they were clearing fields and building a barn. The new colonists were fully prepared for their mission of establishing a settlement. They were well organized. They rose early, worked together, ate together, and, late in the evening, prayed and worshipped together.

It was the strange activities that took place during their prayer meetings that were responsible for their being called "Shakers." During these intense prayer meetings, the worshippers would become so agitated and involved in their prayers, that they would shake and jerk their heads and dance and jump around the room. Of course, this was amazing to those who had never seen such behavior.

As a group, the Shakers were noted for their order and discipline. Their tools were of the highest quality and always well maintained. Their crops and farm animals were superior to any others in the area. The clothes and furniture they made for consumers were of tremendous value. They ate wholesome food and generally lived a healthy existence. The "believers," as they called themselves, did not marry nor have children. They counted on converting others in order to increase their numbers and sustain their beliefs. However, without converts to the religion, the Shakers were doomed to extinction because of their policy of no offspring.

The Shaker community did nearly everything collectively. The whole community really made one big family. They owned property in common, worked in groups, alternated jobs, lived in collective dwellings, ate meals together, and shared the profits made from their consumer goods. The meals were prepared by a group of the believers. The men, women, and children sat in groups at separate tables. The meals were eaten in complete silence. This was a highly disciplined group of devoted people.

While the meals were uninteresting, the Sunday church services and daily prayer meetings were always lively. There was plenty of dancing, singing, and shaking in prayer. Most people in the Troupville area had never encountered anything quite like a Shaker church service.

Word about the arrival of the Shakers spread throughout the area. Many people were curious about the strange things they had heard. People traveled quite a distance just to see and talk with the Shakers, often hoping to see them shake during their prayers. Some neighborly people came by just to offer their help and to welcome their new neighbors to the area.

Soso and Jim were among those who came by the Shaker Heights, the name given to the area where the Shakers lived, to offer their help. They brought a bucket of fish and a jug of apple cider. After exchanging greetings with some of the followers, Elder John came out of his tent and greeted his friends. He thanked Jim for the property that he had sold them. He indicated that they had already started preparing the soil and planting crops on the property that Jim had previously owned. John gracefully accepted the gifts the men brought. He also indicated that he could use their expertise in the areas of sailing and watercraft to help design and build the Shaker community dock on the shore of the bay.

At the direction of Elder John, Soso and Jim went down off the ridge to the stream valley where Third Creek flowed through the Shakers' land. Finding a work party of several Shaker men and other neighbors digging the cribbing and foundation for the main dock, Soso and Jim lent a hand. While they worked they gave advice to the workers and leaders of this project.

Among the other outside helpers was a young man from the nearby village of Palmyra, some twenty-six miles inland from Sodus Bay. The workers on the project enjoyed learning from each other about both the Shaker religion and the waters of the bay. The man from Palmyra who seemed to be the most inquisitive about these new people and their religion was Joe Smith. Even though Joe was only nineteen years old, he was mature and intelligent. He talked about his own religious experiences and those of his neighbors in Palmyra. He told the others of his vision of an angel and his destiny to find buried tablets of gold. He offered to search for such buried treasure on the Shakers' new land. However, his offers were kindly declined. Joe realized full well that the Shakers had overcome plenty of skepticism to establish their new religion, and he saw firsthand how a new religion could promote itself and gain new believers. He would remember these lessons very well.

Ben's New Career

Jamey was surprised to hear that he had a visitor who wanted to see him at the West Point Hotel. With the fall academics of his senior year in full gear, he had to finish his last two afternoon classes before he could go over to the hotel.

Jamey's schedule included engineering and mineralogy in the morning, with geography, history, and ethics in the afternoon. Once again, he was excused from some mineralogy classes to teach mathematics to the plebes.

While the 250 cadets and more than 25 officers, professors, and soldiers on the staff and faculty produced a busy cadet area, the hotel was usually quiet and peaceful during the week. As Jamey approached the registration desk, Ben jumped out from behind a pillar and grabbed his old friend. They hugged one another like old times. The two young men suddenly realized how much they both had grown and matured. The two boyhood friends had turned into men. While they were still close friends, they realized as adults that they didn't need each other's companionship or support as much. They were independent, and they were mature enough to handle their adult responsibilities.

Because of his duties, Jamey could spend only an hour with Ben that afternoon. That was all the time Ben had anyway. He had to catch the next steamboat to Albany. Ben told Jamey all about his new opportunity. Ben had been hired as a banker by the largest bank in New York City. He had decided to leave school and take the position. He was going back to Sodus Bay to see his family before starting work back in New York in about a month.

Ben was ecstatic over the opportunity. It was exactly the type of position that he had hoped for. He liked the idea of staying in the city, and his salary was substantial. Jamey was equally happy for his friend. The two spent the hour discussing their dreams for the future. They sat on the edge of the plain, overlooking the Hudson. The foothills of the Catskill Mountains come right to the waters edge on the west side of the river. They were surrounded by the magnificent river and the huge rock mountain. On that afternoon of 1824, they looked down on the spot where the great chain of the Revolutionary War fifty years earlier had kept the British warships from using the Hudson River and dividing the colonies. It was the ideal spot to think deep thoughts and discuss future plans. The time came for Ben to leave, so Jamey accompanied him to the wharf on the riverbank. As Jamey waved good-bye to Ben, he felt a tingle of homesickness for Troupville and his family. Jamey hadn't been back to Troupville in over a year, and he longed to see his family and Troupville friends.

Homecoming

After the long trip, Ben arrived at Troupville by stagecoach from Lyons, where he had debarked from the canal stage of his travel. It was a bright, sunny October day. He could see two sailboats skimming along the shoreline in the brisk wind. The bay and its surroundings were still breathtaking. Ben hadn't written to anyone about his visit or new job, so his arrival would be a surprise to everyone. He stopped by the Wickham's general store to pass on his greetings. Then he went over to the Davises' house. Jim and Karen Davis were home, and they were surprised and happy to see Ben. Jim volunteered to take Ben across the bay to his family's house. Ben passed on greetings from Jamey. He explained how he and Jamey had spent an afternoon talking during his stop at West Point. Then Jim and Ben sailed Jim's small sloop across the bay.

Ben couldn't believe how much things had changed. The view of the Lummis estate from the shore was magnificent. The stately house overlooked vast, well-kept fields. The dock and boathouse fit perfectly into the landscape. The fall foliage in the area was at its peak. Ben felt overwhelmed by the sheer beauty of his home. He could already feel the warmth and closeness of his family. His absence for over a year from his beloved home had enhanced his emotions for his family. He realized that his next visit to

Sodus Bay might not be for quite a while. He wanted to soak in all that he could before he left.

Jim dropped Ben off at the dock and started back across the bay. Just as he left the dock Jim heard a familiar voice yell, "Uncle Jim, come and see my new friend." Elizabeth Lummis stuck her head around the corner of the boathouse. She was holding a furry, black cat. She couldn't see Ben, who was on shore, from where she was standing.

Jim answered, "Come see my friend. I left him at the dock for you. I have to go home now. See you later."

Elizabeth was six years old and full of energy. She and her cat came running around the corner of the boathouse and ran directly into the arms of her big brother. She was surprised to see her brother. Ben picked up his sister and gave her a big hug and kiss. Elizabeth was delighted to have her brother home. She started telling him all about her new cat and all of the fun things she was doing. The Lummis family would have a happy time for the next few days.

Jim looked back as he sailed out into the bay. Seeing the brother and sister walking up toward the house made Jim miss his own son, Jamey. He promised himself that he would take his family to West Point to see Jamey graduate next summer.

Ben had only ten days at home. He spent time with his parents reminiscing about his childhood and planning his future as an adult. Father and son shared thoughts about abolishing slavery and the Underground Railroad. Ben knew of his father's activities in this cause. He spent plenty of time with Elizabeth. He played with her, read to her, and told her stories about the city. Elizabeth was a smart little girl. She was already reading and writing. She promised to write Ben numerous letters.

Ben spent a whole day fishing and talking with Soso. They took Soso's boat for a sail up the lake past Chimney's Bluffs. Both men hooked a few big trout. Ben told Soso stories about the city and amazed him with tales about its continued growth. Soso reminded Ben of how much he had learned since he had started his first fishing business with Jamey several years before. Ben knew that to be successful he needed to work hard; Soso reminded him that he also needed to be honest and courageous. There would be plenty of obstacles to overcome as a banker in a big city. When they returned from their fishing trip, the two men delivered their catch to two elderly families in Float Bridge. That act alone sent a strong message to Ben Lummis.

Ben spent the last day of his visit helping his father and Soso make repairs on the family's sailboats that had been put up for the winter in the boathouse. Dr. Lummis always kept his boats in perfect condition. Ben enjoyed this one last opportunity to work with his hands. He knew that the next few months would be filled with work of a different variety.

"It sure was nice to be home and see everyone and get to do these enjoyable things. Sometimes, I miss this place so much. But there are parts of New York City I like, too." Ben was slowly saying good-bye to his father and his "uncle" Soso.

"Yes, I remember the city and its people. There certainly is enough to do, but it's different than Sodus Bay. Too many people and not enough nature to suit me." Soso tempered his critical remarks about the city, knowing that Ben had to build his life there.

"Well, I expect that you'll be very busy in your new job. Make sure you write and take good care of yourself. You know that your mother will worry about you, but I know you're going to be fine." Dr. Lummis was proud of and confident in his son.

"You two have been excellent role models for me. I'll do my best. Then when I need to see nature at its finest and most spectacular, I'll come back here." Ben knew he'd miss Sodus Bay, but he hoped to be back many times.

The next morning, Ben left on horseback for the stage line station in Syracuse. Soso accompanied Ben to the station. He was going to meet with several leaders of the Iroquois Indian tribes on a reservation near Syracuse. He planned to see his old friend, James Cooper, who he hoped would be attending the meeting. Soso would then ride Ben's horse back to Lummisville.

The Great Council

After attending the planning meeting in the fall, Soso was called to the Great Council in the spring as a special advisor who knew well the customs, laws, and ways of the whites. All the tribal leaders of the Haudenosaune people came to the Onondagas longhouse. Haudenosaune was the name the Iroquois called themselves. The Onondagas were called the keepers of the central fire and usually hosted the tribal meetings. The Council was headed by the Tadodaho, who was the speaker of the Council and the "keeper of the Iroquois flame that never dies." The leaders of the rest of the Six Nations—Mohawks, keepers of the eastern door; the Senecas, keepers of the western door; the Cayugas, Soso's nation; the Oneidas, and the Tuscaroras, all came from reservations across New York to the Great Council. The Council was called to talk about the rights of the Iroquois people and the white men's violations of their treaties with the Iroquois.

The Tadodaho did not dwell on the problems of the past or even the present. He asked his Council to think about the future of their people. The proceedings were governed by the Iroquois' centuries-old constitution, the Great Law of Peace. These laws for governing the Six Nations included checks and balances that were initiated centuries earlier by the illustrious chief and wise Iroquois leader, Peacekeeper.

The Council heard the opinions of all the participants. Soso talked briefly of how the Iroquois people had to take more time to understand the laws and beliefs of the white man. He also spoke about ways to convince white men that they had much to learn from the Indians. Soso encouraged his people to learn from the whites, but not to forget the ways of the Indians. Medicine men talked of how the new religious laws provided by the great Seneca medicine man, Handsome Lake, would help make the white men more tolerant and understanding of the ways of the Iroquois.

The new tribal spiritual laws discouraged drinking hard liquor, ended magic and witchcraft, and established clear, reasonable punishments for murder and other serious crimes. The Seneca chief and orator, Sa-go-ye-wat-ha or Red Jacket, detailed all the treaty violations. He had been a strong supporter of the white man's ways, but now was very upset over the numerous recent treaty violations. Red Jacket agreed in principle with Soso, but he was not as patient. He pointed out to Soso and the others that, "The Indian has learned from the whites. Why didn't the white men learn from the Indians?"

The Council, with agreement of the Tadodaho, decided to send a delegation to the whitemen's President in Washington. The delegation would explain how the whites had violated the Treaty at Fort Stanwix that had been agreed to by the skillful chief Cornplanter. Even though Cornplanter could not attend the Council, he sent advisors who supported the perspective that the whites were the treaty violators and that something had to be done. The whites had continually taken lands guaranteed to the Iroquois. The whites had agreed not to interfere with the Indians, yet every year new laws took away more Indian lands and freedoms. The delegation would show the white men's President Adams the treaties, demand compliance, and bring back his answer to the Council. The Tadodaho decided that Soso would lead the delegation to the city of Washington. The Council drafted documents to send to President Adams. Soso would wait for the President's reply to their request to see him before traveling to the nation's capital. Accompanying Soso would be two of the strongest chiefs, Red Jacket and Silent Turtle.

Visitor

The letter announcing his planned visit arrived at Soso's on April 15, 1825, the day before James Cooper did. Soso was excited to see his old friend at his door once again. Mac had given his usual warning bark and then happily welcomed the visitor. The two men had plenty to catch up on since they hadn't seen each other in sixteen years. Soso had missed meeting James in the fall as he planned to do on his trip to Syracuse.

James hadn't changed much. He still looked the same and was as humorous and talkative as ever. His fame and wealth, acquired by virtue of the popular novels that he had written, hadn't changed his attitude. James

Cooper was brilliant, but not arrogant. He liked Soso and respected his outlook on life.

Soso was happy for his old friend. He had always liked James. Soso always knew that he would succeed at whatever he did. As expected, the two friends were out fishing and boating that afternoon. James was impressed by all the changes around the bay and the growth of Troupville. He was equally impressed by what hadn't changed. The natural beauty of the area was still present. James Cooper always felt himself a part of nature as he traveled around Sodus Bay.

The afternoon was spent fishing and talking. James wanted to know about the Great Council and the plight of Soso's people. He was upset over the mistreatment of Indians and the violations of the treaties by the government. Soso detailed the proposal that he hoped to give very soon to President John Quincy Adams. James also hoped that the President and Congress would agree to the provisions, but secretly he didn't hold out much hope for change in the way treaties were ignored and Indians mistreated. James was much more pessimistic than the Indians were about making progress in red-white relations.

By the end of the afternoon, James agreed to help Soso prepare for his trip to Washington. James would be staying with Soso for a month or two to learn more about the Iroquois as he worked on another novel about Indians and the frontier. James respected Soso's perspective on the relationship between whitemen and Indians and hoped to learn more about the Iroquois from his conversations with Soso.

That evening Soso and James were invited to the Lummises for dinner. The discussion centered on James' previous novels and his current writing. Even seven-year-old Elizabeth participated in the discussions. She was an avid, precocious reader and already had read some parts of James's novel, *The Spy*. The evening's meal and discussion were perfect closings to James' exciting first day back on Sodus Bay.

The Troupville Postmaster, William Wickham, couldn't help but notice the official postage and the return address on the letter addressed to Soso. The letter had been sent by the Office of the President of the United States. He immediately closed the Post Office and the General Store and went over to Jim Davis's house. As soon as Jim saw William coming down the path, he realized something important was happening. William showed Jim the letter, and the two men immediately climbed into Jim's boat and set sail for

Lummisville. It's not every day that a post office on the rural frontier receives a letter sent by the President of the United States.

After Jim and William docked the boat at Soso's dock, they went up the path toward Soso's house. They met James Cooper, who told them that Soso was out fishing near Briscoe Cove. The three men launched Jim's boat and went looking for Soso. They found their friend wading waist deep in mud trying to catch frogs. The technique of frog catching used by Soso was both humorous and unusual. Soso would quietly sneak up behind a frog and then try to leap for the frog before it leaped to safety. About one of four or five attempts was successful. The failed attempts left Soso sprawled out on the mud bank with nothing but a handful, or face full, of mud. Soso had accumulated a bag of eight frogs by the time the three men found him. The seagulls kept watchful eyes on the proceedings, while continuing their annoying squawks. Some seemed to be laughing at the desperate leaps of the human, while others seemed to cheer him on to success at this strange activity.

It was in this dirty, muddy, smelly condition that Soso opened the letter from the President of the United States. He carefully read the elaborately printed letter.

Dear Ambassador of the Iroquois:

Your proposal for a government inquiry into the current status of Indian treaties has been met with great favor by my staff and me. We will assemble representatives from the Indian Bureau, the Congressional Committee on Indian affairs, and state representatives to discuss the treaties the government still honors. Once this assembly has completed its work, you and representatives of other Indian tribes will be called to an assembly in Washington to learn personally of the treaty status.

Be assured that the United States government will do its best to resolve this situation and take care of all people living on its soil. I have great respect for the Iroquois people and hope to continue our harmonious relationship.

I hope the assembly will work quickly and finish their proceedings by the end of the summer. If this happens, expect an invitation to Washington in the early fall for your delegation.

Sincerely,
John Quincy Adams
President of the United States

The tone and sincerity of the President's letter excited Soso. Even at his most optimistic, Soso had not anticipated so encouraging a response. This letter gave Soso reason to believe progress could be made toward better treatment for all Indian people. He felt a considerable sense of trust in this President. This good news was a cause for celebration and continued hope.

That evening Soso held a party for several friends and neighbors. Jim and Karen Davis, James Cooper, William and Sara Lummis, Joe and Mary Sheldon, and Byram Green enjoyed Soso's fresh fish and frog leg stew. The talk centered on the President's letter to Soso and the prospects for better relations between whites and Indians. In particular, everyone hoped that President Adams would use his influence to change the anti-Indian policies that continued to come from Congress and the Army. Soso enjoyed the exciting evening of hopeful conversation in celebration of the successful accomplishment of the first stage of the mission to improve Indian treatment. His only regret was that none of his Indian friends was there to see the support they had from whites like those assembled at the table.

The other topic of interest during the evening was Jamey Davis's graduation from West Point. The scheduled date was July 1. Jim, Karen, and Susan Davis were planning to leave Troupville on June 10. William, Sara, and Elizabeth were going to travel with Soso, but were planning on leaving June18. They hoped to continue their trip to New York City to see Ben after their visit to West Point. James Cooper wished that he could join his friends, but he had to return home to work on his novel and prepare for a trip to Europe.

Graduation

By June 20, 1825, all the studying and testing were complete and the graduation celebration started. Jamey and many of his classmates welcomed their families and friends. The West Point area was decked out in its finest. The landscape in the area was always breathtaking, but for graduation the buildings and cadet area were equally dressed up. The Davis family members were excited to be a part of the celebration and enjoyed themselves tremendously. They were proud of Jamey, who finished second in academic rank in his class of 37 graduates. He was also one of two company commanders in the battalion of cadets. This gave him the rank of Cadet Captain. The Davises were staying in the hotel right on the Academy grounds. This was an exciting experience for this frontier family.

There were plenty of activities for both visitors and cadets. The cadets marched in parades and conducted demonstrations of military activities every day of the festive week while the families were treated as special guests by Academy personnel and allowed to see all the cadet areas and activities.

The Davises also received a surprise during the week. Jamey introduced Carin Roe to his family as his girlfriend. Jamey hadn't mentioned anything about Carin to his parents before. They certainly enjoyed her company and got to know her and her family during the rest of the week. Carin equally enjoyed the Davises. To her, they were adventurous and exciting, full of the frontier spirit. To them, she was both beautiful and personable. They liked her right from their first meeting.

Jamey and Carin

Jamey could tell he was falling in love with Carin. She was charming and pretty. He thought about her all the time and couldn't wait to see her again, whenever they were apart. They danced together each night of the week during the graduation festivities. Everything was perfect when they were together. Carin was also falling in love with Jamey. She knew how talented and caring he was. She worried that after becoming close to him that he would have to leave, and possibly, she would never see him again. She worried about their future. She wanted him to stay. She wanted to be with him. But she had no idea if the Army would ever accommodate their relationship.

Jamey already knew the location of his first assignment as a brand new Second Lieutenant in the Army. He had to leave immediately after graduation to travel west to St. Louis to an army post called Jefferson Barracks. He was headed to the new frontier, west of the Mississippi River, as a topographic engineer. It had been a tough choice to make for Jamey, engineering or artillery. He enjoyed the technical aspects of both branches. In the end, he had decided that engineering would be more rewarding. He hoped that he had made the right choice. Jamey's first assignment would be mapping and surveying the western expansion of the United States. There would be no room for a wife on the desolate frontier where this assignment would take him. Despite their impending separation and worries about each other, Jamey and Carin had a grand time during the week. Every moment of the week was pure joy. They were together for meals, socializing with their parents, dances, and moonlit walks.

Other Friends

Soso and the Lummises had a hectic trip. They had no time to linger. Averaging an astounding 37 miles a day, they made the 300-mile trip in only eight days. Elizabeth was a precocious child, but, like any other six-year-old, she did not travel well. This was her first long trip, and she wanted to see everything along the way. All the travelers were tired by the time they reached their hotel at Buttermilk Falls, just outside the gate of the Academy.

While Soso and the Lummises didn't share in Jamey's nightlife during the last days of the week, they did have an enjoyable time touring the Academy grounds. The parades were Sara's favorite. She was amazed at the precision and discipline of these young soldiers. The cadets were all polite and respectful. They were handsome and intimidating in their uniforms. Since Jamey was a Company Commander, he was one of the cadets-in-charge of the parade formations. Sara Lummis and all visitors from Sodus Bay were proud of Jamey Davis in his role as leader of the other cadets. In their opinion, he had become a successful young man and would do good things for their country.

The graduation ceremony on July 1 was truly spectacular. One by one, all 37 senior cadets were called forward to receive their graduation salute and commission in the United States Army. Jamey was the second one called forward, since the order was determined by class rank. It was a spectacular day in the Hudson Valley. The bright sun illuminated the magnificent landscape and manicured grounds of the Academy. Nature and the Academy were dressed in their finest. All present that day would remember the moving ceremony for the rest of their lives.

Jamey knew that he would miss his classmates, his professors, and his alma mater. But it was time to move on and put his training and education into practice. After the ceremony, Major Thayer and Captain Davies made a special point to stop and talk with Jamey and his family.

"Lieutenant Davis grew up on the frontier and is now headed to duty on the real frontier. Best of luck in your rugged duties, but be sure to take a mathematics book along. We'd love to have you back here teaching some-day," spoke Charles Davies, who as Mathematics Department Head had to select his faculty from the officers in the Army. Professor Davies knew that Jamey was the best and wanted him back on the faculty as soon as he could get him.

"Yes, sir. I have several mathematics books packed for the trip. I may even try to teach those westerners some math while I'm out there," Jamey responded to his mentor and teacher. Since Jamey already knew how rewarding teaching would be, he hoped that someday he would have the opportunity to come back and teach under Captain Davies.

Sylvanus Thayer also wished him well. "We expect good things from you, Lieutenant Davis. Keep the peace on that wild frontier and keep your-self healthy. Our Army needs smart soldiers like you."

"Yes, sir," Jamey snapped out in his usual response to a superior offi-cer. The West Point spit and polish was well ingrained. "Thank you for all your help."

Then Thayer and Davies shook hands with Jamey and all his guests, thanking them for coming to graduation and supporting Jamey's efforts as a cadet.

Journeys Continue

Soso, the Lummis family, and the Davis family, all left West Point on July 2 in a joyous mood. They headed down to New York City to see Ben Lummis. The steamship was crowded as it slowly but surely chugged the 45 miles down the Hudson. Ben had been unable to get away for Jamey's graduation, but he was waiting at the dock when his visitors arrived that evening.

Jamey's departure from West Point was quite different. He left later on the same day, but headed by steamboat to the north. He was at a loss for words as he tried to say good-bye to Carin. They had promised to write each other often, but no other promises were made. Both of them realized the other's emotions. However, nothing could be done. Jamey was now a Lieutenant in the Army, and the Army was sending him away. Carin understood and could only hope to reestablish their relationship when, and if, her loved one ever returned.

It was an emotional departure. Jamey's eyes filled with tears as he gently kissed Carin for the last time and climbed aboard the steamship. He was leaving behind the woman that he loved and starting a career that he had worked very hard to achieve. As he rode in the boat up the river, he dreamed about a perfect life that contained both Carin and the Army. For now, though, reality meant that he was headed on a long journey westward along the Genesee Road—up the Hudson, west the length of the Erie Canal, overland across Ohio and Indiana, and down the Mississippi River to St. Louis. He wondered what the new frontier was like and what he would be doing in the months and years ahead.

In some ways, Jamey felt fortunate to obtain such an exciting and challenging assignment. Only a few of his classmates were headed west where the real military action was occurring. Ever since the Louisiana Purchase bought the western territories from France in 1804, the US Army had played roles in exploring the territory, taming the west for commerce and navigation, and trying, often unsuccessfully, to keep peace between the settlers and the Indians. Lewis and Clark had completed their famous expedition twenty years before, but little had changed except the scope of the problems. Now there were more settlers, more businesses, and more troubles with the Indians. Duty out west was a challenge, and Jamey hoped he was ready for it.

Several of his classmates were staying at West Point to teach cadets for a year as assistant professors. Jamey had already experienced teaching as an upper-class cadet. While it was something he liked and did well, he knew that he was ready for something else. For now he wanted to taste the real Army. Others of the new Second Lieutenants were on the way to the artillery school in the garrison at Fort Monroe, Virginia. While Jamey enjoyed his artillery training, he had decided on engineering for his branch. One lucky classmate, Tom Hunter, had been assigned to Sacketts Harbor. Jamey would have loved that assignment, but it wasn't offered to him. There he was on the steamboat with only four others of his class heading west to the new frontier. There was real Army work to be done.

Jamey and his former roommate, Horace Smith, were going to Jefferson Barracks, Missouri. The other three officers were headed to even more remote frontier outposts—Fort Snelling, Minnesota; Fort Atkinson, Iowa; and Fort Towson in the Indian Territories. Travel routes to the frontier west were still limited. Jamey could go the northern route, which is what he was taking—west on the Erie Canal, overland through Ohio and Indiana, then south on the Mississippi River. Or he could go the southern route—starting at Baltimore and going overland on the rugged Cumberland Road all the way to St. Louis. The Cumberland Road was rough and steep, and not as fully developed as the northern passage. The Erie Canal was still the most reliable and comfortable route to the West.

Jamey figured that he would get to see and meet Indians from the tribes of the plains. He hoped they would be like Soso. However, he knew that was unlikely. There were serious Indian-related problems on the frontier. He hoped his relationship with Soso would help him understand the Indians he encountered. He planned to show as much compassion as he could for their plight. In his heart, he realized that the United States was building an empire at the expense of the Native American. If it was going to happen, he hoped to be there to show compassion and understanding to the Indians whose lives were being adversely affected. His primary duty was to keep the peace, not to wage war.

New York City

Elizabeth Lummis was amazed by all the activity at the dockside. Bright lights and busy streets were new to the young girl. Even Soso, who had lived in New York City for almost a year eight years before, and William and Sarah Lummis, who were raised in Philadelphia, were impressed with the growth, style, and pace of the huge city. New York City was lively and bustling. The Davises had definitely never seen anything like it. Jim, Karen, and Susan were excited to visit the city where huge oceangoing ships docked every day of the year.

They were staying in the Hotel Franklin, which was in the center of the city, near Ben's bank and apartment. Their first night was spent resting from the boat trip. They would need their rest for the next two days of activity.

After their rest, they visited Ben's bank and other businesses in the area. Then they saw the oceangoing ships, shipyards, museums, and beaches. They ate at fancy restaurants. They met Ben's girlfriend, Carrie, whose father managed the bank where Ben worked. Everyone they met liked Ben, and he was off to an auspicious start in the highly competitive New York City banking world. Sara and William Lummis were proud of their son.

Everyone in the Sodus Bay contingent was tired by the time they began the trip back home. Luckily, it was a restful, uneventful trip. Even the rambunctious Elizabeth was more sedate on the return trip. They were able to take their time and arrived back home on Sodus Bay on July 23, 1825.

Higher Education

The Lummises arrived back home just in time to receive an invitation to attend a ceremony at another college. This time, it was Dr. Lummis who would participate in the festivities. He was invited to give a presentation at the chartering ceremony of Geneva College. Since he had helped the college's founder, Reverend John Henry Hobart, initiate the first classes for the college three years previously and had contributed money for its first academic building, he was considered a special guest. He gladly accepted the invitation and prepared his speech.

Dr. Lummis and Soso had just enough time to make a late night boat trip to Canada. All the traveling had put a strain on several activities that the two men were involved in. The Underground Railroad had slowed considerably, and this worried them. Hired worker Ron Johnson had kept the railroad running while the two men were away. This was a big risk, since Ron didn't have the same contacts or experience that William had for protecting himself and his passengers.

For Soso, this was a special trip to Canada, for it had been a year since he had last seen Betty. After unloading the twelve anxious, but relieved and finally free, fugitive slaves at York harbor, Soso and Mac spent the day with Betty, as Dr. Lummis made business arrangements. Betty was as pretty, personable, and caring as ever. Her happiness and enthusiasm were contagious. Everyone gained energy and renewed their spirits when they were with Betty. This was especially true for Soso. He loved her, but there was still no way that they could be together. Life wasn't fair, but then as an Indian and a black living in the whites' world, Soso and Betty had known that all their lives.

Betty's family of four adopted boys was special. The boys were grow-ing up to be successful young men even though they didn't have a father in the house. All four had part-time jobs in the afternoons and attended school in the mornings. Betty was the schoolteacher, so she knew her boys' needs and personalities quite well. She had developed each of them to their potential. She was proud of them, and they were equally proud of her. They all liked it when Soso came to visit, especially when he brought Mac along.

Geneva College

The 25-mile trip to Geneva was short and simple compared to the fam-ily's previous trip to West Point and New York City. Soso accompanied William, Sarah, and Elizabeth Lummis to Geneva on a cool, bright, fall day. The school grounds of Geneva College were small and meager compared to West Point or Columbia. However, the landscape overlooking Seneca Lake rivaled the beauty of the Hudson River. Several speakers addressed the need for schools of higher education in America. Others, like founder Reverend Hobart, addressed the country's religious needs, since Geneva College was an Episcopal school. Dr. Lummis particularly emphasized the need for education in mathematics and science and held West Point's cur-riculum as a model for consideration and Jamey Davis's success as an example of the power of higher education. Overall, it was a moving cere-mony. Even though Congress had disapproved President Adams' request for funding for the school, there was officially a new school of higher edu-cation in America, Geneva College, and the country would be better off because of it.

After the ceremony, Dr. Lummis, Soso, and Reverend Hobart discussed the situation of higher education in America. Soso was curious about the curriculum, so he discussed this with the Reverend.

"We hope our students get to study many subjects so they understand the past, the present, and the future. It is difficult to tell exactly what will be needed in the future. The world seems to be changing all the time." Reverend Hobart had thought about this subject. "Our graduates must be ready to tackle our complicated world. They can enter business, govern-ment, or become educators themselves."

Dr. Lummis again emphasized the technical side of education. "Just think, in their lifetime there will be faster, bigger boats and trains. We will probably be able to travel across our country in just days instead of weeks. We might be able to send messages very quickly across extended distances. We must be sure our young people understand these complicated ideas and envision these possibilities. They must study the sciences to really understand what can be done to make our world a better place."

The trip to Seneca Lake brought back fond memories for Soso. Geneva College overlooked the lake of the Senecas in the same manner as his old boyhood perch on the hill near his village overlooked the lake of the Cayugas. The two lakes were just fifteen miles apart and looked nearly identical. The deep, clear blue water filled the long, narrow gorges to make two spectacular lakes. The lakes of the Senecas and Cayugas were the largest of a group of narrow, deep bodies of water, called the Finger Lakes. Some of the smaller lakes also held Indian names—Skaneateles, Owasco, Canandaigua, and Keuka. These names made Soso proud. Some of his Native American heritage would be preserved, as long as these delightful places were called by their Indian names. Soso remembered how as a boy he would watch the canoes slowly work their way up or down the lake. In many ways, his world had changed dramatically over the years of his life—new technologies, the wars, and advances in civilization. However, watching the boats slowly move on Seneca Lake made him realize that some parts of the world had changed very little. Most of the real change that he noticed was with himself.

As always happened in his moments of reflection, the realities of his situation began to invade his thoughts. His father, mother, and grandfather were dead. He no longer lived in a world of Indians; instead, his world was that of the white man. This was the reality of the life that he had chosen. He knew it was what he wanted; he didn't regret his decision. Soso at 45 years of age felt that he understood many of the customs and rules of the white man's world. He vowed to continue to make a difference. He was contented, just as long as he remembered and cherished his past as well as his future.

There were still plenty of things in the white man's world that bothered Soso. Power did not come from strength or wisdom. It was derived from possessions. And power was more important than knowledge, dedication, or loyalty. However, Soso also saw the good side of the white man's world. People were never good or bad; they were always both. There was never black or white, there were shades of gray. Soso no longer sensed this as wrong. This situation allowed everyone to contribute and exist. While there were classes of people in the white man's world, there were no outcasts. Everyone's life and opinion counted for something. That is, if you were white.

Frontier

Jefferson Barracks was hardly a fort or even a barracks. It was located nine miles south of St. Louis and consisted of four log buildings that housed a trading post, guard house, horse barn, and commander's quarters. The rest of the officers and soldiers lived in tents or, sometimes during the winter, right in the city of St. Louis. Jamey didn't mind the accommodations. He had a comfortable cot and a small wood stove in his tent. The winter nights were cold, but he made the most of what he had. He would survive.

St. Louis was the center of the fur trade. The city was located on the Mississippi River for a good reason. Steamboats, which had proven their worth on the frontier as well as along the eastern seaboard, took men out to beaver country and carried back the pelts they acquired. Then the pelts were transported down the long river and eventually back East. Otter and beaver pelts still commanded a hefty sum in Europe. The trappers got a small share, then the traders, shippers, processors, businessmen, and governments all profited from the work of the trappers. Everyone was getting rich from the fur trade, except the Indians, who suddenly lost their way of life as the animals they depended on were depleted and disappeared.

The waterfront of the city was lined with taverns where the trappers and rivermen drank, gambled, and fought. St. Louis was a rough town, filled with tough people, who may be rich, but didn't always care for law and order. The toughest survived; the rest didn't.

Despite its wild side, St. Louis had a peaceful, hardworking community of families. It was also the headquarters for many religious missionaries, and Jamey often met up with them when he visited the Indian villages on the western frontier. There were hints of civilization in St. Louis in the form of such things as newspapers, theaters, bookstores, and hairdressers. Businesses and homes went up in one day, but also sometimes fell completely apart during a strong storm or a drunken brawl. Nothing in St. Louis was made to last in order to accommodate instability and change, the two ever-present characteristics of this unruly city.

The pioneer spirit of Lewis and Clark, who had started their western adventure and exploration from this city, was still present. People still talked about the uncharted, unexplored, and dangerous regions west of the Mississippi. They still talked of the great work done by William Clark and Meriwether Lewis. These two men were heroes to the residents of St. Louis and the frontiersmen who used St. Louis as their base of operations. Meriwether Lewis was dead, but William Clark still lived in St. Louis, working as the U.S. Superintendent of Indian Affairs. Even though many residents of St. Louis were suspicious of Clark's lenient and supportive policies towards Indians, they forgave him and treated him as a hero. It turned out that William Clark was a big help to Jamey. He taught Jamey about life on the frontier and how to provide real help to the Indian people. He helped Jamey learn the customs and languages of the plains Indians.

Jamey and his friend, William Clark, had become very sensitive to the issue of resource conservation and care. Jamey noticed how the trappers were making the same mistakes they had made in the East. They completely devastated the animal populations in their areas and never left a sufficient number to breed for the future supply. The Indians had known about conservation, but the greed of the whites prevented them from seeing the devastating pattern. Despite Jamey's pleas, the trappers continued to over-trap, and then moved on to the next available area once they had completely depleted the population. Eventually, this behavior would cause the extinction of the species and the end of the trappers' livelihood.

There was no organized police force in St. Louis or the frontier West. Often the Army had to intercede to keep minimal peace in the worst parts of the town. Jamey hated going to the waterfront district. Whenever he was there on peace-keeping duty, he had fights to break up and crimes to solve. These were not the reasons that he had become a soldier.

Jamey's primary duty was surveying and mapmaking. Those activities took him out of the barracks and onto the frontier. He and his troops faced numerous challenges in the wilds of the West. The frontiersmen and pioneers were tough and aggressive. Sometimes they tried to cooperate with the Indians, but even minor disagreements often escalated into fatal conflicts. Unfortunately for Jamey, the Army was the only law in the West;

therefore, sometimes he was the law, whether he wanted to be or not. Establishing law and order and performing peacekeeping were challenging, demanding jobs.

Jamey's specific mission was to survey and map the new states of Indiana, Missouri, and Illinois; the southern part of the Minnesota Territory; and the southern and eastern portions of the vast Indian Territory. Some of his work built on the maps of Lewis and Clark. It was helpful having William Clark available whenever Jamey needed guidance. The famous explorer was a friend and mentor to the young Army Lieutenant on his first assignment. Jamey's survey party usually consisted of a sergeant, four enlisted soldiers to operate the instruments, and five more soldiers to guard the party while it worked. The eleven soldiers used three small horse-drawn wagons to carry their equipment and supplies. Sometimes they were away from camp for several weeks at a time. It was tough, dangerous duty, but Jamey enjoyed the challenging work.

Jamey's tent was full of sketches, diagrams, and drafts of his surveys and maps. By the end of his first year at St. Louis, he had produced nearly twenty complete maps of areas of the frontier. Some of his most elaborate maps, containing detailed elevation and vegetation information, were sent back to the Army Headquarters in Washington. They were valuable assets for American military forces. William Clark helped Jamey identify areas with the highest need for mapping. The post commander, Major Grim, kept four of Jamey's maps of the local area in his office to orient himself with the terrain and geography of his region of responsibility. Jamey was using his talents in a good cause—mapping the uncharted West.

Several incidents in the field developed Jamey's other special talent, dealing with Indians. For the most part, the Indians were peaceful and in this vast territory were able to stay away from interference of the whites. Although as more and more whites arrived to claim and settle the vast prairie land, they became bolder and more likely to cause problems with the Indians. The settlers, with approval from the government, were generally following a familiar formula—trade with the Indians, corrupt their lifestyle, anger them, fight them, kill them, and steal their land. It seemed like a natural instinct for the American settlers to keep moving westward and, despite treaties, to push the natives out of the way. No power on Earth could satisfy their hunger for more land. No power could stop them, certainly not the Indians, the Army, or the government in Washington. Frontier greed was sweeping through the western lands, just as it had in the East.

Most of the Indian-white incidents involved disputes over land, live-stock, furs, or game. However, each time Jamey was involved in an incident with Indians, he was able to resolve it without resorting to violence. He patiently explained a compromise position that both sides eventually accepted. Jamey had developed quite a reputation as a peacekeeper. However, compromise and peacemaking weren't the usual military solu-tion procedures on the frontier. Quite often, unnecessary force was used against the Indians to solve the problem and teach them the way of the whites in the West—might makes right.

Jamey and William Clark often discussed the proper role of the Army in this remote area. They agreed that the Army was not using its peace-keeping capabilities very wisely. The commanders had been trained to make war, not to keep peace. This difficult role for the Army was beyond the capabilities and often the desires of most Army commanders. The end results were inevitable. The whites and the Indians would be at war until the Indians surrendered their property, rights, and culture. The whites would eventually rule the West. It was a shame that the Indians would pay such a terrible price for the white man's greed, and, of course, it was an even bigger shame that, in the end, the whites would bear an even bigger burden of guilt and lost opportunity. If these two cultures could only learn to coexist and learn from each other, the country and the world would be much better for everyone.

William Clark told Jamey a story of an incident on the famous 'Corps of Discovery' expedition. "We were camped on the mouth of the Columbia, having reached our destination of the great ocean. We faced three alterna-tives for our winter encampment. We could stay on the north or south banks or move back up the river. There were distinct advantages and dis-advantages for the three courses of action. But one thing was certain: we needed to stay together as a group to survive. Meriwether and I decided to put this decision to a vote, like leaders can and should do in a democracy. So we voted, and everyone cast a vote. While there was discussion about the three choices, there was no discussion over the procedure. All affected by the decision voted, and that included the black man, York, and the Indian woman, Sacajawea. Since we all shared equally in the results of the decision, there was no question that everyone should vote to decide." Jamey would never forget this story of equality and leadership. In Jamey's mind, there was still hope for the Indians and blacks as long as people like William Clark still lived. However, there seemed to be few men like William Clark on the frontier.

Jamey enjoyed seeing his West Point classmate, Horace Smith, often, since Horace was the supply officer for his post. Horace's position provided a nice, warm corner of the trading post for his sleeping quarters. For the most part, Horace was too busy ordering food and supplies to go to the field. However, sometimes he would accompany Jamey out on a survey party. Horace was as accomplished at surveying as Jamey, and the two of them made an effective team. One thing for sure, Horace always kept Jamey supplied with good quality paper, pens, ink, and pencils. It helped to have a friend in supply.

Jamey wished his love life had gone as well as his professional career. As promised, he and Carin had exchanged letters for the first few months. However, as he had gotten busier and traveled more, his letter writing diminished. Subsequently, Carin's letter writing also had decreased. He owed her too many letters to count. Now, they were fortunate to exchange letters once a month. Jamey had known that their separation would be difficult. Now he also realized that, despite their love, Carin couldn't wait forever. It was not the way he wanted it. If only he could see her and explain.

Civilization and Bankers

In some ways, New York City was surprisingly similar to St. Louis. It had its bad areas where crime was prevalent and people were out of control. Fortunately, New York had its business and residential areas, too, where what is considered more civil behavior was found.

Ben lived in a well-furnished apartment close to his bank. He had many conveniences of modern civilization. His meals were prepared for him. He had effective coal-fire heat, running water, and oil-fueled lighting lamps. His furniture was both elegant and functional. Compared to Jamey, Ben lived in luxury.

His job was to manage the biggest business accounts held by the bank. He supervised several bookkeepers who helped him keep ledgers and detailed records for these accounts. Ben visited the executives of these businesses quite often. The corporate offices were tall, elaborate buildings. It seemed that the more money his clients made, the more they appreciated and entertained Ben. He was often wined and dined by the richest, most powerful men in America. Ben got to meet and know the city's leaders in business, government, and finance.

It was an exciting time for Ben, but it also had its frustrations. Several of his personal relationships bothered him. He had no true friends in New York City, as he had in Troupville. Everyone was either too busy or too overbearing. The businessmen based decisions strictly on money and power and never on the benefits to the people involved. It was a highly competitive, corrupt system in which he was reluctantly playing a role. He didn't like this part of his job, so he tried not to think about it. However, that was difficult, and Ben was often depressed over his situation. He found out first hand that success and satisfaction didn't necessarily go hand-in-hand.

Disappointment

It had been several months since the letter from the President had been delivered to Soso. There was still no invitation as promised to an assembly on Indian affairs from the President. Soso had written letters to the Tadodaho and Red Jacket about this delay. The Tadodaho advised patience. Red Jacket suggested Soso to go to Washington immediately and demand action. Soso took the middle road by writing the President to ask about the status of the proposed assembly.

The Iroquois had heard the bad news about their native brothers in the new state of Florida. The Seminoles had suffered the worst from the interference and greed of the whites. First, in 1817, General Andrew Jackson had attacked the Seminoles and the black people who were living with them in Florida. While Spain owned Florida it was too weak to do anything. The war motivated Spain to sell Florida to the United States in 1821. Many Indians lost their lives during the war, which was started because run-away slaves had escaped from plantations and hid out with the Seminole tribes.

New President Adams was trying to help the Seminoles and another beleaguered tribe, the Cherokee, but politicians in the state of Georgia were defying him. The state passed laws to force closure of reservations and expulsion of Indians out of the state. Unfortunately, President Adams seemed to be losing the argument. Soso and the other Iroquois leaders were afraid that if Georgia was successful, the same thing could happen in New

York, although they realized that, in many ways, it had already happened. However, in New York there still were some Indians on reservations who enjoyed their lives on their native lands and hoped to live their lives in traditional Indian ways in peaceful co-existence with the whites.

Soso's letter to the President was answered with an invitation for his delegation to come to Washington at the same time that the Seminole delegation was to appear for a special assembly. Soso feared that direct association with the Seminoles could hurt their cause. However, he had waited for this opportunity and felt that a unified front from two tribes might be helpful. He decided to accept the invitation on behalf of the Iroquois and go to Washington to see the American President.

Mission

On July 1, 1826, Silent Turtle, Red Jacket, and Soso met in Syracuse and started their trek to the nation's capital. Red Jacket was especially eager to see the President, because he had recently been stripped of his powers as chief. Red Jacket was the leader of the Iroquois non-Christian alliance. As such, he had many enemies and had many confrontations with other chiefs and government overseers. Previously, he had been recognized as a powerful and popular Iroquois Chief. Now the Christian element in the tribe was trying to usurp his powers and discredit him and his followers. Soso, on the other hand, had always avoided mixing religion and politics, so he was not involved in this controversy. Through this trip to Washington, Red Jacket planned to get the controversy resolved once and for all by appealing directly to the President.

When they arrived in Washington, they were escorted to a small military barracks where the Seminole delegation was staying. They got to meet their counterparts from the southern tribe. Discussions between the two groups of Indians lasted well into the night. It was very interesting for Soso. He had never met Indians from the South. For the most part they all spoke English, although one Seminole chief used a black man from the tribe as a translator. As the discussions continued late into the night, they found that there was substantial similarity between the tribes. Both had suffered at the hands of the whites, but both groups also saw the benefits and inevitability of compromising with the white man's world, just as long as their own culture survived. They were all experienced warriors in the battle of cultures that was raging in America, but they all refused to have their culture conquered by the enemy forces of the whites. Soso was especially impressed with the Seminole chief, Tuckose Emathla, who was called John Hicks by the whites. Tuckose was both wise and determined. Soso could tell immediately that Tuckose was a strong, enlightened leader.

On the next day, the Indian delegations met with Vice President Calhoun and other government officials. The white politicians explained that the United States wanted the Indian tribes to own their land and have the freedom to make their own decisions. However, they also explained that the United States government could not and did not speak for all white men or all governments. The states and other governments could also make laws and take action against the wishes of both the Indians and the federal government.

The following day, the Indians had their opportunity to speak. The three Iroquois and several Seminoles, including Tuckose Emathla, talked to an assembly of congressmen and government officials. Each speaker told of unfair treatment and pointed toward the opportunity for both Indians and whites to learn from each other. Tuckose gave a profound oration about the Indian philosophy of land. Land was to be shared by all creatures, just as the air, the water, the sun and the sky. He explained that all parts of the earth are sacred. But the whites could never understand, despite their intelligence and dominance over the Indians. Most people there wanted a friendly, cooperative relationship to exist between the native and the newly arrived Americans. Somehow they had to make this happen.

The venerable and articulate Red Jacket summed up the Indians' plight by giving his own version of the history of White-Indian relations. "We first knew you as a feeble plant that wanted a little earth on which to grow. We gladly gave it to you. Afterward, when we could have trod you under our feet, we gladly watered and protected you. Now you have grown to a mighty tree, whose top reaches the clouds and whose branches overspread the whole land. Whilst we, who were the tall pine tree of the forest, have become a feeble plant and need your protection in order to grow again. Will you do this for us?"

Among the dignitaries present at the assembly were Congressmen Davy Crockett and Sam Houston and Senator Andrew Jackson. Soso had tremendous admiration for the care and respect displayed by Crockett and Houston. Both men understood the Indians' problems and were willing to do something about them. Soso's feelings for Jackson were just the opposite. Jackson seemed to trivialize the problems, while rudely making fun of the Indians' situation. The Seminoles had good reason for their hatred of Jackson. He had led the military campaign that had killed many of their fellow tribesmen. Jackson showed no remorse for the killings or feelings for the plight of the Indians. He openly stated his disdain for Indians and his desire to rid the country of the evil and savage redman. Soso didn't understand Jackson's hatred, but he would still try somehow to convince Jackson to change.

Part of their last day in Washington was spent with President Adams, who thanked the group for their information but did not seem optimistic about solving their problems. Soso could tell that the President was frustrated over his lack of power to prevent the mistreatment of Indians. The President could not control the prejudice of the people or even the government's imperialistic policies of the western expansion. Soso finally understood how even the most powerful leader was nearly powerless to influence how individuals and groups outside of his control acted. The white chief had the same problems that the Indian chiefs had. Soso realized that overall this was a good situation and the way democracy was supposed to work, but sometimes progress was impeded by the politics of democracy and the misguided actions of small groups of people. Once again, Soso saw the workings of the gray world of the whites, while most Indians continued to live a simpler, more definitive culture

After the meeting with the President, Red Jacket met alone with the President about his removal from tribal office. In this case, the President was able to act quickly, and he appointed Red Jacket an official Iroquois chief in the eyes of the United States government. At least Red Jacket returned home with a sense of accomplishment and official government recognition.

Indians of both tribes returned home to share the feelings of frustration held by the President. The problem was bigger than convincing just one man or one group of people. The Indians had to reeducate the entire country of whites as to their willingness to contribute, their need for freedoms and rights, and the futility of prejudice and discrimination. While Soso was frustrated, he was not going to give up. There was work to be done to gain the respect and understanding of whites, and they had the powerful and caring leader, President Adams, on their side.

Lisa Beth

Elizabeth Lummis was a remarkable little girl. In some ways, she was a typical eight-year-old—rambunctious, inquisitive, and energetic. She enjoyed the out-of-doors. She especially liked fishing and sailing with Soso. She called her favorite fishing companion, "Uncle" Soso. He affectionately called her "Lisa Beth."

She loved animals and was particularly fond of Soso's dog Mac. She enjoyed taking Mac on long walks and throwing sticks in the water for him to retrieve. Soso called Mac a Sodus Bay Retriever, for that seemed to be both his breed and his calling. Mac was tireless when it came to retrieving things thrown onto the bay. Soso was especially thrilled at the way Mac brought back the ducks and geese that he and Jim had shot. Mac was known as a special pet around Float Bridge and Troupville. He was equally well known for being a superb water dog that could find and bring back ducks in the foulest weather and over the greatest distances. But Elizabeth thought of Mac as a friend, and she played with him as often as she could.

In other ways, Elizabeth was quite a bit different than most eight-year-olds. She was an avid reader and could read just about any book found in her father's library. She particularly liked Cooper's *Pioneers*. Stories, like that one about Indians, were her favorite. Soso also gave her a perspective on the story in the *Pioneers* that she had not considered. She was a deep thinker. Elizabeth also wrote very well. She would often compose short stories and poems about her friends and family. Soso was both her favorite topic and the most avid reader of her works. She often gave him presents of her writings about him or other Indians. Everyone knew that Elizabeth was an exceptionally precocious child. Her personality seemed to combine the strong characteristics of her parents. She was studious and brilliant like her father and strong-willed and energetic like her mother.

Sodus Bay hadn't changed much over the past several years. Some growth had occurred in a few spots on the shore. Lummisville continued to grow as the workers on the Lummis farm bought their own land and built houses near the farm. Troupville continued its slow, steady growth. As was usually the case, new families arrived, while some old residents left. Usually the departees moved farther west to find more land and fewer people. To many people, this region of New York was no longer the frontier or the land of opportunity. The Shakers had continued to develop their religious community on the south side of the bay. They had over 85 residents on the homestead. These people had become part of the Sodus Bay community.

Celebration

The biggest change during the year was a name change. Troupville was officially renamed Sodus Point, a name that residents had used for quite some time. The Davises, Lummises, and Soso often had used the name Sodus Point, partially because of their association with West Point. In their minds, the two locations, West Point and Sodus Point, were somewhat similar in form and beauty. One place always reminded them of the other. The main reason for the name, "Sodus Point," was simply that the village really was on a point of land on the west side of Sodus Bay, so it was natural and accurate to call it a point. The name Sodus Point became official in 1826, and the residents celebrated with a ceremony and party. The post office, still under the care of William Wickham, couldn't change its name until December. Nevertheless, the ceremony declaring the name change official took place at the July Fourth celebration.

Soso was proud to share his name with the bay and the village. Most people, even his closest friends, did not realize the name Soso was short for Sosoenodus, son of the silvery waters, and that Sodus was the white man's word for Osoenodus, the silvery waters. It was with great pride that Soso held the secret that his name, the nurturing waters of Sodus Bay, and beautiful village of Sodus Point, all came from the Indian word for the silvery waters that everyone loved.

It was a special year for the citizens of the United States of America. The fiftieth anniversary of American independence was being celebrated around the nation. Settlers from all around the area flocked to Sodus Point to take part in the Independence Day festivities. The entire village was crowded with people who had come from miles away. The celebration was much like the one for the 25th anniversary. The first day's activities started with a parade through the village and ended with a torch and fireworks display. There were contests and games of all kinds for men, women, and children. Once again the shooting contest involved Soso and Jim as the primary contenders. Soso didn't disappoint. As expected, he won the shooting competition for the twentieth time. The runner-up was also no surprise. Even though he was getting old for this sport, 56-year-old Jim finished a close second and almost beat out 46-year-old Soso. The only time that Jim had won the contest in the past was when Soso was unable to compete.

"You must be slipping. I almost had you this year. Just three more hits and your streak would have been over," Jim teased Soso about the margin of victory.

"I know you practiced more than ever this year. But since I had to work so hard for it, this turkey will taste better than ever. You and Karen wouldn't want to come over tomorrow for some of this bird with some special fixings? I've been working on my turkey recipe and am ready to try it out on the runner-up." Soso was happy that he had won, but happier yet that the annual turkey feast would take place once again. Soso enjoyed having his friends over to dinner.

"You know we wouldn't miss it. Karen has a pie and some delicious rolls already baked. We'll be over to help you cook the bird and enjoy the day." Jim was as excited as Soso. This annual turkey feast was tremendous fun for Soso and the Davises.

The celebration went on for three days. The third day featured the horserace from north of Lummisville all around the bay to Sodus Point. The twenty entries in this year's race included old-timers like Byram Greene, Ralph and Joe Sheldon, and James Pollock, but this year's race was dominated by newcomers. The first women—actually 12-year-old Susan Davis— ever to enter the race came in second. Susan Davis took after her brother Jamey. She was a strong, athletic girl. The winner was a 43-year-old distinguished visitor from New York City, General Joseph Swift. General Swift, the first graduate of West Point and a hero during the War of 1812 for his leadership at Sacketts Harbor, had heard stories of the July Fourth celebrations on Sodus Bay from Soso, Jamey, and others. The horserace had always sounded especially exciting to this rugged outdoorsman, so this year he decided to vacation in Sodus Point during the celebration and compete. He was retired from the Army and serving as the port surveyor and manager of New York harbor. He stayed with the Davis family during his visit to Sodus Point. Amazingly, he had brought his own horse all the way from New York City, just to compete in this exciting race.

The winner was apparent from the start. General Swift's horse and riding ability were far superior to those of the other entrants. He took the lead at the start and steadily expanded it to the end. He enjoyed himself immensely and won a few bets from some of the local men who figured such a fancy, fine-bred horse couldn't stand up to the rigors of a 25-mile cross-country race. They were wrong. This horse was bred for endurance— to face the rigors and challenges of the Army's cavalry. Likewise, its rider was trained to face these same challenges. In this case, the rugged frontier had something to learn from an expert from civilized society.

The race for second place was closer. James Pollock was a fine horseman and rode the horse that had won the previous year's race. He was definitely the local favorite. However, Susan Davis, who was four feet, nine inches tall and weighed only 85 pounds, about half the size of the other entrants, had an advantage. Her light weight compensated for her lack of experience. At the end of the race, her fresher, less burdened horse, out sprinted James Pollock's horse to take second place. James was third, with the rest of the field trailing by a wide margin.

Frontier Life

Jefferson Barracks had grown and improved during the two years that Jamey had been there. Several more buildings had been built, including cabins for the officers and a barracks for the soldiers. Life in the fort was actually pleasant at times. Jamey had been saving much of the money that he had earned through his Lieutenant's pay. He only spent as much as the soldiers, who earned just $5 per month. Most of their money was spent by the end of the monthly payday buying whiskey and gambling. Jamey carefully spent his money on clothes, books, and his own supply of chart-making equipment.

Jamey still enjoyed his duties, although at times it seemed as if there were more headaches and problems than enjoyment. The soldiers were a mixed bag. Some of them were recent immigrants; hard-working, family men trying to get a good start on life. Others were criminals, drunks, or misfits. It was a rough job molding such a rag-tag group into an effective military unit. It took tough, hard leaders who weren't shy at imposing discipline and meting out punishment. However, once the members of a unit accepted one another, their leader, and the Army way of life, they could do more than Jamey had ever imagined. For him, the frustration of dealing with a bad soldier was temporary, because soon enough the bad soldier either reformed or was washed out of the Army.

During these years, the Army was taking an active role as a buffer between the white men and the Indians. A long string of small forts kept a military presence across the frontier. At various times during his two years of service, Jamey visited Fort Jessup, Louisiana; Fort Towson and Fort Gibson in the Indian Territories; Fort Swelling, in the Minnesota Territory; and Fort Atkinson at Council Bluffs in Iowa. The Army was beginning to build a network of trails and roads to link these outposts and many others.

These extremely isolated forts were completely self-sufficient. Soldiers there farmed, raised cattle, and kept horses, along with trying to keep the peace.

Jamey found that most Indians he met shared the same sense of values as Soso. In general, he concluded that the plains Indians were similar to those in eastern tribes. The western Indians seemed more nomadic and needed to roam on plenty of land. They were accomplished horsemen. It was obvious to Jamey that the plains Indians had a distinct advantage over the Army soldiers in the area of horsemanship. Most of the Army soldiers were infantrymen, who only occasionally had the chance to ride a horse. The Indians raised finer horses and rode better than the white soldiers. In almost every way, the Indians were individually superior soldiers to the whites. They were better conditioned, better trained, better led, and far superior warriors in both the cavalry and infantry. However, the organization, structure, logistics, communication, size, and technology of the American Army gave it the advantage over the Indian forces in the battles and wars fought on the plains of the West.

Fortunately, Jamey never had to fight in a full-fledged battle. There were incidents in which a few wild, drunken braves harassed Jamey's survey party and had to be chased away. Jamey had to shoot and kill an Indian who had single-handedly attacked a small wagon train that he and his fellow soldiers were guarding. The Indian was probably drunk, but he was ready to kill an innocent woman. There had been no choice. Nevertheless, this incident was tough on Jamey's emotions, and he tried hard to forget about it. He had killed a man, and it bothered him to think about what had happened.

He preferred to remember all the pleasant and good-natured Indians that he had met. As the leader of the survey party, Jamey had the opportunity to meet with chiefs of many tribes to explain his purpose and ask permission to travel across their lands. Jamey met Chief Oshkosh of the Menominee tribe in Wisconsin. He had numerous meetings with the Chippewa, Hole-in-the-Day, who happily escorted Jamey's party north to Lake Superior. Jamey even met the eminent Pawnee chief Petalesharo, who had sincere respect for human life and sought lasting peace between Indians and whites. Jamey also met up with many of the frontier white men who were blazing trails and taming the western wilderness. Peter Ogden led Jamey on his longest expedition, all the way to the Great Salt Lake. Jim

Bridger, William Ashley, Tex Scudder, and William Sublette were among the frontiersmen who met up with Jamey either in St. Louis or further west in the field.

Jamey's toughest time was with the hard-bitten frontiersmen, the greedy trappers, and the foolhardy settlers, who had no respect for the law or Indian treaties. Sometimes, it seemed as if these men went out of their way to provoke Indians. There was still plenty of land, and usually the confrontations with Indians could have been easily avoided. However, trappers and hunters would get drunk or get the Indians drunk, and a fight would inevitably result.

The fur trappers lived an extremely rough life. They were usually in the wilds for eleven months of the year. Then they would come out of the wilderness with their furs during the annual fur rendezvous. During this period, they would sell their fur pelts, collecting as much as $2000 in a good year. Then they would re-provision, buying flour, clothes, ammunition, and new traps. With the rest of the money they would carouse, gamble, and drink. Finally, exhausted and broke, they would return to the wilds for another perilous year of trapping. Jamey did his best to stay away from the fur rendezvous. It was best for those trying to keep the peace to stay out of the way during that wild time of the year when the laws of the land were completely ignored.

It was with mixed feelings that, after two years, Jamey left his assignment at Jefferson Barracks. In the summer of 1827, he was reassigned eastward to continue the survey and map work of the Coast and Geodetic Survey along the eastern seaboard. His new headquarters would be in the nation's capital. He had to prepare himself for a dramatic change in lifestyle. That summer he bid farewell to his friends, colleagues, and soldiers of the West, and headed back East.

Doctor's Orders

For the first time in his life, Soso felt tired, old, and unable to work. He was 46 years old, and he had been very sick during most of the winter. He had lost strength and energy during the illness. There was plenty for him to do during the spring after the ice had left the bay. It was usually his busiest time of the year. Boats needed to be launched and cared for. Crops needed to be planted and nurtured. A half-built knock-about boat in his shop was promised for delivery to Ralph Sheldon by July 1. He also wanted to write letters to the Iroquois tribal leaders to continue to promote their cause. However, he was just too sick to do any of these tasks. He and William Lummis, who was 22 years older than Soso, had always planned to grow old together on the shores of the bay they loved. Now, it seemed to Soso that he had become the older of the two men. Luckily, Soso had Mac to keep him company. Mac sensed that his companion needed extra care. He was always there for Soso, even though at the age of ten, Mac, too, was slowing down.

William and Sara Lummis became concerned about Soso when Elizabeth told them of his condition. During his years as farmer, father, and underground railroad leader, William had always doctored the sick in Sodus Point, Maxwell, Lummisville, and Float Bridge. He would travel for miles and spend days doctoring, if that was what was needed. This time, he carried his medicine bag on a short walk to his neighbor's house. He found Soso too tired to come to the front door. Soso was running a fever. Dr. Lummis hardly recognized the weak, anemic Indian. Ignoring Soso's refusal, the doctor thoroughly examined him. Soso's knees and elbows were severely swollen and sore. While he couldn't be sure, Dr. Lummis believed Soso was suffering from rheumatism.

Dr. Lummis covered Soso in blankets and made him promise to stay in bed. Then he went back home to ask for help from Sara and Elizabeth. They put together a schedule: one of the three of them would stay with Soso at all times. He had Sara prepare meals of milk and vegetables, supplemented by his own special prescription of mineral water. He remembered how his mentor, Dr. Benjamin Rush, had taught him to treat rheumatism. Dr. Lummis had no idea how long it would take for Soso to recover. However, he was confident that his once-strong Indian friend would eventually overcome the disease and resume his normal life.

Recovery

It turned out that Soso was bedridden for about three more weeks. During that time, one of the three Lummises was always at his bedside. The amazing girl, Elizabeth, read numerous stories to him. Their favorite was James Cooper's newly published *Last of the Mohicans*. That book was the result of the research Cooper had done while staying with Soso. Much of

James's information on Indians had been obtained from discussions with Soso. The story made Soso happy. Knowing why Cooper had written the story the way he had, Soso understood and enjoyed even the sad and violent parts. Soso and Elizabeth knew the entire story by heart.

During this time, Elizabeth was also learning French, so, together with Soso, she spent time during those three weeks studying French vocabulary from a book that she had borrowed from Jamey Davis. She enjoyed learning, and languages came easily for her.

The bright girl was always full of questions for Soso. "How do Indians know where to fish and where to hunt?" she asked.

"The same way whites do. By learning nature's ways, and caring enough to pay attention and remember." Soso knew what she meant but had to remind her that the Indians weren't any different than the whites. "I know the depth and forage base of almost every place on this bay. I know that sea trout don't feed in the shady area along the shore during this time of year. But your father knows that, as well. There is no special sense that only Indians have, just knowledge that can learned by anyone who really wants to. Desire, enthusiasm, and hard work are the ingredients of success."

"Do Indians have books about their history and facts about their people?" Lisa Beth continued her questioning.

"No. The books of the whites are far superior to our oral history. We have forgotten so many things that have happened to our people. If Indians had books like those of the whites, there would be great wisdom for all in our world to learn." Soso answered. "Be thankful that you have written words and books to read. We can all learn from one another. Books and written words have made your people strong and smart." These question and answer sessions would last for hours.

By the middle of June, Soso was his old self again. He had regained his strength and energy. He was behind in his work, but he figured that by August 1, Ralph Sheldon would have his new boat. He spent the next month and a half making sure that this would happen along with strengthening his body and enjoying his return to good health. Soso thanked his doctor and the Lummis family for helping during his time of need. His friends had been a blessing during the hard times he had just experienced.

True to his word, Soso launched the knock-about onto Sodus Bay on August 1, 1827. This boat was as well made as his others. The fleet of boats made by Soso not only dominated the boats in use on Sodus Bay but also plied the waters of the entire south shore of Lake Ontario. They were distinct enough in shape and color that boating experts could spot a Soso-built boat from hundreds of yards away.

It wasn't until late fall that Soso returned his attention to the plight of his Indian brothers and sisters living on reservations. He wrote to the tribal chiefs. He wanted to attend the next council meeting to solicit their support in getting other tribes to pull together with the Iroquois to put up a united front against mistreatment by the governments of the whites.

For the most part Soso's letters went unanswered. It seemed to him that the whites had effectively won their prolonged war against the Indians, by dividing the Indian nations. They managed to keep giving small amounts of food, whiskey, and shelter to the Indians, and many Indians seemed to be willing to give up their freedom and their way of life in exchange for these temporary conveniences.

This realization was a blow to Soso. He had held out hope for the possibility that the two cultures would blend to form a stronger, richer way of life. He realized now that the whites' way of life would eventually dominate and overpower that of the Indians. There was little hope for the long-term survival of his people's culture. However, he still hoped to influence and teach whites some of the strong points of the Indian culture, such as the proper care and nurturing of the earth and her living creatures, the strengths of family and community, and the fulfillment of the responsibilities that come with freedom. Soso would never give up fighting for these values and educating those who would listen.

Big City Blues

Ben's life had become truly miserable. He was suffering in both his job and his personal life. The greed of big city business had taken its toll on Ben's good nature and ethics. The banking and business communities of New York City were full of corruption—swindlers took advantage of laborers, customers, and governments. Ben was convinced that he was working for the finest bank in the city, but it still was unpleasant. Financially, he was doing fine. He had accumulated substantial wealth. Socially, he was miserable. After work, he would hide in his apartment, not wanting to see his corrupt associates or clients any more than he had to. He needed a change, and the best his bank could offer him was a similar position with the bank's office in Philadelphia. It was a smaller bank. There was less of an opportunity for advancement. The pay was lower. Realizing that this could make him happier, Ben gladly took the new job.

By the end of September, he had moved all his belongings into an apartment in Philadelphia. He started work in the small accounts division of the bank under the supervision of George Willig. Immediately, Ben's disposition began to improve. He had always liked Philadelphia. It wasn't as crowded or busy as New York. His job was new, different, and occasionally exciting. In managing small accounts, he didn't have to confront as much corruption and greed. He got to see people from all walks of life. Ben was a changed, revitalized man.

He also started getting out and enjoying life again. He toured the city's sites and frequented museums and libraries. He visited his mother and father's old friends and relatives. Sara Lummis was so excited that her son was moving to the city where she grew up that she and Elizabeth planned to visit him in the spring. She wanted to make sure he was happy in his new job.

Ben's new supervisor was a kind, caring gentleman from a well-established Philadelphia family. George Willig took good care of his employees. Ben got to meet George's family and took immediate liking toward them.

Homecoming

Jamey's trip east was like swimming against the current. Most travelers were headed westward to the new promise land. As Jamey met people along the way, they often asked him about St. Louis and other points along the frontier. They were all excited and eager to get a new start on life. Jamey knew firsthand the hardships that they would face and wished them good fortune. They would need it.

Jamey had decided to return to Sodus Point to see his family before traveling to Washington. His arrival was celebrated by a grand party at the hotel. Almost everyone in Sodus Point came by the party to welcome Lieutenant Jamey Davis back from his adventures on the western frontier. Jim and Karen were proud of their son, and the whole community shared in that pride. It was a jubilant celebration. Food and drink were plentiful and delicious. Everyone wanted to talk with Jamey about the wild West and the savage plains Indians. Thanks to the abundance of newspapers and journals with their numerous reporters out West, everyone had read stories about the wild West, the brave gunslingers, the rugged pioneers and frontiersmen, the powerful ranchers, the poor cowboys, and the savage Indians.

Jamey told some stories to those who wanted to hear firsthand his experiences. "The West is a lawless place. One day, this drunken trapper began shooting his pistol at the signs over the storefronts along the street in St. Louis. He kept missing and hitting windows and doors. Everyone was running away from this crazy man. At the same time, a bank was robbed right along the same street. It turned out the drunk accidentally shot two of the robbers, and became a hero. Meanwhile, my unit of Army soldiers chased the leader of the robbers for thirty miles straight west of St. Louis. While we saw him several times, we never got close enough to capture him. The man finally ran into a large hunting party of Indians. He was so scared he stopped dead in his tracks, and then we finally caught up and arrested him. He gladly gave himself up in order to get away from the Indians. After we arrested him, I took him over to the Indians, who were the nicest and friendliest people you could ever know. He was so upset, he swore all the way back to St. Louis."

Every story brought questions from the listeners. Jamey preferred talking about the wisdom of the Indian leaders or the contributions being made by caring individuals like William Clark, but no one really wanted to hear about that. Everyone wanted to know the details of the Indian fights or the wild happenings in St. Louis. The West was thrilling and exciting. Many dreamed of moving out past the Mississippi where land was free and buffalo roamed the prairie.

The next day, Jamey took time to talk individually with Soso about the Indians he had met on the frontier. Soso wondered what Jamey thought of these people. "What were the natives like on the western prairie?" Soso asked.

"Very strong and independent. Superb horsemen, hunters, and trappers. Mostly, they are like the Iroquois, caring and hard working, but not as organized. There were some who were good, some bad. Some you could trust, and others you couldn't. The different tribes were very fascinating. The Menominees, Chippewas, and Pawnee were always friendly. Their culture is similar to the Iroquois. They appreciate and understand nature in ways the whites could never understand." Jamey described them in general, but he preferred to discuss some of the individuals that he had met. "I think that Chief Petalesharo was the most impressive person I met out West. He was a noble leader and perceptive thinker. He was the Indian's equivalent of William Clark."

"I guess there weren't many places to fish. But what kind of animals did they hunt?"

"Soso, you would not believe the size of the buffalo. The Indians try hard to protect the buffalo, but the whites continue to waste many of those majestic beasts. They are big, kind animals. They look awkward, but they are very graceful in their movements. Sometimes they do dumb things, but they are often smarter than their hunters. I wish I could have brought one back to show you, but buffalo were meant to roam the open spaces. There are more buffalo than man can count, but I'm afraid not more than men can kill."

Soso saw that Jamey had learned from his experiences. Soso was delighted that his friend had seen so much and met such interesting people. The good thing was that Jamey's values hadn't changed. He was older, wiser, and more mature. He had become as good a man as he had been a boy.

Jamey spent five days reliving many of things from in his childhood. The weather cooperated enough so that Jamey was able to sail, fish, and hunt on the bay. He rode around the village and along the lake on horseback noticing all the changes that had occurred during the four years that had passed since his last visit. He visited the Lummises and Soso across the bay and was amazed by the changes in Lummisville. Jamey truly enjoyed himself. He was equally proud of his family and village. He wished that he could stay longer, but duty called. Even though he had doubts about the utility of his new job, he intended to do the best he could.

New Job

Washington, D.C. was a confusing place for a newcomer who had spent his entire life in small villages and frontier barracks. Most of the streets were constructed in a crossing pattern with lettered streets in one direction and numbered streets in the other. However, some streets also ran diagonally to connect directly the most important buildings and locations in the city to one another. The problem was that there were so many important buildings in the city that it seemed streets were running every which way. Jamey being a surveyor and engineer appreciated the difficulty of designing a city of this size. It took him a few days to understand the maze that the architects of the city's street system, Frenchman L'Enfant, Surveyor Andrew Ellicott, and the free black scientist, Benjamin Banneker, had designed and constructed. Jamey had studied the work of these famous surveyors during his senior year at West Point. Now he had the opportunity to see firsthand the result of their work. He liked it, but it was a bit confusing to this country boy.

Jamey worked in a small building near the Army Headquarters and several other important buildings in the city. His job was more a caretaker than a surveyor or mapmaker. He and two naval officers were the only ones assigned to the Coast and Geodetic Survey staff. They were there to maintain the existing equipment and maps and to answer questions from Congress about the surveying and mapping that had been completed to date. The coast survey had been abandoned by Congressional order in 1818. Now it was just in a maintenance mode to save and protect the earlier work of the survey. However, no new work was being assigned to this organization. Jamey knew that somebody had to do this work, but why him?

The office storeroom held numerous precision surveying instruments of all types and sizes. Jamey had never seen such high quality, sophisticated equipment. The previous head of the Survey, Ferdinand Hassler, had spent nearly $40,000 for the finest survey equipment in the world. His strategy was to conduct preliminary experiments and concentrate their work in the New Jersey and Long Island regions. However, Congress felt that he was progressing too slowly and had suspended him from his position. Then, they simply ended the work of this important organization. What a waste!

Hassler was upset. According to the experts, the survey was off to a good start. He had plenty of evidence to prove that he had done a fine job and the survey was valuable. Jamey was impressed by what he saw in the office. There were numerous records of the surveys that had already been conducted. Hassler had preceded Jamey at West Point. Although not a graduate of West Point, he had been the Professor of Mathematics until 1810. Hassler was an accomplished scientist and a notable surveyor.

Jamey spent most of his time planning the next surveys to be performed for the eventual continuation of the effort. He also reconnoitered new locations for stations in the Maryland and Virginia areas. The two naval officers had no experience as surveyors, and they tried in vain to construct maps from the data already collected in New Jersey. Mostly they just kept the place clean and organized. That's really all Congress expected them to do.

Probably the biggest benefit of this job to Jamey came from the fact that he had plenty of free time to read mathematics. While he had wanted to keep up his mathematics studies when he was on the frontier, he simply never had the time. Now during the time he was required to sit and care for the equipment, he read his long-neglected mathematics books and checked out additional books from the Congressional library. This enabled him not only to review the material that he had learned at West Point, but also to study new subjects in more advanced fields. He was fortunate to be able to study Hassler's own books on geometry and trigonometry and the new book on descriptive geometry written by his former professor at West Point, Charles Davies. If nothing else, Jamey was gaining knowledge while in his new job. He would have preferred to be actually conducting the coast survey, and several times Jamey appealed to his superior officer somehow to convince Congress to reestablish the organization. For now, that was simply not possible.

The major benefit of his new job was the opportunity to renew his relationship with Carin. He had been unable to see her during his travel from Sodus Point to Washington, since West Point was too far off the route between the two locations and his travel was rushed. Fortunately, Jamie had been able to see his friend, Ben Lummis, for one day in Philadelphia as Jamey passed through. However, Jamie now began writing to Carin several times a week, and she replied regularly. Through this correspondence, they began to rekindle their love for one another. By the end of the year, Jamey couldn't wait to see Carin again. They were trying to make arrangements to see each other when a special surprise was delivered to Jamey. His new Army orders were to go to West Point during the summer of 1828 and prepare to teach mathematics in the fall.

The news of his new assignment couldn't have been better. He was ready to return to his alma mater to teach and to reunite with his friend. Carin had waited patiently for Jamey, and now she wanted to see him more than ever. By the summer, they would be together again. It was remarkably good fortune for Jamey, Carin, and West Point.

Campaign

The presidential election of 1828 contained several ingredients not present in previous elections. Each state had precise controls over the members of the electoral college to insure proper representation of the popular vote, and the two political parties, National Republicans and Democrats, were well organized and fully prepared to help their respective candidates. Even though everyone knew who the candidates would be, the actual campaigns of the two party nominees, incumbent John Quincy Adams and second-time challenger Andrew Jackson, didn't start in earnest until the summer.

The major issues of the campaign were the rights and privileges of the states, care of the eastern laborers, and protection of the western frontiersmen. Adams was a federalist who advocated a stronger central government, while Jackson was a proponent of state's rights and supporter of more rights for the common man. Jackson's supporters were better organized and effectively discredited Adams as an "aristocrat," unconcerned with the American public and its problems.

Dr. Lummis and Soso saw the two candidates in a much different light. Dr. Lummis and other abolitionists in the North knew that state's rights meant continuation of slavery in the South. Jackson's definition of the common man did not include the blacks, slave or free. Soso had a much more personal reason for distrusting Jackson, for he had heard his remarks against Indian rights. Jackson's definition of the common man did not include Indians either. On the other hand, Adams understood that the blacks and Indians' needs for freedom and independence were in the best interests of the entire nation.

This political campaign was the first one to arouse the entire nation's emotions. Newspapers carried the details of the campaign and the candidates' speeches. At the Fourth of July celebration in Sodus Point, Dr.

Lummis and Soso gave speeches in support of Adams and against the policies involving blacks and Indians proposed by Jackson. Many in the Sodus Bay area agreed with the two orators, while others spoke in support of Jackson. Soso and Dr. Lummis could sense that the local mood was for Adams. However, they had no idea about how the rest of the nation felt. They knew that blacks and Indians were small groups without a vote. However, they hoped that others would sympathize with the plights of these two groups and choose a leader who cared for all the people of the nation. This was a lot to expect, but the two remained optimistic right up until election day.

The election results brought bad news. Andrew Jackson won easily. He had carried the southern and western states and Pennsylvania. Even the parts of New York State containing large cities with numerous laborers supported Jackson. Dr. Lummis and Soso were disappointed. They knew this meant more tough times and more discrimination for the country's black and Indian populations. Soso worried that Jackson would take direct and drastic actions against both groups.

Better City Life

In Philadelphia, Ben Lummis couldn't avoid discussions and references to his godfather and namesake Dr. Benjamin Rush. Rush had been a distinguished founding father of Philadelphia. Whenever Ben was introduced as Benjamin Rush Lummis, people wanted to know about their connection. Ben's supervisor at the bank, George Willig, knew the Rush family well.

Sara and Elizabeth's summer trip to Philadelphia was tremendous fun. The two travelers took their time on the trip. They stopped and toured the sights along the way. They were strong, independent people, who enjoyed all the activities and challenges of traveling and touring. They arrived at Philadelphia in time for the Fourth of July celebration. Elizabeth loved the fireworks and parades, but most of all she loved seeing her brother again.

Ben, Elizabeth, and Sarah Lummis had a grand time together. Sara visited her old friends and showed off her children. Ben met many new people and enjoyed his mother and sister's company. In addition to her brother's attention, Elizabeth enjoyed the city's sights, especially the historical points of interest.

"Elizabeth, you sure know a lot about the history of Philadelphia. How did you learn so much?" Ben asked the precocious ten-year-old, who seemed to know Ben Franklin's life history.

"I read the history of Philadelphia with Soso before we left, and on the trip I read a biography of Ben Franklin. Both books were fascinating." Elizabeth's answer didn't surprise her brother. She then added, "Soso told me that you were a good fisherman when you were young. He also said that you learned all about business by selling fish in Troupville when you were my age."

"Yes, I caught many fish with your Uncle Jamey. But I really never knew much about business until I came to the city. In Troupville, everyone was honest and trusting. Unfortunately, that's not the way business works in the city."

"Well, I think you should leave the city and come back to Sodus Bay. I'm sure Uncle Soso has a good job for you. Then I can see you every day." Elizabeth had asked him several times to come back home in the letters that she conscientiously sent to her brother.

"I tell you what. You keep asking me to come back in every letter you send me, and someday I will surprise you." Ben had always thought of returning to his boyhood home, but preferred to keep this tempting thought at a low priority for now. He had a job to do and a career to build. However, he also knew that someday he would return to his roots, his home on Sodus Bay. Philadelphia was different than New York. It was more historic, and life was a bit less chaotic. The slower pace suited Ben.

Reunion of Lovers

West Point hadn't changed much over the past three years. The new class of plebes had arrived on July 1, 1828, just one week before Jamey, but academic classes were still months away. There was plenty to do for a newly arrived faculty member. However, the first thing Jamey wanted to do was to take a trip to a certain farm in New Windsor. He hoped to see the love of his life, Carin Roe.

Jamey borrowed a horse from the Academy's stable and rode out to the Roe farm the very afternoon of his arrival. Carin came to the door. She was as beautiful as he had remembered. No, she was more beautiful than he had ever imagined. There she was, still there for him three years after he had left for the frontier. It was obvious to both of them that they were still in love. That evening was spent enjoying each other's company and telling each other all about the last three years of their lives. By the time Jamey left the Roe farm for the hotel at West Point, he was ecstatic over his assignment to the Academy.

It took Jamey just a few days to get back in the rhythm of West Point. Major Thayer was still the Superintendent, and he personally greeted Jamey and welcomed him back. Jamey also spent time with Professor Davies, discussing the books he had read and the surveying he had done. Professor Davies was pleased to have his bright young protégé on the faculty. He knew that the Mathematics Department was going to benefit. He had two, new, first-class assistants in Jamey Davis and recent graduate, Albert Church, whose first assignment was to stay at West Point and teach.

Jamey's summer was divided equally between his two loves—Carin and mathematics. The young couple had the opportunity to relive many of their previous experiences together. They even spent a lovely day sailing on Mr. Cyler's sloop. Jamey again enjoyed the splendid river and the company of his special friend. It brought back many memories.

Jamey's return was more than a dream come true for Carin. It was as if her whole life had been fulfilled. She had waited patiently for this to happen. She had survived depression when he was far away and out of touch, especially when her letters went unanswered. The waiting was over, and she wanted to stay with Jamey forever.

Once academics started, Jamey was busy teaching during the week. However, after he finished teaching his last calculus class on Saturday morning, he was on his way to Carin's. They enjoyed the weekends together. Their favorite activity was dancing at the inn at Cornwall on Saturday nights. They made a lovely couple as they glided around the dance floor. Their relationship was blooming.

Teaching yearlings, the second year cadets, was a pleasure for Jamey. Calculus was the kind of mathematics that he liked best. He made sure his cadets knew both the applications and the rich history of the subject. He tried to relate his own experiences in the frontier Army to what they were studying. Jamey believed that enthusiasm was the key to teaching and motivation was the key to learning. He told his students about Napoleon's use of mathematics to help him gain advantage over his opponents in both war and peace. Much of the information on Napoleon was taught to Jamey first hand by his old mathematics and engineering professor, Claudius Crozet, who had recently left the Academy and was an engineer in Virginia. Jamey's students liked their instructor. His classroom was full of fun, enthusiasm, and action. His students learned because they saw the relevance of their knowledge. Jamey enjoyed his role, and he was good at it.

He had been thinking about it for quite some time. It was a perfect evening in October, cool and clear with a harvest moon. Jamey and Carin had sat on the porch talking and enjoying each other's company. Then they went for a walk along the edge of the apple orchard. Jamey held Carin's hand as they walked, and, although his heart beat excitedly, he very calmly asked Carin to marry him. She stopped and gently kissed him and said yes. By the time they had returned to the farmhouse, they had decided on an April wedding at the West Point chapel. Jamey and Carin could hardly wait to tell everyone the exciting news and to make the necessary arrangements.

More Romance

It was a strange coincidence that during the same month a similar event happened to Jamey's friend, Ben. After Ben's mother and sister had returned to Sodus Point late in the summer, Ben started spending more social time with George Willig's family. George had several daughters. His oldest, Ann Marie, was seventeen. She had become a mature, charming young lady during the months that Ben had been in Philadelphia. Ben fell in love with her. She fell in love with her handsome and intelligent suitor.

At first, their love was the shy, unspoken, secret kind. Both of them knew of their feelings by the way they looked and talked to one another. However, they had never told each other their feelings, nor did anyone else know. Finally, when Ben needed to escort someone to a big party at the bank president's house, he asked George for permission to invite Ann Marie. At first, George was shocked but then warmed to the idea. He knew that Ann Marie was ready for a life of her own, and George liked Ben very much. The couple went to the party and thoroughly enjoyed their evening together.

"Ann Marie, you are the most beautiful and most charming woman at the party," Ben whispered to his date as they danced for the first time.

"And you are the most handsome and intelligent." Ann Marie had always been impressed by Ben's knowledge. "I feel like we should dance every dance. It makes me feel so alive."

"Of course, we'll dance until we are tired. Then we should talk, because I have so much to say to you," Ben continued to whisper, "and, you should know that you really are the most beautiful woman I have ever seen."

"I bet you say that to all your dates at these fancy parties."

"Yes, but you're the only date I've ever had at a fancy party. And the only one, I ever want to have." Ben was serious about his feelings, and he was surprised at how easily he was able to say the things on his mind. Talking with Ann Marie was easy. She made him feel comfortable, even though he was talking with his first true love.

Just three weeks after their first date, in which time they had two other formal dinner dates, Ben asked Ann Marie for her hand in marriage. Despite their short dating period, they knew that their love was real and forever. She accepted his proposal. Her whole family was thrilled about the news, and permission was granted. Ben wrote a letter to inform his parents of the joyous news. The wedding was set for May in Philadelphia.

Politics

The capital city was alive. It seemed as if everyone in the nation had come to see the popular advocate for the common man, Andrew Jackson, become President of the United States. His inauguration was held on a cold day in March. People had come to celebrate the rise of the common man, the reformation of the political process, and the end of aristocracy. However, for many others it was the end of hope for freedom and the beginning of the end for their homes and property.

Soso and Dr. Lummis could not deny that the Jackson era would bring many advances to the frontier. They looked forward to Jackson's promises of free public education, rights for laborers to form unions, and more suffrage. However, they both vowed to fight against the political system that would harm the slaves and Indians. They decided to go to Washington to influence their government directly. They wanted the government in Washington to consider helping people who were currently mistreated, discriminated against, and valued less than white people.

The plan was for the Sodus Bay contingent of the Davis family, the Lummis family, and Soso to go to West Point for Jamey's wedding in April, then onto Philadelphia for Ben's wedding in May. The Davis family then planned to return to Sodus Point. Soso and Dr. Lummis would continue on to Washington to lobby Congress and the President's staff for action on their issues. Sara and Elizabeth would stay in Philadelphia until the two men returned. Then all four would travel back to Lummisville. This would be a long, rough trip, especially for 71-year-old William. Fortunately, the completion of the Erie Canal and the speed and convenience of the steamship made the trip tolerable—almost pleasurable at times. Transportation had advanced considerably and was much easier to travel than it had been just twenty years before. Technology was changing the world.

Jamey and Carin Davis

The bride was radiant as she walked down the aisle in her lovely, white gown. Jamey smiled as he watched Carin come forward, escorted by her father, Samuel Roe. Guests were assembled in the cadet chapel overlooking the Hudson River. In attendance were Jamey's friends and family from the Sodus Bay area, Carin's friends and family from the Cornwall area, and the staff of the Military Academy. Jamey looked handsome and dignified in the dress uniform of a Second Lieutenant.

The service was exhilarating for everyone. The couple was united in spirit, faith, and commitment. At the conclusion of the ceremony, the new-lyweds kissed and smiled. Among those throwing confetti were Jamey's family; his life-long friends, William and Sara Lummis and Soso; his new in-laws Samuel and Betsy Roe; and his military colleagues Charles Davies and Sylvanus Thayer. Everyone was happy and excited. It was a grand and glorious day in the Hudson Highlands.

Ben and Ann Marie Lummis

Although still frail, Ann Marie was a lovely bride dressed in a long white gown, and Ben a distinguished groom. The Philadelphia Episcopal Church was huge, yet nearly every pew was filled. All of the influential families of Philadelphia were represented. The Sodus Bay contingent sat up front and beamed with joy. George Willig gave away his lovely daughter to Ben Lummis, who gladly took her hand in marriage.

The ceremony and reception were momentous, elegant affairs. After the service, the Willigs hosted a grandiose party. Everyone had a splendid time. Tremendous amounts of food were consumed, and many party-goers danced. William and Sara were proud of their son and happy that he had found such a loving and caring woman to share his life with. They knew that Ben was happy. This was a huge relief for Sara, who had always wor-ried about his stressful city life. Sara wasn't nearly as concerned about Elizabeth. For some reason, she knew that her daughter would always be happy and successful.

Tragedy

Before Soso and William could leave for Washington, William was stricken with a severe stroke. During one of the happiest times of his life, he tragically lost the use of the entire right side of his body. Dr. Lummis was 71 years old and had been fortunate to have had good health his entire life. He had seen his son grow to be a fine, prosperous young man, who was now starting a family of his own. He worried about his young daughter, Elizabeth. While she was highly intelligent, she still needed nurturing and care. Of course, his strong, charming wife Sara would see to that. He retained enough of his faculties to realize that in this condition he would be a tremendous burden on his family. He wanted only one thing—to go back to the bay that he loved and to grow old with his friend, Soso.

After staying a couple of weeks in Philadelphia, the Sodus Bay contingent started the journey back home. Soso canceled his trip to Washington to accompany them. It was a long, depressing trip. Everyone tried to keep up his or her spirits, but William's condition worsened as the trip wore on. By the time they reached Lummisville, it was evident that William was dying. His spirits were raised temporarily when he saw his homestead on the silvery watered bay. After several wearing and deeply emotional days following their return, William fell into a coma.

Sara, Elizabeth, and Soso stayed by his bedside, trying to nurse him back to health. However, the doctors told them it was no use. After several more days of hopeless, nervous waiting, Dr. William Lummis died at his home on Sodus Bay and was buried on his property. He would be sorely missed by all who knew him and the communities that he had served so faithfully and selflessly. The communities of Lummisville, Maxwell, Sodus Point, and Float Bridge deeply mourned his loss. He had been much more than a doctor, farmer, businessman, abolitionist, friend, father, and husband; he had been the community leader, who had helped develop this area from a frontier outpost to a healthy, civilized community. Dr. William Lummis would be fondly remembered and greatly missed.

Recovery and More

All winter long, Soso mourned the loss of his dear friend. They had grown old together on the east side of the bay. Soso was now fifty. He had lived a good, full life and had accomplished a great deal. Losing his friend seemed to take something away from his own life. However, the strength of their friendship slowly revitalized his spirit. The spring thaw of the new year brought renewed hope to everyone along the shore, especially Soso. The ice had been off the bay for a week. Soso had his boat in the water, and he had already caught a mess of the best bullheads that he had ever taken from the cove. Of all the fish he caught, he enjoyed eating bullheads the most. The first meal of bullheads during the spring brought Soso fond memories of his mother. The tender fish were her favorite, and no one could prepare them as well as she could. As usual, Soso shared his catch with his neighbors. They appreciated all the helpful things their Indian friend and favorite neighbor did for them.

Surprise

Soso was alone in his house, except for Mac, eating the last of the bullheads, when he heard a knock on the door. Mac barked once and went back to sleep. Soso opened the door. He couldn't believe his eyes. There stood his beloved Betty with the biggest possible smile on her face. It had been seven years since she had last set foot in Soso's house. Now she was doing it as a free person. She proudly announced to Soso that after all these years she had bought her freedom from her former master. She held aloft the official papers to prove it. She was no longer a fugitive slave, but a free woman able to stay and live in America.

Soso was overwhelmed. He had no idea that such a thing was possible or that Betty could do this. They had written each other faithfully almost every week for the seven years that they had known one another. All that time Betty had kept this possibility a secret from Soso. Now, there she was with all her happiness and enthusiasm, standing in his house as a free person. They embraced. They felt their love for one another erupt. All these years, they had held back their emotional love for one another knowing how hard it would have made their separation. Now they were together forever. Soso wouldn't let anything come between them.

Betty's four adopted sons were now grown men. They had lives of their own. She was free to start anew with the love of her life. Despite his shock over the situation, Soso also was ready to share his life with his true love. He could think of nothing else. It was the happiest day of his life.

The next day, while standing on the shore of the bay, the loving couple was married. It was a simple ceremony attended by Sara and Elizabeth Lummis and Jim and Karen Davis. Betty contributed an additional item usually required in a marriage—a last name. Soso had never taken a white man's name, so he had never used a last name. On the other hand, Betty had acquired a last name from her parents. She was very proud of her name Betty Washington, especially now that her papers of freedom were produced in that name. So from that day on, they were officially Mr. Sosoenodus Washington and Mrs. Betty Washington, husband and wife, a couple together for life.

Whatever hole in Soso's life that was created when William Lummis died was filled to overflowing with his marriage to Betty. Soso cared deeply for Betty. He would provide for her and insure her safety, just as he had once done for his mother. He loved her in a way only a fifty-year-old, successful, caring man could. Betty, on the other hand, gave their marriage vitality and adventure. She was always happy, busy, and ready for new things. Betty had only one hand; however, that never slowed her down. She seemed to be able to do everything that people with no such handicap could. She was intelligent and talented. She also brought a deep religious belief to the marriage. That was something that Soso didn't share with his new wife. Betty was a strong believer in Christianity and attended church service regularly. The white man's religion was something that Soso just didn't understand. Yes, he realized that there were spirits and other things that nature and technology didn't fully explain. Over, the years, he had no longer found much satisfaction or comfort in the Indian spirits. But Soso didn't see how the whites' religion helped explain these things either. Was faith as powerful as knowledge and skill? Faith and spirit didn't control technology or nature. Soso's confusion was real, but he chose to ignore it for now.

It would take everyone a while to get used to the new couple, but there was no doubt that they would play a significant role in the area's future.

One of the first things Betty did was to put a woman's touch on Soso's home. While it had always been well kept, it had never shone and sparkled as it would that summer. Betty added color in the form of curtains, upholstered furniture, a flower garden, a painted fence, and bright shutters on the windows. Soso liked the changes. He felt young again. He fished, worked on his boats, farmed, and hunted with renewed enthusiasm. Life on the east side of Sodus Bay was exceptional in the summer of 1830.

Army Life

The sign over the door read "1LT and Mrs. Jamey Davis." Jamey had just been promoted to First Lieutenant, and the Davises hoped that the small pay raise would help them build a small nest-egg and prosper. The house was small but well built. It was designed for utility, not beauty. It was just what you would expect from an Army-built home. Jamey and Carin's house was located on Academy grounds, less than a half mile from where Jamey worked. It had a small kitchen, a smaller living room, and two tiny bedrooms. There were expectations that the second bedroom would be needed before the year was out.

Jamey and Carin cared for their living quarters as if it was their own. She put up curtains, painted the kitchen, and decorated the living room. All the heat for the house came from a central cooking fireplace. Jamey kept a large pile of logs alongside the house. He built and painted a pretty fence around the yard. They were a happy couple and the prospect of an addition to the family filled them with excitement. So far, Carin's pregnancy had gone fine. She worried that the baby would come during the cold winter months, but Jamey assured her that he would keep the house cozy and warm.

Work had gone equally well for Jamey. He enjoyed the challenges and rewards of teaching. He felt good about the contributions that he was making to his country's future. Cadets were always busy working and studying, but sometimes they disappointed him on their knowledge of basic mathematics. However, they always progressed in their development and eventually improved. As long as he kept his enthusiasm and the cadets stayed motivated, they learned and developed. Jamey felt as if he was making a difference. Not only did he teach the cadets about mathematics, but also he told them about the Army, the frontier, and the Indians. He explained the difference between keeping peace and making war. The nation and the Army would have more capable engineers and effective Army leaders because of Jamey Davis's efforts in the classroom. In a small way, he was helping to improve the Army and to advance the young nation. He faithfully served his country and his fellow man.

During special lessons, Jamey had a game for his cadets to play. He called it speed boards. He had all his cadets at their chalkboards, ready to solve problems. Jamey would read the problem to all the cadets, and they would immediately start work solving it. As soon as the first cadet believed he had the correct solution, he yelled out, "cease work," and all the other cadets would stop their work. Then all the cadets turned around to listen to the cadet who had yelled out the command defend and explain his work. If correct, only that cadet received points. If incorrect, points were deducted and any other cadet could volunteer to explain the correct answer for the points of the problem. It was a fun, lively game. Confident cadets who worked fast did well. Everyone, however, enjoyed the excitement. Jamey knew firsthand that quick thinking on your feet was an essential trait for an Army officer. Jamey was trying to develop that skill in his cadets.

Jamey particularly enjoyed the collection of mathematics books that Sylvanus Thayer and Charles Davies had assembled in the library. There were books in every subject and topic at every level. There were centuries-old classics written by the finest mathematicians in the world; there were modern, up-to-date works from France and England; and there were many of the new American publications. Jamey read as many of them as he could. He loved to learn, and he became a highly skilled mathematician through hard work and dedication to the subject.

As Head of the Mathematics Department, Charles Davies was a task master on the faculty. He kept Jamey busy preparing the less experienced instructors, like the recent West Point graduates, Second Lieutenants Joe Smith, Charles Hackley, and Ormsby Mitchell. Jamey's job was to develop them into effective teachers and confident, competent problem solvers.

Fortunately, teacher and students were up to the task, and a strong faculty team was produced.

A New Davis

It was early afternoon, and Jamey had just finished grading the final tests of the semester when he was told to hurry home. Carin needed him. What perfect timing. His vacation from his teaching duties started just as his son Leonard Soso Davis was born. The Academy Surgeon, Walt Wheaton, and a midwife attended to Carin and Leonard in the small bedroom of the house. Jamey anxiously waited in the living room until mother and son had rested. By late in the evening, he had spent a few minutes with Carin and briefly seen his son sleeping in mother's arms.

As word of the birth spread, it created happiness in Sodus Point, Lummisville, Cornwall, West Point, and Philadelphia. Grandparents Jim and Karen Davis were happy for their son and daughter-in-law. The Lummises in both Lummisville and Philadelphia also celebrated the birth. Soso was honored to have the young boy bear his name.

A New Lummis

In many ways, Ben's life paralleled Jamey's. Ann Marie also was pregnant and due to give birth several months after the birth of Lenny, which was what everyone began calling Leonard Soso Davis. However, Ann Marie was having a difficult time. She was a frail woman who had been sickly for most of her life. The pregnancy had started out fine, but as time progressed more and more troubles developed. She had bad cramps, false contractions, and severe bleeding. She spent the last two months of her pregnancy confined to her bed. All were worried about the imminent birth.

Sara and Elizabeth Lummis traveled to Philadelphia to try to help Ann Marie and Ben through this taxing time. Sara had often helped William doctor his patients. She had assisted during many births and several difficult pregnancies. She wished that William were still alive to help. Even though Ben had obtained the best doctor in Philadelphia, everyone was very concerned for the health of both mother and child. The medical problems persisted to the day of the birth.

Ben, Elizabeth, and Ann Marie's parents, the Willigs, waited, while Sara and Dr. Stephens attended to the expectant mother. Ann Marie was only eighteen years old and looked even younger. Almost everything that could go wrong did. The child was in a difficult position in the womb. The birth canal was infected. After several hours of intense labor, Georgette Lummis, a healthy, but delicate girl was born. Sara cleaned the child and took her out to Ben, Elizabeth, and Mr. and Mrs. Willig.

Even though the baby had been delivered successfully the doctor's work was not done. The labor had completely exhausted Ann Marie. She had lost a tremendous amount of blood and fluids. As time continued after the delivery, the doctor became deeply concerned because the bleeding would not stop. He tried everything he knew to save his patient, but nothing worked. Ann Marie Lummis tragically died later that day.

The family was in deep depression. After the joyous event of holding the baby, the shock of losing the mother was tremendous. Ben cried out in pain at the news of the loss of his wife. The Willigs tearfully took Elizabeth back to their home just a few blocks away so that Sara could comfort her son. Endless questions and senseless thoughts ran through Ben's mind. Why Ann Marie? Why him? How could he continue? What would happen to him and his baby?

The first month after Ann Marie's death was difficult for everyone. Ben was so depressed that he stayed away from work. Sara tried to help, but she eventually felt that she was in the way. The Willigs missed their daughter terribly. Elizabeth was the only one who could cheer up Ben. She tried to keep him occupied. They spent time taking care of Georgette, who was a cute, happy baby.

Fortunately, Georgette Lummis was healthy. She had slight features like her mother, but she ate well and gained strength daily. Both thirteen-year-old Elizabeth and ten-year-old Georgiana Willig, Ann Marie's younger sister, took good care of Georgette. Raising and caring for Georgette became a family enterprise, and the Lummises and the Willigs all did their share.

By the middle of summer, Ben's life had stabilized. Sara and Elizabeth returned to Lummisville. The Willigs kept Georgette much of the time, and Ben stayed alone in his house, except for the few times he kept Georgette overnight. Ben was able to continue his job and restart his life. He had been given a severe blow, but he was slowly recovering, and that was the best anyone could expect.

Farm and Family

Sara and Elizabeth Lummis went from one depressing situation to another. Their farm in Lummisville had suffered greatly during their absence. Without William to organize the activities of the farm, the productivity and upkeep deteriorated. William had been an expert at grafting trees and caring for them. Foreman Ron Johnson had also known these skills but had left the farm to go west in hopes of starting a homestead of his own. The Lummis underground railroad station no longer handled any passengers. It wasn't that Sara hadn't tried to keep up ties with the other stations, but she and William had been gone so much that, without continuity of management, the other contacts became nervous and ineffective. Other stations along the lake had taken their place. The Lummis station had served well but was no longer needed. Betty Washington was just one example of its past importance and success. Its deterioration and loss of the underground railroad station depressed Sara even more.

Sara had another pressing problem. She realized how much potential Elizabeth had for academic achievement. She was an amazingly talented thirteen-year-old. However, without William to teach and nurture her, little significant progress could be made. Although well-schooled as a youth in Philadelphia, Sara was not able to help her daughter, nor was there anyone in the immediate area who could challenge such an advanced student. Sara weighed a couple of alternatives. She and Elizabeth could return to Philadelphia, where Elizabeth could attend a good school for girls. The farm would suffer even further, and she would miss her home. She realized that she enjoyed Sodus Bay and her friends there much more than Philadelphia. The other alternative was to send Elizabeth away to a school, and for her to stay and run the farm. After considerable contemplation, she decided to stay at Lummisville and to send Elizabeth to boarding school. This is something that William had investigated two years before. It was a big step that would temporarily separate mother and child. The separation would be hard, but Sara realized that it was the right thing to do.

The question was where should Elizabeth go. The governments, federal and state, had considered supporting schools for girls, but had decided not to interfere with "God's will for women." So only a few private girl's schools existed, and they were expensive. Sara knew of only two good girl's schools. William had talked to Emma Willard a few years before about her school, the Troy Female Seminary, which was near Albany. Sara also knew of the Female Seminary in Aurora from her ties with the administrators of Geneva College. Aurora was much closer. She could see Elizabeth more often if she went there. Overlooking the lake of the Cayugas, the school was located in an impressive setting near Soso's boyhood home. Elizabeth naturally liked the link of the school to her Uncle Soso. Sara felt that Elizabeth would be comfortable there. It was the toughest decision that she had ever made—Elizabeth would attend the Female Seminary in Aurora.

New School

Soso, Mac, and Sara took Elizabeth to her school. They took their time on the long carriage drive. The forty-mile trip took two days. They spent the first night at Geneva. Sara and Elizabeth stayed with Reverend Hobart's family for the evening. He lived on the campus of Geneva College. Soso spent the night in the hotel in the village. The next day, Soso showed Elizabeth where his old Indian village was located. He was surprised to see that much of the area still looked the same as he remembered it. There were a few houses along the nearby lakeshore but no real villages or large farms.

"This is still a lovely lake and a beautiful spot. I grew up in a longhouse right here in this area." Soso pointed to an area filled with shrubs, bushes, and small trees. "See some of those logs and mounds of dirt. That was part of the long house where Fish Carrier, our chief and wise leader, lived." Soso explained to Elizabeth the details of his former village, which had existed on this same ground some forty years before.

"What happened to the rest of the village? Did all the buildings just fall down or did they burn down?" Elizabeth couldn't imagine a whole village disappearing, unless it was destroyed in a fire, like she heard had happened in Troupville before she was born.

"Slowly, over all these years, the logs and twigs we used on the walls and ceiling just fell down and rotted away. Some things were probably destroyed by visitors, but most were returned to nature's needs over the years. Remember it was forty years ago that I lived here. That's a long time for man-made structures to survive without care and upkeep. It was an exciting village, filled with strong people. We had a large street that ran straight through the village and down to the lakeshore. It was a perfect place to grow up. I was so lucky to call this village home."

Soso had always thought this land was better suited for Indians than for whites. It was rough, marshy, and full of natural dangers and obstacles. It was too bad the Indians couldn't have held onto it. They would have continued to enjoy its closeness to nature, as they had for many centuries before the interference from whites. Now it all seemed wasted. The white men had driven away the Indians, only to ignore the stolen land. Unfortunately, this was typical of the waste produced by the whites' governments and their greedy and powerful leaders. Indians would never tolerate such waste, and through democratic means always picked the most wise and caring people to be their leaders.

Aurora Female Seminary was just a few miles down the east side of the lake from the old Indian village. Elizabeth was nervous as they approached the gate to the school. She saw this as an outstanding opportunity. However, she knew that she would miss her family and friends. She was already a bit homesick. Once she was settled into her room, Soso and Sara left her on her own to meet classmates and teachers. Elizabeth enjoyed meeting everyone and being the center of attention for the evening. Most of her classmates were older, but she would have no problem keeping up with the academic program.

Early the next morning, Soso, Mac, and Sara said their farewells to Elizabeth and left for Lummisville. Sara worried all the way back about her decision. She wanted to do what was best for her daughter. Soso assured her that everything would be fine. This was what Elizabeth needed to help reach her potential. She was talented, and this seminary was the best place to develop that talent. Soso realized that it was nature's way to send the mature nestling out of the nest to fly on her own. It was now Elizabeth's time to spread her capable wings. She would always know her way back to the nest whenever she needed help or nurturing.

Betty awaited Soso's return back in Lummisville. She was still uncomfortable when she was alone. Her papers granting her freedom wouldn't help much if she were kidnapped and whisked away back to the South. She felt perfectly safe when Soso was there. She knew that he would protect her from that fate. She was relieved when he walked through the doorway and they were together again.

While the Lummis farm had deteriorated over the last couple years, Soso's home and farm had flourished. Betty was as good a farmer as she was a homemaker. Between Soso's knowledge of planting and Betty's hard work, their crops were healthier and more plentiful than anyone else's. Soso had learned to graft the best branches of the apple trees to produce healthy trees and good tasting fruit. Betty made the best apple cider and baked the best apple pies in the county. She took tremendous pride in her home and the fields of the farm. Because of the success of his own farm, Soso began spending time helping Sara manage her larger farm and care for her orchards. It was just too big for the field crew she employed, and she couldn't afford to pay any more workers. Despite these problems, with

Soso's help, she managed to start the farm slowly and steadily on the road to recovery.

At first, Mac had been a bit jealous of Betty's arrival and her replacement of him as Soso's best friend. After a while, Mac and Betty's relationship improved. Finally, they established their own warm friendship. However, by then, Mac was an old, tired dog. The winter of 1831-1832 hit him hard. Although Mac went outside only for his necessary duties, he was overcome by the cold weather and failing health. One cold night during the winter, Mac passed away in his sleep. Soso and Betty cried over this loss of a family member. They would miss him. Over the years, Mac had been the perfect companion for Soso on his many adventures. During his younger years, Mac had been bred many times with dogs in the area. Now many of the dogs in the Sodus Bay area looked just like Mac. The Sodus Bay Retriever was a special breed that loved to play and work in the silvery waters of Sodus Bay. Mac, the first of the breed, had left quite a legacy for his offspring.

Boom Times for Ben

Philadelphia was booming. Business was good. The nearby communities were growing and prospering. Ben and his bank were busy. For the most part, he had learned to cope with the loss of his wife and had gone on with the rest of his life and that of his daughter. The Willigs, especially Georgina, took good care of Georgette. Ben faithfully saw his daughter for a couple of hours every evening and cared for her during weekends. Given the circumstances, things were going quite well. He knew that he could survive the loss, and now he had to prosper to care for Georgette.

There had been some changes on the business side for Ben and his bank. He was now involved in bigger businesses, in particular, railroads. On behalf of his bank, he worked closely with the Philadelphia and Germantown Railroad and talented railroad engineer, Matthias Baldwin. They were building a steam locomotive, affectionately named Old Ironsides. Baldwin had built a small-scale model of a locomotive a few years before. However, there were plenty of obstacles in the way of establishing a commercial railroad operation. This project kept Ben fully engaged in an exciting and interesting venture. His health and happiness improved as they progressed toward completion of the project.

The people of Philadelphia were excited over the new invention. The first trial run of the locomotive received plenty of attention from the leaders of the city. Politicians, businessmen, bankers, lawyers, and doctors were among the hundreds of onlookers for the first public display. Old Ironsides looked as powerful as it was. It contained over six tons of metal. The noise it made as it traveled down the tracks pulling fifteen cars at over 25 miles per hour was overpowering. Everyone loved this black metal beast, as it traveled back and forth pulling cars of passengers and freight from Philadelphia to Germantown and back.

Railroads were being experimented with in several other areas of the country. Other places with an "iron horse" locomotive were Baltimore; Honesdale, Pennsylvania; Charleston, South Carolina; and New York City. Coincidentally, Jamey spent part of his summer on a duty from West Point helping John Jervis build an experimental locomotive, appropriately named Experiment. Jervis had designed four swiveling wheels at the front end of the engine for better control. Jamey was helping the engineer with the suspension system. By the end of the summer, the Experiment was running along its tracks on the bank of the Hudson River at phenomenal speeds of nearly fifty miles per hour. Jamey finished his summer work on the railroad by the middle of August and rushed back home to West Point. It had been exciting work, but he had something much more pressing to attend to.

Another Addition

There was more excitement in the Davis household. Lenny was going to have a sibling. Carin was pregnant and due in October, almost two years after Lenny's birth. The Davis family had prospered during that time. Lenny was healthy and active. Jamey was an experienced instructor who helped Charles Davies prepare tests and develop instructors. Carin enjoyed her roles as wife and mother, caring for Jamey and Lenny.

Thankfully, Carin's pregnancy proceeded normally, and on October 18, she gave birth to a baby girl. Both mother and baby were fine. The baby was named Catherine Lummis Davis. Carin chose the name Catherine, and Jamey chose the middle name to honor the family of his friend, Ben Lummis. The baby's crib fit nicely into Lenny's bedroom. The siblings would get to know each other well. Jamey couldn't have been happier.

Summer Vacation

Elizabeth Lummis was an excellent student. She was enthusiastic, intelligent, and hard working. Her teachers were amazed at her progress. Her writing talents were quickly discovered and developed. Her teacher encouraged her to write essays and short stories. Everyone who read her stories knew that someday she would make an outstanding writer and author.

Sara had visited Aurora Seminary several times during the academic year. She was relieved by Elizabeth's adjustment to the school and her new friends. The house and farm in Lummisville were lonely without her, but the extra time spent on the business had enabled Sara to revitalize the farm business. She had hired several new workers, repairs had been made, and the harvest promised to be a good one.

Elizabeth had the summer off from school. Despite her enjoyment of school, she was looking forward to a summer of family, friends, and fishing on Sodus Bay. She hugged her Uncle Soso and Aunt Betty when she arrived back in Lummisville. The next day, Elizabeth and Soso had caught a bucket of fish by noon at their favorite fishing spot on Second Creek. While they fished, she told Soso about the things she had learned and done. She enjoyed telling Soso all about her life. He enjoyed listening. It helped him understand the perspective of the younger generation. Elizabeth was so articulate that Soso felt empowered by their conversations.

"What was your favorite subject?" asked Soso.

"I truly enjoy my language classes. Latin, French, Italian, and English are all so exciting. I wish I could speak more of your language, Uncle Soso. It seems so different and so difficult," Elizabeth answered. "How could a language like yours develop and grow without any written words? Was it easy for you to learn sign language as well as spoken words?"

"Languages come in all varieties—just like people. Languages without written words must be stronger in their spoken form, like the people who have weak muscles, need to have strong minds. The Iroquois language is strong in precision and variety. It is a beautiful language meant to be spoken, but not written. The Indian sign language was merely a necessity to communicate with those who didn't know our language. It contains only the basics."

"I love reading poetry. They express such strong emotions and give such vivid pictures. Some of the stories that I have read were about our area when it was the frontier. There are many delightful poems about our lands and our people." Elizabeth could go on and on about poetry and American literature.

"None is as good as my Lisa Beth's writings." Soso meant what he said. He loved Elizabeth's poetry.

Return Visit

An old friend of Soso and Jim returned to Sodus Bay. It had been 26 years since his last visit to the area. He had heard that his friend from Philadelphia, William Lummis, had passed away. He fondly remembered the two men who had taken him hunting on Sodus Bay. James Audubon had returned to leave them a memento of his last visit and to check out the bird life in the area. Since he had arrived at Sodus Point, he was directed to Jim Davis' house. Despite all those years since the last visit, Jim took one look at the visitor waiting at the door and recognized him immediately. How could he forget an excellent hunting partner and talented artist like James Audubon?

Jim Davis had heard of the exploits of naturalist James Audubon. Now, James took time to tell Jim all about his trips to Europe and the ongoing publication of his wildlife and bird art prints. James detailed many adventures, and Jim listened intently. He showed Jim some of his favorite drawings and color prints. James was just coming from a trip to Florida, so he was able to show Jim drawings of exotic southern birds. Jim was enthralled with the splendor and accuracy of James' work. As Jim already knew from firsthand experience, James Audubon was a genius.

James had a list of birds that he wanted to watch to obtain a better understanding of their behavior. He had seen these birds briefly only a few times before and had crude sketches and descriptions. However, he needed more time watching these species to refine his current sketches. One of the things James had hoped was that Jim or Soso could help him find one of these birds. The list included the gray partridge, the long-eared owl, the northern woodpecker, and the eastern bluebird. Jim had no idea where to find any of these species, but told James that Soso might be able to help. Before they left Jim's house, he showed James the framed picture on the wall in the living room. Even though James had long forgotten all about the pencil drawing of a bald eagle that he had given Jim many years before, he enjoyed seeing how his earlier work was appreciated. James reached into his baggage and presented Jim with a full-colored print of a bald eagle to go with his pencil drawing. It was a spectacular painting, and Jim was astounded by such a magnificent gift.

The trip across the bay was pleasant. The weather was perfect. A light breeze kept the boat traveling at a good clip, yet the waves were small so the ride was smooth. James admired the beauty of the bay. He noticed some of the changes over the past 26 years. Even though there were more houses and people, the feeling of unspoiled nature was still present. Civilization had overtaken and ruined many parts of the east coast of America, but fortunately it hadn't changed the feeling of wild freedom and natural beauty that existed on Sodus Bay. James vaguely remembered their hunting places and recalled the birds they had shot and seen.

By coincidence, Soso was returning by boat from a fishing trip just as Jim and James entered his cove. As Soso and Jim pulled their boats along side one another, Soso recognized Jim's passenger. Soso had always admired James and his work from their brief acquaintance 26 years before. The picture of the snowy owl that James had given Soso still hung over the mantel of the chimney in Soso and Betty's home. Soso knew that James was one of the whites who understood nature as well as any Indian. If only the other white men had this same understanding and appreciation, the world would be a much better place.

They docked the boats, and Soso and James warmly greeted one another. James told Soso about his travels and life-long work of painting the birds of North America. He also asked Soso for help in finding the birds that he sought to watch. James explained in detail the elusive species. Soso gladly accepted the challenge. First, he invited James to stay with him and took him to meet Betty. Jim Davis stayed for dinner and then returned by boat back to Sodus Point. James Audubon and Soso Washington spent the night discussing birds and the beauty of nature. Soso was impressed by James' pictures. They did more much than accurately show the color and features of the birds; somehow they seemed to show their life and function. Before they went to bed, Soso promised to take James to areas where he thought he had seen the birds that James was interested in. James was so excited over the prospects of seeing one of these elusive birds that he could hardly sleep. Getting to see one of these birds would make this trip a remarkable success.

Successful Mission

The two bird watchers, Soso and James, left the dock about two hours before sunrise. They were headed out onto the lake and west toward

Boulder Point, where there was a large boulder about fifty yards offshore. With favorable winds on the clear, moon-lit morning, they easily negotiated the trip through the darkness. It wasn't as dangerous because of the spectacular beacon of light from the Sodus Point Lighthouse that marked the passage. They arrived at Boulder Point just before sunrise. Soso pulled the boat onshore on the east side of the point, and the two men climbed the bank to the top of a low ridge. They positioned themselves so they could see along both sides of the point and out into the lake. They could still see a faint glimmer of light from the lighthouse that they had passed miles down the shore. There they waited. Neither man moved or made a sound as the sun slowly rose and the day blossomed into a clear, bright, radiant morning.

They waited for almost two hours, when Soso whispered to James, "There it is."

James had already seen the bird. He watched intently. Occasionally, the periodic buzzing and drumming of the bird pecking the tree would disrupt the silence. After ten minutes of study, James carefully began sketching. The bird kept pecking for another twenty minutes before it flew away, but by then James had seen what he needed to visualize and better understand the details and habits of the northern woodpecker. He shook Soso's hand and smiled brightly, and then the two excited and satisfied men headed back to Sodus Bay. It had been a successful hunt. James had spent hundreds, even thousands, of hours trying to find that bird, and Soso had given him that gift in just a few hours. It was an unforgettable day.

Once Again

Nearly the same scenario was repeated the next day. This time the early boat trip took them across the bay to First Creek, where, as a teenage boy, Soso had lived with his mother. He had buried his parents on the shore of this winding stream and knew this area well. He took James about one mile up the creek where it was shallow, narrow, twisty, and muddy. Now James knew why they had taken a canoe. Soso's sailboat wouldn't have gotten very far up this creek. They were in position by sunrise. Soso beached the canoe, and the two men stationed themselves on a small, muddy island with just a little solid ground surrounded by a considerable amount of wet, smelly marsh. They could see both heavily wooded banks. They sat as still as people can for over four hours. Birds continually flew overhead. There were flocks of sparrows, dozens of robins, cardinals, blackbirds, and an occasional blue jay. Even a kingfisher periodically appeared to attack the fish in the stream. However, none of the birds on James' list appeared.

Soso decided to try a spot further upstream. Just as the two men boarded the canoe, they were surprised by a blue flash as a small bird darted overhead. Neither man was sure, but both suspected that they had glimpsed one of their targets. They kept still for over an hour just sitting in the canoe. The bird did not return, so they headed in the general direction of its movement, further up the stream. They paddled about a hundred yards and beached the canoe again. They stayed until dark sitting in the muck and mud of the marsh. The mysterious blue bird did not return, so they headed back across the bay.

The bay was perfectly calm. The fires and lantern lights along the shore flickered in unison. The big moon was already high overhead. Its reflection in the water was bright and glimmering. It was an uplifting experience just to be on Great Sodus Bay at a time like this. Soso and James Audubon paddled slowly, so they could prolong the experience.

During the next day, Soso worked the corn and squash fields with Betty. The weeding and trimming had to be done, and he had promised to do it with her. James didn't mind. He spent the day painting and sketching. He hoped that tomorrow would bring him another glimpse, or better yet a prolonged study, of the elusive and mysterious bluebird.

That evening, Soso and Betty hosted James Audubon, Elizabeth and Sara Lummis, and Jim and Karen Davis for supper. After dinner, James entertained them with stories of the many rare and exotic birds he had encountered in France, England, Louisiana, and Florida. He told of royal bird watches and waterfowl hunts. He also explained the challenges of publishing his book of art plates. It was an expensive proposition, and James had worked very hard painting and selling other artwork to support his publishing. Subscriptions to his to-be-published book of plates were set at an astounding price of $1000. James's customers were usually royalty or wealthy businessmen from large cities. As realistic as James's prints were, the people of Sodus Bay experienced nature's real beauty for free and, therefore, had less need for James's artwork.

Everyone had a good time and enjoyed Betty's roasted pheasants and delicious fish stew. Elizabeth fit in fine with the adults. She was a very mature and intelligent fourteen year old. She especially enjoyed James's description of England and the activities of the royal family.

One More Try

Soso and James were in place on a small island in the marsh of First Creek by sunrise the next morning. This time they went just a little farther upstream and camouflaged themselves. Around ten in the morning, another flash of blue darted by in the sky. This time the bird lit on a tree directly across the stream from the bird watchers. The two men gazed in silence as the little bird danced along the branch for about fifteen minutes before it took off through the woods. James was ecstatic as he sketched and refined a previous drawing that he had made of the bluebird. After another hour, the work in the field was done. It was time to celebrate. The two men embraced and danced in the marsh and mud. James had come a long way to visit his friends on Sodus Bay. After seeing these two extraordinary birds, he knew the trip was well worth the time. Sodus Bay was quickly becoming his favorite spot. James never dreamed that he could see these two rare birds in a matter of only three days. Once again it had been a very successful day on Great Sodus Bay.

Special Departure

James had one more day on Sodus Bay, so he decided to spend the last part of it fishing with Soso and Elizabeth. They left Soso's dock in the late afternoon and headed for Elizabeth's favorite spot on Second Creek. They had a good time reeling in bass and telling stories. They stayed a little longer than intended. Soso kept insisting that they stay to catch just a few more fish. Then just about dusk, during a lull in the fishing and the storytelling, it happened. A huge dark shadow appeared from the trees and swept down on the marsh. The three of them sitting in the small boat fishing were overwhelmed as the majestic bird of prey set its wings and dipped for a fish just twenty yards from the boat. James eyes were fixed on the long-eared owl as it carried its prey back to the tree line and disappeared.

James immediately dropped his fishing gear and took up his art work. After several minutes, a smile crossed his face. He realized that Soso had set him up to find his third prize in just four days. As they sailed home, Soso sheepishly admitted that he knew where the owl was all the time. However, Soso also admitted that he was getting worried that the bird wouldn't appear until after dark. Soso had frequently seen the owl just before dark or a bit later in the evening when there was a clear, moon-lit sky.

James left the next day. He was amazed over Soso's knowledge. He found his Native American friend to be as intelligent and advanced in his thinking as anyone he had ever met. He wondered how any man, much less an Indian who had to endure prejudice and discrimination, could become such a talented boat builder, farmer, hunter, fisherman, and community leader, all while keeping his instinctive ties with nature. James wanted to stay longer, but business and personal commitments waited for him in New York City, where, after his business dealings, he was going to depart on an expedition to Maine and the northeast islands of Canada. He left a gift for Elizabeth, a pencil sketch of a long-eared owl swooping down to snatch a fish from the water. It was an experience and a drawing that she would never forget.

Trouble Out West

In 1832, there were more rumors and stories than ever about the situation with the Indians in the West. One week would bring news of progress in the relations between the Cherokees and the whites. The next week would bring news of more fighting. More often than not, Sam Houston would be involved in the good news and President Jackson would be associated with the bad. Soso wasn't surprised. He knew that compassionate white men like Sam Houston could help keep peace, but demanding, uncompromising leaders like Andrew Jackson could undo all the progress with one vicious or irrational decision.

The story of fighting and violence between the Sauk tribal leader, Black Hawk, and the Army troops was particularly frustrating for Soso. As he listened to and read the stories, none of what he learned made sense. For the past three winters, white squatters had violated treaties and taken Indian lands. The squatters took over cabins, fields, and they ruined sacred Indian burial grounds. The patient and wise Sauk Chief, Black Hawk, had tried to keep the peace, but as the whites continued to take his people's land and crops, he had no choice but to organize an Indian Army.

By early 1832, Black Hawk had assembled over 500 braves, capable of defending themselves, if necessary. In complete frustration, they finally took matters into their hands and drove the squatters off their lands in Illinois. The white squatters demanded protection and action from the Army as they retreated from the frontier back to the city of Chicago. The two armies, the whites with 1000 Regular Army soldiers led by General Atkinson, and the Indians with 500 braves led by Black Hawk, skirmished after five Indian emissaries of peace were savagely killed by the whites. Many white soldiers died in the brief fight as they fled to safety. The Indian forces had proven their superiority. However, it was a temporary victory.

The white Army regrouped and gained in strength, even though a cholera outbreak temporarily delayed their build-up. This time General Atkinson with over 1500 well-equipped, well-armed soldiers forcefully attacked the Indians. Black Hawk's braves were forced to withdraw. They got caught between an armed steamboat on the Mississippi River and Atkinson's Army. This time the Indians were massacred. Black Hawk not only lost most of his braves, but also many of the Indian women and children that were traveling with them. Moreover, Black Hawk was also captured. This victory by the whites was complete, and the Indian losses were devastating.

The emotion of this story raged within Soso. The unfairness, mistreatment, and discrimination angered him. This was another case of the white man's power being the only thing that mattered. The whites' Army waged brutal war that not only defeated the Indian warriors but vanquished entire tribes—men, women, and children. Indians fought noble wars; whites fought racial wars to win at all costs. Soso could do little except despair and hope for eventual understanding and change. His faith in the basic justice of man gave him some hope, but this was a clear case of injustice and misuse of power. His people, the Native Americans, who tried to live in peace and harmony, had to suffer and die because the white settlers wouldn't compromise to seek peace and harmony.

Call for Help

The Coast and Geodetic Survey was back in action. The previous head of the survey, Ferdinand Hassler, was re-appointed by Congress as the Superintendent of the Survey. Hassler was 62 years old, but he took to the task with tremendous energy and enthusiasm. He was a brilliant man, who thrived on this kind of challenging, technical job. He planned to take up right where he left off in 1818, some fourteen years before.

Hassler prepared the necessary equipment, renewed the previously completed charts and notes, and took stock of the unfinished projects. Then he started assembling his workers and survey crews. He hired several intelligent hard working men to his first survey team and proceeded to train them in surveying and to educate them in basic mathematics. He soon realized that he needed a skilled assistant to help him with this task. Jamey Davis immediately came to mind. Hassler knew Jamey understood the survey plan from his previous work as caretaker of the Survey, and he also knew that Jamey was a good teacher and an excellent surveyor. He wrote off to Charles Davies at West Point to see if Jamey was available for such duty. Hassler wanted Jamey and, if need be, he would get Congress to help pry Jamey away from his teaching duties at West Point. Hassler was not the kind of man who took no for an answer.

Charles Davies did not want to lose his able assistant, and Jamey enjoyed teaching cadets. The Academy was growing and an exciting, modern mathematics curriculum was evolving. Jamey would have preferred to stay at West Point. However, since duty called, an agreement was finally worked out in which Jamey would spend the next year, all of 1833, working as an Army representative with the Coastal Survey and would then return to West Point to continue his professorship.

On the day after Christmas, Jamey, Carin, Lenny, and Catherine, who was now called Katie, packed all their belongings in their government-issued wagon and left for Washington, DC. Lenny was two years old, and Katie was a toddler. Carin had her hands full watching the children, while Jamey managed the horses that pulled the heavy wagon. The 250-mile trip took over fourteen days of ten hours or more traveling time each day. It was cold, but fortunately there was no snow during their trip.

The Davis family made the trip as much fun as they could. Carin had games for the children, and Jamey took two days during the trip to visit and rest with his friend Ben Lummis in Philadelphia. The two men enjoyed each other's company. They hadn't seen one another in five years. Both had families and successful careers. Ben had endured the losses of his father and wife. However, he had recovered from his suffering. Jamey had endured the wild, untamed West and the hard work of four years at West Point. Both were satisfied with their accomplishments and comfortable with their lifestyles. The two-year olds, Lenny Davis and Georgette Lummis, were natural playmates. Carin and Ben got along fine. They told each other stories about Jamey, who knew he was a prime target, especially for his absent-mindedness. It was a pleasurable break in the long, tedious trip for the Davises and a nice break from a busy working schedule for Ben. The two friends, now nearly thirty years old, promised to see more of each other in the coming years.

New Home

Ferdinand Hassler had found a perfect home for the Davis family. Since Washington was a growing city with new homes being built all the time, Hassler looked until he found a two-bedroom house just like the one Jamey had described to him in a letter. It was close to Jamey's principal workplace, and the rent was reasonable. Jamey's Army-officer salary would be supplemented by the rental amount. It was an ideal situation for Jamey's family, and he knew that he would like this new assignment.

Initially, Carin had strong misgivings about the move, but when she saw the house she felt much better. The house and the neighborhood were much like those that she left at West Point. In addition, there were many facilities nearby that were located only in cities like Washington. Carin looked forward to touring the sights of the nation's capital and enjoying her growing family. Carin's outlook eventually matched her husband's optimism. It was going to be a fun year for the Davises in Washington, DC.

Jamey and Ferdinand Hassler got along well right from the beginning. Both men were expert surveyors and problem solvers. Hassler was determined to make progress on the immense task of surveying and mapping the coastline and boundaries of the United States. He needed several teams of competent workers and assistant surveyors. That was where Jamey was needed. For the next year, he would have to teach and train the men to do the job. With this arrangement, Hassler could spend his time getting the job moving. The two men made a good team, and both were satisfied with their roles.

Intruders

It was still early in the morning at Lummisville when shouts of anger came from the shoreline of Sodus Bay. Soso and Betty couldn't tell exactly what was being shouted or the reason behind the yelling. They were both in the garden when they heard the strange noises. As they came around the house and headed for the shore, they finally understood the words and could see their source. Four men in a small rowboat were yelling disparaging racial remarks aimed at the Indian-black couple. Soso had seen the men a couple times during the previous week or two. They were slave hunters, who claimed to have followed a fugitive slave to the area. Soso figured they were frustrated over the futility of their chase and had decided to vent their frustration on a perfect target for racial hatred—an elderly couple made up of two minorities. Soso believed that the best strategy was to ignore their shouts and stay out of sight. He hoped that they would get bored and go away.

Soso misjudged the levels of frustration and hatred in these men. They stayed in the boat just a few yards off shore all day. The shouts continued, although less frequently as the day progressed, but the insults and remarks were becoming stronger and more personal. Soso decided not to ask for help. His plan was to try to ignore these vile people, as he had always done throughout his life. However, Sara Lummis and Joe Sheldon came by and asked, later demanded, that the hecklers stop their harassment and leave. Finally, at dusk, the men rowed their boat away from Soso's and back to Sodus Point. It had turned out that Jim Davis had lent the boat to the men not knowing their intentions. When they returned, they told Jim their story of the day's events. They started telling him the details and joking about the Indian who didn't even show his face. As had happened before, Jim erupted with rage. He knocked two of the men down and was being pummeled by the other two before a couple of men from the village interceded. The fight quickly broke up, but tempers were still hot.

The four men retreated to the hotel, and Jim eventually calmed down and went home. He told Karen about the incident and then sailed across the bay to Soso's cove. It was fortunate that the moon was bright because Soso was simultaneously headed toward Jim's house. The two saw each other in the middle of the bay.

They brought their boats alongside each other's and discussed the situation. Jim was upset and wanted to take immediate action. His plan was to tell the sheriff and judge about the harassment and have the men arrested. Soso felt a calmer, more tolerant approach was better. He suggested that someone like William Wickham could explain the situation to the men and recommend that they leave the area. Sodus Point may not be a hotbed of abolitionism, but the residents wouldn't tolerate such actions against trusted and respected residents like Soso and Betty and having strangers fighting with one of their community leaders like Jim Davis.

Soso and Jim concluded that little could be done that evening, in any case, so they both returned home. They planned to meet at Jim's house the next morning. Betty was still very nervous and upset. She was afraid to be alone. She had hoped and prayed that this type of thing would never happen. She carefully hid her freedom papers so they would not be stolen or lost. Soso promised not to leave her alone until the men were gone. They went to sleep late in a worried state of mind.

More Trouble

Soso heard a noise and awoke in the darkness of the night just before the flash of light hit his eyes. He jumped from bed and yelled for Betty to hide under the bed. Then he ran through the house toward the work shed. By the time he arrived there, fire was raging, but, fortunately, it was confined to a corner of the work shed building. Soso was able to grab a bucket of water and throw water on the flames. Then he took a horse blanket from the shed and tried to smother the fire. He was making some progress but realized that he would need more help. As he turned to get more water in the bucket, there was Betty handing him another bucket of water to pour on the fire. He threw the damp blanket over more flames. By the time he had smothered what he could, Betty was there with more water. The couple worked at full speed, and by the time the twentieth bucket of water was thrown, the fire was out. They were exhausted, but relieved. They had saved their work shed from destruction.

As it turned out, this was one of the few times in many years that a boat in some stage of development was not in the building. The building was slightly damaged, but it could be repaired. Soso's woodpile of the finest planks and logs of rock elm, white oak, and white pine was unharmed. Soso and Betty sat together nervously guarding their property and wondering what would happen during the next two hours until sunrise.

An investigation in the light of the day showed Soso two sets of footprints and the hoofprints of two horses that had brought the arsonists to his land. They had thrown an oil lamp onto a pile of dried straw on the outside corner of the building. Luckily, Soso had reacted as quickly as he did. A minute or two delay, and the entire building would have been lost.

Soso and Betty cleaned up the mess. Elizabeth had just returned from school the previous week and came by early to see if Soso wanted to go fishing. As she headed for Soso's house, she discovered more damage. Soso's two boats and a canoe docked in the cove had been bashed and broken apart. The boats were sunk alongside the dock. She ran to Soso to report the damage and ask what was happening.

Soso explained to Elizabeth what he knew and had her go tell her mother and Joe Sheldon what had happened and have them come to Soso's. Joe, Sara, and one of Sara's farm hands named Sam arrived at Soso's within minutes. They were angry and disgusted by what they saw. Soso asked Sam to stand watch over his house and property. The plan was for Soso, Betty, Sara, and Elizabeth to travel to Sodus Point and report the crime to Sheriff West and Judge McCarver. Before they left, Joe's son Peter came by with a horse that he had found wandering loose among his father's fruit trees. No one knew where the horse came from, but Soso had an idea that the arsonists might be missing one of theirs.

Things had heated up back at Sodus Point. The four slave hunters had approached both Sheriff West and Judge McCarver. They wanted Jim Davis arrested for assault and Soso Washington arrested for horse stealing. They claimed that the two local men had not only plotted to harass them, but also had harbored the fugitive slave that they had chased from North Carolina.

Jim Davis was fighting mad. He had to be restrained when he heard the ridiculous charges against Soso and himself. Although he knew that Joe West had once caught him aiding the escape of slaves, he had hoped that incident was long forgotten. However, probably because of that incident long ago, Joe was indeed willing to investigate the otherwise ridiculous claims. Joe West couldn't put Jim in jail, since Sodus Point didn't have one. However, Joe did tell him to stay in his house until the investigation was completed. Joe had a guard at Jim's door to prevent his escape.

By the time Soso and the others arrived at Sodus Point, the villagers were in a rage. Most of the locals reckoned that Joe West was way out of line trying to arrest Jim Davis. Joe and Ken were trying to calm the crowd down when Soso and Sara began telling their stories of the previous day and evening's activities. This was too much for the local residents to take. By the time word spread through the village, the four men were in serious trouble. Their safety was in danger. There were calls for lynchings.

The usually competent constable Joe West had lost control of the mob as they rushed the hotel to grab the four southern intruders. The four men had no chance to escape. They were brought out onto the street, where the mob screamed for immediate action. As the mob moved in close to overwhelm them, the four men cowered in fear for their lives. One man finally stood in their defense and shouted over the mob's screams.

It was Soso. He yelled for everyone to stop and listen. When the noise subsided, he both scolded and thanked his friends and neighbors. "It is true. My wife, Jim Davis, and I have been wronged by these four men. We should be angry. However, what you are doing right now is just as wrong. We have laws to take care of these situations. I thank you for protecting our honor, but I ask you to let Constable West and Judge McCarver take charge of these men. I am sure they will do what is right. We must trust their judgment and the laws of our country."

Compromise

There was complete silence. Joe and Ken escorted the four men back to the hotel. Soso and Betty returned to Jim's house to wait for the lawmen. About an hour later Ken came by to talk over the situation with the Davises and Washingtons. The four men had given Joe and Ken the whole story and confessed to harassing Soso and Betty and setting fire to their workshed. All charges against Jim were dropped. Joe was planning to take the men to the jail in Lyons, where they would stand trial in a few days. Ken figured that Soso and Betty would have to testify at the trial.

These complications didn't seem necessary to Soso. If these men were courageous enough to confess and agreed to leave Betty alone, maybe they had learned their lesson. He asked if he could talk to the four men before Joe took them away. Ken agreed, and Soso and his four tormentors talked in private in the hotel room.

When Soso came out of the room, he requested that the four men be released. He believed that they had paid their dues and learned their lesson. Soso would not press charges, and they agreed to leave the area immediately. Joe and Ken were astonished. What about all the harassment and anguish? Didn't Soso want the men to pay for the damage to his building?

Soso reassured them that the arranged punishment would fit the crime. He had an agreement with the men that they would send him money for the damages within six months.

That was exactly how the case ended. Joe escorted the men as far as Arms' Crossroads. Peter Sheldon had delivered the missing horse from Lummisville that morning so that they all could ride away from Sodus Point. It was then time for Soso and Betty Washington and the entire community to forget the ugly incident and get on with their lives. To Soso, that was all that mattered. In his mind, justice had been served. Compromise and understanding had conquered prejudice.

Vacation

In 1833, Lummisville was at its zenith. The entire area was as magnificent as ever. It was also prepared for Ben Lummis's return: fruit trees were in full bloom; grounds were green; waters of the bay were silvery; the lake was a beep blue; the stately Lummis mansion was radiant. Ben returned to the place of his adult dreams and childhood escapades. He and two-year-old Georgette arrived by carriage at Float Bridge at noon on a bright, sunny, summer day. It had been a long, rough trip from Philadelphia for both of them, but their spirits were revitalized when they saw Sara and Elizabeth waiting at the carriage stop.

It had been a long time, but Ben was home again. Sara and Elizabeth were amazed by the changes in Georgette. Ben was surprised by the changes in Elizabeth. She was a beautiful young lady. She had matured and blossomed during her two years at the Aurora Seminary. Ben was not prepared for such a change. Little sister Elizabeth had become a mature fifteen-year-old woman.

All of them were excited as they rode from Float Bridge to Lummisville in an open carriage. Ben wanted Georgette to see everything at once. Sara and Elizabeth wanted to show them the new parts of the farm. It was an exciting and busy afternoon. That evening, the Lummis house was filled with friends and family. The Washingtons, Davises, Sheldons, and Greenes all took part in celebrating Ben's homecoming. He could stay in Lummisville for only three weeks, so he had to make the most of this time with his family.

Ben and Georgette had a marvelous time during these three weeks of vacation. They sailed, swam, and fished. They helped with the vegetable garden, fruit orchard, and farm animals. They talked, walked, sang, and danced. They took time to commune with nature. Ben got to see old friends, and Georgette met new ones. The only problem was that the three weeks went by too quickly.

To temper the sadness involved in their departure, Soso took Ben and Georgette to catch their stage at Float Bridge. Their itinerary called for stagecoach travel to Syracuse, canal boat to Albany, steamboat to New York, and stage and train from New York to Philadelphia. As Ben rode the various modes of transportation, he dreamed about the day when someone could take a train on a direct route all the way from a village like Sodus Point to a city like Philadelphia. If the people that he was working with were successful, such a trip would be possible within his lifetime. Exciting times lay ahead, and it was only his participation in the adventure of railroading that enabled him to return to his business life in the city of Philadelphia and leave the beauty of Sodus Bay behind.

Humiliation

The aftermath of Black Hawk's war was tragic in every respect. The great warrior had temporarily escaped, but he was very quickly surrounded by soldiers and surrendered. He was imprisoned in a filthy, miserable jail on the frontier. Eventually, President Jackson had him transferred to Washington. Black Hawk explained to the President that he had fought to protect his people and revenge their mistreatment. The whites had left him no choice. That didn't matter to Jackson. A broken, hopeless man, Black Hawk also vowed to the President never to fight again. However, to humiliate Black Hawk and to teach all renegade Indians a lesson, Jackson had the chief imprisoned again.

When Soso heard the story of Black Hawk, he felt humiliated. This action was a threat to freedom for virtually all the Native Americans on reservations east of the Mississippi. There was no longer any means to fight the injustice, greed, or power of the white man. The last great warrior of the eastern Indians had been crushed and disgraced. Power had defeated justice. Might had overpowered right. This just confirmed Soso's belief that the Indian way of life was doomed. Soso felt a deep loss, but he vowed to continue somehow to show that Indians could adapt, survive, and contribute in the world of the whites.

Leadership

Sylvanus Thayer had revitalized the Military Academy. During the fifteen years of his leadership, it had grown from a disorganized, training school into a first-class academic institution that rivaled the best schools in the world. There was no way to compare a graduate of 1833 with one of 1817 or earlier. Thayer's plan had been bold, and his implementation brilliant. He was more than the father of the Military Academy, he was the father of technology and technical education in the United States. It was his products, like Jamey Davis, Alex Bache, Horace Smith, and hundreds of others who would lead the technological development of the country over the next fifty years. As Thayer had envisioned, and Thomas Jefferson and George Washington had dreamed, West Point graduates would build the nation's roads, bridges, railroads, canals, buildings, and cities. They would lead businesses, governments, universities, and armies. They would develop and teach in the fields of engineering, science, and mathematics at the college level. They would fight the nation's wars and solve its problems. All this was due to the heroic and brilliant efforts of Sylvanus Thayer.

The heavy burden of leadership and innovation had taken its toll on Thayer. He continually had to fight for everything he and his Academy obtained and produced. Numerous times he took on the War Department, Congress, and the President to get something the Academy needed. He was also tough on his faculty and his cadets. At times, he was criticized for being too stern and too tough. He was the visionary leader and the source of all authority at West Point. However, he felt there was more to be done, and for the first time he couldn't move an obstacle that stood in his way—President Andrew Jackson. Jackson's constant meddling and criticism were just too much to take. So with deep remorse, Thayer resigned as Superintendent of the Academy to return to military engineering, to design the United States coastal defenses, and to use his educational vision to establish other schools and colleges.

In Washington, both Jamey Davis and Ferdinand Hassler were saddened when they heard word of Thayer's resignation. Although in his new job, Thayer would sometimes work with Hassler. Both men admired Thayer's accomplishments and liked him. It would be tough for the Academy to replace such a remarkable man. The new Superintendent would be Major René De Russy, who graduated from West Point in 1812, several years before Thayer's curricular improvements were instituted. Jamey wondered what changes would take place as a result. He had felt comfortable about his return to West Point with Thayer in charge. Now he wondered what he would find when he returned to his teaching job in a few months.

Order and Progress

The Shaker community had grown and matured during its ten years on Sodus Bay. The members' hard work had paid dividends in terms of fertile farmland, well-built homes, and useful facilities such as docks, storage barns, and a blacksmith shop. The community's population had increased to a peak of 150 residents, but had recently declined to about a hundred. Everything in their settlement was clean and orderly. The Shakers got along fine with the other residents of the area. While some people joked about their strange religious practices, everyone respected their hard-working, productive lifestyles. The Shakers were wonderful neighbors. However, since the Shakers did not have children and were no longer attracting young converts, their aging population was decreasing.

New Religion

The people in the Sodus Bay area had heard about the new religion called Mormon, which had been established by a local man—Joseph Smith. Smith had traveled around the area, preaching, teaching, and defending his belief. He had come to the village of Sodus Point at the request of local citizens who were interested in hearing what he had to say.

Smith told his listeners about how the *Book of Mormon* had been given to him by an angel. Smith based his new church on the teachings of Mormon. Mormon was a prophet who explained how a Hebrew tribe had settled in the new continent and had been told by Jesus Christ how to practice the Christian Religion. During his speech at Sodus Point, Jim recognized Joseph Smith as the young boy who had helped the Shakers when they first arrived in the area.

As Jim listened, he was impressed by the passion and enthusiasm exhibited by Joseph and his assistant, Sidney Rigdon. Jim saw some similarity in the discipline and structure of the Shaker and Mormon beliefs and respected those who held such deep religious faith. After the speech, Jim wished Joseph well in his endeavors. Jim was comfortable with his Methodist Christianity and was committed to serve his own church.

"Joseph, you are an enthusiastic and energetic man. Your passion for your religion is tremendous. Good luck in your work." Jim told Smith.

Smith replied, "Religion is one of life's passions, and everyone should have passion in their lives. I can tell that you have deep passion for many good things. You have no need for my religion, but many people do."

"I hope you find those in need. Don't forget that the power of religion is that it tells us how we ought to live our lives. God bless you Joseph Smith. Help your people live good lives."

"And, God bless you and your family, Jim Davis." Joseph Smith then went on to talk to others in the crowd about passion and religion.

Celebrity

It was an astonishing story. Big city newspapers had picked up the some of the details of the racially based incident involving Soso, Betty, and the four slave hunters. They were calling it the "Soso Affair." Most of the newspapers in the North advocated the abolition of slavery, and, thus, they made a big deal out of the incident. Newspapers and magazines such as *Liberator, The Rights of All*, and *New York Evening Post*, carried articles praising Soso's actions, ridiculing the slave hunters, and supporting rights for blacks and Indians.

Writers and leaders in the equal rights movement, like William Bryant, Samuel Cornish, John Chavis, and Morris Brown, not only supported Soso's actions, but also played up his lifetime contributions to his community and nation. Soso was amazed that these people whom he had never seen or met knew so much about him. Certainly, he hadn't sent these famous writers and abolitionists any information. Who was sending them these details? Could such stories help his people or the blacks fight against prejudice and discrimination?

It seemed that almost overnight Soso had become something of a national hero to a small but growing segment of the nation's population. The stories told about his disagreements with and appeals for Indian rights to President Jackson. Headlines and lead-ins to articles about Soso were saying things like: "Indian more civilized than Village, State, or the Nation"; "Indian Hero Sends Away Southern Slave Hunters"; "Call on Indians to Help Abolish Slavery"; "Indian knows Solution, President Doesn't."

All this attention and fame embarrassed Soso and Betty. Their only consolation came from the fact that this publicity might help the black and red people of America and lead to the abolition of slavery and the end of the banishment and mistreatment of Native Americans. Therefore, Soso and Betty endured the personal attention and continued to talk to their friends and neighbors about the issues. If only there were more white people like the authors, editors, and avid readers of these abolitionist journals.

Back Home

The return trip back north for the Davis family was no easier or shorter than their move to the South, just a little over a year before. Jamey, Carin, Lenny, and Katie rumbled along in their heavy, overloaded wagon for twelve days. On this trip there was no time available to stop and rest in Philadelphia to see Ben. Jamey had to get to West Point as soon as possible to take up his teaching duties.

"Are we there yet?" Two-year-old Katie asked again as the wagon slowly entered a small village in northern New Jersey.

"Dad said he'd tell us when we got there, and he didn't say it yet," four-year-old Lenny reminded his sister.

"Let's count the cows in that field," suggested Carin, who had read and told many stories to her two children as they bumped along in the slow wagon. She, more than anyone, suffered on these trips. The two children enjoyed parts of the trip, and Jamey actually loved to travel.

"The last farm had 32 cows. I think there are even more in this field." Of course, the two toddlers didn't really count or understand their father's guess. But any activity that made the time go by was tried. Carin was beginning to wonder if they would ever make it.

Department Head Charles Davies needed Jamey's experience to maintain excellence and growth in the curriculum. Mathematics was the foundation of the West Point engineering program. The Academy had grown to over sixty students per class year. Professor Davies needed someone like Jamey to develop and train his faculty of five officers and two upperclass cadets to provide high quality instruction in small classes to the talented, hard-working cadets. Experienced instructors Edward Ross and Charles Hackley had recently left the Academy, and the only other experienced instructor in the Department was Albert Church. Jamey would definitely be an integral component of the faculty.

It was only by coincidence that the Davis family was able to move back into their previous home on West Point. After they had left, William Owen, instructor in the Natural Philosophy Department, and his new wife had moved into the quarters. They had enjoyed the house as much as the Davises had and maintained everything in fine order. However, William had been itching for an assignment on the western frontier, especially down near Texas. He wanted to be where the action was. William kept writing the War Department asking for reassignment. He finally got his wish just a month before the Davises were to arrive back at the Academy. So the familiar, pleasant, white house with a pretty fence around the yard was available for the Davises. Carin was thrilled to be home. Likewise, Jamey was ready to teach cadets. His assignment with the Coast and Geodetic Survey had been rewarding, but in his heart, Jamey was a mathematics professor.

Temporary Dislocation

The railroad business was booming. In many places, the railroad was an instant success. However, building locomotives and train cars, buying land, and laying track were expensive endeavors. The railroads were very dependent on supportive bankers, and while the banks saw the potential of the railroad, they still regarded them as risky adventures.

It was because of the growing bank-railroad relationship, however, that Ben's bank decided to transfer him to New York City in 1834. Railroads had become big business, and the bank's big business accounts were handled there. This time Ben knew what to expect and how to cope with the pace and lifestyle of New York City. The bad news was the dilemma over how to care for his daughter Georgette. After some consideration of arranging for care in New York City, Ben had no choice but to leave her in Philadelphia with the Willigs. Ben's sister-in-law, Georgiana Willig, was 13 years old and took good care of Georgette. He felt comfortable leaving his daughter under the Willigs' care, but he would miss her tremendously. He promised to return to Philadelphia as often as he could. He also promised himself that his stay in New York City would be temporary. He had definite plans for the future, plans that would eventually take him away from the overcrowded and dirty cities.

Boom Towns

The Erie Canal was in full operation. This safe, reliable, and comfortable mode of transportation brought people, business, and industry to central and western New York. Three major transportation hubs on this waterway had developed over the past several years. These were the fast-growing, fast-paced cities of Syracuse, Rochester, and Buffalo. It seemed almost by coincidence that people congregated and began settling in these three places. It was due to the strength and vision of the strong leaders who had settled in these locations and helped grow the communities along with the physical features or resources of these locations.

Syracuse had been blessed with salt reserves along the lake of the Onondagas. James Geddes began developing that business in addition to his work on the Erie Canal in the Syracuse area. He had no technical training but learned quickly and had become a surveyor for the canal. His friend Joshua Forman also helped in the canal construction. Under their leadership, Syracuse became a city with jobs for workers in textiles, salt manufacturing, banking, and food processing.

Rochester was an even more isolated, unlikely spot for a city to develop. It began as a small mill town, using the Genesee River for power. However, under the leadership of Nathaniel Rochester and because of the convenience of the canal, it steadily grew into a city. People settled in Rochester to work in mills, textile factories, and transportation.

The city of Buffalo grew at the terminus of the canal. This was a natural location for a city to form. There was ample need for people to work on the canal, unload the freight, and distribute the goods. Buffalo was destined to grow. With the help and encouragement of Mr. Buffalo, many settlers on their way west decided to stay in Buffalo, where land was cheap and work plentiful.

Other parts of central and western New York were enjoying growth and prosperity in 1834. It seemed like many of the small villages were destined to grow and become small cities. Places like Geneva, Auburn, Fulton, Oswego, and Batavia were well-known and booming. Everywhere, there were new towns, new roads, new bridges, and new people. It seemed as if the entire region was growing, except possibly Sodus Point. The boom of civilization seemed to bypass the most suitable and sensible spot. Why?

There wasn't a good answer, but it was happening. Sodus Point remained a frontier island in the sea of civilization, growth, and prosperity that swept through the area. The residents didn't mind, so no one paid any attention.

Struggle for Freedom

The newspapers and journals had long forgotten the Soso Affair. They had plenty of new material demonstrative of the nation's mistreatment of Indians and blacks. The latest news reported that several Seminole chiefs had refused to sign the Treaty of Payne's Landing, which had been negoti- ated in 1832. The nation began to follow the exploits of one of the rebel Seminole chiefs named Osceola who had steadfastly refused to sign. The treaty was designed by President Jackson as part of his removal policy to send the Seminoles to the Indian Territories in Oklahoma to join the Creeks and the other eastern tribes banished to reservation life. This was the final piece that Jackson needed to rid the East of all unwanted Indians. The gov- ernment planned to pay for all the Seminole land in Florida a ridiculously low sum of $75,000 and a blanket for each Indian. As part of the Treaty, the blacks and anyone with any black ancestry in the tribe would be sold back into slavery. The Seminole Indians, especially Osceola, responded to this insulting treaty with contempt and scorn. Osceola took his people deeper into the swamps and became fugitives from the whites' Army.

In April, Osceola had once again refused to sign the treaty and was caught by the Army and imprisoned. However, he quickly escaped, and a full-scale war erupted between the Seminoles and the forces of the U.S. Army, which were led by Indian agent General Wiley Thompson.

Neither Thompson nor any other white general, officer, or soldier was prepared for the kind of warfare that the Seminoles would be willing to fight to keep their land and freedom. Osceola and his followers introduced and perfected a highly successful form of guerrilla warfare designed to resist any intrusion or campaign of advancement by the whites. They slipped in and out of the swamps striking out at whatever and whomever they found vulnerable and then disappeared into hiding. The swamps of

Florida were impregnable to the overburdened white soldiers. While the technical superiority of the whites was exploited on the open plains of the West, it was no help in the dense swamp of Florida. The Indian superiority as a warrior, along with their superior tactics and leadership, made this an even fight between two distinctly different armies.

Soso read with a mix of joy and heartbreak the newspaper accounts of the futile attempts of the white men's Army to conquer the out-numbered and out-gunned Seminoles. He knew that in this type of conflict the Indians held the upper hand. The superiority of the whites' weapons and numbers could be offset, at least temporarily, by the Indians' ability to use nature to their advantage. Soso read with great interest as President Jackson lost much of his support in his ridiculous war against the Seminoles over the ownership of the worthless swamps, which were only hospitable to the Seminoles. The whites didn't really want nor need the land. They just didn't want the Indians as neighbors.

Prosperity

In 1834, Ben made more money in New York City than he had made in his entire career as a banker. However, he had not seen his daughter even once during the entire year. So despite his good financial fortune, he was once again depressed over his urban lifestyle. The railroad industry was booming. Ben was in charge of meting out large sums of money at high interest rates to men who would make fortunes. It was only fair that Ben as the banker and one of the risk-takers shared in some of the profits. Engineers continually built better locomotives and train cars, and railroad executives built business empires. President Jackson rode a train down in Baltimore. Everyone wanted to be involved and in tune with this latest technology. The railroad created new and bigger markets and industries for the cities. Farms seemed closer than ever to cities. Clothing, supplies, and equipment were taken to the rural farms, and crops and workers were taken to the markets and industries in the cities. Americans were finding out how to be mobile. Quickly, they were discovering how to profit by their mobility.

The early trains weren't luxurious, but for many people, they were exciting and adventurous. The roadbeds and tracks were often crudely built. The passenger cars usually were made of wood, and their seats were hard and uncomfortable. There were no shock absorbers on the early train cars, so the ride was bumpy and rough. Lighting came from candles and lanterns. Heat came from wood stoves, but most of the warmth escaped through the numerous cracks and holes in the cars. Cold wind blew into the cars, along with smoke and soot from the locomotive. Despite all these hardships, it seemed that everyone loved to ride trains. Actually, it was much faster and often more comfortable than wagons or stagecoaches.

Ben was so busy with his banking work that he was afraid he would have to miss the big event in Sodus Point. After he reconsidered, he decided that both he and Georgette would definitely go there. It was important and exciting. He could hardly believe that his sister Elizabeth was getting married.

Elizabeth was seventeen years old and engaged to marry Bill Ellet, who was a visiting chemistry professor at Geneva College. The two had met at Geneva College several times as Elizabeth traveled back and forth between Lummisville and Aurora. Elizabeth was both extremely intelligent and pretty. She was much more mature than her young age suggested. She was fluent in French, Italian, and German. She could converse with her fiancée about many topics in his own field of chemistry, although science and mathematics were not her favorite subjects. She was already an accomplished author. She had published literary works in several journals and translated an Italian play into English. Her first book of poetry had been published only a month before her wedding. She was especially proud of this work, since it contained several poems about the beauty of Sodus Bay and Lake Ontario.

Even though Bill Ellet, at 29, was substantially older than Elizabeth and an experienced college professor, he was more impulsive and fun-loving than Elizabeth was. His two-year term of visitation at Geneva College was over this year, and he and his new bride would return to his regular school, Columbia College in New York City, for the fall semester. Of course, the Lummises knew Columbia College well because of Ben's three years of attendance there. However, during Ben's stay at Columbia, Ben Lummis had never met Professor Ellet.

The couple's wedding was the first day of June. Ben and Georgette arrived from their travels from New York City and Philadelphia the day before. Georgiana Willig and her father, George, brought Georgette from Philadelphia to New York City via the train so Ben could travel directly to Lummisville from New York with Georgette. Ben and Georgette took the river steamboat to Albany and the canal and stagecoach the rest of the way on their twelve-day, 350-mile journey from New York City to Lummisville.

Preacher Stevens performed the wedding ceremony during a radiant, sun-filled afternoon on the verandah, which was overflowing with people from the Sodus Bay area, Geneva College, and Aurora Seminary. Bill's parents could not make the journey from New York City. However, one dignitary from New York was able to attend. William Bryant, editor of the *New York Evening Post* was there to meet the young woman that he had corresponded with, but never met. Bryant had written and published numerous articles on the Soso Affair and other abolitionist causes. At the reception, Bryant told Soso all about Elizabeth's accurate and detailed reporting of the incident. Bryant was proud of his passionate article entitled, "Sosoenodus, Brave Spirit." Now Soso finally knew who was reporting the inside information about the case. The two men talked about their beliefs in freedom and rights for individuals and the evils of slavery. Soso respected Byrant's dedication to the cause and the victims of prejudice. Bryant respected Soso's wisdom about these complicated issues.

Sara Lummis was revitalized with tremendous energy and enthusiasm to put on her daughter's wedding. Lummisville and her homestead were primed and ready for their guests. The Lummis mansion was magnificent. For that one weekend, everything was perfect. Soso and Betty helped with the arrangements. Ben and Georgette pitched in after they arrived. "Uncle" Soso gave away the bride, and Bill Ellet, the distinguished professor, looking more like a young, nervous boy, took Elizabeth's hand in marriage. It was a grand and glorious day.

Two days after the wedding, Lummisville was back to normal. Sara was used to being alone, but now her family was permanently gone. Soso and Betty were a great help to her, but the farm was really more than she could manage by herself. She had been ill on and off for more than a year. Soso and Betty were the only ones who knew the seriousness of her illness. She even hid it from Ben and Elizabeth. She worried about both of them. She knew Ben was unhappy in the city. Elizabeth was so young. The only things that kept Sara going were the strength and dedication of her friends. Despite everything, she knew that she would be happy and satisfied with her life on the shore of Sodus Bay. She felt contentment and a great peace of mind living on the shore of her beloved silvery-watered bay.

Part IV

More Struggles

New Author

West Point winters were long and gray. However, people were so busy there that they rarely noticed. Cadets had to study and learn. They had to march and train. They had to grow and develop. Everything was still in place from Thayer's system of competition, discipline, and high standards. The professors were busy preparing classes, teaching, grading, and developing cadets. Jamey was busy at work, especially since he and Albert Church were the two principal assistant professors completely responsible for training other instructors. Since about a half of the instructors turned over every year, faculty training was a high priority. The faculty's growth and development were necessary to pave the way for cadet growth and development.

Professor Davies was a tireless worker who demanded the same from his assistants. He didn't teach many cadets, but he was busy writing exams and visiting classes. Another task that kept Professor Davies busy was textbook writing. He had written four mathematics textbooks and was in the process of writing another. Professor Davies knew how busy Jamey was as an instructor and father. However, the Professor had encouraged his talented assistant to write a textbook. Charles Davies knew that Jamey had the ability and tenacity to accomplish such a tremendous task. The country needed mathematics textbooks, since much of the material in the West Point curriculum was beginning to be used in other colleges and universities across the nation. New schools were starting every year. Science and mathematics were becoming regular parts of the curriculum. People were realizing that these technical subjects were helpful for the understanding and development of the new, modern technologies. Jamey's talents were a resource that needed to be developed and put into production.

Because of this considerable need and since this was the first summer that Jamey would be staying at West Point with comparably few duties, Jamey decided to start the task of writing a textbook during the summer. Jamey decided to write the book on the subject he knew most about—surveying. He actually enjoyed the higher-level mathematics topic of differential equations more than surveying, but he decided that would not be an appropriate topic because few students in America would ever study such an esoteric subject. Surveying was taught in many schools and was needed by students considering a career in that important technical profession. Professor Davies approved Jamey's plan and spurred him on to write the best surveying textbook in America.

Jamey spent full days at work in the Mathematics Department all summer long. He spent most of his time preparing the tests to be given in the courses during the next academic year, giving oral entrance and placement exams to new cadets, like the one he had taken, preparing teaching guides, and training new instructors. After work, he would spend an hour or two at home to eat supper with Lenny and Katie. Then Jamey walked back to the Academy's library where he would work on the textbook. It was tough going for the novice writer. He would write and rewrite portions of the book many times over. Sometimes, he would be so dissatisfied with his writings that he would throw sheaves of manuscript away and start a section all over again. Even though Jamey knew all about the practical and theoretical aspects of surveying, this topic had to be explained clearly and succinctly at just the right level so a student could master the important concepts. Jamey was learning firsthand how difficult it was to write a textbook.

By the end of the summer of 1836, Jamey had completed over half the book. He showed the neatly printed copy of what he had written to Charles Davies; his mentor was impressed. This was a fine start to a textbook that would be very helpful for students at West Point and many other schools. Jamey had included many practical examples, instructive questions, and clear explanations. Davies edited the manuscript and recommended the inclusion of several more figures to supplement the exposition. Professor Davies took Jamey across the river to the village of Fishkill to meet with the book publisher, A.S. Barnes. Barnes was also impressed with Jamey's work and offered the novice author the handsome sum of $200 for the copyright to his work. In addition Jamey would receive a three percent royalty on the revenues of all copies sold. Jamey signed a contract and returned to West Point with a $100 advance on the payment of the copyright.

Charles Davies was proud of Jamey. He knew how difficult it was to find the time and energy for such a tremendous task. Charles had important plans for Jamey. He knew that he wouldn't be at West Point forever, and he was grooming Jamey Davis to be his replacement as Department Head. It was a remarkable coincidence that their names were so similar. Charles Davies intended to have Jamey Davis succeed him as the Mathematics Department Head at West Point.

City Life

As always, Mrs. Elizabeth Ellet was the life of the party. All of Professor Bill Ellet's colleagues on the faculty of Columbia enjoyed conversing with the brilliant young woman. And Elizabeth, likewise, enjoyed her new city lifestyle. She had relaxed somewhat her previously serious personality. There was so much to do and see in the city. To Elizabeth, New York City was endless fun and excitement. She had lived there eight months and still saw buildings for the first time and met new people every day. Given the vast resources of Columbia's books and professors, Elizabeth read, discussed, and learned a good deal about many diverse subjects. She was in her element in this urban environment.

While her own life was progressing fine, Elizabeth worried deeply about her brother and mother. She got to see Ben nearly every week. His apartment was a little over a half-hour carriage ride from the Ellet home on the north edge of the city. In her opinion, Ben worked too hard, and his health was suffering as a result. She tried to help her brother by caring for his apartment and including him in many of her own activities. However, he was always too busy to relax fully and enjoy Elizabeth's company.

She finally discovered a way to help to revitalize Ben and to give him an escape from work. She offered to have Georgette and Georgiana come from Philadelphia and stay with her. This way Ben would have the opportunity to be with the pride of his life, his daughter Georgette. Georgette was now five years old and full of energy. She was old enough to miss her father and want his company. Georgina, Georgette's aunt, had practically served as her mother for quite sometime. Elizabeth had enough room in her house for both Georgiana and Georgette to stay there. With this arrangement, Ben could see his daughter for a few hours every day after work, and Elizabeth was able to relieve some of Georgina's responsibility for Georgette.

Worry in Lummisville

Elizabeth's worry over her mother took on an entirely different cast. It was what she didn't know that concerned her. Sara Lummis had never been a consistent letter writer, and now that she was sick, her letter writing was even less frequent. Elizabeth wrote faithfully, knowing that her mother appreciated hearing from her. Soso was Elizabeth's only source of reliable information about her mother, and the news from Soso was not encouraging.

Sara Lummis had expended all her energy to revitalize the farm. The Lummis homestead was again vibrant. The fields were productive and the grounds were well maintained. Soso and Betty had taken over as Sara's business and field managers. Ben and Elizabeth would have been proud of their mother's accomplishments. Dr. William Lummis would have been amazed at all that Sara had done in the seven years since his death. However, the work had taken its toll, and Sara was extremely weak and tired. Soso knew that Sara was ill and needed help. He worried that she was unprepared for the harsh cold of another winter. For the first time in her life, she looked her age—57 years old.

Another Try

The big news around Sodus Bay in 1836 was the new proposed canal that would link the bay to the Erie Canal. Many big names in business in the area had formed a company to build a canal from the Erie Canal in Lyons to the southern shore of Sodus Bay. Local men like Byram Greene and James Pollock were part of this company. Soso and others were disinclined to see that such a venture was possible or profitable. They had seen numerous attempts at this ambitious project fail. Even the initial plans to end the Erie Canal at Sodus Bay had been changed at the last minute to end the canal in Buffalo instead. In addition, railroads were becoming a major competition for canals. However, Soso was impressed by the news that he heard in November. The Sodus Bay Canal Company had bought the 1500 acres of land belonging to the Shakers. During the year, the Shaker community had shrunk to less than fifty believers, and the community leaders figured that it was time to move their flock further west. The Canal Company made an offer the Shakers couldn't refuse. The believers would move out by the following summer to make room for the canal. Things were certainly changing on the shores of Sodus Bay.

Southern Stalemate

Soso continued to follow the exploits of the southern Native Americans, the Seminoles. Osceola and his fellow tribesmen, using effective guerrilla warfare tactics, continued to confound the American military. Andrew Jackson, in the last year of his second term as President, sent more and more men into the field in an attempt to crush the outnumbered Indians. As he had in the past, Jackson gave each general he appointed the mission of conquering and removing the Seminoles from Florida. Each general lasted just a few months before the frustrated President relieved him and sent in another doomed replacement.

During the spring of 1836, the newspapers brought news of the Texans' war for independence from Mexico. This war brought Soso more bad news. His old friend and supporter for Indian rights, Davy Crockett, died in a bloody battle at a place called the Alamo in San Antonio. In Soso's mind, it was a shame that such a strong, yet understanding man should be lost just when the country needed more men like him. Andrew Jackson had run Davy out of Congress and Tennessee for criticizing the Indian movement policies, and now Davy was dead. Why couldn't Jackson see the folly of his hate war against the Indians?

Special Orders

Generals Thompson, Gaines, and, even the celebrated leader, Winfield Scott, had all failed. Late in 1836, Jackson, as a lame-duck President, sent General Jessup south, along with Colonels William Harney and Zachary Taylor. This group was smart enough to insist on enough men, supplies, and time to do the job right. Among the soldiers receiving orders to accompany this new command into the field was First Lieutenant Jamey Davis. His orders for combat action in Florida were delivered to him at West Point on November 10, 1836. The orders relieved him of duties at the Military Academy effective immediately. He had one week to prepare and join the new command group leaving Washington D.C. for Florida on November 20. The only good thing in his orders was the necessary permission for his family to stay in their quarters at West Point until his return from his combat assignment.

Jamey wondered why he was needed in Florida. Many other officers could fight Indians, and he was among only a few who could teach mathematics. It was fortunate that he had finished his surveying textbook, as Barnes was ready to print the first edition. Jamey notified Professor Davies, who upon hearing the news became upset over the impending loss of his principal assistant at just the wrong time. He notified Academy Superintendent Major DeRussy, who had himself spent duty time down in the swamps of Florida ten years before. But nothing could be done to change the order. Jamey had to go. The Army had made its decision. In that case, Jamey was proud to serve and confident that he could help his country as an effective fighting man and strong field leader.

Jamey explained the nature of his new duty to Carin, who was shaken by his impending departure. She worried about his safety. Would he survive? Would he return? How long would he be gone?

Carin was thankful for her family's opportunity to stay at West Point while Jamey was gone. At least she and her children, six-year-old Lenny and five-year-old Katie, would be well cared for at the West Point fortification. She worried about all the dangers that her husband would face in combat. She had heard many terrible stories about the conditions in Florida, and, what's more, she worried about her unborn child. Carin hadn't even had time to tell Jamey about her pregnancy, and she decided that this was not the time to make that announcement. For the time being, this was her secret. She was hopeful that her husband would be home before the baby was born. Every day she prayed for his safety and quick return.

Combat Duty

At times, Jamey rather enjoyed the weather of the Florida swamps. However, he didn't enjoy some of the extras that went with the nice weather. On Christmas day of 1836, he stood waist deep in muddy, insect-infested swamp water. He was supposed to be waiting to ambush an Indian hunting party. As was often the case, the Indians never came. Because of activities like this one, Jamey was on his way to becoming as frustrated as the rest of the 8,000 soldiers deployed in Florida to drive out a few hundred starving Indians, who had already withstood over ten years of continual, but generally ineffective, harassment from white soldiers.

Jamey's Assignment

General Jessup had amassed a large Army to move against the weak, out-numbered, and beleaguered Indians and Blacks that combined to form the remains of the once powerful and prosperous Seminole nation. Despite his huge numerical advantage, Jessup's original plan was to show trust and compassion in order to persuade his opponents to give up without further bloodshed. He planned to use diplomatic and trusted officers like Jamey to negotiate terms of peace with the Seminole leaders.

Jamey's first meeting with the Seminoles took place in a small Indian village. He and five other officers, including Colonel Zachary Taylor, met with Abraham, an emancipated black man and leader of many of the black Seminoles, and Alligator, one of the Seminole chiefs. Jamey was impressed by the wisdom of these two men. They clearly explained that the whites' demands of deportation to the West, placement of Seminoles under the rule of the Creeks, and the revision of all blacks to slavery made no sense and would not be accepted. As they explained, the Seminoles needed very little land to plant crops and could easily stay out of the white man's way in the vast countryside of Florida. Until the whites came to their senses, the Seminoles would be forced to continue their resistance. However, with just a little compromise on the part of the whites, they were ready to peaceful-ly settle this insane war.

While the official position of the negotiating party was that the Indians were uncooperative and belligerent, Jamey saw firsthand a formidable opponent that held the upper hand along with a just cause. In Jamey's opin-ion, the American Army could never really conquer these well-trained and dedicated Native American and black soldiers. The Indians and blacks were on their own land and in their own element. They knew how to fight in the dense underbrush and then disappear into the swamps. Right from the start, Jamey knew he was involved in fighting for an unethical and lost cause. Like everyone else, his morale suffered and frustrations grew. Why fight the Seminoles? It made no sense, unless you were full of hatred and prejudice.

Fun in the City

Elizabeth's plan worked to perfection. The presence of Georgette and Georgiana in New York City completely changed Ben's outlook on life. He enjoyed seeing his daughter and spent as much time as he could with her. Ben, Georgette, Georgiana, Elizabeth, and Bill took advantage of many of the opportunities available in the city. They toured the city's sights. They went swimming at the beach and sailing on the rivers. Most of all, they enjoyed the others' company. On the whole, they were a big, happy family.

Ben's success in managing railroad accounts led to his advancement to the highest management level of the bank. This position gave him greater responsibility and sometimes more flexibility in his schedule. Instead of filling his calendar with appointments, he took time off to be with his family and enjoy life. Ben's supervisor, the bank's president, never complained. He knew that Ben was the lifeblood of the bank. Making the right decisions and keeping his bankers working at peak efficiency, Ben had achieved success in the largest bank in the nation.

In this capacity, Ben had the opportunity to play a key role in the development of a significant invention. Of course, he didn't realize the true potential for the device until much later. One afternoon in the spring of 1837, a fifty-year-old fine arts professor from New York University entered his bank in search of financial backing for the refinement and marketing of a devise to send messages electronically. The professor already had crude devices that coded a message, transmitted it along a wire, and received the message at the end of the wire. The code translated letters and numbers into the dots and dashes of the message signal. This remarkable device was fascinating to Ben. Right in his office, Ben watched intently as his visitor keyed in a signal of beeps and clicks on a funny instrument. At the other end of the wire, a similar apparatus mimicked the input with a clicking and clacking noise. The man claimed to be able to send messages many miles using this equipment, a miraculous power source called a battery, and very long wires.

At the end of an afternoon of deep discussions and amazing demonstrations, Ben had committed his bank to supporting this new, risky technology and this brilliant inventor. Ben advised him to get busy with his patent application, and Samuel Morse left Ben's office a happy man with renewed energy and sufficient support to convince the world that his telegraph, the name he gave his system of transmitters, receivers, and wires, could change the way the world communicated. It was the start of a strong friendship between Ben Lummis and professor-inventor Samuel Morse.

Falling in Love

Something special happened to Ben during that spring of enjoying life. He fell in love with Georgiana. She had developed into a beautiful seventeen-year-old lady. She had cared for his daughter and her niece, Georgette, for six years. She was a mature, yet fun-loving women, much like her late sister Ann Marie. Despite the awkward situation of Georgiana being the sister of his deceased wife, Ben knew that he loved her, just as he had loved her sister. And after spending a wonderful spring with Ben, Georgiana likewise knew that she loved him.

Ben and Georgiana eventually communicated their feelings for one another. In order to make future plans, Ben, Georgiana, and Georgette traveled to Philadelphia during the first week of May. Ben proposed to Georgiana and asked her parents for their blessing as he had done before for their other daughter. The Willigs were pleased with the proposal and happy for their daughter, son-in-law, and granddaughter. While this was an unusual relationship, they knew that this was best for all concerned. They made plans for a July wedding in Philadelphia.

Ben returned to New York City by himself, while Georgiana and Georgette stayed in Philadelphia. Georgiana needed time to make the wedding preparations, and the Willigs wanted to enjoy, for the short time until the wedding, the granddaughter that they had helped raise. It would be a busy two months.

Demonstration

In addition to preparing for the wedding, Ben was helping Samuel Morse promote his invention. Ben had become a believer in the potential of this new system and wanted to make sure it was successful. Sam and Ben agreed to give a public demonstration of the system. Right in front of Ben's bank, Sam set up his telegram system and ran wire around the corner to another receiver some 300 yards away and out of sight from the transmitter. Sam ran one device and Ben the other. Sam's most powerful and reliable battery powered the circuit. They proceeded to show local businessmen, curious on-lookers, newspaper reporters, and several government officials how messages could be sent and received. Once they saw it work, most observers were astounded and convinced of the utility of this marvelous invention. Others were skeptical and confused as to why anyone would waste time sending dots, dashes, clicks, and clacks from one spot to another.

The next day's newspaper accounts reflected these diverse views on the worth of the telegraph. Several papers gave it big headlines with glowing reviews. Others ignored the utility of the demonstration completely, writing about the crowds that had gathered to see a bizarre demonstration given by an eccentric professor. Sam and Ben still had lots of work to do to convince people that the telegraph would change their lives.

Retirement

As it was for most summers, the summer of 1837 brought change to the Department of Mathematics at West Point. The third-year cadets, having completed intense study with the Mathematics Department, entered their engineering study. Several instructors were reassigned to far away posts, ready to perform new military duties. New plebes, fresh from their secondary schooling or time at other colleges, entered the challenging world of the Academy's college-level mathematics program. New instructors, often recent graduates of the Academy, arrived on the faculty to teach protégés the rigors of quantitative problem solving and the foundations to understand the rapid advancing technologies of the nineteenth century. The system of education designed and implemented by Thayer still worked wonders at developing cadets into confident, competent problem solvers and capable professional engineers. The Mathematics Department continued to transform young, generally ignorant boys into mature, knowledgeable students of engineering in just two years. In many ways, for the first two years of study, West Point was a school of mathematics. The last two years contained the engineering. Basic theory and concepts were emphasized.

America counted heavily on this system to produce its technical leaders.

The West Point system was unique in its purpose and implementation. The only other engineering school in America was Rensselaer Polytechnic Institute, which taught very practical, applied engineering. In that environment, mathematics was used but not emphasized. The Ecole Polytechnic in Paris, the school upon which Thayer modeled the West Point system, was different because it taught its students to be specialists, not generalists. Even West Point's harshest critic and frequent antagonist, President Andrew Jackson, freely admitted that West Point had become "the best school in the world." The system of using its own graduates as faculty was dangerous, but necessary at the time, and seemed to be working well. The young military officers on the faculty had a vested interest in the cadets, who would soon be their subordinates in the field Army. Some of the most successful cadets in academics left the Army early in their careers to become civilian scientists, engineers, and professors. Though few in numbers, West Pointers were making an impact as leaders of the growing nation. The Academy's founding fathers, George Washington and Thomas Jefferson, would have been enormously proud of the contributions and role of the Academy. Thayer was justly proud as he watched graduates contribute to the development of the Army and the nation.

On May 31, 1837, another key player in the development of the West Point program left the service of the Academy. Professor Charles Davies, who at forty years of age had headed the largest department at the Academy for fourteen years, was retiring to civilian life. He had plans to continue his textbook writing on a full-time basis. Friend and partner A. S. Barnes would publish Davies' textbooks, so the entire nation could benefit from the genius of this brilliant mathematics educator.

For several years, Charles Davies had planned on turning over his department to Jamey Davis. However, the Army had snatched his assistant away in order to fight a war against a small band of Indians. Fortunately, Professor Davies had another capable alternate to assume that position. Although Albert Church was young and inexperienced at 29, he was intelligent and tireless. Davies felt comfortable leaving the Department under Church's care. However, Church's appointment as Professor of Mathematics left no position for Charles Davies' protégé, Jamey Davis, to assume upon his return. Jamey no longer had the opportunity to return to West Point to instruct mathematics and lead the department. The Seminole

War had cost Jamey the future he had dreamed. His future was just one more tragic victim of this senseless war.

Celebration and Tragedy

Georgiana and Ben were married in a simple ceremony at an Episcopal church in Philadelphia. Georgette made a wonderful flower girl. Georgiana's friends and relatives from Philadelphia were able to attend. Unfortunately, the only relatives of Ben at the festive occasion were his sister, Elizabeth, and her husband, Bill. No one from Lummisville was able to make the long trip. Several of Ben's friends and colleagues from New York City were in attendance. One particular friend, Samuel Morse, gave Ben and Georgiana a spectacular painting that he had made for them as a wedding gift.

Everyone present had a fine time at the church service and the party that followed, although it was nothing near the celebration held for the wedding of Ben and Ann Marie. Unfortunately, there was sobering information from Lummisville that dampened Ben's enthusiasm. Ben realized through letters from both Soso and Jim Davis that his mother was severely ill and suffering. Arthritis and other pains left her bed-ridden and incapacitated. In her condition, travel was completely out of the question. She needed rest and dedicated care just to maintain enough energy to survive. Both Ben and Elizabeth worried about their mother and planned to go to Lummisville immediately after the wedding to help with her care.

The situation in Lummisville was deteriorating. Everyone was depressed over Sara's condition. Every day she lost more strength and hope. The mood of the people of the area was gloomy. With the economy in a state of panic throughout the nation, many of the businesses in the Sodus Bay area had lost everything. The Canal Company had gone bankrupt as land prices fell and they had no cash reserves to make their mortgage payments. There would be no Sodus Bay Canal to link into the Erie Canal. Despite a banner year just the year before, the Lummis farm was now losing money and headed for debt. Sara was too sick to halt the downward trend. She was fighting for her life. Betty and Soso took care of her the best they could. Without their care, she wouldn't have lasted as long as she had.

Just one week after the wedding, Ben, Georgiana, and Georgette Lummis, Elizabeth and Bill Ellet arrived in Lummisville. Sara was unaware that they were coming. Soso was likewise surprised but pleased to see them all. He congratulated the newlyweds and explained as best as he could Sara's condition. She was confined to her bed and spent most of the time resting. It was decided that Soso and Betty would break the news of the group's arrival to Sara before they all went up to see her. When Soso gave Sara the good news of her family's arrival, she was immediately transformed and invigorated. Soso helped her out of bed and into her chair. Betty dressed her in her favorite robe. By the time her family entered the room, Sara was standing and smiling. She warmly and enthusiastically hugged and kissed her family.

To Soso and Betty, Sara's recovery seemed a miracle, but, to the others, she was just a shadow of her former self. The afternoon was spent reminiscing, story telling, and laughing. All eight people stayed in Sara's bedroom for several hours before Sara showed her exhaustion by falling asleep in her chair. The others left, and Ben and Elizabeth picked up their mother and placed her back in bed. She briefly smiled as they laid her down. Then she went sound to sleep.

Ben whispered to his sister, "She is a lovely lady and the best mother we could have. Do you realize how lucky we are?"

Elizabeth replied, "We were blessed with remarkable parents who gave us a comfortable life and taught us well."

"She gave us all strength and courage. She is truly amazing. I'll miss her and remember her forever. Let's go now, so she can sleep in peace."

They quietly left the room. Despite Sara's strong performance, both knew their mother was dying. She was weak, thin, and pale. It truly was a miracle that this seriously ill woman had spent an entire afternoon entertaining her family.

That night was the first time in several months that Soso and Betty were able to sleep together in their own home. During Sara's illness, one of them had stayed awake caring for Sara during the night, while the other one slept. Then the two would trade places during the day. That night Sara had others to care for her.

Elizabeth and Ben took turns that night at their mother's bedside. Several times she woke with a severe coughing spell, but she was never coherent enough to talk to or show recognition of her children. Overnight, Elizabeth and Ben both saw their mother in severe pain and wrestled with their own sorrow and sympathy for her condition. Despite the extra care and renewed energy of the day before, Sara Maxwell Lummis never woke from her night's sleep. She died peacefully on her homestead on the shores of Sodus Bay.

The people of the area mourned their loss. Some, who understood her painful condition, were relieved by the end of her suffering. Others cried and grieved over the loss of this celebrated resident. Soso heard the news from Ben in the morning, and the two of them rowed one of Soso's boats far out into the lake, where the light-blue sky and dark-blue waters seemed to stretch forever. There, as it had happened before for Soso, the two physically and emotionally exhausted men began the recovery over their loss.

Sara was buried next to her husband under the huge tree on the small hill that overlooked the Lummis estate. Her family was there to mourn her loss and celebrate her life.

Decisions

Ben and Elizabeth took several days to recover and reflect. They both faced the reality of deciding what to do with their lives. For Ben, the decision was obvious. He had a new wife and a new opportunity to change his path. Despite his success as a banker, he was much better suited to life as a gentleman farmer like his father. He had endured many years of the city life and made his fortune, just so he could take this opportunity to return to his childhood home. The current economic depression reinforced this decision. His bank, like all others, was in disorder and chaos. There was little reason to go back to the city, except possibly to be sure that his bank maintained support for Samuel Morse and the telegraph. Ben worried that Sam would lose momentum because of the financial depression, but that was a situation beyond Ben's control.

He made his decision. Ben, Georgina, and Georgette would stay in Lummisville and run the farm. He was ready for this new life and excited for his family, who he knew would love living on the shore of Sodus Bay. Ben wrote to his bank, resigning his position, wishing his colleagues success in their future endeavors, and urging continued support for Samuel Morse. He wrote Sam explaining his decision and encouraging his friend to see his great invention through to completion. Ben arranged for his household goods and office furniture to be transported to Lummisville. He was no longer a powerful banker in New York City; now he was a gentleman farmer quietly living on the shores of Sodus Bay.

For Elizabeth, the decision was much tougher. She loved Sodus Bay and her childhood home. However, her and her husband's talents needed facilities that weren't available in Lummisville. Bill had been selected chair of the Chemistry Department at South Carolina College in Columbia. She wanted to stay at the place she called home, but the opportunities of an adventurous and rewarding academic life called her away. She and Bill decided to stay at Lummisville until the beginning of August and then to return to New York City to continue lives in academia and move to the South.

"Ben, you'll have to keep the Lummis homestead going on your own. Bill and I have decided to go to South Carolina. I know you'll like it here. So would I, if I could stay. You, Georgiana, and Georgette will enjoy this charming bay. You make sure that you'll keep a room for us to visit. Our parents made this such a beautiful place." Elizabeth's heart would stay on Sodus Bay, but she and her husband would move on.

"Of course, there will always be a room for you. This is your home, and I'll try to manage this farm and household just like our parents did. Take good care of yourself and continue all the important things you do. We are so proud of you." Ben let Elizabeth know his feelings about her. "You're a great sister. I love you so much."

Soso and Betty deeply mourned the loss of their friend and neighbor. Sara had been such a large part of their lives for several years that her loss left an immense hole. They welcomed Ben and his family back home. It would be hard for both of them for a while, but it was time for Soso and Betty to turn their attention to their own affairs. Ben could take care of the Lummis homestead and farm. Soso needed to refocus on his own family and the development of his farm. He was 57 years old and beginning to slow down.

Thoughts of Home

Charles Davies' letter took three months to reach Jamey, as he toiled in the swamps of Florida. It was the middle of September before Jamey found out that Professor Davies had retired and Albert Church had become Professor of Mathematics. By then, Jamey was extremely frustrated over the

American military and political leaders' lack of understanding of the Seminole situation.

Jamey's depression was intensified when he received Carin's letter, written in June, about Sara passing away. But, he was revitalized by the letter's news that Ben had married Georgina, and he was ecstatic at the news of Carin's pregnancy. With her due date fast approaching, Carin knew that Jamey would never make it home in time, so she had decided to reveal her secret at long last. Since Jamey didn't receive this letter until September, he wondered how everything had gone. The excitement and anticipation were almost too much for him to bear. More than ever, he wished that he could leave the misery and frustration of Florida's swamps and return to his family. He wrote Carin as often as he could, and his next letter contained many questions along with many words of love and kindness for his wife and children.

During the first week of October, 1837, the long awaited letter from Carin arrived. Carin and Jamey had a new baby girl, born on June 30. Carin wrote that both mother and baby were doing fine and waiting patiently for Jamey's return. Jamey was jubilant over the good news. Carin hadn't mentioned the name. He had written and suggested several possibilities for a boy and two for a girl—Joan and Jo Anne. He wondered what Carin had chosen. He immediately wrote to ask his new daughter's name. Until he knew, he thought of her as Baby Davis.

Jamey's excitement was interrupted by the harsh reality of the military campaign. After some initial success in cutting off the Indians from their supplies, General Jessup's progress had slowed. Like his predecessor, new President Martin Van Buren was demanding action. Therefore, Jessup was encouraged by the news that Jamey brought him. The noble chief Osceola was sick. Over the years, Osceola had seen tremendous suffering of his people at the hands of the white men's Army and contagious diseases that had spread among his people. To add to the confusion, the whites were always attempting to grab the blacks living with the Seminoles to make them slaves. It was a mess, and now the Seminole leader was suffering physically from one of those dreaded diseases.

At various times, the whites had befriended Osceola, only later to turn against him. General Jessup had asked for another peace talk, so Osceola reluctantly came out of hiding with his fellow chiefs under the white flag of truce. Osceola was ill, but managed to make it to the negotiations. Jessup, in a desperate and unethical act, used this opportunity to seize the Indian leaders and cart them off to jail. Jessup was finally on the road to victory and conquest of his opponent. Unfortunately, he had violated the rules of war and compromised the ethics of an entire nation just to gain advantage over a hopelessly outnumbered and innocent group of people.

Jamey was outraged by this deceitful act. He went directly to Jessup, who refused to discuss the situation. Fortunately, Jamey was able to relieve his frustrations. His duties now involved caring for and guarding the Indian prisoners. This was better duty than scouting, especially considering that most of Jessup's troops were out in the field to mop up the disorganized, leaderless Indians. Despite their advantage, the American forces managed to destroy only a few abandoned villages on this major operation. Frustrations continued to mount for the American military forces.

Jamey was emotionally drained from the ordeals of war, suffering, and treachery. He didn't understand why this fighting was necessary. He wondered why victory was so important that ethics and moral principles were forgotten. The Seminoles wanted to leave the whites alone, and the only lands they wanted were useless to the whites. The worse thing the Seminoles had ever done was to allow fugitive slaves to live among them. Certainly, that act didn't warrant years of war, famine, and suffering for both Indians and white soldiers.

Jamey had an opportunity to discuss the Seminole's situation with their chief, Osceola. The two of them talked through the iron bars of the prison cell, while Osceola was still weak and suffering from his illness. "Your people have tolerated so much, yet are so strong and determined. How do you do that?" Jamey asked.

"Dedication to the causes of life, liberty, and freedom. We are fighting for our lives and the lives of all our future generations. My people need no motivation or inspiration from me. From me they need leadership and wisdom. That is what I will give them, even from this prison cell." Osceola knew that his days and the days of his people were dwindling, but he wouldn't give up to the evils of the white invaders. The whites had kept up their fighting and harassment long enough to wear out the Indian forces and had almost won the war of attrition. The one thing the whites had that the Seminoles couldn't overcome were the immense numbers of soldiers.

"I respect you and your people as great warriors and strong survivors.

I hope this war will end soon." Jamey was being frank with the prisoner and noble leader whom he respected.

"We are much better citizens of peace than warriors. We were kind, productive, helpful, and cooperative to all our neighbors. Then greedy whites decided to take everything we had. I will never understand the greed that people possess. The white father Jackson must be a man of tremendous hate and evil. The war will be over soon, but the suffering will continue as long as there is so much greed and hate in people."

This was a tough time for Jamey. He had to remain loyal to his country and his profession as a soldier, but he sympathized with his enemy. The horrors of this war were tearing at Jamey's heart. As an Army officer, he was a servant of the people in his country. Why were things so complicated and confusing? The only things that gave Jamey any emotional stability were the letters from Carin and his thought of home. She had written back in embarrassment that she forgot to mention that the new baby's name was Joan. She wrote detailed letters about all the things that were happening. And, of course, Lenny and Katie always included pencil sketches of the most important activity on their minds at the time. Jamey loved his family and couldn't wait to see his beautiful wife and growing children.

Even with many of the Seminole leaders in confinement, the war continued to go badly for the American forces. To top off a miserable week in the field, several Seminole chiefs escaped from their prison. General Jessup was furious. In a fit of rage, he called in Jamey to reprimand him for the lapse in security. Having frequently informed the General about the lack of manpower and supplies to adequately house and secure prisoners, Jamey had a perfect excuse for the escape. The prison was woefully understaffed with guards and other essential positions. Jessup had continually promised him more help, but had never delivered. The General could blame only himself for the escape.

Jamey convinced Jessup to move the Indian prisoners to a more fortified and better supplied fort. General Jessup also placed a higher ranking officer in charge of security. He notified Jamey that from now on he would be in charge of only the welfare and health of the prisoners. Jamey was to insure the prisoners were properly fed, had enough clothes and adequate shelter, and were treated for their diseases and injuries. The best news was that this was a short-term assignment; Jamey would be discharged of his duties on January 1, 1838. At that time, he was to return to West Point to await further orders. The Army had decided that Lieutenant Davis had served in the combat zone long enough. The Army said it was time for him to go home, and Jamey agreed.

Back Home

Ben Lummis didn't notice the harshness of the bitter cold, snowy winter. He was enjoying himself too much to let weather affect his rosy outlook on life. He hadn't been so happy since he had left the Sodus Bay area fifteen years before to go to college. Here on Sodus Bay, he could do the things he loved to do—hunt, fish, farm, and work with his hands. He had time to enjoy life with his wife and child.

The Lummis estate was still magnificent. Ben had bought several thousand more acres of adjacent land. He started constructing a two-mile long road lined on both sides with chestnut tress to connect the estate with the ridge-road highway to Wolcott. The family took many delightful walks and horseback rides around the property. They especially enjoyed the shoreline and the islands. The home itself was equally impressive. The library was spectacular, and Sara had accumulated over the years elaborate furnishings that were still in the house. Everything was perfect.

Soso was a big help to Ben. The two men spent time together fishing, hunting, and talking about farming. Ben was a good businessman, but he needed to learn more about the technical side of the business. Fortunately, he was a quick learner and had an outstanding teacher.

Soso discussed the details of what crops to plant, when to plant them, when to harvest, and how to maintain a healthy farm. The Lummis farm contained apple, pear, and cherry orchards; a vegetable garden of various crops with the largest areas devoted to corn and wheat; and several different farm animals, including cows, chickens, sheep, and ducks. Not only was Ben a quick learner, he also was a hard worker. Soso felt confident that the farm was in good hands and would prosper.

Return Trip

Jamey left the swamps, insects, and misery of war on January 10. Two days before he left, General Jessup promoted Jamey to the rank of captain. Jamey had distinguished himself as a fine leader. Despite his personal frustrations, he had accomplished his missions and taken good care of his soldiers. Recognizing Jamey's contributions, Jessup had personally recommended the promotion. However, this honor was not the primary thing on Jamey's mind. He wanted to get home as soon as he could to see his family and new daughter. First and foremost, Jamey was a family man—a loving husband and caring father. Secondarily, he was an Army officer and mathematics professor. He traveled as fast as he could back to West Point on the crude, but improving transportation system of stagecoaches, trains, ships, and horseback. No one had ever had completed the 1000-mile journey in less time.

On the afternoon of February 2, Jamey entered the West Point gate on horseback. He had rented a horse from the manager of the stagecoach station at Fort Montgomery. He decided to ride the last few miles by horseback because the stage was scheduled for a two-hour wait at Fort Montgomery before continuing north through West Point, and he wasn't going to wait that long. Jamey rode up to the fence that he had built several years before. When he entered his home, he found mother and three children playing in front of the fireplace. He was mugged with hugs and kisses. His baby girl, Joan, smiled and crawled over to this strange visitor. It was an exciting day. This homecoming marked the end of a long ordeal. He promised himself that somehow he would put the entire Seminole War behind him. He needed to forget the evil things that people could inflict on other people. To him, the war had been as disastrous as it had been senseless. Now it was time to heal his emotions and to forget the pain.

Two weeks later, Jamey read in the paper that Osceola had died in his jail cell on January 30. Jamey felt sadness for the wise leader. He had a deep respect for the man, who had kept his dignity up to the very end of his life.

Jamey spent two months waiting for orders from the War Department. The Mathematics Department had sufficient instructors for their courses, so Professor Church had no need of his services, but the Engineering Department did need help, so Jamey taught surveying to twelve third-year cadets. Most of his free time was spent with his family. He wanted to reacquaint himself with his children. There was a lot of catching up to do. Lenny and Katie had grown so much, and little Joan was changing daily. Carin was extremely happy to have her husband home. She had never complained about how tough it was when he was gone. Now she was just thankful to have her husband safely home where he belonged.

After another month of waiting for orders, Jamey wrote to the War Department requesting assignment with either Ferdinand Hassler at the Coast and Geodetic Survey again or duty as an engineer for Colonel Thayer in designing coastal defenses. Both Hassler and Thayer had already written to the War Department with requests for Jamey. However, when his orders finally arrived, they were a surprise—report to Fort Crawford, Wisconsin, for duty as the fort's executive officer by July 1, 1838. His family could travel with him or stay in the quarters at West Point for one more year. The news was devastating. These orders made no sense. Jamey was a first-class mathematician, surveyor, and engineer, but he was not prepared or willing to return to the frontier as an executive officer of a fort with the nonsensical mission of protecting overly aggressive and obnoxious white men by fighting helpless Indians.

Captain Jamey Davis saw no alternative. He resigned his commission after thirteen years of devoted service. It was an emotional decision for this loyal soldier and proud patriot. He decided that he was going to move his family to Sodus Point and have them enjoy the same thrills that he had experienced as a boy. So on July 1, 1838, he arrived with his family at his parent's home in Sodus Point, instead of a frontier fort in Wisconsin. It was the only choice he could have made. He had performed his duty and faithfully served his country. He was thankful to the Army that had given him an education and had allowed his family to grow and prosper. However, he now needed security and stability that the Army was unwilling to give him.

Jim and Karen Davis were excited about having their son and his family back home. Over the past year, Jim had become virtually crippled from his years of hard work. He was 68 years old. Karen wasn't much better. She had a bad leg which hadn't healed after she fell from a run-away carriage three years before. However, both were living as well as possible in their retirement. They certainly never regretted what they had done or the situation they were in now. They spent much of their time sitting on their pretty porch watching the activities on the bay that they loved.

Fortunately, Jim had saved some money over the years, so the couple could live peacefully in their cozy home overlooking the bay. Jamey could tell that Sodus Point had changed some over the years. It wasn't much larger in population, but the homes were older and more settled. The houses, streets, and businesses seemed to fit together in natural harmony. It had been 25 years since the village had been burnt to the ground during the war and thereafter rebuilt. The bay was as beautiful as he remembered. Nature had continued to care for one of her crown jewels—Sodus Bay. Sailboats sped around the silvery waters and darted along the green shoreline. Lenny and Katie were excited by the activity and the beauty of unspoiled nature. Their father had told them all about this place, and now they finally got to see and experience it for themselves. Sodus Bay wasn't just their father's dream; it was real.

Word of Jamey's arrival back home spread fast. By late afternoon, Ben, Georgina, Georgette, Soso, and Betty were on their way across the bay to see the Davis family. It had been a couple of years since Jamey and Ben's families had met in Philadelphia. Everyone hugged and greeted one another. Uncle Soso and Aunt Betty were instant hits with Lenny and Katie. Within a few minutes, Lenny, Katie, and Georgette were playing, and the adults were taking turns holding Joan, who was now nearly a year old and wanted to keep up with her siblings.

The group of friends spent the evening reminiscing and storytelling. Ben and Jamey told their children all about the exploits of the battles during the War of 1812, especially the parts about Jim Davis and Soso Washington. And with the July Fourth celebration of 1838 ready to get underway, the tales of Jim and Soso's shooting abilities and Jamey and Ben's riding skills were told. None of these men had any intention of competing in any of these events this year. It was time for the younger generation to show its prowess.

"Uncle Soso, how do you learn to shoot a gun?" Asked eight-year-old Lenny, who desperately wanted his father to let him shoot.

"It's like learning to fish or ride a horse. You need to know what to do and then practice," Soso replied to his young friend.

"But my father won't let me shoot, so I can't practice."

"Have you learned the important things about how to shoot, or shown him that you are strong and responsible enough to shoot a gun?" Soso advised Lenny.

"No, not yet. I guess I'll have to learn first and get stronger. Then he will let me. Then I'll practice and become a good shot."

"Don't forget to be responsible as well. Then he will have to let you do all those things you want to do." Soso knew that he could only be partially involved in this right of passage between father and son. He didn't want to interfere with that special relationship. Soso also knew that fairly soon, he'd get to see Lenny hold his father's gun and fire his first shot. Lenny was intelligent, responsible, and nearly ready to fire a gun. Lenny may not have known it, but Soso did.

The July Fourth celebration was exhilarating. The nation was 62 years old, and the village's celebration was in its 37th year. With a rebound in the economy, everyone was in good spirits. All agreed that each year the village and the celebration got better.

The Lummis family was happy and pleased that they had decided to stay in Lummisville. The elderly couples, Soso and Betty Washington, Jim and Susan Davis, knew firsthand how lucky they were to live in such a beautiful place. Jamey and Carin spent time enjoying life and not worrying about their unsettled future. Being an officer in the Army was not a lucrative job, and now Jamey needed to earn money to support his growing family and to establish a nest egg for the future. It wouldn't be easy, but he was confident.

After a couple weeks of a relaxing vacation on Sodus Bay, it was time for Jamey to decide the next step in his life. He certainly had no regrets about his past. He had accomplished a great deal. He was a fine husband and father and a responsible citizen. Now it was time to apply his efforts in a new direction. The question was in what direction. He could stay in Sodus Point to fish, sail, build boats, and farm, but that would require an initial investment he didn't have. He could return to city life and work as an engineer or surveyor for a big business, but that would risk his family's enjoyment for a tense, high-pressure job. He could seek a teaching position at a college, and already had an offer from South Carolina College, where Elizabeth and Bill Ellet were, but he didn't want to move to the South. Jamey knew that he could never live in an area where slavery was tolerated. To him, that section of the country was a different and almost foreign world. He hoped that the people of the South would change, but he could never raise his family in such an environment.

Fortunately, while he was contemplating these possibilities, a new opportunity presented itself. Old friend Amos Eaton, senior professor of the engineering school at Rensselaer Polytechnic Institute at Troy, New York, wrote to Jamey seeking his advice on hiring a professor to teach mathematics to the school's engineers. Amos figured that Jamey might know a recent West Point graduate who was good at mathematics and ready to leave the Army. Mailed in early June, the letter finally caught up with Jamey at Sodus Point in late July. Jamey thought the position would be ideal for himself, so he wrote back immediately, explaining his own interest and availability.

After four weeks of waiting, the return letter from Professor Eaton arrived. Jamey was offered the teaching position at Rensselaer. He would be doing many of the same things he had done at West Point. Teaching mathematics was his calling. He regretted having to leave the excitement of his childhood home, but it was time to teach again and look toward the future. Three days later, after a tearful farewell, Jamey and his family were on a canal boat heading east to Albany and then onto Troy to continue their lives in academia.

Southern Life

Bill Ellet enjoyed his position at South Carolina College. The college had students interested in science, so Professor Ellet had recruited two assistants to help him in his innovative new program in chemistry, mineralogy, and geology. He was a busy man and a leader on campus. He liked the friendliness of this small college. He had never fit in well at Columbia, where the pace was too hectic and the number of students overwhelming.

On the other hand, Elizabeth did not adjust to the South as well as Bill. For the most part, she liked the people and the community of Columbia, South Carolina. However, she now lived in a slave state. She was amazed that the same people who were so friendly and educated could even tolerate slavery, much less practice it. In her mind, it seemed as if the residents were confused, brainwashed, and blinded on this issue. The very idea of slavery made her upset. Now she had to see it and live with it every day.

At first, Elizabeth thought she could persuade her neighbors to see the evils of slavery. However, after a short while, she realized that such activity was fruitless. She did have one mechanism to aid her attempts to change those in favor of slavery—the pen. And in Elizabeth's hand, the pen was a mighty weapon. She became one of several anonymous writers, who provided the northern newspapers and magazines with moving articles about the tragic evils of slavery. Her articles and editorials were published anonymously to protect her identity from those who were violent and hostile toward influential abolitionists. In 1838, there seemed to be a growing number of these people. After a while, no one suspected that Elizabeth was an abolitionist; she simply fit into South Carolina society.

Elizabeth was very patriotic. She wanted her country to grow and prosper. She hoped the Union would survive, even with this vast emotional division over the issue of slavery. She realized that all the country's citizens needed to contribute. Slavery wasted considerable resources, as did the limitations on the roles that women could play in the male-dominated society.

Elizabeth was also a feminist. Moreover, she was not the least bit shy about speaking her mind on this subject. She believed women should vote, work, and hold government office. She debated the role of women in society with anyone who dared take on this tremendously intelligent and articulate woman. Once she took up the crusades for rights for blacks via her powerful pen and women through her persuasive speech, she actually enjoyed life in the South. Elizabeth was a fighter who now had plenty of opponents to fight and eventually defeat.

Old Man and His Boy

For all practical purposes, Soso was semi-retired. He had accumulated almost enough money for Betty and him to live comfortably the rest of their lives. He was now 58 years old and, while still physically strong, his illnesses and hard-work had taken their toll.

Soso's workshop contained two half-built canoes and a rowboat. He worked a few hours a day on the boats and seemed to make only slow progress on their completion. He sometimes helped Betty tend their small garden and orchard. They were no longer in the farming business; they planted only enough for themselves and friends. Soso spent most of his time in his boat. He was most comfortable on the water. He knew the bay and its character better than anyone. No matter where he was, he knew the water's depth, the underwater vegetation, and the likelihood of fish being caught. Soso seemed to be able to catch fish whenever he wanted.

Soso often sailed his boat or paddled his canoe across the bay to fish near First Creek. This area was where he had first lived some 45 years before. It was also the place where his parents and grandfather were buried. He often fished in a spot where he could see their graves and think of them while he fished. Soso missed his family. He no longer had any Native American friends nearby. Even though he was an Indian married to a black woman, Soso was most comfortable in the whites' world, yet he still felt as much Indian as he ever had. He knew his people's way of life would not survive the onslaught and discrimination of the whites. The white pioneers, who had pushed the Indians past the Mississippi, would keep pushing. There was no end to their greed. Many men, like Andrew Jackson, had little compassion for or understanding of the strengths of Indian culture. The end of the Indian culture was near. Its only savior was to have its strengths and some of its valued elements absorbed into the new white culture. Soso hoped that was what he had started, and others would continue and eventually succeed.

Soso the Author

Soso had worked for some time trying to find the right words to explain his hull design to other boat builders. Over the years, the late Henry Eckford and friend Levi Johnson had encouraged Soso to write an article about his boat building for the *Ships and Hulls* journal, which Levi edited and published. Finally, Soso began this effort. He had help from Betty, who was a fine writer. She had learned to read and write as a slave and had continued her education in Canada. It was hard work, but after many months Soso and Betty sent the article to Levi. It was well written with considerable technical information on hull design and general shipbuilding procedures. Soso was soon published in the journal. The finest master shipbuilder of the frontier had been published, and now shipbuilders around the world could benefit from his genius. He was proud of his work and happy that he could share ideas with others. Modern communications, publications, and education were excellent examples of powerful innovations and inventions of the white man's world. There were many parts of the whites' culture that Soso admired and valued. Great ideas and inventions spread quickly through writings; whereas, the Indian culture had no mechanisms for such communication and advances.

A Great Loss

It was nearly dark when Soso began his slow, methodical paddle back across the bay from First Creek to Lummisville. It was a hot, windy day, and the west wind was at his back. He had caught a few perch and several frogs that hung in a small creel from the stern of the canoe. Out of a corner of his eye he saw a cloud of smoke bellowing up from Sodus Point. As he looked closer through the fading light of the day, he could see bright red and yellow flames under the smoke that reached high into the air.

Soso turned his canoe in the direction of the fire and started paddling at a faster rate. After a few strokes, he realized exactly where the fire was coming from. His pace quickened even more, and his heart began to race. The sun had just set, and it was getting dark. The fire was out by the time Soso landed his canoe on the shore. Despite the darkness, he could see and smell the thick smoke continuing to rise straight up out of ashy rubble. There was almost nothing left of the Davises' home. The stone fireplace that Soso and Jim had installed when they built the house in 1814 stuck out of the rubble. It was a terrible sight. The smoldering remains were still too hot to be approached, and a large group of villagers stood, grim-faced and exhausted in the road as Soso approached. Some of the men were coated in black from soot and smoke. Others were mesmerized by the sight of the burned out house. But as Soso got closer to the group, he felt an even stronger emotion. By the time fire chief, Walt Matthews, began to explain, Soso knew something was seriously wrong. Walt explained the nature and scope of the fire before he broke the news that Soso's best friends and life-long companions, Jim and Karen Davis, had perished in the fire.

Several villagers had made desperate, unsuccessful attempts to rescue the elderly couple trapped in the flames, but their efforts had been in vain. Jim and Karen Davis, residents of Sodus Point for over forty years, were the unfortunate victims of this terrible tragedy.

Soso stood in disbelief, staring at the destruction. Then he slowly walked back to his canoe and paddled back out to the bay. Soso, through earlier experiences, knew there were no answers or cures to the emptiness and hurt that he felt. But it felt better to work the paddle and to feel the soft warm water of the bay. Soso, lost in his emotions, paddled around the bay and lake for hours. Through the numbness, he recalled his lost loved ones.

He vividly remembered the lives and deaths of his grandfather, father, mother, Ben and Sara Lummis, and now Jim and Karen Davis. He had learned a great deal from the grief that he had experienced over the years. He spent much of the night reflecting on the lives and contributions of his friends and praying to the spirits. The spirits had seemingly always helped him through these tough times. They were always there when he needed emotional help. By the time Soso arrived back home in Lummisville, Betty was frantic with worry. Soso painfully explained the cause of his late return. He and Betty shared their grief as they sat by the edge of the bay talking and crying until sunrise. For Betty, religious faith was strong comfort. Soso knew that her belief in the God of her religion was stronger than his, but now wasn't the time to discuss religion. He wished he had answers. Why had this happened? He took some consolation in the Indian spirits. Once again, these spirits of life and death comforted his grief and restored his strength.

After all the years of being away from his family serving in the Army, Jamey was devastated by the news of his parents' deaths. He had just a month before renewed the richness of his relationship with his parents. They had given him love and support, motivation and encouragement, strength and compassion. Now they were gone. Jamey was comforted by the fact that he and his family had spent time in Sodus Point over the summer. Carin and the children had gotten to know Jim and Karen. And Jim and Karen got to see their son and his family. They had always been proud and supportive, and that consoled him. Now he would have to continue life without them.

Unfortunately, Jamey was too far away to travel back to Sodus Point for the funeral, but he wrote back to Soso to thank him for his letter and to ask him to handle the affairs of the funeral and estate until Christmas. Jamey would try to return to Sodus Point at the winter break, when his school— fondly called RPI—was out for three weeks. That break would enable him to get to Sodus Point, take care of necessary business for a few days, and return to Rensselaer.

The tragic loss led to a gloomy fall and winter around Sodus Bay. In many ways, Jim and Karen Davis had been the heart and soul of Sodus Point. They knew everyone, and everyone knew them. The hurt was still evident when Jamey arrived back in Sodus Point over the Christmas holiday. He joined the entire village in mourning his parents' deaths. He was able to sell their property to pay their debts and funeral expenses. Jim and Karen's life savings had been destroyed by the fire.

It had been a strenuous first semester at RPI. Jamey found the students less motivated and less skilled than those he had taught at West Point. It had been a challenge for him to make all the adjustments—leaving the Army, losing his parents, and teaching in a different environment. Housing for his family in the Troy was also difficult. Patroon Stephen Van Rensselaer was landowner and landlord of all available land in the area. Fortunately, Van Rensselaer had taken a liking to the Davis family and had given them an inexpensive, short-term lease on a small house, but the pay for college teachers was very low and the Davises were just able to make ends meet. There was no Davis family nest egg being built in 1838. These were times when all their energies were focused on survival. Jamey hoped for a better future.

Little Georgette

Ben and Georgiana Lummis continued with the revitalization of the Lummis farm. The mild winter left the orchard and garden in fine shape for a banner crop of fruits and vegetables. Eight-year-old Georgette was a healthy girl who loved to be outside helping her father with farm work or fishing on the bay with her Uncle Soso. Ben was relaxed and comfortable with the slower, albeit rugged life of the rural area of Sodus Bay. While the farm business progressed, Ben worked only as hard as necessary to keep things under control. He also spent plenty of time with Soso and Georgette fishing and boating on Sodus Bay. Georgiana didn't enjoy the water, so she usually stayed home.

While Georgette's appearance favored that of her Aunt, she was not at all scholarly like Elizabeth. However, for Soso, it was like reliving the years when Elizabeth was growing up. The two girls, nearly a generation apart, enjoyed many of the same things. Having Georgette around energized Soso and added to his happiness and health. If he had lived a hundred years earlier, he would have been a wise chief and an important leader of his tribe. Instead, his tribe was scattered and had no need for such a chief. However, Soso was now a leader in the white man's community. While he didn't hold political office or work in an official job, Soso was the advisor and mentor to everyone in the communities surrounding Sodus Bay. They still needed Soso, just like the residents of the settlement of Great Sodus had needed his fish to survive their first year of struggle in 1794.

New Opportunity

Another year of teaching mathematics and watching his children grow helped heal some of Jamey's emotional wounds. Carin was a remarkable wife and mother. The Davis children were smart, well-mannered, and hard workers. Lenny was full of energy for play and learning. Katie, while a year younger, was as big and strong as Lenny. She overcame her position of middle child and often dominated her brother and sister. Only two years old, Joan was ready to keep up with her older brother and sister—or at least get in their way.

As the twin sorrows of losing his parents and his military career faded, Jamey's happy and fun-loving personality began to return. He was an excellent teacher. His students liked him and often thanked him for his efforts. Learning mathematics was necessary to learning engineering, so Jamey was a tremendous addition to the school's faculty. Under Jamey's care, the engineers of RPI would know their mathematics and build a strong foundation for their engineering thinking and problem solving.

By spring, Jamey had started writing another textbook. His first book on surveying had been successful in that West Point still used it, as did RPI and a few other schools. Now he was writing about another mathematics subject, differential equations. This was a more advanced topic that took a good deal of time and effort to translate into readable textbook material. Jamey decided to write most of the book before talking to A.S. Barnes about its publication. It was a risky plan, but he felt confident that he could write an effective and successful book on the subject. Jamey felt that as the country grew and technologies, like the railroad and steamboat, increased, more and more people would become engineers. Certainly, engineers, scientists, and other professionals of the modern world would need to know differential equations.

The day before the Davises were going to leave Troy for a three-week vacation in Sodus Point, a letter in a familiar looking envelope was delivered. Jamey recognized the government postage and envelope and knew right away that the letter was from his former supervisor, Ferdinand Hassler, chief of the Coast and Geodetic Survey.

Ferdinand's letter outlined several refinements that he proposed to implement in the surveys that his agency was conducting and explained that he needed a skilled assistant like Jamey to carry out the plan. Hassler explained that while the salary was low, there was the possibility that his assistant would succeed him as Superintendent with a substantial raise in pay. Hassler was 69 years old, and even he admitted that he would not last forever. Hassler praised Jamey's talents and hoped that he would accept the appointment.

While Jamey loved surveying and treasured his time with the Coast and Geodetic Survey, he realized that accepting this position was not in his or his family's best interests. He liked RPI, he liked teaching, and he liked being close enough to Sodus Bay to take periodic vacations to his childhood home. His new life was getting organized. None of the things he enjoyed were available in the position Hassler offered. Jamey penned and mailed his response. In his letter, Jamey suggested contacting Alex Bache or Horace Smith. Jamey knew both men were excellent surveyors, leaders, and teachers. The duties of the Coast and Geodetic Survey were too important to leave to anyone less that the best available.

Trail of Tears

During the months of 1839, the newspapers covered the developments of General Winfield Scott's efforts to remove the Cherokee Indians from their native lands in Georgia to reservation lands in Oklahoma. The peaceful, unarmed Cherokee were a much easier foe to contend with than the stubborn Seminoles had been. The Cherokees were a sophisticated and peaceful people—gentlemen farmers with tremendous intellect. Their leader, Sequoyah, had developed an alphabet of 86 characters, and the tribe had produced their own newspaper, the *Cherokee Phoenix*, since 1828. They were productive people. None of this mattered to the whites. Many misinformed and uneducated whites thought Indians were savages. The State of Georgia had obtained a court order to have all the Cherokees sent away so the whites could occupy their land. This made the Cherokees prime targets for looters, robbers, and harassers. Whites who despised Indians and sought to take advantage of their vulnerability drove off the Cherokees' livestock, plundered and burned their homes, and tortured and killed many helpless Indians. Finally, General Scott's troops restored order and rounded up the Indians, 15,000 of them, and placed them in prison camps, supposedly for their protection. Then the real reason was revealed. The soldiers prepared groups containing about 1000 Indians for transportation. These groups, one by one, were herded like cattle across Georgia, Tennessee, Kentucky, Illinois, and Missouri, all the way to Oklahoma.

The government's relocation operation was mismanaged from the start. The Indians were mistreated and harassed at every step. Often there was no food or supplies available. Furthermore, the bitter cold weather of the winter months made travel difficult and dangerous. Many Indians became sick or died; yet the soldiers pushed them on. They rushed so much that the Indians were not even allowed to stop to bury or mourn their dead or to care for their sick. This trail of tears lasted all winter as over 4,000 of the 15,000 Cherokees died on this torturous trip.

Some of the terrible news of this tragic escapade appeared in the nation's newspapers. But for the most part, the suffering was ignored by the public. Some newspapers tried to cover up the worst reports, while others put a positive spin on the whole affair. A few newspapers took the opportunity to criticize the Army for their ineptitude. But, the Army was badly served by its political masters. There was an endless supply of conflicting orders and changing policy from Washington, and this confusion caused blunders, hostilities, and atrocities. In general, the nation of whites didn't seem to care that thousands of Native Americans were being robbed, herded, tortured, killed, and confined. They had been desensitized to brutal behavior towards Indians. The Cherokee had even won a Supreme Court ruling to protect their properties, but Andrew Jackson made sure his legacy was not diluted by legal technicalities. The whites wanted the land so the Indians were forced to leave. The American citizens had followed the news of the Seminole Wars for many years, so another story about hassling Indians just didn't merit concern. Those few who did care, white, red, or black, were deeply hurt by this shameful episode of uncivilized brutality.

Soso followed the news the best that he could. To him it was a huge disappointment. It was another dark chapter, maybe the darkest, in red-white relations; relations he had worked so hard to improve. He had hoped for improvement in the nation's policies after Jackson had left the Presidency, but things had not improved under Van Buren. To Soso, Van Buren had no more compassion for Indians than his predecessor had.

Erie Canal

The Erie Canal had steadily improved over its nearly twenty years of existence. The canal boats had become more efficient and comfortable, and the fares had decreased. The travel time and lock efficiency had improved as well. Modern technology was beginning to affect the lives of America's citizens. In 1839, the Davis family could enjoy their excursion from Troy to Sodus Point. While the canal boats moved smoothly along the waterway, the passengers relaxed and socialized on the open, top deck of the boat. As long as the weather was comfortable—no rain or extreme heat—it was pleasant. People talked, sang, played games, or slept. Just six days after leaving Troy, the Davises arrived at Sodus Point well rested and in good spirits.

Back Home

The Davises visited with friends in Sodus Point, before riding by boat with Betty Washington across the bay to the Lummis estate. Betty happened to be at Sodus Point, trading fish, beaver skins, and vegetables for rigging and sails for a boat that Soso was building. The Davis family and their belongings just fit into Betty's little knock-about. The wind was so light it was faster to row the open boat than try to sail it across the bay. Jamey went to work at the oars. He enjoyed the exercise, and the children had fun watching their father steadily row the boat across the smooth, shiny silver water. As Jamey rowed, he told his children all about Uncle Soso and Grandpa Jim. He told them about the fish that they had caught over the years and the ducks and deer they had shot. Lenny and Katie listened intently. They couldn't wait to see their Uncle Soso again. Two-year-old Joan paid no attention to her father and preferred to reach overboard to splash her hands in the warm water of the bay.

Soso and Ben Lummis greeted the Davises at Lummis dock. The two men were talking at the dock, patiently waiting for Betty's return. They had no idea that the Davises would be with her. All were happy to see one another. Lenny was particularly interested in talking to Soso. He wanted to know all about fishing and hunting. Soso wanted to know all about Troy and RPI. Soso was as good a listener as he was a storyteller.

The Davises went up to the Lummis house to meet Georgiana and Georgette, who was Lenny's age. Lenny didn't pay much attention to his girl cousin, but Katie and Georgette immediately began playing with one another and watching Joan. Lenny was at the age where he wanted to do boy things; he had no interest in including girls, especially sisters and cousins, in his activities. The adults caught up on their experiences over the last year. By supper time, Lenny had talked Soso into showing him the partially built boat in the shed and taking him on a fishing trip the next morning. Lenny asked permission from his father for his participation and was ecstatic when he received approval. It was an exciting way to start the summer.

Carin and Georgiana were good friends and got along well. Carin was the more practical and quieter of the two. Georgiana was more spontaneous and humorous. Both were excellent homemakers. They enjoyed being with one another and while their friendship was not as long in duration as their husbands', it was just as meaningful.

The first week of the Davises' visit went by quickly. There was plenty to do on the Lummis farm, along with the water activities of boating, fishing, and swimming. The women and girls—Georgiana, Carin, Betty, Georgette, Katie, and Joan—spent time canning berries, pickling vegetables, and tending the garden. Ben and Jamey worked on maintaining Ben's orchards, boats, and barn. Lenny spent most of the week with Soso. They fished and worked together on the boat in Soso's shed. Lenny was a quick learner, and Soso was a good, patient teacher. It was a productive week for everyone.

As soon as he could, Jamey took a ride across to the west side of the bay. He headed for his favorite spot, the high ground just north of First Creek. It was as spectacular as ever. He stood right where he envisioned the house to be. It would overlook the entire bay. First Creek would enable the boats to be protected from any northeast winds. The land was rich, ready for orchards and gardens. This would be his home, if ever his dreams could come true. All he needed was money. He already had assurance from the landowner, James Pollock, that he would hold the property for four years. The sale price of $300 was agreed to by the two men. This was the year to share his dream with Carin to see if she was as enchanted by this spot as he was.

The second week brought more activities. Ben and Jamey spent the week sailing a circuit of the lake. They delivered fruits, vegetables, flour, and clothing to Canada and returned with a load of prime lumber and wagon wheels. During the trip, the two men had time to reminisce about their past relationship. They were both appreciative of each other. Both men realized that they had plenty to be thankful for. But both saw differences in the other than what they remembered in their youth. Their adult friendship was not as understanding as their childhood friendship had been. Maybe they had been too close as children.

While the men were gone, the women spent the week enjoying the beauty of Sodus Bay. They took a day and sailed around the entire bay. They had a pleasant picnic lunch on Arron Island. Parts of other days were spent on the bay or lake. The young girls caught fish, and they all went swimming in the clear, refreshing water. The beach all along the long narrow sand bar separating the lake and the bay was soft, warm, and fun to play on. Soso and Lenny spent their time attempting to finish the construction of the boat in Soso's shed. The old man and young boy worked to their capacity to form the deck planks and sand down the hull and decking. By the end of the week, the lumber had begun to look like a boat. Soso hoped that they could complete a few more details so that Lenny could experience the launching of the vessel and taste the fruits of his intense labor before he had to return to Troy. Soso was impressed by the enthusiasm and work capacity of this young boy. Lenny reminded Soso of Jamey, who had been Soso's apprentice many years before.

Close Call

By the end of the second week, the women had become a competent boat crew. Always fair sailors, Georgiana and Carin had never spent so much time on the water. Now their crew consisted of eight-year-old Georgette, seven-year-old Katie, and two-year-old Joan. Betty was a part-time crew member and certainly the most knowledgeable sailor in the group. All hands on board learned their duties well and a great time was had by all. However, a slight lapse in concentration on a cruise on the lake nearly resulted in tragedy. Joan loved to lean over the side of the boat and splash the water as the boat glided along. As the women made a sharp turn out in the lake in order to head for shore, the boom was accidentally let loose causing the boat to lurch and turn about too quickly. Joan's momentum sent her over the side into the deep lake water. Most of the others were momentarily thrown down into the boat and didn't notice what had happened. Fortunately, Betty saw Joan's mishap. She wasted no time in jumping into the water after the drowning infant. Joan's screams were answered with mouthfuls of water, as she sunk deeper. Betty took her bearings and dove under the surface after Joan. Luckily the water was clear, and Betty quickly saw Joan struggling and swam toward her. Betty wasn't the best swimmer. She was 54 years old. She was missing her left hand, and she hadn't learned to swim until she was forty. However, she had reacted quickly, and the adrenaline rush of the emergency gave her energy. Within seconds, Betty had brought Joan back to the surface.

By that time, the others saw what was happening, turned the boat around, and headed back for the two swimmers. Betty and Carin hoisted Joan on board, and the young child began sobbing, and, thankfully, breathing. Within a few more minutes, everyone's nerves were calmed, and Joan and Betty began drying off.

This experience left all on board temporarily numb. They were thankful of Joan's recovery but mindful of how close they had been to losing a loved one. Carin hugged Betty and cried, as Georgiana held Joan. The trip home was emotional, and all were happy to get back safely on land. An important lesson on boating safety had been learned by everyone. A more important lesson about life and its value had been reinforced.

Another Soso Original

When Ben and Jamey returned from their trip, they were inspired as the beacon of light from the Sodus Point Lighthouse came into view. It was the welcome sign to all sailors that they were nearing home. No one knew for sure if the lighthouse had saved any lives over its first nineteen years, but everyone agreed it was worth its price and more. It had been a valuable addition to Lake Ontario's southern shoreline. It was the symbol of this proud lakeside village and beautiful harbor. When they reached Soso's house, they were surprised to see the progress made by Soso on the boat in his shed. Soso explained to everyone how much Lenny had helped. Jamey was proud of his son, because he knew that Soso's praise was earned only by hard work and dedication. Everyone was excited by the prospect of putting the boat into the water within the week. The women and girls continued to work in the fields harvesting crops, picking flowers, and enjoying the outdoors. What a magnificent vacation.

While Jamey was gone, Carin had searched across the bay for that special place that he had referred to so often. She found it, and it was just like he had said. The high ground overlooking First Creek was perfect. The spectacular view, the rich soil, and the breath-taking setting made their dream spot like utopia in both their eyes. This would be their dream. If they could own this land, build their house, set up their farm and business, then they would give up their current lives in academics and move to Sodus Point. Carin was just as enthralled over the future possibilities as Jamey was. She dreamed pleasant thoughts about one day living on Sodus Bay and raising her children in this beautiful setting. She shared these thoughts with Jamey when he returned.

But there was one problem looming like a dark cloud over the activities of the summer. Ben and Jamey were having difficulties with their relationships. The two former best friends were finding one another to be strange and different from what they had been during their previous childhood friendship. They began arguing over silly things like loyalty to one another and which of them enjoyed the outdoors of the Sodus Bay area the most. Each blamed the other for their problems, which made things even worse. This was not their typical disposition. Both were usually pleasant, happy people; however, both had become miserable and depressed over this situation. Everyone worried and wondered what was happening to these two friends.

By Tuesday, Lenny and Soso had proceeded far enough along on the boat to schedule the launching for the weekend. This was the day before the scheduled departure of the Davis family back to Rensselaer. However, on Wednesday, Jamey, nervous about the return trip back to Troy and somewhat annoyed with Ben, changed his mind about their departure day and decided to leave the very next day. Lenny was heartbroken that he wouldn't be able to see the boat make its way into the water. He had spent two and half weeks working and hoped to see it float on the bay. However, that wasn't to be. Jamey had made up his mind.

Carin was equally discouraged. She had enjoyed her time at Lummisville and wanted very much to stay the rest of the week. She knew how much the launching of the boat meant to Lenny. Carin asked Jamey to let them stay the extra days, but he was adamant. Jamey had decided that there was no choice—they must leave so he could get back to work at Rensselaer. The vacation was over for the Davis family.

Departure

The day of departure was not one of joy and happiness. The good-byes were emotional and tearful. Lenny, Katie, and Joan cried and begged to stay longer, but Carin and Jamey finally got them onto the carriage of the stagecoach, which took them back to the Erie Canal in Clyde for their ride to Albany.

After the Davises left Lummisville, Ben became remorseful and blamed himself for their abrupt departure. He wished that he hadn't argued with his friend. Ben decided to write Jamey a long letter to try to patch up their differences and asking them to return the next summer for another visit. The same emotions hit Jamey as he rode along the canal with his disappointed family. He too wrote a letter in which he apologized and asked Ben for forgiveness. Jamey thanked his hosts at Lummisville and outlined a plan to return as soon as he could. Their disagreement had been immature and, fortunately, temporary. They were too good of friends to let a little bickering affect their friendship.

Business on the Lake

Ben's farm work was in full gear as he prepared to make his periodic trips around the lake delivering his crops. The fall had been especially busy since he owed several boatloads of crops to businesses in Niagara and ports in Canada. Ben persuaded Soso to make one trip with him. He could always use the help and extra rest, which he got when Soso rode along. Soso's only concern was Betty, but Mrs. Hyde agreed to stay with Betty while Soso was gone. As usual, they left before daybreak and were miles out into the lake before daylight replaced the beacon of the Sodus Point Lighthouse as their source of light and direction.

Soso always looked forward to accompanying Ben on journeys across the lake to deliver the harvest of the orchards. On this trip, the first stop was York, which was a common destination since most of Ben's fruit ended up in Canada on the western part of the lake. The last stop was Niagara, where Ben was able not only to unload all his wares, but also to pick up several new farm instruments that he needed. However, upon arriving at Fort Niagara, Ben found that the instruments that he had bought were not quite ready. It would take another few days before they could load up the equipment. In addition, Ben's boat needed some minor repairs, and it would take a couple days for a haul out to take place and the repairs to be made.

During this unexpected extra time in Niagara, Ben decided to stay in the village and conduct business with local merchants. It was a good time to see what arrangements he could make for selling more of his own products. He could also see if any good deals were available on the things he needed to run his farm. Ben was a savvy businessman and always made the most of every opportunity that presented itself.

Soso's Revelation

Soso decided to spend his few unexpected free days traveling to a nearby Indian reservation. He had been briefly to this reservation once before, and he figured now was a good time to visit some of the Native American people in the area. He heard that Iroquois, especially Cayugas, were plentiful on this reservation. Soso also tried to take advantage of every opportunity that he was presented.

"Ben, I will be gone for a couple days visiting the Indian reservation. I hope to see some people from my tribe. I know you have to leave when the boat is ready, so I'll be back before then. I have missed speaking my native language. This will be an enjoyable trip for me," Soso explained his plans to Ben.

Ben understood. "Enjoy yourself and take care. I'll see you in a few days."

Soso looked forward to seeing people of his tribe. However, when he got there he was surprised and depressed to find the reservation completely run down, dirty, and decaying. Most of the inhabitants were poor, undernourished, and sickly. This was not what he had expected. He had always thought that the white people of Canada, who seemed to understand the Indians better than those in the United States, would take better care of his people, and given the opportunity the Indians would be able to prosper on the bountiful reservation lands.

For Soso this turned out to be a deeply emotional visit. These poor, sickly Indians were his people. He had hoped to be able to relate to them and enjoy his stay. Soso sought to find the cause of the terrible plight. As he talked to the inhabitants of the reservation, he found that they were unhappy in the lifestyle that had been forced upon them. Despite the government's attempts to give them food and supplies, the people didn't know how to build upon this charity. They no longer knew how to take care of themselves. In almost every important way, they had become too dependent on the handouts and could no longer earn their own living or respect themselves for their own contributions.

Off the reservation, there were a few people trying to help the reservation Indians get back on their feet. One special person that Soso met during his stay was the leader of this effort. Actually, Soso was reacquainted with this person, for it was quite amazingly his long-lost sister, Water Lily. What a dramatic surprise and thrill. Soso had not seen her for over 45 years and, eventually, as the years passed, had convinced himself that she was dead. He and his mother, Clear Dawn, had searched for Water Lily and his brother, Perch, for many years after their abduction from the cabin in Great Sodus without success. It turned out that she had been sent to this reservation 37 years before and had lived both on and off the reservation ever since. She had become a strong and successful woman. She had tried to support her people on the reservation in any way she could. Of course, after all these years, the brother and sister didn't immediately recognize one another. It wasn't until their names were mentioned in the introduction that they finally realized their relationship.

Water Lily was as beautiful as Soso remembered. She was two years older than Soso, and he remembered well her look as a sixteen-year-old. The long-lost siblings warmly hugged each other and excitedly caught up on their lives over all these many lost years of separation. It was an exciting reunion for both.

Water Lily recalled that day so long ago when she and her brother had been kidnapped. Despite being held captive together for a few hours, she had never seen Perch or heard of him again after that first day. She had been without her family since that day, and, like Soso, she never found out anything about her missing relatives until now. She had been captured and held by the renegade Indians for two years, before finally being released on the Niagara frontier. She knew that Gar had been involved with these renegades, but she had never seen him. Somehow she had found this reservation and made it her home.

Water Lily was married three months after arriving on the reservation. Her husband had been a white man trapper named Joe Simpson. Joe had been a person of immense kindness and consideration. He had been a devoted husband to Water Lily. They had a son, Joe Junior, in 1804. Joe Jr. had turned out to be very studious and intelligent. He had read many books and studied hard as a young man. Unfortunately, there had been a tragic accident on the reservation several years ago. Both father and son, Joe Sr. and Joe Jr., were consumed in a raging fire that had killed thirty people, mostly children. An old wood stove of the reservation school building had flared up, and scrap wood and paper caught fire. The building had been poorly constructed, and it was consumed so quickly that none of the occu-

pants had been able to escape. The two Simpsons were at the school helping the teacher when the fire started. Lily had been grief-stricken over their
loss.

Joe Jr. and his wife, Scarlet, had a son named Garth Simpson, who was
born in 1821. Garth was now Water Lily's pride and joy. Scarlet had moved
away, going farther west where the rest of her family had been transported
in President Jackson's westward movement of Indians. Scarlet had left
Garth with Water Lily, whom Scarlet knew would take good care of him. So
Lily had raised her grandson Garth for most of his life. Garth was much like
his father, Joe Jr., studious and intelligent. He was also a bit like his grandfather, Joe Sr., considerate and thoughtful. Mostly, he was like his grandmother, Lily, strong and determined.

Garth had grown up spending about half his life on and half off the
reservation. As he had learned about people and about life, he realized that
with his talents he could help the reservation Indians and the people of his
race. Garth Simpson, who was actually three-quarters Indian and one-quar-
ter white, had used his immense talent and dedication to go to college.
Because of his intelligence, he had earned acceptance and a scholarship to
none other than Rensselaer, the engineering school where Jamey Davis was
teaching. Garth was not at the reservation, but back at Rensselaer
Polytechnic Institute, when Soso met Lily, so he did not get to meet his
grandnephew, but Soso heard all about him from Water Lily.

Soso and Lily talked about old times, about their young lives together,
about their parents and brother, and about all the things that had happened
since they had last seen each other. Both had experienced so much in their
lives that were filled with encounters with both Indians and whites. Both of
them were amazed by the accomplishments of the other. Soso was especially excited to hear about Garth's progress in college. He was in his second year at RPI, studying to become an engineer. Lily related Garth's
dreams and hopes of returning to the reservation and helping his people to
regain their dignity. Just like Lily, Garth hoped that he could help return
them to the status they had known before the white men sent them to the
reservation.

Lily told Soso how her deep religious and spiritual beliefs had helped
her during her life. Lily was a devout Roman Catholic, but she still recognized the roles of her childhood Indian spirits and believed that the spirits
and her God had helped her live a successful life. Soso didn't share these

same sentiments. Religion and spiritual guidance had never affected his daily life. He had used spiritual communication only to help ease the pain of losing a loved one, but religion, neither the whites' God nor the Indians' spirits, even the supreme spirit of the Creator, was part of his daily life. Yet at his advanced age, there was something missing—he still sought spiritual peace and understanding. Somehow the realities of the world, knowledge and technology, must have some relation to the needs of the soul, spirit and faith.

It wasn't long after Lily started telling Soso her history that Soso decided that he could also help. He had knowledge that he could share to help revitalize the lives of the reservation Indians. It was a hasty decision, but it was agreed that Soso would stay awhile and work with Lily to see what he could do for the reservation.

She gave him a tour. He met many people, several in poor health and poor spirits. They traveled down crude roads to see crumbling houses and inadequate schools, hospitals, and churches. Soso noticed there were no businesses or industries to employee the residents, nor were there any productive farms. It was a desolate place—no happiness, no future, and no hope. He wanted to change this place and help these people.

Soso returned to Niagara with news for Ben that he wouldn't be returning to Sodus Bay. He told Ben about his encounter with his long-lost sister and his decision to stay on the reservation for a while. He was going to help Water Lily. Soso's hope was that Betty would be able to come and join him, and the two of them would help Lily organize and inspire the Indians of the reservation. Soso would help teach the use of farm equipment and white men's tools to become more productive.

Soso relayed this to Ben and in a letter to Betty, which Ben carried to her. While all this was very sudden and difficult to explain in a letter, he tried to relate the substance of his experiences while at the Niagara reservation. He hoped that Betty would understand and join him.

Soso went right to work in his efforts to help. He first got to know many of the elders, some of whom he had seen when he was young. Some were from his boyhood village or nearby villages in his own Cayuga tribe. He got to talk to them about what they had experienced and how it was very different than the lifestyle that he had lived since they had parted ways. He got to talk more with Water Lily and learn about her, her family, and her life of supporting those less fortunate. Soso took the opportunity to meet the young people on the reservation. He was surprised and pleased to find that the young Indians were still excited about their heritage and their future. They had greater opportunities, expectations, and enthusiasm for life than did the older Indians, who had undergone a significant and devastating change in their lifestyles. Change had left them bitter, frustrated, and disheartened. The young boys and girls played sports, enjoyed activities, and looked forward to a bright future. To the younger Indians, reservation life was natural, and their expectations were based on their own experiences.

Soso was especially pleased to see bagataway sticks and action-packed games. He noticed that there were more rules than what he had as a player many years before. Soso took right to learning the new rules and techniques of the modern bagataway game along with the young children. He was reliving his childhood with a stick in his hands passing the ball to young players on the team that he now helped coach. He was too old to run or play the game. However, it was exciting just to hold the stick and throw the ball.

Soso began seeing how much potential these young people had and at the same time noticed the disappointment and waste that had occurred within the older Indians on the reservation. He was committed to rectifying the situation. He knew firsthand the talents of these people and was sure that they could recover to live better, more productive lives, by building on their Indian heritage.

Lily wrote a letter to Garth at RPI telling him as much as she could about his great uncle, Soso. She explained Soso's relationship with Professor Davis. Similarly, Soso wrote to Jamey detailing his meeting Lily and finding out about his relative attending RPI. As it turned out, Jamey and Garth were already acquainted. RPI was a small school, and most students and faculty knew each other.

During the previous year, Garth had taken Jamey's calculus course, preparing him for engineering in his junior and senior years. Garth had been Jamey's best student. So the two men, upon receiving the letters from Soso and Water Lily, immediately contacted each other at school. They enjoyed learning more about one another and talking about some of the things that the two letters had explained. One thing Jamey was able to do, working with Garth, was to obtain books from the excess, unneeded collection in the library at Rensselaer. The two of them were able to send back nearly a hundrede books to the reservation. Many of these were high school level, which were the type most needed at the reservation school. So it was with great pleasure that the two assembled several boxes of books that were sent to the reservation via the Erie Canal. Garth couldn't wait to return to the reservation next summer to meet Soso. From his grandmother's letter and Jamey's description of Soso, Garth had constructed a powerful image. He dreamed about being like Soso and making contributions to both the white and Indian societies.

Betty didn't quite know what to think of Soso's letter. She had heard Soso talk about his sister and his concern over her fate. So Betty could understand Soso's excitement in finding his sister doing so well in Canada. However, she was confused about Soso's request for her to join him and his desire to stay on at the reservation to help. This was certainly going to be a major disruption in their lives and she, without being there to witness the situation firsthand, did not fully understand Soso's commitment to this effort. Why was it so urgent to be at Niagara? What could Soso and Betty do to help? What would happen to their own farm during their absence? There were many unanswered questions.

Niagara Trip

While still confused about Soso's request, Betty decided to go immediately to Niagara and see him. She packed up some of their excess supplies, farming equipment, household utensils, and some fruit and vegetables and loaded their boat. Then she headed down the lake toward Niagara. However, on her trip, Betty felt the wrath and power of Lake Ontario.

It appeared to be a nice October day as she left Sodus Bay and headed onto the lake. Since the days are rather short in the fall, she started early, at daybreak, in hopes of making the entire hundred-mile trip in two days. Betty realized that progress might be difficult since she was going west and, therefore, would be fighting the prevailing winds the entire way. Her plan was to tack her small boat along the shoreline. When she departed Sodus Bay there was not much wind, but she was still able to make slow progress down the lake. By late afternoon, she had passed the village of Rochester and the river, called Genessee. Not much past Rochester she ran into rougher weather. The lake became choppy from an increasing north-northwest wind. The temperature dropped rapidly, and the seas rose from one and two feet to three or even four feet. This was all Betty's little, overloaded boat could take. It was a tough job sailing through such rough seas, and Betty quickly realized that her sailing abilities were overmatched by the storm.

Taking the safest course of action, she headed into shore and pulled the boat up onto the beach as far she could. Betty had only one hand and was 54 years old, but she was still strong enough to pull the boat far enough onto shore to be out of danger. Fortunately, the boat was on the east side of a small point, which put Betty and her boat out of the worst of the weather. She felt pretty good about her situation and set up camp on the beach for the evening. There were no houses or lights in sight, so she figured that she was not likely to see any people in this area. She had mentally prepared herself for this possibility, so she accepted her fate and made the best of the situation. Despite the howling wind, pelting rain, and cold temperature, Betty finally got some sleep.

The wind stayed north-northwest all night long, and by morning it seemed to have settled down a bit. Betty struggled to get the boat off the shore and with considerable effort was finally able to do it. As she headed out onto the lake, the wind died down a bit more and changed direction, blowing out of the northeast. For a short while, this following wind helped her make rapid progress along the lakeshore.

By noon, it was obvious that the wind was picking up, and she would probably face the problems that she encountered the day before. However, she decided to continue on just a bit farther hoping to complete the journey as soon as she could. She hadn't seen another boat on the lake all day. Betty fought against her fears of the rough water and kept heading down the lake. By mid-afternoon, she ran into much more than just heavy winds.

Huge thunderstorms with dark clouds, heavy rains, and constant thunder and lightning seemed to appear out of nowhere. Betty's biggest problem was the reduced visibility. She could see nothing beyond twenty to thirty feet. Struggling to make headway, she made an error in tacking that caused the boat to dig into the seas. The boat started taking on water and was nearly ready to sink. Fortunately, this happened near shore, and, with skillful maneuvering, Betty was able to steady the boat and head to shore. She made land just about the time the worst of the storm was passing by her location. She had been extremely lucky, and, fortunately, she reached shore safely.

The rain and lake water caused her clothes and supplies to get soaked and some of the fruits, vegetables, and equipment had been washed overboard. Betty was nevertheless able to maintain her composure and found a place out of the weather so that she could pull the boat onto shore without damaging it. This time she barely had enough energy and strength to set up camp for the evening. Again, there were no visible signs of civilization nearby, so she didn't try looking for help. Exhausted, miserable, cold, and wet, she spent a restless night huddled under a small tree near shore hoping and praying for a break in the weather. She knew that she was lucky just to be alive, given the dangerous situation she had experienced. She thanked God for her safety and her life.

The next day's weather was no better. A strong north wind with occasional rain, battered the south shore of the lake. Betty took her time the next day bailing out the boat, drying and re-stowing all the equipment, and preparing herself for the rest of the trip. However, the day was lost for travel. The lake was too rough. By late night, the wind died down, and Betty was able to get a better night's rest. Her confidence and strength were growing as she prepared to do battle with the weather and the waves for another day.

Concerned that Soso would be worried about her, Betty got up early in the morning to find a calmer wind. The waves were still two to three feet, but this day would bring little wind and thankfully it would continue to diminish during the day. Betty left at daybreak, heading toward Niagara. She was still shaken from her ordeal, but fortunately she had a short run of only fifteen to twenty miles. Even in the calm wind, she knew that she could complete her journey. With great relief, five hours later, she arrived at Niagara. Waiting on the dock for her was Soso with a wagon to transport her and the supplies. Both were relieved to see one another. Soso, having seen the weather on the lake the day before and knowing that Betty would have had a tough time making progress in that weather, had been anxiously waiting on the dock for 36 hours. He had hoped that she had pulled onto shore and waited out the weather. Betty explained her ordeal to Soso as the two of them loaded the wagon with the wet supplies that had survived the trip.

The Reservation

Soso was excited about taking the equipment and supplies to the reservation, but it took a while to load the wagon because almost everything was wet. By late afternoon they had loaded the wagon, arranged for storage of

Soso's boat, and started out on the 25-mile overland trip to Lily's house and the reservation.

"Wait until you meet my sister. I'm sure you'll like her. Of course, I didn't even recognize her after 45 years. It's so nice to know she has survived and lived such a productive life." Soso continued to explain the situation to Betty, "Water Lily has done many important things for the reservation, but the people are still in need of help. I think we can make a difference. That's why I've asked you to help me do this."

"Soso, you know that I want to help, but we have left our home at the worse possible time. I hope that Georgette takes good care of the house and the shed over the winter. She's only nine years old, and that's a big responsibility."

"Betty, we can make a difference here. These people need us much more than our home or our neighbors in Lummisville. I hope you understand."

"Yes, Soso, I'm sure they do, and I'm sure we will be able to help during this winter. It's just that I had plans for things around the house. I'll be fine once I'm situated and understand our role." Betty was always organized.

Lily had not come with Soso since she had some business to attend to at the reservation. Soso had originally hoped that they would return that night, but they couldn't make the entire trip that quickly. They stopped and spent the night on the road and arrived at Lily's the following morning. Betty met Water Lily, and the two women began talking about Soso and the things that he had accomplished and experienced during his life. They got to know each other that evening as they talked late into the night. It didn't take long for Betty to understand Soso and Water Lily's hopes about helping the Indians of the reservation. Yes. They could make a difference.

During the course of their discussions, Betty discovered remarkable similarities between Lily and Soso. She also saw an obvious difference. Lily was deeply religious with a strong commitment for service to her Catholic faith. This was something that Betty and Soso had never really discussed. Soso wouldn't let her discuss religion, even though he took her to Float Bridge for the Sunday services of the Methodist Church. Soso had never been deeply involved in either Indian spirits or white man's religions, except in times of extreme need. Lily had become a devout Catholic and had used her religion to help maintain her strength. Betty secretly hoped that Lily's influence would help Soso see the value of religious faith.

Betty, Water Lily, and Soso made an excellent team. All three had their own interests and different groups on the reservation they worked well with. Together they were able to cover most people and many parts of reservation life. Betty was naturally inclined to teach the young adults, men and women, to be productive farmers, home makers, carpenters, and business people. Water Lily continued her enterprise with the elders and leaders of the tribes to establish a political base, arrange for governmental support, and insure financing of activities. Soso worked mostly with the youth. He taught the young boys academic courses, sporting games, woodworking, citizenship, and general teamwork. The girls learned similar skills, along with cooking and sewing.

Together the three of them earned the confidence, pride, and resolution of the reservation communities. They all understood the predicament and the goal: develop modern white man skills while maintaining the cultural Indian roots of the community. While this was difficult, it wasn't impossible. Soso and Lily were examples of this goal. Over the winter, real progress was made.

Revitalization

Betty organized a group that established an icehouse business on the reservation. A cave and entrance building were constructed and insulated in the late fall. All winter long ice was cut, harvested, and stored in this new icehouse. By spring, this operation had stored enough ice to provide one of the reservation communities a year of valuable ice. This would certainly help the standard of living of the entire community. In the spring, she organized several work crews of three or four young adults that began cleaning and fixing public buildings and roads.

Soso worked with the teachers of the two reservation schools. Goals and standards for each student were established in the traditional academic subjects of reading, writing, history, and mathematics. Several Indian elders volunteered their time to teach the Iroquois languages, legends, and beliefs. Soso also organized contests for running, throwing, jumping, and bagataway. This program was especially successful with the older boys and girls. They enjoyed the competition and the physical activity. They were learning modern valuable skills, while maintaining important parts of their Indian heritage. This future generation was the key to survival of the Native Americans and their way of life.

The reservation's leaders had renewed confidence and optimism. They saw the changes that were taking place and liked them. They saw the potential for improvements in the communities. Water Lily helped them organize their governmental support programs to better serve people's needs. New supplies of books, sewing supplies, cooking utensils, medicine, and carpentry tools were substituted for the usual government supplies of rotting food or useless hunting, fishing, and trapping equipment. There were no game animals or fish left in the area, so the aforementioned equipment had no value to the Indians except to trade or sell back to the white men. The benefits of the new kinds of supplies were immediately apparent. People began using the supplies to help themselves and improve their neighborhoods.

By spring, the reservation had been revitalized. The streets, homes, and public buildings were all being cleaned and modernized. By every measure, the reservation was improving and everyone recognized that Water Lily, Betty, and Soso had made the difference.

Religion

There were other changes taking place. Water Lily's devotion to Catholic religion eventually began penetrating Soso's anti-religion shell. Through Water Lily's example, Soso slowly came to realize that the whites' religion was not completely incompatible with Indian spiritual beliefs or with the reality of the technical and material world. Water Lily and Betty discussed a strategy to expose Soso to religious thinking. Water Lily was both persistent and patient. She set the example and then told Soso what she believed, why she believed, and what the church had done for her. Finally, Soso began listening, asking questions, and eventually talking with the reservation's missionary priest, Father John. Soso learned how the whites' religion could help grow his spirit, refresh his mind, and express thanks for God's gifts—nature, technology, and love. Finally, when the time was right, Water Lily and Betty asked Soso to go to church with them. At first, Soso went to see and learn, but then very soon he began to feel the faith and comfort of religion. He began to believe in the power of faith and how it could affect his daily life. Faith, even in small amounts, was empowering and refreshing. Soso was refreshed and re-energized. While not yet ready to believe in all aspects of religion, he felt that he had experienced God and obtained faith.

Dilemma

The winter of 1839-1840 was a rough one in Troy, where Jamey continued to teach students at RPI and, with his wife Carin, raise his family. Jamey was frustrated. While he loved his occupation, he was torn between the profession of teaching and his roots back in Sodus Point. He longed to return to his boyhood home, living near his friends, doing the things he liked best, enjoying nature's beauty, and raising his children as he had been raised. He constantly dreamed of an outdoor life of fishing, hunting, sailing, and farming. It wasn't that he disliked teaching or living in Troy. Teaching was a tremendously rewarding profession, and he was good at it. However, it just wasn't Sodus Point. He continued to dream of a future Davis homestead at First Creek overlooking Sodus Bay.

While he wrestled with this issue, Jamey continued to receive offers to teach at other schools. Harvard offered him a professorship in astronomy. Yale wanted his expertise in engineering. Dartmouth wanted him to teach mathematics. This was a period of tremendous growth in the nation's technical education system. Mathematics, science, and engineering professors were in demand, and experienced West Point graduates like Jamey were sought after by the new schools and programs throughout the country. As a talented and broadly educated applied mathematician, Jamey could teach in virtually every mathematics, science, or engineering program in the nation. He was a well-known textbook author. It felt good being wanted, but none of these offers helped to reduce his frustration since none offered him enough money to begin to save for his dream house. Professor Eaton asked Jamey to continue at RPI, but he couldn't offer him a raise. He declined all the new offers and stayed at RPI. There was no college near Sodus Point, and that is where he wanted to be. If he could only find a position with a high enough salary to save enough money in a few years to buy Pollock's land and build a house, he would take it.

Time to Return

Neither Soso nor Betty had been back to Lummisville for over six months. They had corresponded regularly over that period with Ben and Georgiana and knew that things were fine back home, but both of them were homesick and wanted to return. Georgette had been responsible for watching over things, and the little girl had done a fine job. It was spring, and Lummisville was just a short, two-day, boat trip down the lake. They had to decide when to leave for their return back home. On a cold, but bright and sunny day in late March, they reached their decision. They had spent the day in Niagara, preparing the boat that Betty had sailed down in the fall for a new boating season. The wooden planks were inspected, the fixtures were checked, and the ropes and sails were examined. After working near the water and dreaming of Sodus Bay all day, both agreed it was time to return home. Their work at the reservation had been enjoyable and rewarding, but they could leave now, knowing that what they had started could be continued. Water Lily had the energy and enthusiasm to continue her work without them. The reservation was energized. The only complication was that Soso was still instructing several young men in building a sailboat. He had promised them that he would see them through to the completion of the boat. As of now, they were only halfway through the construction. He needed another three or four weeks to fulfill his promise. So they reluctantly decided that Betty would sail back now, and Soso would travel later using the Erie Canal and overland route to return to Lummisville about a month later, or, if possible, catch a ride with a transport boat heading east when the appropriate time arrived.

There was one young boy whom Soso especially enjoyed teaching. Joe Fox was a bright, enthusiastic teenager from the Seneca tribe. Joe had always looked up to Garth Simpson and wanted to follow in his footsteps. Joe talked to Soso about Garth and his success at Rensselaer. Joe wanted to attend RPI and bring back technical knowledge to the Indians, just like Garth was preparing to do. Soso encouraged Joe to continue to use Garth as a role model.

Betty spent two more days completing her projects and turning over leadership of her activities to others. Mostly, she needed to insure that the workers were able to complete construction projects on public buildings. She spent the last evening thanking her friends and saying her farewells. She didn't have much to take back to Lummisville. It would be an almost empty boat compared to the overflowing load that she had brought down in the fall. On the morning of her departure day, Soso gave her advice about sailing the lake in the early spring. The ice had gone out of the bays only two weeks earlier, so the water in the lake was still extremely cold. Betty waved to Soso and Water Lily, who stood on the dock waving good-bye, and headed out the Niagara River and up the lake toward Sodus Bay.

The day started out sunny, but cold. The wind seemed to be constantly changing direction and speed, which made it difficult to sail. Because of the extreme cold, Betty was wearing heavy clothes and bulky mittens. She had to remain alert as the waves grew and the light boat literally bounced over the big troughs and swells of Lake Ontario. The waves seemed to come from all directions; progress was slow and tedious. When she could, she dreamed of her home and how good it would be to see Sodus Bay and her friends in Lummisville. She had missed her comfortable home and longed for a relaxing summer. Just as she dozed in her dreams, she felt a terrible jolt and heard a frightening noise. It was the rudder of the boat being snapped right off its supports. A big wave had hit at just the wrong angle and the rudder had taken its full force. The entire rudder broke apart and went into the water before she could grab it. Betty now had no way to steer the boat. She should have dropped the sail immediately, but instead she tried to reach overboard to grab a piece of the broken rudder. Just then another wave and gust of wind hit the boat hard, tilting the boat further and vaulting Betty overboard. It was too rough and too cold. Betty never had a chance to catch the boat as it sailed on without her. Quietly she sank into the deep, cold water of the lake.

The boat sailed on for a while, then without its rudder, it began to flutter about. Soon it filled with water. The sail ripped; it was just floating wreckage. From then on, its path was determined by the whims of the currents of the lake.

Soso and Betty had written Ben about their travel plans. Ben and Georgiana had spent a worrisome winter caring for their infant son, Benny, who had been born premature in February. But finally in late spring, he began to show signs of weight gain and development. They hoped that the better weather of summer would help improve their baby's health and relieve their worries.

The Search

Ben anxiously spent the next several days waiting for Betty's arrival in Lummisville. He had planned to go to Albany for a political convention for the election of 1840, but delayed his travel to insure that Betty arrived safely. Finally, his worry over her whereabouts set him in motion. She was over a week late from the travel date stated in the letter. Ben wrote back to Soso, explaining the situation and asking if Betty's travel plans had changed. After contemplating further action, Ben decided to look for Betty by sailing toward Niagara. He took nine-year-old Georgette with him. They sailed slowly along the shore, looking carefully both on shore and in the water. After three days of travel, they arrived at Niagara. Ben and Georgette obtained a carriage ride to the reservation where they found Soso. Soso hadn't yet received Ben's letter expressing concern for Betty, but Soso had been worried since he hadn't received a letter from Betty. Now as he heard that she was missing, he was in a panic with worry. Where could she be? What could have happened?

Soso, Ben, and Georgette returned to Niagara and set off sailing back along the lakeshore. They traveled quickly along the route back to Lummisville. Maybe Betty had been held up along the way, missed meeting Ben, and now had made her destination. Soso prayed that she was safe and that they would find her at home in Lummisville. They sailed quickly along the lakeshore for a day and a half without seeing any sign of her. Arriving at the dock, Soso ran to his house calling for Betty. His worst fears were realized. She was not there. The cold, dark house felt empty and deserted as he searched in vain. His loving wife Betty was missing.

By now it was over two weeks since Betty had left Niagara. Soso tried to think of possible explanations for her disappearance, but nothing made sense. The terrible thought of a water tragedy kept returning to his mind, no matter how hard he tried to block it out. Soso and Ben spent another two weeks carefully searching the lakeshore between Sodus Bay and Niagara in vain. There was no sign of Betty or the boat. After two weeks, Ben ended his searching and returned home to help Georgiana with the farm, but he worried about Soso, who continued the search in other areas of the lake.

Soso continued to pray. In his heart, he hoped for an explanation, but he knew in his mind that it would never come. The reason was beyond understanding, yet he was too mature and educated to believe it was the doings of an evil lake Serpent, which was the traditional Indian explanation for such a tragedy. His new God worked in mysterious ways. Soso now believed in both God and the good spirits of life, both in times of crisis and in times of peace. He still suffered the severe pain of Betty's loss at the same time he was thankful for having loved her and called her his wife.

Exhausted, but determined, Soso searched the Canadian shoreline. He resolved that he would continue to sail completely around the lakeshore until he found something. However, he didn't need to go that far. At first, he refused to believe what he found about 300 yards off shore near the York harbor. It was the boat that Betty had sailed—sunk, rudderless, and empty. The sail was torn and the rudder broken off, but otherwise the boat was structurally sound. Soso could see that the rudder had snapped and the boat sunk with its sail still flying. Whether Betty had stayed with the boat or been thrown overboard, she could not have survived such an ordeal in these cold waters. He no longer needed to search for the boat, but now for her body. Soso finally realized, in both his heart and mind, that he had lost Betty. It wasn't fair that the lake he loved so much could have taken his only greater love away from him. For the first time, he vividly saw a foreboding perspective of Lake Ontario. His prayers were his only defense against loneliness and depression. He kept believing that God had a purpose in mind when he took Betty from him and from her life on Earth. He was convinced—Betty was gone.

Soso continued to search for her body, but it was never found. By July he was completely exhausted and sick. He had continuously sailed the lakeshore for weeks and months, sometimes not eating for days and sleeping on the wet beaches, where he ended one day and began the next. Soso was sixty years old, and the weeks of worry and work had taken their toll. He finally returned to Lummisville and went to bed. Soso had slept for about 24 hours before Georgette noticed his boat at the dock. She went to the door and found it open. Then she noticed Soso asleep in his bed and ran home to tell her parents. For the rest of the summer, the Lummises cared for their seriously-ill neighbor. All Soso could manage to do was rest and pray for the soul of his lost wife. Since he was in no condition to work, his farm decayed and his morale suffered. However, through considerable care from his neighbors, his health and strength slowly returned.

Recovery

By the end of the summer of 1840, Soso was healthy enough to care for himself and started doing jobs around the house. In many ways, he was a new, rebuilt man, ready to be productive. He was mended emotionally as well as physically. During his months of recovery, Soso continued to analyze his beliefs. He began to realize why the whites' religion was both appealing and confusing, for it gave one a guide on how one ought to live and a sense of purpose for life. It was structured. Christ was an excellent role model and teacher. But the whites' religion focused on man, not on all of nature's creatures and components. Such a human-centered faith left Soso with doubts. Why was God like man? Couldn't God be like the fish or the deer or other animals? Couldn't nature's other creatures share their feelings with man and play a role in religion? What is man without the other creatures? Whatever happens to the animals also happens to man. All things are connected. Certainly, the tall mountains, vast oceans, and the bright sun in the sky must all play an important role in life, nature, and religion. The Indian spirits recognized the role of all nature's creatures. The Indians knew that man had to fit into the harmony and order of nature's world. The whites always had man's role as dominating and ruling the world. Soso and his Indian brothers and sisters knew that everything that man did was only done with nature's permission.

Soso did what he had done all his life whenever the ways of the whites and the Indians were in conflict, he forged his own personal religion. In his mind, he combined the structure, teachings, and faith of whites' God and Christ with the breadth and harmony of Mother Nature and the Indian's spirits. He had always been confident that he knew the way one ought to live. Soso now believed in his own kind of religion, where he was comfortable in the whites' church, could pray to God, follow many of the teachings of Christ and the *Bible*, and, at the same time, talk with the Indian spirits that helped Mother Nature care for all things on her Earth. Soso had always been an independent thinker with tolerance for ambiguity. Now he used those traits to forge his own beliefs. He was a believer. He had religion and faith, and it gave him comfort and peace.

At Soso's request, the local Methodist minister from Lyons and the Catholic priest from Clyde, came to Lummisville to conduct jointly a memorial service for Betty. It was a moving ceremony. Prayers were said, passages from the *Bible* were read, and Soso talked with the spirits of life and death. There on the magnificent Lummis estate overlooking Sodus Bay, Betty Washington's husband Soso and her friends paid final tribute to this strong, happy woman. Her cross-shaped grave marker was placed next to those of her friends William and Sara Lummis. Despite beginning life as a slave, Betty had spent an enjoyable and productive seventeen years free from slavery and ten years as Soso's wife. It was Soso's first public appearance in the Sodus Bay area in a year. It felt good to see his friends and neighbors from Lummisville and Sodus Point. They shared their grief over Betty's loss and their memories of her meaningful life with their leader and helpful neighbor, Sosoenodus Washington.

The service was one of celebration for the love and kindness in Betty's life. Soso celebrated Betty's life, while he continued to mourn her loss in his heart. Betty had meant so much to him that he wondered how he could go on. He would never forget her. He vowed that he would live the rest of his life for her. In her remembrance, Soso regained his health, energy, and enthusiasm for life. Soso discovered that his beliefs in God, Mother Nature, and religion could help. Special prayers and *Bible* readings helped him understand his grief and rebuild his spirit. He found that faith could heal wounds of pain and suffering. By late fall, Soso was ready to fish, hunt, farm, and build boats. He was an amazing sixty-year-old man with a brave spirit, kind heart, and keen mind.

Part V

Better Times

Politics

Over the years, politics had become a big issue in America, and even the rural frontier was affected by the actions of the government in Washington. It was a stretch to continue to call Sodus Bay the frontier. The area had grown in population, and the standard of living had improved substantially. There were roads, taverns, and signs of civilization nearly everywhere. The industrial revolution was making its mark, even though the area's primary business was still agriculture. The nearest small cities were thirty and forty miles away in Rochester and Syracuse, but there were several villages in the area. Newark, Sodus, Lyons, Palmyra, and Clyde were the closest centers of population and activity in Wayne County, while Wolcott, Williamson, and Red Creek were growing settlements. The Sodus Bay area was ripe for the introduction of the conveniences of modern civilization and for meeting its potential for growth into a prosperous city. Many residents still believed that a major city would eventually lie on the shores of Sodus Bay. There was just too much potential for growth for this not to happen. However, others had witnessed all the set-backs in developing this area and doubted that substantial growth would ever occur.

During the presidential campaign of 1840, the Whig Party caught the fancy of the American public through novel campaign tactics of catchy slogans, flashy signs, and mass advertisements. The Whig candidate, William Henry Harrison, was elected President and took office in March, 1841. Unfortunately, he died of pneumonia only a month later. Vice President John Tyler succeeded him. This was the first time that this succession procedure had been necessary.

Residents of Sodus Bay area took up sides in many of the political debates over issues of the times. Most people in the area were Whigs because of their agricultural and frontier backgrounds, and they still remembered and supported the expansionist themes that had begun with the Whigs under President Jackson. However, there were more and more Democrats moving into the area, especially as more industries and businesses were established. As always, times were changing. The frontier was now hundreds of miles west of Sodus Bay.

New Party

The Lummises were not enamored with either of the major political parties. They were, however, intrigued by the beginning of a new party based on a platform calling for the abolition of slavery, but not for the abandonment of the Union as many radical abolitionists proposed. This party, called the Liberty Party, had just formed, so its presidential candidate, James Birney, garnered only a few thousand popular votes in the 1840 election. However, the Liberty Party and its cause were building momentum, and Ben Lummis and his sister Elizabeth Ellet were doing all they could to see it succeed. They, along with other supporters, saw this party as a means to the eventual elimination of slavery in the country. Ben had attended its founding meeting in Warsaw, New York in the fall of 1839. However, he had missed the convention at Albany in the spring when he helped Soso search for Betty.

It was not easy to generate support for the Liberty Party, even though many people believed in its platform. Labor unions and factory working conditions held much more interest than did abolition. The slavery laws in the South were firmly fixed in the culture and ethos of the slave states and their citizens, while slave-harboring laws in the northern states were working compromises now accepted by most citizens. The balance of power and sentiment over slavery was delicate, and very few people wanted to rock the boat on slavery issues in fear of causing political turmoil. There were 26 states in the Union: thirteen slave and thirteen free. Still most of the three million black people living in the United States were slaves. The free blacks lived in the North, and the blacks in slavery lived in the South. The average citizen considered slavery abolitionists extremists, and people were leery of the new Liberty Party for that reason. Abolitionist leaders like publisher William Lloyd Garrison and poet John Greenleaf Whittier were just too militant for most people to accept and support. The abolitionist cause had suffered because of radical actions by some of its supporters and intense propaganda against them. Garrison's journal, *The Liberator*, was highly contro-versial; it was banned in many areas of the South. Garrison was an agitator and was frequently involved in fights about slavery. He had been jailed for fighting and inciting a riot on several occasions. Despite his reputation, Garrison was opposed to violent resistance and considered himself a paci-fist who believed in using education and moral persuasion to end slavery. However, his passion for this cause and his radical methods led to his con-flicts and problems with the law. A fellow abolitionist publisher, Elijah Lovejoy, had been killed by citizens in Alton, Illinois, over the anti-slavery articles that he had published in his paper. As part of the nation's mood, threats on abolitionists were common.

These threats didn't stop Ben Lummis from joining the new political party and taking a leadership role. The Liberty Party tried to establish itself as having moderate views on abolition, in order to appeal to the average cit-izen. Ben's letter writing to Elizabeth and Jamey persuaded them to join the Party. Jamey was in an ideal spot to effect political action. Albany, as the capital of New York, became the party headquarters, and Jamey lived just ten miles away. Elizabeth had a much tougher problem. While the Liberty Party was a growing force in New York and several other northern states, it wasn't recognized in South Carolina. Very few people in that state agreed with the party's goal of eliminating slavery and still fewer would dare admit publicly such a belief. Elizabeth had no choice. She would have to contribute silently from afar. Ben also convinced Soso of the value of the cause. Soso, as an Indian, was unable to vote, but he had always realized that Indian rights were related to the rights of the black people. The Liberty Party had the potential to improve the rights for both blacks and Indians, and Soso would do his best to support its activities.

Party leader James Birney was a converted slaveholder from Kentucky. He had freed his slaves and moved to western New York. The Birney fam-ily had been rich, but over the years Birney had spent most of his money in various philanthropic endeavors including abolition. He had been active in many initiatives to help blacks (free and slave) and Indians (free and those confined to reservations). Several years before, he had helped obtain better care and treatment for the Cherokees displaced from Georgia to the west-ern reservations. He had served in several government positions. However, most of his time, energy, and money went to the American Anti-Slavery Society. It was his passion. James had been its secretary and primary spokesman for a number of years. Recently, Elizabeth Ellet had sent him material and articles for publication in the Society's newsletter. After James Birney's first wife died, he married Annie, the daughter of William Fitzhugh of Geneva. The couple enjoyed Sodus Bay, so they often traveled there from their home in Geneva. Of course, whenever James came to Sodus Bay, he spent time at Lummisville with Ben discussing politics and the cause. James also spent time with Soso, and soon the two men became friends and fishing partners.

Both men enjoyed talking about religions and their role in society. Soso was Catholic and James Protestant—both believers in the faith of Christianity. However, both were disappointed in the role that religions were playing in the improvement of society. James had attended the World Anti-Slavery Conference in England in 1840. While in England, he had presented his views on the failure of religions to help with the cause of ending slavery. James, along with fellow abolitionist William Lloyd Garrison, felt that slavery could be defeated if the religions would actively support the abolitionist cause. Similarly, Soso couldn't understand why religions were primarily concerned with converting instead of helping Indians.

Both Soso and James questioned the wisdom of the founding fathers of the country, who had written a constitution that allowed slavery, counted slaves only as parts of people, and gave no rights to Indians. Despite this criticism of the government, they both believed that working within the political system and supporting appropriate changes were the best ways to improve the climate for blacks and Indians. Fellow abolitionist Garrison and his followers thought the government so ill-founded that abolitionists shouldn't seek office or even vote until a new government structure was formed. Soso understood Garrison's passion but preferred Birney's approach of working within the system, which was something that Soso had done successfully all his life.

James Birney was the most impressive man Soso had ever met. He was honest and sincere about his caring for others, completely humble, and extremely articulate. James wasn't a very good fisherman or boatsman, but he could lead and inspire people. Soso always felt good about the prospects of the future after talking with James. James was an optimist and had a vision of a world in which all people were free and equal. If there were only more people like James Birney, Soso knew that the world would be a much better place to live.

James and the other leaders of the Liberty Party supported Soso's efforts to stop government exploitation of Indians. As state governments and the federal government kept violating Indian treaties, the Liberty Party tried to use its influence to prevent future tragedies like the Trail of Tears and restore the terms of valid treaties.

As Soso told James, "We are still dealing with the legacy of the trail of tears. Whites continue to exploit Indians and blacks. Something must to done to save these people and to heal the great divide of our country." To Soso, the culture and character of Native Americans were natural resources that were too valuable to waste or lose.

James Birney was optimistic but cautious. "Soso, some day we will have peace, understanding, harmony, and equality among the races. But, for now, we have to suffer to make everyone understand. I hope we will live to see the day, but I suspect it will be our children or our children's children, who will finally see the fruits of our labors. Meanwhile, we all suffer, but I prefer to consider it just growing pains."

"I hope you are right. I agree, a better world is worth waiting for, and someday it will happen," Soso concluded.

Over the spring, plans were made for a group representing the Liberty Party to lobby the government in Washington, D.C. on behalf of the abolition of slavery. The group would consist of James Birney, Ben Lummis, Jamey Davis, Elizabeth Ellet, Soso Washington, and four other Party leaders—publishers William Cullen Bryant of New York and Wendell Phillips of Boston, Gerrit Smith, and Abby Folsom. Bryant was the editor of the *New York Evening Post* and a popular poet. Phillips was a Harvard lawyer and the most fanatical of the group. Smith, one of the Party's founders, lived in western New York, and Folsom was an activist who frequently traveled and gave lectures against slavery. She lived in Albany and helped at the party headquarters. Birney warned them all to keep Phillips and Folsom under control for the two of them could easily get carried away with their rhetoric and alienate those who weren't so extreme. They planned to meet in Washington by August 1 and spend the month lobbying. They would discuss the five tenets of the Liberty Party platform with politicians who would listen: 1) too much government power is dangerous, 2) liberty is based on freedom and independence, 3) the expansion of slavery must be prevented, 4) the Union must be preserved, and 5) equality for all people, regardless of race, religion, or gender must be obtained. However, those plans were rudely interrupted. In June, James Birney was arrested for harboring slaves and faced a very difficult trial.

The Trial

James knew his harboring trial would be a tough challenge that would consume all his time and effort. He worried that it would adversely affect the Party or its causes. Eight slaves had been found on his property, and there were several witnesses who told the sheriff that they had seen James driving a wagon with several blacks hiding in the back. In reality, there were fifteen slaves on his property at the time of his arrest. The other seven were well hidden in a false room in James' house and never found. He had intended to move all fifteen of them that very night to the next stop on the underground railroad, with their destination in the United States being Lummisville. From there, Soso and Ben had agreed to sail them to Canada. If James Birney were to take the stand, he would have to admit his role in the situation and surely would be found guilty. He was ethically bound to tell the truth. He wasn't as worried about this possibility as he was about his ability to protect the others involved in the underground railroad. What if questions were asked about where the slaves had come from or where they were going? He knew he might have to serve a long jail sentence in order to protect his underground railroad colleagues by refusing to answer the questions, but he figured that was a small price to pay to keep the railroad in business. In order to be acquitted or at least to protect his colleagues, James needed to divert attention from the facts of the case to other, more sensational issues.

James's first step was to hire the best lawyer loyal to the abolitionist cause, S. P. Chase. Chase was a brilliant man, masterful lawyer, and co-founder of the Liberty Party in Ohio. Establishing a legal diversion would be no problem for this shrewd, articulate, dedicated lawyer, who already at age 32 was nicknamed the attorney-general for run-away slaves. James knew that he had hired the right man for the job. Once they laid out their defense plans, he was confident in obtaining acquittal. James insisted that the rest of the Liberty Party organizers continue with their planned visit to Washington. They finally agreed; so Ben, Jamey, and Elizabeth made the arrangements for the trip to Washington. Soso stayed to help James. The rest of the Davis family—Carin, eleven-year-old Lenny, nine-year-old

Catherine, and four-year-old Joan—were going to spend the summer on Sodus Bay with Georgiana, Georgette, and one-year-old Benny. Of course, Lenny's plan was to spend time with his Uncle Soso.

The summer's activities went off pretty much as planned. The very day Birney's trial began in New York State, Ben, Jamey, Elizabeth, William Bryant, Wendell Phillips, and Abby Folsom met in Washington with newly-elected Congressman Samuel Hoar, who was strongly opposed to slavery. They also saw several other congressional leaders. The Washington trip effectively exposed the Liberty Party and its platform to the government leaders. They even met with influential Senators Clay and Calhoun, who were pro-slavery, but were at least willing to listen to the ideas of this new political party. The six Liberty Party representatives were all capable speakers, and the politicians in Washington appreciated their professional approach. The challenge of changing people's minds about such controversial issues would take time, but these initial steps were important.

At the same time, the Party's leader, James Birney, faced an different challenge in a hot, crowded Geneva courtroom. Already, there was tremendous publicity over the case. Newspapers throughout the country had sent reporters to cover this landmark case. It wasn't very often that a former presidential candidate was facing a jail sentence over such a controversial crime. Birney and his lawyer, Chase, had plans to utilize this media attention to their advantage. They knew the reporters liked Birney as an honest, hardworking politician, who had fought an uphill battle as a third-party presidential candidate. They also knew that many of the reporters were not about to support the issue of abolitionism, so that topic as an issue in the case had to be avoided.

The first item on the agenda for the trial was jury selection. As Chase carefully looked over the people in the jury pool, he began the trial with an objection that no blacks (slaves or free) nor Indians were found in the group of potential jurors. Chase launched into an eloquent argument to the people present in the courtroom on the equality of all races and the injustice to his client because blacks and Indians had been excluded from jury duty. Chase's presentation lasted all morning. He was mesmerizing and persuasive. He pointed out that not one black or Indian was even present in the courtroom, yet weren't they considered peers of his client, Birney. The only break in Chase's presentation occurred when the prosecutor casually interrupted with an off-hand comment that no blacks or Indians were available in the county for such duty. Looking around the overheated, crowded courtroom, Judge Baxter decided it would be best to deliberate on the objection and the prosecutor's comment and called for a recess for the entire afternoon.

The collection of newspaper reporters had the beginnings of a momentous story. Chase's detailed argument had been logical, sound, and sensational. There was no one more convincing than S. P. Chase, especially when he was given the points of the argument by James Birney. The reporters wrote their first day's story, pointing out equal rights issues, constitutional rights involving jury selection, and the injustice of trying Birney without any blacks or Indians on the jury. The first day was a success for the Birney-Chase team. The media had bought their argument without starting to look at the facts of the case. The media loved supporting Birney as a political underdog as long as they didn't have to support abolitionism, which was never discussed by Chase in his jury-selection objection and argument.

Day two of the trial began with Judge Baxter asking Chase to conclude his jury-selection arguments. This time Chase had all the details to refute the prosecutor's claim that no blacks or Indians were available. He had numbers and the names of perspective jurors—black, white, and Indian. He clearly pointed out from the county's population demographics what portion of the jury should be white, black, and Indian, and even made a claim that at least one of the eight slaves that had been captured should be on the jury. If anything, Chase was even more convincing of the injustice of the jury selection system during his explanation on day two. Chase's presentation again lasted all morning, and it was as sensational as the first day's presentation. This time the prosecutor's lone interruption had to do with the lack of intelligence and educational level of any of the blacks and Indians who could serve. During this session, there were several times when Judge Baxter lost control of the courtroom. The crowd cheered and clapped during Chase's most eloquent oratory, while Baxter furiously pounded his gravel for attention. Chase cut apart comments the Judge made trying to explain the jury selection procedure. Once again, Baxter decided to recess at noon with the hope that the next day he could regain control of the proceedings. Reporters were delighted with the controversial material that they had at their disposal. Over the course of the next two weeks, nearly every newspaper in the northern part of the country would run critical reports on the first two days of the trial in Judge Baxter's courtroom and the injustice of the nation's jury-selection procedures.

The three local daily newspapers in central New York ran articles in the next day's editions strongly critical of Judge Baxter and very supportive of Birney and Chase. The weekly papers had gone to press with the first day's proceedings. Editors D. M. Keeler of the Wayne Standard, Bill Russell of the Lyons Gazette, and William Cole of the Palmyra Whig, all supported Birney and criticized Baxter. The media-support strategy was working. According to the headlines, the Judge's actions had already prejudiced the case. An editorial in one newspaper called for immediate dismissal. Judge Baxter read the articles and was about ready to end his suffering by dismissing the case, even though it really hadn't even begun. The prosecutor of the case had a similar inclination.

More Courtroom Drama

Day three didn't last very long. Chase opened with information to counter the prosecutor's claim that blacks and Indians were not educated sufficiently to hear the case. While Soso had stayed away from the courtroom on day one upon Chase's request, he was there for days two and three. Chase simply had Soso, as a potential Indian juror, stand and then asked him three questions.

The first question set the stage. "Are you an Indian?"

"Yes," Soso replied.

Then the main point was made. "Have you published an article on shipbuilding in a national journal, designed and led the construction of the hull for the largest steamship in the world, and hold three patents on ship construction?"

"Yes."

Just to insure the point was clear for even the most conservative listeners in the courtroom, Chase asked one more question. "Can you recite Chapter seven, verses one through ten of Genesis?"

"Then the Lord said to Noah, go into the ark, you and all your household, for you alone in this age have I found to be truly just." By the time Soso recited only this first verse of the assigned passage of the *Bible*, Judge Baxter struck his gavel. Baxter then asked the prosecutor if he wished to continue the trial. The prosecutor answered that he did not wish to continue. A humiliated, but relieved, Judge Baxter struck his gavel one last time, proclaiming the case dismissed. James Birney was innocent before any of the facts of the case were ever presented. It had been a remarkable three days.

Just in case they had needed it, Birney and Chase had two more aces up their sleeves. If the Judge had continued the trial, Chase was ready to repeat the procedure that he performed with Soso with both Samuel Cornish, the Black publisher of *Freedom's Journal*, and Garth Simpson, Soso's Indian nephew. Highly educated and articulate, Cornish was currently living in Geneva. Garth had just finished his junior year at RPI. The intelligence and education of blacks and Indians couldn't be questioned, when the examples put forward were Samuel Cornish, Garth Simpson, and Soso Washington.

Birney and Chase celebrated the victory. Things had gone just as they had planned. Soso, Garth, and Samuel joined them in celebration. The five happy men spent the afternoon recounting stories of the trial and then spent the next two weeks fishing on Sodus Bay. Every newspaper in the country ran articles about the trial. Even the southern press couldn't criticize the results very severely. Everything had been so well orchestrated by Birney and Chase that there was little to say in defense of Judge Baxter, the prosecutor, or the jury selection system, especially since the controversial issues of slavery and its abolition had never been mentioned during the proceedings.

The Liberty Party lobbyists read all about the strange and exciting case in the Washington newspapers about ten days after the proceedings were completed. They could hardly contain their ecstasy as they read about the events and the results. This case made their presence in Washington and their message even more powerful. They were now the most popular political visitors in the city. Everyone wanted to talk with them to get their interpretation of the case and of the major players in the trial—James Birney, S. P. Chase, and Sosoenodus Washington.

Reunion

The trip to Washington brought Ben a special surprise. His old friend and former partner, Samuel Morse, was in the nation's capital demonstrating his telegraph to several members of Congress. Sam hoped to convince

Congress to support a large-scale test of the capabilities of his invention in order to gain governmental support for this communication system. Ben and Sam had corresponded regularly over the four years since Ben's retirement as a banker. Ben's letters of encouragement had helped Sam through several disappointments and setbacks. Sam had sent Ben two exquisite paintings that he had produced. Sam was a talented artist as well as a gifted inventor.

As he looked over Sam's new equipment, Ben was impressed with the progress that his friend had made. Sam showed Ben, and the other members of the Liberty Party group, how he had improved his system and explained how many terminals could use the system at once for both private messages and open public announcements. Sam also had developed means to send messages over hundreds of miles, to places all over the country, using more powerful batteries and booster systems at critical locations. Ben was more convinced than ever about the vast potential for this technology. In addition to their own platform, the Liberty Party now became a strong supporter and promoter of the telegraph.

Ben and Sam renewed their friendship, and the members of the Liberty Party delegation were active participants in several demonstrations of the telegraph to members of Congress. It was a huge disappointment to Sam, Ben, and the others when the Congress of 1841 again denied Samuel Morse support for a long-range test and demonstration. Some people just didn't understand modern technology and its potential. The citizens of the world would just have to wait a little longer to communicate directly with their neighbors all over the world. There was only a small group of people who held the knowledge that very soon there would be a big, even earth-shaking, change to the way people communicated with each other.

Summer Fun

It was a spectacular summer on Sodus Bay. The five women of the Lummis and Davis families had a busy, enjoyable summer of fun and work. They farmed—trimming fruit trees and tending vegetable gardens. They fished—the catches were always plentiful and delicious on the dinner table. They played—sailing, swimming, and picnicking.

Lenny practically lived with Soso. The two of them, sixty-year-old Indian and eleven-year-old white boy, helped the Lummis business by sailing the lake and delivering fruits and vegetables to harbors around the lake.

During the first trip, Soso returned Garth back to the Niagara Reservation. It had been exciting to meet with his relative and to see how well-adjusted and successful he was. Garth was the role model that young Indians needed to see. If somehow more Indians could do the things Garth had done, Soso was sure that his people would flourish and respect between the races would increase.

Soso enjoyed being with Lenny as much as Lenny loved being with Soso. The two picked up their friendship right where they had left off the summer before. In addition to their delivery duties, they worked on repairing several boats in Soso's shop and fished nearly every spot on Sodus Bay. Lenny was a quick learner. He was good at making and replacing ribs on boat hulls. He was just as good as Soso in sanding, shaping, and finishing the details of the woodwork on the sailing boats. Soso took Lenny to his stands of rock elm and white oak and showed him the details of nature's ways. He explained how he had harvested wood for all his boats from these areas, yet now these forests were healthier and more productive than when he had first found them. Soso explained to Lenny how nature regenerated itself and how man could live within the rules of nature. These trees were practically part of Soso's family. He had watched them grow, strengthen, and mature. He knew their fathers and mothers. He watched over them. Soso had always cut the trees for their utility. Lenny listened intently as Soso introduced him to nature's ways; Lenny wanted to know more about the perspective of the world that Soso knew.

Lenny was a good sailor who could easily handle a sailing boat by himself and sail in and out of the creeks and coves of the bay. He was also getting the feel of how to fish the bay. He knew which bait to use and when to cast to the surface or near the bottom of the silvery water. His favorite fish were perch, which frequented the shallow shoreline during the hot days of summer. Everyone loved to eat Lenny's delicious perch, which he and Soso cooked over an outdoor fire. It was a summer to remember, and Lenny had the time of his life. Growing up on the shores of Sodus Bay was something special. Learning about life from an expert like Soso was more than special.

Whenever she could get away, Carin took the trip across the bay to revisit their dream location. It was still perfect. Whenever she was there, she dreamed of a bright future with her family growing up on the bay. She confidentially thought that someday this would be her home. Unfortunately, the reality was that they just couldn't afford to buy the land and build a house. Mathematics professors didn't make much money and, with the needs of a growing family, they had never been able to save enough. It wasn't a bad life that she had in Troy, but it wasn't Sodus Point. Carin kept her dream alive and continued to share it with Jamey. Together, somehow, they would make it happen.

Return Home

The Davises left Lummisville on 26 August, the same day that Jamey and Ben left Washington. The two traveling groups—Ben was coming with Jamey to spend a couple weeks in Troy before returning to Lummisville—intended to arrive in Troy at about the same time. Jamey and Ben had enjoyed their time together in Washington. They had regained their strong relationship through a shared dedication to the Liberty Party's cause, but, more importantly, both respected and trusted each other.

Jamey and Ben arrived as scheduled, but Carin and the children ran into a problem. A severe thunderstorm had struck their canal boat as it moved along the route's most exposed and vulnerable leg near Oneida Lake. The storm literally smashed the massive boat, eventually sinking it right on the bank of the canal. This kind of calamity rarely happened on the protected canal. Luckily, Lenny and Catherine were good swimmers, and they abandoned the sinking boat and helped others to shore. Carin kept strong hold of Joan and took her young child to safety. Through swift work of the crew and the passengers, everyone made it safely to the bank of the canal. Some of the cargo and personal baggage were lost, and almost everything that was saved was soaking wet. They spent three days camping on the bank of the canal, waiting for the transportation company to send another boat. Some of the other passengers managed to leave on passing boats, but the Davises were delayed a full week. Jamey and Ben worried over the delay and the unknown status of the Davis family. All were relieved when Carin and the children finally arrived home safely.

Ben spent the next two weeks with the Davises. Ben watched his friend Jamey teach class and enjoy life with his family. He could see that Jamey was successful and an outstanding professor. Ben also knew Jamey longed to return to Sodus Bay. Jamey had a good life in academics, and it would be a big risk for his family if they moved back to the Sodus Bay area without much of a nest egg.

Finally, after over two years of dedicated work, Jamey's differential equations book was complete. Jamey sent the manuscript off to A. S. Barnes for review and publication. Maybe the royalties from this book would provide that nest egg.

Ben offered to help Jamey with the decision of moving to Sodus Bay. Ben couldn't farm all his land, and he didn't need to keep it all. Ben would gladly sell Jamey a fine homestead in Lummisville and even help him build a home. In the meantime, Ben had a small house that was empty since he no longer had a caretaker helping him on the farm. Jamey politely refused Ben's offer. Ben was confused by Jamey's reluctance to consider his proposal, for he knew that this was the only way that the Davises could afford to move back to the Sodus Bay area any time soon. However, Jamey and Carin still dreamed of the Pollock land and wouldn't compromise their dream by accepting such a generous offer, even from their best friend. For now, it was decided that Jamey was still a professor, still dreaming of becoming a fisherman and farmer.

After two weeks, Ben said his good-byes and left on the canal trip west. He longed to return to his home and family. He had missed and worried about them. He couldn't wait to see the silvery waters of the beautiful bay he called home.

Back to Niagara

Ever since Soso had abruptly left the reservation to search for Betty, he and Water Lily had been regular and faithful correspondents. It had been nearly two full years since that fateful day, and much had happened on the reservation since then. The legacy and plan left by Betty and Soso had been followed. The residents of the reservation were much healthier and happier thanks to Betty and Soso, and most definitely thanks to Lily's tremendous efforts. The facilities were better, the schools were improved, and both the old and young people respected their culture, their community, and people of different races.

Lily's March letter was different from the ones that she had previously sent. As usual, she asked Soso to return for a visit, but this time she was adamant that he come to see her. She even proposed the days of April 5 until the end of the month. She indicated that she needed him and asked as a special favor that he do this for her. Of course, Soso couldn't refuse such an emotional request, and he wrote back immediately. They already knew they would see each other over the summer, since he and Lily were planning to go to Troy for Garth's graduation, but now Soso felt that something was wrong. Why did Lily need him now?

As the departure day approached, Soso packed his boat with supplies. He had clothes, carpentry tools, farm equipment, and hunting and trapping gear that he never used anymore. He figured that the reservation Indians had more need for these items than he did. Off he went on his trip remembering, as always, to be careful of the potential fury of the big lake. Once at Niagara, Soso rented a wagon and loaded his supplies for the overland trip to the reservation. He arrived at Lily's very late at night. Lily wasn't home; he immediately sensed a problem. He searched the house and nearby areas, but there was no sign of her. It was a frantic night of searching and worrying, but finally around daybreak Soso discovered that Lily was at the reservation hospital. He found her resting comfortably, but in a very frail and sickly state. Lily smiled at her brother and thanked him for coming to see her. Before she could say more, the missionary priest asked to talk with Soso.

The priest told Soso that Lily was dying. In the doctor's opinion, there was little to do but pray for a miraculous recovery. She wouldn't suffer much and might live another week or two, but the end was near. He also learned the reason that she had wanted Soso to come on this particular date. The reservation elders had a special ceremony planned for her and Soso on April 7, and she wanted to make sure her busy brother would attend.

Soso took Lily back to her home. The next two days were spent in quiet conversation, mixed with considerable sleep for Lily. They talked about their parents, Gar and Clear Dawn, and their grandfather, Trout. Soso tried to stay optimistic, but he could clearly see that Lily was losing the battle. She still was able to think and talk clearly. "Soso, be sure to care for Garth. He is very smart and a good person. But he works too hard and takes too many risks. Show him the ways of the world. You know the ways of the world. Show him the right path."

Soso assured his sister that he would honor her request. "Garth will be fine, and I will help him. You have taught him well. I suspect we will all learn from him before long."

"I have only one regret—and that was losing all those years of knowing my brother, Sosoenodus. If we could have stayed together, we would have been a great pair. Maybe our people could have kept more of their dignity, if we both could have shown them how." Lily faded as she spoke of the past. It had always been the future that gave her the greatest inspiration. But now it was hard to concentrate on the future.

Ceremony

On the afternoon of April 7, Soso returned from a lunch break to find Lily dressed and ready to go to the ceremony. Soso was amazed, but his determined sister had rested for days just so she could go with him. They went, and Lily was full of energy for the entire evening. Soso was shocked to find that he and Lily were made Chiefs of the Cayugas and Elders of the

Iroquois Nation. It was a magnificent traditional ceremony. There was food, singing, and dancing in abundance. Both of them were happy and proud. It had been an exciting and emotional evening. They had been given a great honor.

At the end of the evening, Soso carried his exhausted sister home. She asked him to say the Indian prayer that they had learned together in Iroquois as children and relearned in English at Soso's insistence after he had discovered religion. Together, they slowly and thoughtfully said the words:

> *"Great Spirit and Creator,*
> *Whose voice I hear in the wind,*
> *and whose breath gives life to the world,*
> *I need your strength and wisdom.*
>
> *Help me walk in the beauty you have created,*
> *and let my eyes see clearly the colors of the sunrise.*
> *Let my hands feel the things you have made,*
> *and my ears hear the pleasant sounds of your voice.*
>
> *Make me wise so I understand the ways of the world.*
> *Help me to find and learn the lessons*
> *you have hidden under the rocks and behind the big trees.*
> *Give me strength, not to fight my brother, but to lead others*
> *   to your side.*
>
> *Make me ready to come with you,*
> *so when life fades and the evening sun sets,*
> *my spirit will be ready to serve you*
> *and our world will grow and survive."*

Later that night, Lily died in Soso's arms. She had seen her brother made a chief. She had helped her people regain their dignity. She was proud of her grandson, Garth, and her brother, Soso. She died a happy and fulfilled women. Soso wept the rest of the night, but by morning he recognized how lucky he was to have seen his sister in her glory and to know that she had made a difference.

After the funeral, Soso spent the remainder of the month at the reservation. He wrote Garth and described Lily's last days. He assured Garth that he would still be at RPI for graduation in late May. Despite the hurt over the loss of his sister, Soso enjoyed seeing his friends on the reservation and the happiness and confidence that Lily had restored in them. Soso's young student, Joe Fox, was as enthusiastic as ever. Joe continued to hope and dream for the opportunity to attend RPI. Joe respected Garth and Soso as role models of successful Indians, who helped their people understand and use the whites' technology to help themselves. This was going to be the future of all people, including Indians.

A New and Better Offer

The academic year went smoothly for Jamey. As a good teacher, he made the subjects interesting for his students. Home life was just as successful. Lenny and Catherine were good students. Both excelled academically, and they were happy, responsible children. Carin and Jamey loved their children and were raising them to be hard-working, successful adults.

One day Jamey came home after an enjoyable day at school to find a letter in an envelope that looked like all those he had received from other colleges. Jamey opened the letter, knowing it was another offer. He was right. This letter came from John Yeomans, a friend who knew Jamey's talents quite well. The letter explained that John had been newly appointed as the President of Lafayette College in Pennsylvania and needed an experienced mathematics professor for the growing program. Previous Mathematics Department Chair, McCartney, had resigned when the former President of the College, George Junkin, was ousted. John further explained that even though Lafayette was a liberal arts school and provided a classical education, the mathematics program was going to be emphasized and Jamey was just the right person to revitalize the program. Jamey knew that his talents were well suited to RPI's applied courses that were more like those at West Point. At Lafayette, mathematics was just another course, along with Latin, Greek, philosophy, chemistry, astronomy, and rhetoric. He also knew from Yeomans' letter that Lafayette had been in financial difficulty. In several ways this was the least attractive offer of all those he had received. However, as he read further, he found that in one big way this offer was the best. The salary compensation was more than double that of the other offers. Lafayette College was recruiting the best faculty they could find to re-establish their quality academic program. If Jamey would accept a position as Chair of Mathematics, Natural Philosophy, and Astronomy, he would receive $1000 per year. This was just what he needed to save money for the move to Sodus Point—to fulfill his family's dream. After just two years at this salary, he could buy the Pollock land and build his home in Sodus Point.

He and Carin carefully talked over the details. RPI could not match this offer. Jamey could take the position at Lafayette, while Carin and the children lived on the shores of Sodus Bay with the Lummises. Ben and Georgiana had made that offer to them several times. In two years, he could save nearly $1800, and then he could leave the job, buy the land in Sodus Point for Pollock's price of $300, and have $1500 left with which to build a house and barn. Jamey still hoped that he would also receive royalties for his differential equations book from the publisher, but he had learned there would be no advance payment for such a risky book. Jamey could spend the summers in Lummisville, but the family would be separated for most of the year. It was a high price to pay, but they would be rewarded by a satisfying life on Sodus Bay. Jamey wrote back to John accepting a two-year appointment and requesting that the trustees guarantee his entire salary of $2000 for two years. The decision had finally been made and their future course was set. The Davis family would soon call Sodus Point home.

RPI graduation was hectic for the Davises. Soso was there to see Garth graduate. Jamey was preparing to move to Lafayette College. Carin and the three children were preparing for their move to Lummisville. Jamey's mentor, Amos Eaton, had passed away, and the entire RPI community was mourning his loss. Though it all, Jamey and Carin dreamed of their goal just two years away.

Soso was proud of his grandnephew, Garth Simpson. The two of them had spent two weeks together the previous summer, but they were still learning about each other. Garth was prepared to return to the reservation to help his Indian brothers and sisters. As an engineer, he knew how to build the buildings, roads, and bridges needed to continue the reservation's revitalization. With all the formal education that he had received, Garth would make an outstanding teacher of the children. But most of all, he was an ideal role model for all the Indians, young and old. He was an example of success using the white man's knowledge while maintaining Native American roots. Of course, to Garth, Soso was the perfect role model. The two of them deeply respected one another. Garth gave Soso hope. Soso gave Garth confidence.

Scholarship

Garth explained to Soso the predicament that Joe Fox faced. Joe had been accepted to RPI for the next academic year and had received a partial scholarship from the school. However, Joe still needed almost $200 more per year to fulfill his dream. This was the easiest decision that Soso had ever made. Soso decided to give $900 to RPI to support Joe's education and establish a scholarship for other Native Americans. Soso knew that Joe would give much more than Soso's monetary investment back to the Indians' communities in the future. Soso never felt better about an investment and now knew that his hard work in earning money had been worth it. The future of his people was a bit brighter after RPI accepted $900 for educating Joe Fox and intelligent Indians like him. This was most of Soso's life savings; this decision was a culmination of a lifetime of dedication to the future of his people, the Native American Indians.

After graduation, Garth returned directly to the Niagara Reservation via the Erie Canal. Carin, the Davis children, Soso, and most of the Davises' furniture and possessions departed a week later with a destination of Lummisville. For the next two years the Davis family and Soso would be neighbors, since the Davises would move into the small foreman's house on the Lummis property very close to Soso's. Jamey was the last to leave. He took his academic-related possessions—books, instruments, suits of clothes, and writing desk—and started by steamboat down the Hudson River. He passed right by his old home and school at West Point and landed in New York City. From there, he rented a wagon and team of horses and went overland through New Jersey to Easton, Pennsylvania. Once there, he set up his small apartment and set off for Lummisville so he could arrive by the middle of July and have a short stay with his family. He had to return to Easton by the first of September to start teaching his new students.

New Home

The Davises' temporary home was small, dark, and in need of some repair, but in Carin's eyes it was home. She knew that she could fix it up. She was also confident that she could run her home and raise her children during Jamey's absence. She had done it before, when Jamey was away in the war. At least this time, Jamey's life wasn't in danger.

The house had been vacant for three years, but it was sturdy and had two fireplaces to keep the family warm in the winter. Lenny was twelve years old and very helpful. He was big and strong for his age. Carin knew he could chop wood and care for his sisters when she had to leave the house for a short time. She also had Soso, who was helping to mend fences, repair windows and doors, and insulate the bedrooms. Everything was going to be fine, as long as two years from now, she would see her new house going up on the other side of the bay. Meanwhile, all the Davises, even ten-year-old Katie and five-year-old Joan, would help the Lummises, their generous landlords and best friends, who were letting them live in the house for free.

Georgiana enjoyed having Carin so close. They were good friends. However, the closest relationship between the two families was the friendship and partnership that developed between Lenny Davis and Georgette Lummis. These two now had common interests—boating and fishing. They decided to form a fishing business to deliver fresh fish to inland families and taverns in Wolcott and Clyde, two of the growing Wayne County villages that were closest to Lummisville. With Soso's help, they set up a method to catch plenty of fresh, good eating fish like perch, trout, and bullheads early in the morning. Then by ten in the morning, they were on the road with a small wagon to one of the two communities. They alternated their destination each day. Their parents approved the plan with the provision that they were back by three in the afternoon, which was easy as long as there were no breakdowns. Wolcott was just four miles from Lummisville via a bumpy, but passable road, while Clyde was reachable via eight miles of nice smooth roadway. Their fishing business thrived, they made money, and they became best friends. Sometimes, they let Katie go with them or let her help catch fish, but mostly, this was a two-child operation. Once again, it was a summer of fun, and this year, of substantial profit.

One change that the Davis family had to adjust for was schooling. Lummisville was too small to have its own school, so the Lummisville children either went to a school near Wolcott, actually just three and a half miles from Lummisville, or were home schooled by their parents. Georgiana had always schooled Georgette at home, but this year the Lummises planned to send her to the Wolcott school. Only three-year-old Benny Lummis would be home with his mother and father. The Davises had the same options for Lenny, Katie, and Joan, who would be starting her first year of school. Lenny and Katie had attended an outstanding city school in Troy with good teachers and a challenging curriculum. It would be difficult for a rural one-room school to match their previous experiences. However, after talking to the teacher, Carin decided to send them to school in Wolcott. A group of nine children from Lummisville went to that school, so they all traveled together.

School was enjoyable, but not much of a challenge for the Davis children and Georgette Lummis. They were highly intelligent and, unlike many other children, spent considerable time at home reading and studying with their parents. Carin worried about Lenny's development since, even as young as he was, he had already advanced to a level beyond that of the teacher. However, the teacher recognized his talents and did her best to keep him challenged and progressing. She was excited to have a student as talented as Lenny Davis. Lenny was a dedicated, independent student. He knew that he would have to be both smart and hardworking to achieve his dream of following in his father's footsteps by attending West Point.

Sugaring

The weather was still cold, but it was time for everyone to get out of the house and work. The Davis family was in the business of making and selling maple syrup and sugar. All winter long they had made and prepared their equipment. They had cut and carved hundreds of five-inch long spouts of about a half-inch in diameter to insert in the trees and had constructed dozens of troughs to fasten under the spouts. Then, they had made many buckets to carry the sap back to the boiling fires. Finally, with supreme effort, they had built a big stove to boil the sap to turn it into syrup and sugar. Now it was time to implement their plan.

They worked in two teams. Carin and Joan formed one team, Katie and Lenny the other. Dozens of the big, sap-filled sugar maples were located about a half mile from their house. All told, the Davis family milked nearly a hundred maple trees for their sap during the chilly, but sunny days of March and April. This was one of the best sap seasons ever. These trees were high producers of sweet nectar. The spouts were inserted into holes bored about two inches into the tree. The troughs were hung under the spouts to catch the sap. The troughs were emptied into buckets, and the heavy buckets were carried back to the house. The trees were checked two or three times a day and, after the season was complete, nearly twenty gallons of sap were collected from each tree. Once the children got good at collecting sap, Carin and Soso ran the syrup processing.

In theory, processing the sap into syrup was a simple process—just boil it. But it took a hot fire to keep the big pans of sap boiling, and the fires needed to be tended continually. Then at just the right time, the maple syrup was ready to be poured into containers, cooled, and sent to market. It took about thirty gallons of the watery sap to make just one gallon of the rich, sweet syrup. The Davis family syrup was sent to three different markets—Wickham's store in Sodus Point bought ten gallons, Henry's store in Clyde bought twenty gallons, and Father LeMoyne's mission in Syracuse wanted forty gallons. The rest of the production was given and sold to neighbors or kept for the Davis family to enjoy. Since the bulk rate for quality syrup was 80 cents per gallon, the hard work of the Davis family maple syrup business netted the family over $50 in profit. Every little bit helped, since the family had ventured forth on the risky proposition of buying a new homestead.

Aunt Elizabeth

Ben and Georgiana were excited over the news that Ben's sister, Elizabeth Ellet, was coming to visit during the last week of April and most of May. It had been several years since she had visited, even though Ben had seen her two years before when she joined the Liberty Party lobbying group in Washington. At the tender age of 25, she was one of the most successful and popular women writers in the country. Her books, short stories, articles, translations, reviews, and poems were all bestsellers. She had a special talent for telling interesting stories and finding and presenting the most fascinating facts. She always was working simultaneously on a book, short story, and poem.

Elizabeth lived several different lives at once, and she was happy and successful at all of them. She was a graceful, well-mannered lady who fit suitably into the high society of the wealthy southern plantation owners. She was a sophisticated intellectual who traveled and met with the brightest academics in the country, mostly located in the northeastern cities of Boston, New York, Philadelphia, and Baltimore. Her publishers in New York City and Philadelphia recognized her as a tough, no-nonsense businesswoman who negotiated favorable deals on her publications. A gracious lady, she frequently donated her time and money to help charities caring for disadvantaged women and children. She was a dedicated, passionate, and patriotic abolitionist and feminist who could stir up a crowd with rhetoric or write a provocative article. And she was a loving wife and homemaker for husband Bill Ellet who, as Professor of Chemistry, Mineralogy, and Geology, worked hard. Somehow, her complicated life was just part of her success and striking personality. She was a modern woman, and no one, except possibly her husband, really knew how capable and influential she was.

She arrived in Lummisville via a carriage that took her from the Erie Canal in Clyde to the Lummis Estate. What fond memories the majestic view of the bay brought to her mind. She had written popular poems about the two bodies of water she could see as she rode the last few hundred yards to her family's homestead. The poems were well known in the area and read by all the school children. The Davis children all wanted to hear her read to them her famous poems entitled, "Sodus Bay" and "Lake Ontario." Carin and Georgiana loved her book *Rambles about the Country*. It was exciting to have a celebrity in Lummisville.

It was a superb family reunion. Ben was proud of his sister. Elizabeth, in turn, was happy to be back home with her friends and family. She had corresponded regularly with Soso, so she knew his activities, but it was thrilling to see him again. Of course, she had to meet and learn all about the growing children that she had heard about through letters.

It was a joyous spring of 1843. The children felt as if they had another playmate, while the adults all took to Elizabeth as a warm, charming friend. Several nights were spent reading her poetry and short stories. Other nights were spent in wonderment as she talked about the people she had met and the places she had seen. Elizabeth had spent time with Edgar Allan Poe, while she was in Philadelphia. She told stories of helping him with his reviewing and editing. She also related to the adults his exploits as a drinker, which were legendary in his city of Philadelphia. Elizabeth also corresponded with James Fenimore Cooper and Washington Irving. James Cooper had changed over the years. Soso and Ben had known him when he was young and had always enjoyed his *Leatherstocking Tales*, which included the adventures of Natty Bumppo. But Cooper had suffered as the frontier left New York and moved further west. He was a fish out of water, and his new writings showed it. He was more uncomfortable in the modern, civilized world than Soso. In many ways, Cooper was more of a traditionalist than Soso. This was disappointing to Soso, because he had always liked James Cooper. Soso fully understood that not everyone could adapt. His own father and many of his Indian friends suffered in the same way. Change was usually good for it brought progress, but it was dangerous to those who couldn't cope with its pace or direction. Unfortunately, James Cooper seemed to be that type of person. Soso held out hope that Cooper would regain perspective and contribute to the cause of Indian rights and equality.

The time with Elizabeth went fast. She had the opportunity to sail the bay, see the changes in the area, visit with her old friends, and meet many new ones. Soso and Ben took her on a trip across the lake to Canada to deliver seedlings and farm equipment to York and Toronto. She loved every minute of her stay but needed to leave at the end of May in order to get to a historical society meeting in Chicago where she was the featured speaker. The children would especially miss her nightly readings and storytelling. Elizabeth Lummis Ellet was a treasured and valuable product of the frontier days of Sodus Bay.

New Business

By the time school was out, the Davis children and Georgette were ready to start up their fish business. Their parents did not allow them to run their business during the school year, but all during the winter and spring they made elaborate plans to increase sales and productivity. Lenny, Katie, and Georgette were fully employed in the enterprise and equal partners in the business.

Jamey arrived back in Lummisville in early summer to be with his family after spending the school year at Lafayette. It had been a good year for him. He enjoyed his students and had formed a stronger, more useful, applied mathematics program at the school. His students liked his teaching style, and he had become immensely popular in just a year. The only drawback was that the school continued to struggle financially. He was relieved and happy to be back home with his family. He kept reminding himself that in one short year they would be building their dream house. He had already saved more than enough money to buy the property this summer, so he decided to see James Pollock and negotiate final sale of the land. The additional savings had been safely deposited in a bank earning good interest. The Davises were finally building a nest egg, and they hoped it would soon be hatched.

It was a great day when he held in his hand the deed to the land overlooking First Creek. He and Carin were halfway home.

Everything went well until the end of July, when Georgette and Lenny developed a fever and red rash. They had contracted scarlet fever. Both were extremely sick, with high fevers, sore throats, and dehydration. Doctors were called in from Wolcott and Newark. They treated the two with the best of the modern medical remedies. Nothing seemed to lower their fevers, however. The doctors were nearly helpless, and the parents were frantic as the two children went in and out of consciousness. The families also worried that the other children would catch the fever, and all the other children in the Lummisville area were sent away. Just when things seemed to be at their worst, faint signs of recovery began to appear. They retained some fluids; they regained consciousness. Lenny seemed to gain back his health and strength a little more quickly than Georgette, but both made steady progress. It was a big relief to see them gaining strength and energy. By mid-August, Jamey felt comfortable enough to leave for another year at Lafayette, and the other children were allowed to return to Lummisville. The royalties from his book sales came in handy since they were just enough to pay the doctor's bills for Lenny.

It had been a tough summer for everyone in Lummisville, but they all survived. Moreover, Jamey left knowing that he now owned the most beautiful property on Sodus Bay and, in his mind, the world. He also felt that Lenny and Georgette would recover, although Georgette would need more time to regain her strength. Soso had worried along with his neighbors about the two children. He had slowed up considerably over the past year. It was becoming difficult for him to sail and fish by himself, and he no longer went out onto the lake alone. Seldom traveling over to Sodus Point or to Float Bridge, he spent most of his time at home. It had been a rough summer, since he was happiest when the neighborhood children came by and talked with him, but they had been sent away because of the quarantine. Finally, when the children returned, six-year-old Joan Davis and three-year-old Benny Lummis were his most frequent visitors. When Lenny and Georgette finally felt better, they also came by to see their Uncle Soso. He always had some tarts or pies available. He also had many stories to tell them about his own or their parents' childhood. Soso could see Jamey's intellect in Joan's and Ben's friendly disposition in Benny. It was a tremendous relief to see Lenny and Georgette slowly recover from their bout with the fever.

Soso was the only adult who knew of Lenny's dream to go to West Point. Lenny had not told his father yet. He was holding it as a surprise, if it ever became a real possibility. Soso worried that the aftereffects of the disease would make it difficult for Lenny to develop physically to meet the West Point cadet standards. Only time would tell. Soso prayed for Lenny and the fulfillment of his dream.

Big Trouble

Soso didn't have much money, especially after sending $900 to RPI for the scholarship, or many possessions, but his house, workshop, and farm were valuable and still well maintained. At 63 years old, he considered himself the richest, most fortunate man alive. However, that was soon to change. It was a simple, seemingly harmless mistake. And it was completely out of character for Soso to do something so foolish. However, on a cold, windy night in December, wanting to insure the house stayed warm over the night and into the morning, Soso put several extra logs in the fireplace and went to go to sleep. The flames flared up, just as a gust of wind blew through a crack in a nearby window. In a trice, the fire had jumped to the table and chair where Soso often read and worked. From there, the rug and another chair caught fire. Within a few minutes, the entire living room and kitchen were in flames. Fortunately, Soso wasn't quite asleep so he heard the fire crackle outside his bedroom door. He sensed danger. He quickly dressed and carefully opened the door, but, when he did, the flames jumped into the bedroom. His only retreat was out the bedroom window and, in trying to climb out, he fell hard to the ground. He looked up to see most of his house engulfed in hot, ravaging flames. He crawled about thirty feet from his bedroom window and helplessly stared as the roaring inferno consumed everything he had.

No one saw the flames, but eventually Carin smelled the smoke as she headed for bed. She went outside to investigate and saw, not only Soso's house and workshop on fire, but also the orchard trees near the house were burning as well. She woke up her children and soon everyone in Lummisville was trying to put out the fire. There was no way to save the house or the workshop, but the fires in the trees were extinguished so it wouldn't spread any further. Georgiana and Carin found Soso and took him to the Lummises to warm up and recover. He was in severe shock; he had just seen the most visible product of his entire life's work disappear.

Recovery and Return

Soso was ill for much of the winter. He stayed with the Lummises, and both the Lummis and Davis families cared for him. He was depressed for several months. Benny and Joan were the only ones who could get him to smile or laugh. Soso didn't like being dependent on others for his food and shelter. In early spring, he asked Ben to take him to the Niagara reservation. Soso was not strong or healthy enough to sail the lake by himself—another circumstance that made him depressed. Finally able to get around, he was healthy enough to travel, but he had never returned to the sight of his burned out house and didn't intend to for awhile. Nothing remained but a mound of charred ruins. It was best that he not see what was left; it would only have caused more depression. He wanted to spend about a month or two resting and working with Garth on the reservation. Then he hoped to return to Lummisville for the summer. Everyone agreed that this was a good idea, so Ben took Soso down the lake in early May, got him situated on the reservation, and then returned to Lummisville.

In late May, Jamey Davis arrived back in Lummisville. He was no longer a mathematics professor. He now considered himself a businessman, farmer, fisherman, sailor, and new resident of Sodus Point. He had survived another tumultuous year at Lafayette and was relieved to have escaped from the political and financial problems that unfortunately continued to plague the college. Once again, his teaching had gone fine, but in all the other aspects it had been a year to forget. Letters from Carin had described Soso's tragedy and condition. Jamey still couldn't believe what he saw when he looked at the fire's terrible consequences. Soso's house was a pile of ashes, although most of the mess had been cleaned up by Ben. It had been a horrifying disaster, and he wondered how he could help his friend.

The night of Jamey's first day back in Lummisville, Ben called a meeting of all the Davises and Lummises. He had a plan and wanted to see if others thought it was possible. The Davises were ready to start building their house. Carin had supervised the delivery of the lumber and materials just that week. Jamey was planning to check the materials and pay for the supplies the next day. Jamey was ready to spend his time and energy working with carpenters and getting his home built. Ben's plan was to double the size of the work crews, get volunteers from Sodus Point and Float Bridge, and build two houses simultaneously—the Davises' new one in Sodus Point and a replacement house for Soso right on the spot of the original. Ben had the materials for Soso's house on order and delivery would take place within a week. Soso's new house would be similar to the Davises' new one, but much smaller. Ben would oversee construction at Lummisville, and Jamey would supervise at First Creek. Ben had already talked to people from both villages, and they were all ready to help. This would take quite an effort to organize and complete, and it would be a tremendous example of cooperative community spirit if it could be done. Soso was so respected in the area that it would be no trouble finding more volunteers to help. During that evening, the decision was made to do it, and the plan was finalized. The next day, Ben, Georgiana, Jamey, and Carin set the plan in motion with help from the children to pass the word to all the residents in the area.

It took three more days to get the details worked out. Jamey's analytic mind and experience in practical problem solving enabled a schedule to be made. Work crews and volunteers were scheduled for foundation work, chimney construction, framing, siding, roofing, flooring, and interior work. For four weeks, people from all over the area came and went from the two building sites with tremendous commitment, energy, and enthusiasm. It was as much a community celebration as a work project. Carin and Georgiana kept food and drink available for the workers. Jamey and Ben insured that proper instructions and directions were given and tools and materials were ready for each phase of construction.

The main worker on Jamey's house was master carpenter James Pollock. James knew quality work and made sure everyone on the work teams performed it. One day he even teased Jamey about his work. "Jamey Davis, if Soso could see you now, he'd have you fired. Nails in those joists won't last near as long as bolts. Take time to build this house right. I know the owner very well, and he wouldn't have it otherwise."

James Pollock was right, as usual. Humbled, Jamey responded, "That owner sure is glad he has a friend like you. Please don't tell him. I promise to do right from now on."

James closed the teasing, "You sure don't want this splendid house to fall down during the first nor'easter."

One of the advantages of living on the west side of the bay was that the prevailing winds blew away from shore. The only real wind and wave danger for residents living near First Creek occurred when the wind blew from the northeast. Heavy windstorms from that direction were called nor'easters. While these winds were rare, they were often dangerous. No one on Sodus Bay wanted to experience the fury of a real nor'easter.

Jamey's house was about three days ahead of Soso's, and sometimes crews would come to Sodus Point, work on Jamey's house for a few days, travel to Lummisville, and perform the same job there. After four weeks, both homes were essentially complete. Little things were still left for Jamey and Ben to finish, but both houses were ready for their occupants.

It was nothing short of a miracle. Two superb, well-constructed homes had been built in less than a month. The Davises' dream had come true, and Soso's nightmare would soon be over. The celebration of the miracle was to start at Soso's at noon on July Fourth and move over to the Davises later that day.

Lenny, Katie, and Georgette sailed down to Niagara to pick up Soso and promised to be back on the morning of the Fourth. Ben and Jamey trusted the maturity and skill of their children, but it was a long, complicated trip for the young people to make. Both fathers gave explicit instructions and warnings about the dangers of Lake Ontario before they let their children leave the Lummisville dock. The memory of Betty's unfortunate accident was still on their minds. Everyone was eager for their return so they could witness Soso's reaction upon seeing the new home. It looked quite a bit like his previous house, and all involved hoped that their friend would approve of their handiwork.

More Progress on the Reservation

It had been a pleasant, productive summer on the Indian reservation. Garth had picked up right where his grandmother, Water Lily, had left off. He had improved the schools—both the facilities and the curriculum.

Through his influence and inspiration, several new businesses had started to fulfill community needs. Soso spent the summer recuperating and enjoyed watching his nephew lead his people. As an enthusiastic spectator, he observed bagataway games. He particularly liked watching Joe Fox, who was on vacation from RPI, play this exciting sport. Joe had survived his first year at RPI. He had overcome his weak educational foundation and the prejudice of some of his classmates to become a good student. Over the summer he helped Garth with several community projects. Joe felt terrible about Soso's tragedy and offered to return his scholarship money to Soso. Soso would have none of such talk. He had made a wise investment, and now, more than anything, he wanted to watch it develop. In the fall, Joe would return for his second year at Rensselaer. Soso was pleased with the role he had been able to play in this fine young man's education.

Soso spent time with Garth and Joe teaching them and several other men some of the finer points of boat construction. It was healing time for Soso as he immersed himself in the activities of his new environment, temporarily forgetting the troubles that he had left back in Lummisville. He felt satisfaction in knowing that Garth and Joe were doing such remarkable things for the Native American people. He was getting to see James Birney's prediction of future harmony between the races make slow progress toward fruition.

Garth's major project was the construction of a new hospital. The old one was decayed, cramped, and crowded. He had some financial support from the government, but it was most rewarding to have the residents of the reservation provide most of the materials, money, and work that were needed. Thanks to Garth, the residents of the reservation would become healthier, safer, and more independent people.

Surprise

Soso was surprised to see Lenny, Katie, and Georgette come to the reservation. He was expecting someone to pick him up, but he didn't know who or precisely when it would happen. At 64, Soso was respectful of the big lake. He worried about the safety of the three children. At fourteen years of age, Lenny was fearless; to him Lake Ontario was a challenge. However, Lenny had the benefit of listening to Soso's stories and had learned to respect the lake's power. Even at his young age, Lenny was a responsible sailor. Katie and Georgette were good sailors and helped their captain travel the lake without incident. The three voyagers were happy to see Soso and to meet the Indians of the reservation. They had heard all about the reservation from Soso, but now they saw everything firsthand. While not perfect, it was a flourishing community filled with happy, friendly people.

The three children tried to convince Soso that it was time to leave. They knew they would have to leave the next day in order to be back in time for the Fourth of July festivities. At first Soso was considering staying longer with Garth. However, Lenny secretly told Garth about the surprise they had waiting at Lummisville for Soso, so Garth helped persuade Soso to leave the reservation and head back to Sodus Bay.

The return trip was uneventful. The lake was smooth and a steady west wind kept them on schedule. Soso filled the voyage hours with stories about exploits on the lake. The children enjoyed listening. He told them all about an adventure that happened long ago involving Captain Longknife.

"Just across the lake, about there," Soso spoke and pointed in the direction across the lake toward Canada. "Lenny's and Katie's grandfather Jim and three of his trapper friends had some trouble with a band of fierce Indians that were on the warpath."

"What happened to Grandpa Jim?" asked Katie.

"He and his friends were surrounded and captured by the Indians and put in a cave for two weeks. Then one night, when the Indians were asleep, they made their escape. The first part by boat, the second by foot. Jim and his friend George had to hide from the Indians for three weeks before they made it back to Sodus Bay."

"Why did they capture them? Wasn't Grandpa Jim friends with the Indians?" Georgette asked her Uncle Soso.

"No, this was a long time ago. The Indians and whites were fighting for control of the land, animals and fish, and their ways of life," Soso replied. "But these Indians, the Hurons, were the toughest and fiercest of all. But, even the Hurons, usually left white trappers alone. The reason they attacked the trappers was because Captain Longknife paid them to do it."

"Who was Captain Longknife?" asked Lenny.

"He was a British soldier, who was trying to cause trouble between the redcoats and the Americans. He wanted the trappers killed so it would start a war."

Lenny put closure on this phase of the story. "I know what happened next. Grandpa Jim was safe, but then the War of 1812 started, and you and Grandpa Jim had to save Sodus Point."

That started more stories and more questions about the war and the exploits of their grandfather. Soso had a grand time with the curious children, who loved their uncle and his exciting stories.

The children could tell Soso was getting over the trauma of losing his house. It was good to have Soso back in good health and spirits. He even wanted to see the site of his old house, which was exactly what they intended for him to do.

The timing was nearly perfect. A crowd of about fifty people had already assembled in Soso's yard enjoying the beautiful weather and preparing to celebrate the Fourth of July when word came that Soso was arriving by boat. Everyone hid behind the house while the boat carrying Soso and the three children landed at the dock. Soso had requested this so the children didn't have to invent any stories to execute this part of the plan. Soso slowly walked up the path that used to lead to his house. He wanted to see the rubble and destruction for himself to determine what he had to do to start over again. However, when he came to the clearing he saw a vision. There was a completely new house right where the old one had been. From behind the house came his friends and neighbors, yelling surprise and good wishes. Soso was astounded. He didn't have to start over again; they had already done that for him. What could he say? He was speechless.

What a cheerful celebration. It was exciting for everyone to see the amazement and appreciation reflected in Soso's eyes. The old man cried as everyone told him about his or her role in building the new house. Soso was shown all the rooms and given the details of the construction. He loved it. Then the partying began. Soso's yard was quickly converted into a dance area. Music was played and dancing began. Large amounts of food and drink were consumed. Soso and his friends were joyous in their celebration of the miracle house.

Later in the afternoon, the entire group traveled by boat over to First Creek to celebrate the Davises' housewarming. Over the previous week, Carin and Jamey had worked hard on their dream house, and everyone was invited in to see the results of their efforts. In every respect it was an impressive home. It wasn't nearly as large or as elegant as the Lummis mansion, but it was as big and well built as any house in Sodus Point. It sat up high enough on the small knoll north of First Creek to have an excellent view of the bay. The construction was of the highest quality, thanks mainly to the skills of James Pollock. There was plenty of open land, so the picnicking, dancing, and partying picked up right where it had left off from across the bay. More and more people came, and by evening, most of the citizens of the area were celebrating the Fourth of July at the Davises' new house. What an enjoyable day.

The New Business

Every day was an exciting one for the Davises—new friends to meet, new places to go, and new ideas to consider. Their life was filled with many alternatives, and decisions were needed to establish their business on a solid foundation. Because of the time spent building the house, they did not have a full season of farming. Carin was able to plant a small garden of late season vegetables and that helped put some food on the table. Of course, the children caught plenty of fish, so the Davises ate fresh seafood at every meal. Fried perch were especially delicious at breakfast, which was usually the only meal the entire family ate together. Work dictated the schedule for the rest of the day, and that meant that meals came whenever they were possible. But Carin accepted the disruptions of the hectic summer schedule as long as her family all sat down together for a healthy breakfast.

The children's fish business had been transferred to the west side of the bay. There were more competitors in this area, but also more people to serve, so they managed to restore a decent business. They bought some needed farm equipment with their profits, and they improved their fishing equipment with several purchases as well. The children were doing all that they could to help the family through these lean financial times. Their business was the most exciting and adventurous activity that a young person could do for summer fun.

Ultimately, Jamey wanted to establish a fish and fruit supply company that distributed its products to businesses and markets in the bigger cities of New York, like Rochester, Syracuse, Albany, and even New York City. He planned to use the new railroad system that had just come to central and western New York. New links and stations were being built every day. Currently, the nearest stations were about fifteen miles from the

Davises' farm in the villages of Lyons and Newark. Jamey and Ben both believed that the train would replace the Erie Canal as the best mode of travel and transport. Trains were faster, safer, more reliable, more comfortable, and easier to load than canal boats. Technology had vastly improved the transportation system of America. What changes this 42-year-old former Army officer and mathematics professor had seen—from horse and buggy to the steamboat and locomotive. However, the train supply route was a future plan. For now, he was happy that his children sold fish to inland residents in the nearby villages of Alton, Lyons, and Sodus. The extra money meant extra tools and equipment for the farm that had to be built from scratch, as well.

Jamey spent the rest of the summer and fall planting his orchard. He had a little over thirty acres of cleared land to fill with apple, cherry, and peach trees. Ben had helped him accumulate these seedlings over the past two years. Jamey had studied the latest information on planting trees to make them more productive, on grafting branches to make them produce the best fruit, and on adding fertilizer to keep the ground fertile. He had learned from Ben's mistakes and felt confident that he could grow a healthy, productive orchard. Jamey had to be as efficient as he could, since he didn't have a large farm compared to some others in the area. For instance, Jamey's farm was less than a tenth of the size of Ben's. In one way, Jamey and Ben were competitors, but since Ben marketed his fruits and vegetables in Canada and along the lakeshore, whereas Jamey intended to market inland via the railroad system, they weren't really going to be in any direct competition. In any case, they were close friends, and there was plenty of room in the farming business for both of them.

It was a demanding fall with many long hours of work, but all the Davises were immensely happy. This lifestyle was what they wanted, and now they had it to enjoy. For now, it was just as good as they dreamed it would be.

"What do you like best about our new home?" Jamey asked Carin as they looked out the large window overlooking Sodus Bay. This window was a unique feature of the Davis home. Only the Lummises had a window and an accompanying view of the bay that could compare with it.

"You're the best thing about this house. I can tell you are happy. I'm so glad we did this. This was the right thing to do for us and the children," Carin answered. She continued, "You are working too hard. Promise me you'll slow down and relax some this winter."

"I'll slow down, but only if you do as well."

"We had better let the children in on this slow down, as well. They have been good. We are very lucky to have such hard working, dedicated children. They deserve a nice break this winter."

Election Impact

As the 1844 presidential campaign heated up across the country, its effects were felt on the shores of Sodus Bay. The Liberty Party had nominated James Birney to run again. This time he had a substantially larger political base, and while still a relatively small third party, the Liberty Party hoped to make some impact on the election. People throughout the country knew about Birney and the Liberty Party, even though there were very few Party members. All in all, Birney didn't expect to worry his opponents or win any delegates to the electoral college. For now, he just hoped that the people would listen to the ideas.

Birney had decided to take his campaign national by scheduling appearances in the summer and fall in New England, Pennsylvania, New Jersey, Maryland, Ohio, and Indiana. It was an extremely ambitious schedule and a big political risk since it would take him away from his political stronghold in New York. James needed someone to keep the party issues alive and recruit in New York. For that task, he came to see his friend Ben Lummis. James knew that Ben had the dedication, enthusiasm, and oratorical talents to get the job done. James asked Ben to be the Liberty Party's mouthpiece in New York. A schedule of travel, speeches, debates, and appearances had already been developed. Ben simply had to execute the plan along with handling the criticism, verbal abuse, and possible physical danger that would accompany such a risky and controversial political endeavor.

Ben had spent an exhausting summer working on the farm and helping to build Soso's home. However, he still felt passionately about abolition. He agreed to give it a try and help James Birney become President, the Liberty Party to be heard, and the cause of abolition to be accomplished.

This was a challenging task for a gentleman farmer who had never waged a political campaign or given a political speech. Even though he wasn't running for office himself, he did everything that a candidate would do. His speeches were informative and moving, and his passion for the cause was evident in his voice and words. Ben had learned well from Birney's speeches and the words of the famous black orator, Frederick Douglass. On numerous occasions, Ben had heard the young runaway slave, Douglass, give stirring recollections of his time as a slave, eloquent speeches about the horrors of slavery, and brilliant arguments during debates over slavery. Ben took the best of Douglass and Birney and developed his own effective style as a political spokesperson.

Ben always included supportive commentary on the value and potential of Samuel Morse's telegraph. Federal support for this communication system had become a political issue. Over the summer, the government had withdrawn its support after initially promising $30,000 for an experiment. Samuel had obtained private funding, however, for a test of the telegraph's capability to transmit between Baltimore and Washington. News of the successful demonstration had traveled slowly throughout the rest of the country. Morse had successfully sent the message, "What hath God wrought," from a terminal in Baltimore to a receiver in Washington. It was exactly the impact that the telegraph could make—faster, more reliable communication. No one would have to wait for news to travel slowly from town to town. The way news spread now was from newspaper to newspaper, as editors read issues of neighboring papers containing new information. News spread slowly, like ripples on a pond. Once telegraphs were in position and wires laid to connect them, news could travel instantaneously throughout the country instead of the weeks or months the process now took. With a telegraph system in place, news from Washington could reach the all the citizens of the entire nation immediately. This concept was such a dramatic change that it was hard to imagine. Ben tried to explain its utility and its costs to the concerned citizens and potential voters as he gave his speeches, answered questions, and debated the issues. Somehow the country had to support and implement this enormous technological breakthrough.

Ben learned to like giving speeches and performing in debates. Of course, the verbal attacks and abuse were difficult to take, and sometimes inaccurate reports in the newspapers were very frustrating. However, Ben generally took everything in stride like a strong political leader must do.

A highlight of his circuit came in New York City. In the City's Central Park, he attracted a large, enthusiastic crowd which cheered his words and chanted Birney's name. Ben had accomplished all that James had hoped for and more. Suddenly, Birney was a real presidential candidate in New York State capable of collecting substantial votes and influencing the election.

The 1844 election pitted Whig candidate Henry Clay against a relative unknown, Democrat James Polk. The major issue of the campaign was the annexation of Texas and its eventual status as a slave state. Polk favored annexation and expansion of the country, while Clay initially tried to stay neutral but eventually supported annexation. That made the Liberty Party the only alternative for those who did not support annexation and the expansion of slavery. Even though James Birney received only 60,000 votes nationwide, his candidacy actually determined the outcome of the election. In New York, Birney took 16,000 votes from Clay, who lost the state by only 5,000 votes to Polk. Polk then won the national electoral vote by capturing all 36 electoral votes from New York.

Through the strong efforts of Ben Lummis on behalf of James Birney, the Liberty Party made its mark, and abolition obtained more support. The temporary outcome was not in that direction because the 1844 election resulted in Texas' annexation and in the expansion of slavery into the new states of the southwest.

Best Friends

Little, timid five-year-old Benny was now Soso's constant companion. Because of the difficulties and complications during his birth, Benny was a weak, fragile child who needed constant care. Soso loved watching out for this bright, happy boy. Despite his poor physical condition, Benny had a smile that could brighten anyone's day. He was just what Soso needed to regain purpose and enjoyment in his life. Soso no longer built boats in his workshop. Instead, he made small furniture items right in his house. This way, he kept Benny in a warm, safe environment. Soso was now an accomplished woodworker who could build exquisite desks, shelves, tables, and chairs. The lumber used was the same rock elm that made Soso's boats so distinctive. This good-looking, strong wood was also perfect for fine furniture. Benny liked helping, and Soso always had a piece of wood for him to sand or shape. Benny's frail fingers and hands were talented and creative. Soso was amazed by the abilities of his little helper.

Benny especially liked it when Soso baked tarts and pies. Benny had a sweet tooth and always ate plenty of Soso's baked desserts. He helped Soso wash dishes and clean the house. Benny was learning to read, and Soso often sat with him while the two of them read passages from Benny's children's reader, the *Bible*, or stories and poems written by Aunt Elizabeth.

Technology Comes to the Country

To watch over his two loved ones, Benny and Soso, Ben Lummis built a unique communication system. Samuel Morse had given Ben a small, outdated, telegraph system, so Ben strung wire across the 400 yards of open space between his own house and Soso's. He put a telegraph key at each end to create a two-station system. Ben, Georgina, Georgette, Soso, and even Benny, learned Morse's coding system. People in the two houses passed messages back and forth for both fun and business. Soso kept Ben informed of Benny's activities, and Ben would send messages to Soso for Benny to return home or grant permission for Benny to stay longer. It was fun, exciting, and a big help for the Lummises given the health problems of Soso and Benny. Ben was able to experience firsthand the value of the telegraph. He was a lucky man to have the first telegraph system operating between two houses in western New York.

Samuel Morse was beginning to sell his system to private businesses, which were improving their own communications and making profits on public communications. The federal government, even though many officials were impressed by Morse's demonstrations, was still reluctant to support telegraphs. Samuel Morse was contributing by selling his devices and equipment to businesses, which saw great value and tremendous potential. Morse would have preferred to have his country benefit by public use of his invention, but others had prevented that from happening. He still hoped that someday the government would recognize the value of a public communication system so everyone could benefit.

New Hobby

Ben and Georgiana Lummis were happy that their son liked being with Soso. However, they were worried about both of them. Neither had very good health, but together they seemed to do better. Soso always was doing nice things for the Lummises and his other neighbors. The furniture pieces that he made often appeared as gifts to various families in the area. Soso was building a furniture item as a gift for every family that had helped in building his new house.

The Lummises included Soso in many of their family activities. Over the winter, Ben persuaded Soso to go riding in their ice sleigh. The winter freeze actually made travel across the bay much quicker. On a good day in the winter, the Lummises could travel across the bay to Sodus Point or to the Davises' house on First Creek in less than a half an hour. They would all bundle up in blankets as the two-horse team would pull their big sleigh across the smooth, slippery ice. They were careful to insure Benny and Soso were warm, because their frail health made them susceptible to getting sick in damp, chilly weather. The thrilling sleigh ride across the frozen bay was so inspiring that it invigorated both the sick and the healthy.

The big news of the area was that the Lummises were expecting another child. Georgette and Benny were as happy as Ben and Georgiana. They would soon have a baby brother or sister. Soso was delighted. It looked as if next summer was going to be an exciting and joyous one in Lummisville.

More Work

It was November before Jamey had an opportunity to slow down to a normal pace. He had worked at maximum effort since he had arrived back in Sodus Point in May. There was always more to do and little time to get it done. Although the cold November weather made outdoor farm work impossible, he could work inside his small barn. He needed to build a better wagon, fix up their two fishing and sailing boats, design and build strong containers for transporting fish and fruits to the markets, and build cabinets and shelves for the house. The family had recently received an exquisite dining table with six matching chairs from Soso. They were the most beautiful pieces of furniture that Carin had ever seen, and they were the highlight of the lovely home.

In October the children started attending school. They had to travel one mile to the new Sodus Point school which had two teachers in the small two-room schoolhouse. Once the Davises started attending, there were 44 students. Lenny was more like a teacher than student, just like his father had been 27 years before. He had advanced way past the levels of the teachers. However, he went each day with Katie and Joan, although some afternoons with permission he left school early to hunt or fish. Both girls liked their teachers. Mrs. Susan Malcolm taught the older children and, with the exception of Lenny, Katie was her best student. Joan had class with Miss Mary Ann Grant, who had established the school and had taught for over twelve years. The school had become successful, thanks primarily to her hard work. Sodus Point was a growing village, and schooling for its children was important. Under New York state laws, the school now received public support, and most of the young children in the area attended school.

Just after Christmas, word was sent out that Mrs. Malcolm was ill and wouldn't be able to return for the rest of the year. Volunteers were sought to fill in for her until a new teacher could be hired. Even though there was plenty to do on the farm, Jamey volunteered. He taught the older children's class during January and February, then Carin, with help from Lenny, taught in March until a new teacher arrived. The teaching work didn't affect Jamey's production in his business that much. He still continued his carpentry work in his barn from after school until late at night. The teaching actually gave him a relaxing diversion, although he found teaching young children to be more challenging than college students.

With teaching and farm work, the Davises' lives continued at a frantic pace over the winter months. But they never regretted their decision to move to Sodus Point. They had more than survived; they had prospered. To them, the future was as bright as the glistening reflection of the sun off the smooth sheet of ice that covered Sodus Bay. They awakened each day to a bright, wonderful, and beautiful world.

For the Davis children, it was a winter of immense fun. The hill just south of their house was ideal for sledding. Lenny built sleds for himself and his two sisters. The three of them would race down the hill and slowly climb back up to do it all over again. This activity was repeated until they were exhausted, but no one wanted to be the first to admit he or she was too tired or cold to continue. Seven-year-old Joan usually convinced her big brother or sister to help pull her sled part way up the hill. That way she usually lasted as long as they did.

When he wasn't playing with his sisters, Lenny learned to ice fish and hunt. Lenny bagged his first deer with his musket right before the New Year's celebration. He had seen the deer in the morning near the top of the sledding hill. That afternoon he returned to the hilltop carrying his firearm.

Jamey had taught Lenny about shooting as well as safety, and the father now trusted his son to hunt on his own. Lenny found the trail, tracked the deer, and bagged the small buck with one accurate shot. The New Year's meal of venison was a welcome break from the usual fare of fish and more fish.

A New Christian

The Lummises had never attended regular church services, nor were they strong believers in any religion. Over the years, Georgiana and Georgette occasionally attended a local Episcopal church service, but Ben never went. They read the *Bible* occasionally, but more for educational reading than for religious commitment. The Lummises believed that through education their children would learn enough to make their own choices about religion. They had tried to raise them to be good solid citizens and were seldom worried about their knowing right from wrong. However, this Christmas had special religious significance for the Lummis family. Georgette was joining the Episcopal church. She had taken Soso to the church services in Clyde several times since the summer. At first she waited for him in the carriage while he went inside, then she started attending the service with him. Finally, she participated and asked questions of Soso and the minister. She was mature and intelligent for a fourteen-year-old. She was a young woman with strong feelings. After seeing how the power of religious faith had helped Soso and experiencing it as she attended service, she decided to join the church. She wanted to believe, to serve, and to grow in faith and spirit. She was baptized right after the Christmas service with her family in attendance. Ben and Georgiana were happy for their daughter. This was something that she had wanted and finally obtained. Soso was especially proud, because Georgette had experienced many of the same feelings he had. It was a moving ceremony, and there was a joyous celebration after the service.

Winter Plans and Dreams

Georgette, Georgina, and Soso continued to make the weekly journey to church services in Clyde. Several times, Georgiana and Georgette went by themselves because Soso was ill. Georgette made the trip every Sunday, despite snowstorms that made travel quite difficult. She had found her calling.

Soso continued to play with and teach Benny and support his neighbors. He looked forward to a warm, productive spring so he could enjoy the outdoors. He very much wanted to taste nature's delights. Soso knew he was no longer able to make his own opportunities; he had to wait patiently for them to come to him. So when the opportunities did come, he wanted to be ready to participate. Growing old was natural and even enjoyable when you had patience and wisdom.

Plans for Success

Jamey was anxiously awaiting the summer season, his first full one in the farming business. He had grand plans for a plentiful vegetable garden and an enlarged fruit orchard. Although he knew he would have to wait for his trees to bear fruit, he hoped to see a year of healthy growth in his trees. Over the next year or more, the business would have to be sustained by commercial fishing. He already had five businesses in Rochester and Syracuse that had ordered fish. Now he had to come through by catching sufficient fish, keeping them fresh, and getting them to the markets. James Pollock ran a successful icehouse just a half-mile from the Davises, so Jamey had access to ample amounts of ice. If the family caught enough fish, he was certain they could survive another year or two until the orchard began to produce. The plan was for him, Carin, and Lenny to fillet the fish at a big table built in the barn, pack them with considerable chopped ice in the containers that he had built, and deliver them by wagon to the train station in Lyons all in the same day. This meant that the fish needed to be back at the dock by ten o'clock in the morning. In order to do this, the fishermen—primarily he and Lenny—would have to leave the dock by five o'clock. Carin would pick up the ice at nine o'clock so it would be ready for the filleting. The train would transport the containers of fish on the afternoon routes west to Rochester and east to Syracuse. There the businesses would pick up the fresh fish in the containers for sale the next day. About once every two weeks, the containers would be returned so that Jamey could reuse them. If this plan worked, the Davis fish business would have a productive and profitable summer.

In early spring, Jamey took time to go over to Lummisville to talk with Ben and Soso. He had to travel by horse around the bay because the ice was no longer safe for travel. A thin sheet of ice still covered the bay preventing travel by boat. Jamey wanted to learn all that he could from the two masters. He had respect for their talents and knowledge. Ben knew about successful fruit and vegetable farming, and Soso was the best fisherman ever to cast a line or net into Sodus Bay or Lake Ontario. He hoped their advice would help him avoid mistakes and make for a productive year. They were both more than happy to help him, and they had confidence in his abilities to manage a successful business. They gave him every helpful hint that they knew. Jamey was a brilliant, hard-working, innovative person. Success, in the form of happiness and contribution, although not necessarily power and wealth, usually came to people like Jamey Davis.

First Fish of the Spring

While Jamey was over in Lummisville, he made arrangements to go fishing with Ben and Soso on the first day of open water. The ice was beginning to honeycomb, and the next stiff wind would blow it off the bay, leaving the water ready for the fishermen. It would be just like old times. The three of them pulling in fish and enjoying each other's company. All three were full of anticipation. Jamey worried that the cold water and weather would adversely affect Soso's health, but Soso wouldn't dream of missing this opportunity. He wanted to go with them to remember how nature magically uncovered Sodus Bay every spring, leaving a myriad of fish ready for the taking. This was an opportunity that had come to him, and he was ready to experience it to its fullest.

As for the first day of fishing for the rest of the Davis family, Lenny was planning on leading a fishing party consisting of his mother and two sisters. They would stay on the west side of the bay to see how plentiful the fish were in the areas close to their home. They wouldn't start sending fish to the outside markets for another week, so this was just practice, and the fish caught during the first few days would be sold to local consumers.

Just three days after Jamey returned home from his visit to Lummisville, he awakened to find a stiff, warm southwest wind, and he knew that this was the day the ice would leave the bay. It did. By noon the bay had transformed from a sheet of solid, but mushy, dirty, murky ice into a slivery, dazzling liquid. By the time he loaded his boat with the fishing gear and said his good-byes to Carin and the children, the wind had calmed down and the bay glistened like a shiny glass mirror. The water was ice-cold, but breathtakingly beautiful. He spent an invigorating afternoon traveling across the bay to Lummisville to meet up with his fishing partners.

The three men enjoyed their supper and an evening of storytelling. All three shared common bonds that included deep love and support for their fellow people and mother earth and a sincere appreciation for all the opportunities they had been given. They knew that they had all been fortunate to have the opportunity to live fulfilling, rewarding, and satisfying lives. Best of all, they had become the closest of friends. Jamey and Ben now had similar relationships with Soso that their fathers, Jim and William, had a generation before. Soso was 65 years old; Jamey was 43; and Ben was 41. They were wise, experienced men, who understood the special parts of life.

Their conversation varied from light to serious. They told stories about the old times when Jamey and Ben were inexperienced, but enthusiastic, teenagers running their own fishing business. Soso remembered teaching them patience, the ways of nature, and how to catch fish. Soso related stories to them about their parents. He told them how he had first met their parents, and the similar lessons that he had to give their fathers on fishing and hunting. There was no need to exaggerate; all the stories were delightfully true. That may have been the most amazing element of their lives— there was no need make up artificial stories to be entertained. They were simple people who appreciated their good fortune and understood the responsibilities and obligations it brought. Soso spent time reflecting on some of the important things that he had seen and learned in his life. He was usually a storyteller, but on this night he added more philosophy to his stories.

"Over all my many years of living with the whites, I have seen many changes in the United States and the people of this growing nation. Civilization has improved our way of life. Now we travel fast and safe, over smooth roads, along long canals, in fast steam-powered boats, and on splendid trains. Cities with fancy stores and lovely homes now exist where forests and swamps were all around. The boats that used to sell for $50, cost $250 today. Our orchards and gardens produce so much fruit and vegetables that one farmer can feed an entire village. Most of all, I appreciate the way our schools teach children about the world, even about those places across the oceans we'll never see."

Jamey asked, "But what about the Native American people and their rich and valuable culture? Can they survive?"

"Unfortunately, my people continue to be mistreated and abused. The world has improved, but we still have been pushed away from our lands and our way of life. Not all change means improvement. I chose to join with the whites and their modern, technical world, but many Indians who kept their lifestyles and cultures were punished and destroyed. Civilization is a strange thing. It has helped some and ruined others. But in the long run, it improves more than it destroys. I wouldn't be here with you if I hadn't seen it and believed it. People like Garth and Joe Fox will make sure the Indians learn the good lessons of the whites. If they do, they will survive. I worry about the whites. They are losing a great opportunity to learn from the Indians. I'm counting on people like you to make sure that doesn't happen."

Ben added the obvious. "The Indians and the blacks have suffered greatly for the whites' progress."

Soso concluded, "Prejudice and slavery are the most terrible diseases of our society. They really aren't part of civilization. Somehow, they exist in spite of civilization. Someday, these diseases will be cured and we will see progress for all people. Then our human world will be as beautiful as nature's world."

After so much serious talk, Ben started teasing Soso about getting old and losing his fishing prowess. He bet Soso that he would catch the greater number of fish the next day. Jamey added, "Soso, I hear you're going to bring nets to catch fish, since you lost all your rods. Don't worry, I brought an extra one you can use."

Jamey already knew that Soso had just finished making a new rod for the season. Of course, all three of them knew that Soso was still the best fisherman, but the other two could always hope for a lucky day and a little teasing now was worth the risk of being embarrassed later. It was their only chance to claim superiority over this extraordinary man.

Soso couldn't let Ben's bet and Jamey's comment go unchallenged. He countered, "I have a rod that will bring in more fish tomorrow than all of your rods will catch. At the end of the day, you'll both want me to make you new rods just like mine. As a challenge, I will give my rod to the person catching the most fish tomorrow, but I know that I won't have to make another one for me."

The conversation turned more serious. Soso wanted to make sure both of his friends understood his pride in them and his expectations for their future. He also knew how proud their parents would be, if they were still alive to see the lives their sons were leading and the families they were rais-ing. Now they were friends, but over the years Soso had been their mentor, their teacher, their "uncle," and their supporter. He wanted to let them know how he felt. It was time to be serious.

He spoke to Ben first. "Ben, your legacy is a great one. You have been called, and I have seen you faithfully serve all people. Be sure to guide your family and your friends to follow in your ways. Lead by example, and they, and many others, will follow. Remember to respect nature and her rules. You understand the culture of my people and that will always help you understand the changes and differences you will encounter. Take only what you need, and always return more than you have taken." Here he paused a moment, then continued, "Tomorrow I will teach you humility and respect for your elders. Two lessons you should never forget."

Soso then turned to Jamey. "Jamey, I have seen you do many important things. Now, you must make sure others do the same. Tell them to create lasting ideas, and they will be remembered, as you will be. Remember the balance and symmetry of the perfect hull and the fight and spirit of the most coveted fish. Most of all, remember the magnificence of nature, even when it causes death and destruction, for afterwards there is always life and growth. You are wise and talented in the technical and spiritual ways of the world. Your knowledge and experience give you great wisdom and power. Use them to benefit all the creatures of our earth." Again, a slight pause, "Tomorrow, I will show you how to outsmart fish, which is a challenge that you have not quite mastered despite all your intelligence."

After these words were said, no more challenges were issued, the teasing was concluded, and the philosophizing was over. That evening's final words were about the details of the next day's expedition. They agreed to leave the dock before daybreak with the intention of spending equal time at prime fishing spots near Second Creek, Third Creek, and Float Bridge. They all figured that the light southwest wind would continue, so they expected a clear, pleasant day on the water of their favorite bay.

Where are the Fish?

It was a good day to go fishing. All first days of open water are good days. However, on this day, Ben was worried that Georgiana would go into labor while he was gone. She was due any day. Georgiana assured Ben that she was fine and encouraged him to enjoy the day of fishing. Ben arranged for the midwife to spend the day with Georgiana just in case. Only then did he allow himself to concentrate on the activities of the day—catching fish and enjoying the splendor of nature with his friends.

To these three men, every day was a good day for fishing. It was relatively mild for March on the cold waters of the bay. Just as they had predicted, the wind was light out of the southwest. It took about 35 minutes to sail and row in the dark to a spot off the point on the east side of Second Creek just as it turned light. All signs indicated that it was going to be a superb day for fishing.

Jamey and Ben were pleased to see that Soso was bundled up in warm clothes. They didn't want him to get a chill. All three had their first lines in the water within two minutes of dropping anchor. However, the only fish in the boat after two more minutes belonged to Soso. The aged Indian smiled like a young boy as he reeled in a nice three-pound walleye. Nothing was said, but all three knew that Soso still had the magic touch. A little later, Jamey remarked how he liked the look of Soso's rod, and that brought an even a bigger smile to Soso's face.

After that first fish, however, things were surprisingly slow. No more fish were caught for about an hour, but then they started hitting more walleyes. Within a fifteen-minute period, five more fish were caught. Ben and Jamey each caught two fish, and Soso just one more. After another unsuccessful period of thirty minutes, they decided to move to the next spot as they had planned. It only took twenty minutes to sail a short loop around the point and move up near the mouth of Third Creek. The waters of the bay were sparkling and the bright sun made it feel warm, despite the icy water.

The three lines hit the water, and soon thereafter Soso again brought in the first fish. It was a nice, four-pound trout. This time his skill, luck, and momentum continued. For about thirty minutes, he caught fish after fish. Ben and Jamey mostly watched in amazement as their mentor skillfully and methodically brought in the fish. Eventually the other two men caught one fish each, but by then Soso had over fifteen fish in the boat.

For the rest of the morning, they continued to catch small trout and pike. Soso continued at a pace about double that of his two friends. At noon, they moved to their final spot off the shore of Float Bridge. They ate a lunch of dried and salted venison and fruit as they sailed the boat around another point and up near the southeast corner of the bay. Soso teasingly volunteered lessons for his protégés when they reached their last spot. Jamey tallied the score for the catch thus far. Soso had more than doubled their combined catches, in terms of numbers and pounds of fish. Ben had the largest fish, a fine seven-pound trout.

The Float Bridge spot was productive. Most of the fish taken that afternoon were small pike, with a few perch tossed into the creel. Soso did hook a huge walleye that rivaled Ben's trout for the biggest fish of the day. By the time they returned to the dock, the three men had boated over 250 pounds of fish. Some would be eaten immediately by families and friends, some would be salted and stored away, and some would be sold by Jamey to inlanders living in the Sodus area the following day. As predicted, Soso was the champion fisherman of the day.

Lenny's Big Fish

The other fishing party, consisting of Lenny, Carin, Katie, and Joan, got a much later start. Lenny was ready hours before the planned departure time. He loaded the boat with the rods, nets, bait, and tackle. Then he used the extra time to fish offshore while he waited patiently for the others. Carin tried to move the girls along, but Joan was tired and Katie was slow and methodical and really didn't like the cold weather. Carin made a nice breakfast to eat on the boat, and that seemed to motivate the two girls to climb in and start their day's work. The group was finally assembled and ready for a morning of fishing. As planned, they ventured only a few hundred yards off shore, right along the south shore. They had mixed success and accumulated a varied bag of fish. During the morning, they caught several bullheads, eels, perch, trout, walleyes, and pike. Everyone caught fish, and it was exciting for eight-year-old Joan to keep up with her mother and older brother and sister. Lenny was disappointed that they didn't catch more fish, but this day's experiment showed that the fish were there, and there would be a nice variety to send to their customers.

The highlight of the morning was Lenny's last fish. As soon as he hooked it, he knew it was a big one. It took minutes for him to fight the fish and reel it to the side of the boat. The salmon was so big it scared little Joan, when she looked over the side of the boat. After another three minutes of maneuvering, they finally managed to get a net around the monster and haul it in. It was the biggest fish Lenny had ever seen. The 21-pound salmon dwarfed the other fish they had caught. All the other fish together weighed less than forty pounds. Lenny couldn't wait to show his father his big prize catch.

Tasty Delights

The first fresh fish of the season always tasted the best. After the men landed, they filleted their catch and packed the fish in ice. They selected a few nice trout for the evening meal. Georgiana, despite her pregnancy, insisted on cooking an elaborate meal, and the three gentleman of Sodus Bay ate and drank heartily. They continued the banter that had started the night before. Occasionally, serious discussion took place, and that centered on Georgiana's condition. Ben was concerned that his wife was working too hard and needed to rest in preparation for the delivery. It was a meal and a day to remember. Soso was thankful. Ben and Jamey were happy. Another spring season had opened on Sodus Bay, and, as always, there were plenty of fish for the taking.

Jamey walked with Soso to his house and then sailed back across the bay in the dark of night. Despite his exhaustion, Jamey had been inspired by his day on the bay. He loved his new home and his new life. This day validated the decision that he and Carin had made to return to live on Sodus Bay. Days like this one made him forget all about the worry and exhaustion that came with his new occupation. Being an Army officer was for younger men. Being a mathematics professor was a good profession; being a fisherman-farmer on Sodus Bay gave his family a good life.

By the time Jamey reached home, the day's activities for his family were finished. The Davises had filleted their catch, selected the dinner fare, and packed the rest of the fish on ice. Carin had cooked the best fish fillets of the catch, and the children ate the hearty meal with tremendous satisfaction. The two girls had gone to sleep, and Carin had finally dozed off as she had tried in vain to stay awake to welcome Jamey home. However, the moment Jamey landed his boat, Lenny was there to meet him. Greetings were exchanged between father and son, but Jamey knew that Lenny must have a very good reason to be there. It was very late.

"Got a few fish today. Even Joan caught several perch. Mother got tired and went to bed, but I cleaned and filleted all the fish, except one. How did you do?" Jamey could sense excitement in Lenny's voice.

"We all caught a few. Your Uncle Soso caught more than Ben and I put together. Where's this fish you need to fillet?"

Lenny excitedly showed his father the big salmon he had caught. "I caught this one."

Jamey's reaction was just what Lenny had hoped for. "What a monster. That fish would feed a family for a week. You're quite the fisherman and a great son. Even Soso didn't catch one that big." It was a moment to remember for a proud father and a thoughtful son.

"I really like it here on Sodus Bay. Can we stay here for the rest of our lives?" Lenny was beginning to dream.

"Don't know why we'd move. But there is more to life than fishing. Remember you might have a chance to go to college and learn all about the other things to be done in this world. Who knows, you may go to a place like West Point and become an Army officer and see many places all over our huge world. But for now, let's enjoy our new home. You'd better get to bed now. We'll have a long day tomorrow delivering all these fish. Don't forget, Uncle Soso will be over here to fish with you in a few days." That night Lenny's dreams were filled with visions of fish, West Point uniforms, and exotic places. It had been an exceptional day. Lenny had caught a big fish and heard his father say that he might get to go to West Point.

The Joyous Day

The night of the fishing trip, Georgiana became extremely uncomfortable and felt her delivery was imminent. She lasted the night without waking Ben, who slept soundly from his exhausting day on the water. However, by the next morning, she knew the big day had arrived. She was in labor. She woke Ben, who quickly rode to Float Bridge to get the midwife. By noon, the cutest baby ever born in Lummisville, Rose Lummis, was delivered to her parents. Mother and baby were healthy, and everyone was excited about the new arrival. Nature had blessed the special place called Lummisville and its extraordinary people with the most splendid gift of all, a new life.

Word was sent out, and soon Soso came by to see the proud father, who immediately showed off his baby girl. Over the next couple days, Georgiana recovered her strength, and Rose grew cuter. Benny and Georgette enjoyed the new activities that their sister, Rose, brought the house. Both were going to be good siblings, helping their parents raise their new sister. As predicted, it was looking like a joyous summer on the shores of Sodus Bay.

The day after the birth, Jamey and Carin heard the news and visited their friends in Lummisville. Baby Rose was shown around, and the men celebrated while Carin cared for the baby so Georgiana could get some rest. Soso came over to join the celebration and helped by playing with Benny. Soso wanted to fish again soon, so he had asked if Jamey could join him for a day on the water. However, since Jamey was busy with farm work, Jamey arranged for Lenny to fish with Soso. The plan was for Lenny to meet Soso at First Creek at daybreak in four more days. Jamey could tell that, although Soso was exhausted, he was nevertheless determined to continue his experiences. The long day of fishing had exhausted 43-year-old Jamey. Hopefully, Soso would use the next four days to recover and build energy for another day of fishing on the bay. Jamey knew that Lenny was excited to fish with his Uncle Soso.

Another Fishing Trip

On the arranged day, Soso was on the water several hours before daybreak. He couldn't sleep anyway and was afraid if he did fall asleep he'd sleep for hours. Soso hadn't really slept in days. Life was too exciting, with the fishing trips, the baby being born, the caring for Benny, and the work and chores to be done. Soso decided to take his canoe since there was very little wind, and he didn't want to get stranded trying to row his knock-about. He slowly paddled his small, light-weight canoe across the bay without a worry. He could have done it with his eyes closed, and on this nearly dark night that was just about what it amounted to. However, in the faint moonlight he could see the outlines of the familiar landmarks, and soon he pulled up onto the shore next to First Creek just as he had done so many times before.

Soso knew he had a little time, so he walked along the creek. He loved this spot as much as the Davises. This area had been his first home on Sodus Bay over fifty years before. His parents were buried less than a hundred yards from where he stood. Over the years, Soso had spent many hours at their graves, talking to their spirits and praying for their souls. He spent time thinking of them and his other family members. Lost in thoughts and exhaustion, Soso was startled when Lenny came running down the hill toward the boat. Lenny was never late for fishing, so the two fishermen set off to get a good spot even though daybreak was still a half hour away. They used the Davises' small sailboat and left Soso's canoe on shore.

Lenny and Soso spent the morning fishing near the mouth of the creek and the shallows of the south shore of the bay. It was a productive day. Both caught trout, walleye, and pike. Soso let Lenny take the lead in sailing, spotting the boat, and setting his fishing line. Soso was proud of Lenny. Already he was a smart, careful fisherman who understood nature's ways. Jamey had done a fine job teaching his son the important things in life. Soso considered himself fortunate to have known three generations of Davis men and to have shared many days like this with all three of them. He missed Lenny's grandfather, Jim. But now he had Jamey and Lenny. Soso thanked his God for blessing his life with so much good fortune. Lenny thanked Soso for being such a good teacher.

Just before dark, they returned to shore, unloaded the boat, and filleted the day's catch. It had been a long, full day of outdoor work. The cold, crisp air always felt good and invigorating, but secretly it took away energy and endurance. The wind was picking up, and it was getting colder. Lenny thanked Soso for the gratifying day and asked him to stay for supper. Soso declined, knowing that he still had to make the return trip across the bay. Soso said good-bye and went down to First Creek to find his canoe.

As he approached the canoe, he hesitated. He decided to spend a little more time visiting the graves of his parents and his grandfather. As he had done many times, he prayed for them, and he spoke to them. This was his healing time, and he needed to be soothed and nourished by the memories of his parents and his relatives.

"Clear Dawn, my mother in heaven, you were right, the whites are strong and good. They just needed time to understand and learn. You taught me well, and I love you so."

"Gar, my dedicated father, you also were right. The whites were slow to learn and understand. They could never understand all our ways, nor the ways of nature. But, I have seen them learn many things, and I have seen our own people grow and learn from them."

"I have done what you asked, Grandfáther Trout. I have lived here to catch the big sea trout of Sodus, and I have helped many others, especially the whites, to understand how and why it must be done so that nature is not hurt. You were a splendid fisherman and a better teacher. I thank you for all you did for me."

Soso stayed for a long time, thinking, praying, and talking to his family and the spirits and his God. Finally, he told his family members goodbye, as he always did, and went to find his canoe. Soso was surprised to find it was so dark, the wind was cold and had picked up considerably. He slipped his canoe into the water and began to paddle back across the bay into a stiff northeast wind. A northeast wind was always a danger warning on Sodus Bay. Soso had that feeling of an impending, powerful storm, but in his exhaustion, he let it pass. He was tired and distracted by thoughts of his parents and his own good fortune. He seemed to paddle directly into the stiff wind in a strange, empty trance.

Generally, there was very little to worry about for a boatsman like Soso on Sodus Bay. Nevertheless, the one worthy adversary of any boatsman on the bay was a rising, cold northeast wind bringing a storm across the lake and slamming into the bay. Nor'easters were storms to treat with great respect. There was no mercy in a nor'easter. In the darkness and numbness of his trance, Soso had paddled directly to the middle of the bay, where the storm was raising its greatest rage—four-foot waves of destruction. Off-course, in danger, exhausted, and trapped in a small canoe that was never designed to take on such waves, Soso, like an inexperienced novice, somehow let his exhaustion prevent him from seeing nature's danger signs. Soso had carefully listened to nature for all his life, but for this one time he listened to other voices deep inside his memory. Spirits had temporarily overtaken reality. They were the voices of his departed relatives, answering all his questions and talking with him about all their glorious experiences together.

At this very moment, the silvery waters of Sodus Bay were as powerful and destructive as those of Lake Ontario. Those unrelenting, dangerous waters had taken Betty and so many others. Soso was a tired old man with few defenses left. He thought of his family, he thought of his friends, he prayed, and he remembered Betty. He was barely able to make out the glimmering light of safety coming from the lighthouse on the shore of the lake. But nothing could help him now. He vaguely sensed the danger, but he never saw the wave that hit his canoe. Suddenly he was alone. His canoe was gone. His paddle was gone. It was cold and dark. Soso quietly sank into the waters that he had called home for over fifty years.

Jamey found Soso's body the next morning. It was right where he had been with his canoe the previous morning. In death, Soso had miraculously returned to where he intended to be forever. Jamey held him briefly and cried for his friend, but really he cried for all those people who had known Soso. Then he took Soso's body just seventy yards away to the gravesite next to his parents and grandfather's graves. Jamey buried his friend, his teacher, and his "Uncle Soso" that morning. When he was done, he told his family, who mourned and, in turn, told others. Jamey sailed across the bay and notified the Lummises, who mourned and informed others. Soon enough, even without the efficiency of the telegraph, all the residents of Sodus Bay were mourning Soso's death.

Four days later, during a brief spring storm, the community paid their respects, grieved, and remembered their friend, Soso Washington. Many words were said, but no one mentioned that Soso was an Indian, an outsider, or a savage. Soso had made them all disregard his race and understand the person. As far as anyone knew, Soso had always been their friend, their provider, their leader, their teacher, and their protector. He had left quite a legacy. All were thankful for having known him. Even little baby Rose, who unknowingly smiled and laughed during the solemn service, seemed to know that she, like all those there on that day or those who have come to Sodus Bay since, had plenty of reasons to thank her "Uncle Soso." It was still going to be a joyous summer on Sodus Bay, just like they all had been and just like they always would be.